SWORDS AGAINST DARKNESS

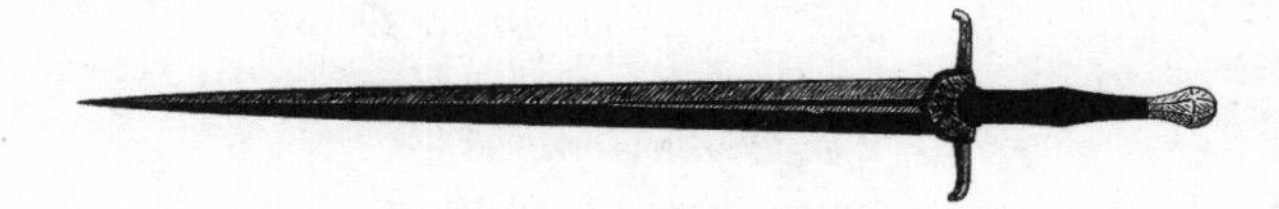

Other Anthologies Edited
by Paula Guran

Embraces
Best New Paranormal Romance
Best New Romantic Fantasy
Zombies: The Recent Dead
The Year's Best Dark Fantasy & Horror: 2010
Vampires: The Recent Undead
The Year's Best Dark Fantasy & Horror: 2011
Halloween
New Cthulhu: The Recent Weird
Brave New Love
Witches: Wicked, Wild & Wonderful
Obsession: Tales of Irresistible Desire
The Year's Best Dark Fantasy & Horror: 2012
Extreme Zombies
Ghosts: Recent Hauntings
Rock On: The Greatest Hits of Science Fiction & Fantasy
Season of Wonder
Future Games
Weird Detectives: Recent Investigations
The Mammoth Book of Angels and Demons
After the End: Recent Apocalypses
The Year's Best Dark Fantasy & Horror: 2013
Halloween: Mystery, Magic & the Macabre
Once Upon a Time: New Fairy Tales
Magic City: Recent Spells
The Year's Best Dark Fantasy & Horror: 2014
Time Travel: Recent Trips
New Cthulhu 2: More Recent Weird
Blood Sisters: Vampire Stories by Women
Mermaids and Other Mysteries of the Deep
The Year's Best Dark Fantasy & Horror: 2015
Warrior Women
Street Magicks
The Mammoth Book of Cthulhu: New Lovecraftian Fiction
Beyond the Woods: Fairy Tales Retold
The Year's Best Dark Fantasy & Horror: 2016
The Mammoth Book of the Mummy

SWORDS AGAINST DARKNESS

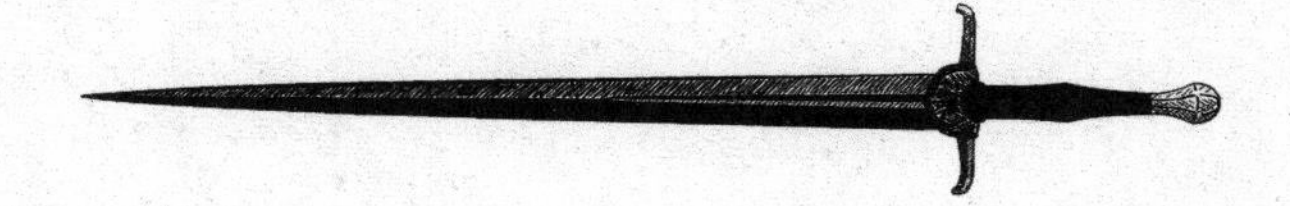

Edited by Paula Guran

PRIME BOOKS

Cover art by Rodrigo Ramos. | Cover design by Sherin Nicole.

Prime Books
Germantown, MD
www.prime-books.com

For more information, contact Prime Books: prime@prime-books.com

Print ISBN: 978-1-60701-485-0
Ebook ISBN: 978-1-60701-486-7

Special thanks to John O'Neill of *Black Gate* (blackgate.com).

Contents

Introduction:
Knowledge Takes Precedence Over Death

Paula Guran

("Sword and sorcery" is sometimes used as a derogatory term for "bad fantasy" or a specific type of bad fantasy. We shall acknowledge but otherwise ignore this usage.)

So. What *is* "sword-and-sorcery" fantasy?

Lin Carter, in his introduction to L. Sprague de Camp's *Literary Swordsmen and Sorcerers: The Makers of Heroic Fantasy* (1976) wrote, among other things, that sword and sorcery "is written primarily to entertain." That's certainly part of it.

Among the many who have defined it one way or another, Darrell Schweitzer described sword-and-sorcery fantasy this way: "In the broadest sense, a sword-and-sorcery story is one about heroic adventures, in a primitive or imaginary-world setting, with supernatural elements." He continues, explaining the definition is both too general and too specific and wonders if "sword and sorcery *ever exist[ed] in the first place*, or was it merely a subset of fantasy defined by its cliché?"

Schweitzer goes on to note (and this is why I chose his definition):

> Much of what was retrospectively lumped together into the "genre" had little in common before that point: Howard's Conan. Clark Ashton Smith's tales of Hyperborea and Zothique. Jack Vance's Dying Earth. Leiber's Fafhrd and the Gray Mouser, de Camp's Poseidonis and Jorian adventures, Moorcock's Elric, Charles Saunders's Imaro, and so on. Those stories have some elements in common, but their *merits*, we suggest, have more to do with their differences. It is precisely because Leiber's or Moorcock's or de Camp's work constitutes an original vision, and is not a retread of Howard, that it is of interest.

It's an interesting theory. Does retaining some tropes, but turning others on their heads keep S&S vital, relevant, and entertaining? Maybe the *best* S&S is not just evolutionary but revolutionary.

All fantasy, including sword and sorcery, has its ancient antecedents in myth and legend. At the least, what came to be known as both the genre and the marketing category of fantasy builds on the past but constantly progresses.

Genres—or subgenres—arise due to public demand. What I mean is: there may be appreciation and critical notice of a literary genre, even a quantity of readers, but it takes sufficient public demand for a particular type of fiction for it to become a marketing category. In order to successfully market a type of fiction, publishers have to produce predictable fiction that the public recognizes as what it wants. *Genrification*. Yes, lots of formulaic garbage results, but the non-garbage is apt to survive and be recognized as something more than the surrounding refuse.

I am briefly looking at the gentrification of fantasy and, specifically sword-and-sorcery fantasy, here. Categories begat opportunities for writers to create. Writers may then subvert or defy the very boundaries that give them opportunity; great originality, even great art may result. (Or not.)

[Note: This introduction and I owe a great deal to "The Making of the American Fantasy Genre" by David Hartwell from *The Secret History of Fantasy*, edited by Peter S. Beagle (Tachyon Publications, 2010). I wish David were still with us for many reasons, the least of which is so I could have picked his brain on the subject.]

In the mid-nineteenth century, fantasy was set apart from adult literature and deemed suitable only for children. In the 1920s and 1930s, pulp magazines were about the only venues through which fantasy (and science fiction) could reach a reading public.

The progenitor of what later came to be known as sword-and-sorcery fantasy was Robert E. Howard (1906-1936). He created the character of Conan the Cimmerian, a barbarian warrior whose adventures first began appearing in *Weird Tales* in 1932. The stories were popular and there was a demand for similar tales. Other writers added their own flavors to the not-yet-seen-as S&S mix.

Aided by the slow death of the pulp magazines in the 1940s, sword and sorcery overall fell out of favor with the reading public. It hadn't disappeared, mind you—in fact, some of the best managed to get published, sometimes lightly disguised as science fiction, during the period—but without enough readers clamoring for it, few opportunities existed.

The Lord of the Rings by J. R. R. Tolkien (1892-1973) was published in three volumes in 1954 and 1955. Not as *fantasy*, but as *general fiction*. Critically acclaimed, it was no bestseller but sold well enough in hardcover. Then, mass-market paperback editions—*as fantasy*—appeared in 1965; it became a publishing phenomenon. A commercial market for fantasy was born.

Publishers, naturally wanting to repeat such sales success, started publishing fantasy of many types. Surprisingly (and to the dismay of many) only the Lancer editions that reprinted Robert E. Howard's Conan stories sold anywhere close to the numbers of Tolkien. Sales for direct imitators of Conan and other more innovative sword-and-sorcery authors—including Fritz Leiber and Michael

Moorcock—were also healthy enough to make publishers happy. Sword & sorcery thrived.

By the start of the seventies, only the sword and sorcery category—or heroic fantasy as it was also called—was selling as well as Tolkien.

There were fewer periodical markets, but what magazines there were published some short S&S fiction. Sword-and-sorcery comics became popular. Reprint anthologies compiling previously published stories appeared, as did original-fiction anthology series with titles like *Flashing Swords, Swords Against Darkness,* and *Sword and Sorceress.*

A film, *Conan the Barbarian* (1982), which had little to do with Howard's creation, was successful enough to be followed by even worse movies of the ilk. Sword and sorcery's rep, already weighed down with too much trash, got worse.

Meanwhile, publishers figured out that readers wanted books that were not only fantasy, but close imitations of Tolkien. Backed by canny marketing, *The Sword of Shannara*, an epic fantasy novel by Terry Brooks become a major bestseller in 1977. The general public had found the next "big thing": big commercial fantasy. Fantasy in general was further codified. (Briefly: virtuous male protagonist aided by mentor overcomes evil. Add magic and top-dollar cover art.) In time, this commercial epic fantasy more or less subsumed sword and sorcery, but S&S was also along for the ride by its own name.

(Generic fantasy that made money meant that higher quality fantasy got published, even though low sales were expected. Publishing still works this way.)

Eventually, the pubic was overwhelmed by too much epic fantasy from the same mold, too much of it of low quality. Publishers became more selective. The number of titles and series were reduced. Other subgenres of fantasy became popular. Generic epic fantasy—some good, some bad—continues to sell well in the twenty-first century, but it doesn't dominate completely. There are still many earlier series being read today even as newer authors are making their mark.

As for S&S, the masses found it in other places. Like gaming. The role-playing game *Dungeons & Dragons* was influenced by many sources. But it owes a considerable debt—as do many games since—to the fiction of Robert E. Howard, Fritz Leiber, Michael Moorcock, and other S&S authors. Even if gamers never heard of such authors, without them video game consoles might never have existed. (And, in turn, gaming has influenced fiction writers.)

Video games are far more popular than books these days. So are films and television—other media often inspired, sometimes unknowingly, by S&S. (And, in turn, film and TV influences fiction writers.) HBO's success with George R. R.

Martin's A Song of Ice and Fire epic fantasy series has brought attention—and thus opportunity for creators.

There is, of course, differences between epic fantasy and S&S. Exceptions are often the rule, but epic fantasy *usually* has grand scale, vast armies, global stakes, and lots of characters. Sword and sorcery *tends* to involve action and only a few characters concerned with more personal, immediate stakes. But many modern epic fantasy authors are using S&S elements and flavors in their fiction. And the "old masters" of S&S are still read and discovered by new readers. An author or a book or a series of books can become a cultural phenomenon if the general public becomes enthralled in a movie or television series or digital video content series. Screen versions of S&S classics are often rumored.

There are those who want S&S to remain as is once was, or kept within a strict definition. That's their prerogative, but they also often wonder why others don't appreciate or even read the "good old stuff." The answer is easy: if you cannot wade through a style of writing or look past elements of racism, sexism, misogyny, and the like or find little to identify with and/or escape into—you are no longer being entertained. You don't read it.

Even though I could not include all the authors I wanted to—particularly Andre Norton, Jennifer Roberson, and Charles R. Saunders—this anthology has examples of many styles and voices of S&S, all of which were published or labeled (by someone or someones other than me) as sword and sorcery. You may find some of the stories not to your liking. If so, you will, I hope, find others that you do enjoy. It is a big book!

The idea is to present a broad range of entertaining stories that can be seen as sword and sorcery. Despite the brief introductions I provide for each story, the aim is not to supply any sort of outline/history of S&S, just information and context.

I've divided the stories into three sections:

- Forging and Shaping: the seminal authors
- Normalizing and Annealing: those who followed and shaped
- Tempering and Sharpening: those who bring something new to the genre

I can debate some of my own categorizations, but the intent is to simply organize and present—not provide profound interpretations or unassailable rules.

The title of this introduction? It is from "Adept's Gambit," a Fafhrd and the Gray Mouser story by Fritz Leiber.

Paula Guran

⚔

Forging & Shaping

Robert E. Howard (1906–1936) is best known as the creator of Conan the Cimmerian (or "Barbarian") and, inadvertently, the father of what came to be known as sword and sorcery. Howard's first Conan story, "The Phoenix and the Sword," was published in Weird Tales *in December 1932. To quote David Drake: "Conan created S&S as a publishing category as surely as Stephen King created horror as a publishing category . . . virtually all of the S&S which appeared after December 1932 was written in some degree with reference to Conan." The literary merit of Howard's work is a matter of debate. His influence on other writers of fantasy and the field itself is, however, indisputable. "The Tower of the Elephant" appeared in* Weird Tales, *March 1933, the third of eighteen Conan stories to be published during Howard's lifetime.*

THE TOWER OF THE ELEPHANT

Robert E. Howard

Chapter 1

Torches flared murkily on the revels in the Maul, where the thieves of the east held carnival by night. In the Maul they could carouse and roar as they liked, for honest people shunned the quarters, and watchmen, well paid with stained coins, did not interfere with their sport. Along the crooked, unpaved streets with their heaps of refuse and sloppy puddles, drunken roisterers staggered, roaring. Steel glinted in the shadows where wolf preyed on wolf, and from the darkness rose the shrill laughter of women, and the sounds of scufflings and strugglings. Torchlight licked luridly from broken windows and wide-thrown doors, and out of those doors, stale smells of wine and rank sweaty bodies, clamor of drinking-jacks and fists hammered on rough tables, snatches of obscene songs, rushed like a blow in the face.

In one of these dens merriment thundered to the low smoke-stained roof, where rascals gathered in every stage of rags and tatters—furtive cut-purses, leering kidnappers, quick-fingered thieves, swaggering bravos with their wenches, strident-voiced women clad in tawdry finery. Native rogues were the dominant element—dark-skinned, dark-eyed Zamorians, with daggers at their girdles and guile in their hearts. But there were wolves of half a dozen outland nations there as well.

There was a giant Hyperborean renegade, taciturn, dangerous, with a broadsword strapped to his great gaunt frame—for men wore steel openly in the Maul. There was a Shemitish counterfeiter, with his hook nose and curled blue-black beard. There was a bold-eyed Brythunian wench, sitting on the knee of a tawny-haired Gunderman—a wandering mercenary soldier, a deserter from some defeated army. And the fat gross rogue whose bawdy jests were causing all the shouts of mirth was a professional kidnapper come up from distant Koth to teach woman-stealing to Zamorians who were born with more knowledge of the art than he could ever attain.

This man halted in his description of an intended victim's charms, and thrust his muzzle into a huge tankard of frothing ale. Then blowing the foam from his fat lips, he said, "By Bel, god of all thieves, I'll show them how to steal wenches: I'll have her over the Zamorian border before dawn, and there'll be a caravan waiting to receive her. Three hundred pieces of silver, a count of Ophir promised me for a sleek young Brythunian of the better class. It took me weeks, wandering among the border cities as a beggar, to find one I knew would suit. And is she a pretty baggage!"

He blew a slobbery kiss in the air.

"I know lords in Shem who would trade the secret of the Elephant Tower for her," he said, returning to his ale.

A touch on his tunic sleeve made him turn his head, scowling at the interruption. He saw a tall, strongly made youth standing beside him. This person was as much out of place in that den as a gray wolf among mangy rats of the gutters. His cheap tunic could not conceal the hard, rangy lines of his powerful frame, the broad heavy shoulders, the massive chest, lean waist and heavy arms. His skin was brown from outland suns, his eyes blue and smoldering; a shock of tousled black hair crowned his broad forehead. From his girdle hung a sword in a worn leather scabbard.

The Kothian involuntarily drew back; for the man was not one of any civilized race he knew.

"You spoke of the Elephant Tower," said the stranger, speaking Zamorian with an alien accent. "I've heard much of this tower; what is its secret?"

The fellow's attitude did not seem threatening, and the Kothian's courage was bolstered up by the ale, and the evident approval of his audience. He swelled with self-importance.

"The secret of the Elephant Tower?" he exclaimed. "Why, any fool knows that Yara the priest dwells there with the great jewel men call the Elephant's Heart, that is the secret of his magic."

The barbarian digested this for a space.

"I have seen this tower," he said. "It is set in a great garden above the level of the city, surrounded by high walls. I have seen no guards. The walls would be easy to climb. Why has not somebody stolen this secret gem?"

The Kothian stared wide-mouthed at the other's simplicity, then burst into a roar of derisive mirth, in which the others joined.

"Harken to this heathen!" he bellowed. "He would steal the jewel of Yara!—Harken, fellow," he said, turning portentously to the other, "I suppose you are some sort of a northern barbarian—"

"I am a Cimmerian," the outlander answered, in no friendly tone. The reply and the manner of it meant little to the Kothian; of a kingdom that lay far to the south, on the borders of Shem, he knew only vaguely of the northern races.

"Then give ear and learn wisdom, fellow," said he, pointing his drinking-jack at the discomfited youth. "Know that in Zamora, and more especially in this city, there are more bold thieves than anywhere else in the world, even Koth. If mortal man could have stolen the gem, be sure it would have been filched long ago. You speak of climbing the walls, but once having climbed, you would quickly wish yourself back again. There are no guards in the gardens at night for a very good reason—that is, no human guards. But in the watch-chamber, in the lower part of the tower, are armed men, and even if you passed those who roam the gardens by night, you must still pass through the soldiers, for the gem is kept somewhere in the tower above."

"But if a man *could* pass through the gardens," argued the Cimmerian, "why could he not come at the gem through the upper part of the tower and thus avoid the soldiers?"

Again the Kothian gaped at him.

"Listen to him!" he shouted jeeringly. "The barbarian is an eagle who would fly to the jeweled rim of the tower, which is only a hundred and fifty feet above the earth, with rounded sides slicker than polished glass!"

The Cimmerian glared about, embarrassed at the roar of mocking laughter that greeted this remark. He saw no particular humor in it, and was too new to civilization to understand its discourtesies. Civilized men are more discourteous than savages because they know they can be impolite without having their skulls split, as a general thing. He was bewildered and chagrined, and doubtless would have slunk away, abashed, but the Kothian chose to goad him further.

"Come, come!" he shouted. "Tell these poor fellows, who have only been thieves since before you were spawned, tell them how you would steal the gem!"

"There is always a way, if the desire be coupled with courage," answered the Cimmerian shortly, nettled.

The Kothian chose to take this as a personal slur. His face grew purple with anger.

"What!" he roared. "You dare tell us our business, and intimate that we are cowards? Get along; get out of my sight!" And he pushed the Cimmerian violently.

"Will you mock me and then lay hands on me?" grated the barbarian, his quick rage leaping up; and he returned the push with an open-handed blow that knocked his tormentor back against the rude-hewn table. Ale splashed over the jack's lip, and the Kothian roared in fury, dragging at his sword.

"Heathen dog!" he bellowed. "I'll have your heart for that!"

Steel flashed and the throng surged wildly back out of the way. In their flight they knocked over the single candle and the den was plunged in darkness, broken by the crash of upset benches, drum of flying feet, shouts, oaths of people tumbling over one another, and a single strident yell of agony that cut the din like a knife. When a candle was relighted, most of the guests had gone out by doors and broken windows, and the rest huddled behind stacks of wine-kegs and under tables. The barbarian was gone; the center of the room was deserted except for the gashed body of the Kothian. The Cimmerian, with the unerring instinct of the barbarian, had killed his man in the darkness and confusion.

CHAPTER 2

The lurid lights and drunken revelry fell away behind the Cimmerian. He had discarded his torn tunic, and walked through the night naked except for a loin-cloth and his high-strapped sandals. He moved with the supple ease of a great tiger, his steely muscles rippling under his brown skin.

He had entered the part of the city reserved for the temples. On all sides of him they glittered white in the starlight—snowy marble pillars and golden domes and silver arches, shrines of Zamora's myriad strange gods. He did not trouble his head about them; he knew that Zamora's religion, like all things of a civilized, long-settled people, was intricate and complex, and had lost most of the pristine essence in a maze of formulas and rituals. He had squatted for hours in the courtyard of the philosophers, listening to the arguments of theologians and teachers, and come away in a haze of bewilderment, sure of only one thing, and that, that they were all touched in the head.

His gods were simple and understandable; Crom was their chief, and he lived on a great mountain, whence he sent forth dooms and death. It was useless to call on Crom, because he was a gloomy, savage god, and he hated weaklings. But he gave a man courage at birth, and the will and might to kill his enemies, which, in the Cimmerian's mind, was all any god should be expected to do.

His sandaled feet made no sound on the gleaming pave. No watchmen passed, for even the thieves of the Maul shunned the temples, where strange dooms had been known to fall on violators. Ahead of him he saw, looming against the sky, the Tower of the Elephant. He mused, wondering why it was so named. No one seemed to know. He had never seen an elephant, but he vaguely understood that it was a monstrous animal, with a tail in front as well as behind. This a wandering Shemite had told him, swearing that he had seen such beasts by the thousands in the country of the Hyrkanians; but all men knew what liars were the men of Shem. At any rate, there were no elephants in Zamora.

The shimmering shaft of the tower rose frostily in the stars. In the sunlight it shone so dazzlingly that few could bear its glare, and men said it was built of silver. It was round, a slim perfect cylinder, a hundred and fifty feet in height, and its rim glittered in the starlight with the great jewels which crusted it. The tower stood among the waving exotic trees of a garden raised high above the general level of the city. A high wall enclosed this garden, and outside the wall was a lower level, likewise enclosed by a wall. No lights shone forth; there seemed to be no windows in the tower—at least not above the level of the inner wall. Only the gems high above sparkled frostily in the starlight.

Shrubbery grew thick outside the lower, or outer wall. The Cimmerian crept close and stood beside the barrier, measuring it with his eyes. It was high, but he could leap and catch the coping with his fingers. Then it would be child's play to swing himself up and over, and he did not doubt that he could pass the inner wall in the same manner. But he hesitated at the thought of the strange perils which were said to await within. These people were strange and mysterious to him; they were not of his kind—not even of the same blood as the more westerly Brythunians, Nemedians, Kothians, and Aquilonians, whose civilized mysteries had awed him in times past. The people of Zamora were very ancient, and, from what he had seen of them, very evil.

He thought of Yara, the high priest, who worked strange dooms from this jeweled tower, and the Cimmerian's hair prickled as he remembered a tale told by a drunken page of the court—how Yara had laughed in the face of a hostile prince, and held up a glowing, evil gem before him, and how rays shot blindingly from that unholy jewel, to envelop the prince, who screamed and fell down, and shrank to a withered blackened lump that changed to a black spider which scampered wildly about the chamber until Yara set his heel upon it.

Yara came not often from his tower of magic, and always to work evil on some man or some nation. The king of Zamora feared him more than he feared death, and kept himself drunk all the time because that fear was more than he could endure sober. Yara was very old—centuries old, men said, and added that he would live for ever because of the magic of his gem, which men called the Heart of the Elephant, for no better reason than they named his hold the Elephant's Tower.

The Cimmerian, engrossed in these thoughts, shrank quickly against the wall. Within the garden someone was passing, who walked with a measured stride. The listener heard the clink of steel. So after all a guard did pace those gardens. The Cimmerian waited, expected to hear him pass again, on the next round, but silence rested over the mysterious gardens.

At last curiosity overcame him. Leaping lightly he grasped the wall and swung himself up to the top with one arm. Lying flat on the broad coping, he looked down into the wide space between the walls. No shrubbery grew near him, though he saw some carefully trimmed bushes near the inner wall. The starlight fell on the even sward and somewhere a fountain tinkled.

The Cimmerian cautiously lowered himself down on the inside and drew his sword, staring about him. He was shaken by the nervousness of the wild at standing thus unprotected in the naked starlight, and he moved lightly around the curve of the wall, hugging its shadow, until he was even with the shrubbery he had noticed. Then he ran quickly toward it, crouching low, and almost tripped over a form that lay crumpled near the edges of the bushes.

A quick look to right and left showed him no enemy in sight at least, and he bent close to investigate. His keen eyes, even in the dim starlight, showed him a strongly built man in the silvered armor and crested helmet of the Zamorian royal guard. A shield and a spear lay near him, and it took but an instant's examination to show that he had been strangled. The barbarian glanced about uneasily. He knew that this man must be the guard he had heard pass his hiding-place by the wall. Only a short time had passed, yet in that interval nameless hands had reached out of the dark and choked out the soldier's life.

Straining his eyes in the gloom, he saw a hint of motion through the shrubs near the wall. Thither he glided, gripping his sword. He made no more noise than a panther stealing through the night, yet the man he was stalking heard. The Cimmerian had a dim glimpse of a huge bulk close to the wall felt relief that it was at least human; then the fellow wheeled quickly with a gasp that sounded like panic, made the first motion of a forward plunge, hands clutching, then recoiled as the Cimmerian's blade caught the starlight. For a tense instant neither spoke, standing ready for anything.

"You are no soldier," hissed the stranger at last. "You are a thief like myself."

"And who are you?" asked the Cimmerian in a suspicious whisper.

"Taurus of Nemedia."

The Cimmerian lowered his sword.

"I've heard of you. Men call you a prince of thieves." A low laugh answered him. Taurus was tall as the Cimmerian, and heavier; he was big-bellied and fat, but his every movement betokened a subtle dynamic magnetism, which was reflected in the keen eyes that glinted vitally, even in the starlight. He was barefooted and carried a coil of what looked like a thin, strong rope, knotted at regular intervals.

"Who are you?" he whispered.

"Conan, a Cimmerian," answered the other. "I came seeking a way to steal Yara's jewel, that men call the Elephant's Heart."

Conan sensed the man's great belly shaking in laughter, but it was not derisive.

"By Bel, god of thieves!" hissed Taurus. "I had thought only myself had courage to attempt that poaching. These Zamorians call themselves thieves—bah! Conan, I like your grit. I never shared an adventure with anyone, but by Bel, we'll attempt this together if you're willing.'

"Then you are after the gem, too?"

"What else? I've had my plans laid for months, but you, I think, have acted on a sudden impulse, my friend."

"You killed the soldier?"

"Of course. I slid over the wall when he was on the other side of the garden. I hid in the bushes; he heard me, or thought he heard something. When he came blundering over, it was no trick at all to get behind him and suddenly grip his neck and choke out his fool's life. He was like most men, half blind in the dark. A good thief should have eyes like a cat."

"You made one mistake," said Conan.

Taurus's eyes flashed angrily.

"I? I, a mistake? Impossible!"

"You should have dragged the body into the bushes."

"Said the novice to the master of the art. They will not change the guard until past midnight. Should any come searching for him now, and find his body, they would flee at once to Yara, bellowing the news, and give us time to escape. Were they not to find it, they'd go on beating up the bushes and catch us like rats in a trap."

"You are right," agreed Conan.

"So. Now attend. We waste time in this cursed discussion. There are no guards in the inner garden—human guards, I mean, though there are sentinels even more deadly. It was their presence which baffled me for so long, but I finally discovered a way to circumvent them."

"What of the soldiers in the lower part of the tower?"

"Old Yara dwells in the chambers above. By that route we will come—and go, I hope. Never mind asking me how. I have arranged a way. We'll steal down through the top of the tower and strangle old Yara before he can cast any of his accursed spells on us. At least we'll try; it's the chance of being turned into a spider or a toad, against the wealth and power of the world. All good thieves must know how to take risks."

"I'll go as far as any man," said Conan, slipping off his sandals.

"Then follow me." And turning, Taurus leaped up, caught the wall and drew himself up. The man's suppleness was amazing, considering his bulk; he seemed almost to glide up over the edge of the coping. Conan followed him, and lying flat on the broad top, they spoke in wary whispers.

"I see no light," Conan muttered. The lower part of the tower seemed much like that portion visible from outside the garden—a perfect, gleaming cylinder, with no apparent openings.

"There are cleverly constructed doors and windows," answered Taurus, "but they are closed. The soldiers breathe air that comes from above."

The garden was a vague pool of shadows, where feathery bushes and low spreading trees waved darkly in the starlight. Conan's wary soul felt the aura of waiting menace that brooded over it. He felt the burning glare of unseen eyes, and he caught a subtle scent that made the short hairs on his neck instinctively bristle as a hunting dog bristles at the scent of an ancient enemy.

"Follow me," whispered Taurus, "keep behind me, as you value your life."

Taking what looked like a copper tube from his girdle, the Nemedian dropped lightly to the sward inside the wall. Conan was close behind him, sword ready, but Taurus pushed him back, close to the wall, and showed no indication to advance, himself. His whole attitude was of tense expectancy, and his gaze, like Conan's, was fixed on the shadowy mass of shrubbery a few yards away. This shrubbery was shaken, although the breeze had died down. Then two great eyes blazed from the waving shadows, and behind them other sparks of fire glinted in the darkness.

"Lions!" muttered Conan.

"Aye. By day they are kept in subterranean caverns below the tower. That's why there are no guards in this garden."

Conan counted the eyes rapidly.

"Five in sight; maybe more back in the bushes. They'll charge in a moment—"

"Be silent!" hissed Taurus, and he moved out from the wall, cautiously as if treading on razors, lifting the slender tube. Low rumblings rose from the shadows and the blazing eyes moved forward. Conan could sense the great slavering jaws, the tufted tails lashing tawny sides. The air grew tense—the Cimmerian gripped his sword, expecting the charge and the irresistible hurtling of giant bodies. Then

Taurus brought the mouth of the tube to his lips and blew powerfully. A long jet of yellowish powder shot from the other end of the tube and billowed out instantly in a thick green-yellow cloud that settled over the shrubbery, blotting out the glaring eyes.

Taurus ran back hastily to the wall. Conan glared without understanding. The thick cloud hid the shrubbery, and from it no sound came.

"What is that mist?" the Cimmerian asked uneasily.

"Death!" hissed the Nemedian. "If a wind springs up and blows it back upon us, we must flee over the wall. But no, the wind is still, and now it is dissipating. Wait until it vanishes entirely. To breathe it is death."

Presently only yellowish shreds hung ghostily in the air; then they were gone, and Taurus motioned his companion forward. They stole toward the bushes, and Conan gasped. Stretched out in the shadows lay five great tawny shapes, the fire of their grim eyes dimmed for ever. A sweetish cloying scent lingered in the atmosphere.

"They died without a sound!" muttered the Cimmerian. "Taurus, what was that powder?"

"It was made from the black lotus, whose blossoms wave in the lost jungles of Khitai, where only the yellow-skulled priests of Yun dwell. Those blossoms strike dead any who smell of them."

Conan knelt beside the great forms, assuring himself that they were indeed beyond power of harm. He shook his head; the magic of the exotic lands was mysterious and terrible to the barbarians of the north.

"Why can you not slay the soldiers in the tower in the same way?" he asked.

"Because that was all the powder I possessed. The obtaining of it was a feat which in itself was enough to make me famous among the thieves of the world. I stole it out of a caravan bound for Stygia, and I lifted it, in its cloth-of-gold bag, out of the coils of the great serpent which guarded it, without awaking him. But come, in Bel's name! Are we to waste the night in discussion?"

They glided through the shrubbery to the gleaming foot of the tower, and there, with a motion enjoining silence, Taurus unwound his knotted cord, on one end of which was a strong steel hook. Conan saw his plan, and asked no questions as the Nemedian gripped the line a short distance below the hook, and began to swing it about his head. Conan laid his ear to the smooth wall and listened, but could hear nothing. Evidently the soldiers within did not suspect the presence of intruders, who had made no more sound than the night wind blowing through the trees. But a strange nervousness was on the barbarian; perhaps it was the lion-smell which was over everything.

Taurus threw the line with a smooth, ripping motion of his mighty arm. The hook curved upward and inward in a peculiar manner, hard to describe, and vanished over the jeweled rim. It apparently caught firmly, for cautious jerking and then hard pulling did not result in any slipping or giving.

"Luck the first cast," murmured Taurus. "I—"

It was Conan's savage instinct which made him wheel suddenly; for the death that was upon them made no sound. A fleeting glimpse showed the Cimmerian the giant tawny shape, rearing upright against the stars, towering over him for the death-stroke. No civilized man could have moved half so quickly as the barbarian moved. His sword flashed frostily in the starlight with every ounce of desperate nerve and thew behind it, and man and beast went down together.

Cursing incoherently beneath his breath, Taurus bent above the mass, and saw his companion's limbs move as he strove to drag himself from under the great weight that lay limply upon him. A glance showed the startled Nemedian that the lion was dead, its slanting skull split in half. He laid hold of the carcass, and by his aid, Conan thrust it aside and clambered up, still gripping his dripping sword.

"Are you hurt, man?" gasped Taurus, still bewildered by the stunning swiftness of that touch-and-go episode.

"No, by Crom!" answered the barbarian. "But that was as close a call as I've had in a life no ways tame. Why did not the cursed beast roar as he charged?"

"All things are strange in this garden," said Taurus. "The lions strike silently—and so do other deaths. But come—little sound was made in that slaying, but the soldiers might have heard, if they are not asleep or drunk. That beast was in some other part of the garden and escaped the death of the flowers, but surely there are no more. We must climb this cord—little need to ask a Cimmerian if he can."

"If it will bear my weight," grunted Conan, cleansing his sword on the grass.

"It will bear thrice my own," answered Taurus. "It was woven from the tresses of dead women, which I took from their tombs at midnight, and steeped in the deadly wine of the upas tree, to give it strength. I will go first—then follow me closely."

The Nemedian gripped the rope and, crooking a knee about it, began the ascent; he went up like a cat, belying the apparent clumsiness of his bulk. The Cimmerian followed. The cord swayed and turned on itself, but the climbers were not hindered; both had made more difficult climbs before. The jeweled rim glittered high above them, jutting out from the perpendicular—a fact which added greatly to the ease of the ascent.

Up and up they went, silently, the lights of the city spreading out further and further to their sight as they climbed, the stars above them more and more dimmed by the glitter of the jewels along the rim. Now Taurus reached up a hand and gripped the rim itself, pulling himself up and over. Conan paused a moment on the very edge, fascinated by the great frosty jewels whose gleams dazzled his eyes—diamonds, rubies, emeralds, sapphires, turquoises, moonstones, set thick as stars in the shimmering silver. At a distance their different gleams had seemed to merge into a pulsing white glare; but now, at close range, they shimmered with a million rainbow tints and lights, hypnotizing him with their scintillations.

"There is a fabulous fortune here, Taurus," he whispered; but the Nemedian answered impatiently. "Come on! If we secure the Heart, these and all other things shall be ours."

Conan climbed over the sparkling rim. The level of the tower's top was some feet below the gemmed ledge. It was flat, composed of some dark blue substance, set with gold that caught the starlight, so that the whole looked like a wide sapphire flecked with shining gold-dust. Across from the point where they had entered there seemed to be a sort of chamber, built upon the roof. It was of the same silvery material as the walls of the tower, adorned with designs worked in smaller gems; its single door was of gold, its surface cut in scales, and crusted with jewels that gleamed like ice.

Conan cast a glance at the pulsing ocean of lights which spread far below them, then glanced at Taurus. The Nemedian was drawing up his cord and coiling it. He showed Conan where the hook had caught—a fraction of an inch of the point had sunk under a great blazing jewel on the inner side of the rim.

"Luck was with us again," he muttered. "One would think that our combined weight would have torn that stone out. Follow me; the real risks of the venture begin now. We are in the serpent's lair, and we know not where he lies hidden."

Like stalking tigers they crept across the darkly gleaming floor and halted outside the sparkling door. With a deft and cautious hand Taurus tried it. It gave without resistance, and the companions looked in, tensed for anything. Over the Nemedian's shoulder Conan had a glimpse of a glittering chamber, the walls, ceiling and floor of which were crusted with great white jewels which lighted it brightly, and which seemed its only illumination. It seemed empty of life.

"Before we cut off our last retreat," hissed Taurus, "go you to the rim and look over on all sides; if you see any soldiers moving in the gardens, or anything suspicious, return and tell me. I will await you within this chamber."

Conan saw scant reason in this, and a faint suspicion of his companion touched his wary soul, but he did as Taurus requested. As he turned away, the Nemedian slipped inside the door and drew it shut behind him. Conan crept about the rim of the tower, returning to his starting-point without having seen any suspicious movement in the vaguely waving sea of leaves below. He turned toward the door—suddenly from within the chamber there sounded a strangled cry.

The Cimmerian leaped forward, electrified—the gleaming door swung open and Taurus stood framed in the cold blaze behind him. He swayed and his lips parted, but only a dry rattle burst from his throat. Catching at the golden door for support, he lurched out upon the roof, then fell headlong, clutching at his throat. The door swung to behind him.

Conan, crouching like a panther at bay, saw nothing in the room behind the stricken Nemedian, in the brief instant the door was partly open—unless it was not a trick of the light which made it seem as if a shadow darted across the gleaming door. Nothing followed Taurus out on the roof, and Conan bent above the man.

The Nemedian stared up with dilated, glazing eyes, that somehow held a terrible bewilderment. His hands clawed at his throat, his lips slobbered and gurgled; then suddenly he stiffened, and the astounded Cimmerian knew that he was dead. And he felt that Taurus had died without knowing what manner of death had stricken him. Conan glared bewilderedly at the cryptic golden door. In that empty room, with its glittering jeweled walls, death had come to the prince of thieves as swiftly and mysteriously as he had dealt doom to the lions in the gardens below.

Gingerly the barbarian ran his hands over the man's half-naked body, seeking a wound. But the only marks of violence were between his shoulders, high up near the base of his bull-neck—three small wounds, which looked as if three nails had been driven deep in the flesh and withdrawn. The edges of these wounds were black, and a faint smell as of putrefaction was evident. Poisoned darts? thought Conan—but in that case the missiles should be still in the wounds.

Cautiously he stole toward the golden door, pushed it open, and looked inside. The chamber lay empty, bathed in the cold, pulsing glow of the myriad jewels. In the very center of the ceiling he idly noted a curious design—a black eight-sided pattern, in the center of which four gems glittered with a red flame unlike the white blaze of the other jewels. Across the room there was another door, like the one in which he stood, except that it was not carved in the scale pattern. Was it from that door that death had come?—and having struck down its victim, had it retreated by the same way?

Closing the door behind him, the Cimmerian advanced into the chamber. His bare feet made no sound on the crystal floor. There were no chairs or tables in the chamber, only three or four silken couches, embroidered with gold and worked in strange serpentine designs, and several silver-bound mahogany chests. Some were sealed with heavy golden locks; others lay open, their carven lids thrown back, revealing heaps of jewels in a careless riot of splendor to the Cimmerian's astounded eyes. Conan swore beneath his breath; already he had looked upon more wealth that night than he had ever dreamed existed in all the world, and he grew dizzy thinking of what must be the value of the jewel he sought.

He was in the center of the room now, going stooped forward, head thrust out warily, sword advanced, when again death struck at him soundlessly. A flying shadow that swept across the gleaming floor was his only warning, and his instinctive sidelong leap all that saved his life. He had a flashing glimpse of a hairy black horror that swung past him with a clashing of frothing fangs, and something splashed on his bare shoulder that burned like drops of liquid hellfire. Springing back, sword high, he saw the horror strike the floor, wheel and scuttle toward him with appalling speed—a gigantic black spider, such as men see only in nightmare dreams.

It was as large as a pig, and its eight thick hairy legs drove its ogreish body over the floor at headlong pace; its four evilly gleaming eyes shone with a horrible intelligence, and its fangs dripped venom that Conan knew, from the burning of his shoulder where only a few drops had splashed as the thing struck and missed, was laden with swift death. This was the killer that had dropped from its perch in the middle of the ceiling on a strand of its web, on the neck of the Nemedian. Fools that they were not to have suspected that the upper chambers would be guarded as well as the lower!

These thoughts flashed briefly through Conan's mind as the monster rushed. He leaped high, and it passed beneath him, wheeled and charged back. This time he evaded its rush with a sidewise leap, and struck back like a cat. His sword severed one of the hairy legs, and again he barely saved himself as the monstrosity swerved at him, fangs clicking fiendishly. But the creature did not press the pursuit; turning, it scuttled across the crystal floor and ran up the wall to the ceiling, where it crouched for an instant, glaring down at him with its fiendish red eyes. Then without warning it launched itself through space, trailing a strand of slimy grayish stuff.

Conan stepped back to avoid the hurtling body—then ducked frantically, just in time to escape being snared by the flying web-rope. He saw the monster's intent and sprang toward the door, but it was quicker, and a sticky strand cast across the door made him a prisoner. He dared not try to cut it with his sword; he knew the stuff would cling to the blade, and before he could shake it loose, the fiend would be sinking its fangs into his back.

Then began a desperate game, the wits and quickness of the man matched against the fiendish craft and speed of the giant spider. It no longer scuttled across the floor in a direct charge, or swung its body through the air at him. It raced about the ceiling and the walls, seeking to snare him in the long loops of sticky gray web-strands, which it flung with a devilish accuracy. These strands were thick as ropes, and Conan knew that once they were coiled about him, his desperate strength would not be enough to tear him free before the monster struck.

All over the chamber went on that devil's game, in utter silence except for the quick breathing of the man, the low scuff of his bare feet on the shining floor, the castanet rattle of the monstrosity's fangs. The gray strands lay in coils on the floor; they were looped along the walls; they overlaid the jewel-chests and silken couches, and hung in dusky festoons from the jeweled ceiling. Conan's steel-trap quickness of eye and muscle had kept him untouched, though the sticky loops had passed him so close they rasped his naked hide. He knew he could not always avoid them; he not only had to watch the strands swinging from the ceiling, but to keep his eye on the floor, lest he trip in the coils that lay there. Sooner or later a gummy loop would writhe about him, python-like, and then, wrapped like a cocoon, he would lie at the monster's mercy.

The spider raced across the chamber floor, the gray rope waving out behind it. Conan leaped high, clearing a couch—with a quick wheel the fiend ran up the wall, and the strand, leaping off the floor like a live thing, whipped about the Cimmerian's ankle. He caught himself on his hands as he fell, jerking frantically at the web which held him like a pliant vise, or the coil of a python. The hairy devil was racing down the wall to complete its capture. Stung to frenzy, Conan caught up a jewel chest and hurled it with all his strength. It was a move toe monster was not expecting. Full in the midst of the branching black legs the massive missile struck, smashing against the wall with a muffled sickening crunch. Blood and greenish slime spattered, and the shattered mass fell with the burst gem-chest to the floor. The crushed black body lay among the flaming riot of jewels that spilled over it; the hairy legs moved aimlessly, the dying eyes glittered redly among the twinkling gems.

Conan glared about, but no other horror appeared, and he set himself to working free of the web. The substance clung tenaciously to his ankle and his hands, but at last he was free, and taking up his sword, he picked his way among the gray coils and loops to the inner door. What horrors lay within he did not know. The Cimmerian's blood was up, and since he had come so far, and overcome so much peril, he was determined to go through to the grim finish of the adventure, whatever that might be. And he felt that the jewel he sought was not among the many so carelessly strewn about the gleaming chamber.

Stripping off the loops that fouled the inner door, he found that it, like the other, was not locked. He wondered if the soldiers below were still unaware of his presence. Well, he was high above their heads, and if tales were to be believed, they were used to strange noises in the tower above them—sinister sounds, and screams of agony and horror.

Yara was on his mind, and he was not altogether comfortable as he opened the golden door. But he saw only a flight of silver steps leading down, dimly lighted by what means he could not ascertain. Down these he went silently, gripping his sword. He heard no sound, and came presently to an ivory door, set with bloodstones. He listened, but no sound came from within; only thin wisps of smoke drifted lazily from beneath the door, bearing a curious exotic odor unfamiliar to the Cimmerian. Below him the silver stair wound down to vanish in the dimness, and up that shadowy well no sound floated; he had an eerie feeling that he was alone in a tower occupied only by ghosts and phantoms.

Chapter 3

Cautiously he pressed against the ivory door and it swung silently inward. On the shimmering threshold Conan stared like a wolf in strange surroundings, ready to fight or flee on the instant. He was looking into a large chamber with a domed golden ceiling; the walls were of green jade, the floor of ivory, partly covered by thick rugs. Smoke and exotic scent of incense floated up from a brazier on a golden tripod, and behind it sat an idol on a sort of marble couch. Conan stared aghast; the image had the body of a man, naked, and green in color; but the head was one of nightmare and madness. Too large for the human body, it had no attributes of humanity. Conan stared at the wide flaring ears, the curling proboscis, on either side of which stood white tusks tipped with round golden balls. The eyes were closed, as if in sleep.

This then, was the reason for the name, the Tower of the Elephant, for the head of the thing was much like that of the beasts described by the Shemitish wanderer. This was Yara's god; where then should the gem be, but concealed in the idol, since the stone was called the Elephant's Heart?

As Conan came forward, his eyes fixed on the motionless idol, the eyes of the thing opened suddenly! The Cimmerian froze in his tracks. It was no image—it was a living thing, and he was trapped in its chamber!

That he did not instantly explode in a burst of murderous frenzy is a fact that measures his horror, which paralyzed him where he stood. A civilized man in his position would have sought doubtful refuge in the conclusion that he was insane; it did not occur to the Cimmerian to doubt his senses. He knew he was face to face with a demon of the Elder World, and the realization robbed him of all his faculties except sight.

The trunk of the horror was lifted and quested about, the topaz eyes stared unseeingly, and Conan knew the monster was blind. With the thought came a thawing of his frozen nerves, and he began to back silently toward the door. But the creature heard. The sensitive trunk stretched toward him, and Conan's horror froze him again when the being spoke, in a strange, stammering voice that never changed its key or timbre. The Cimmerian knew that those jaws were never built or intended for human speech.

"Who is here? Have you come to torture me again, Yara? Will you never be done? Oh, Yag-kosha, is there no end to agony?"

Tears rolled from the sightless eyes, and Conan's gaze strayed to the limbs stretched on the marble couch. And he knew the monster would not rise to attack him. He knew the marks of the rack, and the searing brand of the flame, and tough-souled as he was, he stood aghast at the ruined deformities which his reason told him had once been limbs as comely as his own. And suddenly all fear and repulsion went from him, to be replaced by a great pity. What this monster was, Conan could not know, but the evidences of its sufferings were so terrible and pathetic that a strange aching sadness came over the Cimmerian, he knew not why. He only felt that he was looking upon a cosmic tragedy, and he shrank with shame, as if the guilt of a whole race were laid upon him.

"I am not Yara," he said. "I am only a thief. I will not harm you."

"Come near that I may touch you," the creature faltered, and Conan came near unfearingly, his sword hanging forgotten in his hand. The sensitive trunk came out and groped over his face and shoulders, as a blind man gropes, and its touch was light as a girl's hand.

"You are not of Yara's race of devils," sighed the creature. "The clean, lean fierceness of the wastelands marks you. I know your people from of old, whom I knew by another name in the long, long ago when another world lifted its jeweled spires to the stars. There is blood on your fingers."

"A spider in the chamber above and a lion in the garden," muttered Conan.

"You have slain a man too, this night," answered the other. "And there is death in the tower above. I feel; I know."

"Aye," muttered Conan. "The prince of all thieves lies there dead from the bite of a vermin."

"So—and so!" The strange inhuman voice rose in a sort of low chant. "A slaying in the tavern and a slaying on the road—I know; I feel. And the third will make the magic of which not even Yara dreams—oh, magic of deliverance, green gods of Yag!"

Again tears fell as the tortured body was rocked to and fro in the grip of varied emotions. Conan looked on, bewildered.

Then the convulsions ceased; the soft, sightless eyes were turned toward the Cimmerian, the trunk beckoned.

"Oh man, listen," said the strange being. "I am foul and monstrous to you, am I not? Nay, do not answer; I know. But you would seem as strange to me, could I see you. There are many worlds besides this earth, and life takes many shapes. I am neither god nor demon, but flesh and blood like yourself, though the substance differ in part, and the form be cast in a different mold.

"I am very old, oh man of the waste countries; long and long ago I came to this planet with others of my world, from the green planet Yag, which circles for ever in the outer fringe of this universe. We swept through space on mighty wings that drove us through the cosmos quicker than light, because we had warred with the kings of Yag and were defeated and outcast. But we could never return, for on earth our wings withered from our shoulders. Here we abode apart from earthly life. We fought the strange and terrible forms of life which then walked the earth, so that we became feared, and were not molested in the dim jungles of the east, where we had our abode.

"We saw men grow from the ape and build the shining cities of Valusia, Kamelia, Commoria, and their sisters. We saw them reel before the thrusts of the heathen Atlanteans and Picts and Lemurians. We saw the oceans rise and engulf Atlantis and Lemuria, and the isles of the Picts, and shining cities of civilization. We saw the survivors of Pictdom and Atlantis build their stone-age empires, and go down to ruin, locked in bloody wars. We saw the Picts sink into abysmal savagery, the Atlanteans into apedom again. We saw new savages drift southward in conquering waves from the Arctic circle to build a new civilization, with new kingdoms called Nemedia, and Koth, and Aquilonia and their sisters. We saw your people rise under a new name from the jungles of the apes that had been Atlanteans. We saw the descendants of the Lemurians who had survived the cataclysm, rise again through savagery and ride westward as Hyrkanians. And we saw this race of devils, survivors of the ancient civilization that was before Atlantis sank, come once more into culture and power—this accursed kingdom of Zamora.

"All this we saw, neither aiding nor hindering the immutable cosmic law, and one by one we died; for we of Yag are not immortal, though our lives are as the lives of planets and constellations. At last I alone was left, dreaming of old times among the ruined temples of jungle-lost Khitai, worshiped as a god by an ancient yellow-skinned race. Then came Yara, versed in dark knowledge handed down through the days of barbarism, since before Atlantis sank.

"First he sat at my feet and learned wisdom. But he was not satisfied with what I taught him, for it was white magic, and he wished evil lore, to enslave kings and glut a fiendish ambition. I would teach him none of the black secrets I had gained, through no wish of mine, through the eons.

"But his wisdom was deeper than I had guessed; with guile gotten among the dusky tombs of dark Stygia, he trapped me into divulging a secret I had not intended to bare; and turning my own power upon me, he enslaved me. Ah, gods of Yag, my cup has been bitter since that hour!

"He brought me up from the lost jungles of Khitai where the gray apes danced to the pipes of the yellow priests, and offerings of fruit and wine heaped my broken altars. No more was I a god to kindly jungle-folk—I was slave to a devil in human form."

Again tears stole from the unseeing eyes.

"He pent me in this tower which at his command I built for him in a single night. By fire and rack he mastered me, and by strange unearthly tortures you would not understand. In agony I would long ago have taken my own life, if I could. But he kept me alive—mangled, blinded, and broken—to do his foul bidding. And for three hundred years I have done his bidding, from this marble couch, blackening my soul with cosmic sins, and staining my wisdom with crimes, because I had no other choice. Yet not all my ancient secrets has he wrested from me, and my last gift shall be the sorcery of the Blood and the Jewel.

"For I feel the end of time draw near. You are the hand of Fate. I beg of you, take the gem you will find on yonder altar."

Conan turned to the gold and ivory altar indicated, and took up a great round jewel, clear as crimson crystal; and he knew that this was the Heart of the Elephant.

"Now for the great magic, the mighty magic, such as earth has not seen before, and shall not see again, through a million million of millenniums. By my life-blood I conjure it, by blood born on the green breast of Yag, dreaming far-poised in the great blue vastness of Space.

"Take your sword, man, and cut out my heart; then squeeze it so that the blood will flow over the red stone. Then go you down these stairs and enter the ebony chamber where Yara sits wrapped in lotus-dreams of evil. Speak his name and he will awaken. Then lay this gem before him, and say, 'Yag-kosha gives you a last gift and a last enchantment.' Then get you from the tower quickly; fear not, your way shall be made clear. The life of man is not the life of Yag, nor is human death the death of Yag. Let me be free of this cage of broken blind flesh, and I will once more be Yogah of Yag, morning-crowned and shining, with wings to fly, and feet to dance, and eyes to see, and hands to break."

Uncertainly Conan approached, and Yag-kosha, or Yogah, as if sensing his uncertainty, indicated where he should strike. Conan set his teeth and drove the sword deep. Blood streamed over the blade and his hand, and the monster started convulsively, then lay back quite still. Sure that life had fled, at least life as he understood it, Conan set to work on his grisly task and quickly brought forth something that he felt must be the strange being's heart, though it differed curiously from any he had ever seen. Holding the pulsing organ over the blazing jewel, he pressed it with bold hands, and a rain of blood fell on the stone. To his surprise, it did not run off, but soaked into the gem, as water is absorbed by a sponge.

Holding the jewel gingerly, he went out of the fantastic and came upon the silver steps. He did not look back; he instinctively felt that some transmutation was taking place in the body on the marble couch, and he further felt that it was of a sort not to be witnessed by human eyes.

He closed the ivory door behind him and without hesitation descended the silver steps. It did not occur to him to ignore the instructions given him. He halted at an ebony door, in the center of which was a grinning silver skull, and pushed it open. He looked into a chamber of ebony and jet, and saw, on a black silken couch, a tall, spare form reclining. Yara the priest and sorcerer lay before him, his eyes open and dilated with the fumes of the yellow lotus, far-staring, as if fixed on gulfs and nighted abysses beyond human ken.

"Yara!" said Conan, like a judge pronouncing doom. "Awaken!"

The eyes cleared instantly and became cold and cruel as a vulture's. The tall silken-clad form lifted erect, and towered gauntly above the Cimmerian.

"Dog!" His hiss was like the voice of a cobra. "What do you here?"

Conan laid the jewel on the ebony table.

"He who sent this gem bade me say, 'Yag-kosha gives you a last gift and a last enchantment.'"

Yara recoiled, his dark face ashy. The jewel was no longer crystal-clear; its murky depths pulsed and throbbed, and curious smoky waves of changing color passed over its smooth surface. As if drawn hypnotically, Yara bent over the table and gripped the gem in his hands, staring into its shadowed depths, as if it were a magnet to draw the shuddering soul from his body. And as Conan looked, he thought that his eyes must be playing him tricks. For when Yara had risen up from his couch, the priest had seemed gigantically tall; yet now he saw that Yara's head would scarcely come to his shoulder. He blinked, puzzled, and for the first time that night, doubted his own senses. Then with a shock he realized that the priest was shrinking in stature—was growing smaller before his very gaze.

With a detached feeling he watched, as a man might watch a play; immersed in a feeling of overpowering unreality, the Cimmerian was no longer sure of his own identity; he only knew that he was looking upon the external evidence of the unseen play of vast Outer forces, beyond his understanding.

Now Yara was no bigger than a child; now like an infant he sprawled on the table, still grasping the jewel. And now the sorcerer suddenly realized his fate, and he sprang up, releasing the gem. But still he dwindled, and Conan saw a tiny, pygmy figure rushing wildly about the ebony table-top, waving tiny arms and shrieking in a voice that was like the squeak of an insect.

Now he had shrunk until the great jewel towered above him like a hill, and Conan saw him cover his eyes with his hands, as if to shield them from the glare, as he staggered about like a madman. Conan sensed that some unseen magnetic force was pulling Yara to the gem. Thrice he raced wildly about it in a narrowing circle, thrice he strove to turn and run out across the table; then with a scream that echoed faintly in the ears of the watcher, the priest threw up his arms and ran straight toward the blazing globe.

Bending close, Conan saw Yara clamber up the smooth, curving surface, impossibly, like a man climbing a glass mountain. Now the priest stood on the top, still with tossing arms, invoking what grisly names only the gods know. And suddenly he sank into the very heart of the jewel, as a man sinks into a sea, and Conan saw the smoky waves close over his head. Now he saw him in the crimson heart of the jewel, once more crystal-clear, as a man sees a scene far away, tiny with great distance. And into the heart came a green, shining winged figure with the body of a man and the head of an elephant—no longer blind or crippled. Yara threw up his arms and fled as a madman flees, and on his heels came the avenger. Then, like the bursting of a bubble, the great jewel vanished in a rainbow burst of iridescent gleams, and the ebony table-top lay bare and deserted—as bare, Conan somehow knew, as the marble couch in the chamber above, where the body of that strange transcosmic being called Yag-kosha and Yogah had lain.

The Cimmerian turned and fled from the chamber, down the silver stairs. So mazed was he that it did not occur to him to escape from the tower by the way he had entered it. Down that winding, shadowy silver well he ran, and came into a large chamber at the foot of the gleaming stairs. There he halted for an instant; he had come into the room of soldiers. He saw the glitter of their silver corselets, the sheen of their jeweled sword-hilts. They sat slumped at the banquet board, their dusky plumes waving somberly above their drooping helmeted heads; they lay among their dice and fallen goblets on the wine-stained lapis lazuli floor. And he knew that they were dead. The promise had been made, the word kept; whether sorcery or magic or the falling shadow of great green wings had stilled the revelry, Conan could not know, but his way had been made clear. And a silver door stood open, framed in the whiteness of dawn.

Into the waving green gardens came the Cimmerian, and as the dawn wind blew upon him with the cool fragrance of luxuriant growths, he started like a man waking from a dream. He turned back uncertainly, to stare at the cryptic tower he had just left. Was he bewitched and enchanted? Had he dreamed all that had seemed to have passed? As he looked he saw the gleaming tower sway against the crimson dawn, its jewel-crusted rim sparkling in the growing light, and crash into shining shards.

⚔

The premier Jirel of Joiry story by Catherine Lucille Moore (1911–1987), "Black God's Kiss," appeared in Weird Tales, *October 1934. Jirel, the first heroine of the sword and sorcery, is often cited as the first (or one of earliest) characters to be modeled on Conan. I, however, side with those who see her development as analogous to Conan rather than its descendant. Jirel's willpower, determination, and temperament form the core of Moore's six Jirel stories (one, co-written with Henry Kuttner, combined the swordswoman with Moore's other signature character, Northwest Smith). Moore's use of horror is integral to the tales, and this is especially true in "Hellsgarde" with its nightmarish atmosphere of dread. As Algys Budrys noted in 1970, "the events which occur to Jirel, as she struggles with the half-understood forces of darkness in her quasi-medieval world, are all things that play on the heart of what being you and me is all about." The swordswoman certainly deals with dark forces in "Hellsgarde" (*Weird Tales, *April 1939), the final Jirel of Joiry story.*

HELLSGARDE

C. L. Moore

Jirel of Joiry drew rein at the edge of the hill and sat awhile in silence, looking out and down. So this was Hellsgarde. She had seen it many times in her mind's eye as she saw it now from the high hill in the yellow light of sunset that turned every pool of the marshes to shining glass. The long causeway to the castle stretched out narrowly between swamps and reeds up to the gate of that grim and eerie fortress set alone among the quicksands. This same castle in the marshes, seen at evening from the high hilltop, had haunted her dreams for many nights now.

"You'll find it by sunset only, my lady," Guy of Garlot had told her with a sidelong grin marring his comely dark face. "Mists and wilderness ring it round, and there's magic in the swamps about Hellsgarde. Magic—and worse, if legends speak truth. You'll never come upon it save at evening."

Sitting her horse now on the hilltop, she remembered the grin in his black eyes and cursed him in a whisper. There was such a silence over the whole evening world that by instinct she dared not speak aloud. Dared not? It was no normal silence. Bird-song did not break it, and no leaves rustled. She huddled her shoulders together a little under the tunic of link-mail she wore and prodded her horse forward down the hill.

Guy of Garlot—Guy of Garlot! The hoofbeats thumped out the refrain all the way downhill. Black Guy with his thinly smiling lips and his slanted dark eyes and his unnatural comeliness—unnatural because Guy, within, was ugly as sin itself. It seemed no design of the good God that such sinfulness should wear Guy's dark beauty for a fleshly garment.

The horse hesitated at the head of the causeway which stretched between the marsh pools toward Hellsgarde. Jirel shook the reins impatiently and smiled a one-sided smile downward at his twitching ears.

"I go as loathly as you," she told him. "I go wincing under spurs too, my pretty. But go I must, and you too." And she cursed Guy again in a lingering whisper as the slow hoofbeats reverberated upon the stone arches of the causeway.

Beyond it loomed Hellsgarde, tall and dark against the sunset. All around her lay the yellow light of evening, above her in the sky, below her in the marshy pools beneath which quicksands quivered. She wondered who last had ridden this deserted causeway in the yellow glow of sunset, under what dreadful compulsion.

For no one sought Hellsgarde for pleasure. It was Guy of Garlot's slanting grin that drove Jirel across the marshes this evening—Guy and the knowledge that a score of her best men-at-arms lay shivering tonight in his dripping dungeons with no hope of life save the hope that she might buy their safety. And no riches could tempt Black Guy, not even Jirel's smoothly curving beauty and the promise of her full-lipped smile. And Garlot Castle, high on its rocky mountain peak, was impregnable against even Jirel's masterfully planned attacks. Only one thing could tempt the dark lord of Garlot, and that a thing without a name.

"It lies in Hellsgarde, my lady," he had told her with that hateful smooth civility which his sleek grin so belied. "And it is indeed Hell-guarded. Andred of Hellsgarde died defending it two hundred years ago, and I have coveted it all my life. But I love living, my lady! I would not venture into Hellsgarde for all the wealth in Christendom. If you want your men back alive, bring me the treasure that Andred died to save."

"But what is it, coward?"

Guy had shrugged. "Who knows? Whence it came and what it was no man can say now. You know the tale as well as I, my lady. He carried it in a leather casket locked with an iron key. It must have been small—but very precious. Precious enough to die for, in the end—as I do not propose to die, my lady! You fetch it to me and buy twenty lives in the bargain."

She had sworn at him for a coward, but in the end she had gone. For after all, she was Joiry. Her men were hers to bully and threaten and command, but they were hers to die for too, if need be. She was afraid, but she remembered her men in Garlot's dungeons with the rack and the boot awaiting them, and she rode on.

The causeway was so long. Sunset had begun to tarnish a little in the bright pools of the marsh, and she could look up at the castle now without being blinded by the dazzle beyond. A mist had begun to rise in level layers from the water, and the smell of it was not good in her nostrils.

Hellsgarde—Hellsgarde and Andred. She did not want to remember the hideous old story, but she could not keep her mind off it this evening. Andred had been a big, violent man, passionate and willful and very cruel. Men hated him, but when the tale of his dying spread abroad even his enemies pitied Andred of Hellsgarde.

For the rumor of his treasure had drawn at last besiegers whom he could not overcome. Hellsgarde gate had fallen and the robber nobles who captured the castle searched in vain for the precious casket which Andred guarded. Torture could not loosen his lips, though they tried very terribly to make him speak. He was a powerful man, stubborn and brave. He lived a long while under torment, but he would not betray the hiding-place of his treasure.

They tore him limb from limb at last and cast his dismembered body into the quicksands, and came away empty-handed. No one ever found Andred's treasure.

Since then for two hundred years Hellsgarde had lain empty. It was a dismal place, full of mists and fevers from the marsh, and Andred did not lie easy in the quicksands where his murderers had cast him. Dismembered and scattered broadcast over the marshes, yet he would not lie quiet. He had treasured his mysterious wealth with a love stronger than death itself, and legend said he walked Hellsgarde as jealously in death as in life.

In the two hundred years searchers had gone fearfully to ransack the empty halls of Hellsgarde for that casket—gone and vanished. There was magic in the marshes, and a man could come upon the castle only by sunset, and after sunset Andred's violent ghost rose out of the quicksands to guard the thing he died for. For generations now no one had been so foolhardy as to venture upon the way Jirel rode tonight.

She was drawing near the gateway. There was a broad platform before it, just beyond the place where Andred's drawbridge had once barred the approach to Hellsgarde. Long ago the gap in the causeway had been filled in with rubble by searchers who would reach the castle on horseback, and Jirel had thought of passing the night upon that platform under the gate arch, so that dawn might find her ready to begin her search.

But—the mists between her and the castle had thickened, and her eyes might be playing her false—but were not those the shapes of men drawn up in a double row before the doorway of Hellsgarde? Hellsgarde, that had stood empty and haunted these two hundred years? Blinking through the dazzle of sun on water and the thickening of the mists, she rode on toward the gateway. She could feel the horse trembling between her knees, and with every step he grew more and more reluctant to go on. She set her teeth and forced him ahead resolutely, swallowing her own terror.

They *were* the figures of men, two rows of them, waiting motionless before the gate. But even through the mist and the sun-dazzle she could see that something was wrong. They were so still—so unearthly still as they faced her. And the horse was shying and trembling until she could scarcely force him forward.

She was quite near before she saw what was wrong, though she knew that at every forward step the obscure frightfulness about these guardsmen grew greater. But she was almost upon them before she realized why. They were all dead.

The captain at their front stood slumped down upon the great spear that propped him on his feet, driven through his throat so that the point stood out above his neck as he sagged there, his head dragging forward until his cheek lay against the shaft which transfixed him.

And so stood all the rest, behind him in a double row, reeling drunkenly upon the spears driven through throat or chest or shoulder to prop them on their feet in the hideous semblance of life.

So the company of dead men kept guard before the gateway of Hellsgarde. It was not unfitting—dead men guarding a dead castle in the barren deadlands of the swamp.

Jirel sat her horse before them for a long moment in silence, feeling the sweat gather on her forehead, clenching her hands on the pommel of the saddle. So far as she knew, no other living person in decades had ridden the long causeway to Hellsgarde; certainly no living man had dwelt in these haunted towers in generations. Yet—here stood the dead men reeling against the spears which had slain them but would not let them fall. Why?—how?—when? . . .

Death was no new thing to Jirel. She had slain too many men herself to fear it. But the ghastly unexpectedness of this dead guard! It was one thing to steel oneself to enter an empty ruin, quite another to face a double row of standing dead men whose blood still ran in dark rivulets, wetly across the stones at their feet. Still wet—they had died today, then. Today while she struggled cursing through the wilderness something had slain them here, something had made a jest of death as it propped them on their dead feet with their dead faces toward the causeway along which she must come riding. Had that something expected her? Could the dead Andred have known—?

She caught herself with a little shudder and shrugged beneath the mail, clenching her fingers on the pommel, swallowing hard. (Remember your men—remember Guy of Garlot—remember that you are Joiry!) The memory of Guy's comely face, bright with mockery, put steel into her and she snapped her chin up with a murmured oath. These men were dead—they could not hinder her . . .

Was that motion among the ghastly guard? Her heart leaped to her throat and she gripped the saddle between nervous knees with a reflex action that made the horse shudder. For one of the men in the row before her was slipping silently toward the flagstones. Had the spear-butt slid on the bloody tiles? Had a breeze dislodged his precarious balance? There was no breeze. But with a curious little sigh from collapsing lungs he folded gently downward to his knees, to his side, to a flattened proneness on the stones. And a dark stream of blood trickled from his mouth to snake across the pavement as he lay there.

Jirel sat frozen. It was a nightmare. Only in nightmares could such things happen. This unbearable silence in the dying sunset, no breeze, no motion, no sound. Not even a ripple upon the mirroring waters lying so widely around her below the causeway, light draining from their surfaces. Sky and water were paling as if all life receded from about her, leaving only Jirel on her trembling horse facing the dead men and the dead castle. She scarcely dared move lest the thump of her mount's feet on the stones dislodge the balance of another man. And she thought she could not bear to see motion again among those motionless ranks. She could not bear it, and yet—and yet if something did not break the spell soon the screams gathering in her throat would burst past her lips and she knew she would never stop screaming.

A harsh scraping sounded beyond the dead guardsmen. Her heart squeezed itself to a stop. And then the blood began to thunder through her veins and her heart leaped and fell and leaped again in a frenzied pounding against the mail of her tunic.

For beyond the men the great door of Hellsgarde was swinging open. She gripped her knees against the saddle until her thighs ached, and her knuckles were bone-white upon the pommel. She made no move toward the great sword at her side. What use is a sword against dead men?

But it was no dead man who looked out under the arch of the doorway, stooped beneath his purple tunic with the heartening glow of firelight from beyond reddening his bowed shoulders. There was something odd about his pale, pinched face upturned to hers across the double line of dead defenders between them. After a moment she recognized what it was—he had the face of a hunchback, but there was no deformity upon his shoulders. He stooped a little as if with weariness, but he carried no hump. Yet it was the face of a cripple if she had ever seen one. His back was straight, but could his soul be? Would the good God have put the sign of deformity upon a human creature without cause? But he was human—he was real. Jirel sighed from the bottom of her lungs.

"Good evening to you, my lady," said the hunchback (but he was not humped) in a flat, ingratiating voice.

"*These*—did not find it good," said Jirel shortly, gesturing. And the man grinned.

"My master's jest," he said.

Jirel looked back to the rows of standing dead, her heart quieting a little. Yes, a man might find a grim sort of humor in setting such a guard before his door. If a living man had done it, for an understanding reason, then the terror of the unknown was gone. But the man—

"Your master?" she echoed.

"My lord Alaric of Hellsgarde—you did not know?"

"Know what?" demanded Jirel flatly. She was beginning to dislike the fellow's sidelong unctuousness.

"Why, that my lord's family has taken residence here after many generations away."

"Sir Alaric is of Andred's kin?"

"He is."

Jirel shrugged mentally. It was God's blessing to feel the weight of terror lift from her, but this would complicate matters. She had not known that Andred left descendants, though it might well be so. And if they lived here, then be sure they would already have ransacked the castle from keep to dungeon for that nameless treasure which Andred had died to save and had not yet forsaken, were rumor true. Had they found it? There was only one way to learn that.

"I am nighted in the marshes," she said as courteously as she could manage. "Will your master give me shelter until morning?"

The hunchback's eyes—(but he was no hunchback, she must stop thinking of him so!)—his eyes slid very quickly, yet very comprehensively, from her tanned and red-lipped face downward over the lifting curves of her under the molding chainmail, over the bare brown keens under slim, steel-greaved legs. There was a deeper unctuousness in his voice as he said:

"My master will make you very welcome, lady. Ride in."

Jirel kicked her horse's flank and guided him, snorting and trembling, through the gap in the ranks of dead men which the falling soldier had left. He was a battle-charger, he was used to dead men, yet he shuddered as he minced through these lines.

The courtyard within was warm with the light of the great fire in its center. Around it a cluster of loutish men in leather jerkins looked up as she passed.

"Wat, Piers—up, men!" snapped the man with the hunchback's face. "Take my lady's horse."

Jirel hesitated a moment before she swung from the saddle, her eyes dubious upon the faces around her. She thought she had never seen such brutish men before, and she wondered at the lord who dared employ them. Her own followers were tough enough, reckless, hard fellows without fear or scruple. But at least they were men. These louts around the fire seemed scarcely more than beasts; let greed or anger stir them and no man alive could control their wildness. She wondered with what threats of punishment the lord Alaric held sway here, what sort of man he must be to draw his guard from the very dregs of humanity.

The two who took her horse started at her under shaggy beetle-brows. She flashed them a poison glance as she turned to follow the purple cloak of her guide. Her eyes were busy. Hellsgarde had been a strong fortress in Andred's day; under Alaric it was well manned, but she thought she sensed a queer, hovering sullenness in the very air as she followed her guide across the courtyard, down a passageway, under an arch into the great hall.

The shadows of two hundred haunted years hovered under the lofty roof-beams. It was cold here, damp with the breath of the swamps outside, dark with two centuries of ugly legend and the terrible tradition of murder. But Alaric before the fire in his scarlet tunic seemed pleasantly at home. The great blaze roaring up the chimney from six-foot logs drove back the chill and the dark and the damp a little in a semicircle about the fireplace, and in that semicircle a little company of brightly clad people sat silent, watching Jirel and her guide cross the echoing flags of the great hall toward them.

It was a pleasant scene, warm and firelit and bright with color, but even at a distance, something was wrong—something in the posture of the people crouching before the blaze, something in their faces. Jirel knew a moment of wild wonder if all this were real. Did she really walk a haunted ruin empty two hundred years? Were the people flesh and blood, or only the bright shadows of her own imagination that had so desperately longed for companionship in the haunted marsh?

But no, there was nothing illusive about Alaric in his high-backed chair, his face a pale oval watching her progress. A humped dwarf leaned above his shoulder, fingers suspended over his lute-strings as he stared. On cushions and low benches by the fire a handful of women and girls, two young boys in bright blue, a pair of greyhounds with the firelight scarlet in their eyes—these made up the rest of the company.

Jirel's narrow yellow gaze summed them up as she crossed the hall. Striding smoothly in her thigh-length hauberk, she knew she was a figure on which a man's eyes must linger. Her supple height, the pleasant smooth curves of her under mail, the long, shapely legs beneath the linked metal of her hauberk, the swinging of the long sword whose weight upon its belt pulled in her waist to tigerish slimness—Alaric's eyes missed nothing of all these. Deliberately she tossed the dark cloak back over her shoulders, letting the firelight take the sleek mailed curves of her in a bright glimmer, flash from the shining greaves that clasped her calves. It was not her way to postpone the inevitable. Let Alaric learn in his first long stare how splendid a creature was Joiry's lady. And as for those women at his feet—well, let them know too.

She swaggered to a halt before Alaric, resting a hand on her sword-hilt, tossing back the cloak that had swirled about her as she swung to a stop. His face, half in the shadow of the chair, tilted up to her leanly. Here was no burly brute of a man such as she had half expected on the evidence of the men-at-arms he kept. He was of middle years, his face deeply grooved with living, his nose a hawk-beak, his mouth a sword-gash.

And there was something oddly wrong with his features, a queer cast upon them that made him seem akin to the purple-clad courtier hovering at Jirel's elbow, to the grinning jester who peered across the chair-back. With a little twist of the heart she saw what it was. There was no physical likeness between master and men in any feature, but the shadow of deformity lay upon all three faces, though only the hunchback wore it honestly. Looking at those faces, one would have sworn that each one of the trio went limping through life under the burden of a crooked spine. Perhaps, Jirel thought involuntarily, with a small shudder, the master and the courtier as well as the fool did indeed carry a burden, and if they did she thought she would prefer the jester's to theirs. His at least was honest and of the flesh. But theirs must be of the spirit, for surely, she thought again, God in His wisdom does not for nothing mark a whole and healthy man with a cripple's face. It was a deformity of the soul that looked out of the eyes meeting hers.

And because that thought frightened her she swung her shoulders until the cape swirled wide, and flashed her white teeth in a smile more boldly reckless than the girl behind it felt.

"You must not crave the company of strangers, sir—you keep a discouraging guard before your gate!"

Alaric did not smile. "Honest travelers are welcome here," he said very smoothly. "But the next robbers who ride our causeway will think twice before they storm the gates. We have no gallows here where thieves may swing in chains, but I think the guard before my castle will be warning enough to the next raiders who come."

"A grisly sort of warning," said Jirel. And then, with belated courtesy, "I am Jirel of Joiry. I missed my way in the marsh tonight—I shall be grateful for your hospitality."

"And we for your presence, Lady Jirel."

Alaric's voice was oily, but his eyes raked her openly. She felt other eyes upon her back too, and her red hair stiffened a little at the roots with a prickling uneasiness. "We keep a small court here at Hellsgarde," went on Alaric's voice. "Damara, Ettard, Isoud, Morgaine—all of you, make our guest welcome!"

Jirel swung round with a swirl of her long cloak to face the women, wondering at the subtle slight to their dignity, for Alaric made no effort to introduce them separately.

She thought they crouched a little on their low seats by the fire, looking up with a queer effect of women peering fearfully from under lowered brows, though she could not have said why they seemed so, for they met her eyes squarely. And upon these faces too lay that strange shadow of deformity, not so definitely as upon the men's, but visible in the firelight. All of them were thin creatures with big eyes showing a rather shocking space of whiteness around the staring irises. Their cheek-bones were sharp in the firelight, so that shadows stood hollowly beneath.

The woman who had risen when Alaric said "Damara" was a tall as Jirel, strongly made under the close green gown, but her face too had that queer hollow look and her eyes stared too whitely under wide-open lids. She said in a tight voice:

"Sit down by the fire and warm yourself, lady. We dine in a few minutes."

Jirel sank to the low cushioned stool she dragged forward, one leg doubled under her for instant rising, her sword-hilt and sword-hand free. There was something wrong here. She could feel it in the air.

The two dogs growled a little and shifted away from her on the floor, and even that was—wrong. Dogs had fawned on her always—until now. And the firelight was so red in their eyes . . .

Looking away uneasily from those unnaturally red eyes, she saw the boys' features clearly for the first time, and her heart contracted a little. For naked evil was upon these two young faces. The others wore their shadow of deformity elusively, a thing more sensed than seen. It might be only a trick of her legend-fed imagination that put evil there. But the two young lads had the faces of devils, long faces with high cheekbones and slitted, lusterless eyes. Jirel shuddered a little inwardly. What sort of company had she stumbled into, where the very children and dogs wore evil like a garment?

She drew a deep breath and glanced around the circle of still faces that watched her wordlessly, with an intentness like that of—of beasts prey? Her pride rebelled at that. Joiry was ever the predator, not the prey! She squared her cleft chin and said with determined casualness:

"You have dwelt here long?"

She could have sworn a look went round the semicircle before the fire, a swift, amused glance from face to face as if they shared a secret. Yet not an eye wavered from hers. Only the two boys leaned together a little, and the look of evil brightened upon their wicked young faces. Alaric answered after the briefest possible pause:

"Not long. Nor will we stay long—now." There was a subtle menace in it, though Jirel could not have said why. And again that feeling of knowledge shared ran like a strong current around the circle, a little quiver as if a dreadful amusement were almost stirring in the air. But not a face changed or turned. The eyes were still eager—almost avid—upon the bright, strong face of Jirel with the firelight warming her golden tan and touching her red curls to flame and trembling upon the soft curve of her under-lip. For all the bright clothes of the company around her, she had the sudden feeling that dark robes and dark eyes and dark faces hemmed her in—like shadow around a fire.

The conversation had come to a full stop; the eyes never wavered from her. She could not fathom this strange interest, for it was queer Alaric had not asked anything at all about her coming. A woman alone in this wilderness at night was sufficiently unusual to arouse interest, yet no one seemed concerned to ask how she had come there. Why, then, this concerted, deep interest in the sight of her?

To conquer the little tremor she could not quite ignore she said boldly:

"Hellsgarde of the Marshes has an ugly reputation, my lord. I wonder you dare dwell here—or do you know the old tale?"

Unmistakably this time that quiver of amusement flashed around the circle, though not an eye left hers. Alaric's voice was dry as he answered:

"Yes—yes, we know the tale. We are—not afraid."

And suddenly Jirel was quite sure of a strange thing. Something in his voice and his words told her very surely that they had not come in spite of the terrible old legend, but *because of it*.

No normal people would deliberately seek out a haunted and blood-stained ruin for a dwelling-place, yet there could be no mistaking the implication in Alaric's voice, in the unspoken mirth at her words that ran like a whisper around the circle. She remembered those dead men at the door. What normal person could make a joke so grisly? No, no—this company was as definitely abnormal as a company of monsters. One could not sit with them long even in silence without sensing that. The look of abnormality upon their faces did not lie—it was a sure sign of deformity of the soul.

The conversation had stopped again. To break the nerve-racking silence Jirel said:

"We hear many strange tales of Hellsgarde"—and knew she was talking too much, but could not stop—anything was better than that staring silence—"tales of treasure and—and—is it true that one can come upon Hellsgarde Castle only in the sunset—as I did?"

Alaric paused deliberately for a moment before he answered with a deliberate evasiveness. "There are stranger tales than that of Hellsgarde—and who can say how much of truth is in them? Treasure? There may well be treasure here. Many have come seeking it—and remained, for ever."

Jirel remembered the dead men at the door, and she shot Alaric a yellow glare that would have clanged like the meeting of blades with his stare—had he met it. He was looking up into the shadows of the ceiling, and he was smiling a little. Did he suspect her errand? He had asked no questions . . . Jirel remembered Guy of Garlot's smile as he sent her on this quest, and a murderous wonder began to take shape in her mind. If Guy had known—if he had deliberately sent her into this peril—she let herself sink for a moment into a luxury of picturing that comely smile smashed in by the handle of her sword . . .

They were watching her. She came back with a jerk and said at random:

"How cold the marshes are after sunset!" And she shivered a little, not until that moment realizing the chill of the great hall.

"We find it—pleasant," murmured Alaric, watching her.

The others were watching too, and again she sensed that ripple of subtle amusement running around the circle that closed her out of a secret shared. They were here for a purpose. She knew it suddenly: a strange, unfathomable purpose that bound them together with almost one mind, so that thoughts seemed to flow soundlessly from brain to brain; a purpose that included her now, and in no pleasant way. Danger was in the air, and she alone here by night in the deserted marshes, among these queer, abnormal people who watched her with an avid and unwavering eagerness. Well, she had been in peril before, and hewed her way out again.

A slovenly wench in a ragged smock tiptoed clumsily out of the shadows to murmur in Damara's ear, and Jirel felt with conscious relief the removal of at least one pair of staring eyes as the woman turned to nod. Jirel's gaze was scornful on the girl. A queer household they kept here—the bestial retainers, the sluttish wench in her soiled gown.

Not even Joiry's kitchen maids were so slovenly clad.

Damara turned back to the fire. "Shall we dine now?" she asked.

Every face around the fire brightened magically, and Jirel was conscious of a little loosening of the tension in her own mind. The very fact that the thought of food pleased them made the whole group seem more normal. And yet—she saw it in a moment—this was not even a normal eagerness. There was something a little horrid about the gleam in every eye, the avid hunger on every face. For a little while the thought of food supplanted herself in their interest, and that terrible battery of watchfulness forsook her. It was like an actual weight lifted. She breathed deeper.

Frowsy kitchen scullions and a pair of unwashed girls were carrying in the planks and trestles for the table, setting it up by the fire.

"We dine alone," Alaric was explaining as the group around the fire reshifted itself to make way. It seemed a witless sort of fastidiousness to Jirel, particularly since they let themselves be served by such shamefully unkempt lackeys. Other households dined all together, from lord to stable hands, at the long T-shaped tables where the salt divided noblesse from peasantry. But perhaps Alaric dared not allow those beast-wild men of his even that familiarity. And she was conscious of a tiny disappointment that the company of these staring, strange-faced people was not to be leavened even by the brutish earthliness of their retainers. The men-at-arms seemed scarcely human, but at least it was a normal, open sort of brutality, something she could understand.

When the table was ready Alaric seated her at his right hand, beside the two evil-faced youngsters who sat preternaturally quiet. Young lads of that age were scufflers and squirmers at table in the company she knew. It was another count of eeriness against them that they scarcely moved save to reach for food.

Who were they? She wondered. Alaric's sons? Pages or squires from some noble family? She glanced around the table in deepening bewilderment, looking for signs of kinship on the shadowed faces, finding nothing but that twist of deformity to link the company together. Alaric had made no attempt to introduce any of them, and she could not guess what relationship bound them all together in this close, unspoken communion. She met the eyes of the dwarf at Alaric's elbow and looked quickly away again, angry at his little comprehending grin. He had been watching her.

There was no conversation after the meat was brought in. The whole company fell upon it with such starved eagerness that one might think they had not dined in weeks before now. And not even their food tasted right or normal.

It looked well enough, but there was a subtle seasoning about it that made Jirel gag and lay down her knife after the first taste—a flavor almost of decay, and a sort of burning bitterness she could not put a name to, that lingered on the tongue long after the food itself was swallowed. Everything stank of it, the roast, the bread, the few vegetables, even their bitter wine.

After a brave effort, for she was hungry, Jirel gave up and made not even the pretense of eating. She sat with her arms folded on the table edge, right hand hanging near her sword, watching the ravenous company devour their tainted food. It was no wonder, she realized suddenly, that they ate alone. Surely not even the dull palates of their retainers could accept this revoltingly seasoned meat.

Alaric sat back at last in his high-backed chair, wiping his dagger on a morsel of bread.

"You do not hunger, Lady Jirel?" he asked, tilting a brow at her still-heaping trencher. She could not help her little grimace as she glanced down.

"Not now," she said, with wry humor.

Alaric did not smile. He leaned forward to puck upon his dagger the thick slab of roast before her, and tossed it to the hearth. The two greyhounds streaked from beneath the table to growl over it hungrily, and Alaric glanced obliquely at Jirel, with a hint of a one-sided smile, as he wiped the knife again and sheathed it.

If he meant her to understand that the dogs were included in this queer closed circle of his she caught it. Obviously there had been a message in that act and smile.

When the table had been cleared away and the last glimmer of sunset had faded from the high, narrow slits of the windows, a sullen fellow in frieze went around the hall with a long poletorch, lighting the cressets.

"Have you visited Hellsgarde before, my lady?" inquired Alaric. And as Jirel shook her head, "Let me show you the hall then, and my forefathers' arms and shields. Who knows?—you may find quarterings of your own among our escutcheons."

Jirel shuddered at the thought of discovering even a remote kinship with Hellsgarde's dwellers, but she laid her hand reluctantly on the arm he offered and let him lead her away from the fire out under the echoing vaults of the hall where cressets brought the shadows to life.

The hall was as Andred's murderers must have left it two centuries ago. What shields and armor had not fallen from the walls were thick with rust in the damp air of the marshes, and the tatters of pennons and tapestries had long ago taken on a uniform color of decay. But Alaric seemed to savor the damp and the desolation as a normal man might savor luxury. Slowly he led her around the hall, and she could feel the eyes of the company, who had resumed their seats by the fire, follow her all the way with one unwinking stare.

The dwarf had taken up his lute again and struck occasional chords in the echoing silence of the hall, but except for that there was no sound but the fall of their feet on the rushless flagstones and the murmur of Alaric's voice pointing out the vanished glories of Hellsgarde Castle.

They paused at the side of the big room farthest from the fire, and Alaric said in an unctuous voice, his eyes seeking Jirel's with curious insistence:

"Here on this spot where we stand, lady, died Andred of Hellsgarde two hundred years ago."

Jirel looked down involuntarily. Her feet were planted on the great blotch of a spreading stain that had the rough outline of a beast with questing head and paws outsprawled. It was a broad, stain, black and splattered upon the stone. Andred must have been a big man. He had bled terribly on that day two centuries past.

Jirel felt her host's eyes on her face full of a queer anticipation, and she caught her breath a little to speak, but before she could utter a sound, quite suddenly there was a riot of wind all about them, shrieking out of nowhere in a whirlwind gust that came ravening with such fury that the cressets went out all together in one breath and darkness like a blow fell upon the hall.

In the instant of that blackness, while the whole great hall was black and vocal and bewildering with storm-wind, as if he had been waiting avidly for this moment all evening a man's arm seized Jirel in a grip like death and a mouth came down upon hers in a more savagely violent and intimate kiss than she had ever known before. It all burst upon her so quickly that her impressions confused and ran together into one gust of terrible anger against Alaric as she struggled helplessly against that iron arm and ravenous mouth, while the storm-wind shrieked in the darkness. She was conscious of nothing but the arm, the mouth, the insolent hand. She was not pressed against a man's body, but the strength of the arm was like steel about her.

And in the same moment of seizure the arm was dragging her violently across the floor with irresistible force, never slackening its crushing grip, the kiss in all its revolting intimacy still ravaging her muted mouth. It was as if the kiss, the crush of the arm, the violence of the hand, the howl of the wind and the drag across the room were all but manifestations of a single vortex of violence.

It could not have lasted more than seconds. She had an impression of big, square, wide-spaced teeth against her lips and the queer violence behind them manifest not primarily in the savageness of the kiss or the embrace or the wild drag across the room, but more as if all these were mere incidents to a burning vehemence behind them that beat like heat all around her.

Choking with impotent fury, she tried to struggle, tried to scream. But there was no chest to push for leverage and no body to arch away from, and she could not resist. She could only make the dumb animal sounds in her throat, sealed in behind the storming violation of that mouth.

She had scarcely time to think, it happened so quickly. She was too stunned by the violence and suddenness of the attack even to wonder at the absence of anything but the mouth, the arm, the hand. But she did have the distinct impression of walls closing in around her, as if she were being dragged out of the great open hall into a narrow closet. It was somehow as if that violence beating all about her were confined and made more violent by the presence of close walls very near.

It was all over so quickly that even as that feeling of closing walls dawned upon her she heard the little amazed cries of the others as the cressets were blown out all together. It was as if time had moved faster for her than for them. In another instant someone must have thrown brush on the fire, for the great blaze in the cavern of the chimney roared up with a gush of light and sound, for a moment beating back the darkness in the hall.

And Jirel was staggering alone in the center of the big room. No one was near her, though she could have sworn upon the cross-hilt of her sword that a split second before the heavy mouth had crushed her muted lips. It was gone now as if it had never been. Walls did not enclose her; there was no wind, there was no sound in the great hall.

Alaric stood over the black blotch of Andred's blood at the other side of the hall. She thought she must have known subconsciously after the first moment that it was not he whose lips ravaged her bruised mouth. That flaming vehemence was not in him. No, though he had been the only man near her when the dark closed down, he was not the man whose outrageous kiss still throbbed on her mouth.

She lifted an unsteady hand to those bruised lips and stared around her wildly, gasping for lost breath, half sobbing with fury.

The others were still around the fire, half the width of the room away. And as the light from the replenished blaze leaped up, she saw the blankness of their momentary surprise vanish before one leaping flame of avid hope that for an instant lit every face alike. With long running strides Alaric reached her side. In her dazed confusion she felt his hands on her arms shaking her eagerly, heard him gabbling in a tongue she did not know:

"G'hasta-est? Tai g'hasta? Tai g'hasta?"

Angrily, she shook him off as the other closed round her in an eagerly excited group, babbling all together, *"G'hasta tai? Est g'hasta?"*

Alaric recovered his poise first. In a voice shaking with the first emotion she had heard from him he demanded with almost desperate eagerness.

"What was it? What happened? Was it—was it—?"

But he seemed scarcely to dare name the thing his whole soul longed for, though the tremble of hope was in his voice.

Jirel caught herself on the verge of answering. Deliberately she paused to fight down the dizzy weakness that still swam in her brain, drooping her lids to hide the calculation that came up like a flame behind her yellow eyes. For the first time she had a leverage over these mysterious people. She knew something they frantically desired to know, and she must make full use of the knowledge she scarcely knew she had.

"H-happened?" The stammer was not entirely feigned. "There was a—a wind, and darkness—I don't know—it was all over so quickly." And she glanced up into the gloom with not wholly assumed terror. Whatever that thing had been—it was no human agency. She could have sworn that the instant before the light flared up, walls were closing around her as tightly as a tomb's walls; yet they had vanished more lightly than mist in the glow of the fire. But that mouth upon hers, those big, squarely spaced teeth against her lips, the crush of the brutal arm—nothing could have been more tangible. Yet there had been only the arm, the mouth, the hand. No body . . . With a sudden shudder that made the goose-flesh ripple along her limbs she remembered that Andred had been dismembered before they flung him into the quicksands . . . Andred . . .

She did not know she had said it aloud, but Alaric pounced like a cat on the one word that left her lips.

"Andred? Was it Andred?"

Jirel recovered herself with a real effort, clenching her teeth to stop their chattering.

"Andred? He died two hundred years ago!"

"He will never die until—" One of the young boys with the evil faces said that much before Alaric whirled on him angrily, yet with curious deference.

"Silence! . . . Lady Jirel, you asked me if the legends of Hellsgarde are true. Now I tell you that the tale of Andred is. We believe he still walks the halls where his treasure lies hid, and we—we—" He hesitated, and Jirel saw a strong look of calculation dawn upon his face. He went on smoothly, "We believe there is but one way to find that treasure. Only the ghost of Andred can lead us there. And Andred's ghost has been—elusive, until now."

She could have sworn that he had not meant to say just that when he began to speak. She was surer of it when she saw the little flicker of communication ripple around the circle of faces closing her in. Amusement at a subtle jest in which she did not share . . . it was on every face around her, the hollow-cheeked women's white-rimmed staring eyes brightened, the men's faces twitched a little with concealed mirth. Suddenly she felt smothered by abnormality and mystery and that subtle, perilous amusement without reason.

She was more shaken by her terrifying experience than she would have cared to admit. She had little need to feign weakness as she turned away from them toward the fire, eager to escape their terrible company even though it meant solitude in this haunted dark. She said:

"Let me—rest by the fire. Perhaps it—it—he won't return."

"But he must return!" She thought that nearly every voice around her spoke simultaneously, and eager agreement was bright upon every face. Event the two dogs had thrust themselves forward among the legs of the little crowd around Jirel, and their shadowed eyes, still faintly aglow as if with borrowed firelight, followed the conversation from face to face as if they too understood. Their gazes turned redly up to Alaric now as he said:

"For many nights we have waited in vain for the force that was Andred to make itself known to us. Not until you come does he create that vortex which—which is necessary if we are to find the treasure." Again, at that word, Jirel thought she felt a little current of amusement ripple from listener to listener. Alaric went on in his smooth voice, "We are fortunate to find one who has the gift of summoning Andred's spirit to Hellsgarde. I think there must be in you a kindred fierceness which Andred senses and seeks. We must call him out of the dark again—and we must use your power to do it."

Jirel stared around her incredulously. "You would call—that—up again?"

Eyes gleamed at her with a glow that was not of the firelight. "We would indeed," murmured the evil-faced boy at her elbow. "And we will not wait much longer . . . "

"But—God's Mercy!" said Jirel, "—are all the legends wrong? They say Andred's spirit swoops down with sudden death on all who trespass in Hellsgarde. Why do you talk as if only I could evoke it? Do you want to die so terribly? I do not! I won't endure *that* again if you kill me for it. I'll have no more of Andred's kisses!"

◆ ◆ ◆

There was a pulse of silence around the circle for a moment. Eyes met and looked away again. Then Alaric said:

"Andred resents only outsiders in Hellsgarde, not his own kinsmen and their retainers. Moreover, those legends you speak of are old ones, telling tales of long-ago trespassers in this castle.

"With the passage of years the spirits of the violent dead draw farther and farther away from their death-scenes. Andred is long dead, and he revisits Hellsgarde Castle less often and less vindictively as the years go by. We have striven a long while to draw him back—but you alone succeeded. No, lady, you must endure Andred's violence once again, or—"

"Or what?" demanded Jirel coldly, dropping her hand to her sword.

"There is no alternative." Alaric's voice was inflexible. "We are many to your one. We will hold you here until Andred comes again."

Jirel laughed. "You think Joiry's men will let her vanish without a trace? You'll have such a storming about Hellsgarde walls as—"

"I think not, lady. What soldiers will dare follow when a braver one than any of them was vanished in Hellsgarde? No, Joiry, your men will not seek you here. You—"

Jirel's sword flamed in the firelight as she sprang backward, dragging it clear. The blade flashed once—and then arms like iron pinioned her from behind. For a dreadful moment she thought they were Andred's, and her heart turned over. But Alaric smiled, and she knew. It was the dwarf who had slipped behind her at an unspoken message from his master, and if his back was weak his arms were not. He had a bear's grip upon her and she could not wrench herself free.

Struggling, sobbing curses, kicking hard with her steel-spurred heels, she could not break his hold. There was a murmurous babble all around her of that strange, haunting tongue again, *"L'vraista! Tai g'hasta vrai! El vraist' tai lau!"* and two devil-faced boys dived for her ankles. They clung like ghoulishly grinning apes, pinning her feet to the floor. And Alaric stepped forward to wrench the sword from her hand. He murmured something in their queer speech, and the crowd scattered purposefully.

Fighting hard, Jirel was scarcely ware of their intention before it was accomplished. But she heard the sudden splash of water on blazing logs and the tremendous hissing of steam as the fire went out and darkness fell like a blanket upon the shadowy hall. The crowd had melted away from her into the dark, and now the grip on her ankles suddenly ceased and the great arms that held her so hard heaved in a mighty swing.

Choking with fury, she reeled into the darkness. There was nothing to stop her, and those mighty arms had thrown her hard. She fell and slid helplessly across bare flagstones in black dark, her greaves and empty scabbard clanging upon stone. When she came to a halt, bruised and scratched and breathless, it was a moment before she could collect her senses enough to scramble up, too stunned for even curses.

"Stay where you are Jirel of Joiry," Alaric's voice said calmly out of the blackness. "You cannot escape this hall—we guard every exit with drawn swords. Stand still—and wait."

Jirel got her breath and launched into a blasphemous survey of his ancestry and possible progeny with such vehemence that the dark for several minutes throbbed with her fury. Then she recalled Alaric's suggestion that violence in herself might attract a kindred violence in that strange force called Andred, and she ceased so abruptly that the silence was like a blow upon the ears.

It was a silence full of tense waiting. She could almost feel the patience and the anticipation that beat out upon her from the circle of invisible jailers, and at the thought of what they wanted her blood ran chilly. She looked up blindly into the darkness overhead, certain for a long and dreadful moment that the familiar blast of storm-wind was gathering there to churn the night into chaos out of which Andred's arm would reach . . .

After a while she said in a voice that sounded unexpectedly small in the darkness:

"Y-you might throw me a pillow. I'm tired of standing and this floor's cold."

To her surprise footsteps moved softly and quite surely across stone, and after a moment a pillow hurled out of the darkness to thump softly at her feet. Jirel sank upon it thankfully, only to stiffen an instant later and glare about the dark, the hair prickling on her neck. So—they could see in the darkness! There had been too much certainty in those footsteps and the accurate toss of the pillow to doubt it. She huddled her shoulders together a little and tried not to think.

The darkness was enormous above her. Age upon age went by, with no sound except her own soft breathing to break that quiet pulsing with waiting and anticipation. Her terror grew. Suppose that dreadful storm-wind should come whooping through the hall again; suppose the bodiless arm should seize her and the mouth come ravening down upon her lips once more . . . Coldness crept down her spine.

Yes, and suppose it did come again. What use, for her? These slinking abnormalities who were her jailers would never share the treasure with her which they were so avid to find—so avid that they dared evoke this terror by night and brave a death which legend whispered fearfully of, simply that they might possess it. *It*—did they know, then, what lay in Andred's terribly guarded box? What conceivable thing could be so precious that men would dare this to have it?

And what hope at all for her? If the monstrous thing called Andred did not come tonight—then he would come again some other night, sooner or later, and all nights would find her isolated here as bait for the monster that haunted Hellsgarde. She had boasted without hope when she said her men would follow. They were brave men and they loved her—but they loved living more. No, there was not a man in Joiry who would dare follow where she had failed. She remembered Guy of Garlot's face, and let violence come flooding up in her for a moment. That handsome coward, goading her into this that he might possess the nameless thing he coveted . . . Well, she would ruin his comely face for him with the crosshilt of her sword—if she lived! She was forgetting . . .

Slowly the stars wheeled by the arrow-slit windows high up in the darkness of the walls. Jirel sat hugging her knees and watching them. The darkness sighed above her with vagrant drafts, any one of which might be Andred roaring down out of the night . . .

Well, her captors had made one mistake. How much it might avail her she did not know, but they thought they had disarmed her, and Jirel hugged her greave-sheathed legs in the darkness and smiled a wicked smile, knowing they had not.

It must have been after midnight, and Jirel dozing uneasily with her head on her knees, when a long sigh from the darkness made her start awake. Alaric's voice, heavy with weariness and disappointment, spoke in his nameless language. It occurred to Jirel to wonder briefly that though this seemed to be their mother tongue (for they spoke it under stress and among themselves), yet their speech with her had no taint of accent. It was strange—but she was beyond wondering long about the monstrous folk among whom she had fallen.

Footsteps approached her, walking unerringly. Jirel shook herself awake and stood up, stretching cramped limbs. Hands seized her arms from both sides—at the first grasp, with no groping, though even her dark-accustomed eyes could see nothing. No one bothered to translate Alaric's speech to her, but she realized that they had given up their vigil for the night. She was too drugged with sleep to care. Even her terror had dulled as the endless night hours dragged by. She stumbled along between her captors, making no effort to resist. This was not the time to betray her hidden weapon, not to these people who walked the dark like cats. She could wait until the odds were evener.

No one troubled to strike a light. They went swiftly and unhesitatingly through the blackness, and when stairs rose unexpectedly underfoot Jirel was the only one who stumbled. Up steps, along a cold and echoing hall—and then a sudden thrust that sent her staggering. A stone wall caught her and a door slammed at her back. She whirled, a hot Norman oath smoking on her lips, and knew that she was alone.

Groping, she made out the narrow confines of her prison. There was a cot, a jug of water, a rough door through whose chinks light began to glimmer even as she ran questing hands across the surface. Voices spoke briefly outside, and in a moment she understood. Alaric had summoned one of his apish men to watch her while he and his people slept. She knew it must be a man-at-arms and not one of Alaric's company, for the fellow had brought a lantern with him. She wondered if the guardsman knew how unerringly their masters walked the darkness—of if they cared. But it no longer seemed strange to her that Alaric dared employ such brutish men. She knew well enough now with what ease he could control them—he and his night-sight and his terrible fearlessness.

Silence fell outside. Jirel smiled a thin smile and leaned into the nearest corner, drawing up one knee. The long, thin-bladed knife she carried between greave and leg slid noiselessly from its sheath. She waited with feline patience, her eyes upon the lighted chinks between the door's planks.

It seemed a long while before the guard ceased his muffled pacing, yawned loudly, tested the bar that fastened the door from without. Jirel's thin smile widened. The man grunted and—she had prayed he would—settled down at last on the floor with his back against the panels of her door. She knew he meant to sleep awhile in the certainty that the door could not be opened without waking him. She had caught her own guards at that trick too often not to expect it now.

Still she waited. Presently the even breath of slumber reached her ears, and she licked her lips and murmured, "Gentle Jesu, let him not wear mail" and leaned to the door. Her knife was thin enough to slide easily between the panels . . . He was not wearing mail—and the blade was razor-keen. He must scarcely have felt it, or known when he died. She felt the knife grate against bone and gave it an expert twist to clear the rib it had grazed, and hear the man give a sudden, startled grunt in his sleep, and then a long sigh . . . He must never have awakened. In a moment blood began to gush through the panels of the door in heavy spurts, and Jirel smiled and withdrew her knife.

It was simple enough to lift the bar with that narrow blade. The difficulty was in opening the door against the dead weight of the man outside, but she accomplished that too, without too much noise—and then the lantern sat waiting for her and the hall was so long and empty in the half-dark. She could see the arch of the stairway and knew the way she had come. And she did not hesitate on the way down. She had thought it all out carefully in the darkness of the hall downstairs while she crouched on the cushion and waited for Andred's ravenous storm-blast to come shrieking down above her bent shoulders.

There was no way out. She knew that. Other castles had posterns and windows from which a fugitive might escape, but quicksands surrounded Hellsgarde and the only path to freedom lay along the causeway where Alaric's guard would be watching tonight. And only in minstrel's romances does a lone adventurer escape through a guarded courtyard and a guarded gate.

And too—she had come here for a purpose. It was her duty to find that small treasured box which alone would buy the twenty lives depending on her. She would do that, or die. And perhaps, after all, it was fortunate that the castle had not been empty when she came. Without Alaric, it might never have occurred to her to dare the power of Andred's ghost in order to reach her goal. She realized now that it might well be the only way she would ever succeed. Too many searchers in the past had ransacked Hellsgarde Castle to leave her much hope unless great luck attended her. But Alaric had said it: there was a way—a terrible and deadly perilous way, but the only hope.

And after all, what chance did she have? To sit supinely waiting, a helpless decoy, until the night when Andred's power swooped down to claim her again—or to seek him out deliberately and challenge him to the duel. The end would be the same—she must suffer his presence again, either way. But tonight there was a bare chance for her to escape with the treasure-casket, or at least to find it alone and if she lived to hide it and bargain with Alaric for freedom.

It was a forlorn and futile hope, she knew well. But it was not in her to sit waiting for death, and this way there was at least a bare hope for success. She gripped her bloody knife in one hand and her lantern in the other and went on down the stairs, cat-footed and quick.

Her little circle of light moving with her across the cold flags was so tenuous a defense against the dark. One gust of Andred's storm-wind would puff it out and the darkness would smash in upon her like a blow. And there were other ghosts here than Andred's—small, cold things in the dark just beyond her lantern light. She could feel their presence as she picked her way across the great hall, past the quenched logs of the fireplace, past the crumbling ruins of armor and tapestry, toward the one spot where she thought she might be surest of summoning up the dreadful thing she sought.

It was not easy to find. She ranged back and forth for many minutes with her little circle of light before a corner of that great black splotch she hunted moved into the light; beast-shaped, dark as murder itself upon the flagstones. Andred's life-blood spilled two hundred years ago.

Here once before that ravening ghost had taken her; here if anywhere, surely he would come again. She had her underlip firmly between her teeth as she stepped upon that stain, and she was holding her breath without realizing it. She must have stood there for a full minute, feeling the goose-flesh shudder along her limbs, before she could nerve herself for the thing she must do next. But she had come too far to fail herself now. She drew a deep breath and blew out the lifted lantern.

Darkness crashed upon her with the impact of a physical blow, almost squeezing the breath from her body. And now suddenly fright was past and the familiar winy exultation of tension before battle rushed along her limbs and she looked up into the darkness defiantly and shouted to the great vaults of the ceiling, "Come out of Hell, dead Andred! Come if you dare, Andred the Damned!"

Wind—wind and storm and violence! It snatched the words from her lips and the breath from her throat in one tremendous whirling gust that came rushing out of nowhere. And in the instant of its coming, while the wild challenge still echoed on her lips, a ravenous mouth came storming down to silence hers and a great arm smacked down around her shoulders in a blow that sent her reeling as iron fingers dug agonizingly into her arm—a blow that sent her reeling but would not let her fall, for that terrible drag again was sweeping her across the floor with a speed that ran faster than time itself.

She had ducked her head instinctively when she felt the arm seize her, but not soon enough. The heavy mouth had hers, and again the square, wide-set teeth were bruising her lips and the violence of the monstrous kiss made fury bubble up in her sealed throat as she fought in vain against it.

This time the thing was not such a stunning surprise, and she could sense more clearly what was happening to her. As before, the whole violent fury of the attack burst upon her at once—the mouth seized hers and the arm swept her almost off her feet in the same instant. In that instant the unslackening grip around her shoulders rushed her across the dark floor, blinded in the blackness, deafened by the raving wind, muted and dazed by the terrible vehemence of the mouth and the pain of her iron-clawed arms. But she could sense dimly again that walls were closing around her, closer and closer, like a tomb's walls. And as before she was aware of a tremendous force beating about her, a greater violence than any one manifestation of it upon her body; for the mouth, the gripping hand, the arm, the sweeping drag itself were all but parts of that vortex.

And it was indeed a vortex—it was somehow spinning and narrowing as if the whole force that was Andred were concentrating into one tornado-whirl of savage power. Perhaps it was that feeling of narrowing and vortexing rotation which made walls seem to draw close about her. It was all too dimly sensed a thing to put clearly into words, and yet it was terribly real. Jirel, breathless and bruised and stunned with pain and violence, still knew clearly that here in the midst of the great open hall walls were drawing prison-tight about her.

Savagely she slashed at the arm around her shoulders, at the steel-fingered hand digging her arm to the bone. But the angle was an awkward one and she was too dazed to know if she cut flesh or simply stabbed at disembodied force. And the grip did not slacken; the storming mouth still held hers in a kiss so wild and infuriating that she could have sobbed with pure rage.

Those walls were very near . . . her stumbling knees touched stone. She groped dizzily with her free hand and felt walls dripping-damp, close around her. The forward motion had ceased, and the power which was Andred whirled in one concentrated cone of violence that stopped her breath and sent the darkness reeling around her.

Through the haze of her confusion she knew that this, then, must be his own place to which he had dragged her, a place of stone and damp and darkness somewhere *outside*—for they had reached it too quickly for it to be a real place—and yet it was tangible . . . Stone walls cold against her hands, and what were these round and slipping things underfoot?—things that rattled a little as she stumbled among them—bones? Dear God, the bones of other seekers after treasure, who had found what they sought? For she thought the treasure-box must be here, surely, if it were anywhere at all—here in this darkness unreachable save through the very heart of the whirlwind . . .

Her senses were failing and the whirl that was like the whirl in a tornado's heart seemed to create a vacuum which drew her out of her body in one thin, protesting wisp of self that had no strength to fight . . .

Somewhere a long way off was her body, hanging limp in the clutch of the iron arm, gasping for breath under a kiss that made reality faint about her, still struggling feebly in some tomb-smelling, narrow place where stone walls dripped and bones turned underfoot—the bones of those who had come before her . . .

But she was not there. She was a wispy wraith rooted only tenuously in that fainting body, a wraith that reeled out and out in a thin skein to spin on the whirls of tornado-violence pulling her farther and farther and farther away . . . The darkness was slipping sidewise—the stone walls were a prison no longer, for she was moving up along the great expanding whirl that sucked her out of her body, up and out around widening circles into nighttime distances where space and time were not . . .

Somewhere infinitely far away a foot that was not hers stumbled over something small and square, and a body that was not hers slid to its knees among wet, rattling bones, and a bosom that was not hers bruised itself on the corner of that square something as the tenantless body fell forward among bones upon a wet stone floor. But upon the widening whorls of the vortex the wisp that was Jirel rebelled in its spinning. She must go back—she must remember—there was something—something . . .

For one fleeting instant she was in her body again, crumpled down upon the stones, arms sprawled about a small square thing that was slimy to the touch. A box—a wet leather box thick with fungus, bound with iron. Andred's box, that for two hundred years searchers had hunted in vain. The box that Andred had died for and that she would die for too—was dying for now in the darkness and the damp among the bones, with violence ravening down to seize her again . . .

Dimly, as her senses left her for the second time, she heard a dog bark, high and hysterically, from far above. And another dog answered, and then she heard a man's voice shouting in a tongue she did not know, a wild, exultant shout, choking with triumph. But after that the dizziness of the whirlwind which snatched her out of her body made everything blue, until—until—

Queerly, it was music that brought her back. A lute's strings singing as if madness itself swept wild chords across them. The dwarfed jester's lute, shrieking with music that wakened her out of nowhere into her own fallen body in the dampness and the dark where that hard box-corner bruised her bosom.

And the whirlwind was—uncoiling—from about her. The walls widened until she was no longer aware of their prison closeness and the smell of damp and decay faded from her nostrils. In a dizzy flash of realization she clasped the wet casket to her breast just as the walls faded altogether and she sat up unsteadily, blinking into the dark.

The whirlwind still raved around her, but somehow, strangely, it did not touch her now. No, there was something outside it—some strong force against which it battled—a force that—that—

She was in the dark hall again. Somehow she knew it. And the wild lute-music shrilled and sang, and in some queer way—she saw. It was dark still—but she saw. For a luminous glow was generating itself in a ring around her and by its ghostlight she was aware—scarcely through sight—of familiar faces spinning past her in a wide, whirling ring. A witch dance, round and round . . . Alaric's lined face flashed by, blazing with exultation; Damara's white-ringed eyes glared blindly into the dark. She saw the two boys whirl past, the light of hell itself luminous on their faces. There was a wild bark, and one of the greyhounds loped by her and away, firelight from no earthly flame glaring in its eyes, its tongue lolling in a canine grin of ecstasy. Round and round her through that luminous glow which was scarcely light the mad circle spun. And ever the lute-strings wailed and sang with a wilder music than strings can ever have sung before, and the terrible joy on every face—yes, even upon the dogs'—was more frightening than even Andred's menace had been.

Andred—Andred . . . The power of his volcano-force spun above her now, with a strength that stirred the red hair against her cheeks and a raving of wind through which the lute music screamed high. But it was not the dull force that had overwhelmed her. For this maniac dance that spun round and round through the dark was building up a climax of cumulative strength that she could feel as she knelt there, hugging the slimy box. She thought the very air sang with tension and stress. That circle was reeling counterwise to the spin of Andred's vortexing force, and Andred was weakening. She could feel him slackening above her in the dark. The music shrieked louder above the failing storm-wind and the fearful joy upon those faces whirling past told her why. Somehow they were overpowering him. Something in the dwarf's mad lute-strings, something in the spinning of their dance was breaking down the strength of Andred's centuries-old violence. She could feel it weakening as she crouched there with the casket hugged bruisingly to her bosom.

And yet—was it this precious casket that they fought for? No one had a glance to spare for the crouching girl or the burden she hugged. Every face was lifted raptly, every eye stared blindly and exultantly into the upper dark as if the thing that was Andred was visible and—and infinitely desirable. It was a lust for that thing upon their faces that made joy so vivid there. Jirel's brain had almost ceased recording sensation in the bewilderment of what she watched.

When the dance ended she scarcely knew it. Lulled into a dizzy trance by the mad spinning of the dancers, she was almost nodding on her knees in their center, feeling her brain whirl with their whirling—feeling the motion slow about her so imperceptibly that nothing but the whirl itself registered on her mind. But the dancers were slackening—and with them, the whirl above. The wind no longer raved through the dark; it was a slow sigh now, growing softer and gentler as the circle of dancers ceased to spin . . .

And then there was a great, soft, puffing sigh from the darkness above her that blew out her awareness like a candle flame . . .

Daylight fingering through the arrow-slits touched Jirel's closed lids. She awoke painfully, blinking in the light. Every muscle and bone of her supple body ached from the buffeting of last night's storm and violence, and the cold stones were hard beneath her. She sat up, groping by instinct for her knife. It lay a little distance off, rusting with last night's blood. And the casket—the casket! . . .

Panic swelling in her throat quieted in an instant as she saw that precious, molding thing lying on it side at her elbow. A little thing, its iron hinges rusty, its leather whitened and eaten with rot from two centuries in a nameless, dripping place; but safe, unopened. She picked it up, shaking it experimentally. And she heard the softest shifting within, a sound and weight like finest flour moving gently.

A rustle and a sigh from beyond brought her head up, and she stared around her in the shadows of the halls. In a broad, uneven circle the bodies of last night's dancers lay sprawled. Dead? No, slow breathing stirred them as they lay, and upon the face of the nearest—it was Damara—was a look of such glutted satiety that Jirel glanced away in disgust. But they all shared it. She had seen revelers asleep after a night of drunken feasting with not half such surfeit, such almost obscene satisfaction upon their faces as Alaric's drugged company wore now. Remembering that obscure lusting she had seen in their eyes last night, she wondered what nameless satiety they had achieved in the dark after her own consciousness went out . . .

A footfall sounded upon stone behind her and she spun halfway round, rising on one knee and shifting the knife-hilt firmer in her fist. It was Alaric, a little unsteady on his feet, looking down upon her with a sort of half-seeing abstraction. His scarlet tunic was dusty and rumpled as if he had slept in it all night upon the floor and had only just risen. He ran a hand through his ruffled hair and yawned, and looked down at her with a visible effort at focusing his attention.

"I'll have your horse brought up," he said, his eyes sliding indifferently away from her even as he spoke. "You may go now."

Jirel gaped up at him, her lips parting in amazement over white teeth. He was not watching her. His eyes had shifted focus and he was staring blindly into some delightful memory that had blotted out Jirel's very existence. And upon his face that look of almost obscene satiety relaxed every feature until even his sword-gash mouth hung loose.

"B-but—" Jirel blinked and clutched at the mildewed box she had risked her life for. He came back into focus for an impatient instant to say carelessly:

"Oh—that! Take the thing."

"You—you know what it is? I thought you wanted—"

He shrugged. "I could not have explained to you last night what it was I wanted of—Andred. So I said it was the treasure we sought—you could understand that.

But as for that rotting little box—I don't know or care what lies inside. I've had—a better thing . . . " And his remembering eyes shifted again to escape hers and stare blissfully into the past.

"Then why did you—save me?"

"Save you?" He laughed. "We had no thought of you or your treasure in what we—did—last night. You have served your purpose—you may go free."

"Served—what purpose?"

Impatiently for an instant he brought himself wholly back out of his remembering dream to say:

"You did what we were holding you for—called up Andred into our power. Lucky for you that the dogs sensed what happened after you had slipped off to dare the ghost alone. And lucky for us, too. I think Andred might not have come even to take you, had he sensed our presence. Make no doubt of it—he feared us, and with good reason."

Jirel looked up at him for a long instant, a little chill creeping down her spine, before she said in a shaken whisper:

"What—are you?" And for a moment she almost hoped he would not answer. But he smiled, and the look of deformity deepened upon his face.

"A hunter of undeath," he said softly. "A drinker of undeath, when I can find it . . . My people and I lust after that dark force which the ghosts of the violent dead engender, and we travel far sometimes between—feastings." His eyes escaped hers for an instant to stare gloatingly into the past. Still looking with that unfocused gaze, in a voice she had not heard before from him, he murmured, "I wonder if any man who has not tasted it could guess the utter ecstasy of drinking up the undeath of a strong ghost . . . a ghost as strong as Andred's . . . feeling that black power pouring into you in deep drafts as you suck it down—a thirst that strengthens as you drink—feel—darkness—spreading through every vein more sweetly than wine, more intoxicating . . . To be drunk on undeath—a joy almost unbearable."

Watching him, Jirel was aware of a strong shudder that rose in the pit of her stomach and ran strongly and shakingly along her limbs. With an effort she tore her gaze away. The obscene ecstasy that Alaric's inward-looking eyes dwelt upon was a thing she would not see even in retrospect, through another's words and eyes. She scrambled to her feet, cradling the leather box in her arm, averting her eyes from his.

"Let me go, then," she said in a lowered voice, obscurely embarrassed as if she had looked inadvertently upon something indescribable. Alaric glanced up at her and smiled.

"You are free to go," he said, "but waste no time returning with your men for vengeance against the force we imposed on you." His smile deepened at her little twitch of acknowledgement, for that thought had been in her mind. "Nothing holds us now at Hellsgarde. We will leave today on—another search. One thing before you go—we owe you a debt for luring Andred into our power, for I think he would not have come without you. Take a warning away with you, lady."

"What is it?" Jirel's gaze flicked the man's briefly and fell again. She would not look into his eyes if she could help it. "What warning?"

"Do not open that box you carry."

And before she could get her breath to speak he had smiled at her and turned away, whistling for his men. Around her on the floor Jirel heard a rustling and a sigh as the sleepers began to stir. She stood quiet for an instant longer, staring down in bewilderment at the small box under her arm, before she turned to follow Alaric into the outer air.

Last night was a memory and a nightmare to forget. Not even the dead men still on their ghastly guard before the door could mar her triumph now.

Jirel rode back across the causeway in the strong light of the morning, moving like a rider in a mirage between blue skies and blue reflecting waters. Behind her Hellsgarde Castle was a vision swimming among the mirroring pools of the marsh. And as she rode, she remembered.

The vortex of violence out of which she had snatched this box last night—the power and terror of the thing that had treasured it so long . . . what lay within? Something akin to—Andred? Alaric might not know, but he had guessed . . . His warning still sounded in her ears.

She rode awhile with bent brows, but presently a wicked little smile began to thin the red lips of Joiry's sovereign lady. Well . . . she had suffered much for Guy of Garlot, but she thought now that she would not smash in his handsome, grinning face with her sword-hilt as she had dreamed so luxuriously of doing. No . . . she would have a better vengeance . . . She would hand him a little iron-bound leather box.

⚔

Respected by many writers and readers who appreciate his luxurious, poetic prose, Clark Ashton Smith (1893-1961) remains relatively unknown to the general public. Smith said of his own style:

> *My own conscious ideal has been to delude the reader into accepting an impossibility, or series of impossibilities, by means of a sort of verbal black magic, in the achievement of which I make use of prose-rhythm, metaphor, simile, tone-color, counter-point, and other stylistic resources, like a sort of incantation.*

*Ray Bradbury felt Smith was "a special writer for special tastes; his fame was lonely." Then, too, Smith—unlike his peers Robert E. Howard and H. P. Lovecraft—was not easily imitated nor was his work "franchisable." His stories were not based in an over-arcing mythos and had no recurring protagonist. Although his sword-and-sorcery heroes faced danger with typical valor, they tended to die terrible deaths. This grim tendency is found in epic fantasy today, but was uncommon eight decades ago. His Dying Earth universe of Zothique (the last continent on a dim-sunned Earth) was the first of its kind. "The Dark Eidolon" was the fourth published (*Weird Tales, *January 1935) of the Zothique cycle and is one of the darkest.*

THE DARK EIDOLON

Clark Ashton Smith

Thasaidon, lord of seven hells
Wherein the single Serpent dwells,
With volumes drawn from pit to pit
Through fire and darkness infinite—
Thasaidon, sun of nether skies,
Thine ancient evil never dies,
For aye thy somber fulgors flame
On sunken worlds that have no name,
Man's heart enthrones thee, still supreme,
Though the false sorcerers blaspheme.

—*The Song of Xeethra*

On Zothique, the last continent on Earth, the sun no longer shone with the whiteness of its prime, but was dim and tarnished as if with a vapor of blood. New stars without number had declared themselves in the heavens, and the shadows of the infinite had fallen closer. And out of the shadows, the older gods had returned to man: the gods forgotten since Hyperborea, since Mu and Poseidonis, bearing other names but the same attributes. And the elder demons had also returned, battening on the fumes of evil sacrifice, and fostering again the primordial sorceries.

Many were the necromancers and magicians of Zothique, and the infamy and marvel of their doings were legended everywhere in the latter days. But among them all there was none greater than Namirrha, who imposed his black yoke on the cities of Xylac, and later, in a proud delirium, deemed himself the veritable peer of Thasaidon, lord of Evil.

Namirrha had built his abode in Ummaos, the chief town of Xylac, to which he came from the desert realm of Tasuun with the dark renown of his thaumaturgies like a cloud of desert storm behind him. And no man knew that in coming to Ummaos he returned to the city of his birth; for all deemed him a native of Tasuun. Indeed, none could have dreamt that the great sorcerer was one with the beggar-boy Narthos, an orphan of questionable parentage, who had begged his daily bread in the streets and bazaars of Ummaos. Wretchedly had he lived, alone and despised; and a hatred of the cruel, opulent city grew in his heart like a smothered flame that feeds in secret, biding the time when it shall become a conflagration consuming all things.

Bitterer always, through his boyhood and early youth, was the spleen and rancor of Narthos toward men. And one day the prince Zotulla, a boy but little older than he, riding a restive palfrey, came upon him in the square before the imperial palace; and Narthos implored an alms. But Zotulla, scorning his plea, rode arrogantly forward, spurring the palfrey; and Narthos was ridden down and trampled under its hooves. And afterward, nigh to death from the trampling, he lay senseless for many hours, while the people passed him by unheeding. And at last, regaining his senses, he dragged himself to his hovel; but he limped a little thereafter all his days, and the mark of one hoof remained like a brand on his body, fading never. Later, he left Ummaos, and was forgotten quickly by its people. Going southward into Tasuun, he lost his way in the great desert, and was near to perishing. But finally he came to a small oasis, where dwelt the wizard Ouphaloc, a hermit who preferred the company of honest jackals and hyenas to that of men. And Ouphaloc, seeing the great craft and evil in the starveling boy, gave succor to Narthos and sheltered him. He dwelt for years with Ouphaloc, becoming the wizard's pupil and the heir of his demon-wrested lore. Strange things he learned in that hermitage, being fed on fruits and grain that had sprung not from the watered earth, and wine that was not the juice of terrene grapes. And like Ouphaloc, he became a master in devildom and drove his own bond with the archfiend Thasaidon. When Ouphaloc died, he took the name of Namirrha, and went forth as a mighty sorcerer among the wandering peoples and the deep-buried mummies of Tasuun. But never could he forget the miseries of his boyhood in Ummaos and the wrong he had endured from Zotulla; and year by year he spun over in his thoughts the black web of revenge. And his fame grew ever darker and vaster, and men feared him in remote lands beyond Tasuun. With bated whispers they spoke of his deeds in the cities of Yoros, and in Zul-Bha-Shair, the abode of the ghoulish deity Mordiggian. And long before the coming of Namirrha himself, the people of Ummaos knew him as a fabled scourge that was direr than simoom or pestilence.

Now, in the years that followed the going-forth of the boy Narthos from Ummaos, Pithaim, the father of Prince Zotulla, was slain by the sting of a small adder that had crept into his bed for warmth on an autumn night. Some said that the adder had been purveyed by Zotulla, but this was a thing that no man could verily affirm. After the death of Pithaim, Zotulla, being his only son, was emperor of Xylac, and ruled evilly from his throne in Ummaos. Indolent he was, and tyrannic, and full of strange luxuries and cruelties; but the people, who were also evil, acclaimed him in his turpitude. So he prospered, and the lords of Hell and Heaven smote him not. And the red suns and ashen moons went westward over Xylac, falling into that seldom-voyaged sea, which, if the mariners' tales were true, poured evermore like a swiftening river past the infamous isle of Naat, and fell in a worldwide cataract upon nether space from the far, sheer edge of Earth.

Grosser still he grew, and his sins were as overswollen fruits that ripen above a deep abyss. But the winds of time blew softly; and the fruits fell not. And Zotulla laughed amid his fools and his eunuchs and his lemans; and the tale of his luxuries was borne afar, and was told by dim outland peoples, as a twin marvel with the bruited necromancies of Namirrha.

It came to pass, in the year of the Hyena, and the month of the star Canicule, that a great feast was given by Zotulla to the inhabitants of Ummaos. Meats that had been cooked in exotic spices from Sotar, isle of the east, were spread everywhere; and the ardent wines of Yoros and Xylac, filled as with subterranean fires, were poured inexhaustibly from huge urns for all. The wines awoke a furious mirth and a royal madness; and afterward they brought a slumber no less profound than the Lethe of the tomb. And one by one, as they drank, the revelers fell down in the streets, the houses and gardens, as if a plague had struck them; and Zotulla slept in his banquet-hall of gold and ebony, with his odalisques and chamberlains about him. So, in all Ummaos, there was no man or woman wakeful at the hour when Sirius began to fall toward the west.

Thus it was that none saw or heard the coming of Namirrha. But awakening heavily in the latter forenoon, the emperor Zotulla heard a confused babble, a troublous clamor of voices from such of his eunuchs and women as had awakened before him. Inquiring the cause, he was told that a strange prodigy had occurred during the night; but, being still bemused with wine and slumber, he comprehended little enough of its nature, till his favorite concubine, Obexah, led him to the eastern portico of the palace, from which he could behold the marvel with his own eyes.

Now the palace stood alone at the center of Ummaos, and to the north, west and south, for wide intervals of distance, there stretched the imperial gardens, full of superbly arching palms and loftily spiring fountains. But to eastward was a broad open area, used as a sort of common, between the palace and the mansions of high optimates. And in this space, which had lain wholly vacant at eve, a building towered colossal and lordly beneath the full-risen sun, with domes like monstrous fungi of stone that had come up in the night. And the domes, rearing level with those of Zotulla, were builded of death-white marble; and the huge façade, with multi-columned porticoes and deep balconies, was wrought in alternate zones of night-black onyx and porphyry hued as with dragons' blood. And Zotulla swore lewdly, calling with hoarse blasphemies on the gods and devils of Xylac; and great was his dumbfoundment, deeming the marvel a work of wizardry. The women gathered about him, crying out with shrill cries of awe and terror; and more and more of his courtiers, awakening, came to swell the hub-bub; and the fat castrati diddered in their cloth-of-gold like immense black jellies in golden basins. But Zotulla, mindful of his dominion as emperor of all Xylac, strove to conceal his own trepidation, saying:

"Now who is this that has presumed to enter Ummaos like a jackal in the dark, and has made his impious den in proximity and counterview of my palace? Go forth, and inquire the miscreant's name; but ere you go, instruct the headsman to make sharp his double-handed sword."

Then, fearing the emperor's wrath if they tarried, certain of the chamberlains went forth unwillingly and approached the portals of the strange edifice. It seemed that the portals were deserted till they drew near, and then, on the threshold, there appeared a titanic skeleton, taller than any man of earth; and it strode forward to meet them with ell-long strides. The skeleton was swathed in a loin-cloth of scarlet silk with a buckle of jet, and it wore a black turban, starred with diamonds, whose topmost foldings nearly touched the high lintel. Eyes like flickering marsh-fires burned in its deep eye-sockets; and a blackened tongue like that of a long-dead man protruded between its teeth; but otherwise it was clean of flesh, and the bones glittered whitely in the sun as it came onward.

The chamberlains were mute before it, and there was no sound except the golden creaking of their girdles, the shrill rustling of their silks, as they shook and trembled. And the foot-bones of the skeleton clicked sharply on the pavement of black onyx as it paused; and the putrefying tongue began to quiver between its teeth; and it uttered these words in an unctuous, nauseous voice:

"Return, and tell the emperor Zotulla that Namirrha, seer and magician, has come to dwell beside him."

Hearing the skeleton speak as if it had been a living man, and hearing the dread name of Namirrha as men hear the tocsin of doom in some fallen city, the chamberlains could stand before it no longer, and they fled with ungainly swiftness and bore the message to Zotulla.

Now, learning who it was that had come to neighbor with him in Ummaos, the emperor's wrath died out like a feeble and blustering flame on which the wind of darkness had blown; and the vinous purple of his cheeks was mottled with a strange pallor; and he said nothing, but his lips mumbled loosely as if in prayer or malediction. And the news of Namirrha's coming passed like the flight of evil night-birds through all the palace and throughout the city, leaving a noisome terror that abode in Ummaos thereafter till the end. For Namirrha, through the black renown of his thaumaturgies and the frightful entities who served him, had become a power that no secular sovereign dared dispute; and men feared him everywhere, even as they feared the gigantic, shadowy lords of Hell and of outer space. And in Ummaos, people said that he had come on the desert wind from Tasuun with his underlings, even as the pestilence comes, and had reared his house in an hour with the aid of devils beside Zotulla's palace. And they said that the foundations of the house were laid on the adamantine cope of Hell; and in its floors were pits at whose bottom burned the nether fires, or stars could be seen as they passed under in lowermost night. And the followers of Namirrha were the dead of strange kingdoms, the demons of sky and earth and the abyss, and mad, impious, hybrid things that the sorcerer himself created from forbidden unions.

Men shunned the neighborhood of his lordly house; and in the palace of Zotulla few cared to approach the windows and balconies that gave thereon; and the emperor himself spoke not of Namirrha, pretending to ignore the intruder; and the women of the harem babbled evermore with an evil gossip concerning Namirrha and his concubines. But the sorcerer himself was not beheld by the people of that city, though some believed that he walked forth at will, clad with invisibility. His servitors were likewise not seen; but a howling as of the damned was sometimes heard to issue from his portals; and sometimes there came a strange cachinnation, as if some adamantine image had laughed aloud; and sometimes there was a chuckling like the sound of shattered ice in a frozen hell. Dim shadows moved in the porticoes when there was neither sunlight nor lamp to cast them; and red, eerie lights appeared and vanished in the windows at eve, like a blinking of demoniac eyes. And slowly the ember-colored suns went over Xylac, and were quenched in far seas; and the ashy moons were blackened as they fell nightly toward the hidden gulf. Then, seeing that the wizard had wrought no open evil, and that none had endured palpable harm from his presence, the people took heart; and Zotulla drank deeply, and feasted in oblivious luxury as before; and dark Thasaidon, prince of all turpitudes, was the true but never-acknowledged lord of Xylac. And in time the men of Ummaos bragged a little of Namirrha and his dread thaumaturgies, even as they had boasted of the purple sins of Zotulla.

But Namirrha, still unbeheld by living men and living women, sat in the inner walls of that house which his devils had reared for him, and spun over and over in his thoughts the black web of revenge. And the wrong done by Zotulla to Narthos in old times was the least of those cruelties which the emperor had forgotten.

Now, when the fears of Zotulla were somewhat lulled, and his women gossiped less often of the neighboring wizard, there occurred a new wonder and a fresh terror. For, sitting one eve at his banquet-table with his courtiers about him, the emperor heard a noise as of myriad iron-shod hooves that came trampling through the palace gardens. And the courtiers also heard the sound, and were startled amid their mounting drunkenness; and the emperor was angered, and he sent certain of his guards to examine into the cause of the trampling. But peering forth upon the moon-bright lawns and parterres, the guards beheld no visible shape, though the loud sounds of trampling still went to and fro. It seemed as if a rout of wild stallions passed and re-passed before the façade of the palace with tumultuous gallopings and capricoles. And a fear came upon the guards as they looked and listened; and they dared not venture forth, but returned to Zotulla. And the emperor himself grew sober when he heard their tale; and he went forth with high blusterings to view the prodigy. And all night the unseen hooves rang out sonorously on the pavement of onyx, and ran with deep thuddings over the grasses and flowers. The palm-fronds waved on the windless air as if parted by racing steeds; and visibly the tall-stemmed lilies and broad-petaled exotic blossoms were trodden under. And rage and terror nested together in Zotulla's heart as he stood in a balcony above the garden, hearing the spectral tumult, and beholding the harm done to his rarest flower-beds. The women, the courtiers and eunuchs cowered behind him, and there was no slumber for any occupant of the palace; but toward dawn the clamor of hooves departed, going toward Namirrha's house.

When the dawn was full-grown above Ummaos, the emperor walked forth with his guards about him, and saw that the crushed grasses and broken-down stems were blackened as if by fire where the hooves had fallen. Plainly were the marks imprinted, like the tracks of a great company of horses, in all the lawns and parterres; but they ceased at the verge of the gardens. And though everyone believed that the visitation had come from Namirrha, there was no proof of this in the grounds that fronted the sorcerer's abode; for here the turf was untrodden.

"A pox upon Namirrha, if he has done this!" cried Zotulla. "For what harm have I ever done him? Verily, I shall set my heel on the dog's neck; and the torture-wheel shall serve him even as these horses from Hell have served my blood-red lilies of Sotar and my vein-colored irises of Naat and my orchids from Uccastrog which were purple as the bruises of love. Yea, though he stand the viceroy of Thasaidon above Earth, and overlord of ten thousand devils, my wheel shall break him, and fires shall heat the wheel white-hot in its turning, till he withers black as the seared blossoms." Thus did Zotulla make his brag; but he issued no orders for the execution of his threat; and no man stirred from the palace towards Namirrha's house. And from the portals of the wizard none came forth; or if any came there was no visible sign or sound.

So the day went over, and the night rose, bringing later a moon that was slightly darkened at the rim. And the night was silent; and Zotulla, sitting long at the banquet-table, drained his wine-cup often and wrathfully, muttering new threats against Namirrha. And the night wore on, and it seemed that the visitation would not be repeated. But at midnight, lying in his chamber with Obexah, and fathom-deep in his slumber from the wine, Zotulla was awakened by a monstrous clangor of hooves that raced and capered in the palace porticoes and in the long balconies. All night the hooves thundered back and forth, echoing awfully in the vaulted stone, while Zotulla and Obexah, listening, huddled close amid their cushions and coverlets; and all the occupants of the palace, wakeful and fearful, heard the noise but stirred not from their chambers. A little before dawn the hooves departed suddenly; and afterward, by day, their marks were found on the marble flags of the porches and balconies; and the marks were countless, deep-graven, and black as if branded there by flame.

Like mottled marble were the emperor's cheeks when he saw the hoof-printed floors; and terror stayed with him henceforth, following him to the depths of his inebriety, since he knew not where the haunting would cease. His women murmured and some wished to flee from Ummaos, and it seemed that the revels of the day and evening were shadowed by ill wings that left their umbrage in the yellow wine and bedimmed the aureate lamps. And again, toward midnight, the slumber of Zotulla was broken by the hooves, which came galloping and pacing on the palace-roof and through all the corridors and the halls. Thereafter, till dawn, the hooves filled the palace with their iron clatterings, and they rung hollowly on the topmost domes, as if the coursers of gods had trodden there, passing from heaven to heaven in tumultuous cavalcade.

Zotulla and Obexah, lying together while the terrible hooves went to and fro in the hall outside their chamber, had no heart or thought for sin, nor could they find any comfort in their nearness. In the gray hour before dawn they heard a great thundering high on the barred brazen door of the room, as if some mighty stallion, rearing, had drummed there with his forefeet. And soon after this, the hooves went away, leaving a silence like an interlude in some gathering storm of doom. Later, the marks of the hooves were found everywhere in the halls, marring the bright mosaics. Black holes were burnt in the golden-threaded rugs and the rugs of silver and scarlet; and the high white domes were pitted pox-wise with the marks; and far up on the brazen door of Zotulla's chamber the prints of a horse's forefeet were incised deeply.

Now, in Ummaos, and throughout Xylac, the tale of this haunting became known, and the thing was deemed an ominous prodigy, though people differed in their interpretations. Some held that the sending came from Namirrha, and was meant as a token of his supremacy above all kings and emperors; and some thought that it came from a new wizard who had risen in Tinarath, far to the east, and who wished to supplant Namirrha. And the priests of the gods of Xylac held that their various deities had dispatched the haunting, as a sign that more sacrifices were required in the temples.

Then, in his hall of audience, whose floor of sard and jasper had been grievously pocked by the unseen hooves, Zotulla called together many priests and magicians and soothsayers, and asked them to declare the cause of the sending and devise a mode of exorcism. But, seeing that there was no agreement among them, Zotulla provided the several priestly sects with the wherewithal of sacrifice to their sundry gods, and sent them away; and the wizards and prophets, under threat of decapitation if they refused, were enjoined to visit Namirrha in his mansion of sorcery and learn his will, if haply the sending were his and not the work of another.

Loth were the wizards and the soothsayers, fearing Namirrha, and caring not to intrude upon the frightful mysteries of his obscure mansion. But the swordsmen of the emperor drove them forth, lifting great crescent blades against them when they tarried; so one by one, in a straggling order, the delegation went towards Namirrha's portals and vanished into the devil-builded house.

Pale, muttering and distraught, like men who have looked upon hell and have seen their doom, they returned before sunset to the emperor. And they said that Namirrha had received them courteously and had sent them back with this message:

"Be it known to Zotulla that the haunting is a sign of that which he has long forgotten; and the reason of the haunting will be revealed to him at the hour prepared and set apart by destiny. And the hour draws near: for Namirrha bids the emperor and all his court to a great feast on the afternoon of the morrow."

Having delivered this message, to the wonder and consternation of Zotulla, the delegation begged his leave to depart. And though the emperor questioned them minutely, they seemed unwilling to relate the circumstances of the visit to Namirrha; nor would they describe the sorcerer's fabled house, except in a vague manner, each contradicting the other as to what he had seen. So, after a little, Zotulla bade them go, and when they had gone he sat musing for a long while on the invitation of Namirrha, which was a thing he cared not to accept but feared to decline. That evening he drank even more liberally than was his wont; and he slept a Lethean slumber, nor was there any noise of trampling hooves about the palace to awaken him. And silently, during the night, the prophets and magicians passed like furtive shadows from Ummaos; and no man saw them depart; and at morning they were gone from Xylac into other lands, never to return . . .

Now, on that same evening, in the great hall of his house, Namirrha sat alone, having dismissed the familiars who attended him ordinarily. Before him, on an altar of jet, was the dark, gigantic statue of Thasaidon which a devil-begotten sculptor had wrought in ancient days for an evil king of Tasuun, called Pharnoc. The archdemon was depicted in the guise of a full-armored warrior, lifting a spiky mace as if in heroic battle. Long had the statue lain in the desert-sunken palace of Pharnoc, whose very site was disputed by the nomads; and Namirrha, by his divination, had found it and had reared up the infernal image to abide with him always thereafter. And often, through the mouth of the statue, Thasaidon would utter oracles to Namirrha, or would answer interrogations.

Before the black-armored image there hung seven silver lamps, wrought in the form of horses' skulls, with flames issuing changeably in blue and purple and crimson from their eye-sockets. Wild and lurid was their light, and the face of the demon, peering from under his crested helmet, was filled with malign, equivocal shadows that shifted and changed eternally. And sitting in his serpent-carven chair, Namirrha regarded the statue grimly, with a deep-furrowed frown between his eyes: for he had asked a certain thing of Thasaidon, and the fiend, replying through the statue, had refused him. And rebellion was in the heart of Namirrha, grown mad with pride, and deeming himself the lord of all sorcerers and a ruler by his own right among the princes of devildom. So, after long pondering, he repeated his request in a bold and haughty voice, like one who addresses an equal rather than the all-formidable suzerain to whom he had sworn a fatal fealty.

"I have helped you heretofore in all things," said the image, with stony and sonorous accents that were echoed metallically in the seven silver lamps. "Yea, the undying worms of fire and darkness have come forth like an army at your summons, and the wings of nether genii have risen to occlude the sun when you called them. But, verily, I will not aid you in this vengeance you have planned: for the emperor Zotulla has done me no wrong and has served me well though unwittingly; and the people of Xylac, by reason of their turpitudes, are not the least of my terrestrial worshippers. Therefore, Namirrha, it were well for you to live in peace with Zotulla, and well to forget this olden wrong that was done to the beggar-boy Narthos. For the ways of destiny are strange, and the workings of its laws sometimes hidden; and truly, if the hooves of Zotulla's palfrey had not spurned you and trodden you under, your life had been otherwise, and the name and renown of Namirrha had still slept in oblivion as a dream undreamed. Yea, you would tarry still as a beggar in Ummaos, content with a beggar's guerdon, and would never have fared forth to become the pupil of the wise and learned Ouphaloc; and I, Thasaidon, would have lost the lordliest of all necromancers who have accepted my service and my bond. Think well, Namirrha, and ponder these matters: for both of us, it would seem, are indebted to Zotulla in all gratitude for the trampling he gave you."

"Yea, there is a debt," Namirrha growled implacably. "And truly I will pay the debt tomorrow, even as I have planned . . . There are Those who will aid me, Those who will answer my summoning in your despite."

"It is an ill thing to affront me," said the image, after an interval. "And also, it is not wise to call upon Those that you designate. However, I perceive clearly that such is your intent. You are proud and stubborn and revengeful. Do then, as you will, but blame me not for the outcome."

So, after this, there was silence in the hall where Namirrha sat before the eidolon; and the flames burned darkly, with changeable colors, in the skull-shapen lamps; and the shadows fled and returned, unresting, on the face of the statue and the face of Namirrha. Then, toward midnight, the necromancer arose and went upward by many spiral stairs to a high dome of his house in which there was a single small round window that looked forth on the constellations. The window was set in the top of the dome; but Namirrha had contrived, by means of his magic, that one entering by the last spiral of the stairs would suddenly seem to descend rather than climb, and, reaching the last step, would peer downward through the window while stars passed under him in a giddying gulf. There, kneeling, Namirrha touched a secret spring in the marble, and the circular pane slid back without sound. Then, lying prone on the interior of the dome, with his face over the abyss, and his long beard trailing stiffly into space, he whispered a pre-human rune, and held speech with certain entities who belonged neither to Hell nor the mundane elements, and were more fearsome to invoke than the infernal genii or the devils of earth, air, water, and flame. With them he made his contract, defying Thasaidon's will, while the air curdled about him with their voices, and rime gathered palely on his sable beard from the cold that was wrought by their breathing as they leaned earthward.

Laggard and loth was the awakening of Zotulla from his wine; and quickly, ere he opened his eyes, the daylight was poisoned for him by the thought of that invitation which he feared to accept or decline. But he spoke to Obexah, saying:

"Who, after all, is this wizardly dog, that I should obey his summons like a beggar called in from the street by some haughty lord?"

Obexah, a golden-skinned and oblique-eyed girl from Uccastrog, Isle of the Torturers, eyed the emperor subtly, and said:

"O Zotulla, it is yours to accept or refuse, as you deem fitting. And truly, it is a small matter for the lord of Ummaos and all Xylac, whether to go or to stay, since naught can impugn his sovereignty. Therefore, were it not as well to go?" For Obexah, though fearful of the wizard, was curious regarding that devil-builded house of which so little was known; and likewise, in the manner of women, she wished to behold the famed Namirrha, whose mien and appearance were still but a far-brought legend in Ummaos.

"There is something in what you say," admitted Zotulla. "But an emperor, in his conduct, must always consider the public good; and there are matters of state involved, which a woman can scarcely be expected to understand."

So, later in the forenoon, after an ample and well-irrigated breakfast, he called his chamberlains and courtiers about him and took counsel with them. And some advised him to ignore the invitation of Namirrha; and others held that the invitation be accepted, lest a graver evil than the trampling of ghostly hooves be sent upon the palace and the city.

Then Zotulla called the many priesthoods before him in a body, and sought to resummon the wizards and soothsayers who had fled privily in the night. Among all the latter, there was none who answered the crying of his name through Ummaos; and this aroused a certain wonder. But the priests came in a greater number than before, and thronged the hall of audience so that the paunches of the foremost were straightened against the imperial dais and the buttocks of the hindmost were flattened on the rear walls and pillars. And Zotulla debated with them the matter of acceptance or refusal. And the priests argued, as before, that Namirrha was nowherewise concerned with the sending ; and his invitation, they said, portended no harm nor bale to the emperor; and it was plain, from the terms of the message, that an oracle would be imparted to Zotulla by the wizard; and this oracle, if Namirrha were a true archimage, would confirm their own holy wisdom and reëstablish the divine source of the sending; and the gods of Xylac would again be glorified.

Then, having heard the pronouncement of the priests, the emperor instructed his treasurers to load them down with new offerings; and calling unctuously upon Zotulla and all his household the vicarious blessings of the several gods, the priests departed. And the day wore on, and the sun passed its meridian, falling slowly beyond Ummaos through the spaces of the afternoon that were floored with sea-ending deserts. And still Zotulla was irresolute; and he called his wine-bearers, bidding them pour for him the strongest and most magistral of their vintages; but in the wine he found neither certitude nor decision.

Sitting still on his throne in the hall of audience, he heard, toward middle afternoon, a mighty and clamorous outcry that arose at the palace portals. There were deep wailings of men and the shrillings of eunuchs and women, as if terror passed from tongue to tongue, invading the halls and apartments. And the fearful clamor spread throughout all the palace, and Zotulla, rousing from the lethargy of wine, was about to send his attendants to inquire the cause.

Then, into the hall, there filed an array of tall mummies, clad in royal cerements of purple and scarlet, and wearing gold crowns on their withered craniums. And after them, like servitors, came gigantic skeletons who wore loin-cloths of nacarat orange and about whose upper skulls, from brow to crown, live serpents of banded saffron and ebon had wrapped themselves for head-dresses. And the mummies bowed before Zotulla, saying with thin, sere voices:

"We, who were kings of the wide realm of Tasuun aforetime, have been sent as a guard of honor for the emperor Zotulla, to attend him as is befitting when he goes forth to the feast prepared by Namirrha."

Then with dry clickings of their teeth, and whistlings as of air through screens of fretted ivory, the skeletons spoke:

"We, who were giant warriors of a race forgotten, have also been sent by

Namirrha, so that the emperor's household, following him to the feast, should be guarded from all peril and should fare forth in such pageantry as is meet and proper."

Witnessing these prodigies, the wine-bearers and other attendants cowered about the imperial dais or hid behind the pillars, while Zotulla, with pupils swimming starkly in a bloodshot white, with face bloated and ghastly pale, sat frozen on his throne and could utter no word in reply to the ministers of Namirrha.

Then, coming forward, the mummies said in dusty accents: "All is made ready, and the feast awaits the arrival of Zotulla." And the cerements of the mummies stirred and fell open at the bosom, and small rodent monsters, brown as bitumen, eyed as with accursed rubies, reared forth from the eaten hearts of the mummies like rats from their holes and chittered shrilly in human speech, repeating the words. The skeletons in turn took up the solemn sentence; and the black and saffron serpents hissed it from their skulls; and the words were repeated lastly in baleful rumblings by certain furry creatures of dubious form, hitherto unseen by Zotulla, who sat behind the ribs of the skeletons as if in cages of white wicker.

Like a dreamer who obeys the doom of dreams, the emperor rose from his throne and went forward, and the mummies surrounded him like an escort. And each of the skeletons drew from the reddish-yellow folds of his loin-cloth a curiously pierced archaic flute of silver; and all began a sweet and evil and deathly fluting as the emperor went out through the halls of the palace. A fatal spell was in the music: for the chamberlains, the women, the guards, the eunuchs, and all members of Zotulla's household even to the cooks and scullions, were drawn like a procession of night-walkers from the rooms and alcoves in which they had vainly hidden themselves; and marshaled by the flutists, they followed after Zotulla. A strange thing it was to behold this mighty company of people, going forth in the slanted sunlight toward Namirrha's house, with a cortège of dead kings about them, and the blown breath of skeletons thrilling eldritchly in the silver flutes. And little was Zotulla comforted when he found the girl Obexah at his side, moving, as he, in a thralldom of involitent horror, with the rest of his women close behind.

Coming to the open portals of Namirrha's house, the emperor saw that they were guarded by great crimson-wattled things, half dragon, half man, who bowed before him, sweeping their wattles like bloody besoms on the flags of dark onyx. And the emperor passed with Obexah between the louting monsters, with the mummies, the skeletons and his own people behind him in strange pageant, and entered a vast and multicolumned hall, where the daylight, following timidly, was drowned by the baleful arrogant blaze of a thousand lamps.

Even amid his horror, Zotulla marveled at the vastness of the chamber, which he could hardly reconcile with the mansion's outer length and height and breadth, though these indeed were of most palatial amplitude. For it seemed that he gazed down great avenues of topless pillars, and vistas of tables laden with piled-up viands and thronged urns of wine, that stretched away before him into luminous distance and gloom as of starless night.

In the wide intervals between the tables, the familiars of Namirrha and his other servants went to and fro incessantly, as if a fantasmagoria of ill dreams were embodied before the emperor. Kingly cadavers in robes of time-rotted brocade, with worms seething in their eye-pits, poured a blood-like wine into cups of the opalescent horn of unicorns. Lamias, trident-tailed, and four-breasted chimeras, came in with fuming platters lifted high by their brazen claws. Dog-headed devils, tongued with lolling flames, ran forward to offer themselves as ushers for the company. And before Zotulla and Obexah, there appeared a curious being with the full-fleshed lower limbs and hips of a great black woman and the clean-picked bones of some titanic ape from there upward.

Verily, it seemed to Zotulla that they had gone a long way into some malignly litten cavern of Hell, when they came to that perspective of tables and columns down which the monster had led them. Here, at the room's end, apart from the rest, was a table at which Namirrha sat alone, with the flames of the seven horse-skull lamps burning restlessly behind him, and the mailed black image of Thasaidon towering from the altar of jet at his right hand. And a little aside from the altar, a diamond mirror was upborne by the claws of iron basilisks.

Namirrha rose to greet them, observing a solemn and funereal courtesy. His eyes were bleak and cold as distant stars in the hollows wrought by strange fearful vigils. His lips were like a pale-red seal on a shut parchment of doom. His beard flowed stiffly in black-anointed banded locks across the bosom of his vermilion robe, like a mass of straight black serpents. Zotulla felt the blood pause and thicken about his heart, as if congealing into ice. And Obexah, peering beneath lowered lids, was abashed and frightened by the visible horror that invested this man and hung upon him even as royalty upon a king. But amid her fear, she found room to wonder what manner of man he was in his intercourse with women.

"I bid you welcome, O Zotulla, to such hospitality as is mine to offer," said Namirrha, with the iron ringing of some hidden funereal bell deep down in his hollow voice. "Prithee, be seated at my table."

Zotulla saw that a chair of ebony had been placed for him opposite Namirrha; and another chair, less stately and imperial, had been placed at the left hand for Obexah. And the twain seated themselves; and Zotulla saw that his people were sitting likewise at other tables throughout the huge hall, with the frightful servants of Namirrha waiting upon them busily, like devils attending the damned.

Then Zotulla perceived that a dark and corpse-like hand was pouring wine for him in a crystal cup; and upon the hand was the signet-ring of the emperors of Xylac, set with a monstrous fire-opal in the mouth of a golden bat: even such a ring as Zotulla wore perpetually on his index-finger. And, turning, he beheld at his right hand a figure that bore the likeness of his father, Pithaim, after the poison of the adder, spreading through his limbs, had left behind it the purple bloating of death. And Zotulla, who had caused the adder to be placed in the bed of Pithaim, cowered in his seat and trembled with a guilty fear. And the thing that wore the similitude of Pithaim, whether corpse or an image wrought by Namirrha's enchantment, came and went at Zotulla's elbow, waiting upon him with stark, black, swollen fingers that never fumbled. Horribly he was aware of its bulging, unregarding eyes, and its livid purple mouth that was locked in a rigor of mortal silence, and the spotted adder that peered at intervals with chill orbs from its heavy-folded sleeve as it leaned beside him to replenish his cup or to serve him with meat. And dimly, through the icy mist of his terror, the emperor beheld the shadowy-armored shape, like a moving replica of the still, grim statue of Thasaidon, which Namirrha had reared up in his blasphemy to perform the same office for himself. And vaguely, without comprehension, he saw the dreadful ministrant that hovered beside Obexah: a flayed and eyeless corpse in the image of her first lover, a boy from Cyntrom who had been cast ashore in shipwreck on the Isle of the Torturers. There Obexah had found him, lying behind the ebbing wave, and reviving the boy, she had hidden him awhile in a secret cave for her own pleasure, and had brought him food and drink. Later, wearying, she had betrayed him to the Torturers, and had taken a new delight in the various pangs and ordeals inflicted upon him before death by that cruel, pernicious people.

"Drink," said Namirrha, quaffing a strange wine that was red and dark as if with disastrous sunsets of lost years. And Zotulla and Obexah drank the wine, feeling no warmth in their veins thereafter, but a chill as of hemlock mounting slowly toward the heart.

"Verily, 'tis a good wine," said Namirrha, "and a proper one in which to toast the furthering of our acquaintance: for it was buried long ago with the royal dead, in amphorae of somber jasper shaped like funeral urns; and my ghouls found it, when they came to dig in Tasuun."

Now it seemed that the tongue of Zotulla froze in his mouth, as a mandrake freezes in the rime-bound soil of winter; and he found no reply to Namirrha's courtesy.

"Prithee, make trial of this meat," quoth Namirrha, "for it is very choice, being the flesh of that boar which the Torturers of Uccastrog are wont to pasture on the well-minced leavings of their wheels and racks; and, moreover, my cooks have spiced it with the powerful balsams of the tomb, and have farced it with the hearts of adders and the tongues of black cobras."

Naught could the emperor say; and even Obexah was silent, being sorely troubled in her turpitude by the presence of that flayed and piteous thing which had the likeness of her lover from Cyntrom. And the dread of the necromancer grew prodigiously; for his knowledge of this old, forgotten crime, and the raising of the fantasm, appeared to her a more baleful magic than all else.

"Now, I fear," said Namirrha, "that you find the meat devoid of savor, and the wine without fire. So, to enliven our feasting, I shall call forth my singers and my musicians."

He spoke a word unknown to Zotulla or Obexah, which sounded throughout the mighty hall as if a thousand voices in turn had taken it up and prolonged it. Anon there appeared the singers, who were she-ghouls with shaven bodies and hairy shanks, and long yellow tushes full of shredded carrion curving across their chaps from mouths that fawned hyena-wise on the company. Behind them entered the musicians, some of whom were male devils pacing erect on the hind-quarters of sable stallions and plucking with the fingers of white apes at lyres of the bone and sinew of cannibals from Naat; and others were pied satyrs puffing their goatish cheeks at hautboys formed from the bosom-skin of Negro queens and the horn of rhinoceri.

They bowed before Namirrha with grotesque ceremony. Then, without delay, the she-ghouls began a most dolorous and execrable howling, as of jackals that have sniffed their carrion; and the satyrs and devils played a lament that was like the moaning of desert-born winds through forsaken palace harems. And Zotulla shivered, for the singing filled his marrow with ice, and the music left in his heart a desolation as of empires fallen and trod under by the iron-shod hooves of time. Ever, amid that evil music, he seemed to hear the sifting of sand across withered gardens, and the windy rustling of rotted silks upon couches of bygone luxury, and the hissing of coiled serpents from the low fusts of shattered columns. And the glory that had been Ummaos seemed to pass away like the blown pillars of the simoom.

"Now that was a brave tune," said Namirrha when the music ceased and the she-ghouls no longer howled. "But verily I fear that you find my entertainment somewhat dull. Therefore, my dancers shall dance for you."

He turned toward the great hall, and described in the air an enigmatic sign with the fingers of his right hand. In answer to the sign, a hueless mist came down from the high roof and hid the room like a fallen curtain for a brief interim. There was a babel of sounds, confused and muffled, beyond the curtain, and a crying of voices faint as if with distance.

Then, dreadfully, the vapor rolled away, and Zotulla saw that the leaden tables had gone. In the wide interspaces of the columns, his palace-inmates, the chamberlains, the eunuchs, the courtiers and odalisques and all the others, lay trussed with thongs on the floor, like so many fowls of glorious plumage. Above them, in time to a music made by the lyrists and flutists of the necromancer, a troupe of skeletons pirouetted with light clickings of their toe-bones; and a rout of mummies bowed stiffly; and others of Namirrha's creatures moved with mysterious caperings. To and fro they leapt on the bodies of the emperor's people, in the paces of an evil saraband. At every step they grew taller and heavier, till the saltant mummies were as the mummies of Anakim, and the skeletons were boned as colossi; and louder the music rose, drowning the faint cries of Zotulla's people. And huger still became the dancers, towering far into vaulted shadow among the vast columns, with thudding feet that wrought thunder in the room; and those whereon they danced were as grapes trampled for a vintage in autumn; and the floor ran deep with a sanguine must.

As a man drowning in a noisome, night-bound fen, the emperor heard the voice of Namirrha:

"It would seem that my dancers please you not. So now I shall present you a most royal spectacle. Arise and follow me, for the spectacle is one that requires an empire for its stage."

Zotulla and Obexah rose from their chairs in the fashion of night-walkers. Giving no backward glance at their ministering phantoms, or the hall where the dancers bounded, they followed Namirrha to an alcove beyond the altar of Thasaidon. Thence, by the upward-coiling stairways, they came at length to a broad high balcony that faced Zotulla's palace and looked forth above the city roofs toward the bourn of sunset.

It seemed that several hours had gone by in that hellish feasting and entertainment; for the day was near to its close, and the sun, which had fallen from sight behind the imperial palace, was barring the vast heavens with bloody rays.

"Behold," said Namirrha, adding a strange vocable to which the stone of the edifice resounded like a beaten gong.

The balcony pitched a little, and Zotulla, looking over the balustrade, beheld the roofs of Ummaos lessen and sink beneath him. It seemed that the balcony flew skyward to a prodigious height, and he peered down across the domes of his own palace, upon the houses, the tilled fields and the desert beyond, and the huge sun brought low on the desert's verge. And Zotulla grew giddy; and the chill airs of the upper heavens blew upon him. But Namirrha spoke another word, and the balcony ceased to ascend.

"Look well," said the necromancer, "on the empire that was yours, but shall be yours no longer." Then, with arms outstretched toward the sunset, he called aloud the twelve names that were perdition to utter, and after them the tremendous invocation: *Gna padambis devompra thungis furidor avoragomon.*

Instantly, it seemed that great ebon clouds of thunder beetled against the sun. Lining the horizon, the clouds took the form of colossal monsters with heads and members somewhat resembling those of stallions. Rearing terribly, they trod down the sun like an extinguished ember; and racing as if in some hippodrome of Titans, they rose higher and vaster, coming towards Ummaos. Deep, calamitous rumblings preceded them, and the earth shook visibly, till Zotulla saw that these were not immaterial clouds, but actual living forms that had come forth to tread the world in macrocosmic vastness. Throwing their shadows for many leagues before them, the coursers charged as if devil-ridden into Xylac, and their feet descended like falling mountain crags upon far oases and towns of the outer wastes.

Like a many-turreted storm they came, and it seemed that the world shrank gulfward, tilting beneath the weight. Still as a man enchanted into marble, Zotulla stood and beheld the ruining that was wrought on his empire. And closer drew the gigantic stallions, racing with inconceivable speed, and louder was the thundering of their footfalls, that now began to blot the green fields and fruited orchards lying for many miles to the west of Ummaos. And the shadow of the stallions climbed like an evil gloom of eclipse, till it covered Ummaos; and looking up, the emperor saw their eyes halfway between earth and zenith, like baleful suns that glare down from soaring cumuli.

Then, in the thickening gloom, above that insupportable thunder, he heard the voice of Namirrha, crying in mad triumph:

"Know, Zotulla, that I have called up the coursers of Thamogorgos, lord of the abyss. And the coursers will tread your empire down, even as your palfrey trod and trampled in former time a beggar-boy named Narthos. And learn also that I, Namirrha, was that boy." And the eyes of Namirrha, filled with a vainglory of madness and bale, burned like malign, disastrous stars at the hour of their culmination.

To Zotulla, wholly mazed with the horror and tumult, the necromancer's words were no more than shrill, shrieked overtones of the tempest of doom; and he understood them not. Tremendously, with a rending of staunch-built roofs, and an instant cleavage and crumbling down of mighty masonries, the hooves descended upon Ummaos. Fair temple-domes were pashed like shells of the haliotis, and haughty mansions were broken and stamped into the ground even as gourds; and house by house the city was trampled flat with a crashing as of worlds beaten into chaos. Far below, in the darkened streets, men and camels fled like scurrying emmets but could not escape. And implacably the hooves rose and fell, till ruin was upon half the city, and night was over all. The palace of Zotulla was trodden under, and now the forelegs of the coursers loomed level with Namirrha's balcony, and their heads towered awfully above. It seemed that they would rear and trample down the necromancer's house; but at that moment they parted to left and right, and a dolorous glimmering came from the low sunset; and the coursers went on, treading under them that portion of Ummaos which lay to the eastward. And Zotulla and Obexah and Namirrha looked down on the city's fragments as on a shard-strewn midden, and heard the cataclysmic clamor of the hooves departing toward eastern Xylac.

"Now that was a goodly spectacle," quoth Namirrha. Then, turning to the emperor, he added malignly: "Think not that I have done with thee, however, or that doom is yet consummate."

It seemed that the balcony had fallen to its former elevation, which was still a lofty vantage above the sharded ruins. And Namirrha plucked the emperor by the arm and led him from the balcony to an inner chamber, while Obexah followed mutely. The emperor's heart was crushed within him by the trampling of such calamities, and despair weighed upon him like a foul incubus on the shoulders of a man lost in some land of accursed night. And he knew not that he had been parted from Obexah on the threshold of the chamber, and that certain of Namirrha's creatures, appearing like shadows, had compelled the girl to go downward with them by the stairs, and had stifled her outcries with their rotten cerements as they went.

The chamber was one that Namirrha used for his most unhallowed rites and alchemies. The rays of the lamps that illumed it were saffron-red like the spilt ichor of devils, and they flowed on aludels and crucibles and black athanors and alembics whereof the purpose was hardly to be named by mortal man. The sorcerer heated in one of the alembics a dark liquid full of star-cold lights, while Zotulla looked on unheeding. And when the liquid bubbled and sent forth a spiral vapor, Namirrha distilled it into goblets of gold-rimmed iron, and gave one of the goblets to Zotulla and retained the other himself. And he said to Zotulla with a stern imperative voice: "I bid thee quaff this liquor."

Zotulla, fearing that the draft was poison, hesitated. And the necromancer regarded him with a lethal gaze, and cried loudly: "Fearest thou to do as I?" and therewith he set the goblet to his lips.

So the emperor drank the draft, constrained as if by the bidding of some angel of death, and a darkness fell upon his senses. But, ere the darkness grew complete, he saw that Namirrha had drained his own goblet.

Then, with unspeakable agonies, it seemed that the emperor died; and his soul float free; and again he saw the chamber, though with bodiless eyes. And discarnate he stood in the saffron-crimson light, with his body lying as if dead on the floor beside him, and near it the prone body of Namirrha and the two fallen goblets.

Standing thus, he beheld a strange thing: for anon his own body stirred and arose, while that of the necromancer remained still as death. And Zotulla looked at his own lineaments and his figure in its short cloak of azure samite sewn with black pearls and balas-rubies; and the body lived before him, though with eyes that held a darker fire and a deeper evil than was their wont. Then, without corporeal ears, Zotulla heard the figure speak, and the voice was the strong, arrogant voice of Namirrha, saying:

"Follow me, O houseless phantom, and do in all things as I enjoin thee."

Like an unseen shadow, Zotulla followed the wizard, and the twain went downward by the stairs to the great banquet hall. They came to the altar of Thasaidon and the mailed image, with the seven horse-skull lamps burning before it as formerly. Upon the altar, Zotulla's beloved leman Obexah, who alone of all women had power to stir his sated heart, was lying bound with thongs at Thasaidon's feet. But the hall beyond was deserted, and nothing remained of that Saturnalia of doom except the fruit of the treading, which had flowed together in dark pools among the columns.

Namirrha, using the emperor's body in all ways for his own, paused before the dark eidolon; and he said to the spirit of Zotulla: "Be imprisoned in this image, without power to free thyself or to stir in any wise."

Being wholly obedient to the will of the necromancer, the soul of Zotulla was embodied in the statue, and he felt its cold, gigantic armor about him like a straight sarcophagus, and he peered forth immovably from the bleak eyes that were overhung by its carven helmet.

Gazing thus, he beheld the change that had come on his own body through the sorcerous possession of Namirrha: for below the short azure cloak, the legs had turned suddenly to the hind legs of a black stallion, with hooves that glowed redly as if heated by infernal fires. And even as Zotulla watched this prodigy, the hooves glowed white and incandescent, and fumes mounted from the floor beneath them.

Then, on the black altar, the hybrid abomination came pacing haughtily toward Obexah, and smoking footprints appeared behind it as it came. Pausing beside the girl, who lay supine and helpless regarding it with eyes that were pools of frozen horror, it raised one glowing hoof and set the hoof on her naked bosom between the small breast-cups of golden filigree begemmed with rubies. And the girl screamed beneath that atrocious treading as the soul of one newly damned might scream in hell; and the hoof glared with intolerable brilliance, as if freshly plucked from a furnace wherein the weapons of demons were forged.

At that moment, in the cowed and crushed and sodden shade of the emperor Zotulla, close-locked within the adamantine image, there awoke the manhood that had slumbered unaroused before the ruining of his empire and the trampling of his retinue. Immediately a great abhorrence and a high wrath were alive in his soul, and mightily he longed for his own right arm to serve him, and a sword in his right hand.

Then it seemed that a voice spoke within him, chill and bleak and awful, and as if uttered inwardly by the statue itself. And the voice said: "I am Thasaidon, lord of the seven hells beneath the earth, and the hells of man's heart above the earth, which are seven times seven. For the moment, O Zotulla, my power is become thine for the sake of a mutual vengeance. Be one in all ways with the statue that has my likeness, even as the soul is one with the flesh. Behold! there is a mace of adamant in thy right hand. Lift up the mace, and smite."

Zotulla was aware of a great power within him, and giant thews about him that thrilled with the power and responded agilely to his will. He felt in his mailed right hand the haft of the huge spiky-headed mace; and though the mace was beyond the lifting of any man in mortal flesh, it seemed no more than a goodly weight to Zotulla. Then, rearing he mace like a warrior in battle, he struck down with one crashing blow the impious thing that wore his own rightful flesh united with the legs and hooves of a demon courser. And the thing crumpled swiftly down and lay with the brain spreading pulpily from its shattered skull on the shining jet. And the legs twitched a little and then grew still; and the hooves glowed from a fiery, blinding white to the redness of red-hot iron, cooling slowly.

For a space there was no sound, other than the shrill screaming of the girl Obexah, mad with pain and the terror of those prodigies which she had beheld. Then in the soul of Zotulla, grown sick with that screaming, the chill, awful voice of Thasaidon spoke again:

"Go free, for there is nothing more for thee to do." So the spirit of Zotulla passed from the image of Thasaidon and found in the wide air the freedom of nothingness and oblivion.

But the end was not yet for Namirrha, whose mad, arrogant soul had been loosened from Zotulla's body by the blow, and had returned darkly, not in the manner planned by the magician, to its own body lying in the room of accursed rites and forbidden transmigrations. There Namirrha woke anon, with a dire confusion in his mind, and a partial forgetfulness: for the curse of Thasaidon was upon him now because of his blasphemies.

Nothing was clear in his thought except a malign, exorbitant longing for revenge; but the reason thereof, and the object, were as doubtful shadows. And still prompted by that obscure animus, he arose; and girding to his side an enchanted sword with runic sapphires and opals in the hilt, he descended the stairs and came again to the altar of Thasaidon, where the mailed statue stood as impassive as before, with the poised mace in its immovable right hand, and below it, on the altar, the double sacrifice.

A veil of weird darkness was upon the senses of Namirrha, and he saw not the stallion-legged horror that lay dead with slowly blackening hooves; and he heard not the moaning of the girl Obexah, who still lived beside it. But his eyes were drawn by the diamond mirror that was upheld in the claws of black iron basilisks beyond the altar; and going to the mirror, he saw therein a face that he knew no longer for his own. And because his eyes were shadowed and his brain filled with the shifting webs of delusion, he took the face for that of the emperor Zotulla. Insatiable as Hell's own flame, his old hatred rose within him; and he drew the enchanted sword and began to hew therewith at the reflection. Sometimes, because of the curse laid upon him, and the impious transmigration which he had performed, he thought himself Zotulla warring with the necromancer; and again, in the shiftings of his madness, he was Namirrha smiting at the emperor; and then, without name, he fought a nameless foe. And soon the sorcerous blade, though tempered with formidable spells, was broken close to the hilt, and Namirrha beheld the image still unharmed. Then, howling aloud the half-forgotten runes of a most tremendous curse, made invalid through his own forgettings, he hammered still with the heavy sword-hilt on the mirror, till the runic sapphires and opals cracked in the hilt and fell away at his feet in little fragments.

Obexah, dying on the altar, saw Namirrha battling with his image, and the spectacle moved her to mad laughter like the pealing of bells of ruined crystal. And above her laughter, and above the cursings of Namirrha, there came anon like the rumbling of a swift-driven storm the thunder made by the macrocosmic stallions of Thamogorgos, returning gulfward through Xylac over Ummaos, to trample down the one house that they had spared aforetime.

ⵅ

In the 1940s, when Jack Vance (1916–2013) was writing the stories that would constitute The Dying Earth, *S&S fantasy was so overshadowed by the popularity of science fiction, it barely existed. Jack Vance wrote S&S anyway, coating it with the patina of SF by setting it on a far-future Earth where a depleted and decadent population exists under a failing sun. Full of cynicism and dark humor, the tales had far more sorcery than swordplay, but when S&S was revived and defined, they were considered part of the genre.*

Neil Gaiman discovered Vance at age thirteen and has written: "I loved the way he would digress. I loved the way he would imagine, and most of all I loved the way he wrote it all down: wryly, gently amused, like a god would be amused, but never in a way that made less of what he wrote . . . He's imitable."

"Liane the Wayfarer" was one of six stories in The Dying Earth *(1950). Often called a novel, the book—Vance's first published stories—is really a collection of linked short fiction. "Liane the Wayfarer" also appeared (as "The Loom of Darkness") in the December 1950 issue of* Worlds Beyond. *(The inclusion was, no doubt, promotional as the magazine's publisher, Hillman Periodicals, also published Vance's book. The issue's back cover is an in-house advertisement for* The Dying Earth.*)*

LIANE THE WAYFARER

Jack Vance

Through the dim forest came Liane the Wayfarer, passing along the shadowed glades with a prancing light-footed gait. He whistled, he caroled, he was plainly in high spirits. Around his finger he twirled a bit of wrought bronze—a circlet graved with angular crabbed characters, now stained black.

By excellent chance he had found it, banded around the root of an ancient yew. Hacking it free, he had seen the characters on the inner surface—rude forceful symbols, doubtless the cast of a powerful antique rune . . . Best take it to a magician and have it tested for sorcery.

Liane made a wry mouth. There were objections to the course. Sometimes it seemed as if all living creatures conspired to exasperate him. Only this morning, the spice merchant—what a tumult he had made dying! How carelessly he had spewed blood on Liane's cock comb sandals! Still, thought Liane, every unpleasantness carried with it compensation. While digging the grave he had found the bronze ring.

And Liane's spirits soared; he laughed in pure joy. He bounded, he leapt. His green cape flapped behind him, the red feather in his cap winked and blinked . . . But still—Liane slowed his step—he was no whit closer to the mystery of the magic, if magic the ring possessed.

Experiment, that was the word!

He stopped where the ruby sunlight slanted down without hindrance from the high foliage, examined the ring, traced the glyphs with his fingernail. He peered through. A faint film, a flicker? He held it at arm's length. It was clearly a coronet. He whipped off his cap, set the band on his brow, rolled his great golden eyes, preened himself . . . Odd. It slipped down on his ears. It tipped across his eyes. Darkness. Frantically Liane clawed it off . . . A bronze ring, a hand's-breadth in diameter. Queer.

He tried again. It slipped down over his head, his shoulders. His head was in the darkness of a strange separate space. Looking down, he saw the level of the outside light dropping as he dropped the ring.

Slowly down . . . Now it was around his ankles—and in sudden panic, Liane snatched the ring up over his body, emerged blinking into the maroon light of the forest.

He saw a blue-white, green-white flicker against the foliage. It was a Twk-man, mounted on a dragon-fly, and light glinted from the dragon-fly's wings.

Liane called sharply, "Here, sir! Here, sir!"

The Twk-man perched his mount on a twig. "Well, Liane, what do you wish?"

"Watch now, and remember what you see." Liane pulled the ring over his head, dropped it to his feet, lifted it back. He looked up to the Twk-man, who was chewing a leaf. "And what did you see?"

"I saw Liane vanish from mortal sight—except for the red curled toes of his sandals. All else was as air."

"Ha!" cried Liane. "Think of it! Have you ever seen the like?"

The Twk-man asked carelessly, "Do you have salt? I would have salt."

Liane cut his exultation short, eyed the Twk-man closely.

"What news do you bring me?"

"Three erbs killed Florejin the Dream-builder, and burst all his bubbles. The air above the manse was colored for many minutes with the flitting fragments."

"A gram."

"Lord Kandive the Golden has built a barge of carven mo-wood ten lengths high, and it floats on the River Scaum for the Regatta, full of treasure."

"Two grams."

"A golden witch named Lith has come to live on Thamber Meadow. She is quiet and very beautiful."

"Three grams."

"Enough," said the Twk-man, and leaned forward to watch while Liane weighed out the salt in a tiny balance. He packed it in small panniers hanging on each side of the ribbed thorax, then twitched the insect into the air and flicked off through the forest vaults.

Once more Liane tried the bronze ring, and this time brought it entirely past his feet, stepped out of it and brought the ring up into the darkness beside him. What a wonderful sanctuary! A hole whose opening could be hidden inside the hole itself! Down with the ring to his feet, step through, bring it up his slender frame and over his shoulders, out into the forest with a small bronze ring in his hand.

Ho! and off to Thamber Meadow to see the beautiful golden witch.

Her hut was a simple affair of woven reeds—a low dome with two round windows and a low door. He saw Lith at the pond bare-legged among the water shoots, catching frogs for her supper. A white kirtle was gathered up tight around her thighs; stock-still she stood and the dark water rippled rings away from her slender knees.

She was more beautiful than Liane could have imagined, as if one of Florejin's wasted bubbles had burst here on the water. Her skin was pale creamed stirred gold, her hair a denser, wetter gold. Her eyes were like Liane's own, great golden orbs, and hers were wide apart, tilted slightly.

Liane strode forward and planted himself on the bank. She looked up startled, her ripe mouth half-open.

"Behold, golden witch, here is Liane. He has come to welcome you to Thamber; and he offers you his friendship, his love . . . "

Lith bent, scooped a handful of slime from the bank and flung it into his face.

Shouting the most violent curses, Liane wiped his eyes free, but the door to the hut had slammed shut.

Liane strode to the door and pounded it with his fist.

"Open and show your witch's face, or I burn the hut!"

The door opened, and the girl looked forth, smiling. "What now?"

Liane entered the hut and lunged for the girl, but twenty thin shafts darted out, twenty points pricking his chest. He halted, eyebrows raised, mouth twitching.

"Down, steel," said Lith. The blades snapped from view. "So easily could I seek your vitality," said Lith, "had I willed."

Liane frowned and rubbed his chin as if pondering. "You understand," he said earnestly, "what a witless thing you do. Liane is feared by those who fear fear, loved by those who love love. And you—" his eyes swam the golden glory of her body "—you are ripe as a sweet fruit, you are eager, you glisten and tremble with love. You please Liane, and he will spend much warmness on you."

"No, no," said Lith, with a slow smile. "You are too hasty."

Liane looked at her in surprise. "Indeed?"

"I am Lith," said she. "I am what you say I am. I ferment, I burn, I seethe. Yet I may have no lover but him who has served me. He must be brave, swift, cunning."

"I am he," said Liane. He chewed his lip. "It is not usually thus. I detest this indecision." He took a step forward. "Come, let us—"

She backed away. "No, no. You forget. How have you served me, how have you gained the right to my love?"

"Absurdity!" stormed Liane. "Look at me! Note my perfect grace, the beauty of my form and feature, my great eyes, as golden as your own, my manifest will and power . . . It is you who should serve me. That is how I will have it." He sank upon a low divan. "Woman, give me wine."

She shook her head. "In my small domed hut I cannot be forced. Perhaps outside on Thamber Meadow—but in here, among my blue and red tassels, with twenty blades of steel at my call, you must obey me . . . So choose. Either arise and go, never to return, or else agree to serve me on one small mission, and then have me and all my ardor."

Liane sat straight and stiff. An odd creature, the golden witch. But, indeed, she was worth some exertion, and he would make her pay for her impudence.

"Very well, then," he said blandly. "I will serve you. What do you wish? Jewels? I can suffocate you in pearls, blind you with diamonds. I have two emeralds the size of your fist, and they are green oceans, where the gaze is trapped and wanders forever among vertical green prisms . . . "

"No, no jewels—"

"An enemy, perhaps. Ah, so simple. Liane will kill you ten men. Two steps forward, thrust—thus!" He lunged. "And souls go thrilling up like bubbles in a beaker of mead."

"No. I want no killing."

He sat back, frowning. "What, then?"

She stepped to the back of the room and pulled at a drape. It swung aside, displaying a golden tapestry. The scene was a valley bounded by two steep mountains, a broad valley where a placid river ran, past a quiet village and so into a grove of trees. Golden was the river, golden the mountains, golden the trees—golds so various, so rich, so subtle that the effect was like a many-colored landscape. But the tapestry had been rudely hacked in half.

Liane was entranced. "Exquisite, exquisite . . . "

Lith said, "It is the Magic Valley of Ariventa so depicted. The other half has been stolen from me, and its recovery is the service I wish of you."

"Where is the other half?" demanded Liane. "Who is the dastard?"

Now she watched him closely. "Have you ever heard of Chun? Chun the Unavoidable?"

Liane considered. "No."

"He stole the half to my tapestry, and hung it in a marble hall, and this hall is in the ruins to the north of Kaiin."

"Ha!" muttered Liane.

"The hall is by the Place of Whispers, and is marked by a leaning column with a black medallion of a phoenix and a two-headed lizard."

"I go," said Liane. He rose. "One day to Kaiin, one day to steal, one day to return. Three days."

Lith followed him to the door. "Beware of Chun the Unavoidable," she whispered.

And Liane strode away whistling, the red feather bobbing in his green cap. Lith watched him, then turned and slowly approached the golden tapestry. "Golden Ariventa," she whispered, "my heart cries and hurts with longing for you . . . "

The Derna is a swifter, thinner river than the Scaum, its bosomy sister to the south. And where the Scaum wallows through a broad dale, purple with horse-blossom, pocked white and gray with crumbling castles, the Derna has sheered a steep canyon, overhung by forested bluffs.

An ancient flint road long ago followed the course of the Derna, but now the exaggeration of the meandering has cut into the pavement, so that Liane, treading the road to Kaiin, was occasionally forced to leave the road and make a detour through banks of thorn and the tube-grass which whistled in the breeze.

The red sun, drifting across the universe like an old man creeping to his deathbed, hung low to the horizon when Liane breasted Porphiron Scar, looked across white-walled Kaiin and the blue bay of Sanreale beyond.

Directly below was the market-place, a medley of stalls selling fruits, slabs of pale meat, mollusks from the slime banks, dull flagons of wine. And the quiet people of Kaiin moved among the stalls, buying their sustenance, carrying it loosely to their stone chambers.

Beyond the market-place rose a bank of ruined columns, like broken teeth—legs to the arena built two hundred feet from the ground by Mad King Shin; beyond, in a grove of bay trees, the glossy dome of the palace was visible, where Kandive the Golden ruled Kaiin and as much of Ascolais as one could see from a vantage on the Porphiron Scar.

The Derna, no longer a flow of clear water, poured through a network of dank canals and subterranean tubes, and finally seeped past rotting wharves into the Bay of Sanreale.

A bed for the night, thought Liane; then to his business in the morning.

He leapt down the zig-zag steps—back, forth, back, forth—and came out into the market-place. And now he put on a grave demeanor. Liane the Wayfarer was not unknown in Kaiin, and many were ill-minded enough to work him harm.

He moved sedately in the shade of the Pannone Wall, turned through a narrow cobbled street, bordered by old wooden houses glowing the rich brown of old stump-water in the rays of the setting sun, and so came to a small square and the high stone face of the Magician's Inn.

The host, a small fat man, sad of eye, with a small fat nose the identical shape of his body, was scraping ashes from the hearth. He straightened his back and hurried behind the counter of his little alcove.

Liane said, "A chamber, well-aired, and a supper of mushrooms, wine and oysters."

The innkeeper bowed humbly.

"Indeed, sir—and how will you pay?"

Liane flung down a leather sack, taken this very morning. The innkeeper raised his eyebrows in pleasure at the fragrance.

"The ground buds of the spase-bush, brought from a far land," said Liane.

"Excellent, excellent . . . Your chamber, sir, and your supper at once."

As Liane ate, several other guests of the house appeared and sat before the fire with wine, and the talk grew large, and dwelt on wizards of the past and the great days of magic.

"Great Phandaal knew a lore now forgot," said one old man with hair dyed orange. "He tied white and black strings to the legs of sparrows and sent them veering to his direction. And where they wove their magic woof, great trees appeared, laden with flowers, fruits, nuts, or bulbs of rare liqueurs. It is said that thus he wove Great Da Forest on the shores of Sanra Water."

"Ha," said a dour man in a garment of dark blue, brown and black, "this I can do." He brought forth a bit of string, flicked it, whirled it, spoke a quiet word, and the vitality of the pattern fused the string into a tongue of red and yellow fire, which danced, curled, darted back and forth along the table till the dour man killed it with a gesture.

"And this I can do," said a hooded figure in a black cape sprinkled with silver circles. He brought forth a small tray, laid it on the table and sprinkled therein a pinch of ashes from the hearth. He brought forth a whistle and blew a clear tone, and up from the tray came glittering motes, flashing the prismatic colors red, blue, green, yellow. They floated up a foot and burst in coruscations of brilliant colors, each a beautiful star-shaped pattern, and each burst sounded a tiny repetition of the original tone—the clearest, purest sound in the world. The motes became fewer, the magician blew a different tone, and again the motes floated up to burst in glorious ornamental spangles. Another time—another swarm of motes. At last the magician replaced his whistle, wiped off the tray, tucked it inside his cloak and lapsed back to silence.

Now the other wizards surged forward, and soon the air above the table swarmed with visions, quivered with spells. One showed the group nine new colors of ineffable charm and radiance; another caused a mouth to form on the landlord's forehead and revile the crowd, much to the landlord's discomfiture, since it was his own voice. Another displayed a green glass bottle from which the face of a demon peered and grimaced; another a ball of pure crystal which rolled back and forward to the command of the sorcerer who owned it, and who claimed it to be an earring of the fabled master Sankaferrin.

Liane had attentively watched all, crowing in delight at the bottled imp, and trying to cozen the obedient crystal from its owner, without success.

And Liane became pettish, complaining that the world was full of rock-hearted men, but the sorcerer with the crystal earring remained indifferent, and even when Liane spread out twelve packets of rare spice he refused to part with his toy.

Liane pleaded, "I wish only to please the witch Lith."

"Please her with the spice, then."

Liane said ingenuously, "Indeed, she has but one wish, a bit of tapestry which I must steal from Chun the Unavoidable."

And he looked from face to suddenly silent face.

"What causes such immediate sobriety? Ho, Landlord, more wine!"

The sorcerer with the earring said, "If the floor swam ankle-deep with wine—the rich red wine of Tanvilkat—the leaden print of that name would still ride the air."

"Ha," laughed Liane, "let only a taste of that wine pass your lips, and the fumes would erase all memory."

"See his eyes," came a whisper. "Great and golden."

"And quick to see," spoke Liane. "And these legs—quick to run, fleet as starlight on the waves. And this arm—quick to stab with steel. And my magic—which will set me to a refuge that is out of all cognizance." He gulped wine from a beaker. "Now behold. This is magic from antique days." He set the bronze band over his head, stepped through, brought it up inside the darkness. When he deemed that sufficient time had elapsed, he stepped through once more.

The fire glowed, the landlord stood in his alcove, Liane's wine was at hand. But of the assembled magicians, there was no trace.

Liane looked about in puzzlement. "And where are my wizardly friends?"

The landlord turned his head. "They took to their chambers; the name you spoke weighed on their souls."

And Liane drank his wine in frowning silence.

Next morning he left the inn and picked a roundabout way to the Old Town—a gray wilderness of tumbled pillars, weathered blocks of sandstone, slumped pediments with crumbled inscriptions, flagged terraces overgrown with rusty moss. Lizards, snakes, insects crawled the ruins; no other life did he see.

Threading a way through the rubble, he almost stumbled on a corpse—the body of a youth, one who stared at the sky with empty eye-sockets.

Liane felt a presence. He leapt back, rapier half-bared. A stooped old man stood watching him. He spoke in a feeble, quavering voice: "And what will you have in the Old Town?"

Liane replaced his rapier. "I seek the Place of Whispers. Perhaps you will direct me."

The old man made a croaking sound at the back of his throat. "Another? Another? When will it cease? . . . " He motioned to the corpse. "This one came yesterday seeking the Place of Whispers. He would steal from Chun the Unavoidable. See him now." He turned away. "Come with me." He disappeared over a tumble of rock.

Liane followed. The old man stood by another corpse with eye-sockets bereft and bloody. "This one came four days ago, and he met Chun the Unavoidable . . . And over there behind the arch is still, a great warrior in cloison armor. And there—and there—" he pointed, pointed. "And there—and there—like crushed flies."

He turned his watery blue gaze back to Liane. "Return, young man, return—lest your body lie here in its green cloak to rot on the flagstones."

Liane drew his rapier and flourished it. "I am Liane the Wayfarer; let them who offend me have fear. And where is the Place of Whispers?"

"If you must know," said the old man, "it is beyond that broken obelisk. But you go to your peril."

"I am Liane the Wayfarer. Peril goes with me."

The old man stood like a piece of weathered statuary as Liane strode off.

And Liane asked himself, suppose this old man were an agent of Chun, and at this minute were on his way to warn him? . . . Best to take all precautions. He leapt up on a high entablature and ran crouching back to where he had left the ancient.

Here he came, muttering to himself, leaning on his staff. Liane dropped a block of granite as large as his head. A thud, a croak, a gasp—and Liane went his way.

He strode past the broken obelisk, into a wide court—the Place of Whispers. Directly opposite was a long wide hall, marked by a leaning column with a big black medallion, the sign of a phoenix and a two-headed lizard.

Liane merged himself with the shadow of a wall, and stood watching like a wolf, alert for any flicker of motion.

All was quiet. The sunlight invested the ruins with dreary splendor. To all sides, as far as the eye could reach, was broken stone, a wasteland leached by a thousand rains, until now the sense of man had departed and the stone was one with the natural earth.

The sun moved across the dark-blue sky. Liane presently stole from his vantage-point and circled the hall. No sight nor sign did he see.

He approached the building from the rear and pressed his ear to the stone. It was dead, without vibration. Around the side—watching up, down, to all sides; a breach in the wall. Liane peered inside. At the back hung half a golden tapestry. Otherwise the hall was empty.

Liane looked up, down, this side, that. There was nothing in sight. He continued around the hall.

He came to another broken place. He looked within. To the rear hung the golden tapestry. Nothing else, to right or left, no sight or sound.

Liane continued to the front of the hall and sought into the eaves; dead as dust.

He had a clear view of the room. Bare, barren, except for the bit of golden tapestry.

Liane entered, striding with long soft steps. He halted in the middle of the floor. Light came to him from all sides except the rear wall. There were a dozen openings from which to flee and no sound except the dull thudding of his heart.

He took two steps forward. The tapestry was almost at his fingertips.

He stepped forward and swiftly jerked the tapestry down from the wall.

And behind was Chun the Unavoidable.

Liane screamed. He turned on paralyzed legs and they were leaden, like legs in a dream which refused to run.

Chun dropped out of the wall and advanced. Over his shiny black back he wore a robe of eyeballs threaded on silk.

Liane was running, fleetly now. He sprang, he soared. The tips of his toes scarcely touched the ground. Out the hall, across the square, into the wilderness of broken statues and fallen columns. And behind came Chun, running like a dog.

Liane sped along the crest of a wall and sprang a great gap to a shattered fountain. Behind came Chun.

Liane darted up a narrow alley, climbed over a pile of refuse, over a roof, down into a court. Behind came Chun.

Liane sped down a wide avenue lined with a few stunted old cypress trees, and he heard Chun close at his heels. He turned into an archway, pulled his bronze ring over his head, down to his feet. He stepped through, brought the ring up inside the darkness. Sanctuary. He was alone in a dark magic space, vanished from earthly gaze and knowledge. Brooding silence, dead space . . .

He felt a stir behind him, a breath of air. At his elbow a voice said, "I am Chun the Unavoidable."

Lith sat on her couch near the candles, weaving a cap from frogskins. The door to her hut was barred, the windows shuttered. Outside, Thamber Meadow dwelled in darkness.

A scrape at her door, a creak as the lock was tested. Lith became rigid and stared at the door.

A voice said, "Tonight, O Lith, tonight it is two long bright threads for you. Two because the eyes were so great, so large, so golden . . . "

Lith sat quiet. She waited an hour; then, creeping to the door, she listened. The sense of presence was absent. A frog croaked nearby.

She eased the door ajar, found the threads and closed the door. She ran to her golden tapestry and fitted the threads into the raveled warp.

And she stared at the golden valley, sick with longing for Ariventa, and tears blurred out the peaceful river, the quiet golden forest. "The cloth slowly grows wider . . . One day it will be done, and I will come home . . . "

ᚷ

Leigh Brackett (1915–1978) has been getting more notice lately for her final film work—the first draft script of Star Wars: The Empire Strikes Back*—than her writing of fantasy and science fiction. But our interest here is in her "planetary romance"—which, in this case, is just another name for sword and sorcery set on a fantasy Mars (and, later, other planets beyond our solar system) owing far more to Edgar Rice Burroughs' imaginary Barsoom than to scientific speculation. To quote* The Encyclopedia of Fantasy*: "the development of the sword and sorcery subgenre is as attributable to [Leigh Brackett] as to [Robert] Howard." Her hero, Eric John Stark, made his first appearance in "Queen of the Martian Catacombs" in 1949. As John Clute has written, "Stark concentrates all the virtues of the sword-and-sorcery hero in his lean figure, rather like Robert E. Howard's Conan, though Stark—an orphan of advanced civilization raised by aboriginals of Mercury—is considerably more complex than his mentor." Unusually for the era, in the clash between imperialism and the colonized, Stark sides with the repressed.*

BLACK AMAZON OF MARS

Leigh Brackett

I

Through all the long cold hours of the Norland night the Martian had not moved nor spoken. At dusk of the day before Eric John Stark had brought him into the ruined tower and laid him down, wrapped in blankets, on the snow. He had built a fire of dead brush, and since then the two men had waited, alone in the vast wasteland that girdles the polar cap of Mars.

Now, just before dawn, Camar the Martian spoke.

"Stark."

"Yes?"

"I am dying."

"Yes."

"I will not reach Kushat."

"No."

Camar nodded. He was silent again.

The wind howled down from the northern ice, and the broken walls rose up against it, brooding, gigantic, roofless now but so huge and sprawling that they seemed less like walls than cliffs of ebon stone. Stark would not have gone near them but for Camar. They were wrong, somehow, with a taint of forgotten evil still about them.

The big Earthman glanced at Camar, and his face was sad. "A man likes to die in his own place," he said abruptly. "I am sorry."

"The Lord of Silence is a great personage," Camar answered. "He does not mind the meeting place. No. It was not for that I came back into the Norlands."

He was shaken by an agony that was not of the body. "And I shall not reach Kushat!"

Stark spoke quietly, using the courtly High Martian almost as fluently as Camar.

"I have known that there was a burden heavier than death upon my brother's soul."

He leaned over, placing one large hand on the Martian's shoulder. "My brother has given his life for mine. Therefore, I will take his burden upon myself, if I can."

He did not want Camar's burden, whatever it might be. But the Martian had fought beside him through a long guerilla campaign among the harried tribes of the nearer moon. He was a good man of his hands, and in the end had taken the bullet that was meant for Stark, knowing quite well what he was doing. They were friends.

That was why Stark had brought Camar into the bleak north country, trying to reach the city of his birth. The Martian was driven by some secret demon. He was afraid to die before he reached Kushat.

And now he had no choice.

"I have sinned, Stark. I have stolen a holy thing. You're an outlander, you would not know of Ban Cruach, and the talisman that he left when he went away forever beyond the Gates of Death."

Camar flung aside the blankets and sat up, his voice gaining a febrile strength.

"I was born and bred in the Thieves' Quarter under the Wall. I was proud of my skill. And the talisman was a challenge. It was a treasured thing—so treasured that hardly a man has touched it since the days of Ban Cruach who made it. And that was in the days when men still had the lustre on them, before they forgot that they were gods.

"'Guard well the Gates of Death,' he said, 'that is the city's trust. And keep the talisman always, for the day may come when you will need its strength. Who holds Kushat holds Mars—and the talisman will keep the city safe.'

"I was a thief, and proud. And I stole the talisman."

His hands went to his girdle, a belt of worn leather with a boss of battered steel. But his fingers were already numb.

"Take it, Stark. Open the boss—there, on the side, where the beast's head is carved . . . "

Stark took the belt from Camar and found the hidden spring. The rounded top of the boss came free. Inside it was something wrapped in a scrap of silk.

"I had to leave Kushat," Camar whispered. "I could never go back. But it was enough—to have taken that."

He watched, shaken between awe and pride and remorse, as Stark unwrapped the bit of silk.

Stark had discounted most of Camar's talk as superstition, but even so he had expected something more spectacular than the object he held in his palm.

It was a lens, some four inches across—man-made, and made with great skill, but still only a bit of crystal. Turning it about, Stark saw that it was not a simple lens, but an intricate interlocking of many facets. Incredibly complicated, hypnotic if one looked at it too long.

"What is its use?" he asked of Camar.

"We are as children. We have forgotten. But there is a legend, a belief—that Ban Cruach himself made the talisman as a sign that he would not forget us, and would come back when Kushat is threatened. Back through the Gates of Death, to teach us again the power that was his!"

"I do not understand," said Stark. "What are the Gates of Death?"

Camar answered, "It is a pass that opens into the black mountains beyond Kushat. The city stands guard before it—why, no man remembers, except that it is a great trust."

His gaze feasted on the talisman.

Stark said, "You wish me to take this to Kushat?"

"Yes. Yes! And yet . . . " Camar looked at Stark, his eyes filling suddenly with tears. "No. The North is not used to strangers. With me, you might have been safe. But alone . . . No, Stark. You have risked too much already. Go back, out of the Norlands, while you can."

He lay back on the blankets. Stark saw that a bluish pallor had come into the hollows of his cheeks.

"Camar," he said. And again, "Camar!"

"Yes?"

"Go in peace, Camar. I will take the talisman to Kushat."

The Martian sighed, and smiled, and Stark was glad that he had made the promise.

"The riders of Mekh are wolves," said Camar suddenly. "They hunt these gorges. Look out for them."

"I will."

Stark's knowledge of the geography of this part of Mars was vague indeed, but he knew that the mountain valleys of Mekh lay ahead and to the north, between him and Kushat. Camar had told him of these upland warriors. He was willing to heed the warning.

Camar had done with talking. Stark knew that he had not long to wait. The wind spoke with the voice of a great organ. The moons had set and it was very dark outside the tower, except for the white glimmering of the snow. Stark looked up at the brooding walls, and shivered. There was a smell of death already in the air.

To keep from thinking, he bent closer to the fire, studying the lens. There were scratches on the bezel, as though it had been held sometime in a clamp, or setting, like a jewel. An ornament, probably, worn as a badge of rank. Strange ornament for a barbarian king, in the dawn of Mars. The firelight made tiny dancing sparks in the endless inner facets. Quite suddenly, he had a curious feeling that the thing was alive.

A pang of primitive and unreasoning fear shot through him, and he fought it down. His vision was beginning to blur, and he shut his eyes, and in the darkness it seemed to him that he could see and hear . . .

He started up, shaken now with an eerie terror, and raised his hand to hurl the talisman away. But the part of him that had learned with much pain and effort to be civilized made him stop, and think.

He sat down again. An instrument of hypnosis? Possibly. And yet that fleeting touch of sight and sound had not been his own, out of his own memories.

He was tempted now, fascinated, like a child that plays with fire. The talisman had been worn somehow. Where? On the breast? On the brow?

He tried the first, with no result. Then he touched the flat surface of the lens to his forehead.

The great tower of stone rose up monstrous to the sky. It was whole, and there were pallid lights within that stirred and flickered, and it was crowned with a shimmering darkness.

He lay outside the tower, on his belly, and he was filled with fear and a great anger, and a loathing such as turns the bones to water. There was no snow. There was ice everywhere, rising to half the tower's height, sheathing the ground.

Ice. Cold and clear and beautiful—and deadly.

He moved. He glided snakelike, with infinite caution, over the smooth surface. The tower was gone, and far below him was a city. He saw the temples and the palaces, the glittering lovely city beneath him in the ice, blurred and fairylike and strange, a dream half glimpsed through crystal.

He saw the Ones that lived there, moving slowly through the streets. He could not see them clearly, only the vague shining of their bodies, and he was glad.

He hated them, with a hatred that conquered even his fear, which was great indeed.

He was not Eric John Stark. He was Ban Cruach.

The tower and the city vanished, swept away on a reeling tide.

He stood beneath a scarp of black rock, notched with a single pass. The cliffs hung over him, leaning out their vast bulk as though to crush him, and the narrow mouth of the pass was full of evil laughter where the wind went by.

He began to walk forward, into the pass. He was quite alone.

The light was dim and strange at the bottom of that cleft. Little veils of mist crept and clung between the ice and the rock, thickened, became more dense as he went farther and farther into the pass. He could not see, and the wind spoke with many tongues, piping in the crevices of the cliffs.

All at once there was a shadow in the mist before him, a dim gigantic shape that moved toward him, and he knew that he looked at death. He cried out . . .

It was Stark who yelled in blind atavistic fear, and the echo of his own cry brought him up standing, shaking in every limb. He had dropped the talisman. It lay gleaming in the snow at his feet, and the alien memories were gone—and Camar was dead.

After a time he crouched down, breathing harshly. He did not want to touch the lens again. The part of him that had learned to fear strange gods and evil spirits with every step he took, the primitive aboriginal that lay so close under the surface of his mind, warned him to leave it, to run away, to desert this place of death and ruined stone.

He forced himself to take it up. He did not look at it. He wrapped it in the bit of silk and replaced it inside the iron boss, and clasped the belt around his waist. Then he found the small flask that lay with his gear beside the fire and took a long pull, and tried to think rationally of the thing that had happened.

Memories. Not his own, but the memories of Ban Cruach, a million years ago in the morning of a world. Memories of hate, a secret war against unhuman beings that dwelt in crystal cities cut in the living ice, and used these ruined towers for some dark purpose of their own.

Was that the meaning of the talisman, the power that lay within it? Had Ban Cruach, by some elder and forgotten science, imprisoned the echoes of his own mind in the crystal?

Why? Perhaps as a warning, as a reminder of ageless, alien danger beyond the Gates of Death?

Suddenly one of the beasts tethered outside the ruined tower started up from its sleep with a hissing snarl.

Instantly Stark became motionless.

They came silently on their padded feet, the rangy mountain brutes moving daintily through the sprawling ruin. Their riders too were silent—tall men with fierce eyes and russet hair, wearing leather coats and carrying each a long, straight spear.

There were a score of them around the tower in the windy gloom. Stark did not bother to draw his gun. He had learned very young the difference between courage and idiocy.

He walked out toward them, slowly lest one of them be startled into spearing him, yet not slowly enough to denote fear. And he held up his right hand and gave them greeting.

They did not answer him. They sat their restive mounts and stared at him, and Stark knew that Camar had spoken the truth. These were the riders of Mekh, and they were wolves.

II

Stark waited, until they should tire of their own silence.

Finally one demanded, "Of what country are you?"

He answered, "I am called N'Chaka, the Man-Without-a-Tribe."

It was the name they had given him, the half-human aboriginals who had raised him in the blaze and thunder and bitter frosts of Mercury.

"A stranger," said the leader, and smiled. He pointed at the dead Camar and asked, "Did you slay him?"

"He was my friend," said Stark, "I was bringing him home to die."

Two riders dismounted to inspect the body. One called up to the leader, "He was from Kushat, if I know the breed, Thord! And he has not been robbed." He proceeded to take care of that detail himself.

"A stranger," repeated the leader, Thord. "Bound for Kushat, with a man of Kushat. Well. I think you will come with us, stranger."

Stark shrugged. And with the long spears pricking him, he did not resist when the tall Thord plundered him of all he owned except his clothes—and Camar's belt, which was not worth the stealing. His gun Thord flung contemptuously away.

One of the men brought Stark's beast and Camar's from where they were tethered, and the Earthman mounted—as usual, over the violent protest of the creature, which did not like the smell of him. They moved out from under the shelter of the walls, into the full fury of the wind.

For the rest of that night, and through the next day and the night that followed it they rode eastward, stopping only to rest the beasts and chew on their rations of jerked meat.

To Stark, riding a prisoner, it came with full force that this was the North country, half a world away from the Mars of spaceships and commerce and visitors from other planets. The future had never touched these wild mountains and barren plains. The past held pride enough.

To the north, the horizon showed a strange and ghostly glimmer where the barrier wall of the polar pack reared up, gigantic against the sky. The wind blew, down from the ice, through the mountain gorges, across the plains, never ceasing. And here and there the cryptic towers rose, broken monoliths of stone. Stark remembered the vision of the talisman, the huge structure crowned with eerie darkness. He looked upon the ruins with loathing and curiosity. The men of Mekh could tell him nothing.

Thord did not tell Stark where they were taking him, and Stark did not ask. It would have been an admission of fear.

In mid-afternoon of the second day they came to a lip of rock where the snow was swept clean, and below it was a sheer drop into a narrow valley. Looking down, Stark saw that on the floor of the valley, up and down as far as he could see, were men and beasts and shelters of hide and brush, and fires burning. By the hundreds, by the several thousand, they camped under the cliffs, and their voices rose up on the thin air in a vast deep murmur that was deafening after the silence of the plains.

A war party, gathered now, before the thaw. Stark smiled. He became curious to meet the leader of this army.

They found their way single file along a winding track that dropped down the cliff face. The wind stopped abruptly, cut off by the valley walls. They came in among the shelters of the camp.

Here the snow was churned and soiled and melted to slush by the fires. There were no women in the camp, no sign of the usual cheerful rabble that follows a barbarian army. There were only men—hillmen and warriors all, tough-handed killers with no thought but battle.

They came out of their holes to shout at Thord and his men, and stare at the stranger. Thord was flushed and jovial with importance.

"I have no time for you," he shouted back. "I go to speak with the Lord Ciaran."

Stark rode impassively, a dark giant with a face of stone. From time to time he made his beast curvet, and laughed at himself inwardly for doing it.

They came at length to a shelter larger than the others, but built exactly the same and no more comfortable. A spear was thrust into the snow beside the entrance, and from it hung a black pennant with a single bar of silver across it, like lightning in a night sky. Beside it was a shield with the same device. There were no guards.

Thord dismounted, bidding Stark to do the same. He hammered on the shield with the hilt of his sword, announcing himself.

"Lord Ciaran! It is Thord—with a captive."

A voice, toneless and strangely muffled, spoke from within.

"Enter, Thord."

Thord pushed aside the hide curtain and went in, with Stark at his heels.

The dim daylight did not penetrate the interior. Cressets burned, giving off a flickering brilliance and a smell of strong oil. The floor of packed snow was carpeted with furs, much worn. Otherwise there was no adornment, and no furniture but a chair and a table, both dark with age and use, and a pallet of skins in one shadowy corner with what seemed to be a heap of rags upon it.

In the chair sat a man.

He seemed very tall, in the shaking light of the cressets. From neck to thigh his lean body was cased in black link mail, and under that a tunic of leather, dyed black. Across his knees he held a sable axe, a great thing made for the shearing of skulls, and his hands lay upon it gently, as though it were a toy he loved.

His head and face were covered by a thing that Stark had seen before only in very old paintings—the ancient war-mask of the inland Kings of Mars. Wrought of black and gleaming steel, it presented an unhuman visage of slitted eyeholes and a barred slot for breathing. Behind, it sprang out in a thin, soaring sweep, like a dark wing edge-on in flight.

The intent, expressionless scrutiny of that mask was bent, not upon Thord, but upon Eric John Stark.

The hollow voice spoke again, from behind the mask. "Well?"

"We were hunting in the gorges to the south," said Thord. "We saw a fire . . . " He told the story, of how they had found the stranger and the body of the man from Kushat.

"Kushat!" said the Lord Ciaran softly. "Ah! And why, stranger, were you going to Kushat?"

"My name is Stark. Eric John Stark, Earthman, out of Mercury." He was tired of being called stranger. Quite suddenly, he was tired of the whole business.

"Why should I not go to Kushat? Is it against some law, that a man may not go there in peace without being hounded all over the Norlands? And why do the men of Mekh make it their business? They have nothing to do with the city."

Thord held his breath, watching with delighted anticipation.

The hands of the man in armor caressed the axe. They were slender hands, smooth and sinewy—small hands, it seemed, for such a weapon.

"We make what we will our business, Eric John Stark." He spoke with a peculiar gentleness. "I have asked you. Why were you going to Kushat?"

"Because," Stark answered with equal restraint, "my comrade wanted to go home to die."

"It seems a long, hard journey, just for dying." The black helm bent forward, in an attitude of thought. "Only the condemned or banished leave their cities, or their clans. Why did your comrade flee Kushat?"

A voice spoke suddenly from out of the heap of rags that lay on the pallet in the shadows of the corner. A man's voice, deep and husky, with the harsh quaver of age or madness in it.

"Three men beside myself have fled Kushat, over the years that matter. One died in the spring floods. One was caught in the moving ice of winter. One lived. A thief named Camar, who stole a certain talisman."

Stark said, "My comrade was called Greshi." The leather belt weighed heavy about him, and the iron boss seemed hot against his belly. He was beginning, now, to be afraid.

The Lord Ciaran spoke, ignoring Stark. "It was the sacred talisman of Kushat. Without it, the city is like a man without a soul."

As the Veil of Tanit was to Carthage, Stark thought, and reflected on the fate of that city after the Veil was stolen.

"The nobles were afraid of their own people," the man in armor said. "They did not dare to tell that it was gone. But we know."

"And," said Stark, "you will attack Kushat before the thaw, when they least expect you."

"You have a sharp mind, stranger. Yes. But the great wall will be hard to carry, even so. If I came, bearing in *my* hands the talisman of Ban Cruach . . . "

He did not finish, but turned instead to Thord. "When you plundered the dead man's body, what did you find?"

"Nothing, Lord. A few coins, a knife, hardly worth the taking."

"And you, Eric John Stark. What did you take from the body?"

With perfect truth he answered, "Nothing."

"Thord," said the Lord Ciaran, "search him."

Thord came smiling up to Stark and ripped his jacket open.

With uncanny swiftness, the Earthman moved. The edge of one broad hand took Thord under the ear, and before the man's knees had time to sag Stark had caught his arm. He turned, crouching forward, and pitched Thord headlong through the door flap.

He straightened and turned again. His eyes held a feral glint. "The man has robbed me once," he said. "It is enough."

He heard Thord's men coming. Three of them tried to jam through the entrance at once, and he sprang at them. He made no sound. His fists did the talking for him, and then his feet, as he kicked the stunned barbarians back upon their leader.

"Now," he said to the Lord Ciaran, "will we talk as men?"

The man in armor laughed, a sound of pure enjoyment. It seemed that the gaze behind the mask studied Stark's savage face, and then lifted to greet the sullen Thord who came back into the shelter, his cheeks flushed crimson with rage.

"Go," said the Lord Ciaran. "The stranger and I will talk."

"But Lord," he protested, glaring at Stark, "it is not safe . . . "

"My dark mistress looks after my safety," said Ciaran, stroking the axe across his knees. "Go."

Thord went.

The man in armor was silent then, the blind mask turned to Stark, who met that eyeless gaze and was silent also. And the bundle of rags in the shadows straightened slowly and became a tall old man with rusty hair and beard, through which peered craggy juts of bone and two bright, small points of fire, as though some wicked flame burned within him.

He shuffled over and crouched at the feet of the Lord Ciaran, watching the Earthman. And the man in armor leaned forward.

"I will tell you something, Eric John Stark. I am a bastard, but I come of the blood of kings. My name and rank I must make with my own hands. But I will set them high, and my name will ring in the Norlands!

"I will take Kushat. Who holds Kushat, holds Mars—and the power and the riches that lie beyond the Gates of Death!"

"I have seen them," said the old man, and his eyes blazed. "I have seen Ban Cruach the mighty. I have seen the temples and the palaces glitter in the ice. I have seen *Them*, the shining ones. Oh, I have seen them, the beautiful, hideous ones!"

He glanced sidelong at Stark, very cunning. "That is why Otar is mad, stranger. *He has seen.*"

A chill swept Stark. He too had seen, not with his own eyes but with the mind and memories of Ban Cruach, of a million years ago.

Then it had been no illusion, the fantastic vision opened to him by the talisman now hidden in his belt! If this old madman had seen . . .

"What beings lurk beyond the Gates of Death I do not know," said Ciaran. "But my dark mistress will test their strength—and I think my red wolves will hunt them down, once they get a smell of plunder."

"The beautiful, terrible ones," whispered Otar. "And oh, the temples and the palaces, and the great towers of stone!"

"Ride with me, Stark," said the Lord Ciaran abruptly. "Yield up the talisman, and be the shield at my back. I have offered no other man that honor."

Stark asked slowly, "Why do you choose me?"

"We are of one blood, Stark, though we be strangers."

The Earthman's cold eyes narrowed. "What would your red wolves say to that? And what would Otar say? Look at him, already stiff with jealousy, and fear lest I answer, 'Yes.'"

"I do not think you would be afraid of either of them."

"On the contrary," said Stark, "I am a prudent man." He paused. "There is one other thing. I will bargain with no man until I have looked into his eyes. Take off your helm, Ciaran—and then perhaps we will talk!"

Otar's breath made a snakelike hissing between his toothless gums, and the hands of the Lord Ciaran tightened on the haft of the axe.

"No!" he whispered. "That I can never do."

Otar rose to his feet, and for the first time Stark felt the full strength that lay in this strange old man.

"Would you look upon the face of destruction?" he thundered. "Do you ask for death? Do you think a thing is hidden behind a mask of steel without a reason, that you demand to see it?"

He turned. "My Lord," he said. "By tomorrow the last of the clans will have joined us. After that, we must march. Give this Earthman to Thord, for the time that remains—and you will have the talisman."

The blank, blind mask was unmoving, turned toward Stark, and the Earthman thought that from behind it came a faint sound that might have been a sigh.

Then . . .

"Thord!" cried the Lord Ciaran, and lifted up the axe.

III

The flames leaped high from the fire in the windless gorge. Men sat around it in a great circle, the wild riders out of the mountain valleys of Mekh. They sat with the curbed and shivering eagerness of wolves around a dying quarry. Now and again their white teeth showed in a kind of silent laughter, and their eyes watched.

"He is strong," they whispered, one to the other. "He will live the night out, surely!"

On an outcrop of rock sat the Lord Ciaran, wrapped in a black cloak, holding the great axe in the crook of his arm. Beside him, Otar huddled in the snow.

Close by, the long spears had been driven deep and lashed together to make a scaffolding, and upon this frame was hung a man. A big man, iron-muscled and very lean, the bulk of his shoulders filling the space between the bending shafts. Eric John Stark of Earth, out of Mercury.

He had already been scourged without mercy. He sagged of his own weight between the spears, breathing in harsh sobs, and the trampled snow around him was spotted red.

Thord was wielding the lash. He had stripped off his own coat, and his body glistened with sweat in spite of the cold. He cut his victim with great care, making the long lash sing and crack. He was proud of his skill.

Stark did not cry out.

Presently Thord stepped back, panting, and looked at the Lord Ciaran. And the black helm nodded.

Thord dropped the whip. He went up to the big dark man and lifted his head by the hair.

"Stark," he said, and shook the head roughly. "Stranger!"

Eyes opened and stared at him, and Thord could not repress a slight shiver. It seemed that the pain and indignity had wrought some evil magic on this man he had ridden with, and thought he knew. He had seen exactly the same gaze in a big snow-cat caught in a trap, and he felt suddenly that it was not a man he spoke to, but a predatory beast.

"Stark," he said. "Where is the talisman of Ban Cruach?"

The Earthman did not answer.

Thord laughed. He glanced up at the sky, where the moons rode low and swift. "The night is only half gone. Do you think you can last it out?"

The cold, cruel, patient eyes watched Thord. There was no reply.

Some quality of pride in that gaze angered the barbarian. It seemed to mock him, who was so sure of his ability to loosen a reluctant tongue.

"You think I cannot make you talk, don't you? You don't know me, stranger! You don't know Thord, who can make the rocks speak out if he will!"

He reached out with his free hand and struck Stark across the face.

It seemed impossible that anything so still could move so quickly. There was an ugly flash of teeth, and Thord's wrist was caught above the thumb-joint. He bellowed, and the iron jaws closed down, worrying the bone.

Quite suddenly, Thord screamed. Not for pain, but for panic. And the rows of watching men swayed forward, and even the Lord Ciaran rose up, startled.

"Hark!" ran the whispering around the fire. "Hark how he growls!"

Thord had let go of Stark's hair and was beating him about the head with his clenched fist. His face was white.

"Werewolf!" he screamed. "Let me go, beast-thing! Let me go!"

But the dark man clung to Thord's wrist, snarling, and did not hear. After a bit there came the dull crack of bone.

Stark opened his jaws. Thord ceased to strike him. He backed off slowly, staring at the torn flesh. Stark had sunk down to the length of his arms.

With his left hand, Thord drew his knife. The Lord Ciaran stepped forward. "Wait, Thord!"

"It is a thing of evil," whispered the barbarian. "Warlock. Werewolf. Beast."

He sprang at Stark.

The man in armor moved, very swiftly, and the great axe went whirling through the air. It caught Thord squarely where the cords of his neck ran into the shoulder—caught, and shore on through.

There was a silence in the valley.

The Lord Ciaran walked slowly across the trampled snow and took up his axe again.

"I will be obeyed," he said. "And I will not stand for fear, not of god, man, nor devil." He gestured toward Stark. "Cut him down. And see that he does not die."

He strode away, and Otar began to laugh.

From a vast distance, Stark heard that shrill, wild laughter. His mouth was full of blood, and he was mad with a cold fury.

A cunning that was purely animal guided his movements then. His head fell forward, and his body hung inert against the thongs. He might almost have been dead.

A knot of men came toward him. He listened to them. They were hesitant and afraid. Then, as he did not move, they plucked up courage and came closer, and one prodded him gently with the point of his spear.

"Prick him well," said another. "Let us be sure!"

The sharp point bit a little deeper. A few drops of blood welled out and joined the small red streams that ran from the weals of the lash. Stark did not stir.

The spearman grunted. "He is safe enough now."

Stark felt the knife blades working at the thongs. He waited. The rawhide snapped, and he was free.

He did not fall. He would not have fallen then if he had taken a death wound. He gathered his legs under him and sprang.

He picked up the spearman in that first rush and flung him into the fire. Then he began to run toward the place where the scaly mounts were herded, leaving a trail of blood behind him on the snow.

A man loomed up in front of him. He saw the shadow of a spear and swerved, and caught the haft in his two hands. He wrenched it free and struck down with the butt of it, and went on. Behind him he heard voices shouting and the beginning of turmoil.

The Lord Ciaran turned and came back, striding fast.

There were men before Stark now, many men, the circle of watchers breaking up because there had been nothing more to watch. He gripped the long spear. It was a good weapon, better than the flint-tipped stick with which the boy N'Chaka had hunted the giant lizard of the rocks.

His body curved into a half crouch. He voiced one cry, the challenging scream of a predatory killer, and went in among the men.

He did slaughter with that spear. They were not expecting attack. They were not expecting anything. Stark had sprung to life too quickly. And they were afraid of him. He could smell the fear on them. Fear not of a man like themselves, but of a creature less and more than man.

He killed, and was happy.

They fell away from him, the wild riders of Mekh. They were sure now that he was a demon. He raged among them with the bright spear, and they heard again that sound that should not have come from a human throat, and their superstitious terror rose and sent them scrambling out of his path, trampling on each other in childish panic.

He broke through, and now there was nothing between him and escape but two mounted men who guarded the herd.

Being mounted, they had more courage. They felt that even a warlock could not stand against their charge. They came at him as he ran, the padded feet of their beasts making a muffled drumming in the snow.

Without breaking stride, Stark hurled his spear.

It drove through one man's body and tumbled him off, so that he fell under his comrade's mount and fouled its legs. It staggered and reared up, hissing, and Stark fled on.

Once he glanced over his shoulder. Through the milling, shouting crowd of men he glimpsed a dark, mailed figure with a winged mask, going through the ruck with a loping stride and bearing a sable axe raised high for the throwing.

Stark was close to the herd now. And they caught his scent.

The Norland brutes had never liked the smell of him, and now the reek of blood upon him was enough in itself to set them wild. They began to hiss and snarl uneasily, rubbing their reptilian flanks together as they wheeled around, staring at him with lambent eyes.

He rushed them, before they should quite decide to break. He was quick enough to catch one by the fleshy comb that served it for a forelock, held it with savage indifference to its squealing, and leaped to its back. Then he let it bolt, and as he rode it he yelled, a shrill brute cry that urged the creatures on to panic.

The herd broke, stampeding outward from its center like a bursting shell.

Stark was in the forefront. Clinging low to the scaly neck, he saw the men of Mekh scattered and churned and tramped into the snow by the flying pads. In and out of the shelters, kicking the brush walls down, lifting up their harsh reptilian voices, they went racketing through the camp, leaving behind them wreckage as of a storm. And Stark went with them.

He snatched a cloak from off the shoulders of some petty chieftain as he went by, and then, twisting cruelly on the fleshy comb, beating with his fist at the creature's head, he got his mount turned in the way he wanted it to go, down the valley.

He caught one last glimpse of the Lord Ciaran, fighting to hold one of the creatures long enough to mount, and then a dozen striving bodies surged around him, and Stark was gone.

The beast did not slacken pace. It was as though it thought it could outrun the alien, bloody thing that clung to its back. The last fringes of the camp shot by and vanished in the gloom, and the clean snow of the lower valley lay open before it. The creature laid its belly to the ground and went, the white spray spurting from its heels.

Stark hung on. His strength was gone now, run out suddenly with the battle-madness. He became conscious now that he was sick and bleeding, that his body was one cruel pain. In that moment, more than in the hours that had gone before, he hated the black leader of the clans of Mekh.

That flight down the valley became a sort of ugly dream. Stark was aware of rock walls reeling past, and then they seemed to widen away and the wind came out of nowhere like the stroke of a great hammer, and he was on the open moors again.

The beast began to falter and slow down. Presently it stopped.

Stark scooped up snow to rub on his wounds. He came near to fainting, but the bleeding stopped and after that the pain was numbed to a dull ache. He wrapped the cloak around him and urged the beast to go on, gently this time, patiently, and after it had breathed it obeyed him, settling into the shuffling pace it could keep up for hours.

He was three days on the moors. Part of the time he rode in a sort of stupor, and part of the time he was feverishly alert, watching the skyline. Frequently he took the shapes of thrusting rocks for riders, and found what cover he could until he was sure they did not move. He was afraid to dismount, for the beast had no bridle. When it halted to rest he remained upon its back, shaking, his brow beaded with sweat.

The wind scoured his tracks clean as soon as he made them. Twice, in the distance, he did see riders, and one of those times he burrowed into a tall drift and stayed there for several hours.

The ruined towers marched with him across the bitter land, lonely giants fifty miles apart. He did not go near them.

He knew that he wandered a good bit, but he could not help it, and it was probably his salvation. In those tortured badlands, riven by ages of frost and flood, one might follow a man on a straight track between two points. But to find a single rider lost in that wilderness was a matter of sheer luck, and the odds were with Stark.

One evening at sunset he came out upon a plain that sloped upward to a black and towering scarp, notched with a single pass.

The light was level and blood-red, glittering on the frosty rock so that it seemed the throat of the pass was aflame with evil fires. To Stark's mind, essentially primitive and stripped now of all its acquired reason, that narrow cleft appeared as the doorway to the dwelling place of demons as horrible as the fabled creatures that roam the Darkside of his native world.

He looked long at the Gates of Death, and a dark memory crept into his brain. Memory of that nightmare experience when the talisman had made him seem to walk into that frightful pass, not as Stark, but as Ban Cruach.

He remembered Otar's words—*I have seen Ban Cruach the mighty*. Was he still there beyond those darkling gates, fighting his unimagined war, alone?

Again, in memory, Stark heard the evil piping of the wind. Again, the shadow of a dim and terrible shape loomed up before him . . .

He forced remembrance of that vision from his mind, by a great effort. He could not turn back now. There was no place to go.

His weary beast plodded on, and now Stark saw as in a dream that a great walled city stood guard before that awful Gate. He watched the city glide toward him through a crimson haze, and fancied he could see the ages clustered like birds around the towers.

He had reached Kushat, with the talisman of Ban Cruach still strapped in the blood-stained belt around his waist.

IV

He stood in a large square, lined about with huckster's stalls and the booths of wine-sellers. Beyond were buildings, streets, a city. Stark got a blurred impression of a grand and brooding darkness, bulking huge against the mountains, as bleak and proud as they, and quite as ancient, with many ruins and deserted quarters.

He was not sure how he had come there, but he was standing on his own feet, and someone was pouring sour wine into his mouth. He drank it greedily. There were people around him, jostling, chattering, demanding answers to their questions. A girl's voice said sharply, "Let him be! Can't you see he's hurt?"

Stark looked down. She was slim and ragged, with black hair and large eyes yellow as a cat's. She held a leather bottle in her hands. She smiled at him and said, "I'm Thanis. Will you drink more wine?"

"I will," said Stark, and did, and then said, "Thank you, Thanis." He put his hand on her shoulder, to steady himself. It was a supple shoulder, surprisingly strong. He liked the feel of it.

The crowd was still churning around him, growing larger, and now he heard the tramp of military feet. A small detachment of men in light armor pushed their way through.

A very young officer whose breastplate hurt the eye with brightness demanded to be told at once who Stark was and why he had come there.

"No one crosses the moors in winter," he said, as though that in itself were a sign of evil intent.

"The clans of Mekh are crossing them," Stark answered. "An army, to take Kushat—one, two days behind me."

The crowd picked that up. Excited voices tossed it back and forth, and clamored for more news. Stark spoke to the officer.

"I will see your captain, and at once."

"You'll see the inside of a prison, more likely!" snapped the young man. "What's this nonsense about the clans of Mekh?"

Stark regarded him. He looked so long and so curiously that the crowd began to snicker and the officer's beardless face flushed pink to the ears.

"I have fought in many wars," said Stark gently. "And long ago I learned to listen, when someone came to warn me of attack."

"Better take him to the captain, Lugh," cried Thanis. "It's our skins too, you know, if there is war."

The crowd began to shout. They were all poor folk, wrapped in threadbare cloaks or tattered leather. They had no love for the guards. And whether there was war or not, their winter had been long and dull, and they were going to make the most of this excitement.

"Take him, Lugh! Let him warn the nobles. Let them think how they'll defend Kushat and the Gates of Death, now that the talisman is gone!"

"That is a lie!" Lugh shouted. "And you know the penalty for telling it. Hold your tongues, or I'll have you all whipped." He gestured angrily at Stark. "See if he is armed."

One of the soldiers stepped forward, but Stark was quicker. He slipped the thong and let the cloak fall, baring his upper body.

"The clansmen have already taken everything I owned," he said. "But they gave me something, in return."

The crowd stared at the half healed stripes that scarred him, and there was a drawing in of breath.

The soldier picked up the cloak and laid it over the Earthman's shoulders. And Lugh said sullenly, "Come, then."

Stark's fingers tightened on Thanis' shoulder. "Come with me, little one," he whispered. "Otherwise, I must crawl."

She smiled at him and came. The crowd followed.

The captain of the guards was a fleshy man with a smell of wine about him and a face already crumbling apart though his hair was not yet gray. He sat in a squat tower above the square, and he observed Stark with no particular interest.

"You had something to tell," said Lugh. "Tell it."

Stark told them, leaving out all mention of Camar and the talisman. This was neither the time nor the man to hear that story. The captain listened to all he had to say about the gathering of the clans of Mekh, and then sat studying him with a bleary shrewdness.

"You have proof of all this?"

"These stripes. Their leader Ciaran ordered them laid on himself."

The captain sighed, and leaned back.

"Any wandering band of hunters could have scourged you," he said. "A nameless vagabond from the gods know where, and a lawless one at that, if I'm any judge of men—you probably deserved it."

He reached for wine, and smiled. "Look you, stranger. In the Norlands, no one makes war in the winter. And no one ever heard of Ciaran. If you hoped for a reward from the city, you overshot badly."

"The Lord Ciaran," said Stark, grimly controlling his anger, "will be battering at your gates within two days. And you will hear of him then."

"Perhaps. You can wait for him—in a cell. And you can leave Kushat with the first caravan after the thaw. We have enough rabble here without taking in more."

Thanis caught Stark by the cloak and held him back.

"*Sir,*" she said, as though it were an unclean word. "I will vouch for the stranger."

The captain glanced at her. "You?"

"Sir, I am a free citizen of Kushat. According to law, I may vouch for him."

"If you scum of the Thieves' Quarter would practice the law as well as you prate it, we would have less trouble," growled the captain. "Very well, take the creature, if you want him. I don't suppose you've anything to lose."

Lugh laughed.

"Name and dwelling place," said the captain, and wrote them down. "Remember, he is not to leave the Quarter."

Thanis nodded. "Come," she said to Stark. He did not move, and she looked up at him. He was staring at the captain. His beard had grown in these last days, and his face was still scarred by Thord's blows and made wolfish with pain and fever. And now, out of this evil mask, his eyes were peering with a chill and terrible intensity at the soft-bellied man who sat and mocked him.

Thanis laid her hand on his rough cheek. "Come," she said. "Come and rest."

Gently she turned his head. He blinked and swayed, and she took him around the waist and led him unprotesting to the door.

There she paused, looking back.

"Sir," she said, very meekly, "news of this attack is being shouted through the Quarter now. If it *should* come, and it were known that you had the warning and did not pass it on . . . " She made an expressive gesture, and went out.

Lugh glanced uneasily at the captain. "She's right, sir. If by chance the man did tell the truth . . . "

The captain swore. "Rot. A rogue's tale. And yet . . . " He scowled indecisively, and then reached for parchment. "After all, it's a simple thing. Write it up, pass it on, and let the nobles do the worrying."

His pen began to scratch.

Thanis took Stark by steep and narrow ways, darkling now in the afterglow, where the city climbed and fell again over the uneven rock. Stark was aware of the heavy smells of spices and unfamiliar foods, and the musky undertones of a million generations swarmed together to spawn and die in these crowded catacombs of slate and stone.

There was a house, blending into other houses, close under the loom of the great Wall. There was a flight of steps, hollowed deep with use, twisting crazily around outer corners.

There was a low room, and a slender man named Balin, vaguely glimpsed, who said he was Thanis' brother. There was a bed of skins and woven cloths.

Stark slept.

Hands and voices called him back. Strong hands shaking him, urgent voices. He started up growling, like an animal suddenly awaked, still lost in the dark mists of exhaustion. Balin swore, and caught his fingers away.

"What is this you have brought home, Thanis? By the gods, it snapped at me!"

Thanis ignored him. "Stark," she said. "Stark! Listen. Men are coming. Soldiers. They will question you. Do you hear me?"

Stark said heavily, "I hear."

"Do not speak of Camar!"

Stark got to his feet, and Balin said hastily, "Peace! The thing is safe. I would not steal a death warrant!"

His voice had a ring of truth. Stark sat down again. It was an effort to keep awake. There was clamor in the street below. It was still night.

Balin said carefully, "Tell them what you told the captain, nothing more. They will kill you if they know."

A rough hand thundered at the door, and a voice cried, "Open up!"

Balin sauntered over to lift the bar. Thanis sat beside Stark, her hand touching his. Stark rubbed his face. He had been shaved and washed, his wounds rubbed with salve. The belt was gone, and his blood-stained clothing. He realized only then that he was naked, and drew a cloth around him. Thanis whispered, "The belt is there on that peg, under your cloak."

Balin opened the door, and the room was full of men.

Stark recognized the captain. There were others, four of them, young, old, intermediate, annoyed at being hauled away from their beds and their gaming tables at this hour. The sixth man wore the jeweled cuirass of a noble. He had a nice, a kind face. Grey hair, mild eyes, soft cheeks. A fine man, but ludicrous in the trappings of a soldier.

"Is this the man?" he asked, and the captain nodded.

"Yes." It was his turn to say Sir.

Balin brought a chair. He had a fine flourish about him. He wore a crimson jewel in his left ear, and every line of him was quick and sensitive, instinct with mockery. His eyes were brightly cynical, in a face worn lean with years of merry sinning. Stark liked him.

He was a civilized man. They all were—the noble, the captain, the lot of them. So civilized that the origins of their culture were forgotten half an age before the first clay brick was laid in Babylon.

Too civilized, Stark thought. Peace had drawn their fangs and cut their claws. He thought of the wild clansmen coming fast across the snow, and felt a certain pity for the men of Kushat.

The noble sat down.

"This is a strange tale you bring, wanderer. I would hear it from your own lips."

Stark told it. He spoke slowly, watching every word, cursing the weariness that fogged his brain.

The noble, who was called Rogain, asked him questions. Where was the camp? How many men? What were the exact words of the Lord Ciaran, and who was he?

Stark answered, with meticulous care.

Rogain sat for some time lost in thought. He seemed worried and upset, one hand playing aimlessly with the hilt of his sword. A scholar's hand, without a callous on it.

"There is one thing more," said Rogain. "What business had you on the moors in winter?"

Stark smiled. "I am a wanderer by profession."

"Outlaw?" asked the captain, and Stark shrugged.

"Mercenary is a kinder word."

Rogain studied the pattern of stripes on the Earthman's dark skin. "Why did the Lord Ciaran, so-called, order you scourged?"

"I had thrashed one of his chieftains."

Rogain sighed and rose. He stood regarding Stark from under brooding brows, and at length he said, "It is a wild tale. I can't believe it—and yet, why should you lie?"

He paused, as though hoping that Stark would answer that and relieve him of worry.

Stark yawned. "The tale is easily proved. Wait a day or two."

"I will arm the city," said Rogain. "I dare not do otherwise. But I will tell you this." An astonishing unpleasant look came into his eyes. "If the attack does not come—if you have set a whole city by the ears for nothing—I will have you flayed alive and your body tumbled over the Wall for the carrion birds to feed on."

He strode out, taking his retinue with him. Balin smiled. "He will do it, too," he said, and dropped the bar.

Stark did not answer. He stared at Balin, and then at Thanis, and then at the belt hanging on the peg, in a curiously blank and yet penetrating fashion, like an animal that thinks its own thoughts. He took a deep breath. Then, as though he found the air clean of danger, he rolled over and went instantly to sleep.

Balin lifted his shoulders expressively. He grinned at Thanis. "Are you positive it's human?"

"He's beautiful," said Thanis, and tucked the cloths around him. "Hold your tongue." She continued to sit there, watching Stark's face as the slow dreams moved across it. Balin laughed.

It was evening again when Stark awoke. He sat up, stretching lazily. Thanis crouched by the hearthstone, stirring something savory in a blackened pot. She wore a red kirtle and a necklet of beaten gold, and her hair was combed out smooth and shining.

She smiled at him and rose, bringing him his own boots and trousers, carefully cleaned, and a tunic of leather tanned fine and soft as silk. Stark asked her where she got it.

"Balin stole it—from the baths where the nobles go. He said you might as well have the best." She laughed. "He had a devil of a time finding one big enough to fit you."

She watched with unashamed interest while he dressed. Stark said, "Don't burn the soup."

She put her tongue out at him. "Better be proud of that fine hide while you have it," she said. "There's no sign of attack."

Stark was aware of sounds that had not been there before—the pacing of men on the Wall above the house, the calling of the watch. Kushat was armed and ready—and his time was running out. He hoped that Ciaran had not been delayed on the moors.

Thanis said, "I should explain about the belt. When Balin undressed you, he saw Camar's name scratched on the inside of the boss. And, he can open a lizard's egg without harming the shell."

"What about you?" asked Stark.

She flexed her supple fingers. "I do well enough."

Balin came in. He had been seeking news, but there was little to be had.

"The soldiers are grumbling about a false alarm," he said. "The people are excited, but more as though they were playing a game. Kushat has not fought a war for centuries." He sighed. "The pity of it is, Stark, I believe your story. And I'm afraid."

Thanis handed him a steaming bowl. "Here—employ your tongue with this. Afraid, indeed! Have you forgotten the Wall? No one has carried it since the city was built. Let them attack!"

Stark was amused. "For a child, you know much concerning war."

"I knew enough to save your skin!" she flared, and Balin smiled.

"She has you there, Stark. And speaking of skins . . . " He glanced up at the belt. "Or better, speaking of talismans, which we were not. How did you come by it?"

Stark told him. "He had a sin on his soul, did Camar. And—he was my friend."

Balin looked at him with deep respect. "You were a fool," he said. "Look you. The thing is returned to Kushat. Your promise is kept. There is nothing for you here but danger, and were I you I would not wait to be flayed, or slain, or taken in a quarrel that is not yours."

"Ah," said Stark softly, "but it is mine. The Lord Ciaran made it so." He, too, glanced at the belt. "What of the talisman?"

"Return it where it came from," Thanis said. "My brother is a better thief than Camar. He can certainly do that."

"No!" said Balin, with surprising force. "We will keep it, Stark and I. Whether it has power, I do not know. But if it has—I think Kushat will need it, and in strong hands."

Stark said somberly, "It has power, the Talisman. Whether for good or evil, I don't know."

They looked at him, startled. But a touch of awe seemed to repress their curiosity.

He could not tell them. He was, somehow, reluctant to tell anyone of that dark vision of what lay beyond the Gates of Death, which the talisman of Ban Cruach had lent him.

Balin stood up. "Well, for good or evil, at least the sacred relic of Ban Cruach has come home." He yawned. "I am going to bed. Will you come, Thanis, or will you stay and quarrel with our guest?"

"I will stay," she said, "and quarrel."

"Ah, well." Balin sighed puckishly. "Good night." He vanished into an inner room. Stark looked at Thanis. She had a warm mouth, and her eyes were beautiful, and full of light.

He smiled, holding out his hand.

The night wore on, and Stark lay drowsing. Thanis had opened the curtains.

Wind and moonlight swept together into the room, and she stood leaning upon the sill, above the slumbering city. The smile that lingered in the corners of her mouth was sad and far-away, and very tender.

Stark stirred uneasily, making small sounds in his throat. His motions grew violent. Thanis crossed the room and touched him.

Instantly he was awake.

"Animal," she said softly. "You dream."

Stark shook his head. His eyes were still clouded, though not with sleep. "Blood," he said, "heavy in the wind."

"I smell nothing but the dawn," she said, and laughed.

Stark rose. "Get Balin. I'm going up on the Wall."

She did not know him now. "What is it, Stark? What's wrong?"

"Get Balin." Suddenly it seemed that the room stifled him. He caught up his cloak and Camar's belt and flung open the door, standing on the narrow steps outside. The moonlight caught in his eyes, pale as frost-fire.

Thanis shivered. Balin joined her without being called. He, too, had slept but lightly. Together they followed Stark up the rough-cut stair that led to the top of the Wall.

He looked southward, where the plain ran down from the mountains and spread away below Kushat. Nothing moved out there. Nothing marred the empty whiteness. But Stark said,

"They will attack at dawn."

V

They waited. Some distance away a guard leaned against the parapet, huddled in his cloak. He glanced at them incuriously. It was bitterly cold. The wind came whistling down through the Gates of Death, and below in the streets the watchfires shuddered and flared.

They waited, and still there was nothing.

Balin said impatiently, "How can you know they're coming?"

Stark shivered, a shallow rippling of the flesh that had nothing to do with cold, and every muscle of his body came alive. Phobos plunged downward. The moonlight dimmed and changed, and the plain was very empty, very still.

"They will wait for darkness. They will have an hour or so, between moonset and dawn."

Thanis muttered, "Dreams! Besides, I'm cold." She hesitated, and then crept in under Balin's cloak. Stark had gone away from her. She watched him sulkily where he leaned upon the stone. He might have been part of it, as dark and unstirring.

Deimos sank low toward the west.

Stark turned his head, drawn inevitably to look toward the cliffs above Kushat, soaring upward to blot out half the sky. Here, close under them, they seemed to tower outward in a curving mass, like the last wave of eternity rolling down, crested white with the ash of shattered worlds.

I have stood beneath those cliffs before. I have felt them leaning down to crush me, and I have been afraid.

He was still afraid. The mind that had poured its memories into that crystal lens had been dead a million years, but neither time nor death had dulled the terror that beset Ban Cruach in his journey through that nightmare pass.

He looked into the black and narrow mouth of the Gates of Death, cleaving the scarp like a wound, and the primitive ape-thing within him cringed and moaned, oppressed with a sudden sense of fate.

He had come painfully across half a world, to crouch before the Gates of Death. Some evil magic had let him see forbidden things, had linked his mind in an unholy bond with the long-dead mind of one who had been half a god. These evil miracles had not been for nothing. He would not be allowed to go unscathed.

He drew himself up sharply then, and swore. He had left N'Chaka behind, a naked boy running in a place of rocks and sun on Mercury. He had become Eric John Stark, a man, and civilized. He thrust the senseless premonition from him, and turned his back upon the mountains.

Deimos touched the horizon. A last gleam of reddish light tinged the snow, and then was gone.

Thanis, who was half asleep, said with sudden irritation, "I do not believe in your barbarians. I'm going home." She thrust Balin aside and went away, down the steps.

The plain was now in utter darkness, under the faint, far Northern stars.

Stark settled himself against the parapet. There was a sort of timeless patience about him. Balin envied it. He would have liked to go with Thanis. He was cold and doubtful, but he stayed.

Time passed, endless minutes of it, lengthening into what seemed hours.

Stark said, "Can you hear them?"

"No."

"They come." His hearing, far keener than Balin's, picked up the little sounds, the vast inchoate rustling of an army on the move in stealth and darkness. Light-armed men, hunters, used to stalking wild beasts in the show. They could move softly, very softly.

"I hear nothing," Balin said, and again they waited.

The westering stars moved toward the horizon, and at length in the east a dim pallor crept across the sky.

The plain was still shrouded in night, but now Stark could make out the high towers of the King City of Kushat, ghostly and indistinct—the ancient, proud high towers of the rulers and their nobles, set above the crowded Quarters of merchants and artisans and thieves. He wondered who would be king in Kushat by the time this unrisen sun had set.

"You were wrong," said Balin, peering. "There is nothing on the plain."

Stark said, "Wait."

Swiftly now, in the thin air of Mars, the dawn came with a rush and a leap, flooding the world with harsh light. It flashed in cruel brilliance from sword-blades, from spearheads, from helmets and burnished mail, from the war-harness of beasts, glistened on bare russet heads and coats of leather, set the banners of the clans to burning, crimson and gold and green, bright against the snow.

There was no sound, not a whisper, in all the land.

Somewhere a hunting horn sent forth one deep cry to split the morning. Then burst out the wild skirling of the mountain pipes and the broken thunder of drums, and a wordless scream of exultation that rang back from the Wall of Kushat like the very voice of battle. The men of Mekh began to move.

Raggedly, slowly at first, then more swiftly as the press of warriors broke and flowed, the barbarians swept toward the city as water sweeps over a broken dam.

Knots and clumps of men, tall men running like deer, leaping, shouting, swinging their great brands. Riders, spurring their mounts until they fled belly down. Spears, axes, sword-blades tossing, a sea of men and beasts, rushing, trampling, shaking the ground with the thunder of their going.

And ahead of them all came a solitary figure in black mail, riding a raking beast trapped all in black, and bearing a sable axe.

Kushat came to life. There was a swarming and a yelling in the streets, and soldiers began to pour up onto the Wall. A thin company, Stark thought, and shook his head. Mobs of citizens choked the alleys, and every rooftop was full. A troop of nobles went by, brave in their bright mail, to take up their post in the square by the great gate.

Balin said nothing, and Stark did not disturb his thoughts. From the look of him, they were dark indeed.

Soldiers came and ordered them off the Wall. They went back to their own roof, where they were joined by Thanis. She was in a high state of excitement, but unafraid.

"Let them attack!" she said. "Let them break their spears against the Wall. They will crawl away again."

Stark began to grow restless. Up in their high emplacements, the big ballistas creaked and thrummed. The muted song of the bows became a wailing hum. Men fell, and were kicked off the ledges by their fellows. The blood-howl of the clans rang unceasing on the frosty air, and Stark heard the rap of scaling ladders against stone.

Thanis said abruptly, "What is that—that sound like thunder?"

"Rams," he answered. "They are battering the gate."

She listened, and Stark saw in her face the beginning of fear.

It was a long fight. Stark watched it hungrily from the roof all that morning. The soldiers of Kushat did bravely and well, but they were as folded sheep against the tall killers of the mountains. By noon the officers were beating the Quarters for men to replace the slain.

Stark and Balin went up again, onto the Wall.

The clans had suffered. Their dead lay in windrows under the Wall, amid the broken ladders. But Stark knew his barbarians. They had sat restless and chafing in the valley for many days, and now the battle-madness was on them and they were not going to be stopped.

Wave after wave of them rolled up, and was cast back, and came on again relentlessly. The intermittent thunder boomed still from the gates, where sweating giants swung the rams under cover of their own bowmen. And everywhere, up and down through the forefront of the fighting, rode the man in black armor, and wild cheering followed him.

Balin said heavily, "It is the end of Kushat."

A ladder banged against the stones a few feet away. Men swarmed up the rungs, fierce-eyed clansmen with laughter in their mouths. Stark was first at the head.

They had given him a spear. He spitted two men through with it and lost it, and a third man came leaping over the parapet. Stark received him into his arms.

Balin watched. He saw the warrior go crashing back, sweeping his fellows off the ladder. He saw Stark's face. He heard the sounds and smelled the blood and sweat of war, and he was sick to the marrow of his bones, and his hatred of the barbarians was a terrible thing.

Stark caught up a dead man's blade, and within ten minutes his arm was as red as a butcher's. And ever he watched the winged helm that went back and forth below, a standard to the clans.

By mid-afternoon the barbarians had gained the Wall in three places. They spread inward along the ledges, pouring up in a resistless tide, and the defenders broke. The rout became a panic.

"It's all over now," Stark said. "Find Thanis, and hide her."

Balin let fall his sword. "Give me the talisman," he whispered, and Stark saw that he was weeping. "Give it me, and I will go beyond the Gates of Death and rouse Ban Cruach from his sleep. And if he has forgotten Kushat, I will take his power into my own hands. I will fling wide the Gates of Death and loose destruction on the men of Mekh—or if the legends are all lies, then I will die."

He was like a man crazed. "Give me the talisman!"

Stark slapped him, carefully and without heat, across the face. "Get your sister, Balin. Hide her, unless you would be uncle to a red-haired brat."

He went then, like a man who has been stunned. Screaming women with their children clogged the ways that led inward from the Wall, and there was bloody work afoot on the rooftops and in the narrow alleys.

The gate was holding, still.

Stark forced his way toward the square. The booths of the hucksters were overthrown, the wine-jars broken and the red wine spilled. Beasts squealed and stamped, tired of their chafing harness, driven wild by the shouting and the smell of blood. The dead were heaped high where they had fallen from above.

They were all soldiers here, clinging grimly to their last foothold. The deep song of the rams shook the very stones. The iron-sheathed timbers of the gate gave back an answering scream, and toward the end all other sounds grew hushed. The nobles came down slowly from the Wall and mounted, and sat waiting.

There were fewer of them now. Their bright armor was dented and stained, and their faces had a pallor on them.

One last hammer-stroke of the rams.

With a bitter shriek the weakened bolts tore out, and the great gate was broken through.

The nobles of Kushat made their first, and final charge.

As soldiers they went up against the riders of Mekh, and as soldiers they held them until they died. Those that were left were borne back into the square, caught as in the crest of an avalanche. And first through the gates came the winged battle-mask of the Lord Ciaran, and the sable axe that drank men's lives where it hewed.

There was a beast with no rider to claim it, tugging at its headrope. Stark swung onto the saddle pad and cut it free. Where the press was thickest, a welter of struggling brutes and men fighting knee to knee, there was the man in black armor, riding like a god, magnificent, born to war. Stark's eyes shone with a strange, cold light. He struck his heels hard into the scaly flanks. The beast plunged forward.

In and over and through, making the long sword sing. The beast was strong, and frightened beyond fear. It bit and trampled, and Stark cut a path for them, and presently he shouted above the din, "Ho, there! *Ciaran*!"

The black mask turned toward him, and the remembered voice spoke from behind the barred slot, joyously.

"The wanderer. The wild man!"

Their two mounts shocked together. The axe came down in a whistling curve, and a red sword-blade flashed to meet it. Swift, swift, a ringing clash of steel, and the blade was shattered and the axe fallen to the ground.

Stark pressed in.

Ciaran reached for his sword, but his hand was numbed by the force of that blow and he was slow, a split second. The hilt of Stark's weapon, still clutched in his own numbed grip, fetched him a stunning blow on the helm, so that the metal rang like a flawed bell.

The Lord Ciaran reeled back, only for a moment, but long enough. Stark grasped the war-mask and ripped it off, and got his hands around the naked throat.

He did not break that neck, as he had planned. And the Clansmen who had started in to save their leader stopped and did not move.

Stark knew now why the Lord Ciaran had never shown his face.

The throat he held was white and strong, and his hands around it were buried in a mane of red-gold hair that fell down over the shirt of mail. A red mouth passionate with fury, wonderful curving bone under sculptured flesh, eyes fierce and proud and tameless as the eyes of a young eagle, fire-blue, defying him, hating him . . .

"By the gods," said Stark, very softly. "By the eternal gods!"

VI

A woman! And in that moment of amazement, she was quicker than he.

There was nothing to warn him, no least flicker of expression. Her two fists came up together between his outstretched arms and caught him under the jaw with a force that nearly snapped his neck. He went over backward, clean out of the saddle, and lay sprawled on the bloody stones, half stunned, the wind knocked out of him.

The woman wheeled her mount. Bending low, she took up the axe from where it had fallen, and faced her warriors, who were as dazed as Stark.

"I have led you well," she said. "I have taken you Kushat. Will any man dispute me?"

They knew the axe, if they did not know her. They looked from side to side uneasily, completely at a loss, and Stark, still gasping on the ground, thought that he had never seen anything as proud and beautiful as she was then in her black mail, with her bright hair blowing and her glance like blue lightning.

The nobles of Kushat chose that moment to charge. This strange unmasking of the Mekhish lord had given them time to rally, and now they thought that the Gods had wrought a miracle to help them. They found hope, where they had lost everything but courage.

"A wench!" they cried. "A strumpet of the camps. *A woman*!"

They howled it like an epithet, and tore into the barbarians.

She who had been the Lord Ciaran drove the spurs in deep, so that the beast leaped forward screaming. She went, and did not look to see if any had followed, in among the men of Kushat. And the great axe rose and fell, and rose again.

She killed three, and left two others bleeding on the stones, and not once did she look back.

The clansmen found their tongues.

"Ciaran! Ciaran!"

The crashing shout drowned out the sound of battle. As one man, they turned and followed her.

Stark, scrambling for his life underfoot, could not forbear smiling. Their childlike minds could see only two alternatives—to slay her out of hand, or to worship her. They had chosen to worship. He thought the bards would be singing of the Lord Ciaran of Mekh as long as there were men to listen.

He managed to take cover behind a wrecked booth, and presently make his way out of the square. They had forgotten him, for the moment. He did not wish to wait, just then, until they—or she—remembered.

She.

He still did not believe it, quite. He touched the bruise under his jaw where she had struck him, and thought of the lithe, swift strength of her, and the way she had ridden alone into battle. He remembered the death of Thord, and how she had kept her red wolves tamed, and he was filled with wonder, and a deep excitement.

He remembered what she had said to him once—*We are of one blood, though we be strangers.*

He laughed, silently, and his eyes were very bright.

The tide of war had rolled on toward the King City, where from the sound of it there was hot fighting around the castle. Eddies of the main struggle swept shrieking through the streets, but the rat-runs under the Wall were clear. Everyone had stampeded inward, the victims with the victors close on their heels. The short northern day was almost gone.

He found a hiding place that offered reasonable safety, and settled himself to wait.

Night came, but he did not move. From the sounds that reached him, the sacking of Kushat was in full swing. They were looting the richer streets first. Their upraised voices were thick with wine, and mingled with the cries of women. The reflection of many fires tinged the sky.

By midnight the sounds began to slacken, and by the second hour after the city slept, drugged with wine and blood and the weariness of battle. Stark went silently out into the streets, toward the King City.

According to the immemorial pattern of Martian city-states, the castles of the king and the noble families were clustered together in solitary grandeur. Many of the towers were fallen now, the great halls open to the sky. Time had crushed the grandeur that had been Kushat, more fatally than the boots of any conqueror.

In the house of the king, the flamboys guttered low and the chieftains of Mekh slept with their weary pipers among the benches of the banquet hall. In the niches of the tall, carved portal, the guards nodded over their spears. They, too, had fought that day. Even so, Stark did not go near them.

Shivering slightly in the bitter wind, he followed the bulk of the massive walls until he found a postern door, half open as some kitchen knave had left it in his flight. Stark entered, moving like a shadow.

The passageway was empty, dimly lighted by a single torch. A stairway branched off from it, and he climbed that, picking his way by guess and his memories of similar castles he had seen in the past.

He emerged into a narrow hall, obviously for the use of servants. A tapestry closed the end, stirring in the chill draught that blew along the floor. He peered around it, and saw a massive, vaulted corridor, the stone walls paneled in wood much split and blackened by time, but still showing forth the wonderful carvings of beasts and men, larger than life and overlaid with gold and bright enamel.

From the corridor a single doorway opened—and Otar slept before it, curled on a pallet like a dog.

Stark went back down the narrow hall. He was sure that there must be a back entrance to the king's chambers, and he found the little door he was looking for.

From there on was darkness. He felt his way, stepping with infinite caution, and presently there was a faint gleam of light filtering around the edges of another curtain of heavy tapestry.

He crept toward it, and heard a man's slow breathing on the other side.

He drew the curtain back, a careful inch. The man was sprawled on a bench athwart the door. He slept the honest sleep of exhaustion, his sword in his hand, the stains of his day's work still upon him. He was alone in the small room. A door in the farther wall was closed.

Stark hit him, and caught the sword before it fell. The man grunted once and became utterly relaxed. Stark bound him with his own harness and shoved a gag in his mouth, and went on, through the door in the opposite wall.

The room beyond was large and high and full of shadows. A fire burned low on the hearth, and the uncertain light showed dimly the hangings and the rich stuffs that carpeted the floor, and the dark, sparse shapes of furniture.

Stark made out the lattice-work of a covered bed, let into the wall after the northern fashion.

She was there, sleeping, her red-gold hair the color of the flames.

He stood a moment, watching her, and then, as though she sensed his presence, she stirred and opened her eyes.

She did not cry out. He had known that she would not. There was no fear in her. She said, with a kind of wry humor, "I will have a word with my guards about this."

She flung aside the covering and rose. She was almost as tall as he, white-skinned and very straight. He noted the long thighs, the narrow loins and magnificent shoulders, the small virginal breasts. She moved as a man moves, without coquetry. A long furred gown, that Stark guessed had lately graced the shoulders of the king, lay over a chair. She put it on.

"Well, wild man?"

"I have come to warn you." He hesitated over her name.

"My mother named me Ciara, if that seems better to you." She gave him her falcon's glance. "I could have slain you in the square, but now I think you did me a service. The truth would have come out sometime—better then, when they had no time to think about it." She laughed. "They will follow me now, over the edge of the world, if I ask them."

Stark said slowly, "Even beyond the Gates of Death?"

"Certainly, there. Above all, there!"

She turned to one of the tall windows and looked out at the cliffs and the high notch of the pass, touched with greenish silver by the little moons.

"Ban Cruach was a great king. He came out of nowhere to rule the Norlands with a rod of iron, and men speak of him still as half a god. Where did he get his power, if not from beyond the Gates of Death? Why did he go back there at the end of his days, if not to hide away his secret? Why did he build Kushat to guard the pass forever, if not to hoard that power out of reach of all the other nations of Mars?

"Yes, Stark. My men will follow me. And if they do not, I will go alone."

"You are not Ban Cruach. Nor am I." He took her by the shoulders. "Listen, Ciara. You're already king in the Norlands, and half a legend as you stand. Be content."

"Content!" Her face was close to his, and he saw the blaze of it, the white intensity of ambition and an iron pride. "Are you content?" she asked him. "Have you ever been content?"

He smiled. "For strangers, we do know each other well. No. But the spurs are not so deep in me."

"The wind and the fire. One spends its strength in wandering, the other devours. But one can help the other. I made you an offer once, and you said you would not bargain unless you could look into my eyes. Look now!"

He did, and his hands upon her shoulders trembled.

"No," he said harshly. "You're a fool, Ciara. Would you be as Otar, mad with what you have seen?"

"Otar is an old man, and likely crazed before he crossed the mountains. Besides—I am not Otar."

Stark said somberly, "Even the bravest may break. Ban Cruach himself . . . "

She must have seen the shadow of that horror in his eyes, for he felt her body tense.

"What of Ban Cruach? What do you know, Stark? Tell me!"

He was silent, and she went from him angrily.

"You have the talisman," she said. "That I am sure of. And if need be, I will flay you alive to get it!" She faced him across the room. "But whether I get it or not, I will go through the Gates of Death. I must wait, now, until after the thaw. The warm wind will blow soon, and the gorges will be running full. But afterward, I will go, and no talk of fears and demons will stop me."

She began to pace the room with long strides, and the full skirts of the gown made a subtle whispering about her.

"You do not know," she said, in a low and bitter voice. "I was a girl-child, without a name. By the time I could walk, I was a servant in the house of my grandfather. The two things that kept me living were pride and hate. I left my scrubbing of floors to practice arms with the young boys. I was beaten for it every day, but every day I went. I knew even then that only force would free me. And my father was a king's son, a good man of his hands. His blood was strong in me. I learned."

She held her head very high. She had earned the right to hold it so. She finished quietly,

"I have come a long way. I will not turn back now."

"Ciara." Stark came and stood before her. "I am talking to you as a fighting man, an equal. There may be power behind the Gates of Death, I do not know. But this I have seen—madness, horror, an evil that is beyond our understanding.

"I think you will not accuse me of cowardice. And yet I would not go into that pass for all the power of all the kings of Mars!"

Once started, he could not stop. The full force of that dark vision of the talisman swept over him again in memory. He came closer to her, driven by the need to make her understand.

"Yes, I have the talisman! And I have had a taste of its purpose. I think Ban Cruach left it as a warning, so that none would follow him. I have seen the temples and the palaces glitter in the ice. I have seen the Gates of Death—*not with my own eyes, Ciara, but with his. With the eyes and the memories of Ban Cruach*!"

He had caught her again, his hands strong on her strong arms.

"Will you believe me, or must you see for yourself—the dreadful things that walk those buried streets, the shapes that rise from nowhere in the mists of the pass?"

Her gaze burned into his. Her breath was hot and sweet upon his lips, and she was like a sword between his hands, shining and unafraid.

"Give me the talisman. Let me see!"

He answered furiously, "You are mad. As mad as Otar." And he kissed her, in a rage, in a panic lest all that beauty be destroyed—a kiss as brutal as a blow, that left him shaken.

She backed away slowly, one step, and he thought she would have killed him. He said heavily:

"If you will see, you will. The thing is here."

He opened the boss and laid the crystal in her outstretched hand. He did not meet her eyes.

"Sit down. Hold the flat side against your brow."

She sat, in a great chair of carven wood. Stark noticed that her hand was unsteady, her face the color of white ash. He was glad she did not have the axe where she could reach it. She did not play at anger.

For a long moment she studied the intricate lens, the incredible depository of a man's mind. Then she raised it slowly to her forehead.

He saw her grow rigid in the chair. How long he watched beside her he never knew. Seconds, an eternity. He saw her eyes turn blank and strange, and a shadow came into her face, changing it subtly, altering the lines, so that it seemed almost a stranger was peering through her flesh.

All at once, in a voice that was not her own, she cried out terribly, *"Oh gods of Mars!"*

The talisman dropped rolling to the floor, and Ciara fell forward into Stark's arms.

He thought at first that she was dead. He carried her to the bed, in an agony of fear that surprised him with its violence, and laid her down, and put his hand over her heart.

It was beating strongly. Relief that was almost a sickness swept over him. He turned, searching vaguely for wine, and saw the talisman. He picked it up and put it back inside the boss. A jeweled flagon stood on a table across the room. He took it and started back, and then, abruptly, there was a wild clamor in the hall outside and Otar was shouting Ciara's name, pounding on the door.

It was not barred. In another moment they would burst through, and he knew that they would not stop to enquire what he was doing there.

He dropped the flagon and went out swiftly, the way he had come. The guard was still unconscious. In the narrow hall beyond, Stark hesitated. A woman's voice was rising high above the tumult in the main corridor, and he thought he recognized it.

He went to the tapestry curtain and looked for the second time around its edge.

The lofty space was full of men, newly wakened from their heavy sleep and as nervous as so many bears. Thanis struggled in the grip of two of them. Her scarlet kirtle was torn, her hair flying in wild elf-locks, and her face was the face of a mad thing. The whole story of the doom of Kushat was written large upon it.

She screamed again and again, and would not be silenced.

"Tell her, the witch that leads you, tell her that she is already doomed to death, with all her army!"

Otar opened up the door of Ciara's room.

Thanis surged forward. She must have fled through all that castle before she was caught, and Stark's heart ached for her.

"You!" she shrieked through the doorway, and poured out all the filth of the quarter upon Ciara's name. "Balin has gone to bring doom upon you! He will open wide the Gates of Death, and then you will die!—die!—*die*!"

Stark felt the shock of a terrible dread, as he let the curtain fall. Mad with hatred against conquerors, Balin had fulfilled his raging promise and had gone to fling open the Gates of Death.

Remembering his nightmare vision of the shining, evil ones whom Ban Cruach had long ago prisoned beyond those gates, Stark felt a sickness grow within him as he went down the stair and out the postern door.

It was almost dawn. He looked up at the brooding cliffs, and it seemed to him that the wind in the pass had a sound of laughter that mocked his growing dread.

He knew what he must do, if an ancient, mysterious horror was not to be released upon Kushat.

I may still catch Balin before he has gone too far! If I don't—

He dared not think of that. He began to walk very swiftly through the night streets, toward the distant, towering Gates of Death.

VII

It was past noon. He had climbed high toward the saddle of the pass. Kushat lay small below him, and he could see now the pattern of the gorges, cut ages deep in the living rock, that carried the spring torrents of the watershed around the mighty ledge on which the city was built.

The pass itself was channeled, but only by its own snows and melting ice. It was too high for a watercourse. Nevertheless, Stark thought, a man might find it hard to stay alive if he were caught there by the thaw.

He had seen nothing of Balin. The gods knew how many hours' start he had. Stark imagined him, scrambling wild-eyed over the rocks, driven by the same madness that had sent Thanis up into the castle to call down destruction on Ciara's head.

The sun was brilliant but without warmth. Stark shivered, and the icy wind blew strong. The cliffs hung over him, vast and sheer and crushing, and the narrow mouth of the pass was before him. He would go no farther. He would turn back, now.

But he did not. He began to walk forward, into the Gates of Death.

The light was dim and strange at the bottom of that cleft. Little veils of mist crept and clung between the ice and the rock, thickened, became more dense as he went farther and farther into the pass. He could not see, and the wind spoke with many tongues, piping in the crevices of the cliffs.

The steps of the Earthman slowed and faltered. He had known fear in his life before. But now he was carrying the burden of two men's terrors—Ban Cruach's, and his own.

He stopped, enveloped in the clinging mist. He tried to reason with himself—that Ban Cruach's fears had died a million years ago, that Otar had come this way and lived, and Balin had come also.

But the thin veneer of civilization sloughed away and left him with the naked bones of truth. His nostrils twitched to the smell of evil, the subtle unclean taint that only a beast, or one as close to it as he, can sense and know. Every nerve was a point of pain, raw with apprehension. An overpowering recognition of danger, hidden somewhere, mocking at him, made his very body change, draw in upon itself and flatten forward, so that when at last he went on again he was more like a four-footed thing than a man walking upright.

Infinitely wary, silent, moving surely over the ice and the tumbled rock, he followed Balin. He had ceased to think. He was going now on sheer instinct.

The pass led on and on. It grew darker, and in the dim uncanny twilight there were looming shapes that menaced him, and ghostly wings that brushed him, and a terrible stillness that was not broken by the eerie voices of the wind.

Rock and mist and ice. Nothing that moved or lived. And yet the sense of danger deepened, and when he paused the beating of his heart was like thunder in his ears.

Once, far away, he thought he heard the echoes of a man's voice crying, but he had no sight of Balin.

The pass began to drop, and the twilight deepened into a kind of sickly night.

On and down, more slowly now, crouching, slinking, heavily oppressed, tempted to snarl at boulders and tear at wraiths of fog. He had no idea of the miles he had traveled. But the ice was thicker now, the cold intense.

The rock walls broke off sharply. The mist thinned. The pallid darkness lifted to a clear twilight. He came to the end of the Gates of Death.

Stark stopped. Ahead of him, almost blocking the end of the pass, something dark and high and massive loomed in the thinning mists.

It was a great cairn, and upon it sat a figure, facing outward from the Gates of Death as though it kept watch over whatever country lay beyond.

The figure of a man in antique Martian armor.

After a moment, Stark crept toward the cairn. He was still almost all savage, torn between fear and fascination.

He was forced to scramble over the lower rocks of the cairn itself. Quite suddenly he felt a hard shock, and a flashing sensation of warmth that was somehow inside his own flesh, and not in any tempering of the frozen air. He gave a startled leap forward, and whirled, looking up into the face of the mailed figure with the confused idea that it had reached down and struck him.

It had not moved, of course. And Stark knew, with no need of anyone to tell him, that he looked into the face of Ban Cruach.

It was a face made for battles and for ruling, the bony ridges harsh and strong, the hollows under them worn deep with years. Those eyes, dark shadows under the rusty helm, had dreamed high dreams, and neither age nor death had conquered them.

And even in death, Ban Cruach was not unarmed.

Clad as for battle in his ancient mail, he held upright between his hands a mighty sword. The pommel was a ball of crystal large as a man's fist, that held within it a spark of intense brilliance. The little, blinding flame throbbed with its own force, and the sword-blade blazed with a white, cruel radiance.

Ban Cruach, dead but frozen to eternal changelessness by the bitter cold, sitting here upon his cairn for a million years and warding forever the inner end of the Gates of Death, as his ancient city of Kushat warded the outer.

Stark took two cautious steps closer to Ban Cruach, and felt again the shock and the flaring heat in his blood. He recoiled, satisfied.

The strange force in the blazing sword made an invisible barrier across the mouth of the pass, protected Ban Cruach himself. A barrier of short waves, he thought, of the type used in deep therapy, having no heat in themselves but increasing the heat in body cells by increasing their vibration. But these waves were stronger than any he had known before.

A barrier, a wall of force, closing the inner end of the Gates of Death. A barrier that was not designed against man.

Stark shivered. He turned from the somber, brooding form of Ban Cruach and his eyes followed the gaze of the dead king, out beyond the cairn.

He looked across this forbidden land within the Gates of Death.

At his back was the mountain barrier. Before him, a handful of miles to the north, the terminus of the polar cap rose like a cliff of bluish crystal soaring up to touch the early stars. Locked in between those two titanic walls was a great valley of ice.

White and glimmering that valley was, and very still, and very beautiful, the ice shaped gracefully into curving domes and hollows. And in the center of it stood a dark tower of stone, a cyclopean bulk that Stark knew must go down an unguessable distance to its base on the bedrock. It was like the tower in which Camar had died. But this one was not a broken ruin. It loomed with alien arrogance, and within its bulk pallid lights flickered eerily, and it was crowned by a cloud of shimmering darkness.

It was like the tower of his dread vision, the tower that he had seen, not as Eric John Stark, but as Ban Cruach!

Stark's gaze dropped slowly from the evil tower to the curving ice of the valley. And the fear within him grew beyond all bounds.

He had seen that, too, in his vision. The glimmering ice, the domes and hollows of it. He had looked down through it at the city that lay beneath, and he had seen those who came and went in the buried streets.

Stark hunkered down. For a long while he did not stir.

He did not want to go out there. He did not want to go out from the grim, warning figure of Ban Cruach with his blazing sword, into that silent valley. He was afraid, afraid of what he might see if he went there and looked down through the ice, afraid of the final dread fulfillment of his vision.

But he had come after Balin, and Balin must be out there somewhere. He did not want to go, but he was himself, and he must.

He went, going very softly, out toward the tower of stone. And there was no sound in all that land.

The last of the twilight had faded. The ice gleamed, faintly luminous under the stars, and there was light beneath it, a soft radiance that filled all the valley with the glow of a buried moon.

Stark tried to keep his eyes upon the tower. He did not wish to look down at what lay under his stealthy feet.

Inevitably, he looked.

The temples and the palaces glittering in the ice . . .

Level upon level, going down. Wells of soft light spanned with soaring bridges, slender spires rising, an endless variation of streets and crystal walls exquisitely patterned, above and below and overlapping, so that it was like looking down through a thousand giant snowflakes. A metropolis of gossamer and frost, fragile and lovely as a dream, locked in the clear, pure vault of the ice.

Stark saw the people of the city passing along the bright streets, their outlines blurred by the icy vault as things are half obscured by water. The creatures of vision, vaguely shining, infinitely evil.

He shut his eyes and waited until the shock and the dizziness left him. Then he set his gaze resolutely on the tower, and crept on, over the glassy sky that covered those buried streets.

Silence. Even the wind was hushed.

He had gone perhaps half the distance when the cry rang out.

It burst upon the valley with a shocking violence. *"Stark! Stark!"* The ice rang with it, curving ridges picked up his name and flung it back and forth with eerie crystal voices, and the echoes fled out whispering *Stark! Stark!* until it seemed that the very mountains spoke.

Stark whirled about. In the pallid gloom between the ice and the stars there was light enough to see the cairn behind him, and the dim figure atop it with the shining sword.

Light enough to see Ciara, and the dark knot of riders who had followed her through the Gates of Death.

She cried his name again. "Come back! Come back!"

The ice of the valley answered mockingly, *"Come back! Come back!"* and Stark was gripped with a terror that held him motionless.

She should not have called him. She should not have made a sound in that deathly place.

A man's hoarse scream rose above the flying echoes. The riders turned and fled suddenly, the squealing, hissing beasts crowding each other, floundering wildly on the rocks of the cairn, stampeding back into the pass.

Ciara was left alone. Stark saw her fight the rearing beast she rode and then flung herself out of the saddle and let it go. She came toward him, running, clad all in her black armor, the great axe swinging high.

"Behind you, Stark! Oh, gods of Mars!"

He turned then and saw them, coming out from the tower of stone, the pale, shining creatures that move so swiftly across the ice, so fleet and swift that no man living could outrun them.

He shouted to Ciara to turn back. He drew his sword and over his shoulder he cursed her in a black fury because he could hear her mailed feet coming on behind him.

The gliding creatures, sleek and slender, reedlike, bending, delicate as wraiths, their bodies shaped from northern rainbows of amethyst and rose—if they should touch Ciara, if their loathsome hands should touch her . . .

Stark let out one raging catlike scream, and rushed them.

The opalescent bodies slipped away beyond his reach. The creatures watched him.

They had no faces, but they watched. They were eyeless but not blind, earless, but not without hearing. The inquisitive tendrils that formed their sensory organs stirred and shifted like the petals of ungodly flowers, and the color of them was the white frost-fire that dances on the snow.

"Go back, Ciara!"

But she would not go, and he knew that they would not have let her. She reached him, and they set their backs together. The shining ones ringed them round, many feet away across the ice, and watched the long sword and the great hungry axe, and there was something in the lissome swaying of their bodies that suggested laughter.

"You fool," said Stark. "You bloody fool."

"And you?" answered Ciara. "Oh, yes, I know about Balin. That mad girl, screaming in the palace—she told me, and you were seen from the wall, climbing to the Gates of Death. I tried to catch you."

"Why?"

She did not answer that. "They won't fight us, Stark. Do you think we could make it back to the cairn?"

"No. But we can try."

Guarding each others' backs, they began to walk toward Ban Cruach and the pass. If they could once reach the barrier, they would be safe.

Stark knew now what Ban Cruach's wall of force was built against. And he began to guess the riddle of the Gates of Death.

The shining ones glided with them, out of reach. They did not try to bar the way. They formed a circle around the man and woman, moving with them and around them at the same time, an endless weaving chain of many bodies shining with soft jewel tones of color.

They drew closer and closer to the cairn, to the brooding figure of Ban Cruach and his sword. It crossed Stark's mind that the creatures were playing with him and Ciara. Yet they had no weapons. Almost, he began to hope . . .

From the tower where the shimmering cloud of darkness clung came a black crescent of force that swept across the ice-field like a sickle and gathered the two humans in.

Stark felt a shock of numbing cold that turned his nerves to ice. His sword dropped from his hand, and he heard Ciara's axe go down. His body was without strength, without feeling, dead.

He fell, and the shining ones glided in toward him.

VIII

Twice before in his life Stark had come near to freezing. It had been like this, the numbness and the cold. And yet it seemed that the dark force had struck rather at his nerve centers than at his flesh.

He could not see Ciara, who was behind him, but he heard the metallic clashing of her mail and one small, whispered cry, and he knew that she had fallen, too.

The glowing creatures surrounded him. He saw their bodies bending over him, the frosty tendrils of their faces writhing as though in excitement or delight.

Their hands touched him. Little hands with seven fingers, deft and frail. Even his numbed flesh felt the terrible cold of their touch, freezing as outer space. He yelled, or tried to, but they were not abashed.

They lifted him and bore him toward the tower, a company of them, bearing his heavy weight upon their gleaming shoulders.

He saw the tower loom high and higher still above him. The cloud of dark force that crowned it blotted out the stars. It became too huge and high to see at all, and then there was a low flat arch of stone close above his face, and he was inside.

Straight overhead—a hundred feet, two hundred, he could not tell—was a globe of crystal, fitted into the top of the tower as a jewel is held in a setting.

The air around it was shadowed with the same eerie gloom that hovered outside, but less dense, so that Stark could see the smoldering purple spark that burned within the globe, sending out its dark vibrations.

A globe of crystal, with a heart of sullen flame. Stark remembered the sword of Ban Cruach, and the white fire that burned in its hilt.

Two globes, the bright-cored and the dark. The sword of Ban Cruach touched the blood with heat. The globe of the tower deadened the flesh with cold. It was the same force, but at opposite ends of the spectrum.

Stark saw the cryptic controls of that glooming globe—a bank of them, on a wide stone ledge just inside the tower, close beside him. There were shining ones on that ledge tending those controls, and there were other strange and massive mechanisms there too.

Flying spirals of ice climbed up inside the tower, spanning the great stone well with spidery bridges, joining icy galleries. In some of those galleries, Stark vaguely glimpsed rigid, gleaming figures like statues of ice, but he could not see them clearly as he was carried on.

He was being carried downward. He passed slits in the wall, and knew that the pallid lights he had seen through them were the moving bodies of the creatures as they went up and down these high-flung, icy bridges. He managed to turn his head to look down, and saw what was beneath him.

The well of the tower plunged down a good five hundred feet to bedrock, widening as it went. The web of ice-bridges and the spiral ways went down as well as up, and the creatures that carried him were moving smoothly along a transparent ribbon of ice no more than a yard in width, suspended over that terrible drop.

Stark was glad that he could not move just then. One instinctive start of horror would have thrown him and his bearers to the rock below, and would have carried Ciara with them.

Down and down, gliding in utter silence along the descending spiral ribbon. The great glooming crystal grew remote above him. Ice was solid now in the slots of the walls. He wondered if they had brought Balin this way.

There were other openings, wide arches like the one they had brought their captives through, and these gave Stark brief glimpses of broad avenues and unguessable buildings, shaped from the pellucid ice and flooded with the soft radiance that was like eerie moonlight.

At length, on what Stark took to be the third level of the city, the creatures bore him through one of these archways, into the streets beyond.

Below him now was the translucent thickness of ice that formed the floor of this level and the roof of the level beneath. He could see the blurred tops of delicate minarets, the clustering roofs that shone like chips of diamond.

Above him was an ice roof. Elfin spires rose toward it, delicate as needles. Lacy battlements and little domes, buildings star-shaped, wheel-shaped, the fantastic, lovely shapes of snow-crystals, frosted over with a sparkling foam of light.

The people of the city gathered along the way to watch, a living, shifting rainbow of amethyst and rose and green, against the pure blue-white. And there was no least whisper of sound anywhere.

For some distance they went through a geometric maze of streets. And then there was a cathedral-like building all arched and spired, standing in the center of a twelve-pointed plaza. Here they turned, and bore their captives in.

Stark saw a vaulted roof, very slim and high, etched with a glittering tracery that might have been carving of an alien sort, delicate as the weavings of spiders. The feet of his bearers were silent on the icy paving.

At the far end of the long vault sat seven of the shining ones in high seats marvelously shaped from the ice. And before them, gray-faced, shuddering with cold and not noticing it, drugged with a sick horror, stood Balin. He looked around once, and did not speak.

Stark was set on his feet, with Ciara beside him. He saw her face, and it was terrible to see the fear in her eyes, that had never shown fear before.

He himself was learning why men went mad beyond the Gates of Death.

Chill, dreadful fingers touched him expertly. A flash of pain drove down his spine, and he could stand again.

The seven who sat in the high seats were motionless, their bright tendrils stirring with infinite delicacy as though they studied the three humans who stood before them.

Stark thought he could feel a cold, soft fingering of his brain. It came to him that these creatures were probably telepaths. They lacked organs of speech, and yet they must have some efficient means of communications. Telepathy was not uncommon among the many races of the Solar System, and Stark had had experience with it before.

He forced his mind to relax. The alien impulse was instantly stronger. He sent out his own questing thought and felt it brush the edges of a consciousness so utterly foreign to his own that he knew he could never probe it, even had he had the skill.

He learned one thing—that the shining faceless ones looked upon him with equal horror and loathing. They recoiled from the unnatural human features, and most of all, most strongly, they abhorred the warmth of human flesh. Even the infinitesimal amount of heat radiated by their half-frozen human bodies caused the ice-folk discomfort.

Stark marshaled his imperfect abilities and projected a mental question to the seven.

"What do you want of us?"

The answer came back, faint and imperfect, as though the gap between their alien minds was almost too great to bridge. And the answer was one word.

"Freedom!"

Balin spoke suddenly. He voiced only a whisper, and yet the sound was shockingly loud in that crystal vault.

"They have asked me already. Tell them no, Stark! Tell them no!"

He looked at Ciara then, a look of murderous hatred. "If you turn them loose upon Kushat, I will kill you with my own hands before I die."

Stark spoke again, silently, to the seven. "I do not understand."

Again the struggling, difficult thought. "We are the old race, the kings of the glacial ice. Once we held all the land beyond the mountains, outside the pass you call the Gates of Death."

Stark had seen the ruins of the towers out on the moors. He knew how far their kingdom had extended.

"We *controlled* the ice, far outside the polar cap. Our towers blanketed the land with the dark force drawn from Mars itself, from the magnetic field of the planet. That radiation bars out heat, from the Sun, and even from the awful winds that blow warm from the south. So there was never any thaw. Our cities were many, and our race was great.

"Then came Ban Cruach, from the south . . .

"He waged a war against us. He learned the secret of the crystal globes, and learned how to reverse their force and use it against us. He, leading his army, destroyed our towers one by one, and drove us back . . .

"Mars needed water. The outer ice was melted, our lovely cities crumbled to nothing, so that creatures like Ban Cruach might have water! And our people died.

"We retreated at the last, to this our ancient polar citadel behind the Gates of Death. Even here, Ban Cruach followed. He destroyed even this tower once, at the time of the thaw. But this city is founded in polar ice—and only the upper levels were harmed. Even Ban Cruach could not touch the heart of the eternal polar cap of Mars!

"When he saw that he could not destroy us utterly, he set himself in death to guard the Gates of Death with his blazing sword, that we might never again reclaim our ancient dominion.

"That is what we mean when we ask for freedom. We ask that you take away the sword of Ban Cruach, so that we may once again go out through the Gates of Death!"

Stark cried aloud, hoarsely, *"No!"*

He knew the barren deserts of the south, the wastes of red dust, the dead sea bottoms—the terrible thirst of Mars, growing greater with every year of the million that had passed since Ban Cruach locked the Gates of Death.

He knew the canals, the pitiful waterways that were all that stood between the people of Mars and extinction. He remembered the yearly release from death when the spring thaw brought the water rushing down from the north.

He thought of these cold creatures going forth, building again their great towers of stone, sheathing half a world in ice that would never melt. He thought of the people of Jekkara and Valkis and Barrakesh, of the countless cities of the south, watching for the flood that did not come, and falling at last to mingle their bodies with the blowing dust.

He said again, "No. Never."

The distant thought-voice of the seven spoke, and this time the question was addressed to Ciara.

Stark saw her face. She did not know the Mars he knew, but she had memories of her own—the mountain-valleys of Mekh, the moors, the snowy gorges. She looked at the shining ones in their high seats, and said,

"If I take that sword, it will be to use it against you as Ban Cruach did!"

Stark knew that the seven had understood the thought behind her words. He felt that they were amused.

"The secret of that sword was lost a million years ago, the day Ban Cruach died. Neither you nor anyone now knows how to use it as he did. But the sword's radiations of warmth still lock us here.

"We cannot approach that sword, for its vibrations of heat slay us if we do. But you warm-bodied ones can approach it. And you will do so, and take it from its place. *One of you will take it!*"

They were very sure of that.

"We can see, a little way, into your evil minds. Much we do not understand. But—the mind of the large man is full of the woman's image, and the mind of the woman turns to him. Also, there is a link between the large man and the small man, less strong, but strong enough."

The thought-voice of the seven finished, "The large man will take away the sword for us because he must—to save the other two."

Ciara turned to Stark. "They cannot force you, Stark. Don't let them. No matter what they do to me, don't let them!"

Balin stared at her with a certain wonder. "You would die, to protect Kushat?"

"Not Kushat alone, though its people too are human," she said, almost angrily. "There are my red wolves—a wild pack, but my own. And others." She looked at Balin. "What do *you* say? Your life against the Norlands?"

Balin made an effort to lift his head as high as hers, and the red jewel flashed in his ear. He was a man crushed by the falling of his world, and terrified by what his mad passion had led him into, here beyond the Gates of Death. But he was not afraid to die.

He said so, and even Ciara knew that he spoke the truth.

But the seven were not dismayed. Stark knew that when their thought-voice whispered in his mind,

"It is not death alone you humans have to fear, but the manner of your dying. You shall see that, before you choose."

Swiftly, silently, those of the ice-folk who had borne the captives into the city came up from behind, where they had stood withdrawn and waiting. And one of them bore a crystal rod like a scepter, with a spark of ugly purple burning in the globed end.

Stark leaped to put himself between them and Ciara. He struck out, raging, and because he was almost as quick as they, he caught one of the slim luminous bodies between his hands.

The utter coldness of that alien flesh burned his hands as frost will burn. Even so, he clung on, snarling, and saw the tendrils writhe and stiffen as though in pain.

Then, from the crystal rod, a thread of darkness spun itself to touch his brain with silence, and the cold that lies between the worlds.

He had no memory of being carried once more through the shimmering streets of that elfin, evil city, back to the stupendous well of the tower, and up along the spiral path of ice that soared those dizzy hundreds of feet from bedrock to the glooming crystal globe. But when he again opened his eyes, he was lying on the wide stone ledge at ice-level.

Beside him was the arch that led outside. Close above his head was the control bank that he had seen before.

Ciara and Balin were there also, on the ledge. They leaned stiffly against the stone wall beside the control bank, and facing them was a squat, round mechanism from which projected a sort of wheel of crystal rods.

Their bodies were strangely rigid, but their eyes and minds were awake. Terribly awake. Stark saw their eyes, and his heart turned within him.

Ciara looked at him. She could not speak, but she had no need to. *No matter what they do to me . . .*

She had not feared the swordsmen of Kushat. She had not feared her red wolves, when he unmasked her in the square. She was afraid now. But she warned him, ordered him not to save her.

They cannot force you. Stark! Don't let them.

And Balin, too, pleaded with him for Kushat.

They were not alone on the ledge. The ice-folk clustered there, and out upon the flying spiral pathway, on the narrow bridges and the spans of fragile ice, they stood in hundreds watching, eyeless, faceless, their bodies drawn in rainbow lines across the dimness of the shaft.

Stark's mind could hear the silent edges of their laughter. Secret, knowing laughter, full of evil, full of triumph, and Stark was filled with a corroding terror.

He tried to move, to crawl toward Ciara standing like a carven image in her black mail. He could not.

Again her fierce, proud glance met his. And the silent laughter of the ice-folk echoed in his mind, and he thought it very strange that in this moment, now, he should realize that there had never been another woman like her on all of the worlds of the Sun.

The fear she felt was not for herself. It was for him.

Apart from the multitudes of the ice-folk, the group of seven stood upon the ledge. And now their thought-voice spoke to Stark, saying,

"Look about you. Behold the men who have come before you through the Gates of Death!"

Stark raised his eyes to where their slender fingers pointed, and saw the icy galleries around the tower, saw more clearly the icy statues in them that he had only glimpsed before.

Men, set like images in the galleries. Men whose bodies were sheathed in a glittering mail of ice, sealing them forever. Warriors, nobles, fanatics and thieves—the wanderers of a million years who had dared to enter this forbidden valley, and had remained forever.

He saw their faces, their tortured eyes wide open, their features frozen in the agony of a slow and awful death.

"They refused us," the seven whispered. "They would not take away the sword. And so they died, as this woman and this man will die, unless you choose to save them.

"We will show you, human, how they died!"

One of the ice-folk bent and touched the squat, round mechanism that faced Balin and Ciara. Another shifted the pattern of control on the master-bank.

The wheel of crystal rods on that squat mechanism began to turn. The rods blurred, became a disc that spun faster and faster.

High above in the top of the tower the great globe brooded, shrouded in its cloud of shimmering darkness. The disc became a whirling blur. The glooming shadow of the globe deepened, coalesced. It began to lengthen and descend, stretching itself down toward the spinning disc.

The crystal rods of the mechanism drank the shadow in. And out of that spinning blur there came a subtle weaving of threads of darkness, a gossamer curtain winding around Ciara and Balin so that their outlines grew ghostly and the pallor of their flesh was as the pallor of snow at night.

And still Stark could not move.

The veil of darkness began to sparkle faintly. Stark watched it, watched the chill motes brighten, watched the tracery of frost whiten over Ciara's mail, touch Balin's dark hair with silver.

Frost. Bright, sparkling, beautiful, a halo of frost around their bodies. A dust of splintered diamond across their faces, an aureole of brittle light to crown their heads.

Frost. Flesh slowly hardening in marbly whiteness, as the cold slowly increased. And yet their eyes still lived, and saw, and understood.

The thought-voice of the seven spoke again.

"You have only minutes now to decide! Their bodies cannot endure too much, and live again. Behold their eyes, and how they suffer!

"Only minutes, human! Take away the sword of Ban Cruach! Open for us the Gates of Death, and we will release these two, alive."

Stark felt again the flashing stab of pain along his nerves, as one of the shining creatures moved behind him. Life and feeling came back into his limbs.

He struggled to his feet. The hundreds of the ice-folk on the bridges and galleries watched him in an eager silence.

He did not look at them. His eyes were on Ciara's. And now, her eyes pleaded.

"Don't, Stark! Don't barter the life of the Norlands for me!"

The thought-voice beat at Stark, cutting into his mind with cruel urgency.

"Hurry, human! They are already beginning to die. Take away the sword, and let them live!"

Stark turned. He cried out, in a voice that made the icy bridges tremble:

"I will take the sword!"

He staggered out, then. Out through the archway, across the ice, toward the distant cairn that blocked the Gates of Death.

IX

Across the glowing ice of the valley Stark went at a stumbling run that grew swifter and more sure as his cold-numbed body began to regain its functions. And behind him, pouring out of the tower to watch, came the shining ones.

They followed after him, gliding lightly. He could sense their excitement, the cold, strange ecstasy of triumph. He knew that already they were thinking of the great towers of stone rising again above the Norlands, the crystal cities still and beautiful under the ice, all vestige of the ugly citadels of man gone and forgotten.

The seven spoke once more, a warning.

"If you turn toward us with the sword, the woman and the man will die. And you will die as well. For neither you nor any other can now use the sword as a weapon of offense."

Stark ran on. He was thinking then only of Ciara, with the frost-crystals gleaming on her marble flesh and her eyes full of mute torment.

The cairn loomed up ahead, dark and high. It seemed to Stark that the brooding figure of Ban Cruach watched him coming with those shadowed eyes beneath the rusty helm. The great sword blazed between those dead, frozen hands.

The ice-folk had slowed their forward rush. They stopped and waited, well back from the cairn.

Stark reached the edge of tumbled rock. He felt the first warm flare of the force-waves in his blood, and slowly the chill began to creep out from his bones. He climbed, scrambling upward over the rough stones of the cairn.

Abruptly, then, at Ban Cruach's feet, he slipped and fell. For a second it seemed that he could not move.

His back was turned toward the ice-folk. His body was bent forward, and shielded so, his hands worked with feverish speed.

From his cloak he tore a strip of cloth. From the iron boss he took the glittering lens, the talisman of Ban Cruach. Stark laid the lens against his brow, and bound it on.

The remembered shock, the flood and sweep of memories that were not his own. The mind of Ban Cruach thundering its warning, its hard-won knowledge of an ancient, epic war . . .

He opened his own mind wide to receive those memories. Before he had fought against them. Now he knew that they were his one small chance in this swift gamble with death. Two things only of his own he kept firm in that staggering tide of another man's memories. Two names—Ciara and Balin.

He rose up again. And now his face had a strange look, a curious duality. The features had not changed, but somehow the lines of the flesh had altered subtly, so that it was almost as though the old unconquerable king himself had risen again in battle.

He mounted the last step or two and stood before Ban Cruach. A shudder ran through him, a sort of gathering and settling of the flesh, as though Stark's being had accepted the stranger within it. His eyes, cold and pale as the very ice that sheathed the valley, burned with a cruel light.

He reached and took the sword, out of the frozen hands of Ban Cruach.

As though it were his own, he knew the secret of the metal rings that bound its hilt, below the ball of crystal. The savage throb of the invisible radiation beat in his quickening flesh. He was warm again, his blood running swiftly, his muscles sure and strong. He touched the rings and turned them.

The fan-shaped aura of force that had closed the Gates of Death narrowed in, and as it narrowed it leaped up from the blade of the sword in a tongue of pale fire, faintly shimmering, made visible now by the full focus of its strength.

Stark felt the wave of horror bursting from the minds of the ice-folk as they perceived what he had done. And he laughed.

His bitter laughter rang harsh across the valley as he turned to face them, and he heard in his brain the shuddering, silent shriek that went up from all that gathered company . . .

"Ban Cruach! Ban Cruach has returned!"

They had touched his mind. They knew.

He laughed again, and swept the sword in a flashing arc, and watched the long bright blade of force strike out more terrible than steel, against the rainbow bodies of the shining ones.

They fell. Like flowers under a scythe they fell, and all across the ice the ones who were yet untouched turned about in their hundreds and fled back toward the tower.

Stark came leaping down the cairn, the talisman of Ban Cruach bound upon his brow, the sword of Ban Cruach blazing in his hand.

He swung that awful blade as he ran. The force-beam that sprang from it cut through the press of creatures fleeing before him, hampered by their own numbers as they crowded back through the archway.

He had only a few short seconds to do what he had to do.

Rushing with great strides across the ice, spurning the withered bodies of the dead . . . And then, from the glooming darkness that hovered around the tower of stone, the black cold beam struck down.

Like a coiling whip it lashed him. The deadly numbness invaded the cells of his flesh, ached in the marrow of his bones. The bright force of the sword battled the chill invaders, and a corrosive agony tore at Stark's inner body where the antipathetic radiations waged war.

His steps faltered. He gave one hoarse cry of pain, and then his limbs failed and he went heavily to his knees.

Instinct only made him cling to the sword. Waves of blinding anguish racked him. The coiling lash of darkness encircled him, and its touch was the abysmal cold of outer space, striking deep into his heart.

Hold the sword close, hold it closer, like a shield. The pain is great, but I will not die unless I drop the sword.

Ban Cruach the mighty had fought this fight before.

Stark raised the sword again, close against his body. The fierce pulse of its brightness drove back the cold. Not far, for the freezing touch was very strong. But far enough so that he could rise again and stagger on.

The dark force of the tower writhed and licked about him. He could not escape it. He slashed it in a blind fury with the blazing sword, and where the forces met a flicker of lightning leaped in the air, but it would not be beaten back.

He screamed at it, a raging cat-cry that was all Stark, all primitive fury at the necessity of pain. And he forced himself to run, to drag his tortured body faster across the ice. *Because Ciara is dying, because the dark cold wants me to stop . . .*

The ice-folk jammed and surged against the archway, in a panic hurry to take refuge far below in their many-leveled city. He raged at them, too. They were part of the cold, part of the pain. Because of them Ciara and Balin were dying. He sent the blade of force lancing among them, his hatred rising full tide to join the hatred of Ban Cruach that lodged in his mind.

Stab and cut and slash with the long terrible beam of brightness. They fell and fell, the hideous shining folk, and Stark sent the light of Ban Cruach's weapon sweeping through the tower itself, through the openings that were like windows in the stone.

Again and again, stabbing through those open slits as he ran. And suddenly the dark beam of force ceased to move. He tore out of it, and it did not follow him, remaining stationary as though fastened to the ice.

The battle of forces left his flesh. The pain was gone. He sped on to the tower.

He was close now. The withered bodies lay in heaps before the arch. The last of the ice-folk had forced their way inside. Holding the sword level like a lance, Stark leaped in through the arch, into the tower.

The shining ones were dead where the destroying warmth had touched them. The flying spiral ribbons of ice were swept clean of them, the arching bridges and the galleries of that upper part of the tower.

They were dead along the ledge, under the control bank. They were dead across the mechanism that spun the frosty doom around Ciara and Balin. The whirling disc still hummed.

Below, in that stupendous well, the crowding ice-folk made a seething pattern of color on the narrow ways. But Stark turned his back on them and ran along the ledge, and in him was the heavy knowledge that he had come too late.

The frost had thickened around Ciara and Balin. It encrusted them like stiffened lace, and now their flesh was overlaid with a diamond shell of ice.

Surely they could not live!

He raised the sword to smite down at the whirring disc, to smash it, but there was no need. When the full force of that concentrated beam struck it, meeting the focus of shadow that it held, there was a violent flare of light and a shattering of crystal. The mechanism was silent.

The glooming veil was gone from around the ice-shelled man and woman. Stark forgot the creatures in the shaft below him. He turned the blazing sword full upon Ciara and Balin.

It would not affect the thin covering of ice. If the woman and the man were dead, it would not affect their flesh, any more than it had Ban Cruach's. But if they lived, if there was still a spark, a flicker beneath that frozen mail, the radiation would touch their blood with warmth, start again the pulse of life in their bodies.

He waited, watching Ciara's face. It was still as marble, and as white.

Something—instinct, or the warning mind of Ban Cruach that had learned a million years ago to beware the creatures of the ice—made him glance behind him.

Stealthy, swift and silent, up the winding ways they came. They had guessed that he had forgotten them in his anxiety. The sword was turned away from them now, and if they could take him from behind, stun him with the chill force of the scepter-like rods they carried . . .

He slashed them with the sword. He saw the flickering beam go down and down the shaft, saw the bodies fall like drops of rain, rebounding here and there from the flying spans and carrying the living with them.

He thought of the many levels of the city. He thought of all the countless thousands that must inhabit them. He could hold them off in the shaft as long as he wished if he had no other need for the sword. But he knew that as soon as he turned his back they would be upon him again, and if he should once fall . . .

He could not spare a moment, or a chance.

He looked at Ciara, not knowing what to do, and it seemed to him that the sheathing frost had melted, just a little, around her face.

Desperately, he struck down again at the creatures in the shaft, and then the answer came to him.

He dropped the sword. The squat, round mechanism was beside him, with its broken crystal wheel. He picked it up.

It was heavy. It would have been heavy for two men to lift, but Stark was a driven man. Grunting, swaying with the effort, he lifted it and let it fall, out and down.

Like a thunderbolt it struck among those slender bridges, the spiderweb of icy strands that spanned the shaft. Stark watched it go, and listened to the brittle snapping of the ice, the final crashing of a million shards at the bottom far below.

He smiled, and turned again to Ciara, picking up the sword.

It was hours later. Stark walked across the glowing ice of the valley, toward the cairn. The sword of Ban Cruach hung at his side. He had taken the talisman and replaced it in the boss, and he was himself again.

Ciara and Balin walked beside him. The color had come back into their faces, but faintly, and they were still weak enough to be glad of Stark's hands to steady them.

At the foot of the cairn they stopped, and Stark mounted it alone.

He looked for a long moment into the face of Ban Cruach. Then he took the sword, and carefully turned the rings upon it so that the radiation spread out as it had before, to close the Gates of Death.

Almost reverently, he replaced the sword in Ban Cruach's hands. Then he turned and went down over the tumbled stones.

The shimmering darkness brooded still over the distant tower. Underneath the ice, the elfin city still spread downward. The shining ones would rebuild their bridges in the shaft, and go on as they had before, dreaming their cold dreams of ancient power.

But they would not go out through the Gates of Death. Ban Cruach in his rusty mail was still lord of the pass, the warder of the Norlands.

Stark said to the others, "Tell the story in Kushat. Tell it through the Norlands, the story of Ban Cruach and why he guards the Gates of Death. Men have forgotten. And they should not forget."

They went out of the valley then, the two men and the woman. They did not speak again, and the way out through the pass seemed endless.

Some of Ciara's chieftains met them at the mouth of the pass above Kushat. They had waited there, ashamed to return to the city without her, but not daring to go back into the pass again. They had seen the creatures of the valley, and they were still afraid.

They gave mounts to the three. They themselves walked behind Ciara, and their heads were low with shame.

They came into Kushat through the riven gate, and Stark went with Ciara to the King City, where she made Balin follow too.

"Your sister is there," she said. "I have had her cared for."

The city was quiet, with the sullen apathy that follows after battle. The men of Mekh cheered Ciara in the streets. She rode proudly, but Stark saw that her face was gaunt and strained.

He, too, was marked deep by what he had seen and done, beyond the Gates of Death.

They went up into the castle.

Thanis took Balin into her arms, and wept. She had lost her first wild fury, and she could look at Ciara now with a restrained hatred that had a tinge almost of admiration.

"You fought for Kushat," she said, unwillingly, when she had heard the story. "For that, at least, I can thank you."

She went to Stark then, and looked up at him. "Kushat, and my brother's life. . . " She kissed him, and there were tears on her lips. But she turned to Ciara with a bitter smile. "No one can hold him, any more than the wind can be held. You will learn that."

She went out then with Balin, and left Stark and Ciara alone, in the chambers of the king.

Ciara said, "The little one is very shrewd." She unbuckled the hauberk and let it fall, standing slim in her tunic of black leather, and walked to the tall windows that looked out upon the mountains. She leaned her head wearily against the stone.

"An evil day, an evil deed. And now I have Kushat to govern, with no reward of power from beyond the Gates of Death. How man can be misled!"

Stark poured wine from the flagon and brought it to her. She looked at him over the rim of the cup, with a certain wry amusement.

"The little one is shrewd, and she is right. I don't know that I can be as wise as she . . . Will you stay with me, Stark, or will you go?"

He did not answer at once, and she asked him, "What hunger drives you, Stark? It is not conquest, as it was with me. What are you looking for that you cannot find?"

He shook his head. "I don't know. It doesn't matter." He took her between his two hands, feeling the strength and the splendor of her, and it was oddly difficult to find words.

"I want to stay, Ciara. Now, this minute, I could promise that I would stay forever. But I know myself. You belong here, you will make Kushat your own. I don't. Someday I will go."

Ciara nodded. "My neck, also, was not made for chains, and one country was too little to hold me. Very well, Stark. Let it be so."

She smiled, and let the wine-cup fall.

Ted Giola wrote in an essay, "Fritz Leiber at One Hundred" :

> *[Fafhrd and the Gray Mouser] are depicted as vulnerable, fickle, and down-to-earth in a way that was rare in the 1930s. This was, after all, an era of larger-than-life heroes . . . [and] a simplistic good-versus-evil worldview, not much different than the matchup destined to unfold on European battlefields a few weeks after the publication of the first Fafhrd and Gray Mouser tale. Leiber would have none of this vanilla virtuousness, and in his adventure series he embraced the anti-hero ethos, breaking many of the most cherished rules of genre writing. . . . Leiber's best work comes across as fresh and modern to an almost uncanny degree.*

The nearly seven-foot-tall barbarian Fafhrd and the diminutive, former wizard's apprentice Mouser first appeared in "Two Sought Adventure" (1939). They continued their roguish adventures in more than thirty stories, the last of which was published in 1988. Our novella, "Ill Met in Lankhmar," the story of their first meeting, was published in the April 1970 issue of The Magazine of Science Fiction and Fantasy. *Fritz Leiber (1910-1992), who created the term "sword and sorcery" in 1961, thought his characters were "at the opposite extreme from the heroes of Tolkien. My stuff is at least as equally fantastic as his, but it is an earthier sort of fantasy." The humor, weird wizards, somewhat bawdy encounters with women, and other aspects of the stories were nothing like Howard's Conan stories and marked a new direction for S&S.*

ILL MET IN LANKHMAR

Fritz Leiber

Silent as specters, the tall and the fat thief edged past the dead, noose-strangled watch-leopard, out the thick, lock-picked door of Jengao the Gem Merchant, and strolled east on Cash Street through the thin black nightsmog of Lankhmar, City of Sevenscore Thousand Smokes.

East on Cash it had to be, for west at the intersection of Cash and Silver was a police post with unbribed guardsmen in browned-iron cuirasses and helms, restlessly grounding and rattling their pikes, while Jengao's place had no alley entrance or even window in its stone walls three spans thick and the roof and floor almost as strong and without trap doors.

But tall, tight-lipped Slevyas, master thief candidate, and fat, darting-eyed Fissif, thief second class, brevetted first class for this operation, with a rating of talented in double-dealing, were not in the least worried. Everything was proceeding according to plan. Each carried thonged in his pouch a much smaller pouch of jewels of the first water only, for Jengao, now breathing stentoriously inside and senseless from the slugging he'd suffered, must be allowed, nay, nursed and encouraged, to build up his business again and so ripen it for another plucking. Almost the first law of the Thieves' Guild was never kill the hen that laid brown eggs with a ruby in the yolk, or white eggs with a diamond in the white.

The two thieves also had the relief of knowing that, with the satisfaction of a job well done, they were going straight home now, not to a wife, Aarth forbid!—or to parents and children, all gods forfend!—but to Thieves' House, headquarters and barracks of the all-mighty Guild which was father to them both and mother too, though no woman was allowed inside its ever-open portal on Cheap Street.

In addition there was the comforting knowledge that although each was armed only with his regulation silver-hilted thief's knife, a weapon seldom used except in rare intramural duels and brawls, in fact more a membership token than a weapon, they were nevertheless most strongly convoyed by three reliable and lethal bravos hired for the evening from the Slayers' Brotherhood, one moving well ahead of them as point, the other two well behind as rear guard and chief striking force, in fact almost out of sight—for it is never wise that such convoying be obvious, or so believed Krovas, Grandmaster of the Thieves' Guild.

And if all that were not enough to make Slevyas and Fissif feel safe and serene, there danced along soundlessly beside them in the shadow of the north curb a small, malformed or at any rate somewhat large-headed shape that might have been a small dog, a somewhat undersized cat, or a very big rat. Occasionally it scuttled familiarly and even encouragingly a little way toward their snugly felt-slippered feet, though it always scurried swiftly back into the darker dark.

True, this last guard was not an absolutely unalloyed reassurance. At that very moment, scarcely twoscore paces yet from Jengao's, Fissif tautly walked for a bit on tiptoe and strained his pudgy lips upward to whisper softly in Slevyas' long-lobed ear, "Damned if I like being dogged by that familiar of Hristomilo, no matter what security he's supposed to afford us. Bad enough that Krovas employs or lets himself be cowed into employing a sorcerer of most dubious, if dire, reputation and aspect, but that—"

"Shut your trap!" Slevyas hissed still more softly.

Fissif obeyed with a shrug and occupied himself even more restlessly and keenly than was his wont in darting his gaze this way and that, but chiefly ahead.

Some distance in that direction, in fact just short of the Gold Street intersection, Cash was bridged by an enclosed second-story passageway connecting the two buildings which made up the premises of the famous stonemasons and sculptors Rokkermas and Slaarg. The firm's buildings themselves were fronted by very shallow porticos supported by unnecessarily large pillars of varied shape and decoration, advertisements more than structural members.

From just beyond the bridge there came two low, brief whistles, signal from the point bravo that he had inspected that area for ambushes and discovered nothing suspicious and that Gold Street was clear.

Fissif was by no means entirely satisfied by the safety signal. To tell the truth, the fat thief rather enjoyed being apprehensive and even fearful, at least up to a point. A sense of strident panic overlaid with writhing calm made him feel more excitingly alive than the occasional woman he enjoyed. So he scanned most closely through the thin, sooty smog the frontages and overhangs of Rokkermas and Slaarg as his and Slevyas' leisurely seeming yet un-slow pace brought them steadily closer.

On this side the bridge was pierced by four small windows, between which were three large niches in which stood—another advertisement—three life-size plaster statues, somewhat eroded by years of weather and dyed varyingly tones of dark gray by as many years of smog. Approaching Jengao's before the burglary, Fissif had noted them with a swift but comprehensive overshoulder glance. Now it seemed to him that the statue to the right had indefinably changed. It was that of a man of medium height wearing cloak and hood, who gazed down with crossed arms and brooding aspect. No, not indefinably quite—the statue was a more uniform dark gray now, he fancied, cloak, hood, and face; it seemed somewhat sharper featured, less eroded; and he would almost swear it had grown shorter!

Just below the niche, moreover, there was a scattering of gray and raw white rubble which he didn't recall having been there earlier. He strained to remember if during the excitement of the burglary, with its lively leopard-slaying and slugging and all, the unsleeping watch-corner of his mind had recorded a distant crash, and now he believed it had. His quick imagination pictured the possibility of a hole or even door behind each statue, through which it might be given a strong push and so tumbled onto passersby, himself and Slevyas specifically, the right-hand statue having been crashed to test the device and then replaced with a near twin.

He would keep close watch on all three statues as he and Slevyas walked under. It would be easy to dodge if he saw one start to overbalance. Should he yank Slevyas out of harm's way when that happened? It was something to think about.

Without pause his restless attention fixed next on the porticos and pillars. The latter, thick and almost three yards tall, were placed at irregular intervals as well as being irregularly shaped and fluted, for Rokkermas and Slaarg were most modern and emphasized the unfinished look, randomness, and the unexpected.

Nevertheless it seemed to Fissif, his wariness wide awake now, that there was an intensification of unexpectedness, specifically that there was one more pillar under the porticos than when he had last passed by. He couldn't be sure which pillar was the newcomer, but he was almost certain there was one.

Share his suspicions with Slevyas? Yes, and get another hissed reproof and flash of contempt from the small, dull-seeming eyes.

The enclosed bridge was close now. Fissif glanced up at the right-hand statue and noted other differences from the one he'd recalled. Although shorter, it seemed to hold itself more strainingly erect, while the frown carved in its dark gray face was not so much one of philosophic brooding as sneering contempt, self-conscious cleverness, and conceit.

Still, none of the three statues toppled forward as he and Slevyas walked under the bridge. However, something else happened to Fissif at that moment. One of the pillars winked at him.

The Gray Mouser—for so Mouse now named himself to himself and Ivrian—turned around in the right-hand niche, leaped up and caught hold of the cornice, silently vaulted to the flat roof, and crossed it precisely in time to see the two thieves emerge below.

Without hesitation he leaped forward and down, his body straight as a crossbow bolt, the soles of his ratskin boots aimed at the shorter thief's fat buried shoulder blades, though leading him a little to allow for the yard he'd walk while the Mouser hurtled toward him.

In the instant that he leaped, the tall thief glanced up overshoulder and whipped out a knife, though making no move to push or pull Fissif out of the way of the human projectile speeding toward him. The Mouser shrugged in full flight. He'd just have to deal with the tall thief faster after knocking down the fat one.

More swiftly than one would have thought he could manage, Fissif whirled around then and thinly screamed, "Slivikin!"

The ratskin boots took him high in the belly. It was like landing on a big cushion. Writhing aside from Slevyas' first thrust, the Mouser somersaulted forward, turning feet over head, and as the fat thief's skull hit a cobble with a dull bong he came to his feet with dirk in hand, ready to take on the tall one. But there was no need. Slevyas, his small eyes glazed, was toppling too.

One of the pillars had sprung forward, trailing a voluminous robe. A big hood had fallen back from a youthful face and long-haired head. Brawny arms had emerged from the long, loose sleeves that had been the pillar's topmost section, while the big fist ending one of the arms had dealt Slevyas a shrewd knockout punch on the chin.

Fafhrd and the Gray Mouser faced each other across the two thieves sprawled senseless. They were poised for attack, yet for the moment neither moved.

Each discerned something inexplicably familiar in the other.

Fafhrd said, "Our motives for being here seem identical."

"Seem? Surely must be!" the Mouser answered curtly, fiercely eyeing this potential new foe, who was taller by a head than the tall thief.

"You said?"

"I said, 'Seem? Surely must be!' "

"How civilized of you!" Fafhrd commented in pleased tones.

"Civilized?" the Mouser demanded suspiciously, gripping his dirk tighter.

"To care, in the eye of action, exactly what's said," Fafhrd explained. Without letting the Mouser out of his vision, he glanced down. His gaze traveled from the belt and pouch of one fallen thief to those of the other. Then he looked up at the Mouser with a broad, ingenuous smile.

"Sixty-sixty?" he suggested.

The Mouser hesitated, sheathed his dirk, and rapped out, "A deal!" He knelt abruptly, his fingers on the drawstrings of Fissif's pouch. "Loot you Slivikin," he directed.

It was natural to suppose that the fat thief had been crying his companion's name at the end. Without looking up from where he knelt, Fafhrd remarked, "That . . . ferret they had with them. Where did it go?"

"Ferret?" the Mouser answered briefly. "It was a marmoset!"

"Marmoset," Fafhrd mused. "That's a small tropical monkey, isn't it? Well, might have been, but I got the strange impression that—"

The silent, two-pronged rush which almost overwhelmed them at that instant really surprised neither of them. Each had been expecting it, but the expectation had dropped out of conscious thought with the startlement of their encounter.

The three bravos racing down upon them in concerted attack, two from the west and one from the east, all with swords poised to thrust, had assumed that the two highjackers would be armed at most with knives and as timid or at least cautious in weapons-combat as the general run of thieves and counterthieves. So it was they who were surprised and thrown into confusion when with the lightning speed of youth the Mouser and Fafhrd sprang up, whipped out fearsomely long swords, and faced them back to back.

The Mouser made a very small parry *in carte* so that the thrust of the bravo from the east went past his left side by only a hair's breath. He instantly riposted. His adversary, desperately springing back, parried in turn in carte. Hardly slowing, the tip of the Mouser's long, slim sword dropped under that parry with the delicacy of a princess curtsying and then leaped forward and a little upward, the Mouser making an impossibly long-looking lunge for one so small, and went between two scales of the bravo's armored jerkin and between his ribs and through his heart and out his back as if all were angelfood cake.

Meanwhile Fafhrd, facing the two bravos from the west, swept aside their low thrusts with somewhat larger, down-sweeping parries in seconde and low prime, then flipped up his sword, long as the Mouser's but heavier, so that it slashed through the neck of his right-hand adversary, half decapitating him. Then he, dropping back a swift step, readied a thrust for the other.

But there was no need. A narrow ribbon of bloodied steel, followed by a gray glove and arm, flashed past him from behind and transfixed the last bravo with the identical thrust the Mouser had used on the first.

The two young men wiped and sheathed their swords. Fafhrd brushed the palm of his open right hand down his robe and held it out. The Mouser pulled off right-hand gray glove and shook the other's big hand in his sinewy one. Without word exchanged, they knelt and finished looting the two unconscious thieves, securing the small bags of jewels. With an oily towel and then a dry one, the Mouser sketchily wiped from his face the greasy ash-soot mixture which had darkened it, next swiftly rolled up both towels and returned them to his own pouch. Then, after only a questioning eye-twitch east on the Mouser's part and a nod from Fafhrd, they swiftly walked on in the direction Slevyas and Fissif and their escort had been going.

After reconnoitering Gold Street, they crossed it and continued east on Cash at Fafhrd's gestured proposal.

"My woman's at the Golden Lamprey," he explained.

"Let's pick her up and take her home to meet my girl," the Mouser suggested.

"Home?" Fafhrd inquired politely, only the barest hint of question in his voice.

"Dim Lane," the Mouser volunteered.

"Silver Eel?"

"Behind it. We'll have some drinks."

"I'll pick up a jug. Never have too much juice."

"True. I'll let you."

Several squares farther on Fafhrd, after stealing a number of looks at his new comrade, said with conviction, "We've met before."

The Mouser grinned at him. "Beach by the Mountains of Hunger?"

"Right! When I was a pirate's ship-boy."

"And I was a wizard's apprentice." Fafhrd stopped, again wiped right hand on robe, and held it out. "Name's Fafhrd. Ef ay ef aitch ar dee."

Again the Mouser shook it. "Gray Mouser," he said a touch defiantly, as if challenging anyone to laugh at the sobriquet. "Excuse me, but how exactly do you pronounce that? Faf-hrud?"

"Just Faf-erd."

"Thank you." They walked on.

"Gray Mouser, eh?" Fafhrd remarked. "Well, you killed yourself a couple of rats tonight."

"That I did." The Mouser's chest swelled and he threw back his head. Then with a comic twitch of his nose and a sidewise half-grin he admitted, "You'd have got your second man easily enough. I stole him from you to demonstrate my speed. Besides, I was excited."

Fafhrd chuckled. "You're telling me? How do you suppose I was feeling?"

Later, as they were crossing Pimp Street, he asked, "Learn much magic from your wizard?"

Once more the Mouser threw back his head. He flared his nostrils and drew down the corners of his lips, preparing his mouth for boastful, mystifying speech. But once more he found himself twitching his nose and half grinning. What the deuce did this big fellow have that kept him from putting on his usual acts? "Enough to tell me it's damned dangerous stuff. Though I still fool with it now and then."

Fafhrd was asking himself a similar question. All his life he'd mistrusted small men, knowing his height awakened their instant jealousy. But this clever little chap was somehow an exception. Quick thinker and brilliant swordsman too, no argument. He prayed to Kos that Vlana would like him.

On the northeast corner of Cash and Whore a slow-burning torch shaded by a broad gilded hoop cast a cone of light up into the thickening black night-smog and another cone down on the cobbles before the tavern door. Out of the shadows into the second cone stepped Vlana, handsome in a narrow black velvet dress and red stockings, her only ornaments a silver-sheathed and hilted dagger and a silver-worked black pouch, both on a plain black belt.

Fafhrd introduced the Gray Mouser, who behaved with an almost fawning courtesy, obsequiously gallant. Vlana studied him boldly, then gave him a tentative smile. Fafhrd opened under the torch the small pouch he'd taken off the tall thief. Vlana looked down into it. She put her arms around Fafhrd, hugged him tight, and kissed him soundly. Then she thrust the jewels into the pouch on her belt.

When that was done, he said, "Look, I'm going to buy a jug. You tell her what happened, Mouser."

When he came out of the Golden Lamprey he was carrying four jugs in the crook of his left arm and wiping his lips on the back of his right hand. Vlana was frowning. He grinned at her. The Mouser smacked his lips at the jugs. They continued east on Cash. Fafhrd realized that the frown was for more than the jugs and the prospect of stupidly drunken male revelry. The Mouser tactfully walked ahead, ostensibly to lead the way. When his figure was little more than a blob in the thickening smog, Vlana whispered harshly, "You had two members of the Thieves' Guild knocked out cold and you didn't cut their throats?"

"We slew three bravos," Fafhrd protested by way of excuse.

"My quarrel is not with the Slayers' Brotherhood, but that abominable Guild. You swore to me that whenever you had the chance—"

"Vlana! I couldn't have the Gray Mouser thinking I was an amateur counter-thief consumed by hysteria and blood lust."

"You already set great store by him, don't you?"

"He possibly saved my life tonight."

"Well, he told me that he'd have slit their throats in a wink, if he'd known I wanted it that way."

"He was only playing up to you from courtesy."

"Perhaps and perhaps not. But *you* knew and you didn't—"

"Vlana, shut up!" Her frown became a rageful glare, then suddenly she laughed wildly, smiled twitchingly as if she were about to cry, mastered herself and smiled more lovingly. "Pardon me, darling," she said. "Sometimes you must think I'm going mad and sometimes I believe I am."

"Well, don't," he told her shortly. "Think of the jewels we've won instead. And behave yourself with our new friends. Get some wine inside you and relax. I mean to enjoy myself tonight. I've earned it."

She nodded and clutched his arm in agreement and for comfort and sanity. They hurried to catch up with the dim figure ahead.

The Mouser, turning left, led them a half square north on Cheap Street to where a narrower way went east again. The black mist in it looked solid. "Dim Lane," the Mouser explained.

Fafhrd nodded that he knew.

Vlana said, "*Dim*'s too weak—too *transparent* a word for it tonight," with an uneven laugh in which there were still traces of hysteria and which ended in a fit of strangled coughing. When she could swallow again, she gasped out, "Damn Lankhmar's night-smog! What a hell of a city."

"It's the nearness here of the Great Salt Marsh," Fafhrd explained. And he did indeed have part of the answer. Lying low betwixt the Marsh, the Inner Sea, the River Hlal, and the flat southern grain fields watered by canals fed by the Hlal, Lankhmar with its innumerable smokes was the prey of fogs and sooty smogs. No wonder the citizens had adopted the black toga as their formal garb. Some averred the toga had originally been white or pale brown, but so swiftly soot-blackened, necessitating endless laundering, that a thrifty Overlord had ratified and made official what nature or civilization's arts decreed.

About halfway to Carter Street, a tavern on the north side of the lane emerged from the murk. A gape-jawed serpentine shape of pale metal crested with soot hung high for a sign. Beneath it they passed a door curtained with begrimed leather, the slit in which spilled out noise, pulsing torchlight, and the reek of liquor.

Just beyond the Silver Eel the Mouser led them through an inky passageway outside the tavern's east wall. They had to go single file, feeling their way along rough, slimily bemisted brick and keeping close together.

"Mind the puddle," the Mouser warned. "It's deep as the Outer Sea."

The passageway widened. Reflected torchlight filtering down through the dark mist allowed them to make out only the most general shape of their surroundings. To the right was more windowless, high wall. To the left, crowding close to the back of the Silver Eel, rose a dismal, rickety building of darkened brick and blackened, ancient wood. It looked utterly deserted to Fafhrd and Vlana until they had craned back their heads to gaze at the fourth-story attic under the ragged-guttered roof. There faint lines and points of yellow light shone around and through three tightly-latticed windows. Beyond, crossing the T of the space they were in, was a narrow alley.

"Bones Alley," the Mouser told them in somewhat lofty tones. "I call it Ordure Boulevard."

"I can smell that," Vlana said.

By now she and Fafhrd could see a long, narrow wooden outside stairway, steep yet sagging and without a rail, leading up to the lighted attic. The Mouser relieved Fafhrd of the jugs and went up it quite swiftly.

"Follow me when I've reached the top," he called back. "I think it'll take your weight, Fafhrd, but best one of you at a time."

Fafhrd gently pushed Vlana ahead. With another hysteria-tinged laugh and a pause midway up for another fit of choked coughing, she mounted to the Mouser where he now stood in an open doorway, from which streamed yellow light that died swiftly in the night-smog. He was lightly resting a hand on a big, empty, wrought-iron lamp-hook firmly set in a stone section of the outside wall. He bowed aside, and she went in.

Fafhrd followed, placing his feet as close as he could to the wall, his hands ready to grab for support. The whole stairs creaked ominously and each step gave a little as he shifted his weight onto it. Near the top, one gave way with the muted crack of half-rotted wood. Gently as he could, he sprawled himself hand and knee on as many steps as he could reach, to distribute his weight, and cursed sulfurously.

"Don't fret, the jugs are safe," the Mouser called down gaily.

Fafhrd crawled the rest of the way, a somewhat sour look on his face, and did not get to his feet until he was inside the doorway. When he had done so, he almost gasped with surprise. It was like rubbing the verdigris from a cheap brass ring and finding a rainbow-fired diamond of the first water set in it. Rich drapes, some twinkling with embroidery of silver and gold, covered the walls except where the shuttered windows were—and the shutters of those were gilded. Similar but darker fabrics hid the low ceiling, making a gorgeous canopy in which the flecks of gold and silver were like stars. Scattered about were plump cushions and low tables, on which burned a multitude of candles. On shelves against the walls were neatly stacked like small logs a vast reserve of candles, numerous scrolls, jugs, bottles, and enameled boxes. A low vanity table was backed by a mirror of honed silver and thickly scattered over with jewels and cosmetics. In a large fireplace was set a small metal stove, neatly blacked, with an ornate fire-pot. Also set beside the stove were a tidy pyramid of thin, resinous torches with frayed ends—fire-kindlers—and other pyramids of short-handled brooms and mops, small, short logs, and gleamingly black coal.

On a low dais by the fireplace was a wide, short-legged, high-backed couch covered with cloth of gold. On it sat a thin, pale-faced, delicately handsome girl clad in a dress of thick violet silk worked with silver and belted with a silver chain. Her slippers were of white snow-serpent fur. Silver pins headed with amethysts held in place her high-piled black hair. Around her shoulders was drawn a white ermine wrap. She was leaning forward with uneasy-seeming graciousness and extending a narrow, white hand which shook a little to Vlana, who knelt before her and now gently took the proffered hand and bowed her head over it, her own glossy, straight, darkbrown hair making a canopy, and pressed the other girl's hand's back to her lips.

Fafhrd was happy to see his woman playing up properly to this definitely odd though delightful situation. Then looking at Vlana's long, redstockinged leg stretched far behind her as she knelt on the other, he noted that the floor was everywhere strewn—to the point of double, treble, and quadruple overlaps—with thick-piled, close-woven, many-hued rugs of the finest imported from the Eastern Lands. Before he knew it, his thumb had shot toward the Gray Mouser.

"You're the Rug Robber!" he proclaimed. "You're the Carpet Crimp!—and the Candle Corsair too," he continued, referring to two series of unsolved thefts which had been on the lips of all Lankhmar when he and Vlana had arrived a moon ago.

The Mouser shrugged impassive-faced at Fafhrd, then suddenly grinned, his slitted eyes a-twinkle, and broke into an impromptu dance which carried him whirling and jigging around the room and left him behind Fafhrd, where he deftly reached down the hooded and long-sleeved huge robe from the latter's stooping shoulders, shook it out, carefully folded it, and set it on a pillow.

After a long, uncertain pause, the girl in violet nervously patted with her free hand the cloth of gold beside her and Vlana seated herself there, carefully not too close, and the two women spoke together in low voices, Vlana taking the lead, though not obviously.

The Mouser took off his own gray, hooded cloak, folded it almost fussily, and laid it beside Fafhrd's. Then they unbelted their swords, and the Mouser set them atop folded robe and cloak.

Without those weapons and bulking garments, the two men looked suddenly like youths, both with clear, close-shaven faces, both slender despite the swelling muscles of Fafhrd's arms and calves, he with long red-gold hair falling down his back and about his shoulders, the Mouser with dark hair cut in bangs, the one in brown leather tunic worked with copper wire, the other in jerkin of coarsely woven gray silk.

They smiled at each other. The feeling each had of having turned boy all at once made their smiles for the first time a bit embarrassed. The Mouser cleared his throat and, bowing a little, but looking still at Fafhrd, extended a loosely spread-fingered arm toward the golden couch and said with a preliminary stammer, though otherwise smoothly enough, "Fafhrd, my good friend, permit me to introduce you to my princess. Ivrian, my dear, receive Fafhrd graciously if you please, for tonight he and I fought back to back against three and we conquered."

Fafhrd advanced, stooping a little, the crown of his red-gold hair brushing the bestarred canopy, and knelt before Ivrian exactly as Vlana had. The slender hand extended to him looked steady now, but was still quiveringly a-tremble, he discovered as soon as he touched it. He handled it as if it were silk woven of the white spider's gossamer, barely brushing it with his lips, and still felt nervous as he mumbled some compliments.

He did not sense, at least at the moment, that the Mouser was quite as nervous as he, if not more so, praying hard that Ivrian would not overdo her princess part and snub their guests, or collapse in trembling or tears or run to him or into the next room, for Fafhrd and Vlana were literally the first beings, human or animal, noble, freeman, or slave, that he had brought or allowed into the luxurious nest he had created for his aristocratic beloved—save the two love birds that twittered in a silver cage hanging to the other side of the fireplace from the dais.

Despite his shrewdness and new-found cynicism it never occurred to the Mouser that it was chiefly his charming but preposterous coddling of Ivrian that was keeping doll-like and even making more so the potentially brave and realistic girl who had fled with him from her father's torture chamber four moons ago.

But now as Ivrian smiled at last and Fafhrd gently returned her her hand and cautiously backed off, the Mouser relaxed with relief, fetched two silver cups and two silver mugs, wiped them needlessly with a silken towel, carefully selected a bottle of violet wine, then with a grin at Fafhrd uncorked instead one of the jugs the Northerner had brought, and near-brimmed the four gleaming vessels and served them all four. With another preliminary clearing of throat, but no trace of stammer this time, he toasted, "To my greatest theft to date in Lankhmar, which willy-nilly I must share sixty-sixty with"—he couldn't resist the sudden impulse—"with this great, longhaired, barbarian lout here!" And he downed a quarter of his mug of pleasantly burning wine fortified with brandy.

Fafhrd quaffed off half of his, then toasted back, "To the most boastful and finical little civilized chap I've ever deigned to share loot with," quaffed off the rest, and with a great smile that showed white teeth held out his empty mug.

The Mouser gave him a refill, topped off his own, then set that down to go to Ivrian and pour into her lap from their small pouch the gems he'd filched from Fissif. They gleamed in their new, enviable location like a small puddle of rainbow-hued quicksilver.

Ivrian jerked back a-tremble, almost spilling them, but Vlana gently caught her arm, steadying it, and leaned in over the jewels with a throaty gasp of wonder and admiration, slowly turned an envious gaze on the pale girl, and began rather urgently but smilingly to whisper to her. Fafhrd realized that Vlana was acting now, but acting well and effectively, since Ivrian was soon nodding eagerly and not long after that beginning to whisper back. At her direction, Vlana fetched a blue-enameled box inlaid with silver, and the two of them transferred the jewels from Ivrian's lap into its blue velvet interior. Then Ivrian placed the box close beside her and they chatted on.

As he worked through his second mug in smaller gulps, Fafhrd relaxed and began to get a deeper feeling of his surroundings. The dazzling wonder of the first glimpse of this throne room in a slum, its colorful luxury intensified by contrast with the dark and mud and slime and rotten stairs and Ordure Boulevard just outside, faded, and he began to note the ricketiness and rot under the grand overlay.

Black, rotten wood and dry, cracked wood too showed here and there between the drapes and also loosed their sick, ancient stinks. The whole floor sagged under the rugs, as much as a span at the center of the room. A large cockroach was climbing down a gold-worked drape, another toward the couch. Threads of night-smog were coming through the shutters, making evanescent black arabesques against the gilt. The stones of the large fireplace had been scrubbed and varnished, yet most of the mortar was gone from between them; some sagged, others were missing altogether.

The Mouser had been building a fire there in the stove. Now he pushed in all the way the yellow flaring kindler he'd lit from the fire-pot, hooked the little black door shut over the mounting flames, and turned back into the room. As if he'd read Fafhrd's mind, he took up several cones of incense, set their peaks a-smolder at the fire-pot, and placed them about the room in gleaming, shallow, brass bowls—stepping hard on the one cockroach by the way and surreptitiously catching and crushing the other in the base of his flicked fist. Then he stuffed silken rags in the widest shutter-cracks, took up his silver mug again, and for a moment gave Fafhrd a very hard look, as if daring him to say just one word against the delightful yet faintly ridiculous doll's house he'd prepared for his princess.

Next moment he was smiling and lifting his mug to Fafhrd, who was doing the same. Need of refills brought them close together. Hardly moving his lips, the Mouser explained *sotto voce*, "Ivrian's father was a duke. I slew him, by black magic, I believe, while he was having me done to death on the torture rack. A most cruel man, cruel to his daughter too, yet a duke, so that Ivrian is wholly unused to fending or caring for herself. I pride myself that I maintain her in grander state than ever her father did with all his serving men and maids."

Suppressing the instant criticisms he felt of this attitude and program, Fafhrd nodded and said amiably, "Surely you've thieved together a most charming little palace, quite worthy of Lankhmar's Overlord Karstak Ovartamortes, or the King of Kings at Horborixen."

From the couch Vlana called in her husky contralto, "Gray Mouser, your princess would hear an account of tonight's adventure. And might we have more wine?"

Ivrian called, "Yes, please, Mouse." Wincing almost imperceptibly at that earlier nickname, the Mouser looked to Fafhrd for the go-ahead, got the nod, and launched into his story. But first he served the girls wine. There wasn't enough for their cups, so he opened another jug and after a moment of thought uncorked all three, setting one by the couch, one by Fafhrd where he sprawled now on the pillowy carpets, and reserving one for himself. Ivrian looked wide-eyed apprehensive at this signal of heavy drinking ahead, Vlana cynical with a touch of anger, but neither voiced their criticism.

The Mouser told the tale of counter-thievery well, acting it out in part, and with only the most artistic of embellishments—the ferret-marmoset before escaping ran up his back and tried to scratch out his eyes—and he was interrupted only twice.

When he said, "And so with a whish and a snick I bared Scalpel—" Fafhrd remarked, "Oh, so you've nicknamed your sword as well as yourself?"

he Mouser drew himself up. "Yes, and I call my dirk Cat's Claw. Any objections? Seem childish to you?"

"Not at all. I call my own sword Graywand. All weapons are in a fashion alive, civilized and nameworthy. Pray continue."

And when he mentioned the beastie of uncertain nature that had gamboled along with the thieves (and attacked his eyes!), Ivrian paled and said with a shudder, "Mouse! That sounds like a witch's familiar!"

"Wizard's," Vlana corrected. "Those gutless Guild villains have no truck with women, except as fee'd or forced vehicles for their lust. But Krovas, their current king, though superstitious, is noted for taking *all* precautions, and might well have a warlock in his service."

"That seems most likely; it harrows me with dread," the Mouser agreed with ominous gaze and sinister voice. He really didn't believe or feel what he said—he was about as harrowed as virgin prairie—in the least, but he eagerly accepted any and all atmospheric enhancements of his performance.

When he was done, the girls, eyes flashing and fond, toasted him and Fafhrd for their cunning and bravery. The Mouser bowed and eye-twinklingly smiled about, then sprawled him down with a weary sigh, wiping his forehead with a silken cloth and downing a large drink.

After asking Vlana's leave, Fafhrd told the adventurous tale of their escape from Cold Corner—he from his clan, she from an acting troupe—and of their progress to Lankhmar, where they lodged now in an actors' tenement near the Plaza of Dark Delights. Ivrian hugged herself to Vlana and shivered large-eyed at the witchy parts—at least as much in delight as fear of Fafhrd's tale, he thought. He told himself it was natural that a doll-girl should love ghost stories, though he wondered if her pleasure would have been as great if she had known that his ghost stories were truly true. She seemed to live in worlds of imagination—once more at least half the Mouser's doing, he was sure.

The only proper matter he omitted from his account was Vlana's fixed intent to get a monstrous revenge on the Thieves' Guild for torturing to death her accomplices and harrying her out of Lankhmar when she'd tried freelance thieving in the city, with miming as a cover. Nor of course did he mention his own promise—foolish, he thought now—to help her in this bloody business.

After he'd done and got his applause, he found his throat dry despite his skald's training, but when he sought to wet it, he discovered that his mug was empty and his jug too, though he didn't feel in the least drunk; he had talked all the liquor out of him, he told himself, a little of the stuff escaping in each glowing word he'd spoken.

The Mouser was in like plight and not drunk either—though inclined to pause mysteriously and peer toward infinity before answering question or making remark. This time he suggested, after a particularly long infinity-gaze, that Fafhrd accompany him to the Eel while he purchased a fresh supply.

"But we've a lot of wine left in *our* jug," Ivrian protested. "Or at least a little," she amended. It did sound empty when Vlana shook it. "Besides, you've wine of all sorts here."

"Not this sort, dearest, and first rule is never mix 'em," the Mouser explained, wagging a finger. "That way lies unhealth, aye, and madness."

"My dear," Vlana said, sympathetically patting Ivrian's wrist, "at some time in any good party all the men who are really men simply have to go out. It's extremely stupid, but it's their nature and can't be dodged, believe me."

"But, Mouse, I'm scared. Fafhrd's tale frightened me. So did yours—I'll hear that big-headed, black, ratty familiar a-scratch at the shutters when you're gone, I know I will!"

It seemed to Fafhrd she was not afraid at all, only taking pleasure in frightening herself and in demonstrating her power over her beloved.

"Darlingest," the Mouser said with a small . . . hiccup, "there is all the Inner Sea, all the Land of the Eight Cities, and to boot all the Trollstep Mountains in their sky-scraping grandeur between you and Fafhrd's frigid specters or—pardon me, my comrade, but it could be—hallucinations admixed with coincidences. As for familiars, pish! They've never in the world been anything but the loathy, all-too-natural pets of stinking old women and womanish old men."

"The Eel's but a step, Lady Ivrian," Fafhrd said, "and you'll have beside you my dear Vlana, who slew my chiefest enemy with a single cast of that dagger she now wears."

With a glare at Fafhrd that lasted no longer than a wink, but conveyed "What a way to reassure a frightened girl!" Vlana said merrily, "Let the sillies go, my dear. 'Twill give us chance for a private chat, during which we'll take 'em apart from wine-fumy head to restless foot."

So Ivrian let herself be persuaded and the Mouser and Fafhrd slipped off, quickly shutting the door behind them to keep out the night-smog. Their rather rapid steps down the stairs could clearly be heard from within. There were faint creakings and groanings of the ancient wood outside the wall, but no sound of another tread breaking or other mishap.

Waiting for the four jugs to be brought up from the cellar, the two newly met comrades ordered a mug each of the same fortified wine, or one near enough, and ensconced themselves at the least noisy end of the long serving counter in the tumultuous tavern. The Mouser deftly kicked a rat that thrust black head and shoulders from his hole. After each had enthusiastically complimented the other on his girl, Fafhrd said diffidently, "Just between ourselves, do you think there might be anything to your sweet Ivrian's notion that the small dark creature with Slivikin and the other Guild-thief was a wizard's familiar, or at any rate the cunning pet of a sorcerer, trained to act as go-between and report disasters to his master or to Krovas or to both?"

The Mouser laughed lightly. "You're building bugbears—formless baby ones unlicked by logic—out of nothing, dear barbarian brother, if I may say so. *Imprimis*, we don't really know the beastie was connected with the Guildthieves at all. May well have been a stray catling or a big bold rat—like this damned one!" He kicked again. "But, *secundus*, granting it to be the creature of a wizard employed by Krovas, how could it make useful report? I don't believe in animals that talk—except for parrots and such birds, which only . . . parrot—or ones having an elaborate sign language men can share. Or perhaps you envisage the beastie dipping its paddy paw in a jug of ink and writing its report in big on a floor-spread parchment?

"Ho, there, you back of the counter! Where are my jugs? Rats eaten the boy who went for them days ago? Or he simply starved to death while on his cellar quest? Well, tell him to get a swifter move on and meanwhile brim us again!

"No, Fafhrd, even granting the beastie to be directly or indirectly a creature of Krovas, and that it raced back to Thieves' House after our affray, what could it tell them there? Only that something had gone wrong with the burglary at

Jengao's. Which they'd soon suspect in any case from the delay in the thieves' and bravos' return."

Fafhrd frowned and muttered stubbornly, "The furry slinker might, nevertheless, convey our appearances to the Guild masters, and they might recognize us and come after us and attack us in our homes. Or Slivikin and his fat pal, revived from their bumps, might do likewise."

"My dear friend," the Mouser said condolingly, "once more begging your indulgence, I fear this potent wine is addling your wits. If the Guild knew our looks or where we lodge, they'd have been nastily on our necks days, weeks, nay, months ago. Or conceivably you don't know that their penalty for freelance or even unassigned thieving within the walls of Lankhmar and for three leagues outside them is nothing less than death, after torture if happily that can be achieved."

"I know all about that and my plight is worse even than yours," Fafhrd retorted, and after pledging the Mouser to secrecy told him the tale of Vlana's vendetta against the Guild and her deadly serious dreams of an all-encompassing revenge.

During his story the four jugs came up from the cellar, but the Mouser only ordered that their earthenware mugs be refilled. Fafhrd finished, "And so, in consequence of a promise given by an infatuated and unschooled boy in a southern angle of the Cold Waste, I find myself now as a sober—well, at other times—man being constantly asked to make war on a power as great as that of Karstak Ovartamortes, for as you may know, the Guild has locals in all other cities and major towns of this land, not to mention agreements including powers of extradition with robber and bandit organizations in other countries. I love Vlana dearly, make no mistake about that, and she is an experienced thief herself, without whose guidance I'd hardly have survived my first week in Lankhmar, but on this one topic she has a kink in her brains, a hard knot neither logic nor persuasion can even begin to loosen. And I, well, in the month I've been here I've learned that the only way to survive in civilization is to abide by its unwritten rules—far more important than its laws chiseled in stone—and break them only at peril, in deepest secrecy, and taking all precautions. As I did tonight—not my first hijacking, by the by."

"Certes t'would be insanity to assault the Guild direct, your wisdom's perfect there," the Mouser commented. "If you cannot break your most handsome girl of this mad notion, or coax her from it—and I can see she's a fearless, self-willed one—then you must stoutly refuse e'en her least request in that direction."

"Certes I must," Fafhrd agreed, adding somewhat accusingly, "though I gather you told her you'd have willingly slit the throats of the two we struck senseless."

"Courtesy merely, man! Would you have had me behave ungraciously to your girl? 'Tis measure of the value I was already setting then on your goodwill. But only a woman's man may cross her. As you must, in this instance."

"Certes I must," Fafhrd repeated with great emphasis and conviction. "I'd be an idiot taking on the Guild. Of course if they should catch me they'd kill me in any case for freelancing and highjacking. But wantonly to assault the Guild direct, kill one Guild-thief needlessly, only behave as if I might—lunacy entire!"

"You'd not only be a drunken, drooling idiot, you'd questionless be stinking in three nights at most from that emperor of diseases, Death. Malicious attacks on her person, blows directed at the organization, the Guild requites tenfold what she does other rule-breakings. All planned robberies and other thefts would be called off and the entire power of the Guild and its allies mobilized against you alone. I'd count your chances better to take on single-handed the host of the King of Kings rather than the Thieves' Guild's subtle minions. In view of your size, might, and wit you're a squad perhaps, or even a company, but hardly an army. So, no least giving-in to Vlana in this one matter."

"Agreed!" Fafhrd said loudly, shaking the Mouser's iron-thewed hand in a near crusher grip.

"And now we should be getting back to the girls," the Mouser said.

"After one more drink while we settle the score. Ho, boy!"

"Suits." The Mouser dug into his pouch to pay, but Fafhrd protested vehemently. In the end they tossed coin for it, and Fafhrd won and with great satisfaction clinked out his silver smerduks on the stained and dinted counter also marked with an infinitude of mug circles, as if it had been once the desk of a mad geometer. They pushed themselves to their feet, the Mouser giving the rathole one last light kick for luck.

At this, Fafhrd's thoughts looped back and he said, "Grant the beastie can't paw-write, or talk by mouth or paw, it still could have followed us at distance, marked down your dwelling, and then returned to Thieves' House to lead its masters down on us like a hound!"

"Now you're speaking shrewd sense again," the Mouser said. "Ho, boy, a bucket of small beer to go! On the instant!" Noting Fafhrd's blank look, he explained, "I'll spill it outside the Eel to kill our scent and all the way down the passageway. Yes, and splash it high on the walls too."

Fafhrd nodded wisely. "I thought I'd drunk my way past the addled point."

Vlana and Ivrian, deep in excited talk, both started at the pounding rush of footsteps up the stairs. Racing behemoths could hardly have made more noise. The creaking and groaning were prodigious and there were the crashes of two treads breaking, yet the pounding footsteps never faltered. The door flew open and their two men rushed in through a great mushroom top of night-smog which was neatly sliced off its black stem by the slam of the door.

"I told you we'd be back in a wink," the Mouser cried gaily to Ivrian, while Fafhrd strode forward, unmindful of the creaking floor, crying, "Dearest heart, I've missed you sorely," and caught up Vlana despite her voiced protests and pushings-off and kissed and hugged her soundly before setting her back on the couch again.

Oddly, it was Ivrian who appeared to be angry at Fafhrd then, rather than Vlana, who was smiling fondly if somewhat dazedly.

"Fafhrd, sir," she said boldly, little fists set on her narrow hips, her tapered chin held high, her dark eyes blazing, "my beloved Vlana has been telling me about the unspeakably atrocious things the Thieves' Guild did to her and to her dearest friends. Pardon my frank speaking to one I've only met, but I think it quite unmanly of you to refuse her the just revenge she desires and fully deserves. And that goes for you too, Mouse, who boasted to Vlana of what you would have done had you but known, who in like case did not scruple to slay my very own father—or reputed father—for his cruelties!"

It was clear to Fafhrd that while he and the Gray Mouser had idly boozed in the Eel, Vlana had been giving Ivrian a doubtless empurpled account of her grievances against the Guild and playing mercilessly on the naïve girl's bookish, romantic sympathies and high concept of knightly honor. It was also clear to him that Ivrian was more than a little drunk. A three-quarters empty flask of violet wine of far Kiraay sat on the low table next them.

Yet he could think of nothing to do but spread his big hands helplessly and bow his head, more than the low ceiling made necessary, under Ivrian's glare, now reinforced by that of Vlana. After all, they were in the right. He had promised.

So it was the Mouser who first tried to rebut.

"Come now, pet," he cried lightly as he danced about the room, silk-stuffing more cracks against the thickening night-smog and stirring up and feeding the fire in the stove, "and you too, beauteous Lady Vlana. For the past month Fafhrd has been hitting the Guild-thieves where it hurts them most—in their purses a-dangle between their legs. His highjackings of the loot of their robberies have been like so many fierce kicks in their groins. Hurts worse, believe me, than robbing them of life with a swift, near painless sword slash or thrust. And tonight I helped him in his worthy purpose—and will eagerly do so again. Come, drink we up all." Under his handling, one of the new jugs came uncorked with a pop and he darted about brimming silver cups and mugs.

"A merchant's revenge!" Ivrian retorted with scorn, not one whit appeased, but rather angered anew. "Ye both are at heart true and gentle knights, I know, despite all current backsliding. At the least you must bring Vlana the head of Krovas!"

"What would she do with it? What good would it be except to spot the carpets?" the Mouser plaintively inquired, while Fafhrd, gathering his wits at last and going down on one knee, said slowly, "Most respected Lady Ivrian, it is true I solemnly promised my beloved Vlana I would help her in her revenge, but that was while I was still in barbarous Cold Corner, where blood-feud is a commonplace, sanctioned by custom and accepted by all the clans and tribes and brotherhoods of the savage Northerners of the Cold Waste. In my naïveté I thought of Vlana's revenge as being of that sort. But here in civilization's midst, I discover all's different and rules and customs turned upside-down. Yet—Lankhmar or Cold Corner—one must seem to observe rule and custom to survive. Here cash is all-powerful, the idol placed highest, whether one sweat, thieve, grind others down, or scheme for it. Here feud and revenge are outside all rules and punished worse than violent lunacy. Think, Lady Ivrian, if Mouse and I should bring Vlana the head of Krovas, she and I would have to flee Lankhmar on the instant, every man's hand against us; while you infallibly would lose this fairyland Mouse has created for love of you and be forced to do likewise, be with him a beggar on the run for the rest of your natural lives."

It was beautifully reasoned and put . . . and no good whatsoever. While Fafhrd spoke, Ivrian snatched up her new-filled cup and drained it. Now she stood up straight as a soldier, her pale face flushed, and said scathingly to Fafhrd kneeling before her, "*You count the cost!* You speak to me of things"—she waved at the many-hued splendor around her—"of mere property, however costly, when *honor* is at stake. You gave Vlana *your word*. Oh, is knighthood wholly dead? And that applies to you, too, Mouse, who swore you'd slit the miserable throats of two noisome Guild-thieves."

"I didn't swear *to*," the Mouser objected feebly, downing a big drink. "I merely said I *would have*," while Fafhrd could only shrug again and writhe inside and gulp a little easement from his silver mug. For Ivrian was speaking in the same guilt-showering tones and using the same unfair yet heart-cleaving womanly arguments as Mor his mother might have, or Mara, his deserted Snow Clan sweetheart and avowed wife, big-bellied by now with his child.

In a masterstroke, Vlana tried gently to draw Ivrian down to her golden seat again. "Softly, dearest," she pleaded. "You have spoken nobly for me and my cause, and believe me, I am most grateful. Your words revived in me great, fine feelings dead these many years. But of us here, only you are truly an aristocrat attuned to the highest proprieties. We other three are naught but thieves. Is it any wonder some of us put safety above honor and wordkeeping, and most prudently avoid risking our lives? Yes, we are three thieves and I am outvoted. So please speak no more of honor and rash, dauntless bravery, but sit you down and—"

"You mean they're both *afraid* to challenge the Thieves' Guild, don't you?" Ivrian said, eyes wide and face twisted by loathing. "I always thought my Mouse was a nobleman first and a thief second. Thieving's nothing. My father lived by cruel thievery done on rich wayfarers and neighbors less powerful than he, yet he was an aristocrat. Oh, you're *cowards,* both of you! *Poltroons*!" she finished, turning her eyes flashing with cold scorn first on the Mouser, then on Fafhrd. The latter could stand it no longer. He sprang to his feet, face flushed, fists clenched at his sides, quite unmindful of his down-clattered mug and the ominous creak his sudden action drew from the sagging floor.

"I am not a coward!" he cried. "I'll dare Thieves' House and fetch you Krovas' head and toss it with blood a-drip at Vlana's feet. I swear that, witness me, Kos the god of dooms, by the brown bones of Nalgron my father and by his sword Graywand here at my side!"

He slapped his left hip, found nothing there but his tunic, and had to content himself with pointing tremble-armed at his belt and scabbarded sword where they lay atop his neatly folded robe—and then picking up, refilling splashily, and draining his mug.

The Gray Mouser began to laugh in high, delighted, tuneful peals. All stared at him. He came dancing up beside Fafhrd, and still smiling widely, asked, "*Why not?* Who speaks of fearing the Guild-thieves? Who becomes upset at the prospect of this ridiculously easy exploit, when all of us know that all of them, even Krovas and his ruling clique, are but pygmies in mind and skill compared to me or Fafhrd here? A wondrously simple, foolproof scheme has just occurred to me for penetrating Thieves' House, every closet and cranny. Stout Fafhrd and I will put it into effect at once. Are you with me, Northerner?"

"Of course I am," Fafhrd responded gruffly, at the same time frantically wondering what madness had gripped the little fellow.

"Give me a few heartbeats to gather needed props, and we're off!" the Mouser cried. He snatched from a shelf and unfolded a stout sack, then raced about, thrusting into it coiled ropes, bandage rolls, rags, jars of ointment and unction and unguent, and other oddments.

"But you can't go *tonight,*" Ivrian protested, suddenly grown pale and uncertain-voiced. "You're both . . . in no condition to."

"You're both *drunk*," Vlana said harshly. "Silly drunk—and that way you'll get naught in Thieves' House but your deaths. Fafhrd, where's that heartless reason you employed to slay or ice-veined see slain a clutch of mighty rivals and win me at Cold Corner and in the chilly, sorcery-webbed depths of Trollstep Canyon? Revive it! And infuse some into your skipping gray friend."

"Oh, no," Fafhrd told her as he buckled on his sword. "You wanted the head of Krovas heaved at your feet in a great splatter of blood, and that's what you're going to get, like it or not!"

"Softly, Fafhrd," the Mouser interjected, coming to a sudden stop and drawing tight the sack's mouth by its strings. "And softly you too, Lady Vlana, and my dear princess. Tonight I intend but a scouting expedition. No risks run, only the information gained needful for planning our murderous strike tomorrow or the day after. So no head-choppings whatsoever tonight, Fafhrd, you hear me? Whatever mayhap, hist's the word. And don your hooded robe."

Fafhrd shrugged, nodded, and obeyed. Ivrian seemed somewhat relieved. Vlana too, though she said, "Just the same you're both drunk."

"All to the good!" the Mouser assured her with a mad smile. "Drink may slow a man's sword-arm and soften his blows a bit, but it sets his wits ablaze and fires his imagination, and those are the qualities we'll need tonight. Besides," he hurried on, cutting off some doubt Ivrian was about to voice, "drunken men are supremely cautious! Have you ever seen a staggering sot pull himself together at sight of the guard and walk circumspectly and softly past?"

"Yes," Vlana said, "and fall flat on his face just as he comes abreast 'em."

"Pish!" the Mouser retorted and, throwing back his head, grandly walked toward her along an imaginary straight line. Instantly he tripped over his own foot, plunged forward, suddenly without touching floor did an incredible forward flip, heels over head, and landed erect and quite softly—toes, ankles, and knees bending just at the right moment to soak up impact—directly in front of the girls. The floor barely complained.

"You see?" he said, straightening up and unexpectedly reeling backward. He tripped over the pillow on which lay his cloak and sword, but by a wrenching twist and a lurch stayed upright and began rapidly to accouter himself.

Under cover of this action Fafhrd made quietly yet swiftly to fill once more his and the Mouser's mugs, but Vlana noted it and gave him such a glare that he set down mugs and uncorked jug so swiftly his robe swirled, then stepped back from the drinks table with a shrug of resignation and toward Vlana a grimacing nod.

The Mouser shouldered his sack and drew open the door. With a casual wave at the girls, but no word spoken, Fafhrd stepped out on the tiny porch. The night-smog had grown so thick he was almost lost to view. The Mouser waved four fingers at Ivrian, softly called, "Bye-bye, Misling," then followed Fafhrd.

"Good fortune go with you," Vlana called heartily.

"Oh be careful, Mouse," Ivrian gasped.

The Mouser, his figure slight against the loom of Fafhrd's, silently drew shut the door.

Their arms automatically gone around each other, the girls waited for the inevitable creaking and groaning of the stairs. It delayed and delayed. The night-smog that had entered the room dissipated and still the silence was unbroken. "What can they be doing out there?" Ivrian whispered.

"Plotting their course?" Vlana, scowling, impatiently shook her head, then disentangled herself, tiptoed to the door, opened it, descended softly a few steps, which creaked most dolefully, then returned, shutting the door behind her.

"They're gone," she said in wonder, her eyes wide, her hands spread a little to either side, palms up.

"I'm frightened!" Ivrian breathed and sped across the room to embrace the taller girl.

Vlana hugged her tight, then disengaged an arm to shoot the door's three heavy bolts.

In Bones Alley the Mouser returned to his pouch the knotted line by which they'd descended from the lamp-hook. He suggested, "How about stopping at the Silver Eel?"

"You mean and just *tell* the girls we've been to Thieves' House?" Fafhrd asked, not too indignantly.

"Oh, no," the Mouser protested. "But you missed your stirrup cup upstairs and so did I."

At the word "stirrup" he looked down at his ratskin boots and then crouching began a little gallop in one place, his boot-soles clopping softly on the cobbles. He flapped imaginary reins—"Giddap!"—and quickened his gallop, but leaning sharply back pulled to a stop—"Whoa!"—when with a crafty smile Fafhrd drew from his robe two full jugs.

"Palmed 'em, as 'twere, when I set down the mugs. Vlana sees a lot, but not all."

"You're a prudent, far-sighted fellow, in addition to having some skill at sword taps," the Mouser said admiringly. "I'm proud to call you comrade."

Each uncorked and drank a hearty slug. Then the Mouser led them west, they veering and stumbling only a little. Not so far as Cheap Street, however, but turning north into an even narrower and more noisome alley.

"Plague Court," the Mouser said. Fafhrd nodded.

After several preliminary peepings and peerings, they staggered swiftly across wide, empty Crafts Street and into Plague Court again. For a wonder it was growing a little lighter. Looking upward, they saw stars. Yet there was no wind blowing from the north. The air was deathly still.

In their drunken preoccupation with the project at hand and mere locomotion, they did not look behind them. There the night-smog was thicker than ever. A high-circling nighthawk would have seen the stuff converging from all sections of Lankhmar, north, east, south, west—from the Inner Sea, from the Great Salt Marsh, from the many-ditched grain lands, from the River Hlal—in swift-moving black rivers and rivulets, heaping, eddying, swirling, dark and reeking essence of Lankhmar from its branding irons, braziers, bonfires, bonefires, kitchen fires and warmth fires, kilns, forges, breweries, distilleries, junk and garbage fires innumerable, sweating alchemists' and sorcerers' dens, crematoriums, charcoal burners' turfed mounds, all those and many more . . . converging purposefully on Dim Lane and particularly on the Silver Eel and perhaps especially on the rickety house behind it, untenanted except for attic. The closer to that center it got, the more substantial the smog became, eddy-strands and swirl-tatters tearing off and clinging to rough stone corners and scraggly-surfaced brick like black cobwebs.

But the Mouser and Fafhrd merely exclaimed in mild, muted amazement at the stars, muggily mused as to how much the improved visibility would increase the risk of their quest, and cautiously crossing the Street of the Thinkers, called Atheist Avenue by moralists, continued to Plague Court until it forked. The Mouser chose the left branch, which trended northwest.

"Death Alley."

Fafhrd nodded. After a curve and recurve, Cheap Street swung into sight about thirty paces ahead. The Mouser stopped at once and lightly threw his arm against Fafhrd's chest.

Clearly in view across Cheap Street was a wide, low, open doorway, framed by grimy stone blocks. There led up to it two steps hollowed by the treadings of centuries. Orange-yellow light spilled out from bracketed torches inside. They couldn't see very far in because of Death Alley's angle. Yet as far as they *could* see, there was no porter or guard in sight, nor anyone at all, not a watchdog on a chain. The effect was ominous.

"Now how do we get into the damn place?" Fafhrd demanded in a hoarse whisper. "Scout Murder Alley for a back window that can be forced. You've pries in that sack, I trow. Or try the roof? You're a roof man, I know already. Teach me the art. I know trees and mountains, snow, ice, and bare rock. See this wall here?" He backed off from it, preparing to go up it in a rush.

"Steady on, Fafhrd," the Mouser said, keeping his hand against the big young man's chest. "We'll hold the roof in reserve. Likewise all walls. And I'll take it on trust you're a master climber. As to how we get in, we walk straight through that doorway." He frowned. "Tap and hobble, rather. Come on, while I prepare us."

As he drew the skeptically grimacing Fafhrd back down Death Alley until all Cheap Street was again cut off from view, he explained, "We'll pretend to be beggars, members of *their* guild, which is but a branch of the Thieves' Guild and houses with it, or at any rate reports in to the Beggarmasters at Thieves' House. We'll be new members, who've gone out by day, so it'll not be expected that the Night Beggarmaster and any night watchmen know our looks."

"But we don't look like beggars," Fafhrd protested. "Beggars have awful sores and limbs all a-twist or lacking altogether."

"That's just what I'm going to take care of now," the Mouser chuckled, drawing Scalpel. Ignoring Fafhrd's backward step and wary glance, the Mouser gazed puzzledly at the long tapering strip of steel he'd bared, then with a happy nod unclipped from his belt Scalpel's scabbard furbished with ratskin, sheathed the sword and swiftly wrapped it up, hilt and all, in a spiral, with the wide ribbon of a bandage roll dug from his sack.

"There!" he said, knotting the bandage ends. "Now I've a tapping cane."

"What's that?" Fafhrd demanded. "And why?"

"Because I'll be blind, that's why." He took a few shuffling steps, tapping the cobbles ahead with wrapped sword—gripping it by the quillons, or cross guard, so that the grip and pommel were up his sleeve—and groping ahead with his other hand. "That look all right to you?" he asked Fafhrd as he turned back. "Feels perfect to me. Bat-blind, eh? Oh, don't fret, Fafhrd—the rag's but gauze. I can see through it fairly well. Besides, I don't have to convince anyone inside Thieves' House I'm actually blind. Most Guildbeggars fake it, as you must know. Now what to do with you? Can't have you blind also—too obvious, might wake suspicion." He uncorked his jug and sucked inspiration. Fafhrd copied this action, on principle.

The Mouser smacked his lips and said, "I've got it! Fafhrd, stand on your right leg and double up your left behind you at the knee. Hold! Don't fall on me! Avaunt! But steady yourself by my shoulder. That's right. Now get that left foot higher. We'll disguise your sword like mine, for a crutch cane—it's thicker and'll look just right. You can also steady yourself with your other hand on my shoulder as you hop—the halt leading the blind, always good for a tear, always good theater! But higher with that left foot! No, it just doesn't come off—I'll have to rope it. But first unclip your scabbard."

Soon the Mouser had Graywand and its scabbard in the same state as Scalpel and was tying Fafhrd's left ankle to his thigh, drawing the rope cruelly tight, though Fafhrd's wine-anesthetized nerves hardly registered it. Balancing himself with his steel-cored crutch cane as the Mouser worked, he swigged from his jug and pondered deeply. Ever since joining forces with Vlana, he'd been interested in the theater, and the atmosphere of the actors' tenement had fired that interest further, so that he was delighted at the prospect of acting a part in real life. Yet brilliant as the Mouser's plan undoubtedly was, there did seem to be drawbacks to it. He tried to formulate them.

"Mouser," he said, "I don't know as I like having our swords tied up, so we can't draw 'em in emergency."

"We can still use 'em as clubs," the Mouser countered, his breath hissing between his teeth as he drew the last knot hard. "Besides, we'll have our knives. Say, pull your belt around until yours is behind your back, so your robe will hide it sure. I'll do the same with Cat's Claw. Beggars don't carry weapons, at least in view, and we must maintain dramatic consistency in every detail. Stop drinking now; you've had enough. I myself need only a couple swallows more to reach my finest pitch."

"And I don't know as I like going hobbled into that den of cutthroats. I can hop amazingly fast, it's true, but not as fast as I can run. Is it really wise, think you?"

"You can slash yourself loose in an instant," the Mouser hissed with a touch of impatience and anger. "Aren't you willing to make the least sacrifice for art's sake?"

"Oh, very well," Fafhrd said, draining his jug and tossing it aside. "Yes, of course I am."

"Your complexion's too hale," the Mouser said, inspecting him critically. He touched up Fafhrd's features and hands with pale gray greasepaint, then added wrinkles with dark. "And your garb's too tidy." He scooped dirt from between the cobbles and smeared it on Fafhrd's robe, then tried to put a rip in it, but the material resisted. He shrugged and tucked his lightened sack under his belt.

"So's yours," Fafhrd observed, and stooping on his right leg got a good handful of muck himself, ordure in it by its feel and stink. Heaving himself up with a mighty effort, he wiped the stuff off on the Mouser's cloak and gray silken jerkin too.

The small man got the odor and cursed, but, "Dramatic consistency," Fafhrd reminded him. "It's well we stink. Beggars do—that's one reason folk give 'em coins: to get rid of 'em. And no one at Thieves' House will be eager to inspect us close. Now come on, while our fires are still high." And grasping hold of the Mouser's shoulder, he propelled himself rapidly toward Cheap Street, setting his bandaged sword between cobbles well ahead and taking mighty hops.

"Slow down, idiot," the Mouser cried softly, shuffling along with the speed almost of a skater to keep up, while tapping his (sword) cane like mad. "A cripple's supposed to be *feeble*—that's what draws the sympathy."

Fafhrd nodded wisely and slowed somewhat. The ominous empty doorway slid again into view. The Mouser tilted his jug to get the last of his wine, swallowed awhile, then choked sputteringly. Fafhrd snatched and drained the jug, then tossed it over shoulder to shatter noisily.

They hop-shuffled into Cheap Street, halting almost at once for a richly clad man and woman to pass. The richness of the man's garb was sober and he was on the fat and oldish side, though hard-featured. A merchant doubtless, and with money in the Thieves' Guild—protection money, at least—to take this route at this hour.

The richness of the woman's garb was garish though not tawdry and she was beautiful and young, and looked still younger. A competent courtesan, almost certainly.

The man started to veer around the noisome and filthy pair, his face averted, but the girl swung toward the Mouser, concern growing in her eyes with hothouse swiftness. "Oh, you poor boy! Blind. What tragedy," she said. "Give us a gift for him, lover."

"Keep away from those stinkards, Misra, and come along," he retorted, the last of his speech vibrantly muffled, for he was holding his nose.

She made him no reply, but thrust white hand into his ermine pouch and swiftly pressed a coin against the Mouser's palm and closed his fingers on it, then took his head between her palms and kissed him sweetly on the lips before letting herself be dragged on.

"Take good care of the little fellow, old man," she called fondly back to Fafhrd while her companion grumbled muffled reproaches at her, of which only "perverted bitch" was intelligible.

The Mouser stared at the coin in his palm, then sneaked a long look after his benefactress. There was a dazed wonder in his voice as he whispered to Fafhrd, "Look. *Gold*. A golden coin and a beautiful woman's sympathy. Think you we should give over this rash project and for a profession take up beggary?"

"Buggery even, rather!" Fafhrd answered harsh and low. That "old man" rankled. "Onward we, bravely!"

They upped the two worn steps and went through the doorway, noting the exceptional thickness of the wall. Ahead was a long, straight, high-ceilinged corridor ending in a stairs and with doors spilling light at intervals and wall-set torches adding their flare, but empty all its length.

They had just got through the doorway when cold steel chilled the neck and pricked a shoulder of each of them. From just above, two voices commanded in unison, "Halt!"

Although fired—and fuddled—by fortified wine, they each had wit enough to freeze and then very cautiously look upward.

Two gaunt, scarred, exceptionally ugly faces, each topped by a gaudy scarf binding back hair, looked down at them from a big, deep niche just above the doorway and helping explain its lowness. Two bent, gnarly arms thrust down the swords that still pricked them.

"Gone out with the noon beggar-batch, eh?" one of them observed. "Well, you'd better have a high take to justify your tardy return. The Night Beggarmaster's on a Whore Street furlough. Report above to Krovas. Gods, you stink! Better clean up first, or Krovas will have you bathed in live steam. Begone!"

The Mouser and Fafhrd shuffled and hobbled forward at their most authentic. One niche-guard cried after them, "Relax, boys! You don't have to put it on here."

"Practice makes perfect," the Mouser called back in a quavering voice. Fafhrd's finger-ends dug his shoulder warningly. They moved along somewhat more naturally, so far as Fafhrd's tied-up leg allowed.

"Gods, what an easy life the Guild-beggars have," the other niche-guard observed to his mate. "What slack discipline and low standards of skill! Perfect, my sacred butt! You'd think a child could see through those disguises."

"Doubtless some children do," his mate retorted. "But their dear mothers and fathers only drop a tear and a coin or give a kick. Grown folk go blind, lost in their toil and dreams, unless they have a profession such as thieving which keeps them mindful of things as they really are."

Resisting the impulse to ponder this sage philosophy, and glad they would not have to undergo a Beggarmaster's shrewd inspection—truly, thought Fafhrd, Kos of the Dooms seemed to be leading him direct to Krovas and perhaps head-chopping *would* be the order of the night—he and the Mouser went watchfully and slowly on. And now they began to hear voices, mostly curt and clipped ones, and other noises.

They passed some doorways they'd liked to have paused at, to study the activities inside, yet the most they dared do was slow down a bit more. Fortunately most of the doorways were wide, permitting a fairly long view.

Very interesting were some of those activities. In one room young boys were being trained to pick pouches and slit purses. They'd approach from behind an instructor, and if he heard scuff of bare foot or felt touch of dipping hand—or, worst, heard *clunk* of dropped leaden mock-coin—that boy would be thwacked. Others seemed to be getting training in group tactics: the jostle in front, the snatch from behind, the swift passing of lifted items from youthful thief to confederate.

In a second room, from which pushed air heavy with the reeks of metal and oil, older student thieves were doing laboratory work in lock picking. One group was being lectured by a grimy-handed graybeard, who was taking apart a most complex lock piece by weighty piece. Others appeared to be having their skill, speed, and ability to work soundlessly tested—they were probing with slender picks the keyholes in a half dozen doors set side by side in an otherwise purposeless partition, while a supervisor holding a sandglass watched them keenly.

In a third, thieves were eating at long tables. The odors were tempting, even to men full of booze. The Guild did well by its members.

In a fourth, the floor was padded in part and instruction was going on in slipping, dodging, ducking, tumbling, tripping, and otherwise foiling pursuit. These students were older too. A voice like a sergeant-major's rasped, "Nah, nah, nah! You couldn't give your crippled grandmother the slip. I said duck, not genuflect to holy Aarth. Now this time—"

"Grif's used grease," an instructor called.

"He has, eh? To the front, Grif!" the rasping voice replied as the Mouser and Fafhrd moved somewhat regretfully out of sight, for they realized much was to be learned here: tricks that might stand them in good stead even tonight. "Listen, all of you!" the rasping voice continued, so far-carrying it followed them a surprisingly long way. "Grease may be very well on a night job—by day its glisten shouts its user's profession to all Nehwon! But in any case it makes a thief overconfident. He comes to depend on it and then in a pinch he finds he's forgot to apply it. Also its aroma can betray him. Here we work always dry-skinned—save for natural sweat!—as all of you were told first night. Bend over, Grif. Grasp your ankles. Straighten your knees."

More thwacks, followed by yelps of pain, distant now, since the Mouser and Fafhrd were halfway up the end-stairs, Fafhrd vaulting somewhat laboriously as he grasped curving banister and swaddled sword.

The second floor duplicated the first, but was as luxurious as the other had been bare. Down the long corridor lamps and filigreed incense pots pendant from the ceiling alternated, diffusing a mild light and spicy smell. The walls were richly draped, the floor thick-carpeted. Yet this corridor was empty too and, moreover, *completely* silent. After a glance at each other, they started off boldly. The first door, wide open, showed an untenanted room full of racks of garments, rich and plain, spotless and filthy, also wig stands, shelves of beards and such, and several wall mirrors faced by small tables crowded with cosmetics and with stools before them. A disguising room, clearly.

After a look and listen either way, the Mouser darted in and out to snatch up a large green flask from the nearest table. He unstoppered and sniffed it. A rotten-sweet gardenia-reek contended with the nose-sting of spirits of wine. The Mouser sloshed his and Fafhrd's fronts with this dubious perfume.

"Antidote to ordure," he explained with the pomp of a physician, stoppering the flask. "Don't want to be parboiled by Krovas. No, no, no."

Two figures appeared at the far end of the corridor and came toward them. The Mouser hid the flask under his cloak, holding it between elbow and side, and he and Fafhrd continued onward—to turn back would look suspicious, both drunkenly judged.

The next three doorways they passed were shut by heavy doors. As they neared the fifth, the two approaching figures, coming on arm-in-arm, yet taking long strides, moving more swiftly than the hobble-shuffle, became distinct. Their clothing was that of noblemen, but their faces those of thieves. They were frowning with indignation and suspicion too at the Mouser and Fafhrd.

Just then—from somewhere between the two man-pairs, it sounded—a voice began to speak words in a strange tongue, using the rapid monotone priests employ in a routine service, or some sorcerers in their incantations.

The two richly clad thieves slowed at the seventh doorway and looked in. Their progress ceased altogether. Their necks strained, their eyes widened. They visibly paled. Then of a sudden they hastened onward, almost running, and bypassed Fafhrd and the Mouser as if they were furniture. The incantory voice drummed on without missing a beat.

The fifth doorway was shut, but the sixth was open. The Mouser peeked in with one eye, his nose brushing the jamb. Then he stepped forward and gazed inside with entranced expression, pushing the black rag up onto his forehead for better vision. Fafhrd joined him.

It was a large room, empty so far as could be told of human and animal life, but filled with most interesting things. From knee-height up, the entire far wall was a map of the city of Lankhmar and its immediate surrounds. Every building and street seemed depicted, down to the meanest hovel and narrowest court. There were signs of recent erasure and redrawing at many spots, and here and there little colored hieroglyphs of mysterious import.

The floor was marble, the ceiling blue as lapis lazuli. The side walls were thickly hung, by ring and padlock. One was covered with all manner of thieves' tools, from a huge thick pry-bar that looked as if it could unseat the universe, or at least the door of the Overlord's treasure-vault, to a rod so slim it might be an elf-queen's wand and seemingly designed to telescope out and fish from distance for precious gauds on milady's spindle-legged, ivory-topped vanity table; the other wall had on it all sorts of quaint, gold-gleaming and jewel-flashing objects, evidently mementos chosen for their oddity from the spoils of memorable burglaries, from a female mask of thin gold, breathlessly beautiful in its features and contours, but thickly set with rubies simulating the spots of the pox in its fever-stage, to a knife whose blade was wedge-shaped diamonds set side by side and this diamond cutting-edge looking razor-sharp.

All about were tables set chiefly with models of dwelling houses and other buildings, accurate to the last minutia, it looked, of ventilation hole under roof gutter and ground-level drain hole, of creviced wall and smooth. Many were cut away in partial or entire section to show the layout of rooms, closets, strongrooms, doorways, corridors, secret passages, smoke-ways, and air-ways in equal detail.

In the center of the room was a bare round-table of ebony and ivory squares. About it were set seven straight-backed but well-padded chairs, the one facing the map and away from the Mouser and Fafhrd being higher backed and wider armed than the others—a chief's chair, likely that of Krovas.

The Mouser tiptoed forward, irresistibly drawn, but Fafhrd's left hand clamped down on his shoulder like the iron mitten of a Mingol cataphract and drew him irresistibly back.

Scowling his disapproval, the Northerner brushed down the black rag over the Mouser's eyes again, and with his crutch-hand thumbed ahead; then set off in that direction in most carefully calculated, silent hops. With a shrug of disappointment the Mouser followed.

As soon as they had turned away from the doorway, but before they were out of sight, a neatly black-bearded, crop-haired head came like a serpent's around the side of the highest-backed chair and gazed after them from deepsunken yet glinting eyes. Next a snake-supple, long hand followed the head out, crossed thin lips with ophidian forefinger for silence, and then fingerbeckoned the two pairs of dark-tunicked men who were standing to either side of the doorway, their backs to the corridor wall, each of the four gripping a curvy knife in one hand and a dark leather, lead-weighted bludgeon in the other.

When Fafhrd was halfway to the seventh doorway, from which the monotonous yet sinister recitation continued to well, there shot out through it a slender, whey-faced youth, his narrow hands clapped over his mouth, under terror-wide eyes, as if to shut in screams or vomit, and with a broom clamped in an armpit, so that he seemed a bit like a young warlock about to take to the air. He dashed past Fafhrd and the Mouser and away, his racing footsteps sounding rapid-dull on the carpeting and hollow-sharp on the stairs before dying away.

Fafhrd gazed back at the Mouser with a grimace and shrug, then squatting one-legged until the knee of his bound-up leg touched the floor, advanced half his face past the doorjamb. After a bit, without otherwise changing position, he beckoned the Mouser to approach. The latter slowly thrust half his face past the jamb, just above Fafhrd's.

What they saw was a room somewhat smaller than that of the great map and lit by central lamps that burned blue-white instead of customary yellow. The floor was marble, darkly colorful, and complexly whorled. The dark walls were hung with astrological and anthropomantic charts and instruments of magic and shelved with cryptically labeled porcelain jars and also with vitreous flasks and glass pipes of the oddest shapes, some filled with colored fluids, but many gleamingly empty. At the foot of the walls, where the shadows were thickest, broken and discarded stuff was irregularly heaped, as if swept out of the way and forgot, and here and there opened a large rathole.

In the center of the room and brightly illuminated by contrast was a long table with thick top and many stout legs. The Mouser thought fleetingly of a centipede and then of the bar at the Eel, for the tabletop was densely stained and scarred by many a spilled elixir and many a deep black burn by fire or acid or both.

In the midst of the table an alembic was working. The lamp's flame—deep blue, this one—kept a-boil in the large crystal cucurbit a dark, viscid fluid with here and there diamond glints. From out of the thick, seething stuff, strands of a darker vapor streamed upward to crowd through the cucurbit's narrow mouth and stain—oddly, with bright scarlet—the transparent head and then, dead black now, flow down the narrow pipe from the head into a spherical crystal receiver, larger even than the cucurbit, and there curl and weave about like so many coils of living black cord—an endless, skinny, ebon serpent.

Behind the left end of the table stood a tall, yet hunchbacked man in black robe and hood which shadowed more than hid a face of which the most prominent features were a long, thick, pointed nose with out-jutting, almost chinless mouth just below. His complexion was sallow-gray like clay and a shorthaired bristly, gray beard grew high on his wide cheeks. From under a receding forehead and bushy gray brows, wide-set eyes looked intently down at an age-browned scroll, which his disgustingly small clubhands, knuckles big, short backs gray-bristled, ceaselessly unrolled and rolled up again. The only move his eyes ever made, besides the short side-to-side one as he read the lines he was rapidly intoning, was an occasional farther sidewise glance at the alembic.

On the other end of the table, beady eyes darting from the sorcerer to the alembic and back again, crouched a small black beast, the first glimpse of which made Fafhrd dig fingers painfully into the Mouser's shoulder and the latter almost gasp, not from the pain. It was most like a rat, yet it had a higher forehead and closer-set eyes than either had ever seen in a rat, while its forepaws, which it constantly rubbed together in what seemed restless glee, looked like tiny copies of the sorcerer's clubhands.

Simultaneously yet independently, Fafhrd and the Mouser each became certain it was the beast which had gutter-escorted Slivikin and his mate, then fled, and each recalled what Ivrian had said about a witch's familiar and Vlana about the likelihood of Krovas employing a warlock.

What with the ugliness of the clubhanded man and beast and between them the ropy black vapor coiling and twisting in the great receiver and head, like a black umbilical cord, it was a most horrid sight. And the similarities, save for size, between the two creatures were even more disquieting in their implications.

The tempo of the incantation quickened, the blue-white flames brightened and hissed audibly, the fluid in the cucurbit grew thick as lava, great bubbles formed and loudly broke, the black rope in the receiver writhed like a nest of snakes; there was an increasing sense of invisible presences, the supernatural tension grew almost unendurable, and Fafhrd and the Mouser were hard put to keep silent the open-mouthed gasps by which they now breathed, and each feared his heartbeat could be heard cubits away.

Abruptly the incantation peaked and broke off, like a drum struck very hard, then instantly silenced by palm and fingers outspread against the head. With a bright flash and dull explosion, cracks innumerable appeared in the cucurbit; its crystal became white and opaque, yet it did not shatter or drip. The head lifted a span, hung there, fell back. While two black nooses appeared among the coils in the receiver and suddenly narrowed until they were only two big black knots.

The sorcerer grinned, rolling up the end of the parchment with a snap, and shifted his gaze from the receiver to his familiar, while the latter chittered shrilly and bounded up and down in rapture.

"Silence, Slivikin! Comes now your time to race and strain and sweat," the sorcerer cried, speaking pidgin Lankhmarese now, but so rapidly and in so squeakingly high-pitched a voice that Fafhrd and the Mouser could barely follow him. They did, however, both realize they had been completely mistaken as to the identity of Slivikin. In moment of disaster, the fat thief had called to the witch-beast for help rather than to his human comrade.

"Yes, master," Slivikin squeaked back no less clearly, in an instant revising the Mouser's opinions about talking animals. He continued in the same fifelike, fawning tones, "Harkening in obedience, Hristomilo."

Now they knew the sorcerer's name too.

Hristomilo ordered in whiplash pipings, "To your appointed work! See to it you summon an ample sufficiency of feasters! I want the bodies stripped to skeletons, so the bruises of the enchanted smog and all evidence of death by suffocation will be vanished utterly. But forget not the loot! On your mission, now—depart!"

Slivikin, who at every command had bobbed his head in manner reminiscent of his bouncing, now squealed, "I'll see it done!" and gray lightning-like leaped a long leap to the floor and down an inky rathole.

Hristomilo, rubbing together his disgusting clubhands much as Slivikin had his, cried chucklingly, "What Slevyas lost, my magic has rewon!"

Fafhrd and the Mouser drew back out of the doorway, partly with the thought that since neither his incantation and his alembic, nor his familiar now required his unblinking attention, Hristomilo would surely look up and spot them; partly in revulsion from what they had seen and heard; and in poignant if useless pity for Slevyas, whoever he might be, and for the other unknown victims of the ratlike and conceivably rat-related sorcerer's death spells, poor strangers already dead and due to have their flesh eaten from their bones.

Fafhrd wrested the green bottle from the Mouser and, though almost gagging on the rotten-flowery reek, gulped a large, stinging mouthful. The Mouser couldn't quite bring himself to do the same, but was comforted by the spirits of wine he inhaled during this byplay.

Then he saw, beyond Fafhrd, standing before the doorway to the map room, a richly clad man with gold-hilted knife jewel-scabbarded at his side. His sunken-eyed face was prematurely wrinkled by responsibility, overwork, and authority, framed by neatly cropped black hair and beard. Smiling, he silently beckoned them.

The Mouser and Fafhrd obeyed, the latter returning the green bottle to the former, who recapped it and thrust it under his left elbow with well-concealed irritation.

Each guessed their summoner was Krovas, the Guild's Grandmaster. Once again Fafhrd marveled, as he hobbledehoyed along, reeling and belching, how

Kos or the Fates were guiding him to his target tonight. The Mouser, more alert and more apprehensive too, was reminding himself that they had been directed by the niche-guards to report to Krovas, so that the situation, if not developing quite in accord with his own misty plans, was still not deviating disastrously.

Yet not even his alertness, nor Fafhrd's primeval instincts, gave him forewarning as they followed Krovas into the map room.

Two steps inside, each of them was shoulder-grabbed and bludgeon-menaced by a pair of ruffians further armed with knives tucked in their belts.

They judged it wise to make no resistance, on this one occasion at least bearing out the Mouser's mouthings about the supreme caution of drunken men.

"All secure, Grandmaster," one of the ruffians rapped out.

Krovas swung the highest-backed chair around and sat down, eyeing them coolly yet searchingly. "What brings two stinking, drunken beggar-Guildsmen into the top-restricted precincts of the masters?" he asked quietly.

The Mouser felt the sweat of relief bead his forehead. The disguises he had brilliantly conceived were still working, taking in even the head man, though he had spotted Fafhrd's tipsiness. Resuming his blind-man manner, he quavered, "We were directed by the guard above the Cheap Street door to report to you in person, great Krovas, the Night Beggarmaster being on furlough for reasons of sexual hygiene. Tonight we've made good haul!" And fumbling in his purse, ignoring as far as possible the tightened grip on his shoulders, he brought out the golden coin given him by the sentimental courtesan and displayed it tremble-handed.

"Spare me your inexpert acting," Krovas said sharply. "I'm not one of your marks. And take that rag off your eyes."

The Mouser obeyed and stood to attention again insofar as his pinioning would permit, and smiling the more seeming carefree because of his reawakening uncertainties. Conceivably he wasn't doing quite as brilliantly as he'd thought.

Krovas leaned forward and said placidly yet piercingly, "Granted you were so ordered—and most improperly so; that door-guard will suffer for his stupidity!—why were you spying into a room beyond this one when I spotted you?"

"We saw brave thieves flee from that room," the Mouser answered pat. "Fearing that some danger threatened the Guild, my comrade and I investigated, ready to scotch it."

"But what we saw and heard only perplexed us, great sir," Fafhrd appended quite smoothly.

"I didn't ask you, sot. Speak when you're spoken to," Krovas snapped at him. Then, to the Mouser, "You're an overweening rogue, most presumptuous for your rank."

In a flash the Mouser decided that further insolence, rather than fawning, was what the situation required. "That I am, sir," he said smugly. "For example, I have a master plan whereby you and the Guild might gain more wealth and power in three months than your predecessors have in three millennia."

Krovas' face darkened. "Boy!" he called. Through the curtains of an inner doorway, a youth with dark complexion of a Kleshite and clad only in a black loincloth sprang to kneel before Krovas, who ordered, "Summon first my sorcerer, next the thieves Slevyas and Fissif," whereupon the dark youth dashed into the corridor.

Then Krovas, his face its normal pale again, leaned back in his great chair, lightly rested his sinewy arms on its great padded ones, and smilingly directed at the Mouser, "Speak your piece. Reveal to us this master plan."

Forcing his mind not to work on the surprising news that Slevyas was not victim but thief and not sorcery-slain but alive and available—why did Krovas want him now?—the Mouser threw back his head and, shaping his lips in a faint sneer, began, "You may laugh merrily at me, Grandmaster, but I'll warrant that in less than a score of heartbeats you'll be straining sober-faced to hear my least word. Like lightning, wit can strike anywhere, and the best of you in Lankhmar have age-honored blind spots for things obvious to us of outland birth. My master plan is but this: let Thieves' Guild under your iron autocracy seize supreme power in Lankhmar City, then in Lankhmar Land, next over all Nehwon, after which who knows what realms undreamt will know your suzerainty!"

The Mouser had spoken true in one respect: Krovas was no longer smiling. He was leaning forward a little and his face was darkening again, but whether from interest or anger it was too soon to say.

The Mouser continued, "For centuries the Guild's had more than the force and intelligence needed to make a *coup d'etat* a nine-finger certainty; today there's not one hair's chance in a bushy head of failure. It is the proper state of things that thieves rule other men. All Nature cries out for it. No need slay old Karstak Ovartamortes, merely overmaster, control, and so rule through him. You've already fee'd informers in every noble or wealthy house. Your post's better than the King of Kings'. You've a mercenary striking force permanently mobilized, should you have need of it, in the Slayers' Brotherhood. We Guild-beggars are your foragers. O great Krovas, the multitudes know that thievery rules Nehwon, nay, the universe, nay, more, the highest gods' abode! And the multitudes accept this, they balk only at the hypocrisy of the present arrangement, at the pretense that things are otherwise. Oh, give them their decent desire, great Krovas! Make it all open, honest and aboveboard, with thieves ruling in name as well as fact."

The Mouser spoke with passion, for the moment believing all he said, even the contradictions. The four ruffians gaped at him with wonder and not a little awe. They slackened their holds on him and on Fafhrd too.

But leaning back in his great chair again and smiling thinly and ominously, Krovas said coolly, "In *our* Guild intoxication is no excuse for folly, rather grounds for the extremest penalty. But I'm well aware your organized beggars operate under a laxer discipline. So I'll deign to explain to you, you wee drunken dreamer, that we thieves know well that, behind the scenes, we already rule Lankhmar, Nehwon, all life in sooth—for what is life but greed in action? But to make this an open thing would not only force us to take on ten thousand sorts of weary work others now do for us, it would also go against another of life's deep laws: illusion. Does the sweetmeats hawker show you his kitchen? Does a whore let average client watch her enamel over her wrinkles and hoist her sagging breasts in cunning gauzy slings? Does a conjurer turn out for you his hidden pockets? Nature works by subtle, secret means—man's invisible seed, spider bite, the viewless spores of madness and of death, rocks that are born in earth's unknown bowels, the silent stars acreep across the sky—and we thieves copy her."

"That's good enough poetry, sir," Fafhrd responded with undertone of angry derision, for he had himself been considerably impressed by the Mouser's master plan and was irked that Krovas should do insult to his new friend by disposing of it so lightly. "Closet kingship may work well enough in easy times. But"—he paused histrionically—"will it serve when Thieves' Guild is faced with an enemy determined to obliterate it forever, a plot to wipe it entirely from the earth?"

"What drunken babble's this?" Krovas demanded, sitting up straight. *"What plot?"*

"'Tis a most *secret* one," Fafhrd responded grinning, delighted to pay this haughty man in his own coin and thinking it quite just that the thiefking sweat a little before his head was removed for conveyance to Vlana. "I know naught of it, except that many a master thief is marked down for the knife—and your head doomed to fall!"

Fafhrd merely sneered his face and folded his arms, the still slack grip of his captors readily permitting it, his (sword) crutch hanging against his body from his lightly gripping hand. Then he scowled as there came a sudden shooting pain in his numbed, bound-up left leg, which he had forgotten for a space.

Krovas raised a clenched fist and himself half out of his chair, in prelude to some fearsome command—likely that Fafhrd be tortured. The Mouser cut in hurriedly with, "The Secret Seven, they're called, are its leaders. None in the outer circles of the conspiracy know their names, though rumor has it that they're secret

Guild-thief renegades representing, one for each, the cities of Ool Hrusp, Kvarch Nar, Ilthmar, Horborixen, Tisilinilit, far Kiraay and Lankhmar's very self . . . It's thought they're moneyed by the merchants of the East, the priests of Wan, the sorcerers of the Steppes and half the Mingol leadership too, legended Quarmall, Aarth's Assassins in Sarheenmar, and also no lesser man than the King of Kings."

Despite Krovas' contemptuous and then angry remarks, the ruffians holding the Mouser continued to harken to their captive with interest and respect, and they did not retighten their grip on him. His colorful revelations and melodramatic delivery held them, while Krovas' dry, cynical, philosophic observations largely went over their heads.

Hristomilo came gliding into the room then, his feet presumably taking swift, but very short steps, at any rate his black robe hung undisturbed to the marble floor despite his slithering speed.

There was a shock at his entrance. All eyes in the map room followed him, breaths were held, and the Mouser and Fafhrd felt the horny hands that gripped them shake just a little. Even Krovas' all-confident, world-weary expression became tense and guardedly uneasy. Clearly the sorcerer of the Thieves' Guild was more feared than loved by his chief employer and by the beneficiaries of his skills.

Outwardly oblivious to this reaction to his appearance, Hristomilo, smiling thin-lipped, halted close to one side of Krovas' chair and inclined his hood-shadowed rodent face in the ghost of a bow. Krovas held palm toward the Mouser for silence. Then, wetting his lips, he asked Hristomilo sharply yet nervously, "Do you know these two?"

Hristomilo nodded decisively. "They just now peered a befuddled eye each at me," he said, "whilst I was about that business we spoke of. I'd have shooed them off, reported them, save such action might have broken my spell, put my words out of time with the alembic's workings. The one's a Northerner, the other's features have a southern cast—from Tovilyis or near, most like. Both younger than their now-looks. Freelance bravos, I'd judge 'em, the sort the Brotherhood hires as extras when they get at once several big guard and escort jobs. Clumsily disguised now, of course, as beggars."

Fafhrd by yawning, the Mouser by pitying head shake tried to convey that all this was so much poor guesswork.

"That's all I can tell you without reading their minds," Hristomilo concluded. "Shall I fetch my lights and mirrors?"

"Not yet." Krovas turned face and shot a finger at the Mouser. "How do you know these things you rant about?—Secret Seven and all. Straight simplest answer now—no rodomontades."

The Mouser replied most glibly: "There's a new courtesan dwells on Pimp Street—Tyarya her name, tall, beauteous, but hunchbacked, which oddly delights many of her clients. Now Tyarya loves me 'cause my maimed eyes match her twisted spine, or from simple pity of my blindness—*she* believes it!—and youth, or from some odd itch, like her clients' for her, which that combination arouses in her flesh.

"Now one of her patrons, a trader newly come from Kleg Nar—Mourph, he's called—was impressed by my intelligence, strength, boldness, and close-mouthed tact, and those same qualities in my comrade too. Mourph sounded us out, finally asking if we hated the Thieves' Guild for its control of the Beggars' Guild. Sensing a chance to aid the Guild, we played up, and a week ago he recruited us into a cell of three in the outermost strands of the conspiracy web of the Seven."

"You presumed to do all of this on your own?" Krovas demanded in freezing tones, sitting up straight and gripping hard the chair arms.

"Oh, no," the Mouser denied guilelessly. "We reported our every act to the Day Beggarmaster and he approved them, told us to spy our best and gather every scrap of fact and rumor we could about the Sevens' conspiracy."

"And he told me not a word about it!" Krovas rapped out. "If true, I'll have Bannat's head for this! But you're lying, aren't you?"

As the Mouser gazed with wounded eyes at Krovas, meanwhile preparing a most virtuous denial, a portly man limped past the doorway with help of a gilded staff. He moved with silence and aplomb. But Krovas saw him. "Night Beggar-master!" he called sharply. The limping man stopped, turned, came crippling majestically through the door. Krovas stabbed finger at the Mouser, then Fafhrd. "Do you know these two, Flim?"

The Night Beggarmaster unhurriedly studied each for a space, then shook his head with its turban of cloth of gold. "Never seen either before. What are they? Fink beggars?"

"But Flim wouldn't know us," the Mouser explained desperately, feeling everything collapsing in on him and Fafhrd. "All our contacts were with Bannat alone."

Flim said quietly, "Bannat's been abed with the swamp ague this past ten-day. Meanwhile I have been Day Beggarmaster as well as Night."

At that moment Slevyas and Fissif came hurrying in behind Flim. The tall thief bore on his jaw a bluish lump. The fat thief's head was bandaged above his darting eyes. He pointed quickly at Fafhrd and the Mouser and cried, "There are the two that slugged us, took our Jengao loot, and slew our escort."

The Mouser lifted his elbow and the green bottle crashed to shards at his feet on the hard marble. Gardenia-reek sprang swiftly through the air.

But more swiftly still the Mouser, shaking off the careless hold of his startled guards, sprang toward Krovas, clubbing his wrapped-up sword. If he could only overpower the King of Thieves and hold Cat's Claw at his throat, he'd be able to bargain for his and Fafhrd's lives. That is unless the other thieves wanted their master killed, which wouldn't surprise him at all.

With startling speed Flim thrust out his gilded staff, tripping the Mouser, who went heels over head, midway seeking to change his involuntary somersault into a voluntary one.

Meanwhile Fafhrd lurched heavily against his left-hand captor, at the same time swinging bandaged Graywand strongly upward to strike his right-hand captor under the jaw. Regaining his one-legged balance with a mighty contortion, he hopped for the loot-wall behind him.

Slevyas made for the wall of thieves' tools, and with a muscle-cracking effort wrenched the great pry-bar from its padlocked ring.

Scrambling to his feet after a poor landing in front of Krovas' chair, the Mouser found it empty and the Thief King in a half-crouch behind it, gold-hilted dagger drawn, deep-sunk eyes coldly battle-wild. Spinning around, he saw Fafhrd's guards on the floor, the one sprawled senseless, the other starting to scramble up, while the great Northerner, his back against the wall of weird jewelry, menaced the whole room with wrapped-up Graywand and with his long knife, jerked from its scabbard behind him.

Likewise drawing Cat's Claw, the Mouser cried in trumpet voice of battle, "Stand aside, all! He's gone mad! I'll hamstring his good leg for you!" And racing through the press and between his own two guards, who still appeared to hold him in some awe, he launched himself with flashing dirk at Fafhrd, praying that the Northerner, drunk now with battle as well as wine and poisonous perfume, would recognize him and guess his stratagem.

Graywand slashed well above his ducking head. His new friend not only guessed, but was playing up—and not just missing by accident, the Mouser hoped. Stooping low by the wall, he cut the lashings on Fafhrd's left leg. Graywand and Fafhrd's long knife continued to spare him. Springing up, he headed for the corridor, crying overshoulder to Fafhrd, "Come on!"

Hristomilo stood well out of his way, quietly observing. Fissif scuttled toward safety. Krovas stayed behind his chair, shouting, "Stop them! Head them off!"

The three remaining ruffian guards, at last beginning to recover their fighting-wits, gathered to oppose the Mouser. But menacing them with swift feints of his dirk, he slowed them and darted between—and then just in the nick of time knocked aside with a downsweep of wrapped-up Scalpel Flim's gilded staff, thrust once again to trip him.

All this gave Slevyas time to return from the tools-wall and aim at the Mouser a great swinging blow with the massive pry-bar. But even as that blow started, a very long, bandaged sword on a very long arm thrust over the Mouser's shoulder and solidly and heavily poked Slevyas high on the chest, jolting him backward, so that the pry-bar's swing was short and whistled past harmlessly.

Then the Mouser found himself in the corridor and Fafhrd beside him, though for some weird reason still only hopping. The Mouser pointed toward the stairs. Fafhrd nodded, but delayed to reach high, still on one leg only, and rip off the nearest wall a dozen cubits of heavy drapes, which he threw across the corridor to baffle pursuit.

They reached the stairs and started up the next flight, the Mouser in advance. There were cries behind, some muffled.

"Stop hopping, Fafhrd!" the Mouser ordered querulously. "You've got two legs again."

"Yes, and the other's still dead," Fafhrd complained. "Ahh! Now feeling begins to return to it."

A thrown knife whisked between them and dully clinked as it hit the wall point-first and stone-powder flew. Then they were around the bend.

Two more empty corridors, two more curving flights, and then they saw above them on the last landing a stout ladder mounting to a dark, square hole in the roof. A thief with hair bound back by a colorful handkerchief—it appeared to be a door guards' identification—menaced the Mouser with drawn sword, but when he saw that there were two of them, both charging him determinedly with shining knives and strange staves or clubs, he turned and ran down the last empty corridor.

The Mouser, followed closely by Fafhrd, rapidly mounted the ladder and without pause vaulted up through the hatch into the star-crusted night.

He found himself near the unrailed edge of a slate roof which slanted enough to have made it look most fearsome to a novice roof-walker, but safe as houses to a veteran.

Crouched on the long peak of the roof was another kerchiefed thief holding a dark lantern. He was rapidly covering and uncovering, presumably in some code, the lantern's bull's eye, whence shot a faint green beam north to where a red point of light winked dimly in reply—as far away as the sea wall, it looked, or perhaps the masthead of a ship beyond, riding in the Inner Sea. Smuggler?

Seeing the Mouser, this one instantly drew sword and, swinging the lantern a little in his other hand, advanced menacingly. The Mouser eyed him warily—the dark lantern with its hot metal, concealed flame, and store of oil would be a tricky weapon.

But then Fafhrd had clambered out and was standing beside the Mouser, on both feet again at last. Their adversary backed slowly away toward the north end of the roof ridge. Fleetingly the Mouser wondered if there was another hatch there.

Turning back at a bumping sound, he saw Fafhrd prudently hoisting the ladder. Just as he got it free, a knife flashed up close past him out of the hatch. While following its flight, the Mouser frowned, involuntarily admiring the skill required to hurl a knife vertically with any accuracy.

It clattered down near them and slid off the roof. The Mouser loped south across the slates and was halfway from the hatch to that end of the roof when the faint chink came of the knife striking the cobbles of Murder Alley.

Fafhrd followed more slowly, in part perhaps from a lesser experience of roofs, in part because he still limped a bit to favor his left leg, and in part because he was carrying the heavy ladder balanced on his right shoulder.

"We won't need that," the Mouser called back.

Without hesitation Fafhrd heaved it joyously over the edge. By the time it crashed in Murder Alley, the Mouser was leaping down two yards and across a gap of one to the next roof, of opposite and lesser pitch. Fafhrd landed beside him.

The Mouser led them at almost a run through a sooty forest of chimneys, chimney pots, ventilators with tails that made them always face the wind, black-legged cisterns, hatch covers, bird houses, and pigeon traps across five roofs, four progressively a little lower, the fifth regaining a yard of the altitude they'd lost—the spaces between the buildings easy to leap, none more than three yards, no ladder-bridge required, and only one roof with a somewhat greater pitch than that of Thieves' House—until they reached the Street of the Thinkers at a point where it was crossed by a roofed passageway much like the one at Rokkermas and Slaarg's.

While they crossed it at a crouching lope, something hissed close past them and clattered ahead. As they leaped down from the roof of the bridge, three more somethings hissed over their heads to clatter beyond. One rebounded from a square chimney almost to the Mouser's feet. He picked it up, expecting a stone, and was surprised by the greater weight of a leaden ball big as two doubled-up fingers.

"They," he said, jerking thumb overshoulder, "lost no time in getting slingers on the roof. When roused, they're good."

Southeast then through another black chimney-forest to a point on Cheap Street where upper stories overhung the street so much on either side that it was easy to leap the gap. During this roof-traverse, an advancing front of night-smog, dense enough to make them cough and wheeze, had engulfed them and for perhaps sixty heartbeats the Mouser had had to slow to a shuffle and feel his way, Fafhrd's hand on his shoulder. Just short of Cheap Street they had come abruptly and completely out of the smog and seen the stars again, while the black front had rolled off northward behind them.

"Now what the devil was that?" Fafhrd had asked and the Mouser had shrugged.

A nighthawk would have seen a vast thick hoop of black night-smog blowing out in all directions from a center near the Silver Eel, growing ever greater and greater in diameter and circumference.

East of Cheap Street the two comrades soon made their way to the ground, landing back in Plague Court behind the narrow premises of Nattick Nimblefingers the Tailor.

Then at last they looked at each other and their trammeled swords and their filthy faces and clothing made dirtier still by roof-soot, and they laughed and laughed and laughed, Fafhrd roaring still as he bent over to massage his left leg above and below knee. This hooting and wholly unaffected self-mockery continued while they unwrapped their swords—the Mouser as if his were a surprise package—and clipped their scabbards once more to their belts. Their exertions had burned out of them the last mote and atomy of strong wine and even stronger stenchful perfume, but they felt no desire whatever for more drink, only the urge to get home and eat hugely and guzzle hot, bitter gahveh, and tell their lovely girls at length the tale of their mad adventure.

They loped on side by side, at intervals glancing at each other and chuckling, though keeping a normally wary eye behind and before for pursuit or interception, despite their expecting neither.

Free of night-smog and drizzled with starlight, their cramped surroundings seemed much less stinking and oppressive than when they had set out. Even Ordure Boulevard had a freshness to it.

Only once for a brief space did they grow serious.

Fafhrd said, "You were a drunken idiot-genius indeed tonight, even if I was a drunken clodhopper. Lashing up my leg! Tying up our swords so we couldn't use 'em save as clubs!"

The Mouser shrugged. "Yet that sword-tying doubtless saved us from committing a number of murders tonight."

Fafhrd retorted, a little hotly, "Killing in fight isn't murder."

Again the Mouser shrugged. "Killing is murder, no matter what nice names you give. Just as eating is devouring, and drinking guzzling. Gods, I'm dry, famished, and fatigued! Come on, soft cushions, food, and steaming gahveh!"

They hastened up the long, creaking, broken-treaded stairs with an easy carefulness and when they were both on the porch, the Mouser shoved at the door to open it with surprise-swiftness. It did not budge.

"Bolted," he said to Fafhrd shortly. He noted now there was hardly any light at all coming through the cracks around the door, or noticeable through the lattices—at most, a faint orange-red glow. Then with sentimental grin and in a fond voice in which only the ghost of uneasiness lurked, he said, "They've gone to sleep, the unworrying wenches!" He knocked loudly thrice and then cupping his lips shouted softly at the door crack, "Hola, Ivrian! I'm home safe. Hail, Vlana! Your man's done you proud, felling Guild-thieves innumerable with one foot tied behind his back!"

There was no sound whatever from inside—that is, if one discounted a rustling so faint it was impossible to be sure of it.

Fafhrd was wrinkling his nostrils. "I smell smoke."

The Mouser banged on the door again. Still no response. Fafhrd motioned him out of the way, hunching his big shoulder to crash the portal.

The Mouser shook his head and with a deft tap, slide, and tug removed a brick that a moment before had looked a firm-set part of the wall beside the door. He reached in all his arm. There was the scrape of a bolt being withdrawn, then another, then a third. He swiftly recovered his arm and the door swung fully inward at a touch.

But neither he nor Fafhrd rushed in at once, as both had intended to, for the indefinable scent of danger and the unknown came puffing out along with an increased reek of smoke and a slight sickening sweet scent that though female was no decent female perfume, and a musty-sour animal odor.

They could see the room faintly by the orange glow coming from the small oblong of the open door of the little, well-blacked stove. Yet the oblong did not sit properly upright but was unnaturally a-tilt; clearly the stove had been half overset and now leaned against a side wall of the fireplace, its small door fallen open in that direction.

By itself alone, that unnatural angle conveyed the entire impact of a universe overturned.

The orange glow showed the carpets oddly rucked up with here and there black circles a palm's breadth across, the neatly stacked candles scattered about below their shelves along with some of the jars and enameled boxes, and, above all, two black, low, irregular, longish heaps, the one by the fireplace, the other half on the golden couch, half at its foot.

From each heap there stared at the Mouser and Fafhrd innumerable pairs of tiny, rather widely set, furnace-red eyes. On the thickly carpeted floor on the other side of the fireplace was a silver cobweb—a fallen silver cage, but no love birds sang from it.

There was a faint scrape of metal as Fafhrd made sure Graywand was loose in his scabbard.

As if that tiny sound had beforehand been chosen as the signal for attack, each instantly whipped out sword and they advanced side by side into the room, warily at first, testing the floor with each step.

At the screech of the swords being drawn, the tiny furnace-red eyes had winked and shifted restlessly, and now with the two men's approach they swiftly scattered pattering, pair by red pair, each pair at the forward end of a small, low, slender, hairless-tailed black body, and each making for one of the black circles in the rugs, where they vanished.

Indubitably the black circles were ratholes newly gnawed up through the floor and rugs, while the red-eyed creatures were black rats.

Fafhrd and the Mouser sprang forward, slashing and chopping at them in a frenzy, cursing and human-snarling besides.

They sundered few. The rats fled with preternatural swiftness, most of them disappearing down holes near the walls and the fireplace.

Also Fafhrd's first frantic chop went through the floor and on his third step with an ominous crack and splintering his leg plunged through the floor to his hip. The Mouser darted past him, unmindful of further crackings.

Fafhrd heaved out his trapped leg, not even noting the splinter-scratches it got and as unmindful as the Mouser of the continuing creakings. The rats were gone. He lunged after his comrade, who had thrust a bunch of kindlers into the stove, to make more light.

The horror was that, although the rats were all gone, the two longish heaps remained, although considerably diminished and, as now shown clearly by the yellow flames leaping from the tilted black door, changed in hue—no longer were the heaps red-beaded black, but a mixture of gleaming black and dark brown, a sickening purple-blue, violet and velvet black and ermine white, and the reds of stockings and blood and bloody flesh and bone.

Although hands and feet had been gnawed bone naked, and bodies tunneled heart-deep, the two faces had been spared. That was not good, for they were the parts purple-blue from death by strangulation, lips drawn back, eyes bulging, all features contorted in agony. Only the black and very dark brown hair gleamed unchanged—that and the white, white teeth.

As each man stared down at his love, unable to look away despite the waves of horror and grief and rage washing higher and higher in him, each saw a tiny black strand uncurl from the black depression ringing each throat and drift off, dissipating, toward the open door behind them—two strands of night-smog.

With a crescendo of crackings the floor sagged fully three spans more in the center before arriving at a new temporary stability.

Edges of centrally tortured minds noted details: that Vlana's silver-hilted dagger skewered to the floor a rat, which, likely enough, overeager had approached too closely before the night-smog had done its magic work. That her belt and pouch were gone. That the blue-enameled box inlaid with silver, in which Ivrian had put the Mouser's share of the highjacked jewels, was gone too.

The Mouser and Fafhrd lifted to each other white, drawn faces which were quite mad, yet completely joined in understanding and purpose. No need to tell each other what must have happened here when the two nooses of black vapor had jerked tight in Hristomilo's receiver, or why Slivikin had bounced and squeaked in glee, or the significance of such phrases as "an ample sufficiency of feasters," or "forget not the loot," or "that business we spoke of." No need for Fafhrd to explain why he now stripped off his robe and hood, or why he jerked up Vlana's dagger, snapped the rat off it with a wrist-flick, and thrust it in his belt. No need for the Mouser to tell why he searched out a half dozen jars of oil and after smashing three of them in front of the flaming stove, paused, thought, and stuck the other three in the sack at his waist, adding to them the remaining kindlers and the fire-pot, brimmed with red coals, its top lashed down tight.

Then, still without word exchanged, the Mouser muffled his hand with a small rug and reaching into the fireplace deliberately tipped the flaming stove forward, so that it fell door-down on oil-soaked rugs. Yellow flames sprang up around him.

They turned and raced for the door. With louder crackings than any before, the floor collapsed. They desperately scrambled their way up a steep hill of sliding carpets and reached door and porch just before all behind them gave way and the flaming rugs and stove and all the firewood and candles and the golden couch and all the little tables and boxes and jars—and the unthinkably mutilated bodies of their first loves—cascaded into the dry, dusty, cobweb-choked room below, and the great flames of a cleansing or at least obliterating cremation began to flare upward.

They plunged down the stairs, which tore away from the wall and collapsed and dully crashed in the dark just as they reached the ground. They had to fight their way over the wreckage to get to Bones Alley.

By then flames were darting their bright lizard-tongues out of the shuttered attic windows and the boarded-up ones in the story just below. By the time they reached Plague Court, running side by side at top speed, the Silver Eel's fire-alarm was clanging cacophonously behind them.

They were still sprinting when they took the Death Alley fork. Then the Mouser grappled Fafhrd and forced him to a halt. The big man struck out, cursing insanely, and only desisted—his white face still a lunatic's—when the Mouser cried, panting, "Only ten heartbeats to arm us!"

He pulled the sack from his belt and, keeping tight hold of its neck, crashed it on the cobbles—hard enough to smash not only the bottles of oil, but also the fire-pot, for the sack was soon flaming a little at its base.

Then he drew gleaming Scalpel and Fafhrd Graywand and they raced on, the Mouser swinging his sack in a great circle beside him to fan its flames. It was a veritable ball of fire burning his left hand as they dashed across Cheap Street and into Thieves' House, and the Mouser, leaping high, swung it up into the great niche above the doorway and let go of it.

The niche-guards screeched in surprise and pain at the fiery invader of their hidey hole and had no time to do anything with their swords, or whatever weapons else they had, against the other two invaders.

Student thieves poured out of the doors ahead at the screeching and foot-pounding, and then poured back as they saw the fierce point of flames and the two demon-faced oncomers brandishing their long, shining swords.

One skinny little apprentice—he could hardly have been ten years old—lingered too long. Graywand thrust him pitilessly through as his big eyes bulged and his small mouth gaped in horror and plea to Fafhrd for mercy.

Now from ahead of them there came a weird, wailing call, hollow and hair-raising, and doors began to thus shut instead of spewing forth the armed guards they almost prayed would appear to be skewered by their swords. Also, despite the long, bracketed torches looking newly renewed, the corridor was dark.

The reason for this last became clear as they plunged up the stairs. Strands of night-smog were appearing in the well, materializing from nothing or the air.

The strands grew longer and more numerous and tangible. They touched and clung nastily. In the corridor above they were forming from wall to wall and from ceiling to floor, like a gigantic cobweb, and were becoming so substantial that the Mouser and Fafhrd had to slash them to get through, or so their two maniac minds believed. The black web muffled a little a repetition of the eerie, wailing call, which came from the seventh door ahead and this time ended in a gleeful chittering and cackling insane as the emotions of the two attackers.

Here too doors were thudding shut. In an ephemeral flash of rationality, it occurred to the Mouser that it was not he and Fafhrd the thieves feared, for they had not been seen yet, but rather Hristomilo and his magic, even though working in defense of Thieves' House.

Even the map room, whence counter-attack would most likely erupt, was closed off by a huge oaken, iron-studded door.

They were now twice slashing black, clinging, rope-thick spiderweb for every single step they drove themselves forward. Midway between the map and magic rooms, there was forming on the inky web, ghostly at first but swiftly growing more substantial, a black spider big as a wolf.

The Mouser slashed heavy cobweb before it, dropped back two steps, then hurled himself at it in a high leap. Scalpel thrust through it, striking amidst its eight new-formed jet eyes, and it collapsed like a daggered bladder, loosing a vile stink.

Then he and Fafhrd were looking into the magic room, the alchemist's chamber. It was much as they had seen it before, except some things were doubled, or multiplied even further.

On the long table two blue-boiled cucurbits bubbled and roiled, their heads shooting out a solid, writhing rope more swiftly than moves the black swamp-cobra, which can run down a man—and not into twin receivers, but into the open air of the room (if any of the air in Thieves' House could have been called open then) to weave a barrier between their swords and Hristomilo, who once more stood tall though hunchbacked over his sorcerous, brown parchment, though this time his exultant gaze was chiefly fixed on Fafhrd and the Mouser, with only an occasional downward glance at the text of the spell he drummingly intoned.

At the other end of the table, in the web-free space, there bounced not only Slivikin, but also a huge rat matching him in size in all members except the head.

From the ratholes at the foot of the walls red eyes glittered and gleamed in pairs.

With a bellow of rage Fafhrd began slashing at the black barrier, but the ropes were replaced from the cucurbit heads as swiftly as he sliced them, while the cut ends, instead of drooping slackly, now began to strain hungrily toward him like constrictive snakes or strangle-vines.

He suddenly shifted Graywand to his left hand, drew his long knife and hurled it at the sorcerer. Flashing toward its mark, it cut through three strands, was deflected and slowed by a fourth and fifth, almost halted by a sixth, and ended hanging futilely in the curled grip of a seventh.

Hristomilo laughed cacklingly and grinned, showing his huge upper incisors, while Slivikin chittered in ecstasy and bounded the higher.

The Mouser hurled Cat's Claw with no better result—worse, indeed, since his action gave two darting smog-strands time to curl hamperingly around his sword-hand and stranglingly around his neck. Black rats came racing out of the big holes at the cluttered base of the walls.

Meanwhile other strands snaked around Fafhrd's ankles, knees and left arm, almost toppling him. But even as he fought for balance, he jerked Vlana's dagger from his belt and raised it over his shoulder, its silver hilt glowing, its blade brown with dried rat's-blood.

The grin left Hristomilo's face as he saw it. The sorcerer screamed strangely and importuningly then and drew back from his parchment and the table, and raised clawed clubhands to ward off doom.

Vlana's dagger sped unimpeded through the black web—its strands even seemed to part for it—and betwixt the sorcerer's warding hands, to bury itself to the hilt in his right eye.

He screamed thinly in dire agony and clawed at his face.

The black web writhed as if in death spasm.

The cucurbits shattered as one, spilling their lava on the scarred table, putting out the blue flames even as the thick wood of the table began to smoke a little at the lava's edge. Lava dropped with plops on the dark marble floor.

With a faint, final scream Hristomilo pitched forward, hands still clutched to his eyes above his jutting nose, silver dagger-hilt still protruding between his fingers.

The web grew faint, like wet ink washed with a gush of clear water.

The Mouser raced forward and transfixed Slivikin and the huge rat with one thrust of Scalpel before the beasts knew what was happening. They too died swiftly with thin screams, while all the other rats turned tail and fled back down their holes swift almost as black lightning.

Then the last trace of night-smog or sorcery-smoke vanished and Fafhrd and the Mouser found themselves standing alone with three dead bodies and a profound silence that seemed to fill not only this room but all Thieves' House. Even the cucurbit-lava had ceased to move, was hardening, and the wood of the table no longer smoked.

Their madness was gone and all their rage too—vented to the last red atomy and glutted to more than satiety. They had no more urge to kill Krovas or any other of the thieves than to swat flies. With horrified inner eye Fafhrd saw the pitiful face of the child-thief he'd skewered in his lunatic anger.

Only their grief remained with them, diminished not one whit, but rather growing greater—that and an ever more swiftly growing revulsion from all that was around them: the dead, the disordered magic room, all Thieves' House, all of the city of Lankhmar to its last stinking alleyway and smog-wreathed spire.

With a hiss of disgust the Mouser jerked Scalpel from the rodent cadavers, wiped it on the nearest cloth, and returned it to its scabbard. Fafhrd likewise sketchily cleansed and sheathed Graywand. Then the two men picked up their knife and dirk from where they'd dropped to the floor when the web had dematerialized, though neither so much as glanced at Vlana's dagger where it was buried. But on the sorcerer's table they did notice Vlana's black velvet, silver-worked pouch and belt, the latter half overrun by the hardened black lava, and Ivrian's blue-enameled box inlaid with silver. From these they took the gems of Jengao.

With no more word than they had exchanged back at the Mouser's burned nest behind the Eel, but with a continuing sense of their unity of purpose, their identity of intent, and of their comradeship, they made their way with shoulders bowed and with slow, weary steps which only very gradually quickened out of the magic room and down the thick-carpeted corridor, past the map room's wide door still barred with oak and iron, and past all the other shut, silent doors—clearly the entire Guild was terrified of Hristomilo, his spells, and his rats; down the echoing stairs, their footsteps speeding a little; down the bare-floored lower corridor past its closed, quiet doors, their footsteps resounding loudly no matter how softly they sought to tread; under the deserted, black-scorched guard-niche, and so out into Cheap Street, turning left and north because that was the nearest way to the Street of the Gods, and there turning right and east—not a waking soul in the wide street except for one skinny, bent-backed apprentice lad unhappily swabbing the flagstones in front of a wine shop in the dim pink light beginning to seep from the east, although there were many forms asleep, a-snore and a-dream in the gutters and under the dark porticos—yes, turning right and east down the Street of the Gods, for that way was the Marsh Gate, leading to Causey Road across the Great Salt Marsh, and the Marsh Gate was the nearest way out of the great and glamorous city that was now loathsome to them, indeed, not to be endured for one more stabbing, leaden heartbeat than was necessary—a city of beloved, unfaceable ghosts.

If Leiber deconstructed Conan-style sword and sorcery and Tolkienesque heroic fantasy with Fafhrd and the Gray Mouser, Michael Moorcock annihilated both with Elric of Melniboné. Moorcock's settings are volatile and saturated with dangerous magic. There is no fight between good and evil; there is the struggle of Law and Chaos, maintained in equilibrium by Cosmic Balance. A sorcerer and philosopher, Elric hates his role as emperor of what he sees as a decadent people who live in a land which "fell, in spirit, five hundred years ago." An albino, he is far from rugged and muscle bound. Moorcock's description:

> *It is the color of a bleached skull, his flesh; and the long hair which flows below his shoulders is milk-white. From the tapering, beautiful head stare two slanting eyes, crimson and moody, and from the loose sleeves of his yellow gown emerge two slender hands, also the color of bone.*

Elric relies on his malevolent, sentient, soul-devouring black sword, Stormbringer, for his strength and vitality.

*Elric's first appearance, "The Dreaming City" (*Science Fantasy, *June 1961), ends in utter defeat and bleakness. The second story, "While the Gods Laugh" (*Science Fantasy *#49, October 1961), is set a year later. A young woman's simple mission becomes, for Elric, an existential quest that ends in doom and gloom. Luckily, our anti-hero finds a cheerful companion (who Elric will come to value as his sole true friend) to lighten the angst and melancholy.*

WHILE THE GODS LAUGH

Michael Moorcock

I, while the gods laugh, the world's vortex am;
Maelstrom of passions in that hidden sea
Whose waves of all-time lap the coasts of me,
And in small compass the dark waters cram.

—Mervyn Peake, "Shapes and Sounds," 1941

ONE

One night, as Elric sat moodily drinking alone in a tavern, a wingless woman of Myyrrhn came gliding out of the storm and rested her lithe body against him.

Her face was thin and frail-boned, almost as white as Elric's own albino skin, and she wore flimsy pale green robes which contrasted well with her dark red hair.

The tavern was ablaze with candle-flame and alive with droning argument and gusty laughter, but the words of the woman of Myyrrhn came clear and liquid, carrying over the zesty din.

"I have sought you twenty days," she said to Elric who regarded her insolently through hooded crimson eyes and lazed in a high-backed chair; a silver wine-cup in his long-fingered right hand and his left on the pommel of his sorcerous runesword Stormbringer.

"Twenty days," murmured the Melnibonéan softly, speaking as if to himself; deliberately rude. "A longtime for a beautiful and lonely woman to be wandering the world." He opened his eyes a trifle wider and spoke to her directly: "I am Elric of Melniboné, as you evidently know. I grant no favors and ask none. Bearing this in mind, tell me why you have sought me for twenty days."

Equably, the woman replied, undaunted by the albino supercilious tone. "You are a bitter man, Elric; I know this also-and you are grief-haunted for reasons which are already legend. I ask you no favors but bring you myself and a proposition. What do you desire most in the world?"

"Peace," Elric told her simply. Then he smiled ironically and said: "I am an evil man, lady, and my destiny is hell-doomed, but I am not unwise, nor unfair. Let me remind you a little of the truth. Call this legend if you prefer—I do not care.

"A woman died a year ago, on the blade of my trusty sword." He patted the blade sharply and his eyes were suddenly hard and self-mocking. "Since then I have courted no woman and desired none. Why should I break such secure habits? If asked, I grant you that I could speak poetry to you, and that you have a grace and beauty which moves me to interesting speculation, but I would not load any part of my dark burden upon one as exquisite as you. Any relationship between us, other than formal, would necessitate my unwilling shifting of part of that burden." He paused for an instant and then said slowly: "I should admit that I scream in my sleep sometimes and am often tortured by incommunicable self-loathing. Go while you can, lady, and forget Elric for he can bring only grief to your soul."

With a quick movement he turned his gaze from her and lifted the silver wine-cup, draining it and replenishing it from a jug at his side.

"No," said the wingless woman of Myyrrhn calmly, "I will not. Come with me."

She rose and gently took Elric's hand. Without knowing why, Elric allowed himself to be led from the tavern and out into the wild, rainless storm which howled around the Filkharian city of Raschil. A protective and cynical smile hovered about his mouth as she drew him towards the sea-lashed quayside where she told him her name. Shaarilla of the Dancing Mist, wingless daughter of a dead necromancer—a cripple in her own strange land, and an outcast.

Elric felt uncomfortably drawn to this calm-eyed woman who wasted few words. He felt a great surge of emotion well within him; emotion, he had never thought to experience again, and he wanted to take her finely molded shoulders and press her slim body to his. But he quelled the urge and studied her marble delicacy and her wild hair which flowed in the wind about her head.

Silence rested comfortably between them while the chaotic wind howled mournfully over the sea. Here, Elric could ignore the warm stink of the city and he felt almost relaxed. At last, looking away from him towards the swirling sea, her green robe curling in the wind, she said: "You have heard, of course, of the Dead Gods' Book?"

Elric nodded. He was interested, despite the need he felt to disassociate himself as much as possible from his fellows. The mythical book was believed to contain knowledge which could solve many problems that had plagued men for centuries—it held a holy and mighty wisdom which every sorcerer desired to sample. But it was believed destroyed, hurled into the sun when the Old Gods were dying in the cosmic wastes which lay beyond the outer reaches of the solar system. Another: legend, apparently of later origin, spoke vaguely of the dark ones who had interrupted the Book's sunward coursing and had stolen it before it could be destroyed. Most scholars discounted this legend, arguing that, by this time, the book would have come to light if it did still exist.

Elric made himself speak flatly so that he appeared to be disinterested when he answered Shaarilla. "Why do you mention the Book?"

"I know that it exists," Shaarilla replied intensely, "and I know where it is. My father acquired the knowledge just before he died. Myself—and the book—you may have if you will help me get it."

Could the secret of peace be contained in the book? Elric wondered. Would he, if he found it, be able to dispense with Stormbringer?

"If you want it so badly that you seek my help," he said eventually, "why do you not wish to keep it?"

"Because I would be afraid to have such a thing perpetually in my custody—it is not a book for a woman to own, but you are possibly the last mighty nigromancer left in the world and it is fitting that you should have it. Besides, you might kill me to obtain it—I would never be safe with such a volume in my hands. I need only one small part of its wisdom."

"What is that?" Elric inquired, studying her patrician beauty with a new pulse stirring within him. Her mouth set and the lids fell over her eyes. "When we have the book in our hands—then you will have your answer. Not before."

"This answer is good enough," Elric remarked quickly, seeing that he would gain no more information at that stage. "And the answer appeals to me." Then, half before he realized it, he seized her shoulders in his slim, pale hands and pressed his colorless lips to her scarlet mouth.

Elric and Shaarilla rode westwards, towards the Silent Land, across the lush plains of Shazaar where their ship had berthed two days earlier. The border country between Shazaar and the Silent Land was a lonely stretch of territory, unoccupied even by peasant dwellings; a no-man's land, though fertile and rich in natural wealth. The inhabitants of Shazaar had deliberately refrained from extending their borders further, for though the dwellers in the Silent Land rarely ventured beyond the Marshes of the Mist, the natural borderline between the two lands, the inhabitants of Shazaar held their unknown neighbors in almost superstitious fear. The journey had been clean and swift, though ominous, with several persons who should have known nothing of their purpose warning the travelers of nearing danger. Elric brooded, recognizing the signs of doom but choosing to ignore them and communicate nothing to Shaarilla who, for her part, seemed content with Elric's silence. They spoke little in the day and so saved their breath for the wild love-play of the night.

The thud of the two horses' hooves on the soft turf, the muted creak and clatter of Elric's harness and sword, were the only sounds to break the stillness of the clear winter day as the pair rode steadily, nearing the quaking, treacherous trails of the Marshes of the Mist.

One gloomy night, they reached the borders of the Silent Land, marked by the marsh, and they halted and made camp, pitching their silk tent on a hill overlooking the mist-shrouded wastes. Banked like black pillows against the horizon, the clouds were ominous. The moon lurked behind them, sometimes piercing them sufficiently to send a pale tentative beam down on to the glistening marsh or its ragged, grassy frontiers. Once, a moonbeam glanced off silver, illuminating the dark silhouette of Elric, but, as if repelled by the sight of a living creature on that bleak hill, the moon once again slunk behind its cloud-shield, leaving Elric thinking deeply. Leaving Elric in the darkness he desired.

Thunder rumbled over distant mountains, sounding like the laughter of far-off

Gods. Elric shivered, pulled his blue cloak more tightly about him, and continued to stare over the misted lowlands. Shaarilla came to him soon, and she stood beside him, swathed in a thick woolen cloak which could not keep out all the damp chill in the air.

"The Silent Land," she murmured. "Are all the stories true, Elric? Did they teach you of it in old Melniboné?"

Elric frowned, annoyed that she had disturbed his thoughts. He turned abruptly to look at her, staring blankly through his crimson-irised eyes for a moment and then saying flatly: "The inhabitants are unhuman and feared. This I know. Few men ventured into their territory, ever. None have returned, to my knowledge. Even in the days when Melniboné was a powerful empire, this was one nation my ancestors never ruled—nor did they desire to do so. The denizens of the Silent Land are said to be a dying race, far more evil than my ancestors ever were, who enjoyed dominion over the Earth long before men gained any sort of power. They rarely venture beyond the confines of their territory, nowadays, encompassed as it is by marshland and mountains."

Shaarilla laughed, then, with little humor. "So they are unhuman are they, Elric? Then what of my people, who are related to them? What of me, Elric?"

"You're unhuman enough for me," replied Elric insouciantly, looking her in the eyes.

She smiled. "No compliment," she said, "but I'll take it for one—until your glib tongue finds a better."

That night they slept restlessly and, as he had predicted, Elric screamed agonizingly in his turbulent, terror-filled sleep and he called a name which made Shaarilla's eyes fill with pain and jealousy. That name was Cymoril. Wide-eyed in his grim sleep, Elric seemed to be staring at the one he named, speaking other words in a sibilant language which made Shaarilla block her ears and shudder.

The next morning, as they broke camp, folding the rustling fabric of the yellow silk tent between them, Shaarilla avoided looking at Elric directly but later, since he made no move to speak, she asked him a question in a voice which shook somewhat. It was a question which she needed to ask, but one which came hard to her lips. "Why do you desire the Dead Gods' Book, Elric? What do you believe you will find in it?"

Elric shrugged, dismissing the question, but she repeated her words less slowly, with more insistence.

"Very well then," he said eventually. "But it is not easy to answer you in a few sentences. I desire, if you like, to know one of two things."

"And what is that, Elric?"

The tall albino dropped the folded tent to the grass and sighed. His fingers played nervously with the pommel of his runesword. "Can an ultimate God exist—or not? That is what I need to know, Shaarilla, if my life is to have any direction at all. "The Lords of Law and Chaos now govern our lives. But is there some being greater than them?"

Shaarilla put a hand on Elric's arm. "Why must you know?" she said.

"Despairingly, sometimes, I seek the comfort of a benign God, Shaarilla. My mind goes out, lying awake at night, searching through black barrenness for something—anything—which will take me to it, warm me, protect me, tell me that there is order in the chaotic tumble of the universe; that it is consistent, this precision of the planets, not simply a brief, bright spark of sanity in an eternity of malevolent anarchy."

Elric sighed and his quiet tones were tinged with hopelessness. "Without some confirmation of the order of things, my only comfort is to accept the anarchy. This way, I can revel in chaos and know, without fear, that we are all doomed from the start-that our brief existence is both meaningless and damned. I can accept then, that we are more than forsaken, because there was never anything there to forsake us. I have weighed the proof, Shaarilla, and must believe that anarchy prevails, in spite of all the laws which seemingly govern our actions, our sorcery, our logic. I see only chaos in the world. If the Book we seek tells me otherwise, then I shall gladly believe it. Until then, I will put my trust only in my sword and myself."

Shaarilla stared at Elric strangely. "Could not this philosophy of yours have been influenced by recent events in your past? Do you fear the consequences of your murder and treachery? Is it not more comforting for you to believe in deserts which are rarely just?"

Elric turned on her, crimson eyes blazing in anger, but even as he made to speak, the anger fled him and he dropped his eyes towards the ground, hooding them from her gaze.

"Perhaps," he said lamely. "I do not know. That is the only *real* truth, Shaarilla. I *do not know*."

Shaarilla nodded, her face lit by an enigmatic sympathy; but Elric did not see the look she gave him, for his own eyes were full of crystal tears which flowed down his lean, white face and took his strength and will momentarily from him.

I am a man possessed," he groaned, "and without this devil-blade I carry I would not be a man at all."

◆ ◆ ◆

Two

They mounted their swift, black horses and spurred them with abandoned savagery down the hillside towards the Marsh, their cloaks whipping be-hind them as the wind caught them, lashing them high into the air. Both rode with set, hard faces, refusing to acknowledge the aching uncertainty which lurked within them.

And the horses' hooves had splashed into quaking bogland before they could halt.

Cursing, Elric tugged hard on his reins, pulling his horse back on to firm ground. Shaarilla, too, fought her own panicky stallion and guided the beast to the safety of the turf.

"How do we cross?" Elric asked her impatiently.

"There was a map—" Shaarilla began hesitantly.

"Where is it?"

"It—it was lost. I lost it. But I tried hard to memorize it. I think I'll be able to get us safely across."

"How did you lose it—and why didn't you tell me of this before?" Elric stormed.

"I'm sorry, Elric—but for a whole day, just before I found you in that tavern, my memory was gone. Somehow, I lived through a day without knowing it—and when I awoke, the map was missing."

Elric frowned. "There is some force working against us, I am Sure," he muttered, "but what it is, I do not know." He raised his voice and said to her. "Let us hope that your memory is not too faulty, now. These marshes are infamous the world over, but by all accounts, only natural hazards wait for us." He grimaced and put his fingers around the hilt of his runesword. "Best go first, Shaarilla, but stay dose. Lead the way."

She nodded, dumbly, and turned her horse's head towards the north, galloping along the bank until she came to a place where a great, tapering rock loomed. Here, a grassy path, four feet or so across, led out into the misty marsh. They could only see a little distance ahead, because of the dinging mist, but it seemed that the trail remained firm for some way. Shaarilla walked her horse on to the path and jolted forward at a slow trot, Elric following immediately behind her.

Through the swirling, heavy mist which shone whitely, the horses moved hesitantly and their riders had to keep them on short, tight rein. The mist padded the marsh with silence and the gleaming, watery fens around them stank with foul putrescence. No animal scurried, no bird shrieked above them. Everywhere was a haunting, fear-laden silence which made both horses and riders uneasy.

With panic in their throats, Elric and Shaarilla rode on, deeper and deeper into the unnatural Marshes of the Mist, their eyes wary and even their nostrils quivering for scent of danger in the stinking morass.

Hours later, when the sun was long past its zenith, Shaarilla's horse reared, screaming and whinnying. She shouted for Elric, her exquisite features twisted in fear as she stared into the mist. He spurred his own bucking horse forwards and joined her. Something moved, slowly, menacingly in the dinging whiteness. Elric's right hand whipped over to his left side and grasped the hilt of Stormbringer. The blade shrieked out of its scabbard, a black fire gleaming along its length and alien power flowing from it into Elric's arm and through his body. A weird, unholy light leapt into Elric's crimson eyes and his mouth was wrenched into a hideous grin as he forced the frightened horse further into the skulking mist.

"Arioch, Lord of the Seven Darks, be with me now!" Elric yelled as he made out the shifting shape ahead of him. It was white, like the mist, yet somehow *darker*. It stretched high above Elric's head. It was nearly eight feet tall and almost as broad. But it was still only an outline, Seeming to have no face or limbs—only movement: darting, malevolent movement! But Arioch, his patron god, chose not to hear.

Elric could feel his horse's great heart beating between his legs as the beast plunged forward under its rider's iron control. Shaarilla was screaming something behind him, but he could not hear the words. Elric hacked at the white shape, but his sword met only mist and it howled angrily. The fear-crazed horse would go no further and Elric was forced to dismount.

"Keep hold of the steed," he shouted behind him to Shaarilla and moved on light feet towards the darting shape which hovered ahead of him, blocking his path.

Now he could make out some of its saliencies. Two eyes, the color of thin, yellow wine, were set high in the thing's body, though it had no separate head. A mouthing, obscene slit, filled with fangs, lay just beneath the eyes. It had no nose or ears that Elric could see. Four appendages sprang from its upper parts and its lower body slithered along the ground, unsupported by any limbs. Elric's eyes ached as he looked at it. It was incredibly disgusting to behold and its amorphous body gave off a stench of death and decay. Fighting down his fear, the albino inched forward warily, his sword held high to parry any thrust the thing might make with its arms. Elric recognized it from a description in one of his grimoires. It was a Mist Giant—possibly the only Mist Giant, Bellbane. Even the wisest wizards were uncertain how many existed—one or many. It was a ghoul of the swamp-lands which fed off the souls and the blood of men and beasts. But the Marshes of this Mist were far to the east of Bellbane's reputed haunts.

Elric ceased to wonder why so few animals inhabited that stretch of the swamp. Overhead the sky was beginning to darken.

Stormbringer throbbed in Elric's grasp as he called the names of the ancient Demon-Gods of his people. The nauseous ghoul obviously recognized the names. For an instant, it wavered backwards. Elric made his legs move towards the thing. Now he saw that the ghoul was not white at all. But it had no color to it that Elric could recognize. There was a suggestion of orangeness dashed with sickening greenish yellow, but he did not see the colors with his eyes—he only *sensed* the alien, unholy tinctures. Then Elric rushed towards the thing, shouting the names which now had no meaning to his surface consciousness.

"Balaan—Marthim! Aesma! Alastor! Saebos! Verdelet! Nizilfkm! Haborym! Haborym of the Fires Which Destroy!" His whole mind was torn in two. Part of him wanted to run, to hide, but he had no control over the power which now gripped him and pushed him to meet the horror.

His sword blade hacked and slashed at the shape. It was like trying to cut through water—sentient, pulsating water. But Stormbringer had effect. The whole shape of the ghoul quivered as if in dreadful pain. Elric felt himself plucked into the air and his vision went. He could see nothing—do nothing but hack and cut at the thing which now held him.

Sweat poured from him as, blindly, he fought on.

Pain which was hardly physical—a deeper, horrifying pain, filled his being as he howled now in agony and struck continually at the yielding bulk which embraced him and was pulling him slowly towards its gaping maw. He struggled and writhed in the obscene grasp of the thing. With powerful arms, it was holding him, almost lasciviously, drawing him closer as a rough lover would draw a girl. Even the mighty power intrinsic in the runesword did not seem enough to kill the monster. Though its efforts were somewhat weaker than earlier, it still drew Elric nearer to the gnashing, slavering mouth-slit.

Elric cried the names again, while Stormbringer danced and sang an evil song in his right hand. In agony, Elric writhed, praying, begging and promising, but still he was drawn inch by inch towards the grinning maw.

Savagely, grimly, he fought and again he screamed for Arioch. A mind touched his—sardonic, powerful, evil—and he knew Arioch responded at last! Almost imperceptibly, the Mist Giant weakened. Elric pressed his advantage and the knowledge that the ghoul was losing its strength gave him more power. Blindly, agony piercing every nerve of his body, he struck and struck.

Then, quite suddenly, he was falling.

He seemed to fall for hours, slowly, weightlessly until he landed upon a surface which yielded beneath him. He began to sink.

Far off, beyond time and space, he heard a distant voice calling to him. He did not want to hear it; he was content to lie where he was as the cold, comforting stuff in which he lay dragged him slowly into itself.

Then some sixth sense made him realize that it was Shaarilla's voice calling him and he forced himself to make sense out of her words.

"Elric—the marsh! You're in the marsh. Don't move!"

He smiled to himself. Why should he move? Down he was sinking, slowly, calmly—down into the welcoming marsh . . . *Had there been another time like this; another marsh?*

With a mental jolt, full awareness of the situation came back to him and he jerked his eyes open. Above him was mist. To one side a pool of unnameable coloring was slowly evaporating, giving off a foul odor. On the other side he could just make out a human form, gesticulating wildly. Beyond the human form were the barely discernible shapes of two horses. Shaarilla was there. Beneath him—

Beneath him was the marsh.

Thick, stinking slime was sucking him downwards as he lay spread-eagled upon it, half-submerged already. Stormbringer was still in his right hand. He could just see it if he turned his head. Carefully, he tried to lift the top half of his body from the sucking morass. He succeeded, only to feel his legs sink deeper. Sitting upright, he shouted to the girl.

"Shaarilla! Quickly—a rope!"

"There is no rope, Elric!" She was ripping off her top garment, frantically tearing it into strips.

Still Elric sank, his feet finding no purchase beneath them.

Shaarilla hastily knotted the strips of cloth. She flung the makeshift rope inexpertly towards the sinking albino. It fell short. Fumbling in her haste, she threw it again. This time his groping left hand found it.

The girl began to haul on the fabric. Elric felt himself rise a little and then stop.

"It's no good, Elric—I haven't the strength."

Cursing her, Elric shouted: "The horse—tie it to the horse!"

She ran towards one of the horses and looped the cloth around the pommel of the saddle. Then she tugged at the beast's reins and began to walk it away.

Swiftly, Elric was dragged from the sucking bog and, still gripping Stormbringer was pulled to the inadequate safety of the strip of turf.

Gasping, he tried to stand, but found his legs in-credibly weak beneath him. He rose; staggered, and fell. Shaarilla knelt down beside him. "Are you hurt?"

Elric smiled in spite of his weakness. "I don't think so."

"It was dreadful. I couldn't see properly what was happening. You seemed to disappear and then—then you screamed that-that name!" She was trembling, her face pale and taut.

"What name?" Elric was genuinely puzzled. "What name did I scream?"

She shook her head. "It doesn't matter—but whatever it was—it saved you. You reappeared soon afterwards and fell into the marsh . . . "

Stormbringer's power was still flowing into the albino. He already felt stronger.

With an effort, he got up and stumbled unsteadily towards his horse.

"I'm sure that the Mist Giant does not usually haunt this marsh—it was sent here. By what—or whom—I don't know, but we must get to firmer ground while we can."

Shaarilla said: "Which way—back or forward?"

Elric frowned. "Why, forward, of course. Why do you ask?"

She swallowed and shook her head. "Let's hurry, then," she said.

They mounted their horses and rode with little caution until the marsh and its cloak of mist was behind them.

Now the journey took on a new urgency as Elric realized that some force was attempting to put obstacles in their way. They rested little and savagely rode their powerful horses to a virtual standstill.

On the fifth day they were riding through barren, rocky country and a light rain was falling. The hard ground was slippery so that they were forced to ride more slowly, huddled over the sodden necks of their horses, muffled in cloaks which only inadequately kept out the drizzling rain. They had ridden in silence for some time before they heard a ghastly cackling baying ahead of them and the rattle of hooves.

Elric motioned towards a large rock looming to their right. "Shelter there," he said. "Something comes towards us—possibly more enemies. With luck, they'll pass us."

Shaarilla mutely obeyed him and together they waited as the hideous baying grew nearer.

"One rider—several other beasts," Elric said, listening intently. "The beasts either follow or pursue the rider."

Then they were in sight—racing through the rain. A man frantically spurring an equally frightened horse—and behind him, the distance decreasing, a pack of what at first appeared to be dogs. But these were not dogs—they were half-dog and half-bird, with the lean, shaggy bodies and legs of dogs but possessing birdlike talons in place of paws and savagely curved beaks which snapped where muzzles should have been.

"The hunting dogs of the Dharzi!" gasped Shaarilla. "I thought that they, like their masters, were long extinct!"

"I, also," Elric said. "What are they doing in these parts? There was never contact between the Dharzi and the dwellers of this Land."

"Brought here—by *something*," Shaarilla whispered. "Those devil-dogs will scent us to be sure."

Elric reached for his runesword. "Then we can lose nothing by aiding their quarry," he said, urging his mount forward. "Wait here, Shaarilla."

By this time, the devil-pack and the man they pursued were rushing past the sheltering rock, speeding down a narrow defile. Elric spurred his horse down the slope.

"Ho there!" he shouted to the frantic rider. "Turn and stand, my friend—I'm here to aid you!" His moaning runesword lifted high, Elric thundered towards the snapping, howling devil-dogs and his horse's hooves struck one with an impact which broke the unnatural beast's spine. There were some five or six of the weird dogs left. The rider turned his horse and drew a long saber from a scabbard at his waist. He was a small man, with a broad ugly mouth. He grinned in relief.

"A lucky chance, this meeting, good master!"

This was all he had time to remark before two of the dogs were leaping at him and he was forced to give his whole attention to defending himself from their slashing talons and snapping beaks.

The other three dogs concentrated their vicious attention upon Elric. One leapt high, its beak aimed at Elric's throat. He felt foul breath on his face and hastily brought Stormbringer round in an arc which chopped the dog in two. Filthy blood spattered Elric and his horse and the scent of it seemed to increase the fury of the other dogs" attack. But the blood made the dancing black runesword sing an almost ecstatic tune and Elric felt it writhe in his grasp and stab at another of the hideous dogs. The point caught the beast just below its breastbone as it reared up at the albino. It screamed in terrible agony and turned its beak to seize the blade. As the beak connected with the lambent black metal of the sword, a foul stench, akin to the smell of burning, struck Elric's nostrils and the beast's scream broke off sharply.

Engaged with the remaining devil-dog, Elric caught a fleeting glimpse of the charred corpse. His horse was rearing high, lashing at the last alien animal with flailing hoofs. The dog avoided the horse's attack and came at Elric's unguarded left side. The albino swung in the saddle and brought his sword hurtling down to slice into the dog's skull and spill brains and blood on the wet and gleaming ground. Still somehow alive, the dog snapped feebly at Elric, but the Melnibonéan ignored its futile attack and turned his attention to the little man who had dispensed with one of his adversaries, but was having difficulty with the second. The dog had grasped the saber with its beak, gripping the sword near the hilt.

Talons raked towards the little man's throat as he strove to shake the dog's grip. Elric charged forward, his runesword aimed like a lance to where the devil-dog dangled in mid-air, its talons slashing, trying to reach the flesh of its former quarry. Stormbringer caught the beast in its lower abdomen and ripped upwards, slitting the thing's underparts from crutch to throat. It released its hold on the small man's saber and fell writhing to the ground. Elric's horse trampled it into the rocky ground. Breathing heavily, the albino sheathed Stormbringer and warily regarded the man he had saved. He disliked unnecessary contact with anyone and did not wish to be embarrassed by a display of emotion on the little man's part.

He was not disappointed, for the wide, ugly mouth split into a cheerful grin and the man bowed in the saddle as he returned his own curved blade to its scabbard.

"Thanks, good sir," he said lightly. "Without your help, the battle might have lasted longer. You deprived me of good sport, but you meant well. Moonglum is my name."

"Elric of Melniboné, I," replied the albino, but saw no reaction on the little man's face. This was strange, for the name of Elric was now infamous throughout most of the world. The story of his treachery and the slaying of his cousin Cymoril had been told and elaborated upon in taverns throughout the Young Kingdoms. Much as he hated it, he was used to receiving some indication of recognition from those he met. His albinism was enough to mark him.

Intrigued by Moonglum's ignorance, and feeling strangely drawn towards the cocky little rider, Elric studied him in an effort to discover from what land he came. Moonglum wore no armor and his clothes were of faded blue material, travel-stained and worn. A stout leather belt carried the saber, a dirk and a woolen purse. Upon his feet, Moonglum wore ankle-length boots of cracked leather. His horse-furniture was much used but of obviously good quality. The man himself, seated high in the saddle, was barely more than five feet tall, with legs too long in proportion to the rest of his slight body. His nose was short and uptilted, beneath gray-green eyes, large and innocent-seeming. A mop of vivid red hair fell over his forehead and down his neck, unrestrained. He sat his horse comfortably, still grinning but looking now behind Elric to where Shaarilla rode to join them.

Moonglum bowed elaborately as the girl pulled her horse to a halt. Elric said coldly, "The Lady Shaarilla, Master Moonglum of—"

"Of Elwher," Moonglum supplied. "The mercantile capital of the East—the finest city in the world."

Elric recognized the name. "So you are from Elwher, Master Moonglum. I have heard of the place. A new city, is it not? Some few centuries old. You have ridden far."

"Indeed I have, sir. Without knowledge of the language used in these parts, the journey would have been harder, but luckily the slave who inspired me with tales of his homeland taught me the speech thoroughly."

"But why do you travel these parts—have you not heard the legends?" Shaarilla spoke incredulously.

"Those very legends were what brought me hence—and I'd begun to discount them, until those unpleasant pups set upon me. For what reason they decided to give chase, I will not know, for I gave them no cause to take a dislike to me. This is, indeed, a barbarous land."

Elric was uncomfortable. Light talk of the kind which Moonglum seemed to enjoy was contrary to his own brooding nature. But in spite of this, he found that he was liking the man more and more.

It was Moonglum who suggested that they travel together for a while. Shaarilla objected, giving Elric a warning glance, but he ignored it.

"Very well then, friend Moonglum, since three are stronger than two, we'd appreciate your company. We ride towards the mountains." Elric, himself, was feeling in a more cheerful mood.

"And what do you seek there?" Moonglum inquired.

"A secret," Elric said, and his new-found companion was discreet enough to drop the question.

THREE

So they rode, while the rainfall increased and splashed and sang among the rocks with the sky like dull steel above them and the wind crooning a dirge about their ears. Three small figures riding swiftly towards the black mountain barrier which rose over the world like a brooding God. And perhaps it was a God that laughed sometimes as they neared the foothills of the range, or perhaps it was the wind whistling through the dark mystery of canyons and precipices and the tumble of basalt and granite which climbed towards lonely peaks: Thunder clouds formed around those peaks and lightning smashed downwards like a monster finger searching the earth for grubs. Thunder rattled over the range and Shaarilla spoke her thoughts at last to Elric; spoke them as the mountains came in sight.

"Elric—let us go back, I beg you. Forget the Book—there are too many forces working against us. Take heed of the signs, Elric, or we are doomed!"

But Elric was grimly silent, for he had long been aware that the girl was losing her enthusiasm for the quest she had started.

"Elric—please. We will never reach the Book. Elric, turn back!"

She rode beside him, pulling at his garments until impatiently he shrugged himself clear of her grasp and said: "I am intrigued too much to stop now. Either continue to lead the way—or tell me what you know and stay here. You desired to sample the Book's wisdom once—but now a few minor pitfalls on our journey have frightened you. What was it you needed to learn, Shaarilla?"

She did not answer him, but said instead: "And what was it you desired, Elric? Peace, you told me. Well, I warn you, you'll find no peace in those grim mountains—if we reach them at all."

"You have not been frank with me, Shaarilla," Elric said coldly, still looking ahead of him at the black peaks. "You know something of the forces seeking to stop us."

She shrugged. "It matters not—I know little. My father spoke a few vague warnings before he died, that is all."

"What did he say?"

"He said that He who guards the Book would use all his power to stop mankind from using its wisdom."

"What else?"

"Nothing else. But it is enough, now that I see that my father's warning was truly spoken. It was this guardian who killed him, Elric—or one of the guardian's minions. I do not wish to suffer that fate, in spite of what the Book might do for me. I had thought you powerful enough to aid me—but now I doubt it."

"I have protected you so far," Elric said simply. "Now tell me what you seek from the Book?"

"I am too ashamed."

Elric did not press the question, but eventually she spoke softly, almost whispering. "I sought my wings," she said.

"Your wings—you mean the Book might give you a spell so that you could grow wings!" Elric smiled ironically. "And that is why you seek the vessel of the world's mightiest wisdom!"

"If you were thought deformed in your own land—it would seem important enough to you," she shouted defiantly.

Elric turned his face towards her, his crimson-irised eyes burning with a strange emotion. He put a hand to his dead white skin and a crooked smile twisted his lips. "I, too, have felt as you do," he said quietly. That was all he said and Shaarilla dropped behind him again, shamed.

They rode on in silence until Moonglum, who had been riding discreetly ahead, cocked his overlarge skull to one side and suddenly drew rein. Elric joined him. "What is it, Moonglum?"

"I hear horses coming this way," the little man said. "And voices which are disturbingly familiar. More of those devil-dogs, Elric—and this time accompanied by riders!"

Elric, too, heard the sounds, now, and shouted a warning to Shaarilla.

"Perhaps you were right," he called. "More trouble comes towards us."

"What now?" Moonglum said, frowning.

"Ride for the mountains," Elric replied, "and we may yet outdistance them."

They spurred their steeds into a fast gallop and sped towards the hills.

But their flight was hopeless. Soon a black pack was visible on the horizon and the sharp birdlike baying of the devil-dogs-drew nearer. Elric stared backward at their pursuers. Night was beginning to fall, and visibility was decreasing with every passing moment but he had a vague impression of the riders who raced behind the pack. They were swathed in dark cloaks and carried long spears. Their faces were invisible, lost in the shadow of the hoods which covered their heads.

Now Elric and his companions were forcing their horses up a steep incline, seeking the shelter of the rocks which lay above.

"We'll halt here," Elric ordered, "and try to hold them off. In the open they could easily surround us."

Moonglum nodded affirmatively, agreeing with the good sense contained in Elric's words. They pulled their sweating steeds to a standstill and prepared to join battle with the howling pack and their darkcloaked masters.

Soon the first of the devil-dogs were rushing up the incline, their beak-jaws slavering and their talons rattling on stone. Standing between two rocks, blocking the way between with their bodies, Elric and Moonglum met the first attack and quickly dis-patched three of the animals. Several more took the place of the dead and the first of the riders was visible behind them as night crept closer.

"Arioch!" swore Elric, suddenly recognizing the riders. "These are the Lords of Dharzi—dead these ten centuries. We're fighting dead men, Moonglum, and the too-tangible ghosts of their dogs. Unless I can think of a sorcerous means to defeat them, we're doomed!"

The zombie-men appeared to have no intention of taking part in the attack for the moment. They waited, their dead eyes eerily luminous, as the devil-dogs attempted to break through the swinging network of steel with which Elric and his companion defended themselves. Elric was racking his brains—trying to dredge a spoken spell from his memory which would dismiss these living dead. Then it came to him, and hoping that the forces he had to invoke would decide to aid him, he began to chant:

"Let the Laws which govern all things
Not so lightly be dismissed;
Let the Ones who flaunt the Earth Kings
With a fresher death be kissed."

Nothing happened. "I've failed." Elric muttered hopelessly as he met the attack of a snapping devil-dog and spitted the thing on his sword. But then—the ground rocked and seemed to seethe beneath the feet of the horses upon whose backs the dead men sat. The tremor lasted a few seconds and then subsided.

"The spell was not powerful enough," Elric sighed.

The earth trembled again and small craters formed in the ground of the hillside upon which the dead Lords of Dharzi impassively waited. Stones crumbled and the horses stamped nervously. Then the earth rumbled.

"Back!" yelled Elric warningly. "Back—or we'll go with them!" They retreated—backing towards Shaarilla and their waiting horses as the ground sagged beneath their feet. The Dharzi mounts were rearing and snorting and the remaining dogs turned nervously to regard their masters with puzzled, uncertain eyes. A low moan was coming from the lips of the living dead. Suddenly, a whole area of the surrounding hillside split into cracks, and yawning crannies appeared in the surface. Elric and his companions swung themselves on to their horse, as, with a frightful multi-voiced scream, the dead Lords were swallowed by the earth, returning to the depths from which they had been summoned.

A deep unholy chuckle arose from the shattered pit. It was the mocking laughter of the Earth Kings taking their rightful prey back into their keeping. Whining, the devil-dogs slunk towards the edge of the pit, sniffing around it. Then, with one accord, the black pack hurled itself down into the chasm, following its masters to whatever cold doom awaited them.

Moonglum shuddered. "You are on familiar terms with the strangest people, friend Elric," he said shakily and turned his horse towards the mountains again.

They reached the black mountains on the following day and nervously Shaarilla led them along the rocky route she had memorized. She no longer pleaded with Elric to return—she was resigned to whatever fate awaited them. Elric's obsession was burning within him and he was filled with impatience—certain that he would find, at last, the ultimate truth of existence in the Dead Gods' Book. Moonglum was cheerfully skeptical, while Shaarilla was consumed with foreboding.

Rain still fell and the storm growled and crackled above them. But, as the driving rainfall increased with fresh insistence, they came, at last, to the black, gaping mouth of a huge cave.

"I can lead you no further," Shaarilla said wearily. "The Book lies somewhere beyond, the entrance to this cave."

Elric and Moonglum looked uncertainly at one another, neither of them sure what move to make next. To have reached their goal seemed somehow anticlimactic—for nothing blocked the cave entrance—and nothing appeared to guard it.

"It is inconceivable," said Elric, "that the dangers which beset us were not engineered by something, yet here we are—and no one seeks to stop us entering. Are you sure that this is the *right* cave, Shaarilla?"

The girl pointed upwards to the rock above the entrance. Engraved in it was a curious symbol which Elric instantly recognized.

"The sign of Chaos!" Elric exclaimed. "Perhaps I should have guessed."

"What does it mean, Elric?" Moonglum asked.

"That is the symbol of everlasting disruption and anarchy," Elric told him. "We are standing in territory presided over by the Lords of Entropy or one of their minions. So that is who our enemy is! This can only mean one thing—the Book is of extreme importance to the order of things on this plane—possibly all the myriad planes of the universe. It was why Arioch was reluctant to aid me—he, too, is a Lord of Chaos!"

Moonglum stared at him in puzzlement. "What do you mean, Elric?"

"Know you not that two forces govern the world-fighting an eternal battle?" Elric replied: "Law and Chaos. The upholders of Chaos state that in such a world as they rule, all things are possible. Opponents of Chaos—those who ally themselves with the forces of Law—say that without Law *nothing* material is possible.

"Some stand apart, believing that a balance between the two is the proper state of things, but we cannot. We have become embroiled in a dispute between the two forces. The Book is valuable to either faction, obviously, and I could guess that the minions of Entropy are worried what power we might release if we obtain this Book. Law and Chaos rarely interfere directly in Men's lives—that is why we have not been fully aware of their presence. Now perhaps, I will discover at last the answer to the one question which concerns me—does an ultimate force rule over the opposing factions of Law and Chaos?"

Elric stepped through the cave entrance, peering into the gloom while the others hesitantly followed him.

"The cave stretches back a long way. All we can do is press on until we find its far wall," Elric said.

"Let's hope that its far wall lies not *downwards*," Moonglum said ironically as he motioned Elric to lead on.

They stumbled forward as the cave grew darker and darker. Their voices were magnified and hollow to their own ears as the floor of the cave slanted sharply down.

"This is no cave," Elric whispered, "it's a *tunnel*—but I cannot guess where it leads."

◆ ◆ ◆

For several hours they pressed onwards in pitch darkness, clinging to one another as they reeled forward, uncertain of their footing and still aware that they were moving down a gradual incline. They lost all sense of time and Elric began to feel as if he were living through a dream. Events seemed to have become so unpredictable and beyond his control that he could no longer cope with thinking about them in ordinary terms. The tunnel was long and dark and wide and cold. It offered no comfort and the floor eventually became the only thing which had any reality. It was firmly beneath his feet. He began to feel that possibly he was not moving—that the floor, after all, was moving and he was remaining stationary. His companions clung to him but he was not aware of them. He was lost and his brain was numb. Sometimes he swayed and felt that he was on the edge of a precipice. Sometimes he fell and his groaning body met hard stone, disproving the proximity of the gulf down which he half-expected to fall.

All the while he made his legs perform walking motions, even though he was not at all sure whether he was actually moving forward. And time meant nothing—became a meaningless concept with relation to nothing.

Until, at last, he was aware of a faint, blue glow ahead of him and he knew that he had been moving forward. He began to run down the incline, but found that he was going too fast and had to check his speed. There was a scent of alien strangeness in the cool air of the cave tunnel and fear was a fluid force which surged over him, something separate from himself.

The others obviously felt it, too, for though they said nothing, Elric could sense it. Slowly they moved downward, drawn like automatons towards the pale blue glow below them.

And then they were out of the tunnel, staring awestruck at the unearthly vision which confronted them. Above them, the very air seemed of the strange blue color which had originally attracted them. They were standing on a jutting slab of rock and, although it was still somehow *dark*, the eerie blue glow illuminated a stretch of glinting silver beach beneath them. And the beach was lapped by a surging dark sea which moved restlessly like a liquid giant in disturbed slumber. Scattered along the silver beach were the dim shapes of wrecks—the bones of peculiarly designed boats, each of a different pattern from the rest. The sea surged away into darkness and there was no horizon—only blackness. Behind them, they could see a sheer cliff which was also lost in darkness beyond a certain point. And it was cold—bitterly cold, with an unbelievable sharpness. For though the sea threshed beneath them, there was no dampness in the air—no smell of salt. It was a bleak and awesome sight and, apart from the sea, they were the only things that moved—the only things to make sound, for the sea was horribly silent in its restless movement.

"What now, Elric?" whispered Moonglum, shivering.

Elric shook his head and they continued to stand there for a long time until the albino—his white face and hands ghastly in the alien light said: "Since it is impracticable to return—we shall venture over the sea" His voice was hollow and he spoke as one who was unaware of his words.

Steps, cut into the living rock, led down towards the beach and now Elric began to descend them. The others allowed him to lead them staring around them, their eyes lit by a terrible fascination.

Four

Their feet profaned the silence as they reached the silver beach of crystalline stones and crunched across it. Elric's crimson eyes fixed upon one of the objects littering the beach and he smiled. He shook his head savagely from side to side, as if to clear it. Trembling, he pointed to one of the boats, and the pair saw that it was intact, unlike the others. It was yellow and red—vulgarly gay in this environment and nearing it they observed that it was made of wood, yet unlike any wood they had seen.

Moonglum ran his stubby fingers along its length. "Hard as iron," he breathed. "No wonder it has not rotted as the others have." He peered inside and shuddered. "Well the owner won't argue if we take it," he said wryly.

Elric and Shaarilla understood him when they saw the unnaturally twisted skeleton which lay at the bottom of the boat. Elric reached inside and pulled the thing out, hurling it on to the stones. It rattled and rolled over the gleaming shingle, disintegrating as it did so, scattering bones over a wide area. The skull came to rest by the edge of the beach, seeming to stare sightlessly out over the disturbing ocean.

As Elric and Moonglum strove to push and pull the boat down the beach towards the sea, Shaarilla moved ahead of them and squatted down, putting her hand into the wetness. She stood up sharply, shaking the stuff from her hand.

"This is not water as I know it," she said. They heard her, but said nothing.

"We'll need a sail," Elric murmured. The cold breeze was moving out over the ocean. "A cloak should serve." He stripped off his cloak and knotted it to the mast of the vessel. "Two of us will have to hold this at either edge," he said. "That way we'll have some slight control over the direction the boat takes. It's makeshift—but the best we can manage."

They shoved off, taking care not to get their feet in the sea.

The wind caught the sail and pushed the boat out over the ocean; moving at a faster pace than Elric had at first reckoned. The boat began to hurtle forward as if possessed of its own volition and Elric's and Moonglum's muscles ached as they clung to the bottom ends of the sail.

Soon the silver beach was out of sight and they could see little—he pale blue light above them scarcely penetrating the blackness. It was then that they heard the dry flap of wings over their heads and looked up.

Silently descending were three massive ape-like creatures, borne on great leathery wings. Shaarilla recognized them and gasped.

"Clakars!"

Moonglum shrugged as he hurriedly drew his sword—"A name only—what are they?" But he received no answer for the leading winged ape descended with a rush, mouthing and gibbering, showing long fangs in a slavering snout. Moonglum dropped his portion of the sail and slashed at the beast but it veered away, its huge wings beating, and sailed upwards again.

Elric unsheathed Stormbringer—and was astounded. The blade remained silent, its familiar howl of glee muted. The blade shuddered in his hand and instead of the rush of power which usually flowed up his arm, he felt only a slight tingling. He was panic-stricken for a moment—without the sword, he would soon lose all vitality. Grimly fighting down his fear, he used the sword to protect himself from the rushing attack of one of the winged apes.

The ape gripped the blade, bowling Elric over, but it yelled in pain as the blade cut through one knotted hand, severing fingers which lay twitching and bloody on the narrow deck. Elric gripped the side of the boat and hauled himself upright once more. Shrilling its agony, the winged ape attacked again, but this time with more caution. Elric summoned all his strength and swung the heavy sword in a two-handed grip, ripping off one of the leathery wings so that the mutilated beast flopped about the deck. Judging the place where its heart should be, Elric drove the blade in under the breastbone. The ape's movements subsided.

Moonglum was lashing wildly at two of the winged apes which were attacking him from both sides. He was down on one knee, vainly hacking at random. He had opened up the whole side of a beast's head but, though in pain, it still came at him. Elric hurled Stormbringer through the darkness and it struck the wounded beast in the throat, point first. The ape clutched with clawing fingers at the steel and fell overboard. Its corpse floated on the liquid but slowly began to sink. Elric grabbed with frantic fingers at the hilt of his sword, reaching far over the side of the boat. Incredibly, the blade was sinking with the beast. Knowing Stormbringer's properties as he did, Elric was amazed—once when he had hurled the runesword into the ocean, it had refused to sink. Now it was being dragged beneath the surface as any ordinary blade would be dragged. He gripped the hilt and hauled the sword out of the winged ape's carcass.

His strength was seeping swiftly from him. It was incredible. What alien laws governed this cavern world? He could not guess—and all he was concerned with was regaining his waning strength. Without the runesword's power, this was impossible!

Moonglum's curved blade had disemboweled the remaining beast and the little man was busily tossing the dead thing over the side. He turned, grinning triumphantly, to Elric.

"A good fight," he said.

Elric shook his head. "We must cross this sea speedily," he replied, "else we're lost—finished. My power is gone."

"How? Why?"

"I know not—unless the forces of Entropy rule more strongly here. Make haste—there is no time for speculation."

Moonglum's eyes were disturbed. He could do nothing but act as Elric said.

Elric was trembling in his weakness, holding the billowing sail with draining strength. Shaarilla moved to help him, her thin hands close to his, her deep-set eyes bright with sympathy.

"What *were* those things?" Moonglum gasped, his teeth naked and white beneath his back-drawn lips, his breath coming short.

"Clakars," Shaarilla replied. "They are the primeval ancestors of my people, older in origin than recorded time. My people are thought the oldest inhabitants of this planet."

"Whoever seeks to stop us in this quest of yours had best find some original means." Moonglum grinned. "The old methods don't work." But the other two did not smile, for Elric was half fainting and the woman was concerned only with his plight. Moonglum shrugged, staring ahead.

When he spoke again, sometime later, his voice was excited. "We're nearing land!"

Land it was, and they were traveling fast towards it. Too fast. Elric heaved himself uptight and spoke heavily and with difficulty. "Drop the sail!" Moonglum obeyed him. The boat sped on, struck another stretch of silver beach and ground up it, the prow plowing a dark scar through the glinting shingle. It stopped suddenly, tilting violently to one side so that the three were tumbled against the boat's rail.

Shaarilla and Moonglum pulled themselves upright and dragged the limp and nerveless albino onto the beach. Carrying him between them, they struggled up the beach until the crystalline shingle gave way to thick, fluffy moss, padding their footfalls. They laid the albino down and stared at him worriedly, uncertain of their next actions.

Elric strained to rise, but was unable to do so. "Give me time," he gasped. "I won't die—but already my eyesight is fading. I can only hope that the blade's power will return on dry land."

With a mighty effort, he pulled Stormbringer from its scabbard and he smiled in relief as the evil runesword moaned faintly and then, slowly, its song increased in power as black flame flickered along its length.

Already the power was flowing into Elric's body, giving him renewed vitality. But even as strength returned, Elric's crimson eyes flared with terrible misery.

"Without this black blade," he groaned, "I am nothing, as you see. But what is it making of me? Am I to be bound to it for ever?"

The others did not answer him and they were both moved by an emotion they could not define—an emotion blended of fear, hate and pity-linked with something else . . .

Eventually, Elric rose, trembling, and silently led them up the mossy hillside towards a more natural light which filtered from above. They could see that it came from a wide chimney, leading apparently to the upper air. By means of the light, they could soon make out a dark, irregular shape which towered in the shadow of the gap.

As they neared the shape, they saw that it was a castle of black stone—a sprawling pile covered with dark green crawling lichen which curled over its ancient bulk with an almost sentient protectiveness. Towers appeared to spring at random from it and it covered a vast area. There seemed to be no windows in any part of it and the only orifice was a rearing doorway blocked by thick bars of a metal which glowed with dull redness, but without heat. Above this gate, in flaring amber, was the sign of the Lords of Entropy, representing eight arrows radiating from a central hub in all directions. It appeared to hang in the air without touching the black, lichen-covered stone.

"I think our quest ends here," Elric said grimly. "Here, or nowhere."

"Before I go further, Elric, I'd like to know what it is you seek," Moonglum murmured. "I think I've earned the right."

"A book," Elric said carelessly. "The Dead Gods' Book. It lies within those castle walls—of that I certain. We have reached the end of our journey."

Moonglum shrugged. "I might not have asked," he smiled, "for all your words mean to me. I hope that I will be allowed some small share of whatever treasure it represents."

Elric ginned, in spite of the coldness which gripped his bowels, but he did not answer Moonglum "We need to enter the castle, first," he said instead.

As if the gates had heard him, the metal bars flared to a pale green and then their glow faded back to red and finally dulled into non-existence. The en-trance was unbarred and their way apparently clear.

"I like not *that*," growled Moonglum. "Too easy. A trap awaits us—are we to spring it at the pleasure of whoever dwells within the castle confines?"

"What else can we do?" Elric spoke quietly.

"Go back—or forward. Avoid the castle—do not tempt He who guards the Book!" Shaarilla was gripping the albino's right arm, her whole face moving with fear, her eyes pleading. "Forget the Book, Elric!"

"Now?" Elric laughed humorlessly. "Now—after this journey? No, Shaarilla, not when the truth is so close. Better to die than never to have tried to secure the wisdom in the Book when it lies so near."

Shaarilla's clutching fingers relaxed their grip and her shoulders slumped in hopelessness. "We cannot do battle with the minions of Entropy . . . "

"Perhaps we will not have to." Elric did not believe his own words but his mouth was twisted with some dark emotion, intense and terrible.

Moonglum glanced at Shaarilla. "Shaarilla is right," he said with conviction. "You'll find nothing but bitterness, possibly death, inside those castle walls. Let us, instead, climb yonder steps and attempt to reach the surface." He pointed to some twisting steps which led towards the yawning rent in the cavern roof.

Elric shook his head. "No. You go if you like."

Moonglum grimaced in perplexity. "You're a stubborn one, friend Elric. Well, if it's all or nothing—then I'm with you. But personally, I have always preferred compromise."

Elric began to walk slowly forward towards the dark entrance of the bleak and towering castle. In a wide, shadowy courtyard a tall figure, wreathed in scarlet fire, stood awaiting them.

Elric marched on, passing the gateway. Moonglum and Shaarilla nervously followed.

Gusty laughter roared from the mouth of the giant and the scarlet fire fluttered about him. He was naked and unarmed, but the power which flowed from him almost forced the three back. His skin was scaly and of smoky purple coloring. His massive body was alive with rippling muscle as he rested lightly on the balls of his feet. His skull was long, slanting sharply backwards at the forehead and his eyes were like slivers of blue steel, showing no pupil. His whole body shook with mighty, malicious joy.

"Greetings to you, Lord Elric of Melniboné—I congratulate you for your remarkable tenacity!"

"Who are you?" Elric growled, his hand on his sword.

"My name is Orunlu the Keeper and this is a stronghold of the Lords of Entropy." The giant smiled cynically. *"You need not finger your puny blade so nervously, for you should know that I cannot harm you now. I gained power to remain in your realm only by making that vow."*

Elric's voice betrayed his mounting excitement. "You cannot stop us?"

"I do not dare to—since my oblique efforts have failed. But your foolish endeavors perplex me somewhat, I'll admit. The Book is of importance to us—but what can it mean to you? I have guarded it for three hundred centuries and have never been curious enough to seek to discover why my Masters place so much importance upon it—why they bothered to rescue it on its sunward course and incarcerate it on this boring ball of earth populated by the capering, briefly lived clowns called Men."

"I seek in it the Truth," Elric said guardedly.

"*There is no Truth but that of Eternal struggle,*" the scarlet-flamed giant said with conviction.

"What rules above the forces of Law and Chaos?" Elric asked. "What controls your destinies as it controls mine?"

The giant frowned. *"That question, I cannot answer. I do not know. There is only the Balance."*

"Then perhaps the Book will tell us who holds it." Elric said purposefully. "Let me pass—tell me where it lies."

The giant moved back, smiling ironically. "It lies in a small chamber in the central tower. I have sworn never to venture there, otherwise I might even lead the way. Go if you like—my duty is over."

Elric, Moonglum, and Shaarilla stepped towards the entrance of the castle, but before they entered, the giant spoke warningly from behind them.

"I have been told that the knowledge contained in the Book could swing the Balance on the side of the forces of Law. This disturbs me—but, it appears, there is another possibility which disturbs me even more."

"What is that?" Elric said.

"It could create such a tremendous impact on the multiverse that complete entropy would result. My Masters do not desire that, for it could mean the destruction of all matter in the end. We exist only to fight—not to win, but to preserve the Eternal struggle."

"I care not," Elric told him. "I have little to lose, Orunlu the Keeper."

"Then go."

The giant strode across the courtyard into blackness.

Inside the tower, light of a pale quality illuminated winding steps leading upwards. Elric began to climb them in silence, moved by his own doom-filled purpose. Hesitantly, Moonglum and Shaarilla followed in his path, their faces set in hopeless acceptance.

On and upward the steps mounted, twisting tortuously towards their goal, until at last they came to the chamber, full of blinding light, many-colored and scintillating, which did not penetrate outwards at all but remained confined to the room which housed it.

Blinking, shielding his red eyes with his arm, Elric pressed forward and, through slitted pupils saw the source of the light lying on a small stone dais in the center of the room.

Equally troubled by the bright light, Shaarilla and Moonglum followed him into the room and stood in awe at what they saw.

It was a huge book—the Dead Gods' Book, its covers encrusted with alien gems from which the light sprang. It gleamed, it throbbed with light and brilliant color.

"At last," Elric breathed, "At last—the Truth!" He stumbled forward like a man made stupid with drink, his pale hands reaching for the thing he had sought with such savage bitterness. His hands touched the pulsating cover of the Book and, trembling, turned it back.

"Now, I shall learn," he said, half-gloatingly. With a crash, the cover fell to the floor, sending the bright gems skipping and dancing over the paving stones.

Beneath Elric's twitching hands lay nothing but a pile of yellowish dust.

"No!" His scream was anguished, unbelieving. "No!" Tears flowed down his contorted face as he ran his hands through the fine dust. With a groan which racked his whole being, he fell forward, his face hitting the disintegrated parchment, Time had destroyed the Book—untouched, possibly forgotten, for three hundred centuries. Even the wise and powerful Gods who had created it had perished—and now its knowledge followed them into oblivion.

They stood on the slopes of the high mountain, staring down into the green valleys below them. The sun shone and the sky was clear and blue. Behind them lay the gaping hole which led into the stronghold of the Lords of Entropy.

Elric looked with sad eyes across the world and his head was lowered beneath a weight of weariness and dark despair. He had not spoken since his companions had dragged him sobbing from the chamber of the Book. Now he raised his pale face and spoke in a voice tinged with self-mockery, sharp with bitterness—a lonely voice: the calling of hungry seabirds circling cold skies above bleak shores. "Now," he said, "I will live my life without ever knowing why I live it—whether it has purpose or not. Perhaps the Book could have told me. But would I have believed it, even then? I am the eternal skeptic—never sure that my actions are my own; never certain that an ultimate entity is not guiding me.

"I envy those who know. All I can do now is to continue my quest and hope, without hope, that before my span is ended, the truth will be presented to me."

Shaarilla took his limp hands in hers and her eyes were wet.

"Elric—let me comfort you."

The albino sneered bitterly. "Would that we'd never met, Shaarilla of the Dancing Mist. For a while, you gave me hope—I had thought to be at last at peace with myself. But, because of you, I am left more hopeless than before. There is no salvation in this world—only malevolent doom. Goodbye." He took his hands away from her grasp and set off down the mountainside.

Moonglum darted a glance at Shaarilla and then at Elric. He took something from his purse and put it in the girl's hand.

"Good luck," he said, and then he was running after Elric until he caught him up.

Still striding, Elric turned at Moonglum's approach and, despite his brooding misery said: "What is it, friend Moonglum? Why do you follow me?"

"I've followed you thus far, Master Elric, and I see no reason to stop," grinned the little man. "Besides, unlike yourself, I'm a materialist. We'll need to eat, you know."

Elric frowned, feeling a warmth growing within him. "What do you mean, Moonglum?"

Moonglum chuckled. "I take advantage of situations of any kind, where I may," he answered. He reached into his purse and displayed something on his outstretched hand which shone with a dazzling brilliancy. It was one of the jewels from the cover of the Book. "There are more in my purse," he said, "And each one worth a fortune." He took Elric's arm. "Come, Elric—what new lands shall we visit so that we may change these baubles into wine and pleasant company?"

Behind them, standing stock still on the hillside, Shaarilla stared miserably after them until they were no longer visible. The jewel Moonglum had given her dropped from her fingers and fell, bouncing and bright, until it was lost amongst the heather. Then she turned—and the dark mouth of the cavern yawned before her.

⚔

Normalizing & Annealing

During the 1970s, the marketing terms "high fantasy" and "heroic fantasy" were often applied to S&S fiction, but by any name it was the dawning of a second golden age for sword-and-sorcery fiction. There were opportunities for novels and venues for short fiction. Tanith Lee—who became an extremely prolific author in several genres—was published in both long and short forms. Her first novel for adults, The Birthgrave *(1975), was S&S of a new kind. As David Forbes has written:*

> *It is a Sword and Sorcery epic, thunderously bloody and sensual . . . Yet it is also a deeper story of character and identity: a feminist work of a piece with the questions sweeping through its time. . . . It was innovative for Lee to turn the focus of the story not just on a woman . . . but on one who, by the end, is well on her way to becoming the sort of secret-clad sorceress that usually plays the villain's part.*

Lee also wrote shorter sword-and-sorcery stories. In 1979 and 1980 she wrote six short stories about Cyrion, a mysterious swordsman, that were published in various anthologies and magazines. In 1982 they were collected—along with new material—in Cyrion. *James Lecky sums up the collection and character in a 2009 review:*

> *Tanith Lee's stories of the mysterious swordsman Cyrion are as entertaining as they come . . . . Angelically handsome, devilishly clever, and with a past shrouded in mystery, Cyrion could be likened to a quasi-medieval James Bond or, perhaps more accurately, like a medieval cross between James Bond and Sherlock Holmes. Never stuck for a solution to a problem, no matter how thorny or potentially fatal. Cyrion takes it all in his cool, handsome stride. . . . there is no threat he cannot meet and no enemy he cannot conquer.*

A HERO AT THE GATES

Tanith Lee

The city lay in the midst of the desert.

At the onset it could resemble a mirage; next, one of the giant mesas that were the teeth of the desert, filmy blue with distance and heat. But Cyrion had found the road which led to the city, and taking the road, presently the outline of the place came clear. High walls and higher towers within, high gates of hammered bronze. And above, the high and naked desert sky that reflected back from its sounding-bowl no sound at all from the city, and no smoke.

Cyrion stood and regarded the city. He was tempted to believe it a desert too, one of those hulks of men's making, abandoned centuries ago as the sands of the waste crept to their threshold. Certainly, the city was old. Yet it had no aspect of neglect, none of the indefinable melancholy of the unlived-in house.

Intuitively, Cyrion knew that as he stood regarding the city from without, so others stood noiselessly within, regarding Cyrion.

What did they perceive? This: a young man, tall and deceptively slim, deceptively elegant, which elegance itself was something of a surprise, for he had been months traveling in the desert, on the caravan routes and the rare and sand-blown roads. He wore the loose dark clothing of a nomad, but with the generous hood thrust back to show he did not have a nomad's pigmentation. At his side a sword was sheathed in red leather. The sunlight struck a silver-gold burnish on the pommel of the sword that was also the color of his hair. His left hand was mailed in rings which apparently no bandit had been able to relieve him of. If the watchers in the city had remarked that Cyrion was as handsome as the Arch-Demon himself, they would not have been the first to do so.

Then there came the booming scraping thunder of two bronze gates unbarred and dragged inward on their runners. The way into the city was exposed—yet blocked now by a crowd. Silent they were, and clad in black, the men and the women; even the children. And their faces were all the same, and gazed at Cyrion in the same way. They gazed at him as if he were the last bright day of their lives, the last bright coin in the otherwise empty coffer.

The sense of his dynamic importance to them was so strong that Cyrion swept the crowd a low, half-mocking bow. As he swept the bow, from his keen eyes' corner, Cyrion saw a man walk through the crowd and come out of the gate.

The man was as tall as Cyrion. He had a hard face, tanned but sallow, wings of black hair beneath a shaved crown, and a collar of swarthy gold set with gems. But his gaze also clung on Cyrion. It was like a lover's look. Or the starving lion's as it beholds the deer.

"Sir," said the black-haired man, "what brings you to this, our city?"

Cyrion gestured lazily with the ringed left hand. "The nomads have a saying: 'After a month in the desert, even a dead tree is an object of wonder.' "

"Only curiosity, then," said the man.

"Curiosity; hunger, thirst, loneliness, exhaustion," enlarged Cyrion. By looking at Cyrion, few would think him affected by any of these things.

"Food we will give you, drink and rest. Our story we may not give. To satisfy the curious is not our fate. Our fate is darker and more savage. We await a savior. We await him in bondage."

"When is he due?" Cyrion inquired.

"You, perhaps, are he."

"Am I? You flatter me. I have been called many things, never savior."

"Sir," said the black-haired man, "do not jest at the wretched trouble of this city, nor at its solitary hope."

"No jest," said Cyrion, "but I hazard you wish some service of me. Saviors are required to labor, I believe, in behalf of their people. What do you want? Let us get it straight."

"Sir," said the man, "I am Memled, prince of this city."

"Prince, but not savior?" interjected Cyrion, his eyes widening with the most insulting astonishment.

Memled lowered his gaze. "If you seek to shame me with that, it is your right. But you should know, I am prevented by circumstance."

"Oh, indeed. Naturally."

"I bear your gibe without complaint. I ask again if you will act for the city."

"And I ask you again what I must do."

Memled raised his lids and directed his glance at Cyrion once more.

"We are in the thrall of a monster, a demon-beast. It dwells in the caverns beneath the city, but at night it roves at will. It demands the flesh of our men to eat; it drinks the blood of our women and our children. It is protected through ancient magic, by a pact made a hundred years before between the princes of the city (cursed be they!) and the hordes of the Fiend. None born of the city has power to slay the beast. Yet there is a prophecy. A stranger, a hero who ventures to our gates, will have the power."

"And how many heroes," said Cyrion gently, "have you persuaded to an early death with this enterprise, you and your demon-beast?"

"I will not lie to you. Upward of a score. If you turn aside, no one here will speak ill of you. Your prospects of success would be slight, should you set your wits and sword against the beast. And our misery is nothing to you."

Cyrion ran his eyes over the black-clad crowd. The arid faces were all still fixed towards his. The children, like miniature adults, just as arid, immobile, noiseless. If the tale were true, they had learned the lessons of fear and sorrow early, nor would they live long to enjoy their lessoning.

"Other than its dietary habits," Cyrion said, "what can you tell me of your beast?"

Memled shivered. His sallowness increased.

"I can reveal no more. It is a part of the foul sorcery that binds us. We may say nothing to aid you, do nothing to aid you. Only pray for you, if you should decide to pit your skill against the devil."

Cyrion smiled. "You have a cool effrontery, my friend, that is altogether delightful. Inform me then merely of this. If I conquer your beast, what reward is there—other, of course, than the blessing of your people?"

"We have our gold, our silver, our jewels. You may take them all away with you, or whatever you desire. We crave safety, not wealth. Our wealth has not protected us from horror and death."

"I think we have a bargain," said Cyrion. He looked at the children again. "Providing the treasury tallies with your description."

It was noon, and the desert sun poured its merciless light upon the city. Cyrion walked in the company of Prince Memled and his guard—similarly black-clad men, but with weighty blades and daggers at their belts, none, presumably, ever stained by beast-blood. The crowd moved circumspectly in the wake of their prince. Only the rustle of feet shuffling the dust was audible, and no speech. Below the bars of overhanging windows, here and there, a bird cage had been set out in the violet shade. The birds in the cages did not sing.

They reached a marketplace, sun-bleached, unpeopled and without merchandise of any sort. A well at the market's center proclaimed the water which would, in the first instance, have caused the building of a city here. Further evidence of water lay across from the market, where a broad stairway, flanked by stone columns, led to a massive battlemented wall and doors of bronze this time plated by pure flashing gold. Over the wall-top, the royal house showed its peaks and pinnacles, and the heads of palm trees. There was a green perfume in the air, heady as incense in the desert.

The crowd faltered in the marketplace. Memled, and his guard conducted Cyrion up the stairway. The gold-plated doors were opened. They entered a cool palace, blue as an under-sea cave, buzzing with slender fountains, sweet with the scent of sun-scorched flowers.

Black-garmented servants brought chilled wine. The food was poor and did not match the wine. Had the flocks and herds gone to appease the demon-beast? Cyrion had spied not a goat nor a sheep in the city. For that matter, not a dog, nor even the sleek lemon cats and striped marmosets rich women liked to nurse instead of babies.

After the food and drink, Memled, near wordless yet courteous, led Cyrion to a treasury where wealth lay as thick as dust, and spilling on the ground.

"I would have thought," said Cyrion, fastidiously investigating ropes of pearls and chains of rubies, "such stuff might have bought you a hero, had you sent for one."

"This, too, is our limitation. We may not send. He must come to us, by accident."

"As the nomads say," said Cyrion charmingly, innocently. " 'No man knows the wall better than he who built it.' "

At that instant, something thundered in the guts of the world.

It was a fearful bellowing cacophony. It sounded hot with violence and the lust for carnage. It was like a bull, or a pen of bulls, with throats of brass and sinews of molten iron, roaring in concert underground. The floor shook a little. A sapphire tumbled from its heap and fell upon another heap below.

Cyrion seemed interested rather than disturbed.

Certainly, there was nothing more than interest in his voice as he asked Prince Memled: "Can that be your beast, contemplating tonight's dinner?"

Memled's face took on an expression of the most absolute anguish and despair. His mouth writhed. He uttered a sudden sharp cry, as if a dreaded, well-remembered pain had seized him. He shut his eyes.

Intrigued, Cyrion observed: "It is fact then, you cannot speak of it? Calm yourself, my friend. It speaks very ably for itself."

Memled covered his face with his hands, and turned away.

Cyrion walked out through the door. Presently, pallid, but sufficiently composed, Memled followed his hero-guest. Black guards closed the treasury.

"Now," said Cyrion, "since I cannot confront your beast until it emerges from its caverns by night, I propose to sleep. My journey through the desert has been arduous, and, I am sure you agree, freshness in combat is essential."

"Sir," said Memled, "the palace is at your disposal. But, while you sleep, I and some others shall remain at your side."

Smiling, Cyrion assured him, "Indeed, my friend, you and they will not."

"Sir, it is best you are not left alone. Forgive my insistence."

"What danger is there? The beast is no threat till the sun goes down. There are some hours yet."

Memled seemed troubled. He spread his hand, indicating the city beyond the palace walls. "You are a hero, sir. Certain of the people may bribe the guard. They may enter the palace and disrupt your rest with questions and clamor."

"It seemed to me," said Cyrion, "your people are uncommonly quiet. But if not, they are welcome. I sleep deeply. I doubt if anything would wake me till sunset, when I trust you, Prince, or another, will do so."

Memled's face, such an index of moods, momentarily softened with relief. "That deeply do you sleep? Then I will agree to let you sleep alone. Unless, perhaps a girl might be sent to you?"

"You are too kind. However, I decline the girl. I prefer to select my own ladies, after a fight rather than before."

Memled smiled his own stiff and rusty smile. Behind his eyes, sluggish currents of self-dislike, guilt and shame stirred cloudily.

The doors were shut on the sumptuous chamber intended for Cyrion's repose. Aromatics burned in silver bowls. The piercing afternoon sun was excluded behind shutters of painted wood and embroidered draperies. Beyond the shut doors, musicians made sensuous low music on pipes, drums, and ghirzas. All was conducive to slumber. Though not to Cyrian's.

In contrast to his words, he was a light sleeper. In the city of the beast, he had no inclination to sleep at all. Privacy was another case. Having secured the chamber doors on the inside, he prowled soundlessly, measuring the room for its possibilities. He prised open a shutter, and scanned across the blistering roofs of the palace into the dry green palm shade of the gardens.

All about, the city kept its tongueless vigil. Cyrion thoughtfully felt of its tension. It was like a great single heart, poised between one beat and the next. A single heart, or two jaws about to snap together—

"Cyrion," said a voice urgently.

To see him spin about was to discover something of the nature of Cyrion. A nonchalant idler at the window one second, a coiled spring let fly the split second after. The sword was ready in his bare right hand. He had drawn too fast almost for a man's eye to register. Yet he was not even breathing quickly. And, finding the vacant chamber before him, as he had left it, no atom altered in his stance.

"Cyrion," cried the voice again, out of nothing and nowhere. "I pray heaven you had the cunning to lie to them, Cyrion."

Cyrion appeared to relax his exquisite vigilance. He had not.

"Heaven, no doubt, enjoys your prayers," he said. "And am I to enjoy the sight of you?"

The voice was female, expressive, and very beautiful.

"I am in a prison," said the voice. There was the smallest catch in it, swiftly mastered. "I speak to warn you. Do not credit them, Cyrion."

Cyrion began to move about the room. Casually and delicately he lifted aside the draperies with his sword.

"They offered me a girl," he said reflectively.

"But they did not offer you certain death."

Cyrion had completed his circuit of the room. He looked amused and entertained.

He knelt swiftly, then stretched himself flat. A circular piece was missing in the mosaic pattern of the floor. He set one acute eye there and looked through into a dim area, lit by one murky source of light beyond his view. Directly below, a girl lay prone on the darkness which must itself be a floor, staring up at him from luminous wild eyes. In the half-glow she was more like a bloom of light herself than a reality; a trembling crystalline whiteness on the air, hair like the gold chains in the treasury, a face like that of a carved goddess, the body of a beautiful harlot before she gets in the trade—still virgin—and at her waist, her wrists, her ankles, drawn taut to pegs in the ground, iron chains.

"So there you are."

"It is a device of the stonework that enabled you to hear me and I you. In former days, princes would sit in your room above, drinking and making love, listening to the cries of those being tortured in this dungeon, and sometimes they would peer through to increase their pleasure. But either Memled has forgotten, or he thought me past crying out. I glimpsed your shadow pass over the aperture. Earlier, the jailer spoke your name to me. Oh, Cyrion, I am to die, and you with me."

She stopped, and tears ran like drops of silver from her wild eyes.

"You have a captive audience, lady," said Cyrion.

"It is this way," she whispered. "The beast they have pretended to seek rescue from is, in fact, the familiar demon of the city. They love the brute, and commit all forms of beastliness in its name. How else do you suppose they have amassed such stores of treasure, here in the wilderness? And once a year they honor the beast by giving to it a beautiful maiden and a notable warrior. I was to have been the bride of a rich and wise lord in a city by the sea. But I am thought beautiful; Memled heard of me. Men of this city attacked the caravan in which I rode, and carried me here, to this, where I have lingered a month. You arrived by unlucky destiny, unless some of Memled's sorcery enticed you here, unknowingly. Tonight, we shall share each other's fate."

"You are their prisoner, I am not. How do they plan to reconcile me to sacrifice?"

"That is but too simple. At dusk a hundred men will come. You do not seem afraid, but even fearless, before a hundred men you cannot prevail. They will take your sword, stun you, bind you. There is a trick door in the western wall that gives on a stairway. Through the door and down the stair they will thrust you. Below are the caverns where the beast roams, bellowing for blood. I too must pass that way to death."

"A fascinating tale," said Cyrion, "What prompts you to tell it me?"

"Are you not a hero?" the girl demanded passionately. "Have you not promised to slay the beast for them, to be their savior, though admittedly in return for gold. Can you not instead be your own savior, and mine?"

"Forgive me, lady," said Cyrion, in a tone verging subtly on naiveté, "I am at a loss. Besides, our dooms seem written with a firm hand. Perhaps we should accept them."

Cyrion rose from the mosaic. On his feet he halted, just aside from the hole.

After a moment, the girl screamed: "You are a coward, Cyrion. For all your looks and your fine sword, for all your nomad's garments, the wear of those they name the Lions of the Desert—for all that—*coward* and *fool*."

Cyrion seemed to be considering.

After a minute, he said amiably: "I suppose I might open the trick door now, and seek the monster of my own volition, sword in hand and ready. Then, if I slay him, I might return for you, and free you."

The girl wept. Through her tears she said, with a knife for a voice: "If you are a *man*, you will do it."

"Oh no, lady. Only if I am your notion of a man."

The stair was narrow, and by design lightlessly invisible—save that Cyrion had filched one of the scented tapers from the room above to give him eyes. The trick door had been easy to discover, an ornamental knob that turned, a slab that slid. Thirty steps down, he passed another kind of door, of iron, on his right. Faintly, beyond the door, he heard a girl weeping.

The stair descended through the western wall of the palace, and proceeded underground. Deep in the belly of the caverns that sprawled, as yet unseen, at the end of the stair, no ominous rumor was manifested. At length, the stair reached bottom, and ceased. Ahead stretched impenetrable black, and from the black an equally black and featureless silence.

Cyrion advanced, the taper held before him. The dark toyed with the taper, surrendering a miniature oasis of half-seen things, such as trunks of rock soaring up towards the ceiling. The dark mouthed Cyrion. It licked him, rolled him around on its tongue. The lit taper was just a garnish to its palate; it liked the light with Cyrion, as a man might like salt with his meat.

Then there came a huge wind from out of the nothing ahead. A metallic heated blast, as if from a furnace. Cyrion stopped, pondering. The beast, closeted in the caverns, had sighed? An instant after, it roared.

Above, in the treasury, the roaring had seemed to stagger the foundations of the house. Here, it peeled even the darkness, and dissected it like a fruit. The broken pieces of the dark rattled on the trunks of rock. Shards erupted from the rock and rained to the ground. The caverns thrummed, murmured, fell dumb.

The dark did not re-congeal.

There was a new light. A flawless round of light, pale, smoky red. Then it blinked. Then there were two. Two flawless rounds of simmering raw rose. Two eyes. Cyrion dropped the taper and put his heel on it.

This beast you witnessed by its own illumination. It swelled from the black as the eyes brightened with its interest. It was like no other beast; you could liken it to nothing else. It was like itself, unique. Only its size was comparable to anything. To a tower, a wall—one eye alone, that rosy window, could have fit tall Cyrion in its socket.

So radiant now, those eyes, the whole cavern was displayed, the mounting rocks, the floor piled with dusts, the dust curtains floating in the air. From the dust, the beast lifted itself. It gaped its mouth. Cyrion ducked, and the blast of burning though non-incendiary breath rushed over his head. It was not fetid breath, simply very hot. Cyrion planted his sword point down in the dust, and indolently leaned on it. He looked like a marvelous statue. For someone who could move like lightning, he had chosen now to become stone, and the pink fires settled on his pale hair, staining it the color of diluted wine.

In this fashion Cyrion watched the demon-beast, by the light of its vast eyes, slink towards him. He watched, motionless, leaning on his sword.

Then a sinewy taloned forefoot, lengthy as a column, struck at him, and Cyrion was no longer in that spot, motionless, leaning on his sword, as he had been an instant before. Away in the shadow, Cyrion stood again unmoving, sword poised, negligently waiting. Again, the batting of scythe-fringed death; again missing him.

The jaws clashed, and slaver exploded forth, like a waterfall. Cyrion was gone, out of reach. Stone had returned to lightning. The fourth blow was his. He neither laughed at the seriousness of his mission nor frowned. No meditation was needed, the target no challenge, facile . . .

Cyrion swung back his arm, and sent the sword plummeting, like a straight white rent through the cavern. It met the beast's left eye, shattered it like pink glass, plunged to the brain.

Like a cat, Cyrion sprang to a ledge and crouched there.

Black ichor spouted to the cavern's top. Now, once more gradually, the light faded. The thunderous roaring ebbed like a colossal sea withdrawing from these dry caves beneath the desert.

On his ledge, Cyrion waited, pitiless and without triumph, for the beast, in inevitable stages, to fall, to be still, to die.

In the reiterated blackness—blind, but remembering infallibly his way, as he remembered all things, once disclosed—Cyrion went to the demon-beast and plucked out his sword, and returned with it up the pitchy stairway to the iron dungeon door set in the wall.

The iron door was bolted from without. He shot the bolts and pushed open the door.

He paused, just inside the prison, sword in hand, absorbing each detail. A stone box the prison was, described by dull fluttering torches. The girl lay on the floor, pegged and chained as he had regarded her through the peephole. He glanced towards the peephole, which was barely to be seen against the torch murk.

"Cyrion," the girl murmured, "the beast's black blood is on your sword, and you live."

Her white and lovely face was turned to him, the rich strands of golden hair swept across the floor, her silken breasts quivered to the tumult of her heart. Her tears fell again, but now her eyes were yielding. They showed no amazement or inquisition, only love. He went to her, and, raising his sword a second time, chopped the head from her body.

Thirty steps up, a door crashed wide. Cyrion stooped gracefully, straightened, took the thirty steps in a series of fine-flexed leaps. He stepped through the trick door and was in the upper chamber, the sword yet stark in his bare right hand. And in his left hand, mailed with rings, a woman's head held by its shining hair.

Opposite, in the forced doorway of the chamber, Memled stared with a face like yellow cinders.

Then he collapsed on his knees, and behind him, the guards also dropped down.

Memled began to sob. The sobs were rough, racking him. He plainly could not keep them back, and his whole body shuddered.

Cyrion remained where he was, ignoring his bloody itinerary. Finally Memled spoke.

"After an eternity, heaven has heard our lament, replied to our entreaty. You, the hero of the city, after the eternity, our savior. But we were bound by the hell-pact, and could neither warn nor advise you. How did you fathom the truth?"

"And what is the truth?" asked Cyrion, with unbelievable sweetness, as he stood between blotched blade and dripping head.

"The truth—that the monster is illusion set to deceive those heroes who would fight for us, set to deceive by the bitch-sorceress whose head you have lopped.

Year in and out, she has drained us, roaming by night, feasting on the flesh and blood of my people, unrelenting and vile she-wolf that she was. And our fragile chance, a prophecy, the solitary weakness in the hell-pact—that only if a heroic traveler should come to the gates and agree to rid us of our torment, might we see her slain. But always she bewitched and duped these heroes, appearing in illusory shackles, lying that we would sacrifice her, sending each man to slay a phantom beast that did not exist save while her whim permitted it. And then the hero would go to her, trustingly, and she would seize him and murder him too. Over a score of champions we sent to their deaths in this manner, because we were bound and could not direct them where the evil lay. And so, again, sir hero, how did you fathom truth in this sink of witchery?"

"Small things," said Cyrion laconically.

"But you will list them for me?" Memled proffered his face, all wet with tears, and brimming now with a feverish joy.

"Her proximity to me, which seemed unlikely if she were what she claimed. Her extreme beauty which had survived a month's imprisonment and terror, and her wrists and ankles which were unchafed by her chains. That, a stranger to this place, she knew so much of its by-ways and its history. More interesting, that she knew so much of me—besides my name, which I did not see why a jailer should have given her—for instance, that I wore a nomad's garment, and that she thought me presentable, though she could not have seen me herself. She claimed she beheld my shadow pass over the peephole, but no more. She knew all our bargain, too, yours and mine, as if she had been listening to it. Would you hear more?"

"Every iota of it!"

"Then I will cite the beast, which patently was unreal. So huge a voice it could make the floors tremble, and yet the house was still intact. And the creature itself so untiny it could have shaken the city to flour, but confined in a cavern where it had not even stirred the dust. And then, the absence of bones, and its wholesome breath, meant to impress by volume and heat, and which smelled of nothing else. A cat which chews rats will have a fouler odor. And this thing, which supposedly ate men and drank their blood and was big enough to fill the air with stink, clean as a scoured pot on the stove. Lastly, I came above and saw the peephole would show nothing of what went on in this room, let alone a shadow passing. And I noticed too, the lady's sharp teeth, if you like."

Memled got to his feet. Halfway to Cyrion, he checked and turned to the guards.

"Inform the city our terror has ended."

The guards, round-eyed, rushed away.

Memled came to Cyrion, glaring at the head, which Cyrion had prudently set down in a convenient bowl, and which was beginning to crumble to a sort of rank powder.

"We are free of her," Memled cried. "And the treasury is yours to despoil. Take all I have. Take—take this, the royal insignia of the city," and he clutched the collar of swarthy gold at his throat.

"Unnecessary," said Cyrion lightly. He wiped his sword upon a drapery. Memled paid no heed. Cyrion sheathed the sword. Memled smiled, still rusty, but his face vivid with excitement. "The treasury, then," suggested Cyrion.

Cyrion dealt cannily in the treasury. The light of day was gone by now, and by the smooth amber of the lamps, Cyrion chose from among the ropes of jewels and skeins of metal, from the cups and gemmy daggers, the armlets and the armor. Shortly, there was sufficient to weigh down a leather bag, which Cyrion slung upon his back. Memled would have pressed further gifts on him. Cyrion declined.

"As the nomads say," said Cyrion, " 'three donkeys cannot get their heads into the same bucket.' I have enough."

Outside in the city, now ablaze with windows under a sky ablaze with stars, songs and shouting of celebration rose into the cool hollow of the desert night.

"A night without blood and without horror," said Memled.

Cyrion walked down the palace stairway. Memled remained on the stair, his guards scattered loosely about him. In the marketplace a fire burned, and there was dancing. The black clothes were all gone; the women had put on their finery and earrings sparkled and clinked as they danced together. The men drank, eying the women.

Near the edge of the group, two children poised like small stones, dressed in their best, and Cyrion saw their faces.

A child's face, incorrigible calendar of the seasons of the soul. Men learn pretense, if they must. A child has not had the space to learn.

Cyrion hesitated. He turned about, and strolled back towards the steps of the palace, and softly up the steps.

"One last thing, my friend, the prince," he called to Memled.

"What is that?"

Cyrion smiled. "You were too perfect and I did not quite see it, till just now a child showed me." Cyrion swung the bag from his shoulder exactly into Memled's belly. Next second the sword flamed to Cyrion's hand, and Memled's black-winged head hopped down the stair.

Around the fire, the dancers had left off dancing. The guards were transfixed in stammering shock, though no hand flew to a blade. Cyrion wiped his own blade, this time on Memled's already trembling torso.

"That one, too," said Cyrion.

"Yes, sir," said the nearest of the guard, thickly. "There were the two of them."

"And they dined nightly over who should batten on the city, did they not, your prince-demon and his doxy. He could not avoid the prophecy, either, of a hero at the gates. He was obliged to court me, and, in any event, reckoned the lady would deal with me as with the others. But when she did not, he was content I should have killed her, if he could escape me and keep the city for himself to feed him. He rendered himself straightly. He never once uttered for his own demonic side. He acted as a man, as Memled, the prince—fear and joy. He was too good. Yet I should never have been sure but for the children's agonized blankness down there, in the crowd."

"You are undeniably a hero, and heaven will bless you," said the guard. It was easy to see he was a true human man, and the rest of them were human too. Unpredictable and bizarre was their relief at rescue, as with all true men, who do not get their parts by heart beforehand, when to cry or when to grin.

Cyrion laughed low at the glittering sky. "Then bless me, heaven."

He went down the stair again. Both children were howling now, as they had not dared do formerly, untrammeled, healthy. Cyrion opened the leather bag, and released the treasure on the square, for adults and children alike to play with.

Empty-handed, as he came, Cyrion went away into the desert, under the stars.

C. J. Cherryh (1942–) is another prolific author who debuted with a sword-and-sorcery novel. Gate of Ivrel *(1976) won her the John W. Campbell Award for Best New Writer in 1977. Three more novels were added to what came to be known as the Morgaine Cycle. Despite protagonist Morgaine's mission to save the entire universe and her travel through time and space, it doesn't always read like science fiction. The other protagonist, Nhi Vanye i Chya, starts out as the exiled bastard son of an aristocrat, a young, untried warrior living in a culture similar to the Japanese shogun period.*

The story included here is from an entirely different SF/fantasy series. "A Thief in Korianth," is an earlier (1981) novelette version of the author's 1985 novel Angel with the Sword. *The story, when expanded, turned into SF. Its setting became a planet that is a backwater cut off from the rest of the thirty-third century human universe—which provided a premise for a singular female hero—Gillian—to be living a far-future but male-dominated hierarchal society in which a girl's puberty makes her an instant target for rape. The novelette, written for a* Flashing Swords *anthology, stays true to fantasy. Gillian is a resourceful, shrewd liar and thief who knows her way around the streets. Her desire for riches stems primarily from a maternal instinct to protect her younger sister*

A THIEF IN KORIANTH

C. J. Cherryh

1

The Yliz river ran through Korianth, a sullen, muddy stream on its way to the nearby sea, with stone banks where it passed through the city . . . gray stone and yellow water, and gaudy ships which made a spider tangle of masts and riggings above the drab jumbled roofs of the dockside. In fact all Korianth was built on pilings and cut with canals more frequent than streets, the whole pattern of the lower town dictated by old islands and channels, so that buildings took whatever turns and bends the canals dictated, huddled against each other, jammed one up under the eaves of the next—faded paint, buildings like ancient crones remembering the brightness of their youths, decayed within from overmuch of wine and living, with dulled, shuttered eyes looking suspiciously on dim streets and scummed canals, where boat vendors and barge folk plied their craft, going to and fro from shabby warehouses. This was the Sink, which was indeed slowly subsiding into the River—but that took centuries, and the Sink used only the day, quick pleasures, momentary feast, customary famine. In spring rains the Yliz rose; tavern keepers mopped and dockmen and warehousers cursed and set merchandise up on blocks; then the town stank considerably. In summer heats the River sank, and the town stank worse.

There was a glittering world above this rhythm, the part of Korianth that had grown up later, inland, and beyond the zone of flood: palaces and town houses of hewn stone (which still sank, being too heavy for their foundations, and developed cracks, and whenever abandoned, decayed quickly). In this area too were temples . . . temples of gods and goddesses and whole pantheons local and foreign, ancient and modern, for Korianth was a trading city and offended no one permanently. The gods were transients, coming and going in favor like dukes and royal lovers. There was, more permanent than gods, a king in Korianth, Seithan XXIV, but Seithan was, if rumors might be believed, quite mad, having recovered after poisoning. At least he showed a certain bizarre turn of behavior, in which he played obscure and cruel jokes and took to strange religions, mostly such as promised sybaritic afterlives and conjured demons.

And central to that zone between, where town and dockside met on the canals, lay a rather pleasant zone of mild decay, of modest townsmen and a few dilapidated palaces. In this web of muddy waterways a grand bazaar transferred the wealth of the Sink (whose dark warrens honest citizens avoided) into higher-priced commerce of the Market of Korianth.

It was a profitable place for merchants, for proselytizing cults, for healers, interpreters of dreams, prostitutes of the better sort (two of the former palaces were brothels, and no few of the temples were), palm readers and sellers of drinks and sweetmeats, silver and fish, of caged birds and slaves, copper pots and amulets and minor sorceries. Even on a chill autumn day such as this, with the stench of hundreds of altars and the spices of the booths and the smokes of midtown, that of the river welled up. Humanity jostled shoulder to shoulder, armored guard against citizen, beggar against priest, and furnished ample opportunity for thieves.

Gillian glanced across that sea of bobbing heads and swirling colors, eased up against the twelve-year-old girl whose slim, dirty fingers had just deceived the fruit merchant and popped a first and a second handful of figs into the torn seam of her cleverly sewn skirt. Gillian pushed her own body into the way of sight and reached to twist her fingers into her sister's curls and jerk. Jensy yielded before the hair came out by the roots, let herself be dragged four paces into the woman-wide blackness of an alley, through which a sickly stream of something threaded between their feet.

"Hsst," Gillian said. "Will you have us on the run for a fistful of sweets? You have no judgment."

Jensy's small face twisted into a grin. "Old Haber-shen's never seen me." Gillian gave her a rap on the ear, not hard. The claim was truth: Jensy was deft. The double-sewn skirt picked up better than figs. "Not here," Gillian said. "Not in *this* market. There's high law here. They cut your hand off, stupid snipe."

Jensy grinned at her; everything slid off Jensy. Gillian gripped her sister by the wrist and jerked her out into the press, walked a few stalls down. It was never good to linger. They did not look the best of customers, she and Jensy, ragged curls bound up in scarves, coarse sacking skirts, blouses that had seen good days—before they had left some goodwoman's laundry. Docksiders did come here, frequent enough in the crowds. And their faces were not known outside the Sink; varying patterns of dirt were a tolerable disguise.

Lean days were at hand; they were not far from winter, when ships would be scant, save only the paltry, patched coasters. In late fall and winter the goods were here in midtown, being hauled out of warehouses and sold at profit. Dockside was slim pickings in winter; dockside was where she preferred to work—given choice. And with Jensy—

Midtown frightened her. This place was daylight and open, and at the moment she was not looking for trouble; rather she made for the corner of the fish market with its peculiar aromas and the perfumed reek of Agdalia's gilt temple and brothel.

"Don't want to," Jensy declared, planting her feel.

Gillian jerked her willy-nilly. "I'm not going to leave you there, mousekin. Not for long."

"I hate Sophonisba."

Gillian stopped short, jerked Jensy about by the shoulder and looked down into the dirty face. Jensy sobered at once, eyes wide. "Sophonisba never lets the customers near you."

Jensy shook her head, and Gillian let out a breath. *She* had started that way; Jensy would not. She dragged Jensy to the door, where Sophonisba held her usual post at the shrine of the tinsel goddess—legitimacy of a sort, more than Sophonisba had been born to. Gillian shoved Jensy into Sophonisba's hands . . . overblown and overpainted, all pastels and perfumes and swelling bosom—it was not lack of charms kept Sophonisba on the market street, by the Fish, but the unfortunate voice, a Sink accent and a nasal whine that would keep her here forever. *Dead ear*, Gillian reckoned of her in some pity, for accents came off and onto Gillian's tongue with polyglot facility; Sophonisba probably did not know her affliction—a creature of patterns, reliable to follow them.

"Not in daylight," Sophonisba complained, painted eyes distressed. "Double cut for daylight. Are you working *here*? I don't want any part of that. Take yourselves elsewhere."

"You know I wouldn't bring the king's men down on Jensy; mind her, old friend, or I'll break your nose."

"Hate you," Jensy muttered, and winced, for Sophonisba gripped her hair. She meant Sophonisba. Gillian gave her a face and walked away, free. The warrens or the market—neither plate was safe for a twelve-year-old female with light fingers and too much self-confidence; Sophonisba could still keep a string on her—and Sophonisba was right to worry: stakes were higher here, in all regards.

Gillian prowled the aisles, shopping customers as well as booths, lingering nowhere long, flowing with the traffic. It was the third winter coming, the third since she had had Jensy under her wing. Neither of them had known hunger often while her mother had been there to care for Jensy—but those days were gone, her mother gone, and Jensy—Jensy was falling into the pattern. Gillian saw it coming. She had nightmares, Jensy in the hands of the city watch, or knifed in some stupid brawl, like their mother. Or something happening to herself, and Jensy growing up in Sophonisba's hands.

Money. A large amount of gold: that was the way out she dreamed of, money that would buy Jensy into some respectable order, to come out polished and fit for midtown or better. But that kind of money did not often flow accessibly on dockside, in the Sink. It had to be hunted here; and she saw it—all about her—at the risk of King's-law, penalties greater than the dockside was likely to inflict: the Sink took care of its own problems, but it was apt to wink at pilferage and it was rarely so inventively cruel as King's-law. Whore she was not, no longer, never again; whore she had been, seeking out Genat, a thief among thieves; and the apprentice had passed the master. Genat had become blind Genat the beggar—dead Genat soon after—and Gillian was free, walking the market where Genat himself seldom dared pilfer.

If she had gold enough, then Jensy was out of the streets, out of the way of things that waited to happen.

Gold enough, and she could get more: gold was power, and she had studied power zealously, from street bravos to priests, listening to gossip, listening to rich folk talk, one with the alleys and the booths—she learned, did Gillian, how rich men stole, and she planned someday—she always had—to be rich.

Only three years of fending for two, and this third year that saw Jensy filling out into more than her own whipcord shape would ever be, *that* promised what Jensy would be the fourth year, when at thirteen she became a mark for any man on the docks—

This winter or never, for Jensy.

Gillian walked until her thin soles burned on the cobbles. She looked at jewelers' booths—too wary, the goldsmiths, who tended to have armed bullies about them. She had once—madly—entertained the idea of approaching a jeweler, proposing her own slight self as a guard: truth, no one on the streets could deceive her sharp eyes, and there would be no pilferage; but say to them, *I am a better thief than they, sirs?*—that was a way to end like Genat.

Mistress to such, instead? There seemed no young and handsome ones—even Genat had been that—and she, moreover, had no taste for more such years. She passed the jewelers, hoping forlornly for some indiscretion.

She hungered by afternoon and thought wistfully of the figs Jensy had fingered; Jensy had them, which meant Jensy would eat them. Gillian was not so rash as in her green years. She would not risk herself for a bit of bread or cheese. She kept prowling, turning down minor opportunities, bumped against a number of promising citizens, but each was a risk, and each deft fingering of their purses showed nothing of great substance.

The hours passed. The better classes began to wend homeward with their bodyguards and bullies. She began to see a few familiar faces on the edges of the crowd, rufflers and whores and such anticipating the night, which was theirs. Merchants with more expensive goods began folding up and withdrawing with their armed guards and their day's profits.

Nothing—no luck at all, and Sophonisba would not accept a cut of bad luck; Gillian had two coppers in her own purse, purloined days ago, and Sophonisba would expect one. It was the streets and no supper if she was not willing to take a risk.

Suddenly a strange face cut the crowd, making haste: that caught her eye, and like the reflex of a boxer, her body tended that way before her mind had quite weighed matters, so she should not lose him. This was a stranger; there was a fashion to faces in Korianth, and this one was not Korianthine—Abhizite, she reckoned, from upriver. Gillian warmed indeed; it was like summer, when gullible foreigners came onto the docks carrying their traveling funds with them and giving easy opportunity to the light-fingered trade.

She bumped him in the press at a corner, anticipating his move to dodge her, and her razor had the purse strings, her fingers at once aware of weight, her heart thudding with the old excitement as she eeled through the crowd and alleyward.

Heavy purse—it was too soon missed; her numbing blow had had short effect. She heard the bawl of outrage, and suddenly a general shriek of alarm. At the bend of the alley she looked back.

Armored men. Bodyguards!

Panic hit her; she clutched the purse and ran the dark alley she had mapped in advance for escape, ran with all her might and slid left, right, right, along a broad back street, down yet another alley. They were after her in the twilight of the maze, cursing and with swords gleaming bare.

It was no ordinary cutpursing. She had tripped something, indeed. She ran until her heart was nigh to bursting, took the desperate chance of a stack of firewood to scamper to a ledge and into the upper levels of the midtown maze.

She watched them then, she lying on her heaving belly and trying not to be heard breathing. They were someone's hired bravos for certain, scarred of countenance, with that touch of the garish that bespoke gutter origins.

"Common cut-purse," one said. That rankled. She had other skills.

"Someone has to have seen her," said another. "Money will talk, in the Sink." They went away. Gillian lay still, panting, opened the purse with trembling fingers. A lead cylinder stamped with a seal; lead, and a finger-long sealed parchment, and a paltry three silver coins.

Bile welled up in her throat. They had sworn to search for her even into the impenetrable Sink. She had stolen something terrible; she had ruined herself; and even the Sink could not hide her, not against money, and such men.

Jensy, she thought, sick at heart. If passersby had seen her strolling there earlier and described Jensy—their memories would be very keen, for gold. The marks on the loot were ducal seals, surely; lesser men did not use such things. Her breath shuddered through her throat. Kings and dukes. She had stolen lead and paper, and her death. She could not read, not a word—not even to know *what* she had in hand.

—and Jensy!

She swept the contents back into the purse, thrust it into her blouse and, dropping down again into the alley, ran.

2

The tinsel shrine was closed. Gillian's heart sank, and her vision blurred. Again to the alleys and behind, thence to a lower-story window with a red shutter. She reached up and rapped it a certain pattern with her knuckles.

It opened. Sophonisba's painted face stared down at her; a torrent of abuse poured sewer-fashion from the dewy lips, and Jensy's dirty-scarfed head bobbed up from below the whore's ample bosom.

"Come *on*," Gillian said, and Jensy scrambled, grimaced in pain, for Sophonisba had her by the hair.

"My cut," Sophonisba said.

Gillian swallowed air, her ears alert for pursuit. She fished the two coppers from her purse, and Sophonisba spat on them. Heat flushed Gillian's face; the next thing in her hand was her razor.

Sophonisba paled and sniffed. "I know you got better, slink. The whole street's roused. Should I take such risks? If someone comes asking here, should I say lies?"

Trembling, blind with rage, Gillian took back the coppers. She brought out the purse, spilled the contents: lead cylinder, parchment, three coins. "Here. See? Trouble, trouble and no lot of money."

Sophonisba snatched at the coins. Gillian's deft fingers saved two, and the other things, which Sophonisba made no move at all to seize.

"Take your trouble," Sophonisba said. "And your brat. And keep away from here."

Jensy scrambled out over the sill, hit the alley cobbles on tier slippered feet. Gillian did not stay to threaten. Sophonisba knew her—knew better than to spill to king's-men . . . or to leave Jensy on the street. Gillian clutched her sister's hand and pulled her along at a rate a twelve-year-old's strides could hardly match.

They walked, finally, in the dark of the blackest alleys and, warily, into the Sink itself. Gillian led the way to Threepenny Bridge and so to Rat's Alley and the Bowel. They were *not* alone, but the shadows inspected them cautiously: the trouble that lurked here was accustomed to pull its victims into the warren, not to find them there; and one time that lurkers did come too close, she and Jensy played dodge in the alley. "Cheap flash," she spat, and: "Bit's Isle," marking herself of a rougher brotherhood than theirs. They were alone after.

After the Bowel came the Isle itself, and the deepest part of the Sink. There was a door in the alley called Blindman's, where Genat had sat till someone knifed him, She dodged to it with Jensy in tow, this stout door inconspicuous among others, and pushed it open

It let them in under Jochen's stairs, in the wine-smelling backside of the Rose. Gillian caught her breath then and pulled Jensy close within the shadows of the small understairs pantry. "Get Jochen," she bade Jensy then. Jensy skulked out into the hall and took off her scarf, stuffed that in her skirts and passed out of sight around the corner of the door and into the roister of the tavern.

In a little time she was back with fat Jochen in her wake, and Jochen mightily scowling.

"You're in trouble?" Jochen said. "Get out if you are."

"Want you to keep Jensy for me."

"Pay," Jochen said. "You got it?"

"How much?"

"How bad the trouble?"

"For her, none at all. Just keep her." Gillian turned her back—prudence, not modesty—to fish up the silver from her blouse, not revealing the purse. She held up one coin. "Two days' board and close room."

"You *are* in trouble."

"I want Nessim. Is he here?"

He always was by dark. Jochen snorted. "A cut of what's going."

"A cut if there's profit; a clear name if there's not; get Nessim."

Jochen went. "I don't want to be left," Jensy started to say, but Gillian rapped her ear and scowled so that Jensy swallowed it and looked frightened. Finally a muddled old man came muttering their way and Gillian snagged his sleeve. The reek of wine was strong; it was perpetual about Nessim Hath, excommunicate priest and minor dabbler in magics. He read, when he was sober enough to see the letters; that and occasionally effective magics—wards against rats, for one—made him a livelihood and kept his throat uncut.

"Upstairs," Gillian said, guiding sot and child up the well-worn boards to the loft and the private cells at the alleyside wall. Jensy snatched the taper at the head of the stairs and they went into that room, which had a window.

Nessim tottered to the cot and sat down while Jensy lit the stub of a candle. Gillian fished out her coppers, held them before Nessim's red-rimmed eyes and pressed them into the old priest's shaking hand.

"Read something?" Nessim asked.

Gillian pulled out the purse and knelt by the bedside while Jensy prudently closed the door. She produced the leaden cylinder and the parchment. "Old man," she said, "tell me what I've got here."

He gathered up the cylinder and brought his eyes closely to focus on it, frowning. His mouth trembled as did his hands, and he thrust it back at her. "I don't know this seal. Lose this thing in the canal. Be rid of it."

"You know it, old man."

"I don't." She did not take it from him, and he held it, trembling. "A false seal, a mask seal. Some thing some would know—and not outsiders. It's no good, Gillian."

"And if some would hunt a thief for it? It's good to someone." Nessim stared at her. She valued Nessim, gave him coppers when he was on one of his lower periods: he drank the money and was grateful. She cultivated him, one gentle rogue among the ungentle, who would not have failed at priesthood and at magics if he did not drink and love comforts; now he simply had the drink.

"Run," he said. "Get out of Korianth. Tonight."

"Penniless? This should be worth something, old man."

"Powerful men would use such a seal to mask what they do, who they are. Games of more than small stakes."

Gillian swallowed heavily. "You've played with seals before, old man; read me the parchment."

He took it in hand, laid the leaden cylinder in his lap, turned the parchment to all sides. Long and long he stared at it, finally opened his purse with much trembling of his hands, took out a tiny knife and cut the red threads wrapped round, pulled them from the wax and loosed it carefully with the blade.

"Huh," Jensy pouted. "*Anyone* could cut it." Gillian rapped her ear gently as Nessim canted the tiny parchment to the scant light. His lips mumbled, steadied, a thin line. When he opened his mouth they trembled again, and very carefully he drew out more red thread from his pouch, red wax such as scribes used. Gillian held her peace and kept Jensy's, not to disturb him in the ticklish process that saw new cords seated, the seal prepared—he motioned for the candle and she held it herself while he heated and replaced the seal most gingerly.

"No magics," he said then, handing it back. "No magics of mine near this thing. Or the other. Take them. Throw them both in the River."

"Answers, old man."

"Triptis. Promising—without naming names—twenty thousand in gold to the shrine of Triptis."

Gillian wrinkled her nose and took back parchment and cylinder. "Abhizite god," she said. "A dark one." The sum ran cold fingers over her skin. "Twenty thousand. That's—*gold*—twenty thousand. How much do rich men have to spend on temples, old thief?"

"Rich men's *lives* are bought for less."

The fingers went cold about the lead. Gillian swallowed, wishing Jensy had stayed downstairs in the pantry. She held up the lead cylinder. "Can you breach that seal, old man?"

"Wouldn't."

"You tell me why."

"It's more than a lead seal on that. Adepts more than the likes of me; I know my level, woman; I know what not to touch, and you can take my advice. Get out of here. You've stolen something you can't trade in. They don't need to see you, do you understand me? This thing can be traced."

The hairs stirred to her nape. She sat staring at him. "Then throwing it in the river won't do it, either."

"They might give up then. Might. Gillian, you've put your head in the jaws this time."

"Rich men's lives," she muttered, clutching the objects in her hand. She slid them back into the purse and thrust it within her blouse. "I'll get rid of it. I'll find some way. I've paid Jochen to keep Jensy. See he does, or sour his beer."

"Gillian—"

"You don't want to know," she said. "I don't want either of you to know." There was the window, the slanting ledge outside; she hugged Jensy, and old Nessim, and used it.

3

Alone, she traveled quickly, by warehouse roofs for the first part of her journey, where the riggings and masts of dockside webbed the night sky, by remembered ways across the canal. One monstrous old warehouse squatted athwart the canal like a misshapen dowager, a convenient crossing that avoided the bridges. Skirts hampered; she whipped off the wrap, leaving the knee breeches and woolen hose she wore beneath, the skirt rolled and bound to her waist with her belt. She had her dagger, her razor and the cant to mark her as trouble for ruffians—a lie: the nebulous brotherhood would hardly back her now, in her trouble. They disliked long looks from moneyed men, hired bullies and noise on dockside. If the noise continued about her, she might foreseeably meet with accident, to be found floating in a canal—to quiet the uproar and stop further attentions.

But such as she met did not know it and kept from her path or, sauntering and mocking, still shied from brotherhood cant. Some passwords were a cut throat to use without approval, and thieves out of the Sink taught interlopers bitter lessons.

She paused to rest at the Serpentine of midtown, crouched in the shadows, sweating and hard-breathing, dizzy with want of sleep and food. Her belly had passed the point of hurting. She thought of a side excursion—a bakery's back door, perhaps—but she did not dare the possible hue and cry added to what notoriety she already had. She gathered what strength she had and set out a second time, the way that led to the tinsel shrine and one house that would see its busiest hours in the dark.

Throw it in the canal: she dared not. Once it was gone from her, she had no more bargains left, nothing. As it was she had a secret valuable and fearful to someone. *There comes a time,* Genat had told her often enough, *when chances have to be taken—and taken wide.* It was not Sophonisba's way.

Panting, she reached the red window, rapped at it; there was dim light inside and long delay—a male voice, a curse, some drunken converse. Gillian leaned against the wall outside and slowed her breathing, wishing by all the gods of Korianth (save one) that Sophonisba would make some haste. She rapped again finally, heart racing as her rashness raised a complaint within—male voice again. She pressed herself to the wall, heard the drunken voice diminish—Sophonisba's now, shrill, bidding someone out. A door opened and closed.

In a moment steps crossed the room and the shutter opened. Gillian showed herself cautiously, stared up into Sophonisba's white face. "Come on out here," Gillian said.

"Get out of here," Sophonisba hissed, with fear stark in her eyes. "*Out*, or I call the watch. There's *money* looking for you."

She would have closed the shutters, but Gillian had both hands on the ledge and vaulted up to perch on it; Gillian snatched and caught a loose handful of Sophonisba's unlaced shift. "Don't do that, Sophie. If you bring the watch, we'll both be sorry. You know me. I've got something I've got to get rid of. Get dressed."

"And lose a night's—"

"Yes. Lose your nose if you don't hurry about it." She brought out the razor, that small and wicked knife of which Sophonisba was most afraid. She sat polishing it on her knee while Sophonisba sorted into a flurry of skirts. Sophonisba paused once to look; she let the light catch the knife and Sophonisba made greater haste. "Fix your hair," Gillian said.

"Someone's going to come back here to check on me if I don't take my last fee front—"

"Then fix it on the way." Steps were headed toward the door. "Haste! Or there'll be bloodletting."

"Get down," Sophonisba groaned. "I'll get rid of her." Gillian slipped within the room and closed the shutters, stood in the dark against the wall while Sophonisba cracked the door and handed the fee out, heard a gutter dialogue and Sophonisba pleading indisposition. She handed out more money finally, as if she were parting with her life's blood, and closed the door. She looked about with a pained expression. "You owe me, you owe me—"

"I'm carrying something dangerous," Gillian said.

"It's being tracked, do you understand? Nessim doesn't like the smell of it."

"O gods."

"Just so. It's trouble, old friend. Priest trouble."

"Then take it to priests."

"Priests expect donations. I've the scent of *gold*, dear friend. It's rich men pass such things back and forth, about things they don't want authority to know about."

"Then throw it in a canal."

"Nessim's advice. But it doesn't take the smell off my hands or answer questions when the trackers catch me up—or *you*, now, old friend."

"What do you want?" Sophonisba moaned. "Gillian, please—"

"Do you know," she said softly, reasonably, "if *we* take this thing—we, dear friend—to the wrong party, to someone who isn't disposed to reward us, or someone who isn't powerful enough to protect us so effortlessly that protection costs him nothing—who would spend effort protecting a whore and a thief, eh, Sophie? But some there are in this city who shed gold like gods shed hair, whose neighborhoods are so well protected others hesitate to meddle in them. Men of birth, Sophie. Men who might like to know who's paying vast sums of gold for favors in this city."

"Don't tell me these things."

"I'll warrant a whore hears a lot of things, Sophie. I'll warrant a whore knows a lot of ways and doors and windows in Korianth, who's where, who has secrets—"

"A whore is told a lot of lies. I can't help you."

"But you can, pretty Sophonisba." She held up the razor. "I daresay you know names and such—even in the king's own hall."

"No!"

"But the king's mad, they say; and who knows what a madman might do? What other names do you know?"

"I don't know *anyone*, I swear I don't."

"Don't swear; we've gods enough here. We improvise, then, you and I." She flung the shutter open. "Out, out with you."

Sophonisba was not adept at ledges. She settled herself on it and hesitated. Gillian thought of pushing her; then, fearing noise, took her hands and lei her down gently, followed after with a soft thud. Sophonisba stood shivering and tying her laces, the latter unsuccessfully.

"Come on," Gillian said.

"I don't walk the alleys," Sophonisba protested in dread; Gillian pulled her along nonetheless, the back ways of the Grand Serpentine.

They met trouble. It was inevitable. More than once gangs of youths spotted Sophonisba, like dogs a stray cat, and came too close for comfort. Once the cant was not password enough, and they wanted more proof: Gillian showed that she carried, knife-carved in her shoulder, the brotherhood's initiation, and drunk as they were, they had sense to give way for that. It ruffled her pride. She jerked Sophonisba along and said nothing, seething with anger and reckoning she should have cut one. She could have done it and gotten away; but not with Sophonisba.

Sophonisba snuffled quietly, her hand cold as ice.

They took to the main canalside at last, when they must, which was at this hour decently deserted. It was not a place Gillian had been often; she found her way mostly by sense, knowing where the tall, domed buildings should lie. She had seen them most days of her life from the rooftops of the Sink.

The palaces of the great of Korianth were walled, with gardens, and men to watch them. She saw seals now and then that she knew, mythic beasts and demon beasts snarling from the arches over such places.

But one palace there was on the leftside hill, opposed to the great gold dome of the King's Palace, a lonely abode well walled and guarded.

There were guards, gilt-armed guards, with plumes and cloaks and more flash than ever the rufflers of midtown dared sport. Gillian grinned to herself and felt Sophonisba's hand in hers cold and limp from dread of such a place.

She marked with her eye where the guards stood, how they came and went and where the walls and accesses lay, where trees and bushes topped the walls inside and how the wall went to the very edge of the white marble building. The place was defended against armed men, against that sort of threat; against—the thought cooled her grin and her enthusiasm—guilded Assassins and free-lancers; a prince must worry for such things.

No. It was far from easy as it looked. Those easy ways could be set with traps; those places too unguarded could become deadly. She looked for the ways less easy, traced again that too-close wall.

"Walk down the street," she told Sophonisba. "Now. Just walk down the street."

"You're mad."

"Go."

Sophonisba started off, pale figure in blue silks, a disheveled and unlaced figure of ample curves and confused mien. She walked quickly as her fear would urge her, beyond the corner and before the eyes of the guards at the gate.

Gillian stayed long enough to see the sentries' attention wander, then pelted to the wall and carefully, with delicate fingers and the balance Genat had taught, spidered her way up the brickwork.

Dogs barked the moment she flung an arm over. She cursed, ran the crest of the thin wall like a trained ape, made the building itself and crept along the masonry—*too much of ornament, my lord!*—as far as the upper terrace.

Over the rim and onto solid ground, panting. Whatever had become of Sophonisba, she had served her purpose.

Gillian darted for a further terrace. Doors at the far end swung open suddenly; guards ran out in consternation. Gillian grinned at them, arms wide, like a player asking tribute; bowed. They were not amused, thinking of their hides, surely. She looked up at a ring of pikes, cocked her head to one side and drew a conscious deep breath, making obvious what they should see; that it was no male intruder they had caught.

"Courier," she said, "for Prince Osric."

4

He was not, either, amused.

She stood with a very superfluous pair of men-at-arms gripping her wrists so tightly that the blood left her hands and the bones were about to snap, and the king's bastard—and sole surviving son—fingered the pouch they had found in their search of her.

"Courier," he said.

They were not alone with the guards, he and she. A brocaded troop of courtiers and dandies loitered near, amongst the porphyry columns and on the steps of the higher floor. He dismissed them with a wave of his hand; several seemed to feel privileged and stayed.

"For whom," the prince asked, "are you a courier?"

"Couriers bring messages," she said. "I decided on my own to bring you this one. I thought you should have it."

"Who are you?"

"A freelance assassin," she said, promoting herself, and setting Prince Osric back a pace. The guards nearly crushed her wrists; they went beyond pain.

"Jisan," Osric said.

One of the three who had stayed walked forward, and Gillian's spine crawled; she knew the look of trouble, suspected the touch of another brotherhood, more disciplined than her own. "I was ambitious," she said at once. "I exaggerate."

"She is none of ours," said the Assassin. A dark man he was, unlike Osric, who was white-blond and thin; this Jisan was from southern climes and not at all flash, a drab shadow in brown and black beside Osric's glitter.

"Your name," said Osric.

"Gillian," she said; and recalling better manners and where she was: "—majesty."

"And how come by this?"

"A cut-purse . . . found this worthless. It fell in the street. But it's some lord's seal."

"No lord's seal. Do you read, guttersnipe?"

"Read, I?" The name rankled; she kept her face calm. "No, lord."

He whisked out a dagger and cut the cords, unfurled the parchment. A frown came at once to his face, deepened, and his pale eyes came suddenly up to hers. "Suppose that someone read it to you."

She sucked a thoughtful breath, weighed her life, and Jensy's. "A drunk clerk read it—for a kiss; said it was something he didn't want to know; and I think then—some great lord might want to know it; but which lord, think I? One lord might make good use and another bad, one be grateful and another not—might make rightest use of something dangerous—might be glad it came here in good loyal hands, and not where it was supposed to go; might take notice of a stir in the lowtown, bully boys looking for that cut-purse to cut throats, armed men and some of them not belonging hereabouts. King's wall's too high, majesty, so I came here."

"Whose bravos?" Jisan asked.

She blinked. "Wish I knew that; I'd like to know."

"You're that cut-purse," he said.

"If I were, would I say yes, and if I weren't, would I say yes? But I know that thing's better not in my hands and maybe better here than in the River. A trifle of reward, majesty, and there's no one closer mouthed than I am; a trifle more, majesty, and you've all my talents at hire: no one can outbid a prince, not for the likes of me; I know I'm safest to be bribed once and never again."

Osric's white-blue eyes rested on her a very long, very calculating moment. "You're easy to kill. Who would miss you?"

"No one, majesty. No one. But I'm eyes and ears and Korianthine—" Her eyes slid to the Assassin. "And I go places where *he* won't."

The Assassin smiled. His eyes did not. Guild man. He worked by hire and public license.

And sometimes without.

Osric applied his knife to the lead cylinder to gently cut it. "No," Gillian said nervously. And when he looked up, alarmed: "I would not," she said. "I have been advised—the thing has some ill luck attached."

"Disis," Osric called softly, and handed the cylinder into the hands of an older man, a scholarly man, whose courtier's dress was long out of mode. The man's long, lined face contracted at the touch of it in his hand.

"Well advised," that one said. "Silver and lead—a confining. I would be most careful of that seal, majesty; I would indeed."

The prince took the cylinder back, looked at it with a troubled mien, passed it back again. Carefully then he took the purse from his own belt, from beside his dagger. "Your home?" he asked of Gillian.

"Dockside," she said.

"All of it?"

She bit her lip. "Ask at the Anchor," she said, betraying a sometime haunt, but not Sophonisba's, not the Rose either. "All the Sink knows Gillian." And that was true.

"Let her go," Osric bade his guards. Gillian's arms dropped, relief and agony at once. He tossed the purse at her feet, while she was absorbed in her pain. "Come to the garden gate next time. Bring me word—and *names*."

She bent, gathered the purse with a swollen hand, stood again and gave a shy bow, her heart pounding with the swing of her fortunes. She received a disgusted wave of dismissal, and the guards at her right jerked her elbow and brought her down the hall, the whole troop of them to escort her to the door.

"My knives," she reminded them with a touch of smugness. They returned them and hastened her down the stairs. She did not gape at the splendors about her, but she saw them, every detail. In such a place twenty thousand in gold might be swallowed up. *Gillian* might be swallowed up, here and now or in the Sink, later. She knew. She reckoned it.

They took her through the garden, past handlers and quivering dogs the size of men, and there at the garden gate they let her go without the mauling she had expected. Princes' favor had power even out of princes' sight, then; from what she had heard of Osric, that was wise of them.

They pitched the little bundle of her skirt at her feet, undone. She snatched that up and flung it jauntily over her shoulder, and stalked off into the alleys that were her element.

She had a touch of conscience for Sophonisba. Likely Sophonisba had disentangled herself by now, having lied her way with some small skill out of whatever predicament she had come to, appearing in the high town: *forgive me, lord; this lord he brought me here, he did, and turned me out, he did, and I'm lost, truly, sir*... Sophonisba would wait till safe daylight and find her way home again, to nurse a grudge that money would heal. And she...

Gillian was shaking when she finally stopped to assess herself. Her wrists felt maimed, the joints of her hands swollen. She crouched and slipped the knives back where they belonged, earnestly wishing she had had the cheek to ask for food as well. She rolled the skirt and tied it in the accustomed bundle at her belt. Lastly—for fear, lastly—she spilled the sack into her cupped hand, spilled it back again quickly, for the delight and the terror of the flood of gold that glinted in the dim light. She thrust it down her blouse, at once terrified to possess such a thing and anxious until she could find herself in the Sink again, where she had ratholes in plenty. This was not a thing to walk the alleys with.

She sprang up and started moving, alone and free again, and casting furtive and careful glances all directions, most especially behind.

Priests and spells and temple business. Of a sudden it began to sink into her mind precisely what services she had agreed to, to turn spy; Triptis's priests bought whores' babes, or any else that could be stolen. That was a thief's trade beneath contempt; a trade the brotherhood stamped out where it found it obvious: grieving mothers were a noise, and a desperate one, bad for business. It was *that* kind of enemy she dealt with.

Find me names, the lord Osric had said, with an Assassin standing on one side and a magician on the other. Suddenly she knew who the old magicker had been: Disis, the prince had called him; Aldisis, more than dabbler in magics—part and parcel of the prince's entourage of discontents, waiting for the mad king to pass the dark gates elsewhere. The prince had had brothers and a sister, and now he had none; now he had only to wait.

Aldisis the opener of paths. His ilk of lesser station sold ill wishes down by the Fish, and some of those worked; Aldisis had skills, it was whispered.

And Jisan cared for those Aldisis missed.

Find me names.

And what might my lord prince do with them? Gillian wondered, without much wondering; and with a sudden: *What but lives are worth twenty thousand gold? And what but high-born lives?*

She had agreed with no such intention; she had priest troubles and hunters on her trail, and she did not need to know their names, not from a great enough distance from Korianth. One desperate chance—to sell the deadly information and gamble it was not Osric himself, to gamble with the highest power she could reach and hope she reached above the plague spot in Korianth . . . for gold, to get her and Jensy out of reach and out of the city until the danger was past. Dangerous thoughts nibbled at her resolve, the chance she had been looking for, three years on the street with Jensy—a chance not only of one purse of gold . . . but of others. She swore at herself for thinking of it, reminded herself what she was; but there was also what she might be. Double such a purse could support Jensy in a genteel order: learning and fine clothes and fine manners; freedom for herself, to eel herself back dockside and vanish into her own darknesses, gather money, and power . . . No strange cities for her, nothing but Korianth, where she knew her way, all the low and tangled ways that took a lifetime of living to learn of a city—no starting over elsewhere, to play whore and teach Jensy the like, to get their throats cut in Amisent or Kesirn, trespassing in another territory and another brotherhood.

She skipped along, the strength flooding back into her, the breath hissing regularly between her teeth. She found herself again in familiar territory, known alleys; found one of her narrowest boltholes and rid herself of the prince's purse, all but one coin, itself a bit of recklessness. After that she ran and paused, ran and paused, slick with sweat and light-headed with fortune and danger and hunger.

The Bowel took her in, and Blindman's—home territory indeed; her sore, slippered feet pattered over familiar cobbles; she loosed her skirt and whipped it about her, mopped her face with her scarf and knotted that about her waist, leaving her curls free. The door to the Rose was before her. She pushed it open.

And froze to the heart.

5

All the Rose was a shambles, the tables broken, a few survivors or gawkers milling about in a forlorn knot near the street-side door. There was chill in the air, a palpable chill, like a breath of ice. Fat Jochen lay stark on the floor by the counter, with all his skin gone gray and his clothes . . . faded, as if cobweb composed them.

"Gods," Gillian breathed, clutching at the luck piece she bore, easygoing Agdalia's. And in the next breath: "Jensy," she murmured, and ran for the stairs.

The door at the end of the narrow hall stood open, moonlight streaming into a darkened room from the open window. She stopped, drew her knife—clutched the tawdry charm, sick with dread. From her vantage point she saw the cot disheveled, the movement of a shadow within, like a lich robed in cobwebs.

"Jensy!" she shouted into that dark.

The wraith came into the doorway, staggered out, reached.

Nessim. She held her hand in time, only just, turned the blade and with hilt in hand gripped the old man's sticklike arms, seized him with both hands, heedless of hurts. He stammered something. There was a silken crumbling in the cloth she held, like something moldered, centuries old. The skin on Nessim's poor face peeled in strips like a sun-baked hinterlander's.

"Gillian," he murmured. "They wanted you."

"Where's Jensy?"

He tried to tell her, pawed at the amulet he had worn; it was a crystal, cracked now, in a peeling hand. He waved the hand helplessly. "Took Jensy," he said. He was bald, even to the eyebrows.

"I saved myself—saved myself—had no strength for mousekin. Gillian, run away."

"Who, blast you, Nessim!"

"Don't know. Don't know. But Triptis. Triptis's priests . . . ah, go, go, Gillian." Tears made tracks down his seared cheeks. She thrust him back, anger and pity confounded in her. The advice was sound; they were without power, without patrons. Young girls disappeared often enough in the Sink without a ripple.

Rules changed. She thrust past him to the window and out it, onto the creaking shingles, to the eaves and down the edge to Blindman's. She hit the cobbles in a crouch and straightened. They were looking for her. For her, not Jensy. And Nessim had survived to give her that message.

Triptis.

She slipped the knife into her belt and turned to go, stopped suddenly at the apparition that faced her in the alley.

"Gillian," the shadow said, unfolding upward out of the debris by Goat's Alley. Her hand slipped behind her to the dagger; she set her back against solid brick and flicked a glance at shadows . . . others, at the crossing of Sparrow's. More around the corner, it was likely.

"Where is it?" the same chill voice asked.

"I sell things," she said. "Do you want it back? You have something I want."

"You can't get it back," the whisper said. "Now what shall we do?" Her blood went colder still. They knew where she had been. She was followed; and no one slipped up on Gillian, no one.

Seals and seals, Nessim had said.

"Name your price," she said.

"You gained access to a prince," said the whisper. "You can do it again."

Osric, she thought. Her heart settled into a leaden, hurting rhythm. *It was Osric it was aimed at.*

"We also," said the whisper, "sell things. You want the child Jensy. The god has many children. He can spare one."

Triptis; it was beyond doubt; the serpent-god, swallowing the moon once monthly; the snake and the mouse. *Jensy!*

"I am reasonable," she said.

There was silence. If the shadow smiled, it was invisible. A hand extended, open, bearing a tiny silver circlet. "A gift you mustn't lose," the whisper said.

She took the chill ring, a serpent shape, slipped it onto her thumb, for that was all it would fit. The metal did not warm to her flesh but chilled the flesh about it.

A second shadow stepped forward, proffered another small object, a knife the twin of her own.

"The blade will kill at a scratch," the second voice said. "Have care of it."

"Don't take off the ring," the first whispered.

"You could hire assassins," she said.

"We have," the whisper returned.

She stared at them. "Jensy comes back alive," she said. "To this door. No cheating."

"On either side."

"You've bid higher," she said. "What proof do you want?"

"Events will prove. Kill him."

Her lips trembled. "I haven't eaten in two days; I haven't slept— "

"Eat and sleep," the shadow hissed, "in what leisure you think you have. We trust you." They melted backward, shadow into shadow, on all sides. The metal remained cold upon her finger. She carried it to her lips, unconscious reflex, thought with cold panic of poison, spat onto the cobbles again and again. She was shaking.

She turned, walked into the inn of the Rose past Jochen's body, past Nessim, who sat huddled on the bottom of the steps. She poured wine from the tap, gave a cup to Nessim, drank another herself, grimacing at the flavor. Bread on the sideboard had gone hard; she soaked it in the wine, but it had the flavor of ashes; cheeses had molded: she sliced off the rind with a knife from the board and ate. Jochen lay staring at the ceiling. Passers-by thrust in their heads and gaped at a madwoman who ate such tainted things; another, hungrier than the rest, came in to join the pillage, and an old woman followed.

"Go, run," Nessim muttered, rising with great difficulty to tug at her arm, and the others shied from him in horror; it was a look of leprosy.

"Too late," she said. "Go away yourself, old man. Find a hole to hide in. I'll get Jensy back."

It hurt the old man; she had not meant it so. He shook his head and walked away, muttering sorrowfully of Jensy. She left, then, by the alleyway, which was more familiar to her than the street. She had food in her belly, however tainted; she had eaten worse. She walked, stripped the skirt aside and limped along, feeling the cobbles through the holes that had worn now in her slippers. She tucked the skirt in a seam of itself, hung it about her shoulder, walked with more persistence than strength down Blindman's.

Something stirred behind her; she spun, surprised nothing, her nape prickling. A rat, perhaps; the alleys were infested this close to the docks. Perhaps it was not. She went, hearing that something behind her from time to time and never able to surprise it

She began to run, took to the straight ways, the ways that no thief liked to use, broke into the streets and raced breathlessly toward the Serpentine, that great canal along which all the streets of the city had their beginnings. Breath failed her finally and she slowed, dodged late walkers and kept going. If one of the walkers was that one who followed her . . . she could not tell.

The midtown gave way to the high; she retraced ways she had passed twice this night, with faltering steps, her breath loud in her own ears. It was late, even for prowlers. She met few but stumbled across one drunk or dead in the way, leapt the fallen form and fled with the short-range speed of one of the city's wary cats, dodged to this course and that and came out again in the same alley from which she and Sophonisba had spied out the palace.

The garden gate, Prince Osric had instructed her. The ring burned cold upon her finger. She walked into the open, to the very guards who had let her out not so very long before.

6

The prince was abed. The fact afforded his guards no little consternation—the suspicion of a message urgent enough to make waking him advisable; the suspicion of dangerous wrath if it was not. Gillian, for her part, sat still, wool-hosed ankles crossed, hands folded, a vast fear churning at her belly. They had taken the ring. It had parted from her against all the advice of him who had given it to her; and it was not pleasing them that concerned her, but Jensy.

They had handled it and had it now, but if it was cold to them, they had not said, had not reacted. She suspected it was not. It was hers, for her.

Master Aldisis came. He said nothing, only stared at her, and she at him; him she feared most of all, his sight, his perception. His influence. She had nothing left, not the ring, not the blades, not the single gold coin. The scholar, in his night robe, observed her and walked away. She sat, the heat of exertion long since fled, with her feet and hands cold and finally numb.

"Mistress Gillian," a voice mocked her.

She looked up sharply, saw Jisan standing by a porphyry column. He bowed as to a lady. She sat still, staring at him as warily as at Aldisis.

"A merry chase, mistress Gillian."

Alarm might have touched her eyes. It surprised her, that it had been he.

"Call the lord prince," the Assassin said, and a guard went.

"Who is your contract?" she asked.

He smiled. "Guildmaster might answer," he said. "Go ask."

Patently she could not. She sat still, fixed as under a serpent's gaze. Her blades were in the guards' hands, one more knife than there had been. They suspected something amiss, as it was their business to suspect all things and all persons; Jisan knew. She stared into his eyes.

"What game are you playing?" he asked her plainly.

"I've no doubt you've asked about."

"There's some disturbance down in lowtown. A tavern with a sudden . . . unwholesomeness in it. Dead men. Would you know about that, mistress Gillian?"

"I carry messages," she said.

His dark eyes flickered. She thought of the serpent-god and the mouse. She kept her hands neatly folded, her feet still. This was a man who killed. Who perhaps enjoyed his work. She thought that he might.

A curse rang out above, echoing in the high beams of the ceiling. Osric. She heard every god in the court pantheon blasphemed and turned her head to stare straight before her, smoothed her breeches, a nervousness—stood at the last moment, remembering the due of royalty, even in night dress.

Called from some night's pleasure? she wondered. In that case he might be doubly wrathful; but he was cold as ever, thin face, thin mouth set, white-blue eyes as void of the ordinary. She could not imagine the man engaged in so human a pastime. Maybe he never did, she thought, the wild irrelevance of exhaustion. Maybe that was the source of his disposition.

"They sent me back," she said directly, "to kill you."

Not many people surely had shocked Osric; she had succeeded. The prince bit his lips, drew a breath, thrust his thin hands in the belt of his velvet robe. "Jisan?" he asked.

"There are dead men," the Assassin said, "at dockside."

"Honesty," Osric murmured, looking at her, a mocking tone.

"Lord," she said, at the edge of her nerves. "Your enemies have my sister. They promise to kill her if I don't carry out their plans."

"And you think so little of your sister, and so much of the gold?"

Her breath nigh strangled her; she swallowed air and kept her voice even. "I know that they will kill her and me whichever I do; tell me the name of your enemies, lord prince, that you didn't tell me the first time you sent me out of here with master Jisan behind me. *Give me names,* lord prince, and I'll hunt your enemies for my own reasons, and kill them or not as you like."

"You should already know one name, thief."

"A god's name? Aye, but gods are hard to hunt, lord prince." Her voice thinned; she could not help it. "Lend me master Aldisis's company instead of master Jisan's, and there's some hope. But go I will; and kill me priests if you haven't any better names."

Osric's cold, pale eyes ran her up and down, flicked to Jisan, back again. "For gold, good thief?"

"For my *sister,* lord prince. Pay me another time."

"Then why come here?"

"Because they'd know." She slid a look toward the guards, shifted weight anxiously. "A ring; they gave me a ring to wear, and they took it."

"Aldisis!" the prince called. The mage came, from some eavesdropping vantage among the columns or from some side room.

An anxious guard proffered the serpent ring, but Aldisis would not touch it;

waved it away. "Hold it awhile more," Aldisis said; and to Osric: "They would know where that is. And whether she held it."

"My sister," Gillian said in anguish. "Lord, give it back to me. I came because they'd know if not; and to find out their names. Give me their names. It's almost morning."

"I might help you," said Osric. "Perhaps I might die and delight them with a rumor."

"Lord," she murmured, dazed.

"My enemies will stay close together," he said. "The temple—or a certain lord Brisin's palace . . . likely the temple; Brisin fears retaliation; the god shelters him. Master Aldisis could explain such things. You're a bodkin at best, mistress thief. But you may prick a few of them; and should you do better, that would delight me. Look to your reputation, thief."

"Rumor," she said.

"Chaos," muttered Aldisis.

"You advise me against this?" Osric asked.

"No," said Aldisis. "Toward it."

"You mustn't walk out the front gate this time," Osric said, "mistress thief, if you want a rumor."

"Give me what's mine," she said. "I'll clear your walls, lord, and give them my heels; and they'll not take me."

Osric made a sign with his hand; the guards brought her her knives, her purse and her ring, while Osric retired to a bench, seated himself, with grim stares regarded them all. "I am dead," he said languidly. "I shall be for some few hours. Report it so and ring the bells. Today should be interesting."

Gillian slid the ring onto her finger; it was cold as ever.

"Go!" Osric whispered, and she turned and sped from the room, for the doors and the terrace she knew.

Night opened before her; she ran, skimmed the wall with the dogs barking, swung down with the guards at the gate shouting alarm—confused, and not doing their best. She hit the cobbles afoot as they raced after her, and their armor slowed them; she sprinted for known shadows and zigged and zagged through the maze.

She stopped finally, held a hand to a throbbing side and fetched up against a wall, rolled on a shoulder to look back and find pursuit absent.

Then the bells began out of the dark—mournful bells, tolling out a lie that must run through all of Korianth: the death of a prince.

She walked, staggering with exhaustion, wanting sleep desperately; but the hours that she might sleep were hours of Jensy's life. She was aware finally that she had cut her foot on something; she noted first the pain and then that she left a small spot of blood behind when she walked. It was far from crippling; she kept moving.

It was midtown now. She went more surely, having taken a second wind.

And all the while the bells tolled, brazen and grim, and lights burned in shuttered windows where all should be dark, people wakened to the rumor of a death.

The whole city must believe the lie, she thought, from the Sink to the throne, the mad monarch himself believed that Osric had died; and should there not be general search after a thief who had killed a prince?

She shivered, staggering, reckoning that she ran ahead of the wave of rumor: that by dawn the name of herself and Jensy would be bruited across the Sink, and there would be no more safety.

And behind the doors, she reckoned, rumor prepared itself, folk yet too frightened to come out of doors—never wise for honest folk in Korianth.

When daylight should come . . . it would run wild—mad Seithan to rule with no hope of succession, an opportunity for the kings of other cities, of upcoast and upriver, dukes and powerful men in Korianth, all to reach out hands for the power Seithan could not long hold, the tottering for which all had been waiting for more than two years . . .

This kind of rumor waited, to be flung wide at a thief's request. This kind of madness waited to be let loose in the city, in which all the enemies might surface, rumors in which a throne might fall, throats be cut, the whole city break into riot . . . A prince might die indeed then, in disorder so general.

Or . . . a sudden and deeper foreboding possessed her . . . a king might. A noise in one place, a snatch in the other; thief's game in the market. She had played it often enough, she with Jensy.

Not for concern for her and her troubles that Osric risked so greatly . . . but for *Osric's* sake, no other.

She quickened her pace, swallowing down the sickness that threatened her; somehow to get clear of this, to get away in this shaking of powers before two mites were crushed by an unheeding footstep.

She began, with the last of her strength, to run.

7

The watch was out in force, armed men with lanterns, lights and shadows rippling off the stone of cobbles and of walls like the stuff of the Muranthine Hell, and the bells still tolling, the first tramp of soldiers' feet from off the high streets, canalward.

Gillian sped, not the only shadow that judged the neighborhood of the watch and the soldiers unhealthy; rufflers and footpads were hieing themselves to cover apace, with the approach of trouble and of dawn. She skirted the canals that branched off the Serpentine, took to the alleys again and paused in the familiar alley off Agdalia's Shrine, gasping for breath in the flare of lanterns. A door slammed on the street: Agdalia's was taking precautions. Upper windows closed. The trouble had flowed thus far, and folk who did not wish to involve themselves tried to signify so by staying invisible.

The red-shuttered room was closed and dark; Sophonisba had not returned . . . had found some safe nook for herself with the bells going, hiding in fear, knowing where her partner had gone, perhaps witness to the hue and cry after. *Terrified,* Gillian reckoned, and did not blame her.

Gillian caught her breath and took to that street, forested with pillars, that was called the Street of the Gods. Here too the lanterns of the watch showed in the distance, and far away, dimly visible against the sky . . . the palace of the king upon the other hill of the fold in which Korianth nestled, the gods and the king in close association.

From god to god she passed, up that street like an ascent of fancy, from the bare respectability of little cults like Agdalia's to the more opulent temples of gods more fearsome and more powerful. Watch passed; she retreated at once, hovered in the shadow of the smooth columns of a Korianthine god, Ablis of the Goldworkers, one of the fifty-two thousand gods of Korianth. He had no patronage for her, might, in fact, resent a thief; she hovered fearfully, waiting for ill luck; but perhaps she was otherwise marked. She shuddered, fingering that serpent ring upon her thumb, and walked farther in the shadow of the columns.

It was not the greatest temple nor the most conspicuous in this section, that of Triptis. Dull black-green by day, it seemed all black in this last hour of night, the twisted columns like stone smoke, writhing up to a plain portico, without window or ornament.

She caught her breath, peered into the dark that surrounded a door that might be open or closed; she was not sure.

Nor was she alone. A prickling urged at her nape, a sense of something that lived and breathed nearby; she whipped out the poisoned blade and turned.

A shadow moved, tottered toward her. "Gillian," it said, held out a hand, beseeching.

"Nessim," she murmured, caught the peeling hand with her left, steadied the old man. He recoiled from her touch.

"You've something of them about you," he said.

"What are you doing here?" she hissed at him. "Old man, go back—get out of here."

"I came for mousekin," he said. "I came to try, Gillian." The voice trembled. It was, for Nessim, terribly brave.

"You would die," she said. "You're not in their class, Nessim."

"Are you?" he asked with a sudden straightening, a memory, perhaps, of better years. "You'd do what? *What* would you do?"

"You stay out," she said, and started to leave; he caught her hand, caught the hand with the poisoned knife and the ring. His fingers clamped.

"No," he said. "No. Be rid of this."

She stopped, looked at his shadowed, peeling face. "They threatened Jensy's life."

"They know you're here. You understand that? With this, they know. Give it to me."

"Aldisis saw it and returned it to me. *Aldisis* himself, old man. Is your advice better?"

"My reasons are friendlier."

A chill went over her. She stared into the old man's eyes. "What should I do?"

"Give it here. Hand it to me. I will contain it for you . . . long enough. They won't know, do you understand me? I'll do that much."

"You can't light a candle, old trickster."

"Can," he said. "Reedlight's easier. I never work more than I have to."

She hesitated, saw the fear in the old man's eyes. A friend, one friend. She nodded, sheathed the knife and slipped off the ring. He took it into his hands and sank down in the shadows with it clasped before his lips, the muscles of his arms shaking as if he strained against something vastly powerful.

And the cold was gone from her hand.

She turned, ran, fled across the street and scrambled up the stonework of the paler temple of the Elder Mother, the Serpent Triptis's near neighbor . . . up, madly, for the windowless temple had to derive its light from some source; and a temple that honored the night surely looked upon it somewhere.

She reached the crest, the domed summit of the Mother, set foot from pale marble onto the darker roof of the Serpent, shuddering, as if the very stone were alive and threatening, able to feel her presence.

To steal from a god, to snatch a life from his jaws . . .

She spun and ran to the rear of the temple, where a well lay open to the sky, where the very holy of the temple looked up at its god, which was night. That was the way in she had chosen. The sanctuary, she realized with a sickness of fear, thought of Jensy and took it nonetheless, swung onto the inside rim and looked down, with a second impulse of panic as she saw how far down it was, a far, far drop.

Voices hailed within, echoing off the columns, shortening what time she had; somewhere voices droned hymns or some fell chant.

She let go, plummeted, hit the slick stones and tried to take the shock by rolling . . . sprawled, dazed, on cold stone, sick from the impact and paralyzed.

She heard shouts, outcries, struggled up on a numbed arm and a sprained wrist, trying to gain her feet. It was indeed the sanctuary; pillars of some green stone showed in the golden light of lamps, pillars carved like twisting serpents, even to the scales, writhing toward the ceiling and knotting in folds across it. The two greatest met above the altar, devouring a golden sun, between their fanged jaws, above her.

"Jensy," she muttered, thinking of Nessim and his hands straining about that thing that they had given her.

She scrambled for the shadows, for safety if there was any safety in this lair of demons.

A man-shaped shadow appeared in that circle of night above the altar; she stopped, shrank back farther among the columns as it hung and dropped as she had.

Jisan. Who else would have followed her, dark of habit and streetwise? He hit the pavings hardly better than she, came up and staggered, felt of the silver-hiked knife at his belt; she shrank back and back, pace by pace, her slippered feet soundless.

And suddenly the chanting was coming this way, up hidden stairs, lights flaring among the columns; they hymned Night, devourer of light, in their madness beseeched the day not to come—forever Dark, they prayed in their mad hymn. The words crept louder and louder among the columns, and Jisan lingered, dazed.

"Hsst!" Gillian whispered; he caught the sound, seemed to focus on it, fled the other way, among the columns on the far side of the hall.

And now the worshipers were within the sanctuary, the lights making the serpent columns writhe and twist into green-scaled life, accompanied by shadows. They bore with them a slight, tinseled form that wept and struggled. Jensy, crying! she never would.

Gillian reached for the poisoned blade, her heart risen into her throat. Of a sudden the hopelessness of her attempt came down upon her, for they never would keep their word, never, and there was nowhere to hide: old Nessim could not hold forever, keeping their eyes blind to her.

Or they knew already that they had been betrayed.

She walked out among them. "We have a bargain!" she shouted, interrupting the hymn, throwing things into silence. "I kept mine. Keep yours."

Jensy struggled and bit, and one of them hit her. The blow rang loud in the silence, and Jensy went limp.

One of them stood forward. "He is dead?" that one asked. "The bargain is kept?"

"What else are the bells?" she asked.

There was silence. Distantly the brazen tones were still pealing across the city.

It was near to dawn; stars were fewer in the opening above the altar. Triptis's hours were passing.

"Give her back," Gillian said, feeling the sweat run down her sides, her pulse hammering in her smallest veins. "You'll hear no more of us."

A cowl went back, showing a fat face she had seen in processions. No priest, not with that gaudy dress beneath; Duke Brisin, Osric had named one of his enemies; she thought it might be. And they were not going to honor their word.

Someone cried out; a deep crash rolled through the halls; there was the tread of armored men, sudden looks of alarm and a milling among the priests like a broken hive. Jensy fell, dropped; and Gillian froze with the ringing rush of armored men coming at her back, the swing of lanterns that sent the serpents the more frenziedly twisting about the hall. "Stop them," someone was shouting.

She moved, slashed a priest, who screamed and hurled himself into the others who tried to stop her. Jensy was moving, scrambling for dark with an eel's instinct, rolling away faster than Gillian could help her.

"Jisan!" Gillian shouted to the Assassin, hoping against hope for an ally; and suddenly the hall was ringed with armed men, and herself with a poisoned bodkin, and a dazed, gilt child, huddled together against a black wall of priests.

Some priests tried to flee; the drawn steel of the soldiers prevented; and some died, shrieking. Others were herded back before the altar.

"Lord," Gillian said nervously, casting about among them for the face she hoped to see; and he was there, Prince Osric, in the guise of a common soldier; and Aldisis by him; but he had no eyes for a thief.

"Father," Osric hailed the fat man, hurled an object at his feet, a leaden cylinder. The king recoiled pace by pace, his face white and trembling, shaking convulsively so that the fat quivered upon it. The soldiers' blades remained leveled toward him, and Gillian seized Jensy's naked shoulder and pulled her back, trying for quiet retreat out of this place of murders, away from father and son, mad king who dabbled in mad gods and plotted murders.

"Murderer," Seithan stammered, the froth gathering at his lips. "Killed my legitimate sons . . . every one; killed me, but I didn't die . . . kin-killer. Kin-killing bastard . . . I have loyal subjects left; you'll not reign."

"You've tried *me* for years, honored father, majesty. *Where's my mother?*"

The king gave a sickly and hateful laugh.

There was movement in the dark, where no priest was . . . a figure seeking deeper obscurity; Gillian took her own cue and started to move.

A priest's weapon whipped up, a knife poised to hurl; she cried warning . . . and suddenly chaos, soldiers closed in a ring of bright weapons, priests dying in a froth of blood, and the king . . . The cries were stilled. Gillian hugged Jensy against her in the shadows, seeing through the forest of snakes the sprawled bodies, the bloody-handed soldiers, Osric—king in Korianth.

King! the soldiers hailed him, that made the air shudder; he gave them orders, that sent them hastening from the slaughter here.

"The palace!" he shouted, urging them on to riot that would see throats cut by the hundreds in Korianth.

A moment he paused, sword in hand, looked into the shadows, for Jensy glittered, and it was not so easy to hide. For a moment a thief found the courage to look a prince in the eye, wondering, desperately, whether two such motes of dust as they might not be swept away. Whether he feared a thief's gossip, or cared.

The soldiers had stopped about him, a warlike knot of armor and plumes and swords.

"Get moving!" he ordered them, and swept them away with him, running in their haste to further murders.

Against her, Jensy gave a quiet shiver, and thin arms went round her waist. Gillian tore at a bit of the tinsel, angered by the tawdry ornament. Such men cheated even the gods. A step sounded near her. She turned, dagger in hand, faced the shadow that was Jisan. A knife gleamed in his hand.

He let the knife hand fall to his side.

"Whose are you?" she asked. He tilted his head toward the door, where the prince had gone, now king.

"Was," he said. "Be clever and run far, Gillian thief; or lie low and long. There comes a time princes don't like to remember the favors they bought. Do you think King Osric will want to reward an assassin? Or a thief?"

"You leave first," she said. "I don't want you at my back."

"I've been there," he reminded her, "for some number of hours."

She hugged Jensy the tighter. "Go," she said. "Get out of my way."

He went; she watched him walk into the beginning day of the doorway, a darkness out of darkness, and down the steps.

"You all right?" she asked of Jensy.

"Knew I would be," Jensy said with little-girl nastiness; but her lips shook. And suddenly her eyes widened, staring beyond.

Gillian looked, where something like a rope of darkness twisted among the columns, above the blood that spattered the altar; a trick of the wind and the lamps, perhaps. But it crossed the sky, where the stars paled to day, and moved against the ceiling. Her right hand was suddenly cold.

She snatched Jensy's arm and ran, weaving in and out of the columns the way

Jisan had gone, out, out into the day, where an old man huddled on the steps, rocking to and fro and moaning.

"Nessim!" she cried. He rose and cast something that whipped away even as he collapsed in a knot of tatters and misery. A serpent-shape writhed across the cobbles in the beginning of day . . .

. . . and shriveled, a dry stick.

She clutched Jensy's hand and ran to him, her knees shaking under her, bent down and raised the dry old frame by the arms, expecting death; but a blistered face gazed back at her with a fanatic's look of triumph. Nessim's thin hand reached for Jensy, touched her face.

"All right, mousekin?"

"Old man," Gillian muttered, perceiving something she had found only in Jensy; he would have, she vowed, whatever comfort gold could buy, food, and a bed to sleep in. A mage; he was that. And a man.

Gold, she thought suddenly, recalling the coin in her purse; and the purse she had buried off across the canals.

And one who had dogged her tracks most of the night.

She spat an oath by another god and sprang up, blind with rage.

"Take her to the Wyvern," she bade Nessim and started off without a backward glance, reckoning ways she knew that an Assassin might not, reckoning on throat-cutting, on revenge in a dozen colors.

She took to the alleys and began to run by alleys a big man could never use, cracks and crevices and ledges and canal verges.

And made it. She worked into the dark, dislodged the stone, took back the purse and climbed catwise to the ledges to lurk and watch.

He was not far behind to work his big frame into the narrow space that took hers so easily, to work loose the self-same stone.

Upon her rooftop perch she stood, gave a low whistle . . . shook out a pair of golden coins and dropped them ringing at his feet, a grand generosity, like the prince's.

"For your trouble," she bade him, and was away.

⚔

Karl Edward Wagner's Kane, in the author's words, is "not a sword and sorcery hero; he is a gothic hero-villain from the tradition of . . . novels of the eighteenth and early nineteenth centuries." Kane "could master any situation intellectually, or rip heads off if push came to shove." So long as he eludes death by violence, "time can not wither his physical being." Kane is not a sorcerer—but his "power so defies human comprehension that men call it magic." He amorally "serves himself and no other gods or obscure values," and, wearied with immortality, he combats ennui by seeking adventure.

Writing in the 1970s and 1980s, Wagner saw the women in his Kane stories as "very independent characters," far from "helpless-girl stereotypes," and never "simpering girls in diaphanous gowns." True, but re-reading the Kane stories in 2016, I found more than a touch of misogyny. Of course, not all is as it always seems in a Kane story. In "Undertow," for instance, a stereotypical barbarian hero thinks *he is saving a beautiful woman from an evil sorcerer.*

UNDERTOW

Karl Edward Wagner

Prologue

"She was brought in not long past dark," wheezed the custodian, scuttling crablike along the rows of silent, shrouded slabs. "The city guard found her, carried her in. Sounds like the one you're asking about."

He paused beside one of the waist-high stone tables and lifted its filthy sheet. A girl's contorted face turned sightlessly upward—painted and rouged, a ghastly strumpet's mask against the pallor of her skin. Clots of congealed blood hung like a necklace of dark rubies along the gash across her throat.

The cloaked man shook his head curtly within the shadow of his hood, and the moon-faced custodian let the sheet drop back.

"Not the one I was thinking of," he murmured apologetically. "It gets confusing sometimes, you know, what with so many, and them coming and going all the while." Sniffling in the cool air, he pushed his rotund bulk between the narrow aisles, careful to avoid the stained and filthy shrouds. Looming over his guide, the cloaked figure followed in silence.

Low-flamed lamps cast dismal light across the necrotorium of Carsultyal. Smoldering braziers spewed fitful, heavy fumed clouds of clinging incense that merged with the darkness and the stones and the decay—its cloying sweetness more nauseating than the stench of death it embraced. Through the thick gloom echoed the monotonous drip-drip-drip of melting ice, at times chorused suggestively by some heavier splash. The municipal morgue was crowded tonight—as always. Only a few of its hundred or more slate beds stood dark and bare; the others all displayed anonymous shapes bulging beneath blotched sheets—some protruding at curious angles, as if these restless dead struggled to burst free of the coarse folds. Night now hung over Carsultyal, but within this windowless subterranean chamber it was always night. In shadow pierced only by the sickly flame of funereal lamps, the nameless dead of Carsultyal lay unmourned—waited the required interval of time for someone to claim them, else to be carted off to some unmarked communal grave beyond the city walls.

"Here, I believe," announced the custodian. "Yes. I'll just get a lamp."

"Show me," demanded a voice from within the hood. The portly official glanced at the other uneasily. There was an aura of power, of blighted majesty about the cloaked figure that boded ill in arrogant Carsultyal, whose clustered, star-reaching towers were whispered to be overawed by cellars whose depths plunged farther still. "Light's poor back here," he protested, drawing back the tattered shroud.

The visitor cursed low in his throat—an inhuman sound touched less by grief than feral rage.

The face that stared at them with too wide eyes had been beautiful in life; in death it was purpled, bloated, contorted in pain. Dark blood stained the tip of her protruding tongue, and her neck seemed bent at an unnatural angle. A gown of light-colored silk was stained and disordered. She lay supine, hands clenched into tight fists at her side.

"The city guard found her?" repeated the visitor in a harsh voice.

"Yes, just after nightfall. In the park overlooking the harbor. She was hanging from a branch—there in the grove with all the white flowers every spring. Must have just happened—said her body was warm as life, though there's a chill to the sea breeze tonight. Looks like she done it herself—climbed out on the branch, tied the noose, and jumped off. Wonder why they do it—her as pretty a young thing as I've seen brought in, and took well care of, too."

The stranger stood in rigid silence, staring at the strangled girl.

"Will you come back in the morning to claim her, or do you want to wait upstairs?" suggested the custodian.

"I'll take her now."

The plump attendant fingered the gold coin his visitor had tossed him a short time before. His lips tightened in calculation. Often there appeared at the necrotorium those who wished to remove bodies clandestinely for strange and secret reasons—a circumstance which made lucrative this disagreeable office. "Can't allow that," he argued. "There's laws and forms—you shouldn't even be here at this hour. They'll be wanting their questions answered. And there's fees . . . "

With a snarl of inexpressible fury, the stranger turned on him. The sudden movement flung back his hood. The caretaker for the first time saw his visitor's eyes. He had breath for a short bleat of terror, before the dirk he did not see smashed through his heart.

Workers the next day, puzzling over the custodian's disappearance, were shocked to discover, on examining the night's new tenants for the necrotorium, that he had not disappeared after all.

I. Seekers in the Night

There—he heard the sound again.

Mavrsal left off his disgruntled contemplation of the near-empty wine bottle and stealthily came to his feet. The captain of the *Tuab* was alone in his cabin, and the hour was late. For hours the only sounds close at hand had been the slap of waves on the barnacled hull, the creak of cordage, and the dull thud of the caravel's aged timbers against the quay. Then had come a soft footfall, a muffled fumbling among the deck gear outside his half-open door. Too loud for rats—a thief, then?

Grimly Mavrsal unsheathed his heavy cutlass and caught up a lantern. He catfooted onto the deck, reflecting bitterly over his worthless crew. From cook to first mate, they had deserted his ship a few days before, angered over wages months unpaid. An unseasonable squall had forced them to jettison most of their cargo of copper ingots, and the *Tuab* had limped into the harbor of Carsultyal with shredded sails, a cracked mainmast, a dozen new leaks from wrenched timbers, and the rest of her worn fittings in no better shape. Instead of the expected wealth, the decimated cargo had brought in barely enough capital to cover the expense of refitting. Mavrsal argued that until refitted, the *Tuab* was unseaworthy, and that once repairs were complete, another cargo could be found (somehow), and then wages long in arrears could be paid—with a bonus for patient loyalty. The crew cared neither for his logic nor his promises and defected amidst stormy threats.

Had one of them returned to carry out . . . ? Mavrsal hunched his thick shoulders truculently and hefted the cutlass. The master of the *Tuab* had never run from a brawl, much less a sneak thief or slinking assassin.

Night skies of autumn were bright over Carsultyal, making the lantern almost unneeded. Mavrsal surveyed the soft shadows of the caravel's deck, his brown eyes narrowed and alert beneath shaggy brows. But he heard the low sobbing almost at once, so there was no need to prowl about the deck.

He strode quickly to the mound of torn sail and rigging at the far rail. "All right, come out of that!" he rumbled, beckoning with the tip of his blade to the half-seen figure crouched against the rail. The sobbing choked into silence. Mavrsal prodded the canvas with an impatient boot. "Out of there, damn it!" he repeated.

The canvas gave a wriggle and a pair of sandaled feet backed out, followed by bare legs and rounded hips that strained against the bunched fabric of her gown. Mavrsal pursed his lips thoughtfully as the girl emerged and stood before him. There were no tears in the eyes that met his gaze. The aristocratic face was defiant, although the flared nostrils and tightly pressed lips hinted that her defiance was a mask. Nervous fingers smoothed the silken gown and adjusted her cloak of dark brown wool.

"Inside." Mavrsal gestured with his cutlass to the lighted cabin.

"I wasn't doing anything," she protested.

"Looking for something to steal."

"I'm not a thief."

"We'll talk inside." He nudged her forward, and sullenly she complied.

Following her through the door, Mavrsal locked it behind him and replaced the lantern. Returning the cutlass to its scabbard, he dropped back into his chair and contemplated his discovery.

"I'm no thief," she repeated, fidgeting with the fastenings of her cloak.

No, he decided, she probably wasn't—not that there was much aboard a decrepit caravel like the *Tuab* to attract a thief. But why had she crept aboard? She was a harlot, he assumed—what other business drew a girl of her beauty alone into the night of Carsultyal's waterfront? And she *was* beautiful, he noted with growing surprise. A tangle of loosely bound red hair fell over her shoulders and framed a face whose pale-skinned classic beauty was enhanced rather than flawed by a dust of freckles across her thin-bridged nose. Eyes of startling green gazed at him with a defiance that seemed somehow haunted. She was tall, willowy. Before she settled the dark cloak about her shoulders, he had noted the high, conical breasts and softly rounded figure beneath the clinging gown of green silk. An emerald of good quality graced her hand, and about her neck she wore a wide collar of dark leather and red silk from which glinted a larger emerald.

No, thought Mavrsal—again revising his judgment—she was too lovely, her garments too costly, for the quality of street tart who plied these waters. His bewilderment deepened. "Why were you on board, then?" he demanded in a manner less abrupt.

Her eyes darted about the cabin. "I don't know," she returned.

Mavrsal grunted in vexation. "Were you trying to stow away?"

She responded with a small shrug. "I suppose so." The sea captain gave a snort and drew his stocky frame erect. "Then you're a damn fool—or must think I'm one! Stow away on a battered old warrior like the *Tuab*, when there's plainly no cargo to put to sea, and any eye can see the damn ship's being refitted! Why, that ring you're wearing would book passage to any port you'd care to see, and on a first-class vessel! And to wander these streets at this hour! Well, maybe that's your business, and maybe you aren't careful of your trade, but there's scum along these waterfront dives that would slit a wench's throat as soon as pay her! Vaul! I've been in port three days and four nights, and already I've heard talk of enough depraved murders of pretty girls like you to—"

"Will you stop it!" she hissed in a tight voice. Slumping into the cabin's one other chair, she propped her elbows onto the rough table and jammed her fists against her forehead. Russet tresses tumbled over her face like a veil, so that Mavrsal could not read the emotions etched there. In the hollow of the cloak's parted folds, her breasts trembled with the quick pounding of her heart.

Sighing, he drained the last of the wine into his mug and pushed the pewter vessel toward the girl. There was another bottle in his cupboard; rising, he drew it out along with another cup. She was carefully sipping from the proffered mug when he resumed his place.

"Look, what's your name?" he asked her.

She paused so tensely before replying, "Dessylyn."

The name meant nothing to Mavrsal, although as the tension waxed and receded from her bearing, he understood that she had been concerned that her name would bring recognition.

Mavrsal smoothed his close-trimmed brown beard. There was a rough-and-ready toughness about his face that belied the fact that he had not quite reached thirty years, and women liked to tell him his rugged features were handsome. His left ear—badly scarred in a tavern brawl—gave him some concern, but it lay hidden beneath the unruly mass of his hair. "Well, Dessylyn," he grinned. "My name's Mavrsal, and this is my ship. And if you're worried about finding a place, you can spend the night here."

There was dread in her face. "I can't."

Mavrsal frowned, thinking he had been snubbed, and started to make an angry retort.

"I dare not . . . stay here too long," Dessylyn interposed, fear glowing in her eyes.

Mavrsal made an exasperated grimace. "Girl, you sneaked aboard my ship like a thief, but I'm inclined to forget your trespassing. Now, my cabin's cozy, girls tell me I'm a pleasant companion, and I'm generous with my coin. So why wander off into the night, where in the first filthy alley some pox-ridden drunk is going to take for free what I'm willing to pay for?"

"You don't understand!"

"Very plainly I don't." He watched her fidget with the pewter mug for a moment, then added pointedly, "Besides, you can hide here."

"By the gods! I wish I could!" she cried out. "If only I *could* hide from him!"

Brows knit in puzzlement, Mavrsal listened to the strangled sobs that rose muffled through the tousled auburn mane. He had not expected so unsettling a response to his probe. Thinking that every effort to penetrate the mystery surrounding Dessylyn only left him further in the dark, he measured out another portion of wine—and wondered if he should apologize for something.

"I suppose that's why I did it," she was mumbling. "I was able to slip away for a short while. So I walked along the shore, and I saw all the ships poised for flight along the harbor, and I thought how wonderful to be free like that! To step on board some strange ship, and to sail into the night to some unknown land—where *he* could never find me! *To be free!* Oh, I knew I could never escape him like that, but still when I walked by your ship, I wanted to try! I thought I could go through the motions—pretend I was escaping him!

"Only I know there's no escape from Kane!"

"Kane!" Mavrsal breathed a curse. Anger toward the girl's tormentor that had started to flare within him abruptly shuddered under the chill blast of fear.

Kane! Even to a stranger in Carsultyal, greatest city of mankind's dawn, that name evoked the specter of terror. A thousand tales were whispered of Kane; even in this city of sorcery, where the lost knowledge of pre-human Earth had been recovered to forge man's stolen civilization, Kane was a figure of awe and mystery. Despite uncounted tales of strange and disturbing nature, almost nothing was known for certain of the man save that for generations his tower had brooded over Carsultyal. There he followed the secret paths along which his dark genius led him, and the hand of Kane was rarely seen (though it was often felt) in the affairs of Carsultyal. Brother sorcerers and masters of powers temporal alike spoke his name with dread, and those who dared to make him an enemy seldom were given long, to repent their audacity.

"Are you Kane's woman?" he blurted out.

Her voice was bitter. "So Kane would have it. His mistress. His possession. Once, though, I was my own woman—before I was fool enough to let Kane draw me into his web!"

"Can't you leave him—leave this city?"

"You don't know the power Kane commands! Who would risk his anger to help me?"

Mavrsal squared his shoulders. "I owe no allegiance to Kane, nor to his minions in Carsultyal. This ship may be weathered and leaky, but she's mine, and I sail her where I please. If you're set on—"

Fear twisted her face. "Don't!" she gasped. "Don't even hint this to me! You can't realize what power Kane—

"What was that!"

Mavrsal tensed. From the night sounded the soft buffeting of great leathery wings. Claws scraped against the timbers of the deck outside. Suddenly the lantern flames seemed to shrink and waver; shadow fell deep within the cabin.

"He's missed me!" Dessylyn moaned. "He's sent it to bring me back!"

His belly cold, Mavrsal drew his cutlass and turned stiffly toward the door. The lamp flames were no more than a dying blue gleam. Beyond the door a shuffling weight caused a loosened plank to groan dully.

"No! Please!" she cried in desperation. "There's nothing you can do! Stay back from the door!"

Mavrsal snarled, his face reflecting the rage and terror that gripped him. Dessylyn pulled at his arm to draw him back.

He had locked the cabin door; a heavy iron bolt secured the stout timbers. Now an unseen hand was drawing the bolt aside. Silently, slowly, the iron bar turned and crept back along its mounting brackets. The lock snapped open. With nightmarish suddenness, the door swung wide.

Darkness hung in the passageway. Burning eyes regarded them. Advanced.

Dessylyn screamed hopelessly. Numb with terror, Mavrsal clumsily swung his blade toward the glowing eyes. Blackness reached out, hurled him with irresistible strength across the cabin. Pain burst across his consciousness, and then was only the darkness.

II. "Never, Dessylyn"

She shuddered and drew the fur cloak tighter about her thin shoulders. *Would there ever again be a time when she wouldn't feel this remorseless cold?*

Kane, his cruel face haggard in the glow of the brazier, stood hunched over the crimson alembic. *How red the coals made his hair and beard; how sinister was the blue flame of his eyes . . .* He craned intently forward to trap the last few drops of the phosphorescent elixir in a chalice of ruby crystal.

He had labored sleepless hours over the glowing liquid, she knew. Hours precious to her because these were hours of freedom—a time when she might escape his loathed attention. Her lips pressed a tight, bloodless line. The abominable formulae from which he prepared the elixir! Dessylyn thought again of the mutilated corpse of the young girl Kane had directed his servant to carry off. Again a spasm slid across her lithe form.

"Why won't you let me go?" she heard herself ask dully for the . . . *how many times had she asked that?*

"I'll not let you go, Dessylyn," Kane replied in a tired voice. "You know that."

"Someday I'll leave you."

"No, Dessylyn. You'll never leave me."

"Someday."

"Never, Dessylyn."

"Why, Kane!"

With painful care, he allowed a few drops of an amber liqueur to fall into the glowing chalice. Blue flame hovered over its surface.

"Why!"

"Because I love you, Dessylyn."

A bitter sob, parody of laughter, shook her throat. "You love me." She enclosed a hopeless scream in those slow, grinding syllables.

"Kane, can I ever make you understand how utterly I loathe you?"

"Perhaps. But I love you, Dessylyn." The sobbing laugh returned.

Glancing at her in concern, Kane carefully extended the chalice toward her. "Drink this. Quickly—before the nimbus dies."

She looked at him through eyes dark with horror. "Another bitter draught of some foul drug to bind me to you?"

"Whatever you wish to call it."

"I won't drink it."

"Yes, Dessylyn, you will drink it."

His killer's eyes held her with bonds of eternal ice. Mechanically she accepted the crimson chalice, let its phosphorescent liqueur pass between her lips, seep down her throat.

Kane sighed and took the empty goblet from her listless grip. His massive frame seemed to shudder from fatigue, and he passed a broad hand across his eyes. Blood rimmed their dark hollows.

"I'll leave you, Kane."

The sea wind gusted through the tower window and swirled the long red hair about his haunted face. "Never, Dessylyn."

◆ ◆ ◆

III. At the Inn of the Blue Window

He called himself Dragar . . .

Had the girl not walked past him seconds before, he probably would not have interfered when he heard her scream. Or perhaps he would have. A stranger to Carsultyal, nonetheless the barbarian youth had passed time enough in mankind's lesser cities to be wary of cries for help in the night and to think twice before plunging into dark alleys to join in an unseen struggle. But there was a certain pride in the chivalric ideals of his heritage, along with a confidence in the hard muscle of his sword arm and in the strange blade he carried.

Thinking of the lithe, white limbs he had glimpsed—the patrician beauty of the face that coolly returned his curious stare as she came toward him—Dragar unsheathed the heavy blade at his hip and dashed back along the street he had just entered.

There was moonlight enough to see, although the alley was well removed from the nearest flaring streetlamp. Cloak torn away, her gown ripped from her shoulders, the girl writhed in the grasp of two thugs. A third tough warned by the rush of the barbarian's boots, angrily spun to face him, sword streaking for the youth's belly.

Dragar laughed and flung the lighter blade aside with a powerful blow of his sword. Scarcely seeming to pause in his attack, he gashed his assailant's arm with an upward swing, and as the other's blade faltered, he split the thug's skull. One of the two who held the girl lunged forward, but Dragar sidestepped his rush, and with a sudden thrust sent his sword ripping into the man's chest. The remaining assailant shoved the girl against the barbarian's legs, whirled, and fled down the alley.

Ignoring the fugitive, Dragar helped the stunned girl to her feet. Terror yet twisted her face, as she distractedly arranged the torn bodice of her silken gown. Livid scratches streaked the pale skin of her breasts, and a bruise was swelling out her lip. Dragar caught up her fallen cloak and draped it over her shoulders.

"Thank you," she breathed in a shaky whisper, speaking at last.

"My pleasure," he rumbled. "Killing rats is good exercise. Are you all right, though?"

She nodded, then clutched his arm for support.

"The hell you are! There's a tavern close by, girl. Come—I've silver enough for a brandy to put the fire back in your heart."

She looked as if she might refuse, were her knees steadier. In a daze, the girl let him half-carry her into the Inn of the Blue Window. There he led her to an unoccupied booth and called for brandy.

"What's your name?" he asked, after she had tasted the heady liqueur.

"Dessylyn."

He framed her name with silent lips to feel its sound. "I'm called Dragar," he told her. "My home lies among the mountains far south of here, though it's been a few years since last I hunted with my clansmen. Wanderlust drew me away, and since then I've followed this banner or another's—sometimes just the shadow of my own flapping cloak. Then, after hearing tales enough to dull my ears, I decided to see for myself if Carsultyal is the wonder men boast her to be. You a stranger here as well?"

She shook her head. When the color returned to her cheeks, her face seemed less aloof.

"Thought you might be. Else you'd know better than to wander the streets of Carsultyal after nightfall. Must be something important for you to take the risk."

The lift of her shoulders was casual, though her face remained guarded. "No errand . . . but it was important to me."

Dragar's look was questioning.

"I wanted to . . . oh, just to be alone, to get away for a while. Lose myself, maybe—I don't know. I didn't think anyone would dare touch me if they knew who I was."

"Your fame must be held somewhat less in awe among these gutter rats than you imagined," offered Dragar wryly.

"All men fear the name of Kane!" Dessylyn shot back bitterly.

"Kane!" The name exploded from his lips in amazement. *What had this girl to do . . . ?* But Dragar looked again at her sophisticated beauty, her luxurious attire, and understanding dawned. Angrily he became aware that the tavern uproar had become subdued on the echo of his outburst. Several faces had turned to him, their expressions uneasy, calculating.

The barbarian clapped a hand to his sword hilt. "Here's a man who doesn't fear a name!" he announced. "I've heard something of Carsultyal's most dreaded sorcerer, but his name means less than a fart to me! There's steel in this sword that can slice through the best your world-famed master smiths can forge, and it thrives on the gore of magicians. I call the blade Wizard's Bane, and there are souls in Hell who will swear that its naming is no boast!"

Dessylyn stared at him in sudden fascination.

And what came after, Dessylyn?

I . . . I'm not sure . . . My mind—I was in a state of shock, I suppose. I remember holding his head for what seemed like forever. And then I remember sponging off the blood with water from the wooden lavabo, and the water was so cold and so red, so red. I must have put on my clothes . . . Yes, and I remember the city and walking and all those faces . . . All those faces . . . they stared at me, some of them. Stated and looked away, stared and looked compassionate, stared and looked curious, stared and made awful suggestions . . . And some just ignored me, didn't see me at all. I can't think which faces were the most cruel . . . I walked, walked so long . . . I remember the pain . . . I remember my tears, and the pain when there were no more tears . . . I remember . . . My mind was dazed . . . My memory . . . I can't remember . . .

IV. A Ship Will Sail . . .

He looked up from his work and saw her standing there on the quay—watching him, her face a strange play of intensity and indecision. Mavrsal grunted in surprise and straightened from his carpentry. She might have been a phantom, so silently had she crept upon him.

"I had to see if . . . if you were all right," Dessylyn told him with an uncertain smile.

"I am—aside from a crack on my skull," Mavrsal answered, eying her dubiously.

By the dawnlight he had crawled from beneath the overturned furnishings of his cabin. Blood matted his thick hair at the back of his skull, and his head throbbed with a deafening ache, so that he had sat dumbly for a long while, trying to recollect the events of the night. *Something* had come through the door, had hurled him aside like a spurned doll. And the girl had vanished . . . carried off by the demon? Her warning had been for him; for herself she evidenced not fear, only resigned despair.

Or had some of his men returned to carry out their threats? Had too much wine, the blow on his head . . . ? But no, Mavrsal knew better. His assailants would have robbed him, made certain of his death—had any human agency attacked him. She had called herself a sorcerer's mistress, and it had been sorcery that spread its black wings over his caravel. Now the girl had returned, and Mavrsal's greeting was tempered by his awareness of the danger which shadowed her presence.

Dessylyn must have known his thoughts. She backed away, as if to turn and go.

"Wait!" he called suddenly.

"I don't want to endanger you any further."

Mavrsal's quick temper responded. "Danger! Kane can bugger with his demons in Hell, for all I care! My skull was too thick for his creature to split, and if he wants to try his hand in person, I'm here to offer him the chance!" There was gladness in her wide eyes as Dessylyn stepped toward him. "His necromancies have exhausted him," she assured the other. "Kane will sleep for hours yet."

Mavrsal handed her over the rail with rough gallantry. "Then perhaps you'll join me in my cabin. It's grown too dark for carpentry, and I'd like to talk with you. After last night, I think I deserve to have some questions answered, anyway."

He struck fire to a lamp and turned to find her balanced at the edge of a chair, watching him nervously. "What sort of questions?" she asked in an uneasy tone.

"Why?"

"Why what?"

Mavrsal made a vague gesture. "Why everything. Why did you get involved with this sorcerer? Why does he hold to you, if you hate him so? Why can't you leave him?"

She gave him a sad smile that left him feeling naïve. "Kane is . . . a fascinating man; there is a certain magnetism about him. And I won't deny the attraction his tremendous power and wealth held for me. Does it matter? It's enough to say that there was a time when we met and I fell under Kane's spell. It may be that I loved him once—but I've since hated too long and to deeply to remember.

"But Kane continues to love me in his way. *Love!* His is the love of a miser for his hoard, the love of a connoisseur for some exquisitely wrought carving, the love a spider feels for its imprisoned prey! I'm his treasure, his possession—and what concern are the feelings of a lifeless object to its owner? Would the curious circumstance that his prized statue might hate him lessen the pleasure its owner derives from its possession?

"And leave him?" Her voice broke. "By the gods, don't you think I've tried?"

His thoughts in a turmoil, Mavrsal studied the girl's haunted face. "But why accept defeat? Past failure doesn't mean you can't try again. If you're free to roam the streets of Carsultyal at night, your feet can take you farther still. I see no chain clamped to that collar you wear."

"Not all chains are visible."

"So I've heard, though I've never believed it. A weak will can imagine its own fetters."

"Kane won't let me leave him."

"Kane's power doesn't reach a tenth so far as he believes."

"There are men who would dispute that, if the dead cared to share the wisdom that came to them too late."

Challenge glinted in the girl's green eyes as they held his. Mavrsal felt the spell of her beauty, and his manhood answered. "A ship sails where its master wills it—may the winds and the tides and perils of the sea be damned!"

Her face craned closer. Tendrils of her auburn hair touched his arm. "There is courage in your words. But you know little of Kane's power."

He laughed recklessly. "Let's say I'm not cowed by his name."

From the belt of her gown, Dessylyn unfastened a small scrip. She tossed the leather pouch toward him.

Catching it, Mavrsal untied the braided thong and dumped its contents onto his palm. His hand shook. Gleaming gemstones tumbled in a tiny rainbow, clattered onto the cabin table. In his hand lay a fortune in rough-cut diamonds, emeralds, other precious stones.

Through their multihued reflections his face framed a question.

"I think there is enough to repair your ship, to pay her crew . . . " She paused; brighter flamed the challenge in her eyes. "Perhaps to buy my passage to a distant port—if you dare!"

The captain of the *Tuab* swore. "I meant what I said, girl! Give me another few days to refit her, and I'll sail you to lands where no man has ever heard the name of Kane!"

"Later you may change your mind," Dessylyn warned. She rose from her chair. Mavrsal thought she meant to leave, but then he saw that her fingers had loosened other fastenings at her belt. His breath caught as the silken gown began to slip from her shoulders.

"I won't change my mind," he promised, understanding why Kane might go to any extreme to keep Dessylyn with him.

V. Wizard's Bane

"Your skin is like the purest honey," proclaimed Dragar ardently. "By the gods, I swear you even taste like honey!"

Dessylyn squirmed in pleasure and hugged the barbarian's shaggy blond head to her breasts. After a moment she sighed and languorously pulled from his embrace. Sitting up, she brushed her slim fingers through the tousled auburn wave that cascaded over her bare shoulders and back, clung in damp curls to her flushed skin.

Dragar's calloused hand imprisoned her slender wrist as she sought to rise from the rumpled bed. "Don't prance away like a contrite virgin, girl. Your rider has dismounted but for a moment's rest—then he's ready to gallop through the palace gates another time or more, before the sun drops beneath the sea."

"Pretty, but I have to go," she protested. "Kane may grow suspicious . . . "

"Bugger Kane!" cursed Dragar, pulling the girl back against him. His thick arms locked about her, and their lips crushed savagely. Cupped over a small breast, his hand felt the pounding of her heart, and the youth laughed and tilted back her feverish face. "Now tell me you prefer Kane's effete pawings to a man's embrace!"

A frown drifted like a sudden thunderhead. "You underestimate Kane. He's no soft-fleshed weakling." The youth snarled in jealousy. "A foul sorcerer who's skulked in his tower no one knows how long! He'll have dust for blood, and dry rot in his bones! But go to him if you prefer his toothless kisses and withered loins!"

"No, dearest! Yours are the arms I love to lie within!" Dessylyn cried, entwining herself about him and soothing his anger with kisses. "It's just that I'm frightened for you. Kane isn't a withered graybeard. Except for the madness in his eyes, you would think Kane a hardened warrior in his prime. And you've more than his sorcery to fear. I've seen Kane kill with his sword—he's a deadly fighter!"

Dragar snorted and stretched his brawny frame. "No warrior hides behind a magician's robes. He's but a name—an ogre's name to frighten children into obedience. Well, I don't fear his name, nor do I fear his magic, and my blade has drunk the blood of better swordsmen than your black-hearted tyrant ever was!"

"By the gods!" whispered Dessylyn, burrowing against his thick shoulder. "Why did fate throw me into Kane's web instead of into your arms!"

"Fate is what man wills it. If you wish it, you are my woman now."

"But Kane . . . "

The barbarian leaped to his feet and glowered down at her. "Enough sniveling about Kane, girl! Do you love me or not?"

"Dragar, beloved, you know I love you! Haven't these past days . . . "

"These past days have been filled with woeful whimperings about Kane, and my belly grows sick from hearing it! Forget Kane! I'm taking you from him, Dessylyn! For all her glorious legend and over-mighty towers, Carsultyal is a stinking pesthole like every other city I've known. Well, I'll waste no more days here.

"I'll ride from Carsultyal tomorrow, or take passage on a ship, perhaps. Go to some less stagnant land, where a bold man and a strong blade can win wealth and adventure! You're going with me."

"Can you mean it, Dragar?"

"If you think I lie, then stay behind."

"Kane will follow."

"Then he'll lose his life along with his love!" sneered Dragar.

With confident hands, he slid from its scabbard his great sword of silver-blue metal. "See this blade," he hissed, flourishing its massive length easily. "I call it Wizard's Bane, and there's reason to the name. Look at the blade. It's steel, but not steel such as your secretive smiths forge in their dragon-breath furnaces. See the symbols carved into the forte. This blade has power! It was forged long ago by a master smith who used the glowing heart of a fallen star for his ore, who set runes of protection into the finished sword. Who wields Wizard's Bane need not fear magic, for sorcery can have no power over him. My sword can cleave through the hellish flesh of demons. It can ward off a sorcerer's enchantments and skewer his evil heart!

"Let Kane send his demons to find us! My blade will shield us from his spells, and I'll send his minions howling in fear back to his dread tower! Let him creep from his lair if he dares! I'll feed him bits of his liver and laugh in his face while he dies!"

Dessylyn's eyes brimmed with adoration. "You can do it, Dragar! You're strong enough to take me from Kane! No man has your courage, beloved!"

The youth laughed and twisted her hair. "No man? What do you know of men?

Did you think these spineless city-bred fops, who tremble at the shadow of a senile cuckold, were men? Think no more of slinking back to Kane's tower before your keeper misses you. Tonight, girl, I'm going to show you how a man loves his woman!"

But why will you insist it's impossible to leave Kane?

I know.

How can you know? You're too fearful of him to try.

I know.

But how can you say that?

Because I know.

Perhaps this bondage is only in your mind, Dessylyn.

But I know Kane won't let me leave him.

So certain—is it because you've tried to escape him? Have you tried, Dessylyn? Tried with another's help—and failed, Dessylyn?

Can't you be honest with me, Dessylyn?

And now you'll turn away from me in fear!

Then there was another man?

It's impossible to escape him—and now you'll abandon me!

Tell me, Dessylyn. How can I trust you if you won't trust me?

On your word, then. There was another man . . .

VI. Night and Fog

Night returned to Carsultyal and spread its misty cloak over narrow alleys and brooding towers alike. The voice of the street broke from its strident daylight cacophony to a muted rumble of night. As the stars grew brighter through the sea mists, the streets grew silent, except for fitful snorts and growls like a hound uneasy in his sleep. Then the lights that glimmered through the shadow began to slip away, so stealthily that their departure went unnoticed. One only knew that the darkness, the fog, the silence now ruled the city unchallenged. And night, closer here than elsewhere in the cities of mankind, had returned to Carsultyal.

They lay close in each other's arms—sated, but too restless for sleep. Few were their words, so that they listened to the beating of their hearts, pressed so close together as to make one sound. Fog thrust tendrils through chinks in the bolted shutters, brought with it the chill breath of the sea, lost cries of ships anchored in the night.

Then Dessylyn hissed like a cat and dug her nails so deep into Dragar's arm that rivulets of crimson made an armlet about the corded muscle. Straining his senses against the night, the barbarian dropped his hand to the hilt of the unsheathed sword that lay beside their bed. The blade glinted blue—more so than the wan lamplight would seem to reflect.

From the night outside . . . Was it a sudden wind that rattled the window shutters, buffeted the streamers of fog into swirling eddies? A sound . . . Was that the flap of vast leathery wings?

Fear hung like a clinging web over the inn, and the silence about them was so desolate that theirs might have been the last two hearts to beat in all of haunted Carsultyal.

From the roof suddenly there came a slithering metallic scrape upon the slate tiles.

Wizard's Bane pulsed with a corposant of blue witchfire. Shadows stark and unreal cringed away from the lambent blade.

Against the thick shutters sounded a creaking groan of hideous pressure. Oaken planks sagged inward. Holding fast, the iron bolts trembled, then abruptly smoldered into sullen rubrous heat. Mist poured past the buckling timbers, bearing with it a smell not of any sea known to man.

Brighter pulsed the scintillant glare of the sword. A nimbus of blue flame rippled out from the blade and encircled the crouching youth and his terrified companion. Rippling blue radiance, spreading across the room, struck the groaning shutters.

A burst of incandescence spat from the glowing iron bolts. Through the night beyond tore a silent snarl—an unearthly shriek felt rather than heard—a spitting bestial cry of pain and baffled rage.

The shutters sprang back with a grunting sigh as the pressure against them suddenly relented. Again the night shuddered with the buffet of tremendous wings. The ghost of sound dwindled. The black tide of fear ebbed and shrank back from the inn.

Dragar laughed and brandished his sword. Eyes still dazzled, Dessylyn stared in fascination at the blade, now suffused with a sheen no more preternatural than any finely burnished steel. It might all have been a frightened dream, she thought, knowing well that it had not been.

"It looks like your keeper's sorcery is something less than all powerful!" scoffed the barbarian. "Now Kane will know that his spells and coward's tricks are powerless against Wizard's Bane. No doubt your ancient spellcaster is cowering under his cold bed, scared spitless that these gutless city folk will some day find courage enough to call his bluff! And against that, he's probably safe."

"You don't know Kane," moaned Dessylyn.

With gentle roughness, Dragar cuffed the grim-faced girl. "Still frightened by a legend? And after you've seen his magic defeated by the star-blade! You've lived within the shadow of this decadent city too long, girl. In a few hours we'll have light, and then I'll take you out into the real world—where men haven't sold their souls to the ghosts of elder races!"

But her fears did not dissolve under the barbarian's warm confidence. For a timeless period of darkness Dessylyn clung to him, her heart restlessly drumming, shuddering at each fragment of sound that pierced the night and fog.

And through the darkened streets echoed the clop-clop of hooves.

Far away, their sound so faint it might have been imagined. Closer now, the fog-muffled fall of iron-shod hooves on paving bricks. Drawing ever closer, a hollow, rhythmic knell that grew deafening in the absolute stillness. Clop-Clop Clop-Clop Clop-Clop CLOP-CLOP CLOP-CLOP. Approaching the inn unhurriedly. Inexorably approaching the mist-shrouded inn.

"What is it?" he asked her, as she started upright in terror.

"I know that sound. It's a black, black stallion, with eyes that burn like living coals and hooves that ring like iron!"

Dragar snorted.

"Ah! And I know his rider!"

CLOP-CLOP CLOP-CLOP. Hoofbeats rolled and gobbled across the courtyard of the Inn of the Blue Window. Echoes rattled against the shutters... *Could no one else hear their chill thunder?*

CLOP-CLOP CLOP. The unseen horse stamped and halted outside the inn's door. Harness jingled. *Why were there no voices?*

From deep within the chambers below echoed the dull chink of the bolt and bars falling away, clattering to the floor. A harsh creak as the outer door swung open. *Where was the innkeeper?*

Footfalls sounded on the stairs—the soft scuff of boot leather on worn planks. Someone entered the hallway beyond their door; strode confidently toward their room.

Dessylyn's face was a stark mask of terror. Knuckles jammed against her teeth to dam a rising scream were stained red with drawn blood. Dread-haunted eyes were fixed upon the door opposite.

Slipping into a fighting crouch, Dragar spared a glance for the bared blade in his taut grasp. No nimbus of flame hovered about the sword, only the deadly gleam of honed steel, reflected in the unnaturally subdued lamplight.

Footsteps halted in front of their door. It seemed he could hear the sound of breathing from beyond the threshold.

A heavy fist smote the door. Once. A single summons. A single challenge.

With an urgent gesture, Dessylyn signed Dragar to remain silent.

"Who dares . . . !" he growled in a ragged voice.

A powerful blow exploded against the stout timber. Latch and bolt erupted from their setting in a shower of splinters and wrenched metal. All but torn from its hinges, the door was hurled open, slammed resoundingly against the wall.

"Kane!" screamed Dessylyn.

The massive figure strode through the doorway, feral grace in the movements of his powerful, square-torsoed frame. A heavy sword was balanced with seeming negligence in his left hand, but there was no uncertainty in the lethal fury that blazed in his eyes.

"Good evening," sneered Kane through a mirthless smile.

Startled despite Dessylyn's warning, Dragar's practiced eye swiftly sized up his opponent. So the sorcerer's magic had preserved the prime of his years after all . . . At about six feet Kane stood several inches shorter than the towering barbarian, but the enormous bands of muscle that surged beneath leather vest and trousers made his weight somewhat greater. Long arms and the powerful roll of his shoulders signaled a swordsman of considerable reach and strength, although the youth doubted if Kane could match his speed. A slim leather band with a black opal tied back his shoulder-length red hair, and the face beneath the close-trimmed beard was brutal, with a savagery that made his demeanor less lordly than arrogant. And his blue eyes burned with the brand of killer.

"Come looking for your woman, sorcerer?" grated Dragar, watching the other's blade. "We thought you'd stay hidden in your tower, after I frightened off your slinking servants!"

Kane's eyes narrowed. "So that's . . . Wizard's Bane, I believe you call it. I see the legends didn't lie when they spoke of the blade's protective powers. I shouldn't have spoken of it to Dessylyn, I suppose, when I learned that an enchanted sword had been brought into Carsultyal. But then, its possession will compensate in some part for the difficulties you've caused me."

"Kill him, Dragar, my love! Don't listen to his lies!" Dessylyn cried.

"What do you mean?" rumbled the youth, who had missed Kane's inference.

The warrior wizard chuckled dryly. "Can't you guess, you romantic oaf? Don't you understand that a clever woman has used you? Of course not—the chivalrous barbarian thought he was defending a helpless girl. Pity I let Laroc die after persuading him to tell me of her game. He might have told you how innocent his mistress—"

"Dragar! Kill him! He only means to take you off guard!"

"To be sure! Kill me, Dragar—if you can! That was her plan, you know. Through my . . . sources . . . I learned of this formidable blade you carry and made mention of it to Dessylyn. But Dessylyn, it seems, has grown bored with my caresses. She paid a servant, the unlamented Laroc, to stage an apparent rape, trusting that a certain lout would rush in to save her. Well plotted, don't you think? Now poor Dessylyn has a bold defender whose magic blade can protect her against Kane's evil spells. I wonder, Dessylyn—did you only mean to go away with this thickheaded dolt, or did you plan to goad me into this personal combat, hoping I'd be slain and the wealth of my tower would be yours?"

"Dragar! He's lying to you!" moaned the girl despairingly.

"Because if it was the latter, then I'm afraid your plotting wasn't as intelligent as you believed," concluded Kane mockingly.

"Dragar!" came the tortured choke.

The barbarian, emotions a fiery chaos, risked an agonized glance at her contorted face.

Kane lunged.

Off guard, Dragar's lightning recovery deflected Kane's blade at the last possible instant, so that he took a shallow gash across his side instead of the steel through his ribs. "Damn you!" he cursed.

"But I am!" laughed Kane, parrying the youth's flashing counterattack with ease. His speed was uncanny, and the awesome power of his thick shoulders drove his blade with deadly force.

Lightning seemed to flash with the ringing thunder of their blades. Rune-stamped star-metal hammered against the finest steel of Carsultyal's far-fanned forges, and their clangor seemed the cries of two warring demons—harsh, strident with pain and rage.

Sweat shone on Dragar's naked body, and his breath spat foam through his clenched teeth. A few times only had he crossed blades with an opponent his equal in strength, and then the youth's superior speed had carried the victory. Now, as in some impossible nightmare, he faced a skilled and cunning swordsman whose speed was at least his equal—and whose strength seemed somewhat greater. After his initial attack had been deftly turned away, Dragar's swordplay became less reckless, less confident. Grimly he set about wearing down his opponent's endurance, reasoning that the sorcerer's physical conditioning could not equal that of a hardened mercenary.

In all the world there was no sound but their ringing blades, the desperate rush of their bodies, the hoarse gusts of their breath. Everywhere time stood frozen, save for the deadly fury of their duel, as they leaped and lunged about the bare-timbered room.

Dragar caught a thin slash across his left arm from a blow he did not remember deflecting. Kane's left-handed attack was dangerously unfamiliar to him, and only his desperate parries had saved him from worse. Uneasily he realized that Kane's sword arm did not falter as the minutes dragged past and that more and more he was being confined to the defensive. Wizard's Bane grew ragged with notches from the Carsultyal blade, and its hilt slippery with sweat. Kane's heavier sword was similarly scarred from their relentless slash, parry, thrust.

Then as Kane deflected Dragar's powerful stroke, the youth made a quick thrust with the turning blade—enough so that its tip gashed diagonally across Kane's brow, severing his headband. A shallow cut, but blood flowed freely, matted the clinging strands of his unbound hair. Kane gave back, flung the blood and loose hair from his eyes.

And Dragar lunged. Too quick for Kane to parry fully, his blade gored a furrow the length of the sorcerer's left forearm. Kane's long sword faltered. Instantly the barbarian hammered at his guard.

The sword left Kane's grip as it clumsily threw back the star-blade. For a fraction of a second it turned free in midair. Dragar exulted that he had at last torn the blade from Kane's grasp—as he raised his arm for a killing stroke.

But Kane's right hand caught up the spinning blade with practiced surety. Wielding the sword with skill scarcely inferior to his natural sword arm, Kane parried Dragar's flashing blow. Then, before the startled barbarian could recover, Kane's sword smashed through Dragar's ribs.

The force of the blow hurled the stricken youth back against the bed. Wizard's Bane dropped from nerveless fingers and skidded across the wide oaken planks.

From Dessylyn's throat came a cry of inexpressible pain. She rushed to him and cradled Dragar's head against her lap. Desperately she pressed ineffectual fingers against the pulsing wound in his chest. "Please, Kane!" she sobbed. "Spare him!"

Kane glanced through burning eyes at the youth's ruined chest and laughed. "I give him to you, Dessylyn," he told her insolently. "And I'll await you in my tower—unless, of course, you young lovers still plan on running off together."

Blood trailing from his arm—and darker blood from his sword—he stalked from the room and into the night mists.

"Dragar! Dragar!" Dessylyn moaned, kissing his haggard face and blood-foamed lips. "Please don't die, beloved! Onthe, don't let him die!"

Tears fell from her eyes to his as she pressed her face against his pallid visage. "You didn't believe him, did you, Dragar? What if I did engineer our meeting, dearest! Still I love you! It's true that I love you! I'll always love you, Dragar!"

He looked at her through glazing eyes. "Bitch!" he spat, and died.

◆ ◆ ◆

How many times, Dessylyn?
How many times will you play this game?
(But this was the first!)
The first? Are you sure, Dessylyn?
(I swear it! . . . How can I be sure?)
And how many after?
How many circles, Dessylyn?
(Circles? Why this darkness in my mind?)
How many times, Dessylyn, have you played at Lorelei?
How many are those who have known your summoning eye?
How many are those who have heard your siren cry, Dessylyn?
How many souls have swum out to you, Dessylyn?
And perished by the shadows that hide below,
And are drawn down to Hell by the undertow?
How many times, Dessylyn?
(I can't remember . . .)

VII. "He'll Have to Die . . ."

"You know he'll have to die."

Dessylyn shook her head. "It's too dangerous."

"Clearly it's far more dangerous to let him live," Mavrsal pointed out grimly. "From what you've told me, Kane will never permit you to leave him—and this isn't like trying to get away from some jealous lord. A sorcerer's tentacles reach farther than those of the fabled Oraycha. What good is it to escape Carsultyal, only to have Kane's magic strike at us later? Even on the high sea his shadow can follow us."

"But we might escape him," murmured Dessylyn. "The oceans are limitless, and the waves carry no trail."

"A wizard of Kane's power will have ways to follow us."

"It's still too dangerous. I'm not even sure Kane can be killed!" Dessylyn's fingers toyed anxiously with the emerald at her throat; her lips were tightly pressed.

Angrily Mavrsal watched her fingers twist the wide silk and leather collar. Fine ladies might consider the fashion stylish here in Carsultyal, but it annoyed him that she wore the ornament even in bed. "You'll never be free of Kane's slave collar," he growled, voicing his thought, "until that devil is dead."

"I know," breathed the girl softly, more than fear shining in her green eyes.

"Yours is the hand that can kill him," he continued. Her lips moved, but no sound issued.

Soft harbor sounds whispered through the night as the *Tuab* gently rocked with the waves. Against the quay, her timbers creaked and groaned, thudded against the buffers of waste hemp cordage. Distantly, her watch paced the deck; low conversation, dimly heard, marked the presence of other crewmen—not yet in their hammocks, despite a hard day's work. In the captain's cabin a lamp swung slowly with the vessel's roll, playing soft shadows back and forth against the objects within. Snug and sheltered from the sea mists, the atmosphere was almost cozy—could the cabin only have been secure against a darker phantom that haunted the night.

"Kane claims to love you," Mavrsal persisted shrewdly. "He won't accept your hatred of him. In other words, he'll unconsciously lower his guard with you. He'll let you stand at his back and never suspect that your hand might drive a dagger through his ribs."

"It's true," she acknowledged in a strange voice.

Mavrsal held her shoulders and turned her face to his. "I can't see why you haven't tried this before. Was it fear?"

"Yes. I'm terrified of Kane."

"Or was it something else? Do you still feel some secret love for him, Dessylyn?"

She did not reply immediately. "I don't know."

He swore and took her chin in his hand. The collar, with its symbol of Kane's mastery, enraged him—so that he roughly tore it from her throat. Her fingers flew to the bared flesh.

Again he cursed. "Did Kane do that to you?"

She nodded, her eyes wide with intense emotion.

"He treats you as a slave, and you haven't the spirit to rebel—or even to hate him for what he does to you!"

"That's not true! I hate Kane!"

"Then show some courage! What can the devil do to you that's any worse than your present lot?"

"I just don't want you to die, too!"

The captain laughed grimly. "If you'd remain his slave to spare my life, then you're worth dying for! But the only death will be Kane's—if we lay our plans well. Will you try, Dessylyn? Will you rebel against this tyrant—win freedom for yourself, and love for us both?"

"I'll try, Mavrsal," she promised, unable to avoid his eyes. "But I can't do it alone."

"Nor would any man ask you to. Can I get into Kane's tower?"

"An army couldn't assail that tower if Kane wished to defend it."

"So I've heard. But can I get inside? Kane must have a secret entrance to his lair."

She bit her fist. "I know of one. Perhaps you could enter without his knowing it."

"I can if you can warn me of any hidden guardians or pitfalls," he told her with more confidence than he felt. "And I'll want to try this when he won't be as vigilant as normal. Since there seem to be regular periods when you can slip away from the tower, I see no reason why I can't steal inside under the same circumstances."

Dessylyn nodded, her face showing less fear now. "When he's deep into his necromancies, Kane is oblivious to all else. He's begun again with some of his black spells—he'll be so occupied until tomorrow night, when he'll force me to partake of his dark ritual."

Mavrsal flushed with outrage. "Then that will be his last journey into the demonlands—until we send him down to Hell forever! Repairs are all but complete. If I push the men and rush reprovisioning, the *Tuab* can sail with the tide of another dawn. Tomorrow night it will be, then, Dessylyn. While Kane is exhausted and preoccupied with his black sorcery, I'll slip into his tower.

"Be with him then. If he sees me before I can strike, wait until he turns to meet my attack—then strike with this!" And he drew a slender dirk from a sheath fixed beneath the head of his bunk.

As if hypnotized by his words, by the shining sliver of steel, Dessylyn turned the dagger about in her hands, again and again, staring at the flash of light on its keen edge. "I'll try. By Onthe, I'll try to do as you say!"

"He'll have to die," Mavrsal assured her. "You know he'll have to die."

VIII. Drink a Final Cup . . .

Spread out far below lay Carsultyal, fog swirling through her wide brick streets and crooked filthy alleys, hovering over squalid tenements and palatial manors—although her arrogant towers pierced its veil and reared toward the stars in lordly grandeur. Born of two elements, air and water, the mist swirled and drifted, sought to strangle a third element, fire, but could do no more than dim with tears its thousand glowing eyes. Patches of murky yellow in the roiling fog, the lights of Carsultyal gained the illusion of movement, so that one might be uncertain at any one moment whether he gazed down into the mist-hung city or upward toward the cloud-buried stars.

"Your mood is strange tonight, Dessylyn," Kane observed, meticulously adjusting the fire beneath the tertiary alembic.

She moved away from the tower window. "Is it strange to you, Kane? I marvel that you notice. I've told you countless times that this necromancy disgusts me, but always before have my sentiments meant nothing to you."

"Your sentiments mean a great deal to me, Dessylyn. But as for demanding your attendance here, I only do what I must."

"Like that?" she hissed in loathing, and pointed to the young girl's mutilated corpse.

Wearily Kane followed her gesture. Pain etching his brow, he made a sign and barked a stream of harsh syllables. A shadow crossed the open window and fell over the vivisected corpse. When it withdrew, the tortured form had vanished, and a muffled slap of wings faded into the darkness.

"Why do you think to hide your depraved crimes from my sight, Kane? Do you think I'll forget? Do you think I don't know the evil that goes into compounding this diabolical drug you force me to drink?"

Kane frowned and stared into the haze of phosphorescent vapor which swirled within the cucurbit. "Are you carrying iron, Dessylyn? There's asymmetry to the nimbus. I've told you not to bring iron within the influence of this generation."

The dagger was an unearthly chill against the flesh of her thigh. "Your mind is going, Kane. I wear only these rings."

He ignored her to lift the cup and hurriedly pour in a measure of dark, semi-congealed fluid. The alembic hissed and shivered, seemed to burst with light within its crimson crystal walls. A drop of phosphorescence took substance near the receiver. Kane quickly shifted the chalice to catch the droplet as it plunged.

"Why do you force me to drink this, Kane? Aren't these chains of fear that hold me to you bondage enough?"

His uncanny stare fixed her, and while it might have been the alchemical flames that made it seem so, she was astonished to see the fatigue, the pain that lined his face. It was as if the untold centuries whose touch Kane had eluded had at last stolen upon him. His hair billowed wildly, his face was shadowed and sunken, and his skin seemed imparted with the sick hue of the phosphorescent vapors.

"Why must you play this game, Dessylyn? Does it please you to see to what limits I go to hold you to me?"

"All that would please me, Kane, is to be free of you."

"You loved me once. You will love me again."

"Because you command it? You're a fool if you believe so. I hate you, Kane. I'll hate you for the rest of my life. Kill me now, or keep me here till I'm ancient and withered. I'll still die hating you."

He sighed and turned from her. His words were breathed into the flame. "You'll stay with me because I love you, and your beauty will not fade, Dessylyn. In time you may understand. Did you ever wonder at the loneliness of immortality? Have you ever wondered what must be the thoughts of a man cursed to wander through the centuries? A man doomed to a desolate, unending existence—feared and hated wherever men speak his name. A man who can never know peace, whose shadow leaves ruin wherever he passes. A man who has learned that every triumph is fleeting, that every joy is transient. All that he seeks to possess is stolen away from him by the years. His empires will fall, his songs will be forgotten, his loves will turn to dust. Only the emptiness of eternity will remain with him, a laughing skeleton cloaked in memories to haunt his days and nights.

"For such a man as this, for such a curse as this—is it so terrible that he dares to use his dark wisdom to hold something which he loves? If a hundred bright flowers must wither and die in his hand, is it evil that he hopes to keep one, just *one*, blossom for longer than the brief instant that Time had intended? Even if the flower hated being torn from the soil, would it make him wish to preserve its beauty any less?"

But Dessylyn was not listening to Kane. The billow of a tapestry, where no wind had blown, caught her vision. Could Kane hear the almost silent rasp of hidden hinges? No, he was lost in one of his maddened fits of brooding.

She tried to force her pounding heart to pulse less thunderously, her quick breath to cease its frantic rush. She could see where Mavrsal stood, frozen in the shadow of the tapestry. It seemed impossible that he might creep closer without Kane's unnatural keenness sensing his presence. The hidden dirk burned her thigh as if it were sheathed in her flesh. Carefully she edged around to Kane's side, thinking to expose his back to Mavrsal.

"But I see the elixir is ready," announced Kane, breaking out of his mood. Administering a few amber drops to the fluid, he carefully lifted the chalice of glowing liqueur.

"Here, drink this quickly," he ordered, extending the vessel.

"I won't drink your poisoned drugs again."

"Drink it, Dessylyn." His eyes held hers.

As in a recurrent nightmare—and there were other nightmares—Dessylyn accepted the goblet. She raised it to her lips, felt the bitter liqueur touch her tongue.

A knife whirled across the chamber. Struck from her languid fingers, the crystal goblet smashed into a thousand glowing shards against the stones.

"No!" shouted Kane in a demonic tone. "No! *No!*" He stared at the pool of dying phosphorescence in stunned horror.

Leaping from concealment, Mavrsal flung himself toward Kane—hoping to bury his cutlass in his enemy's heart before the sorcerer recovered. He had not reckoned on Kane's uncanny reflexes.

The anguished despair Kane displayed burst into inhuman rage at the instant he spun to meet his hidden assailant. Weaponless, he lunged for the sea captain. Mavrsal swung his blade in a natural downward slash, abandoning finesse in the face of an unarmed opponent.

With blurring speed, Kane stepped under the blow and caught the other's descending wrist with his left hand. Mavrsal heard a scream escape his lips as his arm was jammed to a halt in mid swing—as Kane's powerful left hand closed about his wrist and shattered the bones beneath the crushed flesh. The cutlass sailed unheeded across the stones.

His face twisted in bestial fury, Kane grappled with the sea captain. Mavrsal, an experienced fighter at rough and tumble, found himself tossed about like a frail child. Kane's other hand circled its long fingers about his throat, choking off his breath. Desperately he sought to break Kane's hold, beat at him with his mangled wrist, as Kane with savage laughter carried him back against the wall, holding him by his neck like a broken puppet.

Red fog wavered in his vision—pain was roaring in his ears . . . Kane was slowly strangling him, killing him deliberately, taunting him for his helplessness.

Then he was falling.

Kane gasped and arched his back inward as Dessylyn drove her dagger into his shoulder. Blood splashed her sweat-slippery fist. As Kane twisted away from her blow, the thin blade lodged in the scapula and snapped at the hilt.

Dessylyn screamed as his backhand blow hurled her to the stones. Frantically she scrambled to Mavrsal's side, where he lay sprawled on the floor—stunned, but still conscious.

Kane cursed and fell back against his worktable, overturning an alembic that burst like a rotted gourd. "Dessylyn!" he groaned in disbelief. Blood welled from his shoulder, spread across his slumped figure. His left shoulder was crippled, but his deadliness was that of a wounded tiger. "Dessylyn!"

"What did you expect?" she snarled, trying to pull Mavrsal to his feet.

A heavy flapping sound flung foggy gusts through the window. Kane cried out something in an inhuman tongue.

"If you kill Mavrsal, better kill me this time as well!" cried Dessylyn, clinging to the sea captain as he dazedly rose to his knees.

He cast a calculating eye toward the fallen sword. Too far.

"Leave her alone, sorcerer!" rasped Mavrsal. "She's guilty of no crime but that of hating you and loving me! Kill me now and be done, but you'll never change her spirit!"

"And I suppose you love her, too," said Kane in a tortured voice. "You fool. Do you know how many others I've killed—other fools who thought they would save Dessylyn from the sorcerer's evil embrace? It's a game she often plays. Ever since the first fool . . . only a game. It amuses her to taunt me with her infidelities, with her schemes to leave with another man. Since it amuses her, I indulge her. But she doesn't love you."

"Then why did she bury my steel in your back?" Despair made Mavrsal reckless.

"She hates you, sorcerer—and she loves me! Keep your lies to console you in your madness! Your sorcery can't alter Dessylyn's feelings toward you—nor can it alter the truth you're forced to see! So kill me and be damned—you can't escape the reality of your pitiful clutching for something you'll never hold!"

Kane's voice was strange, and his face was a mirror of tormented despair. "Get out of my sight!" he rasped. "Get out of here, both of you!

"Dessylyn, I give you your freedom. Mavrsal, I give you Dessylyn's love. Take your bounty, and go from Carsultyal! I trust you'll have little cause to thank me!"

As they stumbled for the secret door, Mavrsal ripped the emerald-set collar from Dessylyn's neck and flung it at Kane's slumping figure. "Keep your slave collar!" he growled. "It's enough that you leave her with your scars about her throat!"

"You fool," said Kane in a low voice.

"How far are we from Carsultyal?" whispered Dessylyn.

"Several leagues—we've barely gotten underway," Mavrsal told the shivering girl beside him.

"I'm frightened."

"Hush. You're done with Kane and all his sorcery. Soon it will be dawn, and soon we'll be far beyond Carsultyal and all the evil you've known there."

"Hold me tighter then, my love. I feel so cold."

"The sea wind is cold, but it's clean," he told her. "It's carrying us together to a new life."

"I'm frightened."

"Hold me closer, then."

"I seem to remember now . . . "

But the exhausted sea captain had fallen asleep. A deep sleep—the last unblighted slumber he would ever know.

For at dawn he awoke in the embrace of a corpse—the moldering corpse of a long-dead girl, who had hanged herself in despair over the death of her barbarian lover.

⚔

Katherine Kurtz's debut novel, Deryni Rising, *was published in 1970 by Ballantine Books—the first book to be published under their Adult Fantasy imprint that was not a reissue of an older work. There was nothing like it at the time: a "historical" fantasy based on medieval politics and a strong faith similar to Catholicism, featuring a race of psychics—the Deryni—who practice magic. This type of non-Tolkien secondary-world historical fantasy is common now, but Kurtz seems to be the first to write it. Ursula R. Le Guin disparaged the novel's prose in her essay "From Elfland to Poughkeepsie," but from 1970 until sometime in the nineties, Kurtz's fiction was popular and widely read. As Kari Sperring has written:*

> *Modern accounts of historical fantasy focus on the men who followed her, notably [Guy Gavriel] Kay and [George R. R.] Martin . . . Her books are entertaining and well-paced and convey a very strong sense of a realistic world . . . Her characters are memorable. She remains one of the best writers on faith and magic within fantasy. And she changed the shape of our genre. She was the first, and, as such, she deserves to be more widely recognized and studied.*

The Deryni series consists of five trilogies, one stand-alone novel, various short stories (and one collection of them), and two reference books. The most recent Deryni novel is The King's Deryni *(2014).*

"Swords Against the Marluk" (1977) was the first Deryni short story and was published in Lin Carter's Flashing Swords #4: Barbarians and Black Magicians.

SWORDS AGAINST THE MARLUK

Katherine Kurtz

They had not anticipated trouble from the Marluk that summer. In those days, the name of Hogan Gwernach was little more than legend, a vague menace in far-off Tolan who might or might not ever materialize as a threat to Brion's throne. Though rumored to be a descendant of the last Deryni sorcerer-king of Gwynedd, Gwemach's line had not set foot in Gwynedd for nearly three generations—not since Duchad Mor's ill-fated invasion in the reign of Jasher Haldane. Most people who knew of his existence at all believed that he had abandoned his claim to Gwynedd's crown.

And so, late spring found King Brion in Eastmarch to put down the rebellion of one of his own earls, with a young, half-Deryni squire named Alaric Morgan riding at his side. Rorik, the Earl of Eastmarch, had defied royal writ and begun to overrun neighboring Marley—a move he had been threatening for years—aided by his brash son-in-law, Rhydon, who was then only *suspected* of being Deryni. Arban Howell, one of the local barons whose lands lay along the line of Rorik's march, sent frantic word to the king of what was happening, then called up his own feudal levies to make a stand until help could arrive.

Only, by the time the royal armies did arrive, Brion's from the capital and an auxiliary force from Claibourne in the north, there was little left to do but assist Arban's knights in the mop-up operation. Miraculously, Arban had managed to defeat and capture Earl Rorik, scattering the remnants of the rebel forces and putting the impetuous Rhydon to flight. Only the formalities remained to be done by the time the king himself rode into Arban's camp.

Trial was held, the accused condemned, the royal sentence carried out. The traitorous Rorik, his lands and titles attainted, was hanged, drawn, and quartered before the officers of the combined armies, his head destined to be returned to his old capital and displayed as a deterrent to those contemplating similar indiscretions in the future. Rhydon, who had assisted his father-in-law's treason, was condemned in absentia and banished. Loyal Arhan Howell became the new Earl of Eastmarch for his trouble, swearing fealty to King Brion before the same armies which had witnessed the execution of his predecessor only minutes before.

And so the rebellion ended in Eastmarch. Brion dismissed the Claibourne levies with thanks, wished his new earl godspeed, then turned over command of the royal army to his brother Nigel. Nigel and their uncle, Duke Richard, would see the royal levies back to Rhemuth. Brion, impatient with the blood and killing of the past week, set out for home along a different route, taking only his squire with him.

It was late afternoon when Brion and Alaric found a suitable campsite. Since their predawn rising, there had been little opportunity for rest; and accordingly, riders and horses both were tired and travel-worn when at last they stopped. The horses smelled the water up ahead and tugged at their bits as the riders drew rein.

"God's wounds, but I'm tired, Alaric!" the king sighed, kicking clear of his stirrups and sliding gratefully from the saddle. "I sometimes think the aftermath is almost worse than the battle. I must be getting old."

As Alaric grabbed at the royal reins to secure the horses, Brion pulled off helmet and coif and let them fall as he made his way to the edge of the nearby stream. Letting himself fall facedown, he buried his head in the cooling water. The long black hair floated on the current, streaming down the royal back just past his shoulders as he rolled over and sat up, obviously the better for wear. Alaric, the horses tethered nearby, picked up his master's helm and coif and laid them beside the horses, then walked lightly toward the king.

"Your mail will rust if you insist upon bathing in it, Sire," the boy smiled, kneeling beside the older man and reaching to unbuckle the heavy swordbelt.

Brion leaned back on both elbows to facilitate the disarming, shaking his head in appreciation as the boy began removing vambraces and gauntlets.

"I don't think I shall ever understand how I came to deserve you, Alaric." He raised a foot so the boy could unbuckle greaves and spurs and dusty boots. "You must think me benighted, to ride off alone like this, without even an armed escort other than yourself, just to be away from my army."

"My liege is a man of war and a leader of men," the boy grinned, "but he is also a man unto himself, and must have time away from the pursuits of kings. The need for solitude is a familiar one to me."

"You understand, don't you?"

Alaric shrugged. "Who better than a Deryni, Sire? Like Your Grace, we are also solitary men on most occasions—though our solitude is not always by choice."

Brion smiled agreement, trying to imagine what it must be like to be Deryni like Alaric, a member of that persecuted race so feared still by so many. He allowed the boy to pull the lion surcoat off over his head while he thought about it, then stood and shrugged out of his mail hauberk. Discarding padding and singlet as well, he stepped into the water and submerged himself with a sigh, letting the water melt away the grime and soothe the galls of combat and ill-fitting harness and too many hours in the saddle. Alaric joined him after a while, gliding eel-like in the dappled shadows. When the light began to fail, the boy was on the bank without a reminder and pulling on clean clothes, packing away the battle-stained armor, laying out fresh garb for his master. Reluctantly, Brion came to ground on the sandy bottom and climbed to his feet, slicked back the long, black hair.

There was a small wood fire waiting when he had dressed, and wild rabbit spitted above the flames, and mulled wine in sturdy leather traveling cups. Wrapped in their cloaks against the growing night chill, king and squire feasted on rabbit and ripe cheese and biscuits only a little gone to mold after a week in the pack. The meal was finished and the camp secured by the time it was fully dark, and Brion fell asleep almost immediately, his head pillowed on his saddle by the banked fire. After a final check of the horses, Alaric slept, too.

It was sometime after moonrise when they were awakened by the sound of hoofbeats approaching from the way they had come. It was a lone horseman—that much Brion could determine, even through the fog of sleep he was shaking off as he sat and reached for his sword. But there was something else, too, and the boy Alaric sensed it. The lad was already on his feet, sword in hand, ready to defend his master if need be. But now he was frozen in the shadow of a tree, sword at rest, his head cocked in an attitude of more than listening.

"Prince Nigel," the boy murmured confidently, returning his sword to its sheath. Brion, used by now to relying on the boy's extraordinary powers, straightened and peered toward the moonlit road, throwing his cloak around him and groping for his boots in the darkness.

"A Haldane!" a young voice cried.

"Haldane, ho!" Brion shouted in response, stepping into the moonlight to hail the newcomer. The rider reined his lathered horse back on its haunches and half fell from the saddle, tossing the reins in Alaric's general direction as the boy came running to meet him.

"Brion, thank God I've found you!" Nigel cried, stumbling to embrace his older brother. "I feared you might have taken another route!"

The prince was foam-flecked and grimy from his breakneck ride, and his breath came in ragged gasps as he allowed Brion to help him to a seat by the fire. Collapsing against a tree trunk, he gulped the wine that Brion offered and tried to still his trembling hands. After a few minutes, and without attempting to speak, he pulled off one gauntlet with his teeth and reached into a fold of his surcoat. He took a deep breath as he withdrew a folded piece of parchment and gave it over to his brother.

"This was delivered several hours after you and Alaric left us. It's from Hogan Gwernach."

"The Marluk?" Brion murmured. His face went still and strange, the gray Haldane eyes flashing like polished agate, as he held the missive toward the firelight.

There was no seal on the outside of the letter—only a name, written in a fine, educated hand: Brion Haldane, Pretender of Gwynedd. Slowly, deliberately, Brion unfolded the parchment, let his eyes scan it as his brother plucked a brand from the fire and held it close for light. The boy Alaric listened silently as the king read.

"To Brion Haldane, Pretender of Gwynedd, from the Lord Hogan Gwernach of Tolan, Festillic Heir to the Thrones and Crowns of the Eleven Kingdoms. Know that We, Hogan, have determined to exercise that prerogative of birth which is the right of Our Festillic Ancestors, to reclaim the Thrones which are rightfully Ours. We therefore give notice to you, Brion Haldane, that your stewardship and usurpation of Gwynedd is at an end, your lands and Crown forfeit to the House of Festil. We charge you to present yourself and all members of your Haldane Line before Our Royal Presence at Cardosa, no later than the Feast of Saint Asaph, there to surrender

yourself and the symbols of your sovereignty into Our Royal Hands. Sic dicto, Hoganus Rex Regnorum Undecim."

"King of the Eleven Kingdoms?" Alaric snorted, then remembered who and where he was. "Pardon, Sire, but he must be joking!"

Nigel shook his head. "I fear not, Alaric. This was delivered by Rhydon of Eastmarch under a flag of truce."

"The treasonous dog!" Brion whispered.

"Aye." Nigel nodded. "He said to tell you that if you wished to contest this," he tapped the parchment lightly with his fingernail, "the Marluk would meet you in combat tomorrow near the Rustan Cliffs. If you do not appear, he will sack and burn the town of Rustan, putting every man, woman, and child to the sword. If we leave by dawn, we can just make it."

"Our strength?" Brion asked.

"I have my vanguard of eighty. I sent sixty of them ahead to rendezvous with us at Rustan and the rest are probably a few hours behind me. I also sent a messenger ahead to Uncle Richard with the main army. With any luck at all, he'll receive word in time to turn back the Haldane levies to assist. Earl Ewan was too far north to call back, though I sent a rider anyway."

"Thank you. You've done well."

With a distracted nod, Brion laid a hand on his brother's shoulder and got slowly to his feet. As he stood gazing sightlessly into the fire, the light gleamed on a great ruby in his ear, on a wide bracelet of silver clasped to his right wrist. He folded his arms across his chest against the chill, bowing his head in thought. The boy Alaric, with a glance at Prince Nigel, moved to pull the king's cloak more closely around him, to fasten the lion brooch beneath his chin as the king spoke.

"The Marluk does not mean to fight a physical battle. You know that, Nigel," he said in a low voice. "Oh, there may be battle among our various troops in the beginning. But all of that is but prelude. Armed combat is not what Hogan Gwernach desires of me."

"Aye. He is Deryni," Nigel breathed. He watched Brion's slow nod in the firelight.

"But, Brion," Nigel began, after a long pause. "It's been two generations since a Haldane king has had to stand against Deryni magic. Can you do it?"

"I—don't know." Brion, his cloak drawn close about him, sank down beside his brother once again, his manner grave and thoughtful. "I'm sorry if I appear preoccupied, but I keep having this vague recollection that there is something I'm supposed to do now. I seem to remember that Father made some provision, some preparation against this possibility, but—"

He ran a hand through sable hair, the firelight winking again on the silver at his wrist, and the boy Alaric froze, head cocked in a strained listening attitude, eyes slightly glazed. As Nigel nudged his brother lightly in the ribs, the boy sank slowly to his knees. Both pairs of royal eyes stared at him fixedly.

"There is that which must be done," the boy whispered, "which was ordained many years ago, when I was but a babe and you were not yet king, Sire."

"My father?"

"Aye. The key is—the bracelet you wear upon your arm." Brion's eyes darted instinctively to the silver. "May I see it, Sire?"

Without a word, Brion removed the bracelet and laid it in the boy's left hand. Alaric stared at it for a long moment, his pupils dilating until they were pools of inky blackness. Then, taking a deep breath to steel himself for the rush of memories he knew must follow, he bowed his head and laid his right hand over the design incised in the silver. Abruptly he remembered the first time he had seen the bracelet He had been just four when it happened, and it was mid-autumn. He had been snuggled down in his bed, dreaming of some childhood fantasy which he would never remember now, when he became aware of someone standing by his couch—and that was not a dream.

He opened his eyes to see his mother staring down at him intently, golden hair spilling bright around her shoulders, a loose-fitting gown of green disguising the thickening of her body from the child she carried. There was a candle in her hand, and by its light he could see his father standing gravely at her side. He had never seen such a look of stern concentration upon his father's face before, and that almost frightened him.

He made an inquisitive noise in his throat and started to ask what was wrong, but his mother laid a finger against her lips and shook her head. Then his father was reaching down to pull the blankets back, gathering him sleepily into his arms. He watched as his mother followed them out of the room and across the great hall, toward his father's library. The hall was empty even of the hounds his father loved, and outside he could hear the sounds of horses stamping in the yard—perhaps as many as a score of them—and the low-voiced murmur of the soldiers talking their soldier-talk.

At first, he thought the library was empty. But then he noticed an old, gray-haired man sitting in the shadows of his father's favorite armchair by the fireplace, an ornately carved staff cradled in the crook of his arm. The man's garments were rich and costly, but stained with mud at the hem. Jewels winked dimly in the crown of his leather cap, and a great red stone gleamed in his right earlobe. His cloak of red leather was clasped with a massive enameled brooch bearing the figure of a golden lion.

"Good evening, Alaric," the old man said quietly, as the boy's father knelt before the man and turned his son to face the visitor.

His mother made a slight curtsy, awkward in her condition, then moved to stand at the man's right hand, leaning heavily against the side of his chair. Alaric thought it strange, even at that young age, that the man did not invite his mother to sit down—but perhaps the man was sick; he was certainly very old. Curiously, and still blinking the sleep from his eyes, he looked up at his mother. To his surprise, it was his father who spoke.

"Alaric, this is the king," his father said in a low voice. "Do you remember your duty to His Majesty?"

Alaric turned to regard his father gravely, then nodded and disengaged himself from his father's embrace, stood to attention, made a deep, correct bow from the waist. The king, who had watched the preceding without comment, smiled and held out his right hand to the child. A silver bracelet flashed in the firelight as the boy put his small hand into the king's great, scarred one.

"Come and sit beside me, boy," the king said, lifting Alaric to a position half in his lap and half supported by the carven chair-arms. "I want to show you something."

Alaric squirmed a little as he settled down, for the royal lap was thin and bony, and the royal belt bristled with pouches and daggers and other grown-up accouterments fascinating to a small child. He started to touch one careful, stubby finger to the jewel at the end of the king's great dagger, but before he could do it, his mother reached across and touched his forehead lightly with her hand. Instantly, the room took on a new brightness and clarity, became more silent, almost reverberated with expectation. He did not know what was going to happen, but his mother's signal warned him that it was in that realm of special things of which he was never to speak, and to which he must give his undivided attention. In awed expectation, he turned his wide child-eyes upon the king, watched attentively as the old man reached around him and removed the silver bracelet from his wrist.

"This is a very special bracelet, Alaric. Did you know that?"

The boy shook his head, his gray eyes flicking from the king's face to the flash of silver. The bracelet was a curved rectangle of metal as wide as a man's hand, its mirror-sheen broken only by the carved outline of a heraldic rose. But it was the inside which the king turned toward him now—the inner surface, also highly polished but bearing a series of three curiously carved symbols which the boy did not recognize—though at four, he could already read the scriptures and simple texts from which his mother taught him.

The king turned the bracelet so that the first sigil was visible and held his fingernail beneath it. With a piercing glance at the boy's mother, he murmured the word, *"One!"* The room spun, and Alaric had remembered nothing more of that night.

But the fourteen-year-old Alaric remembered now. Holding the bracelet in his hands, the old king's successor waiting expectantly beside him, Alaric suddenly knew that this was the key, that he was the key who could unlock the instructions left him by a dying man so many years before. He turned the bracelet in his hands and peered at the inside—he knew now that the symbols were runes, though he still could not read them—then raised gray eyes to meet those of his king.

"This is a time which your royal father anticipated, Sire. There are things which I must do, and you, and," he glanced uneasily at the bracelet before meeting Brion's eyes again, "and somehow he knew that I would be at your side when this time arrived."

"Yes, I can see that now," Brion said softly. " *'There will be a half-Deryni child called Morgan who will come to you in his youth,'* my father said. *'Him you may trust with your life and with all. He is the key who unlocks many doors.'*" He searched Alaric's eyes carefully. "He knew. Even your presence was by his design."

"And was the Marluk also his design?" Nigel whispered, his tone conveying resentment at the implied manipulation, though the matter was now rendered academic.

"*Ancient mine enemy,*" Brion murmured. His face assumed a gentle, faraway air. "No, he did not cause the Marluk to be, Nigel. But he knew there was a possibility, and he planned for *that*. It is said that the sister of the last Festillic king was with child when she was forced to flee Gwynedd. The child's name was—I forget—not that it matters. But his line grew strong in Tolan, and they were never forced to put aside their Deryni powers. The Marluk is said to be that child's descendant."

"And full Deryni, if what they say is true," Nigel replied, his face going sullen. "Brion, we aren't equipped to handle a confrontation with the Marluk. He's going to be waiting for us tomorrow with an army and *his full Deryni powers*. And us? We'll have eighty men of my vanguard, maybe we'll have the rest of the Haldane levies, *if* Uncle Richard gets back in time, and you'll have—what?—to stand against a full Deryni lord who has good reason to want your throne!"

Brion wet his lips, avoiding his brother's eyes. "Alaric says that Father made provisions. We have no choice but to trust and see. Regardless of the outcome, we must try to save Rustan town tomorrow. Alaric, can you help us?"

"I—will try, Sire."

Disturbed by the near-clash between the two brothers, and sobered by the responsibility Brion had laid upon him, Alaric laid his right forefinger beneath the first rune, grubby fingernail underscoring the deeply carved sign. He could feel the Haldane eyes upon him as he whispered the word, *"One!"*

The word paralyzed him, and he was struck deaf and blind to all externals, oblivious to everything except the images flashing through his mind—the face of the old king seen through the eyes of a four-year-old boy—and the instructions, meaningless to the four-year-old, now re-engraving themselves in the young man's mind as deeply as the runes inscribed on the silver in his hand.

A dozen heartbeats, a blink, and he was in the world again, turning his gray gaze on the waiting Brion. The king and Nigel stared at him with something approaching awe, their faces washed clean of whatever doubts had remained until that moment. In the moonlight, Alaric seemed to glow a little.

"We must find a level area facing east," the boy said. His young brow furrowed in concentration. "There must be a large rock in the center, living water at our backs, and—and we must gather wildflowers."

It was nearing first-light before they were ready. A suitable location had been found in a bend of the stream a little way below their camp, with water tumbling briskly along the northern as well as the western perimeter. To the east stretched an unobstructed view of the mountains from behind which the sun would shortly rise. A large, stream-smoothed chunk of granite half the height of a man had been dragged into the center of the clearing with the aid of the horses, and four lesser stones had been set up to mark the four cardinal compass points.

Now Alaric and Nigel were laying bunches of field flowers around each of the cornerstones, in a pattern which Alaric could not explain but which he knew must be maintained. Brion, silent and withdrawn beneath his crimson cloak, sat near the center stone with arms wrapped around his knees, sheathed sword lying beside him. A knot of blazing pine had been thrust into the ground at his right to provide light for what the others did, but Brion saw nothing, submerged in contemplation of what lay ahead. Alaric, with a glance at the brightening sky, set a small drinking vessel of water to the left of the center stone and dropped to one knee beside the king. An uneasy Nigel snuffed out the torch and drew back a few paces as Alaric took up the bracelet and laid his finger under the second rune.

"Two!"

There was a moment of profound silence in which none of the three moved, and then Alaric looked up and placed the bracelet in the king's hand once more.

"The dawn is nearly upon us, Sire," he said quietly. "I require the use of your sword."

"Eh?"

With a puzzled look, Brion glanced at the weapon and picked it up, wrapped the red leather belt more tidily around the scabbard, then scrambled to his feet. It had been his father's sword, and his grandfather's. It was also the sword with which he had been consecrated king nearly ten years before. Since that day, no man had drawn it save himself.

But without further query, Brion drew the blade and formally extended it to Alaric across his left forearm, hilt first. Alaric made a profound bow as he took the weapon, appreciating the trust the act implied, then saluted the king and moved to the other side of the rock. Behind him, the eastern sky was ablaze with pink and coral.

"When the rim of the sun appears above the horizon, I must ward us with fire, my liege," he said. "Please do not be surprised or alarmed at anything which may happen."

Brion nodded, and as he and Nigel drew themselves to respectful attention, Alaric turned on his heel and strode to the eastern limit of the clearing. Raising the sword before him with both hands, he held the cross-hilt level with his eyes and gazed expectantly toward the eastern horizon. And then, as though the sun's movement had not been a gradual and natural thing, dawn was spilling from behind the mountains.

The first rays of sunlight on sword turned the steel to fire. Alaric let his gaze travel slowly up the blade, to the flame now blazing at its tip and shimmering down its length, then extended the sword in salute and brought it slowly to ground before him. Fire leaped up where blade touched sun-parched turf—a fire which burned but did not consume—and a ribbon of flame followed as he turned to the right and walked the confines of the wards.

When he had finished, he was back where he began, all three of them standing now within a hemisphere of golden light. The boy saluted sunward once again, with hands that shook only a little, then returned to the center of the circle. Grounding the now-normal blade, he extended it to Nigel with a bow, the hilt held cross-wise before him. As the prince's fingers closed around the blade, Alaric turned back toward the center stone and bowed his head. Then he held his hands outstretched before him, fingers slightly cupped—gazed fixedly at the space between them.

Nothing appeared to happen for several minutes, though Alaric could feel the power building between his hands. King and prince and squire stared until their eyes watered, then blinked in astonishment as the space between Alaric's hands began to glow. Pulsating with the heartbeat of its creator, the glow coalesced in a sphere of cool, verdant light, swelling to head-size even as they watched. Slowly, almost reverently, Alaric lowered his hands toward the stream-smoothed surface of the center stone; watched as the sphere of light spread bright across the surface.

He did not dare to breathe, so tenuous was the balance he maintained. Drawing back the sleeve of his tunic, he swept his right hand and arm across the top of the stone like an adze, shearing away the granite as though it were softest sand. Another pass to level the surface even more, and then he was pressing out a gentle hollow with his hand, the stone melting beneath his touch like morning frost before the sun.

Then the fire was dead, and Alaric Morgan was no longer the master mage, tapping the energies of the earth's deepest forge, but only a boy of fourteen, staggering to his knees in exhaustion at the feet of his king and staring in wonder at what his hands had wrought. Already, he could not remember how he had done it.

Silence reigned for a long moment, finally broken by Brion's relieved sigh as he tore his gaze from the sheared-off stone. A taut, frightened Nigel was staring at him and Alaric, white-knuckled hands gripping the sword hilt as though it were his last remaining hold on reality. With a little smile of reassurance, Brion laid a hand on his brother's. He felt a little of the tension drain away as he turned back to the young man still kneeling at his feet.

"Alaric, are you all right?"

"Aye, m'lord."

With a weak nod, Alaric brought a hand to his forehead and closed his eyes, murmuring a brief spell to banish fatigue. Another deep breath and it was done. Smiling wanly, he climbed to his feet and took the bracelet from Brion's hands once more, bent it flat and laid it in the hollow he had made in the rock. The three runes, one yet unrevealed, shone in the sunlight as he stretched forth his right hand above the silver.

" '*I form the light and create darkness,*' " the boy whispered. " '*I make peace and create evil: I the Lord do all these things.*' "

He did not physically move his hand, although muscles and tendons tensed beneath the tanned skin. Nonetheless, the silver began to curve away, to conform to the hollow of the stone as though another, invisible hand were pressing down between his hand and the metal. The bracelet collapsed on itself and grew molten then, though there was no heat given off. When Alaric removed his hand a few seconds later, the silver was bonded to the hollow like a shallow, silver bowl, all markings obliterated save the third and final rune. He laid his finger under the sign and spoke its name.

"Three!"

This time, there was but a fleeting outward hint of the reaction triggered: a blink, an interrupted breath immediately resumed. Then he was taking up the vessel of water and turning toward Brion, gesturing with his eyes for Brion to extend his hands. Water was poured over them, the edge of Alaric's cloak offered for a towel. When the king had dried his hands, Alaric handed him the rest of the water. "Pour water in the silver to a finger's depth. Sire," he said softly. Brion complied, setting the vessel on the ground when he had finished. Nigel, without being told, moved to the opposite side of the stone and knelt, holding the sword so that the long, cross-shadow of the hilt fell across rock and silver.

"Now," Alaric continued, "spread your hands flat above the water and repeat after me. Your hands are holy, consecrated with chrism at your coronation just as a priest's hands are consecrated. I am instructed that this is appropriate."

With a swallow, Brion obeyed, his eyes locking with Alaric's as the boy began speaking.

"I, Brion, the Lord's Anointed . . . "

"I, Brion, the Lord's Anointed . . . "

" . . . bless and consecrate thee, O creature of water . . . "

" . . . bless and consecrate thee, O creature of water . . . by the living God, by the true God, by the holy God . . . by that God Who in the beginning separated thee by His word from the dry land . . . and Whose Spirit moved upon thee."

"Amen," Alaric whispered.

"Amen," Brion echoed.

"Now, dip your fingers in the water," Alaric began, "and trace on the stone—"

"I know this part!" Brion interrupted, his hand already parting the water in the sign of a cross. He, too, was being caught up in that web of recall established so many years before by his royal father, and his every gesture, every nuance of phrasing and pronunciation, was correct and precise as he touched a moistened finger to the stone in front of the silver.

"Blessed be the Creator, yesterday and today, the Beginning and the End, the Alpha and the Omega."

A cross shone wetly on the stone, the Greek letters drawn haltingly but precisely at the east and west aspects.

"His are the seasons and the ages, to Him glory and dominion through all the ages of eternity. Blessed be the Lord. Blessed be His Holy Name."

The signs of the Elementals glistened where Brion had drawn them in the four quadrants cut by the cross—Air, Fire, Water, Earth—and Brion, as he recognized the alchemical signs, drew back his hand as though stung, stared aghast at Alaric.

"How—?" He swallowed. "How did I know that?"

Alaric permitted a wan smile, sharing Brion's discomfiture at being compelled to act upon memories and instructions which he could not consciously remember.

"You, too, have been schooled for this day, Sire," he said. "Now, you have but to carry out the rest of your father's instructions, and take up the power which is rightfully yours."

Brion bowed his head, sleek, raven hair catching the strengthening sunlight. "I—am not certain I know how. From what we have seen and done so far, there must be other triggers, other clues to aid me, but—" He glanced up at the boy. "You must give me guidance, Alaric. You are the master here—not I."

"No, you are the master, Sire," the boy said, touching one finger to the water and bringing a shimmering drop toward Brion's face.

The king's eyes tracked on the fingertip automatically, and as the droplet touched his forehead, the eyes closed. A shudder passed through the royal body and Brion blinked. Then, in a daze, he reached to his throat and unfastened the great lion brooch which held his cloak in place. He hefted the piece in his hand as the cloak fell in a heap at his feet and the words came.

"Three drops of royal blood on water bright,
To gather flame within a bowl of light.
With consecrated hands, receive the Sight
Of Haldane—'tis thy sacred, royal Right."

The king glanced at Alaric unseeing, at Nigel, at the red enameled brooch heavy in his hand. Then he turned the brooch over and freed the golden clasp-pin from its catch, held out a left hand which did not waver.

"Three drops of royal blood on water bright," he repeated. He brought the clasp against his thumb in a swift, sharp jab.

Blood welled from the wound and fell thrice upon the water, rippling scarlet, concentric circles across the silver surface. A touch of tongue to wounded thumb, and then he was putting the brooch aside and spreading his hands above the water, the shadow of the cross bold upon his hands. He closed his eyes.

Stillness. A crystalline anticipation as Brion began to concentrate. And then, as Alaric extended his right hand above Brion's and added his strength to the spell, a deep, musical reverberation, more felt than heard, throbbing through their minds. As the sunlight brightened, so also brightened the space beneath Brion's hands, until finally could be seen the ghostly beginnings of crimson fire flickering on the water. Brion's emotionless expression did not change as Alaric withdrew his hand and knelt.

"Fear not, for I have redeemed thee," Alaric whispered, calling the words from memories not his own. "*I have called thee by name, and thou art mine. When thou*

walkest through the fire, thou shalt not be burned: neither shall the flame kindle upon thee."

Brion did not open his eyes. But as Alaric's words ended, the king took a deep breath and slowly, deliberately, brought his hands to rest flat on the silver of the bowl. There was a gasp from Nigel as his brother's hands entered the flames, but no word or sound escaped Brion's lips to indicate the ordeal he was enduring. Head thrown back and eyes closed, he stood unflinching as the crimson fire climbed his arms and spread over his entire body. When the flames died away, Brion opened his eyes upon a world which would never appear precisely the same again, and in which he could never again be merely mortal.

He leaned heavily on the altar-stone for just a moment, letting the fatigue drain away. But when he lifted his hands from the stone, his brother stifled an oath. Where the royal hands had lain, the silver had been burned away. Only the blackened silhouettes remained etched indelibly in the hollowed surface of the rock. Brion blanched a little when he saw what he had done, and Nigel crossed himself. But Alaric paid no heed—stood, instead, and turned to face the east once more, extending his arms in a banishing spell. The canopy of fire dissipated in the air.

They were no longer alone, however. While they had worked their magic, some of the men of Nigel's vanguard had found the royal campsite—an even dozen of his crack commanders and tacticians—and they were gathered now by the horses in as uneasy a band as Alaric had ever seen. Brion did not notice them immediately, his mind occupied still with sorting out his recent experience, but Alaric saw them and touched Brion's elbow in warning. As Brion turned toward them in surprise, they went to their knees as one man, several crossing themselves furtively. Brion's brow furrowed in momentary annoyance.

"Did they see?" he murmured, almost under his breath.

Alaric gave a careful nod. "So it would appear, Sire. I suggest you go to them immediately and reassure them. Otherwise, the more timid among them are apt to bolt and run."

"From me, their king?"

"You are more than just a man now, Sire," Alaric returned uncomfortably. "They have seen that with their own eyes. Go to them, and quickly."

With a sigh, Brion tugged his tunic into place and strode across the clearing toward the men, automatically pulling his gauntlets from his belt and beginning to draw them on. The men watched his movements furtively as he came to a halt perhaps a half-dozen steps from the nearest of them. Noting their scrutiny, Brion froze in the act of pulling on the right glove; then, with a smile, he removed it and held his hand toward them, the palm exposed. There was no mark upon the lightly calloused skin.

"You are entitled to an explanation," he said simply, as all eyes fastened on the hand. "As you can see, I am unharmed. I am sorry if my actions caused you some concern. Please rise."

The men got to their feet, only the chinking of their harness breaking the sudden stillness which had befallen the glade. Behind the king, Nigel and Alaric moved to back him, Nigel bearing the royal sword and Alaric the crimson cloak with its lion brooch. The men were silent, a few shifting uneasily, until one of the bolder ones cleared his throat and took a half-step nearer.

"Sire."

"Lord Raison?"

"Sire," the man shifted from one foot to the other and glanced at his comrades. "Sire, it appears to us that there was magic afoot," he said carefully. "We question the wisdom of allowing a Deryni to influence you so. When we saw—"

"What *did* you see, Gerard?" Brion asked softly.

Gerard Raison cleared his throat. "Well, I—we—when we arrived. Sire, you were holding that brooch in your hand," he gestured toward the lion brooch which Alaric held, "and then we saw you prick your thumb with it." He paused. "You looked—not yourself. Sire, as though—something else was commanding you." He glanced at Alaric meaningfully, and several other of the men moved a little closer behind him, hands creeping to rest on the hilts of their weapons.

"I see," Brion said. "And you think that it was Alaric who commanded me, don't you?"

"It appeared so to us, Majesty," another man rumbled, his beard jutting defiantly.

Brion nodded. "And then you watched me hold my hands above the stone, and Alaric hold his above my own. And then you saw me engulfed in flame, and that frightened you most of all."

The speaker nodded tentatively, and his movement was echoed by nearly every head there. Brion sighed and glanced at the ground, looked up at them again.

"My lords, I will not lie to you. You were witness to very powerful magic. And I will not deny, nor will Alaric, that his assistance was used in what you saw. And Alaric is, most definitely, Deryni."

The men said nothing, though glances were exchanged.

"But there is more that I would have you know," Brion continued, fixing them all with his Haldane stare. "Each of you has heard the legends of my House—how we returned to the throne of Gwynedd when the Deryni Imre was deposed. But if you consider, you will realize that the Haldanes could not have ousted Deryni lords without some power of their own."

"Are you Deryni, then, Sire?" asked one bold soul from the rear ranks.

Brion smiled and shook his head. "No—or at least, I don't believe I am. But the Haldanes have very special gifts and abilities, nonetheless, handed down from father to son—or sometimes from brother to brother." He glanced at Nigel before continuing. "You know that we can Truth-Read, that we have great physical stamina. But we also have other powers, when they are needed, which enable us to function almost as though we were, ourselves, Deryni. My father, King Maine, entrusted a few of these abilities to me before his death, but there were others whose very existence he kept secret, for which he left certain instructions with Alaric Morgan *unknown even to him*—and which were triggered by the threat of Hogan Gwernach's challenge which we received last night. Alaric was a child of four when he was instructed by my father—so that even he would not remember his instructions until it was necessary—and apparently I was also instructed.

"The result, in part, was what you saw. If there was a commanding force, another influence present within the fiery circle, it was my father's. The rite is now fulfilled, and I am my father's successor *in every way*, with all his powers and abilities."

"Your late *father* provided for all of this?" one of the men whispered.

Brion nodded. "There is no evil in it, Alwyne. You knew my father well. You know he would not draw down evil."

"Aye, he would not," the man replied, glancing at Alaric almost involuntarily. "But what of the Deryni lad?"

"Our fathers made a pact, that Alaric Morgan should come to Court to serve me when he reached the proper age. That bargain has been kept. Alaric Morgan serves me and the realm of Gwynedd."

"But, he is Deryni, Sire! What if he is in league with—"

"He is in league with *me*!" Brion snapped. "He is my liege man, just as all of you, sworn to my service since the age of nine. In that time, he has scarcely left my side. Given the compulsions which my father placed upon him, do you really believe that he could betray me?"

Raison cleared his throat, stepping forward and making a bow before the king could continue.

"Sire, it is best we do not discuss the boy. None of us here, Your Majesty included, can truly know what is in his heart. You are the issue now. If you were to reassure us, in some way, that you harbor no ill intent, that you have not allied yourself with the Dark Powers—"

"You wish my oath to that effect?" Brion asked. The stillness of his response was, itself, suddenly threatening. "You would be that bold?"

Raison nodded carefully, not daring to respond by words, and his movement was again echoed by the men standing at his back. After a frozen moment, Brion made a curt gesture for his brother to kneel with the royal sword. As Nigel held up the cross hilt, Brion laid his bare right hand upon it and faced his waiting knights.

"Before all of you and before God, and upon this holy sword, I swear that I am innocent of your suspicions, that I have made no dark pact with any evil power, that the rite which you observed was benevolent and legitimate. I further swear that I have never been, nor am I now, commanded by Alaric Morgan or any other man, human or Deryni; that he is as innocent as I of any evil intent toward the people and crown of Gwynedd. This is the word of Brion Haldane. If I be forsworn, may this sword break in my hour of need, may all succor desert me, and may the name of Haldane vanish from the earth."

With that, he crossed himself slowly, deliberately—a motion which was echoed by Alaric, Nigel, and then the rest of the men who had witnessed the oath. Preparations to leave for Rustan were made in total silence.

They met the Marluk while still an hour's ride from Rustan and rendezvous with the rest of Nigel's vanguard. All morning, they had been following the rugged Llegoddin Canyon Trace—a winding trail treacherous with stream-slicked stones which rolled and shifted beneath their horses' hooves. The stream responsible for their footing ran shallow along their right, had crossed their path several times in slimy, fast-flowing fords that made the horses lace back their ears. Even the canyon walls had closed in along the last mile, until the riders were forced to go two abreast. It was a perfect place for an ambush; but Alaric's usually reliable knack for sensing danger gave them almost no warning.

It was cool in the little canyon, the shade deep and refreshing after the heat of the noonday sun, and the echo of steel-shod hooves announced their progress long before they actually reached the end of the narrows. There the track made a sharp turn through the stream again, before widening out to an area of several acres. In the center waited a line of armed horsemen, nearly twice the number of Brion's forces.

They were mailed and helmed with steel, these fighting men of Tolan, and their lances and war axes gleamed in the silent sunlight. Their white-clad leader sat a heavy sorrel destrier before them, lance in hand and banner bright at his back. The blazon left little doubt as to his identity—Hogan Gwernach, called the Marluk. He had quartered his arms with those of Royal Gwynedd.

But there was no time for more than first impressions. Even as Alaric's lips moved in warning, and before more than a handful of Bunn's men could clear the stream and canyon narrows, the Marluk lowered his lance and signaled the attack. As the great-horses thundered toward the stunned royal party, picking up momentum as they came, Brion couched his own lance and set spurs to his horse's sides. His men, overcoming their initial dismay with commendable speed, galloped after him in near-order, readying shields and weapons even as they rode.

The earth shook with the force of the charge, echoed with the jingle of harness and mail, the creak of leather, the snorting and labored breathing of the heavy war-horses. Just before the two forces met, one of Brion's men shouted, *"A Haldane!"*—a cry which was picked up and echoed instantly by most of his comrades in arms. Then all were swept into the melee, and men were falling and horses screaming riderless and wounded as lances splintered on shield and mail and bone.

Steel clanged on steel as the fighting closed hand-to-hand, cries of the wounded and dying punctuating the butcher sounds of sword and ax on flesh. Alaric, emerging unscathed from the initial encounter, found himself locked shield to shield with a man twice his age and size, the man pressing him hard and trying to crush his helm with a mace. Alaric countered by ducking under his shield and wheeling to the right, hoping to come at his opponent from the other side, but the man was already anticipating his move and swinging in counterattack. At the last possible moment, Alaric deflected the blow with his shield, reeling in the saddle as he tried to recover his balance and strike at the same time. But his aim had been shaken, and instead of coming in from behind on the man's temporarily open right side, he only embedded his sword in the other's high cantle.

He recovered before the blade could be wrenched from his grasp, gripping hard with his knees as his charger lashed out and caught the man in the leg with a driving foreleg. Then, parrying a blow from a second attacker, he managed to cut the other's girth and wound his mount, off-handedly kicking out at yet a third man who was approaching from his shield side. The first knight hit the ground with a yelp as his horse went down, narrowly missing death by trampling as one of his own men thundered past in pursuit of one of Brion's wounded.

Another strike, low and deadly, and Alaric's would-be slayer was, himself, the slain. Drawing ragged breath, Alaric wheeled to scan the battle for Brion, and to defend himself from renewed attack by the two men on foot.

The king himself was in little better circumstances. Though still mounted and holding his own, Brion had been swept away from his mortal enemy in the initial clash, and had not yet been able to win free to engage with him. Nigel was fighting at his brother's side, the royal banner in his shield hand, but the banner only served to hamper Nigel and to tell the enemy where Gwynedd's monarch was. Just now, both royal brothers were sore beset, half a dozen of the Marluk's knights belaboring them from every side but skyward. The Marluk, meantime, was busily slaying a hundred yards away—content, thus far, to spend his time slaughtering some of Brion's lesser warriors, and shunning Brion's reputed superior skill. As Brion and Nigel beat back their attackers, the king glanced across the battlefield and saw his enemy, dispatched one of his harriers with a brutal thrust, raised his sword and shouted the enemy's name:

"Gwernach!"

The enemy turned in his direction and jerked his horse to a rear, circled his sword above his head. His helmet was gone, and pale hair blew wild from beneath his mail coif.

"The Haldane is mine!" the Marluk shouted, spurring toward Brion and cutting down another man in passing. "Stand and fight, usurper! Gwynedd is mine by right!"

The Marluk's men fell back from Brion as their master pounded across the field, and with a savage gesture, Brion waved his own men away and urged his horse toward the enemy. Now was the time both had been waiting for—the direct, personal combat of the two rival kings. Steel shivered against steel as the two men met and clashed in I lie center of the field, and the warriors of both sides drew back to watch, their own hostilities temporarily suspended.

For a time, the two seemed evenly matched. The Marluk took a chunk out of the top of Brion's shield, but Brion divested the Marluk of a stirrup, and nearly a foot. So they continued, neither man able to score a decisive blow, until finally Brion's sword found the throat of the Marluk's mount. The dying animal collapsed with a liquid scream, dumping its rider in a heap. Brion, pursuing his advantage, tried to ride down his enemy then and there.

But the Marluk rolled beneath his shield on the first pass and nearly tripped up Brion's horse, scrambling to his feet and bracing as Brion wheeled viciously to come at him again. The second pass cost Brion his mount, its belly ripped out by the Marluk's sword. As the horse went down, Brion leaped clear and whirled to face his opponent.

For a quarter hour the two battled with broadsword and shield, the Marluk with the advantage of weight and height, but Brion with youth and greater agility in his favor. Finally, when both men could barely lift their weapons for fatigue, they drew apart and leaned on heavy swords, breath coming in short, ragged gasps. After a moment, golden eyes met steely gray ones. The Marluk flashed a brief, sardonic grin at his opponent.

"You fight well, for a Haldane," the Marluk conceded, still breathing heavily. He gestured with his sword toward the waiting men. "We are well matched, at least in steel, and even were we to cast our men into the fray again, it would still come down to the same—you against me."

"Or my power against yours," Brion amended softly. "That is your eventual intention, is it not?"

The Marluk started to shrug, but Brion interrupted.

"No, you would have slain me by steel if you could," he said. "To win by magic exacts greater payment, and might not give you the sort of victory you seek if you would rule my human kingdom and not fear for your throne. The folk of Gwynedd would not take kindly to a Deryni king after your bloody ancestors."

The Marluk smiled. "By force, physical or arcane—it matters little in the long reckoning. It is the victory itself which will command the people after today. But you, Haldane, your position is far more precarious than mine, dynastically speaking. Do you see yon riders, and the slight one dressed in blue?"

He gestured with his sword toward the other opening of the clearing from which he and his men had come, where half a score of riders surrounded a pale, slight figure on a mouse-gray palfrey.

"Yonder is my daughter and heir, Haldane," the Marluk said smugly. "Regardless of the outcome here today, she rides free—you cannot stop her—to keep my name and memory until another time. But you—your brother and heir stands near, his life a certain forfeit if I win." He gestured toward Nigel, then rested the tip of his sword before him once more. "And the next and final Haldane is your Uncle Richard, a childless bachelor of fifty. After him, there are no others."

Brion's grip tightened on the hilt of his sword, and he glared across at his enemy with something approaching grudging respect. All that the Marluk had said was true. There were no other male Haldanes beyond his brother and his uncle, at least for now. Nor was there any way that he or his men could prevent the escape of the Marluk's heir. Even if he won today, the Marluk's daughter would remain a future menace. The centuries-long struggle for supremacy in Gwynedd would not end here—unless, of course, Brion lost.

The thought sobered him, cooled the hot blood racing through his veins and slowed his pounding heart. He must answer this usurper's challenge, and now, and with the only card he had left. They had fought with force of steel before, and all for naught. Now they must face one another with other weapons.

Displaying far more confidence than he felt, for he would never play for higher stakes than life and crown, Brion let fall his shield and helm and strode slowly across half the distance separating him from his mortal enemy. Carefully, decisively, he traced an equal-armed cross in the dust with the tip of his sword, the first arm pointing toward the Marluk.

"I, Brion, Anointed of the Lord, King of Gwynedd, and Lord of the Purple March, call thee forth to combat mortal, Hogan Gwernach, for that thou hast raised hostile hand against me and, through me, against my people of Gwynedd. This I will defend upon my body and my soul, to the death, so help me, God."

The Marluk's face had not changed expression during Brion's challenge, and now he, too, strode to the figure scratched in the dust and laid his sword tip along the same lines, retracing the cross.

"And I, Hogan Gwernach, descendant of the lawful kings of Gwynedd in antiquity, do return thy challenge, Brion Haldane, and charge that thou art base pretender to the throne and crown thou holdest. And this I will defend upon my body and my soul, to the death, so help me, God."

With the last words, he began drawing another symbol in the earth beside the cross—a detailed, winding interlace which caught and held Brion's concentration with increasing power. Only just in lime, Brion recognized the spell for what it was and, with an oath, dashed aside the Marluk's sword with his own, erasing the symbol with his boot. He glared at the enemy standing but a sword's length away, keeping his anger in check only with the greatest exertion of will.

If I let him get me angry, he thought, *I'm dead.*

Biting back his rage, he forced his sword-arm to relax.

The Marluk drew back a pace and shrugged almost apologetically at that—he had not really expected his diversion to work so well—then saluted with his sword and backed off another dozen paces. Brion returned the salute with a sharp, curt gesture and likewise withdrew the required distance. Then, without further preliminaries. In extended his arms to either side and murmured the words of a warding spell. As answering fire sprang up crimson at his back, the Marluk raised a similar defense, blue fire joining crimson to complete the protective circle. Beneath the canopy of light thus formed, arcs of energy began to crackle sword to sword, ebbing and flowing, as arcane battle was joined.

The circle brightened as they fought, containing energies so immense that all around it would have perished had the wards not held it in. The very air within grew hazy, so that those without could no longer see the principals who battled there. So it remained for nearly half an hour, the warriors of both sides drawing mistrustfully together to watch and wait. When, at last, the fire began to flicker erratically and die down, naught could be seen within the circle but two ghostly, fire-edged figures in silhouette, one of them staggering drunkenly.

They could not tell which was which. One of them had fallen to his knees and remained there, sword upraised in a last, desperate, warding-off gesture. The other stood poised to strike, but something seemed to hold him back. The tableau remained frozen that way for several heartbeats, the tension growing between the two; but then the kneeling one reeled sidewards and let fall his sword with a cry of anguish, collapsing forward on his hands to bow his head in defeat. The victor's sword descended as though in slow motion, severing head from body in one blow and showering dust and victor and vanquished with blood. The fire dimmed almost to nonexistence, and they could see that it was Brion who lived.

Then went up a mighty cheer from the men of Gwynedd. A few of the Marluk's men wheeled and galloped away across the field toward the rest of their party before anyone could stop them, but the rest cast down their weapons and surrendered immediately. At the mouth of the canyon beyond, a slender figure on a gray horse turned and rode away with her escort. There was no pursuit.

Brion could not have seen them through the haze, but he knew. Moving dazedly back to the center of the circle, he traced the dust-drawn cross a final time and mouthed the syllables of a banishing spell. Then, as the fiery circle died away, he gazed long at the now-empty canyon mouth before turning to stride slowly toward his men. They parted before him as he came, Gwynedd and Tolan men alike.

Perhaps a dozen men remained of Brion's force, a score or less of the Marluk's, and there was a taut, tense silence as he moved among them. He stopped and looked around him, at the men, at the wounded lying propped against their shields, at Nigel and Alaric still sitting upon their blood-bespattered war-horses, at the bloody banner still in Nigel's hand. He stared at the banner for a long time, no one daring to break the strained silence. Then he let his gaze fall on each man in turn, catching and holding each man's attention in rapt, unshrinking thrall.

"We shall not speak of the details of this battle beyond this place," he said simply. The words crackled with authority, compulsion, and Alaric Morgan, of all who heard, knew the force behind that simple statement. Though most of them would never realize that fact, every man there had just been touched by the special Haldane magic.

Brion held them thus for several heartbeats, no sound or movement disturbing their rapt attention. Then Brion blinked and smiled and the otherworldliness was no more. Instantly, Nigel was springing from his horse to run and clasp his brother's arm. Alaric, in a more restrained movement, swung his leg over the saddle and slid to the ground, walked stiffly to greet his king.

"Well fought, Sire," he murmured, the words coming with great difficulty.

"My thanks for making that possible, Alaric," the king replied, "though the shedding of blood has never been my wish."

He handed his sword to Nigel and brushed a strand of hair from his eyes with a blood-streaked hand. Alaric swallowed and made a nervous bow.

"No thanks are necessary, Sire. I but gave my service as I must." He swallowed again and shifted uneasily, then abruptly dropped to his knees and bowed his head. "Sire, may I crave a boon of you?"

"A boon? You know you have but to ask, Alaric. I pray you, stand not upon ceremony."

Alaric shook his head, brought his gaze to meet Brion's. "No, this I will and must do, Sire." He raised joined hands before him. "Sire, I would reaffirm my oath of fealty to you."

"Your oath?" Brion began. "But, you have already sworn to serve me, Alaric, and have given me your hand in friendship, which I value far more from you than any oath."

"And I, Sire," Alaric nodded slightly. "But the fealty I gave you before was such as any liegeman might give his lord and king. What I offer now is fealty for the powers which we share. I would give you my fealty as Deryni."

There was a murmuring around them, and Nigel glanced at his brother in alarm, but neither king nor kneeling squire heard. A slight pause, a wry smile, and then Brion was taking the boy's hands between his own blood-stained ones, gray eyes meeting gray as he heard the oath of the first man to swear Deryni fealty to a human king in nearly two centuries.

"I, Alaric Anthony, Lord Morgan, do become your liegeman of life and limb and earthly worship. And faith and truth I will bear unto you, *with all the powers at my command*, so long as there is breath within me. This I swear upon my life, my honor, and my faith and soul. If I be forsworn, may my powers desert me in my hour of need."

Brion swallowed, his eyes never leaving Alaric's. "And I, for my part, pledge fealty to you, Alaric Anthony, Lord Morgan, to protect and defend you, and any who may depend upon you, with all the powers at my command, so long as there is breath within me. This I swear upon my life, my throne, and my honor as a man. And if I be forsworn, may dark destruction overcome me. This is the promise of Brion Donal Cinhil Urien Haldane, King of Gwynedd, Lord of the Purple March, and friend of Alaric Morgan."

With these final words, Brion smiled and pressed Alaric's hands a bit more closely between his own, then released them and turned quickly to take back his sword from Nigel. He glanced at the stained blade as he held it before him.

"I trust you will not mind the blood," he said with a little smile, "since it is through the shedding of this blood that I am able to do what I do now."

Slowly he brought the flat of the blade to touch the boy's right shoulder.

"Alaric Anthony Morgan," the sword rose and crossed to touch the other shoulder, "I create thee Duke of Corwyn, by right of thy mother," the blade touched the top of his head lightly and remained there. "And I confirm thee in this title, for thy life and for the surviving issue of thy body, for so long as there shall be Morgan seed upon the earth." The sword was raised and touched to the royal lips, then reversed and brought to ground. "So say I, Brion of Gwynedd. Arise, Duke Alaric."

Okay. I admit this is not exactly *a sword-and-sorcery story. Perhaps I should have chosen a tale of the dark-skinned swordswoman Tarma and fair sorceress Kethry from Mercedes Lackey's Vows and Honor series. But those are only slightly connected to Lackey's Valdemar universe and Valdemar has been a gateway drug to S&S and other fantasy for many young folks, mostly girls. It is difficult to keep track of how many novels Lackey (1950–) has published since her debut in 1985. Including those she has co-written, I think there are more than one hundred with five more scheduled for 2017. The Heralds of Valdemar series is high fantasy—magic, quests, heroism, average people called to greatness, good fighting evil—usually with teen protagonists (often abused or at least misunderstood) trying to find themselves. And then there are the Companions, magical horses (well, creatures that look like white with bright blue eyes and silver hooves) that Choose a virtuous, MindGifted Herald with whom they form mind-to-mind bonds. The Valdemar books might be considered "sword and sorcery lite," but if you are unacquainted with them, I think you can see from this tale how certain youthful readers are seduced by Lackey. If they outgrow Lackey, they don't necessarily outgrow fantasy—or sword and sorcery.*

OUT OF THE DEEP: A VALDEMAR STORY

Mercedes Lackey

Now *this* was a forest!

Trees crowded the road, overshadowing it, overhanging it. You didn't need a hat even at midday; you almost needed a torch instead to see by. Herald-Intern Alain still couldn't get used to all of the *wilderness* around him—trees that weren't pruned into symmetrical and pleasing shapes, wildflowers that were really wild, ragged, and insect-nibbled. All of his life—except for the brief course in Wilderness Survival—he'd never seen a *weed*, much less a wilderness. He kept expecting to wake up and find that all of this was a fever-dream.

By all rights, he shouldn't be out here, league upon league away from Haven on his Internship Circuit. He was a Prince, after all, and Princes of Valdemar had never gone out of Haven for their Internships, much less out into the furthermost West of the Kingdom, where there were no Guardsmen to rescue you if you got into trouble, and often nowhere to shelter if nature decided to have a bash at you. He *should* have been serving his Internship beside one of the Heralds who helped the City Guard, the Watch, and the city judges.

There was just one teeny, tiny problem with that.

:Actually,: his Companion Vedalia observed, *:There are seven rather tall and vigorous problems with that. And four slender and attractive ones as well.:*

Alain sighed. It wasn't the easiest thing in the world, being the youngest of twelve royal children who had *all* been Chosen.

:It wasn't the easiest thing in the world trying to find things for all of those young and eager Heralds to do,: Vedalia pointed out. *:It wouldn't take more than a candlemark for any of you to figure out that he'd been set make-work. As it was—:*

As it was, it was just bad luck that Alain was not only the youngest of his sibs, he was the youngest by less than a candlemark. Queen Felice was not only the most fecund Consort in the history of Valdemar, she had the habit of having her children in lots. Three sets of twins and two sets of triplets, to be precise. The Heir, whose real name was Tanivel but who they all called Vel for short, was the eldest of his set of twins. Alain was the youngest of his. And in between—

:It is rather a good thing that your mother was never Chosen,: Vedalia observed. *:I'm not sure her poor Companion would have gotten much exercise, much less attention . . . :*

It was true enough that until after Alain had been born, no one in the Court could remember her in any state other than expecting. The fact that she actually possessed a waist had come as a complete surprise to everyone except the King. Everyone wanted to know—and no one dared ask—both the "why" and the "how" of it.

The "how" was easy; multiples ran in her family. Felice was one of a set of twins, and not one of her sisters had ever given birth to less than twins. Her family history held that it had something to do with a blessing placed on them, but by what—well, there were several versions.

The real question was "why"—having had Vel and Vixen (his twin's name was Lavenna, but no one ever called her that) she could have stopped with the traditional "heir and a spare." Certainly most women would have called a halt at the next lot, which were triplets. Not Felice. Rumor had it that she was trying to fill all the extra rooms in the newly rebuilt Heralds' Collegium with her own offspring.

Only Alain had dared to ask his mother what no one else would. She'd hugged him then looked him straight in the eye and said, "Marriages of state. You're *Heralds*, all of you. You don't need a spouse to be loved."

Now, Alain knew his blunt-spoken mother well enough to read between the lines. Shockingly blunt in this case . . . except . . . well Felice had not made a love-match with King Chalinel; she cared deeply for him, but theirs had been a marriage made in the Council chamber. She knew very well that the way to cement the loyalty of a powerful noble house was to marry into it; the way to ensure a foreign alliance was to send (or send for) a bride or groom. Neither she nor the King would force one of their children into a marriage he or she did not want; they would consent to any marriage, even to a beggar, where love was. But this way . . . if an alliance had to be made, there would be someone available to make it at the altar.

Vanyel Ashkevron had made his terrible sacrifice decades ago; Queen Elspeth was Alain's great-great-grandmother. Valdemar's borders had expanded as more and more independent nobles sought to come under the banner of those who had defeated the Karsites. Those nobles—some no better than robber-barons—had no traditional ties to the Valdemaran throne, and no real understanding of what Heralds (the backbone of Valdemaran authority) were and did. One of the obvious solutions was Felice's. After all, it had worked for her family. Her father had gone from an uneasy ally to a doting grandfather who would no more dream of a disloyal thought than jump off the top of his own manor.

And all of his grandchildren—Chosen. That truly brought it home to him and every one of his people what Heralds were and what they did. The lesson was painless and thorough, and the Baron soon was accustomed to having white-clad Heralds coming and going on his lands.

Both Heralds' Collegium and Valdemar had benefited by the arranged marriage with Felice—for now eleven other Heralds, whose skills would be useful outside the capitol, would be freed up by Felice's brood for those other duties while the Princes and Princesses took over.

All of the ten eldest had done well in their classes. Alain and his twin sister Alara had run through the Collegium curriculum like a hot needle through ice. How not? They'd listened to ten siblings as they recited their lessons, they'd practiced weapons-work and archery with ten older siblings, watched and listened with ten siblings. King Chalinel often said that intelligence in the family just kept increasing with each set of children and culminated with Alain and Alara. Alain didn't know about *that*—all of his sibs were clever . . .

:But you and Alara made it through a year early, and Kristen, Kole, and Katen lagged behind because they lost a year to the scarlet fever. With five of you going into Internship at once, there was something of a problem, since we don't like to Intern relatives with relatives,: said Vedalia.

Which was, of course, why he was out on Circuit in the wilderness. No one wanted to risk the health of the triplets after that near-miss with fever, which meant they had to stay within the confines of Haven.

And there were only four Haven Internships available. The four Haven Internships had gone to his other siblings, yes, because of the triplets' uncertain health, but also because they all had Gifts that were useful in those internships. To create a new position just for Alain would have been wrong—

:Yes, well my so-called Gift probably had something to do with why I'm out here, on the edge of the Kingdom, and not somewhere else,: Alain observed.

Vedalia's tone turned sharp. :There is nothing wrong with your Gift,: he said. *:It's as strong as anyone in the Collegium has got, and stronger than your sister's.:*

:And a fat lot of good Animal Mindspeech would have been, Interning with the Lord-Martial's Herald,: he retorted. *:What would I do, interrogate the Cavalry horses? What else can I do? Nothing that a weakly Gifted Herald can't. I don't even have enough ordinary Mindspeech to talk to Herald Stedrel—and he's got the strongest Mindspeech of any Herald anyone's ever heard of!:* He couldn't help it; a certain amount of bitterness crept into his thoughts. He hated not being able to MindSpeak other Heralds—when he could Hear a tree-hare chattering at ten leagues away.

Vedalia was silent so long that Alain thought the conversation was over.

:Look around you,: Vedalia said. *:Listen to the birdsong in the trees. Feel that free wind in your hair. Take a deep breath of air that no human has been breathing but you. Think about all you're learning from the wild things. Are you really so unhappy that your Gift brought you here?:*

Well, put that way . . .

:Hmm. I suppose not.:

:And admit it; it's a relief to be away from Alara for the first time in your life.:

Alain laughed aloud; Herald Stedrel looked back over his shoulder and smiled at him, then turned his attention back to the trail ahead.

It *was* a relief to be away from Alara, who thought she had to have the last word in everything they did, who bossed him as if she was five years, not half a candlemark, older than he. It was a relief to be away from all of his siblings, and from the Court, and all the burdens of royal birth. And so far, although no one could call circuit-riding in the hinterlands a pleasure-jaunt, he'd been enjoying it. He would probably change his mind as soon as winter set in and they were riding with snow up to Vedalia's hocks, but right now, he was enjoying it.

Out here, no one knew he was a Prince. He could flirt with pretty village girls, he could swim naked by moonlight, he could dance at fairs and sing rude songs and no one would make a face or take him aside to remind him that he must act with more decorum. Stedrel actually encouraged him to kick up his heels within reason. He might even try the experiment some time of getting really and truly drunk, though he'd have to wait until he was pretty sure he wouldn't be needed.

:You'll regret it,: Vedalia laughed.

:Probably. But at least I'll have tried it. And maybe I'll try a few more things, too—:

:Tch. Sixteen, and delusions of immortality,: Vedalia teased.

:Doesn't that go with being sixteen?: he retorted.

No, on second consideration, he wouldn't trade being out here for any of the Internships his sibs had. He wished Alara joy of the Lord Martial, who thought that women in general were useless and good only as decoration, and female Heralds in particular were a nuisance. She wouldn't get around *him* by speaking in a slightly higher, more breathy voice and acting hurt, or by turning bossy either.

Maybe that was the point. Internships were supposed to teach you about really being a Herald.

He wondered just what he was supposed to learn out here.

:A good question. Now find the answer to it.: Vedalia tossed his head and Alain smiled.

Then he asked Vedalia to move up alongside of Stedrel's Lovell. "Is there anything I should know about the next village, sir?" he asked respectfully, drawing a smile from the taciturn Herald.

"This'll be our first fishing village, Alain," Stedrel told him. "Do you remember your classes about the Lake Evendim fisher-folk?"

Alain nodded, but not because he recalled his classes as such; one of his yearmates had been from Lake Evendim, and had regaled them all with stories about "home." "Not exactly Holderkin, are they, sir," he responded tentatively.

Sted just snorted. "Not exactly, no. But at least if one of the girls sneaks you off into the water-caves you won't find yourself facing a father, a priest, and a wedding next day." He grinned when Alain blushed. "And unless you have the stamina of a he-goat," the older Herald continued wickedly, as Alain's flushes deepened, "You won't flirt the way you have been with more than one girl at a time."

"They—wouldn't!" Alain choked.

"They would, both together," Sted replied. "Or even three—if you're monumentally stupid enough to put that to the test. With the men out on the boats so much, and fishing being the hazardous occupation that it is, the girls get—"

"Lonely?" Alain said, tactfully.

Sted laughed.

:Thinking of another experiment to try, Chosen?: Vedalia asked innocently.

Alain spluttered, but held his tongue—not the least because he was thinking that very thing. And none of his sibs would be around to tease him and cross-examine him about it afterwards, either.

But when they finally came out of the woods—abruptly, for the trail ended on a rocky cliff-face that dropped steeply down to the gray-green waters the lake—any tentative plans he might have been making vanished abruptly.

The little village that they were making for was built in a river-valley cutting through the cliff, making a narrow and gravel-strewn perch for the Evendim longhouses he'd heard so much about, and a harbor for the fishing boats. The boats should have been out this time of day; instead, they were pulled up on the gravel beach, and the place was in an uproar. They must have been expected, because the moment they came into view, someone spotted them and set up a shout.

Shortly the two Companions were surrounded by what seemed to be every ambulatory person in the entire village. The anxiety in the air was as thick as the smoke from the fires where great racks of fish were being smoked and preserved. Alain hung back, sensing that someone a great deal senior to *him* was who was called for at this moment, but he needn't have bothered with such diffidence. It was clear that the villagers knew the senior Herald here, and two of the more prosperous-looking men fastened themselves to Companion Lovell's reins and began babbling a confused tale of raiders . . .

Alain couldn't make head or tail of it, but Sted seemed to have no trouble. Then again, this was his circuit, and he knew these people. To Alain's ears, their accent, thick enough at the best of times, rendered excited speech incomprehensible.

Then Vedalia came to the rescue.

:Some sort of bandits or raiders have destroyed the next village up the coast,: Vedalia supplied. *:The indications are that the bandits came in by water rather than overland, which is something new, and did so while the men were out fishing. The men returned to find their houses burned out, their women and children gone, and anyone older than forty or younger than four dead in the ashes.:*

Alain felt the blood drain from his face. This was over and above a mere raid. This was an atrocity. And why kill anyone they didn't take? Unless it was to prevent the survivors from telling something?

:The folk here just got warning from the men, who took their boats up and down the coast to warn everyone else. They're afraid to go out fishing now.:

But if they didn't, it wouldn't be long before they were all starving. Without fish, there was nothing to eat and nothing to trade to the farmers farther inland.

:Exactly so—: Vedalia shut up, as Stedrel began speaking calmly, confidently,

and his manner soothed some of the agitation. Alain paid close attention; this was a master at work.

"This happened yesterday? Is there any attempt at pursuit?" he asked.

"Half the men—but it's a big lake—" said one of the men at Lovell's reins, waving at the water.

Big lake? That was an understatement. Even from the top of the cliff it had been impossible to see the other side, and the curve of the shore was imperceptible.

"Defenses first, then," Sted said firmly—turning attention to that without making it obvious that he felt the captives were beyond help.

:They are. There's nothing we can do for them,: Vedalia said glumly. Alain bit his lip; his heart wanted to launch some sort of rescue, but how? With no troops, and no ships—out on a trackless expanse of water—

:The only way to track them might be to FarSee—neither of you have that Gift.:

So they would have to wait until a Herald with that Gift could reach them.

"I wouldn't think that this village is very defensible," Sted began, giving orders—cleverly phrased as suggestions—to safeguard the people of this place.

:Solenbay,: Vedalia supplied.

"Have you anywhere that people can go to hide if raiders appear?" he wanted to know. "These raiders won't know the lay of the land, they won't know where to look, and I doubt if they would linger very long to search."

The babbling died to whispers, and anxious eyes were locked on Sted's face.

"The water-caves," suggested one girl promptly, from the back of the crowd, and blushed.

"Good. If there are any that are particularly hard to find?" Stedrel prompted.

The girl giggled nervously, and Alain had a shrewd notion that she knew the location of every water-cave within walking distance of the village. "Reckon I know some that no one else does," she offered, turning such a deep crimson that she looked sunburnt.

"That be why we can't find you, half nights, Savvy?" asked an older woman—not unkindly, but knowingly.

"Perhaps if you moved all your valuables and stores there now, you'd have only yourselves to get into hiding," Sted suggested, and got nods, some reluctant, all around. "Obviously the main thing is to save you, but I doubt these raiders are going to appear over the horizon within the next day or two, and we should save as much as we can from them."

"I can't see us fighting them off," said one of the other men (who seemed to be one of the village leaders) with a defeated air. "We're fisherfolk, not fighters."

"So save everything that you can in the caves," Sted agreed.

"The ones farthest from here?" Alain ventured. "That way the ones nearest wouldn't be crammed so full people wouldn't fit."

"Good thought," Sted seconded. "Now, I suppose there's no reason why you couldn't spare the young women and children with the swiftest feet and keenest sight to keep watch along the coast?"

"With a horn for each—or something to build a signal fire?" added Alain, and got another approving glance from Sted.

"But the chores—" objected one of the men. "The cleaning, the cooking—" But the ones who were at risk here were nodding vigorously. "No reason why we can't eat common out of the big fish-kettle till this is over," pointed out one old man. "Only takes *one* set of hands for fish-stew, cooking all day." "And if the choice is dirty floors and unmade beds or being carried off, dirty floors we'll have, Matt Runyan," said another woman sharply. "As for the rest—well, we'll barrel up the fish as it's finished smoking and move it into hiding. *Let* 'em have a few racks of fish, I say. Better fish than our children."

"And when they come, find no one, and burn the place out?" the same man objected.

"They'd do that anyway!" shouted a haggard-looking fellow who Alain realized must be one of the now-bereft fisherfolk from the village that had been destroyed. "What's more important, your *things* or your people? You can rebuild *housen*. You tell me how to bring back your wives and kiddies!"

"I'll be sending word of this to Haven anyway," Stedrel pointed out. "As soon as I've got a moment of quiet."

That quieted some of the agitation, as they all recalled that Stedrel was so powerful a Mindspeaker he could send directly to Haven itself, and every receptive mind along the way. Help would not be far off—two or three fortnights at most.

"The King will send troops, and when they get here, you'll be able to go back to life as usual. And we'll be able to scour the coast for the missing." That last as a sop to the men from the destroyed village. They surely knew it was an offer unlikely to bear fruit, but they looked hopeful anyway.

"Soonest begun's soonest done," one of the women said briskly. "We've only got two wagons for the whole village. Let's get our traps moved before sunset!" Within moments, the women, young and old, were heading purposefully towards their family longhouses, followed a little reluctantly by the men.

"Savvy!" Sted called after the girl who had confessed to knowing where most of the water-caves were. She turned back abruptly.

"Sir?" she responded.

"Go to that longhouse over there—" Sted pointed at one where a bevy of women were already moving bundles, barrels, and boxes out briskly to be piled beside the door. "When they're ready to take a load out, guide them to the farthest cave you know of—"

"I'll take her up behind, pillion," Alain offered quickly. "That way we can come back for the next load while the first is still unloading."

"Good. I want you to keep each longhouse's goods in a separate cave, that way when this is over there won't be any quarrels over what belongs to who." Sted smiled encouragingly at her, and the girl returned his smile shyly.

There was some objection to the choice of cave as the wagon-load set off: "We're ready *first*," grumbled the oldest dame, "Don't see why we should be goin' the farthest."

"But milady, the farther away the cave is, the less likely it will be that it will be discovered," Alain pointed out, thinking quickly. "You're getting the *choice* spot, not the worst one." The old woman gave him a quick look, but nodded with reluctant satisfaction, and made no further complaints.

He would never have believed it, but the longhouses were stripped of every portable object—and some he wouldn't have considered portable—by twilight. The two village mules were ready to drop before it was over, but they were made much of and given an extra ration. The village was substantially deserted now, with only a handful of the very old and the very young remaining behind. In order to get everything moved, the wagons had simply been unloaded at the flat spot nearest to each family's cave before returning for another load. Now all of the able-bodied were lowering their goods down the cliff walls to be stored; they would work all night, if necessary.

As darkness fell, Sted looked around the empty street down the middle of the village. "I'm going to go somewhere quiet and contact Haven," he told Alain. "See what you can do to make yourself useful."

Sted and his Companion drifted off in the twilight. As gloom descended on the street, it occurred to Alain that the most immediately useful thing he could do would be to light the village lamps, so that the returning villagers would have lights beckoning them homeward. There were lamps outside the door of each longhouse, lamps with fat wicks and large reservoirs of oil that by the smell could only come from fish. He got a spill and ventured into the first of the longhouses.

He had never seen anything like it; there was a central hearth with a cone-shaped metal hood over it, and a metal chimney reaching up to the roof. For the rest, it seemed to be one enormous room with cupboards lining all four walls. There were no windows, only slits covered with something that wasn't glass just under the eaves, like clerestory windows, but smaller.

It must be very dark in here during the day.

He knew why there weren't any windows, and why, as much as possible, the Evendim folk spent their time out-of-doors. When winter storms closed in, the coast was hellish; storms swept in over the water with fangs of ice and claws of snow. During the five Winter Moons it was hardly possible to set foot outside these houses, and it would have been folly to give the wind that the fisherfolk called "the Ice-Drake" any way to tear into the shelter of their homes.

But winter was moons away, and the present danger was not from nature but from man. Alain lit the spill at the remains of the fire, and went out to light the lanterns.

When he had done the last of them, he found a couple of old men, limbs knotted with age, slowly stacking wood in a firepit at the center of the village and he ran to help.

From that moment until late that night he worked, as hard as he had ever worked in his life, and despite being a Prince, he was no stranger to physical labor. He carried wood and water, the enormous iron kettle, and all the ingredients for the great pot of fish-stew that would be cooking night and day for as long as this crisis lasted. He took a torch out to the drying racks for an old woman, rolled up empty barrels and brought a keg of salt and a bag of herbs, and helped her stack smoked fish in layers with salt and herbs. There were no fresh fish to spread upon the racks, but he helped her layer the fires for the next day, when the men *would* go out. With aching muscles and sore feet he put babies and toddlers to bed, persuaded them to stay there, then helped their grandmothers and grandfathers to their beds when old bodies could do no more. Then he waited, getting off his feet at last, with Vedalia beside him, watching the stew to see that it didn't burn. He'd taken Vedalia's tack and packs off him, but had no idea where he should be stabled or where the two Heralds should stay. So he heaped tack and packs beside the fire and used them as props for his back. As full as that kettle was, it would be a long time cooking, and he needn't actually watch it, just stir it from time to time to keep what was on the bottom from sticking and burning. He wished he could have a bath; even his hair felt full of smoke, and his eyes gritty.

Slowly, slowly, the folk of the village began trickling back in, weary, too weary to think past the next footstep. They didn't seem to notice him sitting by the fire; they trudged into their houses to seek what they'd left of their beds, leaving him standing guard beside tomorrow's dinner.

And he could hardly keep his eyes open.

:You sleep,: Vedalia said. *:I'll wake you if it needs stirring—or anything comes.:*

"No—I'm still on duty," Alain protested.

:Just close your eyes then to rest them,: Vedalia suggested. It seemed a sensible suggestion; they were sore, irritated by all the smoke he'd been standing in. He let his lids fall for just a moment.

When he opened them again, it was because there was a rooster crowing in his ear. He jerked awake and startled it and the two chickens scratching around his feet into flight.

It was dawn, and there was a young girl stirring the pot with a great wooden paddle. Someone had draped a cloak over him, and he had curled up with Vedalia's saddle as a pillow. His packs were nowhere to be seen, but Vedalia dozed hip-shot beside him.

The Companion snorted and stirred as Alain sat up, opening his brilliant blue eyes. *:Stedrel was here and took our packs, but he didn't see any reason to wake you. There's a Waystation just outside of the village. If you'll just drape my saddle on me, we'll go wake him.:*

They didn't have to; they hadn't gotten past the last longhouse when he and his Companion appeared on the road before them. "You might as well turn back around," Sted called cheerfully. "We have to organize the coast-watch now, and we'll both be a part of it."

Wishing mightily for more sleep, and trying not to feel disgruntled at Sted's announcement, Alain sighed and did as he was told. At least there was food waiting—a communal kitchen set up by all the grannies to dole out cold smoked fish and bread to anyone who stuck out a hand. The men, trusting blindly that Sted would see to the protection of their families and village, took to the boats with their breakfasts in their pockets and more of the same for eating later.

Before a candlemark was out, the village resembled a ghost town. One set of elderly women minded children and babies—but Sted had cunningly assigned every child too small to run to someone big enough to pick it up and carry it. Several of the adult women were to carry babies—and were put to fashioning slings that let them have one slung on the back, one on the front, and one on each hip. That left the older children and some of the adult women—and a few of the grannies and granthers that were still spry enough to sprint—on coast-watch.

And now came the shock for Alain. This was not the only village at risk—

Which, when the men returned, Sted made very plain.

"We've done what we can for you," he told the villagers, once the men returned with holds full of fish and the catch was distributed on the smoking racks. "Help is coming, and it will come here first, in three days' time. I reached a Herald riding with a troop of the Guard no farther away than that. Now Alain and I have to do the same for the rest of the villages."

He'd chosen his moment well; in the first flush of success, or perhaps because of exhaustion, no one objected.

"I will go north along the coast; Alain will go south and west," Sted announced. "We'll do for them what we've done for you. If you can hold out for three days, all will be well."

Alain had gone quite still with shock. He would be going out alone? He looked at Sted in silent appeal, but the older Herald was already mounting and preparing to ride to the next village. "Herald Stedrel?" he faltered.

The Herald just gave him a sobering look, and he shut his mouth on any objections.

:Let's go,: Vedalia said. *:If we push, we can make the next village by sundown.:*

They pushed—and found that place in as much of an uproar as the first, and having had a full day to stew over the warnings, people were ready to greet *anything* that looked like help with full cooperation. Either they were not necessarily expecting Stedrel, or they were so grateful to see the uniform that they were willing to overlook the youthful face. In either case, no one objected to a single aspect of the plan.

The water-caves here were nearer and larger; evacuation of goods and stores took place by torch- and moonlight, and this village had a leader in the form of one indomitable old woman. Once given a plan, she was perfectly prepared to see it carried out. Conscious of the passing of time, Alain decided to move on that very night. He'd always understood that it was possible for a Herald to sleep in the saddle; now he found out the truth of it. It wasn't exactly *sleep*, but it was no worse than his night beside the kettle. He reached the third village at dawn, finding it in as desperate a state as the previous two.

And in coming closer to hysteria. So much so that he decided to organize the coast-watchers *first*. And it was a good thing that he did.

For it was no more than a candlemark after the youngsters had set off than wild horn-calls sounded in the middle distance, and all the careful plans fell to pieces.

After the first moment of blank incomprehension, while people, interrupted in mid-task, stared silently at the west, someone screamed.

Then all hell broke loose. No one seemed to know where to go, or what to do, despite Alain's instructions only two candlemarks ago. They dashed in all directions, some to their homes, some to the woods, some to snatch up belongings, and some dropping them. Five people managed to keep their heads: Alain, Vedalia, and three of the village elders.

"Get them to the caves!" Alain shouted over the screaming, the weeping, as people milled in panic around him. "We have to get them to the caves!"

The elders began picking up children, shoving them into random arms, shouting at those who had frozen with fear to rouse them, and shoving them in the right direction. Once little groups were moving towards safety, Vedalia encouraged them by charging at them with lashing hooves and bared teeth, looking utterly demonic.

Alain headed off those going in the opposite direction, screaming at them, even going so far as to swat a couple of those lagging behind with the flat of his blade until they disappeared into the trees in the direction of the caves—

Then he returned to chivvy another group into safety.

He had not a moment to spare to look for the enemy—as they sailed swiftly into the harbor he got nothing more than a glimpse of ships, long, lean, fast-looking to his land-accustomed eyes. He sensed, more than heard or saw, the moment when the raiders came ashore. Vedalia was hot on the heels of another group of stragglers; he went back to chase a few more away from a chest they were trying to haul off.

He never realized how close the raiders were, that they were charging up the street at a run, until it was too late. He never even got a chance to defend himself. There was just a shout behind him, and he half-turned, and then—

—he woke in darkness, head reeling, stomach heaving, pain shooting through his skull; his hands were tied in front of him, and his ankles bound together. He'd been tossed on a pile of what felt like rope, and he was just about to lose what little he had in his stomach. He managed to roll over to the side before throwing up, and managed to roll away from the mess he'd made. The floor beneath the ropes on which he lay was moving.

From the way his head hurt, someone had coshed him, and done so with enthusiasm and some expertise. Enthusiasm, because they'd given him a concussion for certain—given the way that his stomach churned and the deck (it must be a ship's deck) beneath him felt as if it was spinning as well as rising and falling. Expertise, because he wasn't dead.

He was trussed up, but hastily; evidently his captors trusted to the hit on the head to keep him quiet. And he was in darkness, because it was night, but he was also under a tarp draped between two bulky objects. Around him were foreign noises, the rushing and splashing of water, sounds of creaking, the groaning of wood, men shouting. The air was damp and cool and smelled of open water.

At least they hadn't shoved him into the hold.

Well, perhaps there wasn't any room in the hold. He was probably the least valuable object the raiders had taken.

Right. I'm on a ship, a captive, and—

Only then did he realize that there was a conspicuous *absence* in his thoughts.

—in trouble. I can't hear Vedalia.

He must be leagues away from the village, if he couldn't hear his Companion. Leagues away, and no way for anyone to track him.

"—and I don' know what th' *hell* ye wanted with the Herald!" someone said, just coming into earshot. "He's no good to us—a woman or a kiddie we could use, but him?"

"Look, if we kill him, we get more trouble than we can handle," said a second voice. "Kill one of them white-coats, and the rest *never* give up comin' after you!"

You've got that right, Alain thought—though what good that would do him if he was dead—

"If we left him, gods only know what he'd manage to do—him or that horse. And gods know how close their people are. I thought, we take him, though, they won't dare come after us with everything they've got. Even if they got ships ready to sail, you bet they'd hang back. They won't risk our killing him. If we held him till we were safe out of reach, I figured we *stayed* safe."

His heart plummeted and his spirit went cold. *Gods help me. Bandits who think.*

"So now what?" asked the first voice, sounding a little mollified.

"We sail a little farther, we make sure there's nothing chasing us, then we dump him." The second voice sounded utterly indifferent. "We could probably get a ransom for him, but that'd put us in their reach again."

Alain felt his heart falter, and the panic he had been holding off until that moment rise up and seize him. He wanted to scream, but he could only whimper a little, a pathetic whine lost in the sounds the ship made. And inside, he began screaming silently—and futilely—for help. He couldn't *help* himself—it was an automatic reaction.

But even as he shrieked at the top of his mental voice, some part of him despaired and *knew* it was useless. Maybe in the woods, even if there was no human with Mindspeech near enough to help, he could have summoned elk, a mountain-cat, wolves to his aid. But this was the vast water, with nothing in it but fish. Still his mind yammered as if anything that *could* help him was likely to hear him . . .

:?:

The response, faint as it was, stopped his mental gibbering in its tracks. *:What?:* he called back.

:??: came the return—stronger! There was a sense of something he hadn't expected; behind that startled query was intelligence. Maybe enough to help him?

He fought back pain and nausea and focused all of his strength behind something more coherent.

:Help me! Please!: he Sent, and added overtones of his situation; easy enough to do since it was all very physical.

The response was not a single voice, but a chorus.

:Landwalker? Yes, Landwalker!:

:Landwalker. Net-bound.:

:Brother to Weeps-On-Shore.:

:Captive to——: What followed was emotion, and senses, rather than words—a sense of something destructive, a taste of blood, and anger on the part of the speaker. Whatever these creatures were, they knew his captors, and they had no love for them.

:Yes. They must not have him.:

:Enough. They must be stopped.:

:Call the Deep One.:

:Yes! The Deep One will know! The Deep One will rid the face of the waters of them!:

:Call the Deep One!:

Well, it was very nice that they saw his enemies as their own, but they hadn't answered him. He chose this moment to insert his own plea.

:Please? Help me?:

But at that moment, the tarp was ripped aside. He blinked up at four shadowed faces interposed between him and a star-filled sky.

Someone else, just out of sight, spoke. "Right. We're safe enough. Over the side with him."

Fear and nausea warred within him, but he had no time to react—four sets of hands seized shoulders and ankles, there was a moment of futile struggle as they heaved him up—

Then flying weightless through the air—just enough time for a last gulp of air—

Then he hit the water like a stone.

He managed to keep his breath, and he sank for a moment, the cold water hitting him a blow that made him choke back a gasp that would have lost him that precious breath. With bound hands and feet, disoriented in the black water, he thrashed, trying to find the surface, the air, the precious air, and not knowing where it was.

:We come, Walker!:

Miraculously he was surrounded by large, fleshy bodies, warm, slick bodies that bore him suddenly up to the surface and held him there as he gasped for breath.

He couldn't see them—the moon must have set—so he had only the sense that they were larger than he was, slick and not scaly like a fish. As they thrust under his arms with oblong heads and long snouts, they used those rounded, bulbous heads to keep him afloat. Others went to work on the ropes tying his hands and feet. They had sharp teeth, too, in those snouts—they took it in turns to slice at his bonds, slicing into his hands, though he sensed apology every time tooth met flesh and he gasped with pain.

:It's all right,: he managed, and conveyed the sense that he would rather be free and wounded than bound and whole. He got amused concurrence and a renewed assault on his bonds. They must be the terror of the fish, these creatures; veritable wolves of the water.

Just as the final rope parted on his hands, there was a stirring among his rescuers, a rush of excitement.

:The Deep One comes!: cried one voice, and then another—

And suddenly he was alone in the water, paddling frantically. *:Wait!:* he called after them. *:Wait, I don't—I can't—:*

:Peace, little Walker.:

The Mindvoice was like none he had ever heard before; huge, deep, with a kind of echo. It swept through his mind and made him shiver and catch his breath, knowing in his bones he was in the presence of something—monumental.

:Peace. Be still. I come.: He felt something, a pressure in the water beneath him, and then—

Then something bigger than the biggest ship he had ever seen rose up beneath him like a floor. And he felt himself in a Presence.

:Yes, little Walker. I uphold you. Well for you that you cannot see me, else your fear would make a dumb beast of you, and render you lawful prey . . .

It had the same sort of slick, resilient hide as the others had, this creature whose back held him, supported him, in just a few thumb-breadths of water. He couldn't see anything of it, but the sense of something so huge he couldn't even imagine it held him silent.

:So, tell me, Walker-On-Land, what is it that should cause the Bright Leapers to come to your aid and call upon me?:

:I don't know, my lord,: Alain said humbly. :I just—asked for help.:

:Just asked for help. Never has a Walker asked help of us. Perhaps that is reason enough. But what of these others?: The Mindvoice lost its sense of amusement, and Alain shivered again. ***:The Leapers say that they must be stopped. Their tree-float tastes of blood and pain, their minds of ravening. I know what they have done to the Leapers—but what else have they done to their own kind?:*** *

As briefly as possible, Alain outlined to the vast creature beneath his hands just what it was that the raiders had done, and he felt an anger as enormous as creature itself slowly rousing.

:So. Bad enough to make war, but those who make it upon the infant and the aged . . . the wisdom of the people and the hope . . . : A pause. ***:Yes. I can see. But this is between you and your kind, and although I wish to follow the wishes of the Leapers, I must have a price from you.:***

:A price?: It didn't matter; whatever it wanted, it could have, if it would put an end to these marauding bandits. *:Is it—:* he gulped. *:—me you want, oh Lord of the Deep?:*

The surface beneath his hands vibrated; in a moment, he recognized it as laughter. ***:No, little Walker, be you ever so tasty, you are too noble for my eating. Besides, I would not cause the Weeper-On-The-Shore, your White Spirit-Brother, to dissolve in grief. No. Before I act in the affairs of Walkers . . . a vow from you, Walker, brother to the White Spirit. That you reveal me to no one. Ever.:***

:You have it,: he promised, not entirely sure why this creature wanted it, nor what he was exchanging the vow for, but willing enough to give it. *:None shall know. Not even my Companion.:*

:Then I shall act.:

He felt the great bulk beneath him begin to move, felt it rise until he was completely out of the water. He balanced on this hill of flesh, and the air of its passing flowed around him, chilling him so that he shivered. The resilient flesh beneath him undulated slowly.

Lights appeared on the horizon, lights too yellow and unwinking to be stars.

They were lanterns, lanterns hung on the rail of the ship that had taken him and on its sister-ships in the raiding fleet. Swiftly as these ships sailed, the creature beneath Alain was faster.

Now he sensed other minds around him, the minds of the smaller creatures that had initially been his rescuers. They exchanged no words, only feelings of excitement and some of the same anger that the greater creature felt. And with that came glimpses of the cause of that anger—the wanton slaughter of these creatures by the men of the swift, agile ships.

:Stay with the Leapers, Walker, and observe.:

The bulk that supported him slipped from beneath him, plunging him into the water again as it disappeared. But before he could panic, the others were around him, one under each outstretched arm. And before the ship sailed away from where they waited in the water, something black and terrible surged up out of the waves beside it—

—and crashed down on it before the few sailors manning the sails and tiller had a chance to do more than register the presence of something beside them.

The ship disintegrated with a horrible sound of shattering timber and the screams of the men aboard.

The men on the other ships had that much warning—enough to know their doom, not enough to avoid it. Again and again, the huge bulk leapt from the waves and smashed down on their ships, splintered them as a wanton child would splinter a toy, but with anger no child could ever feel.

How many died instantly, how many were left to flounder in the water he would never find out, for the smaller swimmers left him again and the huge one rose beneath him and carried him quickly away.

:There are more of them yet, clinging to bits of their tree-floater, but I will hunt tonight, Walker,; said the voice with grim satisfaction. ***:When you are safe I shall return, and oh, I shall dine well . . . so remember your vow.:***

:I will,: he pledged fervently, with a shudder, and felt the creature's amusement.

:Come. I hunger. The sooner the Leapers can take you ashore, the sooner I may feed.:

Again the huge bulk rose out of the water with him atop it, and sped—in what direction? He could not tell. He could only cling to it as best he could, exhausted, cold, shivering, aching in head and limb, and hope this *thing* that had spoken of dining on men would take him home.

And yet—and yet—

He was afraid of it—but it was more respect than fear.

:Speak with me, Walker. Tell me of your life. I have never met one who could Speak to my thoughts, and I have lived long . . . long.:

So throughout that long night, that strange journey, he spoke with the unseen creature that bore him. It was not ignorant of the ways of humans, but Heralds and Companions were new and fascinating to it. He came to understand that it was his despised Gift of Animal Mindspeech that had saved him; the creature could *hear* the strong thoughts of others, but imperfectly. Only Alain had ever been able to converse with it, and with the ones called the Bright Leapers.

Gradually, respect entirely replaced fear—

Though he did not forget what it intended to do when it returned to the shattered wrecks to hunt. And he was torn; the men were guilty of murder, robbery, rapine—and certainly their lives would have been forfeit had their fate come upon them from the hands of Selenay's Guard. But to be devoured after candlemarks of terror, floating on the face of the water—

:Their fate is what it will be. Perhaps they will drown before I return; drowned

or living, they will serve me well. It is neither you, nor I, to whom they must answer for their deeds. I do but send them quickly to that judgment.:

There was nothing he could say to that; and in the end, perhaps this was no worse than imprisonment, perhaps a trial, and in the end, the axe or rope . . .

:But the dawn is near, and so is the shore,: the creature continued. ***:No Walker has yet seen me, nor shall they—not those who I let live, at least. I go to hunt; the Leapers will see you to your friends.:*** There was a sense of a smile in its Mindvoice. *:Begin to call when I leave you, so that your Spirit-Brother will cease to lament. His weeping tears at my heart even now.:*

The creature slowed and stopped, and slowly submerged, dropping him again into the water. A moment later, it was gone—it could probably swim faster under the water than above it, and had only kept to the surface for his benefit. The water felt warm after the chill of wet garments in rushing air; the Bright Leapers were soon around him, holding him up.

:Move your limb from out the dead-skin you wear, so we can take it in our mouths and pull you,: said one. After a moment he puzzled out that they meant him to pull his hands and arms up into his sleeves so they could take the ends in their mouths. He did as they asked, and soon they were towing him between two of them, with the others swimming alongside, occasionally leaping into the air, apparently just for the sheer exuberance of living. Remembering what the Deep One had said, he began to MindCall Vedalia. And as the sky before them grew light, and the water reflected it back in dull silver, he heard Vedalia answer.

What passed between them was too deep for words, and he was glad to be towed and not swimming, for he couldn't have swum and wept at the same time.

And as the sun itself appeared on the horizon, it seemed that the Leapers were not going to have to take him to shore after all, for there were boats coming to meet them—and although Vedalia could not have fit in them, Sted was in the prow of the foremost, his white uniform shining in the early light.

The Leapers—he saw now that they *looked* like fish, but with sleek, brown hides, merry eyes, and mouths frozen into a perpetual grin—now made good their name, for all those who surrounded the two who towed him flung themselves into the air in graceful arcs. From the distant boats a cheer arose, made faint by distance—and by the water in his ears, perhaps.

He grayed-out for a moment—it was a good thing that his caretakers were competent and kept him from drowning—for when he came to himself, there were two bright-eyed heads holding him up, with his arms across what might have been their necks if they'd had such a thing. And the foremost boat was coming alongside. Many hands reached down to haul him aboard, which was a good thing, because now that he was safe, the last of his energy ran out, and he felt as weak as a newborn kitten.

But he was not so exhausted that he didn't notice the fishermen bowing to the Bright Leapers, and calling out their thanks as he was hauled aboard. "You know these creatures?" he said, surprised.

"They are the Wave-Wise," said one of the fishermen, wrapping a rough woolen blanket about his shoulders. "Some say they are the spirits of those of us who drowned and never came home to be buried on land. We never molest them, and if one should be tangled in a net, we cut the net to let him free. Better to lose a catch than drown a brother."

:Deep-Speaker!: one called, bobbing with its head above the water, making a chattering sound and nodding as it MindSpoke. *:Tell your friends that we know where the Netted Ones are, and we will guide them there!:*

The Netted Ones? The kidnapped women?

:Yes! Yes! And now the Deep One feeds, there are none to keep them netted!:

"Dear gods—" he grabbed the fisherman by the collar. "Listen—your Wave-Wise are wiser than you guess! They say they know where the women and children are that were stolen away, and will guide you there!"

Pandemonium broke out among the boats, as the Bright Leapers cavorted and word passed from vessel to vessel. All wanted to go, but the crew of the boat that held Sted and Alain reluctantly agreed to turn back with them.

Then, and only then, did Alain lie back, his shivering easing, a flask of some herb cordial that Sted had pressed into his hand, sheer exhaustion flattening him against the support of rope and blankets that Sted had rigged for him.

Sted, who spoke but seldom, had been babbling ever since he was brought aboard out of sheer relief. Since most of what he was saying had been variations on "Thank the gods you're safe!" Alain hadn't paid a lot of attention.

Now, though—"Vedalia said you were rescued by those fish—or whatever they are," Sted was saying.

"Not fish—I s'ppose they must be something like a Pelagiris-creature, a kyree or whatever," Alain replied, hoping he sounded as exhausted as he felt. "They said the only reason they could hear me, and I could hear them, was my Gift."

"But how did you get away?" Sted asked.

Alain tried to laugh and coughed instead, taking a sip of the cordial. "I didn't. The bastards only kept me long enough to be sure you weren't chasing them with boats full of Guards. Then they tossed me overboard. But I'd been yelling like a scared baby, and the—they call themselves Bright Leapers—the Bright Leapers heard me." He held out his wrists so Sted could see the cuts from their teeth.

"Got the ropes off, then towed me back. I suppose I was rescued for the novelty of listening to me talk while I was brought back as much as anything else. I got the impression that these water-creatures, the intelligent ones, spend a lot of their time just—playing, learning, being curious. So much for the honor and glory of being a Herald! My real value seems to have been that I could tell a good story!"

He might be exhausted, but he was choosing his words very carefully. He was telling the exact truth, just not all of it . . . and as long as he stuck to the exact truth, Sted was not likely to wonder what he was trying to hide.

Sted chuckled, and so did the fisherman nearest them, the man at the tiller. "We've always honored the Wave-Wise, but if they bring us to the captives, they'll be getting a share of our catches from now on," the fisherman said. "As for stories, I expect you'll be tired of telling this one long before anyone gets tired of hearing it. There've been other tales of the Wave-Wise rescuing fisherfolk, but never like this one."

"And I fervently hope there never is again," Alain said emphatically. "I pray that no one ever meets the sort of things I did last night."

He closed his eyes and Sted's urging, and felt consciousness rapidly slipping away. But—did he hear the far-off echo of an appreciative—and sated—chuckle at that last?

:No, of course not.:

:Of course not,: he agreed, and slept.

⚔

Michael Shea's (1946–2014) first published novel, A Quest for Simbilis *(1974), was an authorized sequel to Jack Vance's two Dying Earth books. (When Vance's* Cugel's Saga *appeared in 1983, it took the series in a new direction and Shea's novel was no longer considered part of the canon.) Shea's* Nifft the Lean *(1982)—four connected novellas—was influenced by Vance, Clark Ashton Smith, Fritz Leiber, and H. P. Lovecraft. Considered by some to be one of the more important works of modern sword and sorcery, it won the World Fantasy Award for best novel in 1983. Nifft later appeared in* The Mines of Behemoth *(1997) and in* The A'rak *(2000). Shea also authored three other non-Nifft novels and over thirty shorter works. "Epistle from Lebanoi," the final Nifft story, was published in 2012.*

EPISTLE FROM LEBANOI

Michael Shea

Long hast thou lain in dreams of war—
Lift from the dark your eyeless gaze!
Stand beneath the sky once more,
Where seas of suns spill all ablaze!
—Gothol's invocation of his
long-drowned father, Zan-Kirk

I

From Lebanoi
Nifft the Lean, traveler and entrepreneur at large,
Salutes Shag Margold, Scholar

I am to ship out to the Ingens Cluster, but it seems the craft I've passage on is finding the refitting of a gale-damaged mast slow work. Writing—even to you, old friend—is tedious toil, but since the alternative is the restless fidgets, write I will. And in truth, what's passed here merits some memorial.

Well then—I disembarked here at Lebanoi from a Lulumean carrack a fortnight ago. I know you are aware that for all the lumber towns along this forested coast, and all the flumes you'll find in them, Lebanoi's Great Flume is justly preeminent. Standing at dockside, staring up its mighty sweep to the peaks, I gave this fabled structure its due of honest awe.

Then, bent on some ale, I repaired to a tavern, where I found out right quick about the native fiber of some of these lumbering folk! They can thump a bar, and bray and scowl with the best, these logger-lads! No dainty daisies these, be sure of that, when they come down the mountain for their spree!

I sat with a pint in the Peavey Inn—an under-Flume inn, one of countless grog-dens built high up within the massy piers which prop that mighty channel of water-borne timber. In many of these inns and taverns—clumped up right against the Flume's underbelly and reached by zigzags of staircases—you can hear just above you, through the ceiling, the soft rumble of rivering timber as you sit imbibing.

And thus sat I, assaying the domestic stout, till a bit of supper should restore my land-legs for the long ascent to Upflume—Lebanoi's smaller sister city on the higher slopes halfway up the Flume's length.

But here came trouble, a come-to-blows brewing. For behold, a bare-armed lout, all sinewed and tattooed—axes and buck-saws inked upon his arms—stood next to me at the bar, and he began booming gibes at me which he thinly guised as jests.

"Your braid's divine!" he cried. "Do they not call that style a 'plod's-tail,' honest traveler?"

My hair was clubbed in the style of the Jarkeladd nomads. I keep it long to unbind in polite surroundings to mask the stump that's all that remains of my left ear—lost, as you know Shag, down among the Dead.

Soon, I knew, after initial insults, the lout would mock my ear, for his eye already dwelt on it. I decided that this slur, when it came, would trigger my clouting him.

Beaming in his face, I cried, "Why thank you! Your own dense curls, Sir, merit equal praise! Sawdust and shavings besprinkle your coiffure! How stylish to resemble—as you do—a broom that's used to scour a saw-mill's floor!"

He sneered and plucked a phial out of his vest, tapped dust into his cup, and drank it off. Even swamp-despising woodsmen buy swamp spices—this one "whiff," unless I missed my guess, productive of raw energy, no more.

"Another thing, fine foreigner," brayed my lout, "that I adore your doublet, and your hose! Garments so gay they would not shame a *damsel*!"

This bellicose buffoon would blanch to face such men as wear the Ephesian mode I wore. I grant, the costume does not shun display. The snake-scale appliqué upon my hose, the embroidered dragon coiled upon my codpiece, my doublet harlequinned with beadwork—all my clothes artfully entertained the cultivated eye with rich invention.

Of course, I would straightway don self-effacing garb once I should find an inn, and stroll the town to learn its modes. The seasoned traveler travels to behold, not be beheld. But, until I did so, a bustling port like Lebanoi might sanely be expected to extend sophisticated sufferance to the modes of the far-flung cultures whom her trade invites!

"No doubt," I said, "your celibate sojourns in the woods make even stumps and knotholes seem to sport a womanly allure. No doubt even alley curs arouse your lust, so be that they have tails to wag, and furry arses."

Oddly, though his mates looked to be loggers like himself, they seemed in the main unmoved by our exchange, and unconcerned by gibes from me that mocked their trade. Their cool interest set my nerves on edge.

"Where did you hear," brayed Lout, "we lacked for lasses? You were mis-told, or likelier mis-*heard*! Yes, half-heard with your half-a-brace of ears! 'Tis very meet that you should mention arses—that puckered hole you sport athwart your head resembles one!"

All knew my blow was coming, yet showed no concern beyond any man's casual interest in a developing brawl . . .

Well, I clouted him, and brought him down, then backed away a bit, and let my hand hover in the general direction of my sword-hilt. An older, gnarlier woodsman, giving a sardonic eye to my stunned adversary on the floor, addressed me.

"Think nothing of it, stranger! Here now my lads—someone prop him at a table and pour him another flagon."

"Please!" I interjected. "Permit me to buy his drink—by way of amends!"

This was generally well received. The older man, Kronk, stood me a flagon. "Wabble's not a bad sort, but he's dim, and in his cups. He took you for a spice magnate, merely by your costly gear. Too dim to see that your style—no offense—is much too lively even for an Up-flume entrepreneur."

We talked. I learned that tree-jacks dabbled in spice trade even as Up-flumers did, in the long years since the Witches' War had damaged Rainbowl Crater, and reduced the output of Lebanoi's mills.

I took a thankful leave of him, keen to have some daylight left to learn the city a bit more, and to dress myself less noticeably.

Stairs and catwalks threaded the maze of under-Flume construction. I made my way a good half mile farther inland from the dockside, or farther "up-flume" as the saying is here. I mounted a level rooftop, scooted well back into the Flume's shadow, and disrobed. I stowed my gaudier gear, and donned a leather jerkin and woolen hose. Bound up my hair, and hid it in a Phrygian cap.

I rested and enjoyed the view, the golden sinking of the day. Above me hummed the Flume's boxed flood, the softly knocking bones of trees that colossal conduit carried down to the wharf-side mills. I looked upwards along its mighty sweep, ascending on its titan legs the skorse-clad mountains . . .

All Lebanoi was bathed in rosy westering light. Her mills and yards and manses and great halls glowed every mellow hue of varnished wood. Her houses thronged the gentler coastal hills. And they were so etched by the slanting sunbeams that I could trace the carven vines and leaves that filigreed the gables of even the more distant buildings.

The rumble of the rivering logs above me, the shriek of saws from the mills, the creak of tackle, the shouts and thumps of cargo from the shipyards—all blended in a pleasing song of energy and enterprise. Despite her wounds from the Witches' War, the city still prospered.

But I'd just tasted the tensions at work here. Where factions are at odds, outsiders best go lightly. Best to head inland to the town of Up-flume, obtain my spice, and ship out tomorrow. It meant harvesting at night, but by all reports spice-gathering went on in the swamp at all hours.

And so, I mounted from the Flume's underside to its top. This, of course, forms a wide wooden highway which streams with traffic up-Flume and down, and in the late sun its whole great sweep showed clear. Far up I saw where the Flume's high terminus lay shattered, just below great Rainbowl Crater's fractured wall—Lebanoi's two great wounds, suffered in the Witches' War . . .

My own goal lay but half as far—just four miles up, where Lebanoi's smaller sister-city filled a shallow valley under the Flume's crossing: Up-Flume, where the spice swamp lay.

I flagged a dwarf-plod shay. "Are spicers ready-found at night?" I asked my teamster, a white-haired woman, as she sped us up-flume. She slant-eyed me, wryly marking an innocent abroad. "Readily found, at double rate, and like to take you roundabout if you don't watch 'em close."

I tipped her for the warning.

As we reached Up-Flume, the full moon was just rising as the red sun sank to sea. At Up-flume, one took ramps that zigzagged down through a three- and four-tiered city of dwellings densely built amid the Flume's pilings, and jutting out an eighth mile to either side on tiered platforms. Down amid the swampwaters themselves could be seen here and there the bow and stern-lights of spicers' boats out harvesting amid the darkening bogs.

Descending, I was accosted on the stairs by more than a few would-be guides, and courteously deflected all of them. It might behoove me to try them later, but first I meant to try my hand alone.

On the swampside docks, a punt-and-pole was readily rented for a high fee and a hefty deposit, and in this narrow vessel I set off cautiously along the swamp's meandering shoreline, where my pole—with careful probing—found mucky purchase.

No accident my being here at the full moon's rising. A full moon is prescribed, both for one's searching and for the spices' potency, which is held to peak when bathed in lunar light.

But the density of vegetation here—big shaggy trees all spliced with scaly vines, overarching a boskage of glossy shrubs and dense thickets—provided an eerie matrix for all the furtive movement everywhere about me. The swamp teemed with spicers all hunting discreetly, taut, intent, and sly. On all sides the feculent waters chuckled and tremored with their stealthy investigations. Foliage flustered or twitched or whispered here and there, and you glimpsed the sheen of swift hulls crossing moonlit patches of black water and then ducking quick back into the darkness again.

But soon I knew I could not move so discreetly, however deftly I poled through the shadowy margins. My punt was rented, and the sight of it drew defter boatmen gliding to my gunnels.

"What spice, what spice, Sir? Five lictors in my pocket brings you to it!"

At my outset, I firmly declined their insistence. Before my coming to Lebanoi, costly consultations with two different spice connoisseurs had provided me with sketches of the herbs I sought. These drawings had looked detailed enough on receipt, but proved useless compared to the intricate, moonlit weeds and worts I scanned.

So at length, I named to these solicitors the growths I sought. "Sleight Sap, Spiny Vagary, and Obfusc Root."

The spice-hustlers showed me knowing smiles at this, and their price rose to twenty or even thirty lictors. What I sought were inducers of trance, confused logic, and ready belief. All these herbal attributes inescapably pointed to thievery as their seeker's aim.

I resolved to search on solo, and stoutly forbade myself to be discouraged. The full moon neared zenith, which made my sketches easy to scan, but did nothing to improve their correspondence to the jungled growths around me

And then, a new difficulty. I became aware of a furtive follower—that sensation one gets of cautious, incremental movements at one's back. Now astern of me, now to my right or my left, it seemed that something in the middle distance always moved in concert with me. Thrice I diverged, at ever sharper angles, and each time, soon sensed him once more astern.

At the moon-drenched middle of a large pool, I drove my pole in the muck and, thus anchored, turned my face towards his approach, and waited. At length, he edged out into view. "He" surely, so hugely thewed his arms and shoulders showed, his cask-like torso. Shy though, he seemed—pausing, then gingerly poling forward again, as though doubting his welcome.

But at length he came to rest, his raft rim almost touching my gunnel. His massy shoulders were torqued out of line, his huge arms hung a bit askew, and his gnarled body seemed constantly straining to straighten itself. So thick was his neck his whole head seemed a stump, his ears a ragged lichen, his brows a shaggy shelf. Yet for all the brute strength in the shape of him, his eyes were meek and blinking.

"Friend, you are in danger here." His voice, an abyssal echo, came eerily distinct from his great chest.

I felt a strange conviction from his calm utterance, which I resisted. "Does this danger come from you yourself, Sir, or from some other quarter?"

"Another quarter. It comes from Gothol, who is, in a manner of speaking, my half-brother."

Again his deep resonance somehow invited my trust against my will. But indeed his words were full of somber implications which, as I sorted them out, prickled along my spine.

"If it comes from Gothol, it also comes, then, from . . . "—my throat, for a moment, would not give passage to the name. The deformed giant courteously waited, despite an air of growing unease. "Ahem . . . Comes also, then, from Zan-Kirk, who *begot* Gothol on the demon Heka-Tong."

"Just so, my friend. That great mage indeed did sire Gothol thus, down in the sub-World."

"So . . . if you speak of him as your half-brother," I ventured to continue, "then might you not, Sir, be born of Zan-Kirk's consort, Hylanais . . . ?" I stood in some suspense, fearing that perhaps my mouth had outrun my wit. I had asked, in effect, if he had not been born of the witch's defiant coupling with a nameless vagabond abroad in the wilderness, done in vengeance for her mighty consort's sub-World dalliance with the demon Heka-Tong . . .

"Born of Hylanais, yes, and named by her Yanîn—but truly, hark me, Sir—"

"Delighted. My name is Nifft, called the Lean, of Karkmahn-Ra."

"I greet you, Nifft, but in all truth we stand in *danger* even now. For Gothol *is at hand.* And Zan-Kirk—even now quite near to us—will himself follow hard upon Gothol's coming!

"In fact, good Nifft, we have *no time* to flee. If you'll permit me, I will take the liberty of hiding you. We truly have no time—see there?"

His gnarled arm swept up-flume. Up at the fractured Rainbowl Crater—up from behind the low rampart that repaired the lowest fraction of its gaping wound—a golden star had risen . . .

Or comet? It moved at a steady, easy pace down . . . down towards us, sinking smoothly through the night sky in an arc that arched along the Flume's great lanterned length. This gliding, golden star looked likely to alight quite near us. Urgently, the deformed brute asked me: "To preserve your safety, Sir, would you permit me a rather brusque liberty with your person?"

The comet sank nearer and nearer—now there was no doubt it would alight near where we stood. "Well," I said, "I suppose if you think it—"

"Thank you Sir!" His huge arm plucked me from my punt and hurled me into the air, hurled me high into the branches of the great tree shadowing us.

I was plunged into the black cloud of its leaves, where I bruisingly impacted with its boughs, which I desperately embraced. My launcher's voice rose after me, soft but distinct:

"I'll be at hand my friend, but we must not be seen. A dire work which we cannot prevent is to be done here, and witnesses will surround us who must not see you. You must lie still, and watch, and harken. On our lives, don't betray our presence here!"

II

But my dear Shag, let us leave me—I assure you I don't mind—leave me up in those boughs for a moment, up in the tree where Yanîn has just tossed me. Because it occurs to me that just now you might be wondering, "Hylanais? Zan-Kirk? And who might these be?"

They were long faithful lovers, these two mages. In the use of their powers they were beneficent, and their thaumaturgies were often helpful to the cities of that coast, for their powers were wielded in controversion of all mishap or malevolence that might befall Kolodria.

Their concord was Lebanoi's blessing, as was their discord nearly Lebanoi's undoing.

They were faithful to one another, these two, until Zan-Kirk's ambition urged him to an exploit that could truly test his power. And thus it was, in a moment fatal to Lebanoi's peace, that Zan-Kirk resolved to descend to the Sub-World, and there to couple with the Demoness Heka-Tong. This would be an eroto-chthonic feat unequaled in thaumaturgy's annals, and it may actually be the case that the sorcerer fatuously expected his mate's approval of this exploit for its daring.

Instead, her wrath and reproach are well chronicled in Shallows ballads. In one, the sorceress most movingly expostulates:

Ah Zan-Kirk, had we not a vow
That all-encircled us as now
This sky, these green-clad mountains do?
Thour't all to me—not I to you?
Go then—rut as suits thy will!
But know, therewith our vow dost kill.
Thereafter, from unplighted troth,
I fly bird-free, and nothing loath
To try the love of any man
That please mine eye, where-ere it scan.
And should I choose conceive, I shall,
And so, of all we've shared, ends all!

Thus a Chilite lay reports her rage. Zan-Kirk answered this with equal rage. This was to be an exploit, in no way erotic. It was a Feat, to which he, as a hero, had a right. At her threatened infidelity, he thundered,

Shouldst thou do me adultery
What spawn thou hast in bastardy
Shall choke its life out in my grip,
And I thy bitch's bowels shall rip!

—spoke thus, and wheeled his dragon-mount up and away through the dawn-lit sky, south to Magor Ingens, the hell-vent through which he descended to his infernal exploit upon the vast, fuliginous body of the Narn Heka-Tong. This was a coupling that required seven years for its accomplishment, and at the end of that term Gothol—who at present bestrides the sky above us—was born full-grown in all his power.

In these years of betrayal Hylanais embraced a nomad's path. Cloaked or cowled, she appears here and there in the popular record of song and penny-sheet poetry, from which it seems she wandered up and down through the length of Kolodria, and even across the Narrows into Lulume, and in the course of these peregrinations she committed a retaliatory infidelity with a hulking rural simpleton chance-met on a country lane.

However impregnated, she bore a man-child some few years before Zan-Kirk accomplished his swiving of the Narn Heka-Tong. The warlock must perforce abide with the Narn as she lay in brood, but Zan-Kirk's rage at Hylanais caused him to leave the Narn-son, Gothol, too abruptly, before that potent nursling had been molded to the mage's will.

Rumors winged with terror flocked ahead of Zan-Kirk's return to Lebanoi, for he came to destroy his "faithless" mate. He raised a demon army and led it up from the Sub-World through the Taarg Vortex. The march of this subworld army through *our* world—through Sordon Head, and thence across Kolodria's southern tip—left a wake of slaughter and nightmare still traceable seven generations later. Perhaps to still the panic his advent might spread, he sent ahead nuncios to Lebanoi to proclaim that it was Rainbowl Crater he came to "protect," and the city itself had naught to fear from him if it offered him no opposition.

Hylanais was amply forewarned. She scorned to draw her forces from the sub-Worlds. Those she recruited were warriors who had proven their greatness in their dying. She went to the Cidril Steppes and raised the Orange Brotherhood from the plains where they'd fallen, holding off the K'ouri Hordes. These she called up from the blanketing earth where they'd lain three hundred years. In Lulume she raised the Seven Thousand from their tombs in Halasspa, which they saved from the Siege of Giants by their valiant but fatal sortie from that city's walls.

She rushed her forces overland. Her dead army's march still echoes eerily in the mountain folks' traditions, but of physical scars they left none. All passions were quelled in them but the soul-fire of warriors. They advanced without hungers, or hurtfulness.

Hylanais arrived just before her wrathful mate. Her forces took the high ground just beneath the crater's wall. Rainbowl is closely flanked by neighboring peaks, but sea-ward the crater presents an almost sculpted rim, like an immense chalice of glossy stone. Beautifully carven by nature, it had spillways cut from its base to feed the Flume, which like a titanic wooden nursling suckled from the crater's mother waters.

Shortly after the witch had deployed, the warlock drew his forces up below her. Her lich army's shadowy sockets stared down into the Subworld legion's sulfurous orbs.

Rainbowl Crater's catastrophe is almost universally ascribed to Zan-Kirk's ungoverned fury, for it seems he was one of those men who thinks fidelity their *mate's* sacred duty, not his own. Raging upslope he came, in his fury conjuring a lightning-storm so ill-controlled as to wildly overleap his hated consort, and strike great Rainbowl's wall instead.

Thus, battle was never joined. A thunderous din of broken stone deafened half the world, and the crater's towering rim fragmented. Colossal shards of stone hung in the air, then thundered down the slope, just ahead of the down-rushing waters unpent by the blast.

The avalanching rubble entombed those martial legions of the dead. The great wave swept the demons down, and drowned Upflume Valley and half its population in a demon-clogged flood.

Though no direct witness is recorded, the Elder Fiske's lines are surely close to the truth as best we can reconstruct it:

Now Rainbowl, a chalice with moon-silvered rim
Gigantically balanced above the mad din
Of up-swarming demons and down-swarming dead—
Now Rainbowl is ambushed by black thunder-heads.
White tridents of lightning lash Rainbowl's curved wall,
And the stone is all fractures, is starting to fall . . .

The wall is all fragments hung loose in the sky
Thrust out by a water-wall half a mile high.
On the dead who so long in their first tombs have lain
The stone crashes down and entombs them again,
And the following wave smites the demon array
And washes them wheeling and wailing away.

And thus it came to be that under the landslide of Rainbowl's broken wall, the witch's army of the Raised Dead lay once more entombed, and that downslope a great swamp was created in Upflume Valley, and buried in the muck of that swamp, a host of demons lay ensorcelled. The subsequently famed "swamp-spice" which flourished in that fen—the herbs and weeds and worts of various and subtle potencies—sprang from the sub-World nimbus that corona'd those drowned demons.

III

I hope you will not have forgotten, Shag, that we left me hugging the high branches of a tree in that same swamp, on a torchlit night with the full moon at zenith, nor have forgotten the slow-sinking golden comet that was descending, arching down towards us.

I hugged the boughs and peered up through the foliage. The comet slowed and slowed still more as it sank, sank nearer . . . until it paused midair perhaps two hundred feet above the swamp, about of a height with the top of the Flume.

And, coming to rest in the air, it was a comet no more, but an airborne raft of carven logs with cressets blazing all around its rim. Amidships stood a man of more than human stature, half again a tall man's height, heroically muscled, and clad in a golden corselet and brazen greaves.

So regal seemed his ownership of the very air he stood on! Already he'd conjured a rapt multitude, for atop the Flume a torch-bearing crowd gazed up at him, while all the rooftops and stairways of the under-Flume city had sprouted hundreds more folk, all clutching lights and lanterns.

A sorcery breathed from this giant. Though he hung so high above us, his face blazed eerily visible. His carven features, the leonine curlings of his golden mane, and his eyes! His eyes beamed down a radiant tenderness upon our upturned faces.

He seemed to behold his enraptured worshipers with a rapture of his own. His voice filled the sky in tones of tenderness—it plucked our spines like lute-strings, and woke plangent melodies within our minds, even though, for me at least, what he uttered was the most brazen inversion of historical truth that it would be possible to speak.

"Beloved Lebanites! Dear friends! My sisters and my brothers! When Rainbowl burst two hundred years ago, a dire vandalism was done against you! Zan-Kirk—my Sire, and still beloved by me—was cut down by his traitorous consort Hylanais, as he was in the very act of bringing back to Lebanoi her greatness and her ancient grandeur!

"Oh Hylanais! Thou misguided witch! You were self-ensorceled by your spite against my father, who was your loving mate! Just when our city was to taste of greatness, you struck the chalice from her hand—you or your bastard spawn! You shattered Rainbowl and our hope, and sealed Zan-Kirk within this boggy tomb where he now lies with his doomed army . . .

"But hear me now, O Lebanites! Even this, the Rainbowl's breakage, was not the true loss of your greatness, not the *whole* loss. After all, your mills perhaps produce less wealth, but still you have sufficiency of trade!

"No! Lebanoi lost her *true* greatness far longer ago than the shattering of Rainbowl! Lebanoi's true greatness fled with the Rainbowl's *creation*! Lebanoi lost her strength and glory half a millennium ago! Her greatness fled when the Sojourners in their fiery vessel departed. For it was the flame of their star-seeking craft that *melted* great Rainbowl from the mountain's living stone! That *created* Rainbowl for our lasting benefit! But that boon, though great, was too little recompense for the loss of the Sojourners themselves—our loss of them amidst the distant stars!"

Ah Shag, even I—crouched like a lemur in my tree—was moved by the vision he conjured, for I had heard of the Sojourners, those grand Ancients, those bold travelers who in their daring had leapt off the earth itself and out into the vastness of the star-fields . . . The Narn-son spoke on:

"But note well, my friends! The Sojourners left us with the means to our reunion with them! The Rainbowl is a beacon, my people! It is a bell! When it is sounded, it will call the Sojourners *back* to us! And—oh hear me, my countrymen—the art of its sounding is now *known* to us.

"For my great Sire, Zan-Kirk, descended to the subworld because only in those sulfurous deeps could the lore be found to *send* a summons that might reach the stars, and call our mighty forebears home. Call them home to share with us their harvest of star-spanning lore, of trans-galactic discovery!"

The Narn-son was eloquent, I can't deny it. His tones were pure and plangent. My heart cried assent: *A beacon! A bell! Yes, kindle it, sound it! Bring those starry navigators back home to us!*

At the same time, I sensed there was a reason that he was using the sorcery of his voice up here, *in the swamp*, instead of down in Lebanoi proper, where he could have swayed far more folk just as powerfully. I began to realize there was something in the swamp itself he wanted. Uneasiness began to crawl up my back on tiny ants' feet.

And now the Narn-son gazed down upon the swamp below. He spread his hands towards the waters, and apostrophized the murky pools in their beds of black growth:

"My father, I have come for you!"

He brought his torch-rimmed raft down now, gently descending towards the swamp itself, until it hung hovering just above the largest pond—a small black lake in truth, that opened out beside the tree I crouched in. And as Gothol sank towards this tarn, he reached out his fist and opened it palm-down. A white spark drifted down from his hand, and when it touched the water, a dim, pale light overspread the pool, and seemed—so faintly!—to thin the utter blackness of the deep.

The Narn-son's raft settled onto the surface. He was below me now, and I could see that at the raft's center sat a low golden chair, like a squat throne. Under the raft's weight the water flexed like crawling skin, and chuckled and muttered in the mucky marges of the fen.

Gothol solemnly addressed the tarn, speaking as if to the water itself, or to someone in it. His voice was mellow and tender, but by its sheer size it made the swamp seem smaller:

Father who art sunk in sleep,
Who art shepherd of the drowned—
Bestir thy flock to quit the deep!
Come sound the Bell thou sought'st to sound.

Ascend the lofty shrine of stone
Whence giants of our race adjourned!
What seas of stars have they o'erflown?
What whirling worlds of wonders learned?

Their ark sailed incandescent floods
Past archipelagos of flame!
Unto what power have these, our blood,
In all their wanderings attained?

Unto what wisdom have they grown
That left with wisdoms we have lost?
What rescues might to them be known
Whom vast galactic gales have tossed?

Long hast thou lain in dreams of war—
Lift from the dark your eyeless gaze!
Stand beneath the sky once more
Where seas of suns spill all ablaze!
And call, with me, those sailors home
Whose ships those seas of suns have roamed!

The waters' blackness relented further. Moonlight in spiderweb filaments lay like glowing nets on bulky shapes upon the silty bottom.

Gothol cast a torch into the water. Its flame—undimmed—shrank to a blood-rose of light as it sank. Deep in the smoky muck it settled by one of those shapes, beside its head, the red glow revealing an eyeless face of leather and stark teeth.

The Narn-son spoke a syllable. That blind face stirred. The gaunt jaw moved.

Gothol gestured at the water. A circle of foam began to spin, and a vortex sank from this, sharp-tipped—a whirling foam-fang that struck and somehow seized the sodden lich.

A gangly stick-figure was plucked up to the surface, to lie spinning on a slow wheel of foam. It was the black, shriveled form of a man in loose-hung armor. Gothol, with a slight lift of his head and his right hand, made it rise dripping from the wheeling foam, and hang in the air before him. He reached out his arms, and embraced it.

It lay, a crooked black swamp-rotted root, against the giant's burnished corselet. He carried it to the low golden chair, and enthroned it. The dripping mummy lay slack against the carven gold.

"Father," the Narn-son said.

Torchlit, he was a dreadful object, this bony remnant of a big-framed man, though dwarfed by him who'd called him Father. The trellis of his ribs showed through his rusted mail. His crusted sword hung from his caved-in loins. His knob-kneed legs rose from his rotted boots like dead saplings from old pots. He wore a helmet with the beaver up, swamp-weed dangling from its rusted hinges.

The giant leaned near. "Father, greet your bereaved son, un-orphaned now by your return." He touched the mailed chest—which expanded—and the eye-sockets, in which two orange sparks kindled.

The shrunk ribs heaved. With crackly, whistly labor, Zan-Kirk leaned forward and began to cough—slow, endless coughs that sounded like hammerblows fracturing ice. He wrenched his mummied jaws apart, and spat a black clot into the black waters.

Then slowly, slowly the wizard raised his hand before his face, and higher yet, till he could fan his stark-boned fingers out against the zenithed moon, and thus he held them back-lit, gazing at them for many moments.

He turned at last the glow of his empty orbits to his son's eyes. His voice emerged in rusty gasps: "Plucked . . . like a root . . . from my sleep . . . How dare you . . . *puppet* me . . . like this?"

"I wake you, Sire, to serve your *own* great Work, suspended by my step-dam's sorcery. I wake you to enthrone you at my side, that we *together* might recall the Sojourners to their primeval home. That we *together* might embrace the gods that they have certainly become."

"Enthrone me!" hissed the lich. "*Use* me, rather . . . You want my army . . . What of Hylanais? . . . Does she live?" His long-drowned voice was all whispers and gasps, but when he spoke the name of Hylanais, it came out crackling like a blaze.

I think I did not fully credit that this charnel thing had life, until I heard him speak the witch's name, and heard his words come scorched from him, as in the furnace of that warlock's wrath.

The golden giant smiled sadly. "Father, I do not know. I only rejoice at your new life, and the work we shall do together."

"*Life* . . . These cold sparks . . . gnawing my dead bones? . . . *Life?*" And yet Zan-Kirk rose, and with a noise of wet wood crackling, strode stiffly left and right across the raft. Found—with a groan—enough strength in his arm-bones to wrench his rusted blade from its scabbard, and slice the air with it: stroke, and counter-stroke . . .

When he spoke again, there was a bit more timbre, and more purpose in his voice, though still a hissing voice it was. "For my allegiance . . . two conditions . . . First . . . If we win . . . you and I . . . stand forth as *equals* . . . before the Sojourners . . . for their bounty . . .

"Second . . . the demon-bitch . . . Hylanais, if she . . . walks the earth . . . I shall be free . . . be helped at need . . . to work her death . . . in agony . . . Do you *accept* . . . these terms?"

"Great Sire," the giant boomed, "your demands are branded on my heart-of-hearts, so inward to my purpose are they now."

Zan-Kirk nodded. The phosphorescence of his sockets flared. He walked to the raft's rim and raised his sword. He flourished it, and its blade glowed red, as from a forge. Two-handed, he propelled it point-first down into the waters.

The sword came ablaze as it dove, and burned a red track through the murk. It transfixed the muddy bottom and burned there still, revealing heaped on every side a bulky litter of uncanny forms, trunked and limbed and skulled in every bestial shape: his demon army, so long drowned.

Now the entire swamp-floor came a-boil with movement. Clawed paws and spiny tentacles thrust upward amid smoky blooms of silt, while a smutty lambency of green and orange stole like fever-glow across the whole drowned grave.

The raft rocked as the first shape erupted from the water: a huge one, its wide, black bat-wings drizzling mud as their labor held it poised upon the air. Submissively it offered Zan-Kirk back his sword, hilt first. Zan-Kirk seized the sword, and mounted the brute's shoulders.

Gothol swept his raft aloft again. The torch-bearing crowds on the Flume and on the rooftops of the town beneath it were crying aloud, all astir with movement that knew not yet where to flow. The Narn-son hovered high, the demon-borne wizard beside him, and suddenly my leafy perch began to tremor. There were deep movements of the muck my tree was rooted in. The whole swamp-floor began to quake.

A noise of torn water and of muddy suction rose. Brute shapes erupted and lurched from the fen. They were demon-shapes in lumbering cavalcade that seemed to take form as they climbed, shedding the muck that blurred their vile bodies as they moved upslope.

Gothol, aloft, sent his mellow voice down upon the terrified throngs on the Flume and the rooftops. "Look, beloved Lebanites! Behold, and fear not! See how submissive these monsters move! Hark! They go silent! See! They go docile! They are my father's slaves and mine! They go to work a wonder for you all! They go up to Rainbowl, and there will abide, to heal her wound, and work your city's weal! They go but to repair the Rainbowl's wound!"

Beloved Lebanites indeed! What could the citizens, those torch-clutching thousands *do*, after all? What but stand, and tremble where they stood?

The dripping, malformed army trudged endlessly up from the fen. The swamp's floor convulsed, as my tree tilted near to toppling, while other trees around me crashed into the water.

Those mud-slick shapes moved in strange unison, their ascending column seemed cohesive as a fluid. From high on his broad-winged brute, Zan-Kirk bent down on them the eyeless fire of his gaze, while Gothol, like a captain who waves forth his troop, swept summit-ward his moon-bright blade . . .

You know how much I've seen of the sub-Worlds, Shag. Demons are dire in the snarling seethe of their dissension. To see their eerie concord here, as they climbed dripping from the swamp, oh, worse than demonlike it was, this homicidal unison! Against such a tide, what could stand?

I watched the very last of them lurch dripping from the fen, their line so long now: half a mile of greasy thew and burnished carapace, of drooling maw and spiky mandible, they toiled and rippled peak-ward past the Flume's huge legs.

Then, far up in the rubble-slope beneath the Rainbowl's wound, something moved. A sharp noise echoed down of shifted stone. And there once more—the moonlight betrayed that something *moved* in that high rubble.

Those stones were big as battle-chariots, as drayers' vans, and suddenly one of them sprang hammering down half a furlong before it came again to rest.

Yet . . . what *was* it which thrust that boulder free? It was something too small to see at first. Too small until it writhed up from the rubble and stood swaying in the moonlight, and was visible then only by its blackness amid the pallid boulders: it was a little human figure, gaunt and dark as some long-withered root.

Such a paltry apparition! So slight a thing to rise, and stand, and face downslope as if to challenge the demon legion climbing up to meet it.

Below my high perch in the branches, Yanîn emerged from his leafy covert. He pointed at the small far shape of darkness, and in a tone of awe and joy he said, "You see her there, Nifft? Hylanais, my most precious mother! Two hundred years of burial she's endured! Alas! I could not choose but leave her lie! I was not yet grown strong enough to face the war of the Dead with the Demons!"

Then that far, high, moon-bleached landslide moved again, and three more boulders tipped from their lodgements. Two came soon to rest, the third went banging farther down, and three—then four, five, six more lean dark forms stood up with Hylanais.

One of these shapes pulled what looked to be an ancient pike out of the rubble. The others heaved against more stones which, though they seemed propelled by such slight force, all lurched like mighty hammers down, in their turn displacing further stones.

Now scores of these black, crooked shapes stood toiling in the rubble of great Rainbowl's wall, all of them shifting other boulders, till the crack and bang of tumbled stone rose to an unremitting roar, rose like a noise of war, like the clang and clash of gathered shields colliding, while the gaunt shapes standing up from the rubble suddenly numbered in the hundreds.

I watched these meager figures sprouting like weeds from that lofty rock-slide—all looking so frail amidst the mighty stones they moved—and then I regarded the demon horde already half a mile upslope of us, a single viscous mass it seemed of sinew, scale and talon, of fang, beak, spike and claw . . .

I asked Yanîn, "Do you think the witch's risen dead—those troops *twice* killed already—can stand against this demon mass? Or against Gothol and Zan-Kirk, who marshal them?"

He aimed his eyes up at me—as nearly as his wrenched frame could manage this. "Stand against these demons? Stand against Zan-Kirk and his Narn-son? Why certainly! But they will not do so! Our dead allies have more urgent work to do!"

"What work's more urgent than killing those demons?"

"Why, the Rainbowl's repair of course!"

"Repair? How repair?"

"By restoring the broken stone to the cleft."

"But first things first! These demons!"

"Who repairs the Bell can sound it—no one else!"

I gazed up disbelieving at the gigantic rubble of those stones, and chose to ask a more urgent question. "But who then will oppose these demons, and the two great mages that command them?"

"Who? Why, you and I!"

"You and I?"

"We'll have some help, of course."

" . . . I rejoice to hear it."

"Now I must take the liberty of asking you to come down and, ah, sit astride my shoulders."

"Hmm. It would seem in that case that I am to be the one taking the liberty . . . "

Yet before I descended, I could not help but pause, an awe-struck witness. For already the dark, shrunken dead, so slight and frail on their far height, were in fact hoisting those great stones—in pairs and threes—and bringing them up to the great cleft. This mere work of portage, like the labor of ants, had the impact of a witnessed wonder.

But even more miraculous was the laying of each stone in contact with the ruptured wall. As each boulder touched the stone it had been part of, it flowed like a liquid into that substance and extended it. Already the ashlar patch was half masked by restored native granite. The antlike dead touched boulder after boulder to the base of the patch, and reborn rock rose like poured fluid in a conic cup.

"My friend!" called Yanîn from below me. "Look where the Narn-son and Zan-Kirk fly to the witch to work her harm! Make haste!"

And there indeed were Gothol on his blazing raft, and the wizard on his wide-winged brute, sweeping up in advance of their monstrous troops. They were less than two miles below the witch and her lichfield of gaunt laborers. The moonlight glinted on the Narn-son's blade, while the warlock's brightest feature were the blazing coals that were his eyes . . .

I swung down from my tree. Yanîn crouched before me and I mounted his shoulders. "All I can do in aid is yours—forgive the liberty," I said.

"You're light as a leaf. Grip the collar of my jerkin."

I did so. "And, ahem, exactly how are we to—"

"Aerially," he said. And leapt straight into the sky.

IV

"Leapt," while accurate, is too weak a term. Such was the speed of our ascent my frame seemed to contract to half its volume, my ribcage too compressed to allow the intake of a breath.

At our apex, and the start of our descent, I could breathe again, had breath and awe to spare for what stretched out below us: the dark might of the demon army toiling upslope. An army they truly seemed; despite their multiplicity of shape, the mute unison of their movement was sinister in the extreme.

Within the wind-rush of our plunge (whose angle I anxiously gauged, fearing we might not come down far enough in advance of that dire vanguard) Yanîn's rumbled words rose plain to me:

"You may doubt that we'll have help. Be comforted! I have many friends in this forest."

I rejoiced to hear it, but scanning the wooded slopes, could see no sign of any allies amid those trees. Here came the treetops, and hard earth beneath.

"Hold tight," Yanîn gritted.

Twigs whipped my head and shoulders, and the arse-and-spine-numbing impact was reduced by a second, lesser leap skyward, one that just cleared the crests of several trees, and plunged us again to the mountainside some furlongs higher upslope.

And as soon as I had dismounted his shoulders, and shaken the numbness from my legs and arse, I could feel through my footsoles the tramp of the ascending demon columns climbing towards us.

Yanîn seized my right shoulder in his huge hand, and an icy rill went through my bone and sinew—the pulse of sorcery.

"Thus I endow your touch with power. We must run zig and zag across the front of their advance! Strike every trunk with the flat of your hand and say: *Root and branch! Arise! Advance!*"

This will not seem much to do—the pair of us running crosswise to the slope, striking tree after tree and crying the words aloud. And indeed, I was awed to wake so much power so quickly. Each skorse, as we struck and invoked it, shuddered and shook its great crest like a brandished lance. Tore out its roots from the soil and rock and stood upon them.

Every skorse sinks a tripod of taproots. Each one we woke writhed and wrenched them free, and with a gigantic, staggery strength surged down toward the demon-horde.

In truth they were titans, but lurching and lumbering ones. To strike, they must make a stand on their roots, and make great lateral strokes with their lower and largest boughs. The demons they connected with, they bashed to bloody tatters, but such was their weighty momentum, recovery from each stroke was slow. Meanwhile demons, of course, are agile as lizards or rats. Demons are limber as maggots in meat.

The head of their up-rushing column was compacted at first, and thus at the outset, the slaughter those timber titans wrought was grand and glorious: neighboring trees, with opposing strokes of their branches, scissored whole streams of demon-meat between them . . .

It could not last. Zan-Kirk—though flown far peak-wards to engage his hated spouse—wheeled back astride his winged brute, and with a gesture caused his demons to disperse in a hundred branching paths upslope.

Now, they were flooding upwards in a swath a quarter-mile broad, and from a column, had become a rising inundation.

"We must defend the crater—hold tight!" I mounted his shoulders again and once more Yanîn leapt into the sky. Our arc was flatter, would bring us down on the rubble-slope where Hylanais toiled. The witch's work was stunningly advanced. She was airborne on wings she'd conjured, transparent and invisible in their vibration as a dragonfly's. Her dead were an ant-swarm, dwarfed by the boulders that they hoisted, up from the diminishing rubble-slope and onto the steep pitch of the crater wall—twin streams of these great stones, balanced on their bone-lean shoulders, they carried up the rupture's either side.

Their progress gave us hope. The crude repair of ashlar that had stood so long impounding its meager reservoir was swallowed up and twice overtopped. Two hundred feet of the wound was seamlessly closed in the glittery gray rock they lofted, shard by shard. For to touch one of these boulders to the patch at any point was to see it snatched into the reborn wall like water into a sponge—to see the fragment meld with the broken rim, and the whole mend incrementally rise.

And in their toil, it seemed the dead soldiers grew brighter, for the stone they wrestled scoured the rusted greaves and corselets they wore, such that their armor began to flash brazen and silver in the blaze of moonlight, and their long-empty sockets seemed to gleam with it too.

Those twice-dead warriors—tireless—ant-swarmed the boulders upslope either side of the breach, like a V-shaped bucket brigade, but of course the upper third of the crater's great wound yawned widest of all. Those skeletal conscripts twice resurrected by the witch—two hundred years ago, and now—toiled like the heroes they were, but we already saw that once arrived at the crater, the best we could do against the ascending demons would be too little. If they reached the breach in their thousands, they would usurp the crater's repair . . . We apexed, and now we were plunging again

Even as we dove, we saw Hylanais overwhelmed. She was zigging and zagging on her blur of wings, and retreating ever higher from her army, because Gothol on his raft, and Zan-Kirk on his demon, flanked her left and right, and flung bolt after bolt of raw thaumaturgic energy at her, while her fierce dodges and deflections plainly cost her all the strength she had. Even as we plunged to the crater's rubble-slope, we saw we'd land with but scant lead on the up-rushing hellspawn.

Yanîn's great torqued mass—like a spring—somehow diminished our impact with Rainbowl. Here was the rubble-slope much shrunk by the energy of the dead heroes, yet it seemed a work that could not be accomplished before the demons swarmed up from the trees.

Yanîn said, "Take arms against them when they come, my friend. I must give myself to one task alone. Good luck."

He lifted the boulder next to the one he stood on—it was as big as a mail-coach!—and thrust it into the air. Astonished, I watched it arc high, high up the cone, strike the patch, and melt into it.

A hellish din! Now five thousand demons erupted from the treeline not many furlongs downslope from us, while bolts of crackling energy split the sky between the three combatant wizards high above us. Yanîn, in swift series, hurled three huge stones arcing a quarter-mile through the air to merge with—and incrementally augment—the stony poultice on great Rainbowl's wound.

The demons poured from the trees, crossed the open slopes, muscling and lurching and scrabbling through moonlight, clawing and seething, gaunt-limbed and rasp-tongued and thorn-furred and fungus-eyed they came, their unearthly stench—an almost solid thing—welling forth from them like a kind of miasmic vanguard.

It was time to turn to. I had a good sword, though I sorely disliked lacking a shield . . .

Here they came closing, closing—I had just time for another glance behind me at Yanîn. There seemed to be two of him, so incessant and swift were his workings. I saw no less than three huge boulders strung through the air along the same trajectory, and he launched yet a fourth along that same parabola just before the first of the series impacted with the patch, and swelled it . . .

And here were the demons now. As I set my blade sweeping through that thorny surf of claws and jaws, I saw with great relief hundreds of the dead army leave off their relay of rocks, draw their blades, and turn with us to hew this demon-flux.

Dead allies! I can see them still, sharp-etched in moonlight! Though their gaunt jaws seemed to gnaw the air, though leather their flesh and their limbs scarce more than bones—though they had mere moonlight for eyes in their sockets—the smell that came off those twice-dead warriors was not of the grave, not at all! Not of the tomb, though they'd lain twice entombed. The smell that came off these dead warriors was of ice and stone and midnight wind, all laced with the lovely bitter smell of steel . . .

We lifted our blades and on came the demons. A beetle-backed one with triple barbed bug-jaws had at me, and I blessed this chance for a shield. I sheared off his up-reaching jaws with a cross-stroke, sliced five of his legs out from under, and as he buckled down before me, hacked out a great square of his leathery carapace, and ripped it free of his back—a shield!

But no, Shag—I'll spare you the details of my own small doings, and show you the grand tides in flux here, the whole sea of war in its surgings.

Full half of the twice-raised dead had come down off the crater and—raising a skullish hiss, a windy war-cry from their leathery lungs—swept down in a scything line that bagged the demon onslaught in a vast net of bony, tireless limbs and whistling swordblades.

Up on the crater their twice-dead brethren in two chain-lines passed wall-wrack back up to the wall. Aloft, Hylanais was blasted, scorched and thunderbolted from two sides by her risen mate and his subworld scion. Though scathed with blazing energies, the witch remained impossibly aloft, her wings a blur, though her wearied sorcery was all shield-work now, all incandescent hemispheres she deployed left and right of her to contain and cancel her husband's and the Narnson's bolts and blazes.

While through it all Yanîn's brute energy launched huge stones moonward that plunged, plunged, plunged into the great wound, the healed rock rising in the gap like pale wine in a goblet.

When you are sunk in combat on a grand scale, you can feel a touch of the eternal. When did this all-engulfing turmoil start? How could it ever end?

But end it did! It ended with the hurling of a single stone. Just as my eye chanced to be turned that way, Yanîn launched a mighty boulder, and I saw—astonished—that it was the final fragment of Rainbowl's collapse.

It arced up, up through the moonlight—big as a three-storey manse it was!—and as it soared, dead silence fell upon that whole infernal battlefield, for it soared up to an almost perfectly completed crater, and fell into the one little notch of vacancy that remained, high up upon the crater's crown.

It seemed that Hylanais had never doubted this would come to pass, for she had shot aloft, and already she hung there, centered high above the bowl, as that last fragment found its niche.

And then quite leisurely—for an odd paralysis seemed to befall both Zan-Kirk and his son—she stretched out her hand, and dropped a tiny clot of light down into the high, gigantic basin.

What an audience we were in that moment! A true and single audience, united by our sudden stillness and our rapt attention. Furiously though the demon army and its generals had fought to reach the crater and to kindle there the summons to the Sojourners, we had beaten them.

And now every one of us—human, demon, dead and living—raptly awaited what would answer the summons. A dire and various audience we were, to be sure: claws, clubs, blades, and fangs all cocked to rend and slay, but all our eyes, human and hellish, were in unison now fixed aloft; a host of living warriors, hilts gripped, lifted axes taking the moonlight; a host of dead warriors in a killing frenzy, to whom this moment was the more apocalyptic for their having lain so long in death before waking to possess it . . . But all of these awaiting the outcome, all now realizing that whatever would spring from the witch's spark, it would befall every one of us.

None in all that host but the airborne—none but the witch, and the warlock, and the Narn-son—could see what that little clot of radiance illuminated as it dropped inside the crater. But every one of us reckoned—from the speed of its plunge—the rate of its unseen journey to the imagined crater floor.

And such a concord was there in that monstrous throng's silent reckonings, that a single shudder moved across the whole grim host of us upon the mountainside—every corpse, and demon, and every living soul of us shuddered just one heartbeat before the crater erupted.

It was the eruption, huge and silent, of a perfect inverted cone of rose-red light up to the stars.

The full moon had somewhat declined from zenith, and the rubescent beam, spreading as it rose, just nicked the lunar rim, painting there a red ellipse like a bloody thumbprint . . .

Still that impossible stillness held us all. Rapt, our eyes or empty sockets scanned aloft as that great chalice of light beamed up at the stars . . . and as something began to *fill* that chalice.

Indistinct it was at first, a kind of granulation within the rosy cup of radiance . . . until these contents began to seem more like the substance of the cup itself.

Faces! Tier upon tier of them spiraling upwards and outwards, these were the vast chalice's substance! They were a towering tribunal—rank on widening rank of faces rising toward the stars, every one of them preternaturally distinct within their dizzying distances, and every one of them gazing down on Lebanoi, upon her war-torn slopes, her sprawling butchery of man and demon.

It froze us even stiller than before—every one of us it froze. Something in the unearthly concord of those sky-borne gazes unutterably diminished us, annihilated us with the sad austerity of their ageless, alien regard.

Within their great cyclone of sentience they grieved, that sad tribunal of the Sojourners. It was grief with a shudder in it they showed us, as they gazed down on the wide, bleeding wreckage we'd spread for their welcome.

That witnessing host roofed our world, and their somber regard showed us starkly the inferno that our bodies blazed in. My flesh felt thin as a shadow sheathing my bones, while the eyes of the Sojourners seemed to gaze down into a pit centuries deep, upon some holocaust of remote antiquity.

Beheld by that tribunal, we felt ourselves to be the briefest of echoes from some distant past, a rumor roaming the reverberant corridors through which had thronged a great host long ago . . .

That high tribunal of skyborn faces! The gravity of them had turned us to stone in mid-slaughter. Stunned we stood, sword-arms hanging slack. It was among the strangest moments of my life, Shag! To stand arms-length from demons and to think no more of them than that they were residents like me on this strange earth! But in truth, no more than that they seemed when this host—eyes immutable as constellations—paved the night sky . . .

The somber knowledge of that multitude! Knowing our future as well as our past . . . It seemed they had gathered to witness our metamorphosis. To witness this strange crescendo our old world—once theirs—was rising towards.

I felt it through my legs: whatever was to come of this, would not be long in coming.

A true thought, that one. Yanîn leapt prodigiously aloft, and stood astride the Flume just below its shattered terminus. Looking back down upon the mingled army of demons just emerged from the trees, and of dead still climbing from their fen, he bellowed, "Come up! Climb up! Come see and be seen!"

Those demons in their homicidal fever required no prompting to come up. That wry-framed giant with his equine eyes—had he sided with the warlock? It was the witch had my allegiance from the first. But did Hylanais's son embrace the subworld?

I looked up at the witch's army on the crater wall—those twice-dead veterans of sorcerous war. My allegiance went to them completely, such that it made the hair stir on my neck to see that demon column—shields and axes high—come foaming up the mountainside at them.

"Let them come to you!" Hylanais from astride her winged demon called down: "Wrack and dark ruin upon you both!" and she gestured obscenely, first at Gothol on his raft, then at Zan-Kirk astride his monster.

Come they did, and hurtling up the steep terrain those subworld soldiers—so variously limbed and bodied—looked agile as insects swarming up a wall. They looked every bit as swift as the dead that were avalanching to meet them, and deploying to fill the whole slope below Rainbowl.

You must keep in mind, Shag, how moon-drenched it was, how stark white-and-black; the twice-killed soldiers, bare bone showing everywhere, plunging down against the muck-dark demons baying their hunger as they climbed . . .

But the collision of their ranks astonished every combatant—living, dead and demon alike. For as those warfronts, those harrows of hammering steel, collided high on the slope, the astonishment of it filled every eye for sixty leagues around, and half a dozen other cities saw it.

For colors bloomed as blazing rich as any tropic jungle at full noon—this in the night, mind you, in moonlight only!

The battle lines seemed to merge and swell as impossible night-blazing colors erupted everywhere from the hillside. From our post just below Rainbowl's wall we saw what caused this profusion. For as every demon with one of the dead collided, the both of them exploded into a branching, blossoming skeleton, its every bone a limb that flowered, blossomed purple, saffron, blood-red and cerulean . . .

Branching and budding and blooming, a rainbow growth overspread that battlefield, and climbed the Flume's mighty legs. A forestation of hues that blazed even in darkness, knit from every shape of branch, leaf, tendril, limb and frond.

So like an earthquake was this efflorescence to my astonished mind, that it was almost detachedly I watched as Gothol's raft—the Narn-son's wrath proclaimed in his raised fist—and Zan-Kirk's hairy-winged mount both plummeted to the earth. As he plunged, Gothol stood mute. The warlock barked one hoarse curse at his mate: "Forever the dark then, witch!"

On impact came their writhe of metamorphosis . . . and both those grim, dire men were . . . flower trees!—their legs gnarled roots, and their arms all blossoms scooping up the moonlight and the air . . .

And as these two, so the hosts they led also rippled with mountain-wide metamorphosis, and their forest of lifted blades and brandished lances were trunks and boughs and branches multifoliate, and the screams and butchering grunts of war sank to the wide whisper of foliage rattling, muttering and whispering in the night wind off the sea . . .

The Sojourners, that watching host which filled the sky—all those faces softened with something like assent, and then grew vague, grew smoky, and dispersed, and left just moon-drenched night behind.

I stood still staring, straining still to see that host of unsuspected witnesses, straining still to feel their cosmic fellowship—undreamed of, and then so briefly known.

"Would you not like to see where they have gone?" Though softly spoken, the depth of Yanîn's voice at my ear caused me a tremor.

I weighed my answer. "I would like to, but only if I could certainly return here from there. For this strange world is marvel enough for me."

We two looked about us. Shaggy with blossom the whole upper Flume had grown. The crater wall and its under-slope, that had been so starkly stony for so long, was growing even as we watched, growing ever more richly encrusted with color and form. Judging by the vernal riot of blossoming, foliate and fronded forms emerging everywhere, there was just no telling what might spring up next . . .

James Enge's first story was published in Black Gate *(Summer 2005). His fiction features Morlock Ambrosius, a Maker (wizard) and Seer, who has (so far) been featured in six novels and a number of short stories. The hunchbacked, often drunk, Morlock is a skilled swordsman, but not truly a warrior. Tim Pratt, of* Locus, *has written of Enge's work:*

> *One of Enge's great virtues as a writer is weirdness—he's not afraid to do the unexpected, and his imagination is formidable. But there's an underlying emotional power here, too. The author excels at depicting the bonds of friendship, the pain of betrayal, and the tragedy of well-laid plans going awry, and that emotional payload is what makes this novel into more than just an entertaining adventure story about a guy with a magical sword who fights monsters.*

PAYMENT DEFERRED

James Enge

There is the house whose people sit in darkness;
dust is their food and clay their meat.
—The Epic of Gilgamesh
(English translation: N. K. Sandars)

The thug's first thrust sent his sword screeching past Morlock Ambrosius's left ear. He retreated rather than parry Morlock's riposte; then he thrust again in the same quadrant as before.

While the thug was still extended for his attack, Morlock deftly kicked him in the right knee. With a better swordsman this would have cost Morlock, but he had the measure of his opponent. The thug went sideways, squawking in dismay, into a pile of garbage.

The point of Morlock's blade, applied to the thug's wrist, persuaded him to release his sword. The toe of Morlock's left shoe, applied to the thug's chin, persuaded him to keep lying where he was.

"What's your story, Slash?" Morlock asked.

"Whatcha mean?"

Morlock's sword point shifted to the thug's throat. "I'm in Sarkunden for an hour. You pick me out of a street crowd, follow me into an alley, and try to kill me. Why?"

"Y're smart, eh? See a lot, eh?"

"Yes."

"Dontcha like it, eh? Dontcha like to fight, eh?"

"No."

"Call a Keep, hunchback!" the thug sneered. "Maybe, I dunno, maybe I oughta—" He raised his hand theatrically to his mouth and inhaled deeply, as if he were about to cry out.

Morlock's sword pressed harder against the thug's neck, just enough to break the skin. The shout never issued from the thug's mouth, but the thug sneered triumphantly. He'd made his point: Morlock, as an imperial outlaw, wanted to see the Keepers of the Peace—squads of imperial guards detailed to policing the streets—even less than this street punk with a dozen murders to his credit. (Morlock knew this from the cheek rings in the thug's face. The custom among the water gangs was one cheek ring per murder. Duels and fair fights did not count.)

"Ten days' law—that's what you got, eh?" the thug whispered. "Ten days to reach the border; then if they catch you inside it—zzccch! When'd your time run out, uh, was it twenny days ago? Thirty?"

"Two months."

"Sure. Call a Keep, scut-face. By sunrise they'll have your head drying on a stake upside the Kund-Way Gate."

"I won't be calling the Keepers of the Peace," Morlock agreed. The crooked half-smile on his face was as cold as his ice-gray eyes. "What will I do instead?"

"You can't kill me, crooky-boy—" the thug began, with suddenly shrill bravado.

"I *can* kill you. But I won't. I'll cut your tendons and pull your cheek rings. I can sell the metal for drinking money at any bar in this town, as long as the story goes with it. And I'll make sure everyone knows where I last saw you."

"There's a man; he wants to see you," said the thug, giving in disgustedly.

"Dead?"

"Alive. But I figure: the Empire pays more for you dead than this guy will alive."

"You're saying he's cheap."

"Cheap? He's riding his horse, right, and you cross the road after him and step in his horse-scut. He's gonna send a greck after you to charge you for the fertilizer. You see me?"

"I see you." Morlock briefly weighed his dangers against his needs. "Take me to this guy. I'll let you keep a cheek ring, and one tendon, maybe."

"Evil scut-sucking bastard," hissed the thug, unmistakably moved with gratitude.

"The guy's" house was a fortresslike palace of native blue-stone, not far inside the western wall of Sarkunden. Morlock and the limping thug were admitted through a heavy bronze door that swung down to make a narrow bridge across a dry moat. Bow slits lined the walls above the moat; through them Morlock saw the gleam of watching eyes.

"Nice place, eh?" the thug sneered.

"I like it."

The thug hissed his disgust at the emblems of security and anyone who needed them.

They waited in an unfinished stone anteroom with three hard-faced guards until an inner door opened and a tall fair-haired man stepped through it. He glanced briefly in cold recognition at the thug, but his eyes lit up as they fell on Morlock.

"Ah! Welcome, sir. Welcome to my home. Do come in."

"Money," said the thug in a businesslike tone.

"You'll be paid by your gang leader. That was the agreement."

"I better be," said the thug flatly. He walked back across the bronze doorbridge, strutting to conceal his limp.

"Come in, do come in," said the householder effusively. "People usually call me Charis."

Morlock noted the careful phrasing and replied as precisely, "I am Morlock Ambrosius."

"I know it, sir—I know it well. I wish I had the courage to do as you do. But few of those-who-know can afford to be known by their real names."

Those-who-know was a euphemism for practitioners of magic, especially solitary adepts. Morlock shrugged his crooked shoulders, dismissing the subject.

"I had a prevision you were coming to Sarkunden," said the sorcerer who called himself Charis, "and—yes, thank you, Veskin, you may raise the bridge again—I wanted to consult with you on a matter I have in hand. I hope that gangster didn't hurt you, bringing you in—I see you are limping."

"It's an old wound."

"Ah. Well, I'm sorry I had to put the word out to the water gangs, but they cover the town so much more thoroughly than the Keepers of the Peace. Then there was the matter of your—er—status. I hope, by the way, you aren't worried about that fellow shopping you to the imperial forces?"

"No."

Charis's narrow blond eyebrows arched slightly. "Your confidence is justified, "he admitted, "but I don't quite see its source."

Morlock waved a hand. "This place—your house. No ordinary citizen would be allowed to have a fortress like this within the town's walls. You are not a member of the imperial family. So I guess you have a large chunk of the local guards in your pocket, and have had for at least ten years."

Charis nodded. "Doubly astute. You've assessed the age of my house to the year, and you're aware of its political implications. Of course, you were in the Emperor's service fairly recently, weren't you?"

"Yes, but let's not dwell on it."

Charis dwelled on it. Knotting his eyebrows theatrically, he said, "Let's see, what was it that persuaded him to exile you?"

"I had killed his worst enemy and secured his throne from an usurpation attempt."

"Oh, my God. Well, there you are. I don't claim your own level of political astuteness, you understand, but if I had been there to advise you I would have said, 'Don't do it!' I never do anything for anybody that they can't repay, and I never allow anybody to do anything for me that I can't repay. Gratitude is painless enough in short bursts, but few people can stand it on a day-to-day basis."

They ascended several flights of stairs, passing several groups of servants who greeted Charis with every appearance of cheerful respect. Finally they reached a tower room ringed with windows, with a fireplace in its center and two liveried pages in attendance. Charis seated Morlock in a comfortable chair and planted himself in its twin on the other side of the fireplace. He gestured negligently and the pages stood forward.

"May I offer you something?" Charis asked. "A glass of wine? The local grapes are particularly nasty, as you must know, but there's a vineyard in northern Kaen I've come to favor lately. I'd like your opinion on their work."

"I'm not a vintner. Some water for me, thanks."

This remark set Charis's eyebrows dancing again. "But surely . . . " he said, as the demure dark-eyed servant at his side handed him a glass-lined drinking cup."

I don't drink when I'm working, and I gather you want me to do a job. What is it?"

Charis leaned back in his chair. "Let me begin to answer by asking a question: What do you think is the *most* remarkable thing about this remarkable house of mine?"

Morlock accepted a cup of water from a bold-eyed blond-haired page. He drank deeply as he mulled the question over, then replied, "I suppose the fact that all the servants are golems."

The comment caught his host in midswallow. Morlock watched with real interest as Charis choked down his wine, his astonishment, and an obvious burst of irritation more or less simultaneously.

"May I ask how you knew that?" Charis said carefully, when he was free for speech.

"From the fact that all the servants we've met, including your guards, have been golems, I deduced that your entire staff consisted of golems."

"Yes, but surely, sir, you understand the intent of my question: How did you *know* they were golems? For I think, sir, as a master in the arts of Making, you will admit they are excellent work—*extremely* lifelike." Charis's frank and inquisitive look had something of a glare in it. Clearly he had made the golems himself and was vexed because they had not deceived Morlock.

"Mostly the eyes," Morlock said. "The golems are well made, I grant you, and the life-scrolls must be remarkably complicated and various. But you can't quite get a natural effect with clay eyes."

Charis turned his gaze from Morlock to the dark-haired modest page at his left hand. Morlock watched the struggle in his host's face as he realized the truth of the observation.

"What would you use?" Charis asked finally. "If I may be so bold."

"Molten glass for the eyes proper—the eyeball and the cornea. I'd slice up some gems and use a fan-ring assembly for the irises. You're using black mirror-tube for the visual canals? I think that would work very well."

"You can't use glass," Charis said sharply, sitting on the edge of his chair. "I've tried it. The vivifying spell induces some flexibility in the material, but it's not sufficient."

"It would be necessary to keep it molten until the vivifying spell is activated," Morlock replied.

"It seems to me, frankly, that the problems are completely insuperable."

"I can show you," Morlock said indifferently.

"Frankly, you'll have to. That will have to be part of the deal. Frankly."

"What deal are you offering?"

Charis leapt to his feet, walked impatiently all around the room, and threw himself back down in his chair. "You have me at a disadvantage," he remarked. "As you no doubt intended."

"We both have something the other needs."

"Thank God! I thought for a moment—no matter what I thought. As you guessed: except for myself, all my household are golems. I do business every day in the city—a very large business in very small spells—and, frankly, when I come home I detest the human race. But I have the normal human desire for a sociable life."

Morlock, who had none of these problems, inclined his head to acknowledge them. "And the golems are your solution."

"A most effective one, by and large. Except that I will never be able to look one of the damned things in the eyes again!"

"That can be fixed," Morlock pointed out. "Also, there must have been something else, or you wouldn't have been looking for me."

"Yes. Yes. As you noticed, I've been at some pains to give each of my golems a distinctive character, physically and otherwise. A desert of a thousand identical faces and minds would hardly satisfy my social instincts."

"No golem has a mind," Morlock observed. "A limited set of responses can be incorporated into any life-scroll."

"A difference that is no difference, sir. What does it matter to me whether they really have minds or not? If they *seem* to have minds, my social instincts will be satisfied."

Morlock thought this unlikely, but did not say so. "Then?"

"The trouble is that, since *I* inscribed their life-scrolls, nothing they say or do can ever surprise me. You see? The illusion that they have identities collapses. My social instincts are not satisfied. Frankly, it's dull."

"Then. You would have me make a new set of lifelike golems, at least some of whose responses you will not expect."

"In an unthreatening and even charming way. Play fair, now."

"I can't undertake to provide charm," Morlock said. "We can rule out danger, insubordination, and incivility."

"Very well. I'm sure I can trust your esthetic instincts. Also, you must show me your method of constructing their eyes."

Morlock nodded.

"The question arises, 'What can I do for you?' I take it that mere gold will not . . . ? No."

Morlock shook his head. "I understand the Sarkunden garrison still runs scouting missions into the Kirach Kund," he said, naming the mountain pass to the north of Sarkunden.

"Ye-e-es," Charis said slowly.

"I can't remain in the empire, as you know. I can't go west—"

"No one goes into the Wardlands."

"In any case, I can't. I dislike Anhi and Tychar, and therefore would not go east."

"You intend to cross the Kirach Kund!"

"Yes. It is done from time to time, I believe."

"By armed companies. Nor do they always survive."

Morlock lifted his wry shoulders in a shrug. "I have done it. But I was once taken prisoner by the Khroi and am reluctant to risk it again."

"The Khroi take only prey, never prisoners. You will excuse my being so downright, but we live in the Khroi's shadow, here, and we know something about them."

"They made an exception for me, once. They may not make the same mistake again. It would be better for me if I knew what the imperial scouts know—what hordes are allied to each other, which are at war, where the latest fighting is, where dragon-cavalry has been seen."

"I see." Charis's face twisted. "I have never meddled with strictly military matters before. It will strain my relationship with the garrison commander."

Morlock lifted his crooked shoulders in a shrug. "You could hire a number of human servants. If—"

"No!" Charis shouted. "No people! I won't have it!" His nostrils flared with hatred; he neglected to move his eyebrows expressively.

"Very well," he said at last. "I'll get you your news. You make me my golems." And they settled down to haggle over details.

On the appointed day, Charis strode into Morlock's workroom, unable to disguise his feelings of triumph. "Oh, Morlock, you must come and see this. Say, you've been cleaning up in here!"A shrug from the crooked shoulders. "My work's done. I hope you like your golems."

"They're *marvelous*. I'm so grateful. One of them speaks nothing but Kaenish! And I don't know a word!"

A smile was a rare crooked thing on Morlock's dark face. "You'll have to learn, I guess."

"Wonderful. But come along to my workshop. The guardsman will be along presently, and I badly want to show you this before you depart. Oh, do leave that," he said, as the other began to reach for the sword belt hanging on the wall. "You won't want it, and there's no place for it in my room."

They went together to Charis's workshop. Body parts fashioned in clay of various shades lay scattered all over the room. There was a positive clutter of arms on the worktable—Charis had mentioned to Morlock at supper last night that he was "on an arm jag," and now it could be seen what he meant.

Charis worked by inspiration, crafting dozens of arms or legs, for instance, as the mood took him, getting a feel for the body part and creating subtle differences between the members in the series. In the end he would construct golems like jigsaw puzzles out of pieces he had already made, and improvise a life-scroll that suited the body. His other skills as a sorcerer were quite minor, as he freely admitted, but his pride as a golem maker was fully justified.

So far, though, irises had defeated him. In everything else he had proved a ready pupil to Morlock, even in the manipulation of globes of molten glass, a difficult magic. But creating the fan-ring assemblies of paper-thin sheets of gem had proved the most challenging task of Making he had ever undertaken.

His latest efforts lay on the worktable, two small rings of purple amethyst flakes, glittering among the chaos of clay arms. He watched anxiously as the other bent down to examine them.

"Hm." A hand reached out. "An aculeus, please." Charis quickly handed over the needlelike probe. The skilled hands made the artificial irises expand, contract, expand again. Finally the maker's form straightened (insofar as it ever could, Charis thought, glancing scornfully at the crooked shoulders), saying, "Excellent. You should have no trouble now making lifelike eyes for your golems."

Charis sighed in relief. "I'm so glad to hear you say so. Really, I'm deeply in your debt."

A shrug. "You can pay me easily, with news from the pass."

"I'm afraid that would hardly cover it," Charis said regretfully, and pushed him over, onto the table. The clay arms instantly seized him and held him, a long one wrapping itself like a snake across his mouth, effectively gagging him. Charis carefully swept the artificial irises off the table into his left hand and, moving back, commanded, "Table: stand."

The table-shaped golem tipped itself vertically and, unfolding two stumpy human legs from under one of its edges, stood. Its dozens of mismatched arms still firmly held Morlock's struggling form.

"I'm sorry about this—I really am," Charis said hastily, in genuine embarrassment. "When push came to shove, though, it occurred to me that my relationship with the garrison commander simply couldn't take the strain of fishing for secret military information. You've no idea how stuffy he is. Also, I'm not convinced the news would be as useful to you as you think, and you might hold a grudge against me. You've given me so much, and I'm afraid—that is, I don't like to think about you holding a grudge, that's all. So this is better—not for you, I quite see that. But for me. Guardsmen!"

From a side door three imperial guardsmen entered, the fist insignia of Keepers of the Peace inscribed on their breastplates. They eyed the inhuman golem and its struggling victim with distaste and fear.

"Have it let him go," the senior guard directed. "We'll take him in."

"Are you out of your mind?" Charis exploded. "This man is the most powerful maker in the worlds, and a dangerous swordsman besides. If you think that he is going to quietly walk between you to his place of execution, you—Look here:

let's not quarrel. You'll get your reward whether you bring him in dead or alive. I simply can't risk his surviving to take revenge on me, don't you see? Cut his head off here. That's what we agreed. Don't worry about the golem; it was made for this purpose."

"They say Ambrosius's blood is poison," one of the other guardsmen offered quaveringly. "They say—"

"Gentlemen, it is your own blood you ought to be concerned about," Charis remarked. "This man is lethal. He has been condemned to death by the Emperor himself. You have him helpless. I've paid you well to come here, and you'll be paid even better when you bring his head to your captain. What more needs to be said?"

The senior guard nodded briskly and said, "Tervin: your sword."

"Hey!" shouted the junior addressed. "I'm not going to—"

"No. I am. But I'm not going to use my own sword. I paid a hundred eagles for that thing, and I don't want it wrecked if his blood eats metal, like they say. Your weapon's standard issue. Give it to me."

Tervin silently surrendered his sword; the senior guard stepped forward and remarking, in a conversational tone, "In the name of the Emperor," lopped off the head of the struggling victim. The sword bit deeply into the table-golem; several of the arms fell with the severed head to the floor.

The senior guard leapt back immediately to avoid the gush of poisonous Ambrosial blood, then took another step back when he saw that there was no gush of blood. The headless form in the table-golem's arms continued its useless struggle.

"No," croaked Charis, his throat dry. "This can't be happening."

He stepped forward, as if against his own will, and touched the gleaming edge of the severed neck. It was clay. He reached down into the open throat and drew out a life-scroll inscribed in Morlock Ambrosius's peculiar hooked style. The body ceased to move.

"They told me you were cheap," Morlock's voice sounded behind and below him.

He turned and, looking down, met the calm gray gaze of the severed head that looked like Morlock's.

"They told me you were cheap," the severed head remarked again, "so I expected this. I am somewhere you can't reach me. Have the information ready when I send for it and I'll hold no grudges. But do not betray me again."

"I won't," whispered Charis, knowing he would have nightmares about this moment as long as he lived. "I promise. I promise I won't." Then he turned away from the suddenly lifeless head to soothe the frightened guards with gold.

That night the unbeheaded and authentic Morlock lay dreaming in the high cold hills north of Sarkunden, but he wasn't aware of it. To him it seemed he was lying, wrapped in his sleeping cloak, watching the embers of his fire, wondering why he was still awake.

An old woman walked into the cool red circle of light around Morlock's dying campfire. He could not see her face. She bent down and took the book of palindromes from Morlock's backpack and flipped through it until she reached the page for that day. She carried it over and showed it to him. Her index finger pointed to a palindrome: *Molh lomolov alinio cret. Terco inila vo lomolhlom.*

Which might be rendered: *Blood red as sunset marks the road north. Son walks east into the eastering sun.*

He looked up from the book to her face. He still could not see it. He wasn't able to see it, he realized suddenly, because he never had seen it. Then he awoke.

He opened his eyes to find the book of palindromes open in his hand. It was his index finger resting on the palindrome he had read in his dream.

Morlock got up and restowed the book in his pack. Then he settled down and built up the fire to make tea: he doubted he would sleep any more that night.

He was caught up in some conflict he didn't understand with a seer whose skill surpassed his own. Any omen or vision he received was doubly important because of this, but it was doubly suspect as well.

He much preferred Making to Seeing: the subtleties of vision were often lost on him. In a way, he had made the book of palindromes so that he would have some of the advantages of Seeing through an instrument of Making. He thought the omen pointing him northward was a real omen, and it was possible that this one was, too. But it was possible that one or both had been sent by his enemy to mislead him.

Morlock drank his tea and thought the matter over all night. By sunrise he had struck camp and was walking along the crooked margin of the mountains eastward, keeping his eyes open for he knew not what.

⚔

"The Swords of Her Heart" is the only story original to this volume. It adheres closely to some of the grand traditions of sword and sorcery, but has its own entertaining twists, turns, humor, and style. The author has previously penned S&S gaming-related fiction. There are two protagonists: Brimm, a failed scholar, and the ever-optimistic Snoori. This is the first tale to feature them. I hope to see more.

THE SWORDS OF HER HEART

John Balestra

"And precisely why should I go with you to Atlantis?" Brimm asked, his voice tinged with amazement. "You nearly got me killed in the den of the Voorhi. I blame the arrack. Sober, I would never have listened to your ridiculous notions of beast-men hoarding gold."

"I still think we gave up too soon, Brimm." Snoori wiped ale froth from his yellow beard and went on. "The Voorhi probably had the gold hidden under those enormous heaps of dung."

"Then it can stay there!" Brimm arched an eyebrow, and leaned back in the teetering wooden chair, toying with his ancient dagger—he held it between his long index fingers, its dulled point not quite penetrating his pale skin. "The only thing the beast-men hoarded was fleas. And I nearly froze in those mountains."

"It wasn't so bad."

"You were born with your own coat of fat and fur."

"It's not fur. I'm simply gifted of a little more body hair than some men."

Snoori scowled at his flagon of ale and Brimm glanced about the tavern. There were but two others in the low-ceilinged, sag-floored old tavern: an old man in a bearskin cloak muttering sadly over a goblet and the heavy-browed woman who brought the ale. She licked her lips and winked at Brimm when he glanced her way. Brimm shivered, partly from the night's chill and partly from pondering what he might have to do to pay for a pallet in the tavern loft. "How about a fire, innkeeper?" he called. "It's fearful cold in here."

"Why, you have your candles!" she said, her voice creaking at her own wit. "But you may have your fire, if you pay for its making! Two groats!"

A shared leg of tough mutton and two ales had depleted Brimm's resources. He had not even a groat.

Struck by a thought, Snoori looked up at him, his flaring mustaches lifted by a smile. "You wish warmth? Atlantis is warm! It is far to the south, just west of the Pillars of the Gods, and everyone who trades there basks in the glory of the sun!"

Brimm snorted. "Some are sacrificed to the glory of the sun god, from what I've heard."

He shrugged. "They're more likely to be sacrificed to Poseidon. Occasionally someone is chained to sea rocks as the tide rises. Crabs as big as calves eat them." He raised a finger to forestall Brimm's inevitable reaction. "*But—!* We need not run afoul of priests and their acolytes! Remember, as a boy I went to Atlantis with my uncle. I have seen it with my own eyes! And truly it is *such* a pleasantly warm place—hot springs bubble through the island. The very ground is warm to the touch!"

Watching the cold plume of his own breath quiver the candle flame, Brimm tugged his father's tattered red velvet cloak closer about his slender shoulders. The thought of going to a warm land had a certain appeal. He was tired of Hyperborea, no less weary of Hypexa, Hyperborea's sprawling, biggest, most malodorous port city. He had been tired of Hyperborea for most of his twenty-two years. He was raised in the shipyards of Hypexa, though his mother—who had given him his fine-boned features, onyx eyes, and shiny jet-black hair—was said to have been Thracian. Brimm looked like a foreigner in this land; was often treated like one. He felt no loyalty to Hyperborea's ice-bound mountains, its rocky shores noisy with querulous sea birds and walruses, nor to the blond ruffians who made up its seafarers. Was he not a refined man of the world—had he not studied with Urgus himself, in far Keltia?

A man of the world? He shrugged ruefully, amused at himself. In truth he'd seen little of the great world, only Keltia and a few other ports.

Atlantis was supposedly bristling with castles painted in leaf of gold. He had seen the Atlantean triremes, passing Hypexa by: grand triple-decked ships of mahogany trimmed in ornately carved ivory, figureheads of Poseidon gazing at the horizons with eyes of burnished emerald. The sun was indeed said to be friendly on the vast island of Atlantis, and the women were rumored to be friendlier to men of the north than their own mincing, decadent husbands.

Yes. Atlantis had a certain appeal . . .

But Snoori planned a skulk into some Atlantean fastness after "easy treasure," and in Brimm's opinion, if ever treasure was easy to find, it had already been found and spent.

Still—Brimm was a Svell, son of Hosly Svell, with a blood-born obligation to take to the sea. Brimm's name, in fact, was Brimir Svell—his first name meaning "rover." But most called him Brimm the Savant—a nickname not without irony, thanks to their doubts that he was truly a savant who had studied with Urgus. Yet it was so. It was also true that he had been expelled after seven seasons, not quite two years, for breaking into the great sorcerer's Arct Scrolls. Did Urgus praise Brimm for his acumen in discovering the secret room? Did he appreciate Brimm's cunning in persuading the guardian—hippogriffs love fresh fish, and meat still bloody—to admit him into the Arct Chamber?

No! Instead, the intractable old sorcerer had cursed him for his temerity, smiting him with blindness in one eye and a painful limp, a curse lasting an entire year. The maladies had passed away at midnight of the anniversary of his expulsion. A torment, yes, but it was the dismissal that hurt more.

Still—Brimm could now see with two clear eyes; he could stride with steady steps, and just as important, he was one of the few living men schooled to keenness with an Atlantean piercer. His father had taught Brimm well, as Hosly Svell had been taught by his own father; for Brimm's grandfather had made his fortune as a mercenary employed by King Squen, Lord of the Fifth Kingdom of Atlantis. Brimm's father insisted that the slender, finally turned, silver-hued piercer was the only sword of its kind north of Atlantis—and few remained in Atlantis itself, the metal's secret having been lost with the death of its forger. The blade was his father's only patrimony, apart from the cloak and the chipped old iron dagger. Hosly Svell gambled, drank, and whored away his shipbuilding profits, yet had affected to look down upon Brimm for being cast out of his apprenticeship.

Brimm sighed. It was true, Father had traded a solid gold orb for his son's place in the halls of Urgus, and Brimm had squandered his chances. Perhaps indeed, Brimm had been beaten, as Urgus told him, by his first real battle. *"You have been defeated in battle: defeated by your own youth. Maturity is the first bridge to win across, and you were driven back; defeated by a protracted boyhood . . . "*

There had been nothing for it but to prove himself in other tests, in other places. Even one-eyed and limping, he had won three duels with experienced warriors. A Kelt and two Hyperboreans went down before the piercer. They were strong, fierce, and slow men with clumsy broadswords and axes of iron. He had carved them almost at his leisure.

But the duels had left nothing but a sense of sickened obligation. Urgus had sent him on his way with a bag of silver pieces—the silver had been doled out by the handful as compensation to the widows of his felled opponents, and now he had no funds for dueling, nor any desire for it.

Fighting as a mercenary, perhaps defending ships from occasional pirates—that he could do with a will. But so far the shipmasters had looked on him and laughed. He was tall and lean, more like a willow than an oak; he carried a weapon that, to their eyes, looked like a slender saber made of some light metal meant for jewelry, sure to break at the first clash. Fragile the piercer was not, he swore; it was in fact stronger than iron, and sharper than iron ever could be. But they only laughed and waved him away. To Brimm, it was as if in dismissing his sword, they dismissed Brimir Svell; he was too much like his sword. His father had waved him away, on his deathbed. *"Take the sword, take your great-grandfather's dagger, take my seafaring cloak—and go."*

Brooding over such things awoke pangs within Brimm. He shook his head. Best not to think on it. He needed something to keep his mind busy . . .

"Very well, then, Snoori. What is this new absurdity you call a plan?"

Excitement in Snoori's eyes joined with reflected candlelight as he leaned forward to whisper eagerly across the table. "On the north side of the great island of Atlantis are impassible cliffs made of sheer green glass coughed up from a forgotten volcano—but there is one place where rise the ramparts, jutting right over the sea. This is the outer wall of the city of Poseidonia. It is circled with fields and orchards and a river jumping with fish. And there, in an old palace, is beauteous Cleito, a princess who has offered ten bushels of gold to any force of ten men who will become the Swords of her Heart: the champions who will destroy the minor demon of the piddling sorcerer who keeps her bound in a cavern. Now, all one has to do is join this band, help them slay a demon and, perhaps, an odious old man, and they each will receive a bushel of gold and . . . " He paused dramatically. " . . . a helmet full of pearls!" He cleared his throat. "Oh and the bravest of her champions will win her hand—that's just by the by. Why do you look at me that way?"

"I cannot believe you are once more babbling on about winning the hands of princesses." Brimm shook his head. "Gods! How many times at the temple of edification, when you should have been learning your letters, you maundered on about such myths!"

"But I have heard the tale from many a sailor! Just yesterday I had it from the captain of a certain ship that it's all quite true! And even if it is not all true, why, there are ten kingdoms in Atlantis, each with a king who sits at the Atlantean council—and each king needs good men! We could carry spears and bask in the sun and drink the king's wine! Meanwhile—what harm to visit Poseidonia and see if the treasure for the ten is indeed on offer?"

"We have no way to get to Atlantis, even should I agree on such a foolish expedition," Brimm grumbled. He sipped the dregs of his ale and put his empty flagon down in disgust. "After paying our score here, we are now without funds."

"I am the friend of your boyhood, one of the few who could bear your prideful ways. Would I invite you along on an adventure an adventure *guaranteed* to bring riches—had I no means to get us there?"

"What means do you have?" Brimm asked suspiciously.

"Ah . . . as to that . . . I have an arrangement with the very captain I mentioned! He needs mercenaries to protect his ship. He needs them tonight, so badly he'll take anyone, even you and your pretty sword! He assures me there will be free food, wine every night, and we may sit at our ease the whole way to Atlantis."

"Snoori, you have turned me into a galley slave," Brimm said bitterly. "Had I more slack in my chain I would strangle you with it."

The sun was high. They were overdue for their noon gruel, and for the cupful of water that kept them from dying of thirst. Great green waves lifted as if to stare into the galley, and then sank back; clouds curdled on the horizon; dolphins followed their wake, making their mad laughing sounds at the two rows of chained men, as if to say *We are free to leap, to cavort, and you must hunch in the sun on a sweat-stained bench.* The manacles were hot from the sunlight, burning Brimm's wrists. Once when the galley rose on the waves so that he could see the dolphins, he glimpsed a green-skinned nereid, naked but for a filigree of foam, riding one of the dolphins as it arched from the sea; she too laughed at him before vanishing into the billows.

"I was quite surprised Captain Zenk had his brute strike us from behind," Snoori admitted, nodding, when the row-master had stalked past. "And truly astounded that he chained us to the oars," he added, putting his back into the stroke as he saw the burly, bow-legged row-master approaching with his whip. "I knew it was a *galley* but he said we would merely act as lookouts, and fight if necessary. It's *all* quite surprising. I thought myself a better judge of men."

"Or perhaps I might not strangle you," murmured Brimm, as if savoring a new concept. "Perhaps I'll strangle that great whip-bearing ape, then take over the ship and leave you chained at the oars. That might be more satisfying."

"Brimm, Brimm, you abuse me! The winds have been fair, we are indeed headed toward Atlantis, and we haven't had to row *constantly*."

"We have rowed most of four days—it feels like four years!" Normally Brimm was slow to indulge in complaints but this was Snoori's doing and he deserved to hear it. Or so Brimm told himself. "My hands are raw. My back is aching. Sunburn blackens me. I am abased! I; am a scholar, not a slave!"

" . . . And they *do* give us wine in the evening."

"That swill? The rank spoilage from their kegs." He was constantly sick to his stomach but couldn't tell if it was from the fish stew, the sour wine, the ever-thickening stench of bilge—or the rising waves. Up the face of one enormous wave they sailed, down another, up and down perpetually. He had sailed beyond sight of land with his father, when a boy, to deliver wave coursers to Keltia and Iberia, and had fared well enough; but as the son of the shipmaster he had lolled in the shade of the sails, taking lessons in navigation and cordage. Now he was fallen to the lowest station of men, apart from the cockeyed boy who emptied their stool pots. Chained at the oars in front of him were aging cutthroats, scooped from the gutters of Hypexa; rowing behind him were several witless farmhands, caught by a thump on the head as he had been.

"Have I no more wit than a gaping farmhand?" he murmured aloud. Perhaps he was at fault as much as Snoori. He should have known better.

If it had been a trireme, at least he'd have been under a deck cover, sheltered from the sun. But this was but a pentekontor, a two-masted, square-sailed vessel rowed by fifty men, twenty-five to a side; there was a slightly raised deck between, and the shade of the sails scarcely reached Brimm and Snoori.

A shadow did fall over him then—that of the row-master. "Keep *rhythm*, dog!" snarled the row-master, and on the word "rhythm" snapped the very tip of his whip betwixt Brimm's shoulder blades, not so hard as to damage the muscles of a useful slave, but with an exacting flick that stung like a wasp, doubly painful because it struck sunburned skin.

Brimm hissed between grinding teeth, and fell into rhythm. It was not easy to row with Snoori at his side. Snoori was broad shouldered but short-legged, coming not quite up to Brimm's shoulder. There was a saying that a tall man and a small man could not row well together, and now he saw it was so.

As he struggled to row with Snoori, Brimm noticed the ship's captain, Zenk—a swarthy man in a red turban and yellow silk—making his way to the prow of the vessel, now and then missing stride as the ship rolled. But what held Brimm's gaze was the sword borne awkwardly in Zenk's yellow sash. It was Brimm's own piercer.

But the Atlantean piercer must be used properly. The tubby, oafish Captain Zenk wouldn't be able to cut a melon with the blade, Brimm was sure, let alone an enemy.

The night Snoori and Brimm had come aboard, Zenk had greeted them affably enough, then pointed to the prow. They had turned to look, and the row-master had cracked them firmly on their heads from behind, using an oar as a club, wielding it in one vigorous swing. Down they went—and so went Brimm's sword, his dagger, his cloak, and his freedom.

"I'll show you how that sword is used, you strutting boar," Brimm muttered, watching him.

But first he must lay his hands on the blade—hands confined by iron chains. He had already tried magicking them off with Rootsun's Efficacious Unchainer, but—judging from the lack of results—he had failed to memorize the spell properly. His erstwhile master, Urgus, had hectored him for his "lackadaisical, feeble, haphazard efforts at memorization" and not for the first time Brimm feared Urgus had been right about him. Of course, he had never envisaged himself in chains. Why then learn an unchaining spell? He had not anticipated Captain Zenk.

But other spells had a certain fascination for him . . . Rootsun's Divulger of the Feminine Mind, Lurania's Guaranteed Charisma Enhancer, Urgus's own Summoning for the Smiting of Enemies . . . But suppose he persuaded an elemental to smite Captain Zenk? How would it get him out of these chains? It might end up sinking the ship and him with it.

And so he sighed, and waited. Time seemed to slow; it dragged by, measured only by the steady creak of the oars—and then a spindly, coughing rower chained near the prow gave a final gasp, lunged against his chains, and collapsed. His brother, who had been kidnapped with him, cried out for help. The row-master took a quick look, unchained the spindly man, and tossed him headfirst over the side. His brother sobbed, and was beaten for it.

Brimm decided he would complain no further. It was a waste of energy—and he had come to this vessel of his own accord.

Fatigue and monotony and rising temperatures melted the days together. Two weeks passed. Occasionally, when a strong following wind pushed them rapidly enough, they were allowed to walk the decks a few at a time, to keep their muscles from cramping up and becoming useless. But even then they were kept on long chains, like hounds on leashes, and watched closely by a hulking much-scarred Hyperborean brute armed with a spiked hammer.

Once as he worked the oars, feeling the sea was the measure of his mounting despair, Brimm called out to the conventional gods of his people: that triumvirate of giants, Apollon, and his sons Boreas and Chione. But they did not respond; they never had, perhaps because Brimm had never sacrificed to them.

Brimm recalled that Urgus had jeered at the usual gods like Wotan and Apollon, saying they were mere *egregores*, creations of the human mind. Urgus insisted there were only a handful of *true* "titanic beings"—that was his term for them—like the goddess of fertility, the Red Lord of war, and the sea king whom the Atlanteans called Poseidon. These were intermediary entities, emanations of the Unnameable Lord above all, the secret god who over-arched all things, whose true name was known to but a few, and who, at any rate, held himself remote from mankind. Below the Unameable and the titanic beings were the elementals, and below them the invisible spirits, who sometimes showed themselves to mankind and could occasionally be treated with, and even controlled . . .

But Urgus himself had claimed to worship only the unnameable one. He did not practice rituals of submission to the Titanic Beings. "You're best being ignored by them," he said.

"Oh, Unnameable Lord," murmured Brimm, late afternoon, "you who Urgus spoke of only by touching the Sign of Nine Points—can you not help us this once?"

It seemed to his disordered senses that the sun briefly flared in the sky. But Brimm only hung his head, fearing madness was creeping up on him.

Soon after, when the row-master had gone to the other side of the ship to harangue the portside oarsmen, Snoori whispered, "Brimm—you see the storm clouds there, off to the west?"

"What of it? They are not coming this way."

"But what if they could? What if they changed their minds? Did you not tell me you learned a spell to *draw* a storm?"

"Why . . . " He almost lost rowing rhythm, considering it. Did he indeed remember the incantation? Had he the energy of spirit required to summon an air elemental? "Perhaps. If I ponder it. But—were I to summon a storm it might well send us to the bottom in our chains. What good would it do us?"

"Look yonder—to the south. Do you see that streak of blue?"

"That cloud bank?"

"I have been to Atlantis, you remember. It was just once, trading with my uncle. That streak of blue on the horizon—why that is the ramparts of Poseidonia—one of the ten kingdoms of Atlantis."

"The land of your mythical 'Poseidonian princess,'" Brimm sniffed. "We will see the docks, and no more of Atlantis than that."

"Just so. If the captain fetches up to the docks of Poseidonia, he will never unchain us, unless it is to sell us into worse conditions. But—if the ship is driven carefully, there are sandbars just under those ramparts. My uncle's ship ran aground on them. In about an hour, with the diminishing tide . . . "

"We would capsize in these waves and drown."

Snoori sighed. "Perhaps you're right."

"But on the other hand—" Brimm was in a desperate mood "—if indeed we merely ran aground. Then . . . "

◆ ◆ ◆

Dusk was upon them when the sails were raised, and the rowers were given a rest and their thin fishy stew. The other rows were bemused by the murmured incantations of the lean Hyperborean with long black hair, the sunburn turning his pale skin the color of cherries. Clearly he had surrendered to madness. Only one of them, an old, blue-dyed Pict, recognized his hand-motions as magical passes. The Pict only shrugged. He had tried calling on his own gods. But it was useless, for they reigned far from here. As far as the Pict could tell, the Hyperborean's hand motions only succeeded in making his chains clink.

But Brimm was scarcely aware of the chains, or the galley to which they bound him. He was in a state of mystical trance, the deep inward focus that Urgus had taught him; in his weakened state his spirit energy was not at its most potent, in the somatic sense—but fury too is tinder for a blaze, and of fury he had an abundance. He expanded the flickering rainbow of his emanation, and drew on the electricity in the air to expand it further; he firmed it, then extended unseen fingers toward the flaring, brooding storm to the west. His unseen fingers beckoned. They could be seen only by a creature of astral form . . .

Brimm spoke the name of the aerial elemental, Zirrish: he who was known to revel in storms. Brimm promised two ritual sacrifices, the lives of two men, if Zirrish should bring the storm hither and turn the ship with a precision that would glorify Zirrish in the stories Brimm would tell of the air god's glorious power . . .

There was a pause. Then—thunder responded, from just overhead.

For a moment Brimm thought the thunder a rebuke. Then the waves from the west rose, rearing up as the storm changed directions; black clouds rushing toward them on long crooked legs of blue-white lightning.

Onward the storm came, with unnatural haste, and Captain Zenk gave orders to shorten sail—but it was no use, the ship's hull itself was driven ahead of the storm, and men cowered in terror as lightning stampeded toward them; as ragged bolts flashed about them and the ship plowed a new furrow in the sea, turning to the southeast, toward the sandbars beneath the northerly ramparts of Atlantis . . .

Snapped from his trance by a flash of lightning and a wall of pelting rain, Brimm struggled with his own rising fear. Already lightning had struck one of the two masts, and set it afire; already the ship's timbers were working, intermittently spitting water. The aft was lifted, the prow dipped, the galley surging headlong toward the cliffs of Atlantis. Oars snapped off; men groaned and cried out, each to his own gods.

"This was a ghastly mistake!" Brimm cried—but Snoori was huddled with his head under his arms, terrified of the lightning and the high, sharp-peaked waves looming over them; the onrushing cliffs of glassy stone ahead.

Then they struck the sandbar at just the angle planned. Everyone on board was tossed and jolted, slaves in their chains howling with terror at the impact, the burning mast snapping to fall into the sea.

But the ship held together, taking little brinewater, and in seconds the storm diminished, pounding thunderously away like one of the great angry mammoths that yet roamed upper Hyperborea. The darkness thickened, but the galley steadied. Waves still assaulted it and the tide had only just dropped. Reavers and scavengers might come upon them, Brimm thought, and make short work of the crew to take its cargo of furs and northern iron and Hyperborean ale.

The ship must be pulled free of the sandbar. As the waves slackened, crewmen brought levers and tools to use to force it off the bar.

As Brimm and Snoori had calculated, the row-master and the Hyperborean brute hurried to unchain the oarsmen—their collective muscle would be needed to free the ship. They were meant to work at the incentive of a snapping whip and threat of the blade.

Unchained, stretching his limbs with the row-master's whip cracking over his head, Brimm saw his chance. The row-master and the brute were turned away, shouting at other men, and the captain had gone to the rail to assess their position—Zenk standing only a stride away, with his back to Brimm.

It was the work of a hate-energized moment to snatch his silver piercer from the captain's waistband.

Zenk turned in startlement, just in time to receive the sword's thrust through his heart. Brimm shouted at the sky, "Zirrish! I offer these, my enemies, to thee!" He added a few arcane words, dedicating Zenk's lifeforce to Zirrish.

Captain Zenk gawped down at the blade in his chest and then sank to the deck, eyes glassy. Brimm pulled the blade free with an expert motion.

The row-master roared and rushed at Brimm—but Snoori tackled the whip-wielder's bowed legs, knocking him to the deck. With a swift stroke, Brimm struck the slaver's head from his shoulders. Snoori snatched up the whip and snapped it in the faces of the crew, driving them back. The rowers took pieces of shattered oars and used them as clubs, battering the crew.

The Brute was swinging his great spiked hammer at Brimm who ducked easily under it, pivoting and lunging in one motion, to slash the tip of his light, powerful blade at the Brute's throat. It struck quick and deep, and the great vein there spurted blood, which arced over the rail into the sea, as Brimm muttered again to Zirrish, offering up another life. The air about him whispered and hissed in pleasure . . . as the Brute raised his hammer again, and staggered toward Brimm, who only had to back away, staying out of the range of that whirling hammer, until the Brute had lost enough blood. The scarred Hyperborean fell heavily to his knees, then forward onto his face, twitching.

The other slaves gasped—and then cheered. They rushed headlong at the retreating crew, who as one man jumped over the rails into the sea. Brimm found his old dagger and cloak—the row-master had used the one to pick his teeth and the other to wipe his sweat—and called for Snoori.

Javelins were caught up from their racks and thrown after the swimming crew; Snoori plucked one for himself, and then ran to Brimm at the rail. "What now?"

A one-eyed Hyperborean oarsman, mane and beard of flowing red, roared in triumph and urged the freed rowers to declare him their new captain. He extolled himself as a former pirate and wise in the ways of the sea. "And if I'm to have a ship to captain and you to share we must move it from the sandbar!"

But before the matter was decided, Brimm and Snoori were over the rail, dropping feet first into the sea. They were scarcely under water before they found footing and lurched across the sandbar, the waves up to their chins, with the confidence of true Hyperboreans.

Snoori knew the way to spiral stone stairs below the blue-painted ramparts of Poseidonia. His first journey here had brought him to the sandbars, and with his uncle he had gone up the stairway to the well-defended gates, the two of them seeking aid for their grounded vessel. As Snoori's uncle was a trader who had business with Atlantis, his ship was, in due course, pulled off the sandbar.

But the two wet, bedraggled escaped slaves who presented themselves now at those same gates seemed to the guards more like undesirables. None of the guards remembered Snoori. His journey here had taken place nine years ago.

And so . . .

"From a slave galley to a dungeon. Thank you, Snoori."

"I was *astonished* they didn't remember me, Brimm! Of course I didn't have a beard then and they spoke only to my uncle and . . . Could you conjure up some gold? We could bribe our way out."

"There is no such spell that actually works, Snoori. If there were, I'd have used it long ago. Why am I explaining this to you? You know, there *is* enough slack in these dungeon chains to strangle you with . . . "

"You wouldn't! The faithful friend of your youth! You're not so crass!"

It was morning, something Brimm surmised only thanks to the spare shaft of dawn light slanting through the dungeon's single high window. The morning light illuminated a sweating stone wall slathered with some slick green growth, and a rat-sized roach scuttling to a crack in a corner. The air reeked of urine and moldy straw. They were sitting on the damp straw, their arms numb from half a night pinioned over their shoulders, and Brimm had spent hours wracking his brains for a suitable spell.

Again, he was bereft of his sword. How long before that bastard of a jailer sold it?

"A sword," Brimm growled. "I much prefer them to magic. The piercer always works. One can use it to shave, as well as cut throats; it can be used to stir a pot, or to pry at a stone wall."

"Are you becoming delirious?" Snoori asked, as if merely curious.

There was a rattling at the door, which then squeaked open, and a bear-like man in a yellowing tunic came in: the jailer, carrying a lantern in one hand and keys in the other. He led the way for two men in gold-threaded gray-black livery. One of the men was red faced, gray bearded, and hawk eyed. His beard was coated in fragrant unguents. The other, younger, clean-shaven man had the raptor-eyed look too. He was probably the bearded man's son. Their eyes were lined with kohl.

The younger man raised a lace kerchief to his nose as he approached the staring prisoners. He looked doubtfully from one to the other. "I am Fress—this is my father Remnon. We are the king's sacred retainers. Are you the fools who asked to serve the princess?"

Their weapons returned to them, each awarded an ill-fitting helmet of thin iron and oak, Brimm and Snoori stood beside Remnon and Fress and gazed down upon the fabled land of ten kingdoms.

Atlantis was not quite a continent; yet it was enormous, a very big island shaped like a slightly off-center diamond; a land big enough to be divided into ten distinct fiefdoms of various sizes. The kingdoms were now ruled by the descendants—or so the rulers claimed—of the demigods who had ruled Atlantis after its establishment by Poseidon.

Several of those kingdoms, including Squema, Thothia, and Poseidonia, spread out before Brimm and Snoori as if on a map, for they stood upon the high bricked road just under the walls of the city. Also called Poseidonia, the hoary city of mossy, settling blocks at their back was splayed along the upper stone rim overlooking succeeding valleys that receded, each flatter and lower, to the several circular inner canals that gave Atlantis one of its geographical distinctions. To the east the cliffs of Atlantis parted, and here a deep inlet entered the island from the sea. The inlet was wide enough for three ships abreast and flowed into a channel connecting the ring-like canals—one canal inside the next—that curved to follow the island's natural outer walls of volcanic glass. Dug out centuries before by legions of slaves and linked by a transverse channel, the canals contacted each of the kingdoms; thus, each King had his own port. On the beetling prominences overlooking the inlet stood catapults, in the distance seeming to Brimm like insects poised to leap. Mechanisms like gigantic crossbows stood beside the catapults, pointed warningly out to sea; countless warships and merchant vessels anchored along the canals within, or moved with stately ease to Inner Atlantis, slowly propelled by galley oarsmen.

Much of the land was lost in the haze of distance; But immediately below Brimm and Snoori, terraced orchards and fields of velvety green hugged the canals; rustic castles of wood and stone—none coated in gold—rose atop stony bosses of land clustered round by hamlets emitting a haze of dun woodsmoke. Low walls of piled black stone divided fields and borders.

Separated from the canals by a curving causeway was a dark lake within the crater of a volcanic vent. Even now, hot vapors rose fitfully from it; sulfurous bubbles burst on its bleak surface to exhale a yellow mist that rose to blur the sun into a coppery oval. Lifted on gray stone buttresses overlooking the lake, in the shadow of the outer rim of the island, rested the partly tumbled ruin of an ancient palace.

"There lies the palace Great Poseidon erected for his mortal love, Cleito!" said Remnon, pointing at the palace with a trembling finger. Remnon wore the livery of King Merz: gold sea dragons embroidered on flat black silk. His speech was High Atlantean, a variant of the cruder language spoken by most of those who lived and wandered 'round the Great Sea—but the accent seemed quaint to Brimm.

"Cleito, you say?" Brimm frowned. "But surely that is the name of the princess we are asked to rescue? It cannot be the same one! If that is the palace of a Cleito she lived centuries in the past."

"Of course it's not *her*, oaf," declared the younger retainer. "She is the great-great-granddaughter, and then some, of Poseidon's love. She is Cleito the Ninth."

"The *eleventh*, Fress!" his father corrected irritably, wincing.

Fress scratched his head. "I thought it was the ninth. Are you sure?"

Brimm gazed uneasily at the palace. The rectilinear, blocky ruins seemed to squirm in the rising vapors of the lake. "Perhaps, after all, we might simply sign on with good King Merz—we should be happy to guard his palace."

"The king has all the help he needs—except at the old palace of Poseidon, yonder."

"Does King Merz have a harem?" Snoori asked, trying to make it sound like innocent curiosity.

Remnon shot Snoori a glare. "You will never get near enough to *that* to so much as smell the perfume, that I assure you!"

"The sun tilts high, Father," said Fress. "We'd best be off."

"Yes. The eight who've already come are drinking good wine and devouring sausages as they await us. With you two, we have the Ten who count themselves the Swords of Her Heart, and we need delay no more. We'll take a cart from the stables to the cliff road!"

Their guides strode toward the stables. Brimm hesitated, and caught Snoori's arm. "Snoori—perhaps we might dash down the hillside here, and find another employer in some other kingdom."

"I haven't eaten since yesterday—and they spoke of sausages and wine! Come on! Besides—the treasure!" Snoori hurried after them. Sighing and pondering the insatiable demands of friendship, Brimm followed.

What remained of the repast was scattered across a block of fallen stone, which served as a table, outside the palace gates. The sausages and wine were mostly depleted, but Brimm and Snoori managed a small meal from the scraps and the dregs of several bronze goblets. Remnon and Fress waited impatiently until they finished, then waved them into the Hall of Supplicants, where the rest of the Ten awaited . . .

The Hall of Supplicants was a high-ceilinged chamber alive with shadows and echoes. Twitching yellow light from a few torch sconces scarcely penetrated the darkness. The sound of their boot-steps came back to them as Brimm and Snoori strode to join the others waiting at the high metal doors at the other end of the hall. The cracked blocks of the walls were carved of red granite; the pilasters along the walls were trimmed in red coral and volcanic glass, some of it fallen about the bases of the square columns; in a panel along the upper walls porphyry glittering with quartz was carved to represent the waves of the sea. Dust and rubble hid the corners of the marble floor.

The squirming shadows hid most of the sagging ceiling; Brimm could faintly make out a patchily intact mosaic of something like a giant squid, watched over by a bearded man wearing a diadem. Poseidon?

The eight soldiers raggedly assembled before the high doors seemed to be from everywhere but Atlantis. There were two northern nomads, with their high cheekbones, dark skin, almond eyes; they were clad only in rancid beast-furs, their weapons hammers of bronze and stone. The company included one sleek, armored man of Ur, wielder of a short curved iron sword and stubby spears, his bronze helmet topped with the silver disk of the moon god, his face masked. There was an ebon warrior of the far south, his face ornately decorated with scars. He was clad in a long red robe. He towered over the rest of them, but his flint-tipped spear was longer than he was tall. Beside him was a painted, intricately garbed, ruddy-skinned warrior wearing a headpiece resembling a feathery snake—he hailed from the far western continents, where rose mighty civilizations centered around stepped pyramids; there was a blue-dyed Pict armed with a stone-tipped club and a bronze dagger. The other three looked to be ragtag vagabonds, peering fearfully about them as they hefted cast-off Atlantean battleaxes.

The door before them was of the same silvery metal, Brimm judged, as his own slender sword, but less polished. It had once been inset with gems, but they'd evidently been pried away by thieves and only scratched indentations remained.

The palace was in large part a ruin; everything about it spoke of disuse and abandonment and fear. A rankness caught at Brimm's nostrils, carried by a faint draft from under the slightly bent metal doors. Rotting fish?

"So, we leave you now to your holy task!" declaimed Remnon portentously. "Once we have gone, the doors will open and you will behold Cleito! You will see the sea demon that holds her in its clutches; this is the fiend you must defeat! There are many of you, and thus you are likely to win the day! We have shall go and, ah, count out the gold and pearls, to be divided among you—and now—"

"Hold!" Brimm cried out. His doubts were gathering force—he had noticed Fress's curious smile, quickly hidden under his be-ringed hand, at the mention of counting out gold and pearls. "No need for such haste!" insisted Brimm. "Indeed, Fress there looks doughty enough and wears a fine sword! Why should he not join us and partake of the treasure? Surely we are to have casualties. There will be enough gold for those who remain!"

"Ah, no," Fress said, blinking at Brimm in alarm. "My sword is purely ornamental. It's for ritualistic purposes only. Mere costumery! Not even sharp!"

"I shall loan you my dagger!"

"No, no, I thank you! You see, the door of the throne room opens of its own accord. It will open quite soon—and sadly, Father and I are not permitted to remain!"

Remnon cleared his throat. "And now, we must bid you goodbye! May the good fortune of the gods attend you all!"

"Stop!" Brimm called, his voice harsh with warning. "You shall not depart! If we face this, so shall you. We have need of your knowledge."

Remnon took his son's upper arm and tugged him back from the door. The two retainers backed away. "That is not possible. But—again—best of luck to you all!"

"Stop them!" Brimm shouted.

Snoori nodded. "I too mistrust them."

The Ten exchanged frowns and turned dark looks at the Atlanteans. Suddenly the black warrior from the South made several quick bounds and took up a stance behind the retainers, his spear jabbing. Remnon and Fress came to a sudden confused halt. Brimm drew his sword and joined the black warrior—and together they herded their protesting guides to the metal doors. Which at that moment creaked wide open.

Forcing the protesting Atlanteans along, the Ten stepped forward, for, despite their doubts, none of them were cowards and all still hoped treasure might be found.

They were in a smaller room now—it was high ceilinged but a third the size of the Hall of Supplicants. Brimm saw no throne. Nor were there torches; a flaring, dipping blue light emanated from vents near the floor. There were no furnishings, no columns; nothing except the ripe stench, and a few dimly perceived mosaics on the walls. The mosaics showed nereids and mermen frolicking in the waves beneath unfamiliar astrological configurations. The floor—at least, nearer the doors—looked to be of some brown and gray material. Then Brimm realized it was the dried residue of old blood on white marble.

The high metal doors closed behind them and, whirling as a group to look, each man saw there were no handles, no knobs, no visible means of opening them. They murmured and cursed, each in his native language.

"Father, what has happened?" Fress wailed, clutching his groin as if to prevent his bladder giving way. "This is not seemly—this is not *possible*! The door opens not from this side!"

"Silence," the old man muttered. "Let me think. Somewhere there must be a way . . ."

The floor began to quake—and a metallic grinding noise brought everyone around to stare at the far end of the rectangular chamber. There, the dirty marble was separating, gradually parting, halves shunting aside into the walls. The stench of oceanic decay was palpable now.

The Ten stared in dull amazement as a shimmering pool of indigo was gradually revealed, its shuddering surface giving off more of the sickly blue light. From the center of the pool, gratingly lifted by some ancient, rusting mechanical device, rose a throne, on which was seated a strange but beautiful woman. Her throne, almost too big for her, was of gold-streaked marble arrayed roundabout with broken coral branches, streaming water as it rose. On her head was a crown of coral tipped with emeralds, dripping with sparkling water. She herself was the color of green olives, her full lips crimson; the whites of her large pupilless oval eyes were speckled with gold like polished opal; her slick green-black hair draped wetly over her bare shoulders; her small hands, nails crusted with ruby dust, rested placidly on the arms of the throne. She wore an iridescent gown that clung to her firm breasts and slim waist, the gown greatly expanding, fanning out widely below to hide her hips, her legs, the entire lower part of the throne.

"Behold!" Fress said, his voice a squeak of awe, shaking hands clutched before his face. "Princess Cleito! The sacred consort of Poseidon!"

"And . . . you may as well know," said Remnon grimly. "That is Cleito herself—not her descendant. She was mortal, and there was only one way she could live on, without the blessing of Poseidon. For when she strayed from him, he cursed her . . . and now you—" he pointed his long-nailed finger at Brimm "—have cursed us all! At least my son and I would have lived—but now—!"

Remnon turned a shaking hand toward the ancient princess on the throne before them—and fell to his knees. *"Cleito!"* cried the king's retainer. "Take these others, but spare my son and your faithful servant Remnon! We have brought you many a succulent hero—as did my father and his father before him! Spare us in their memory!"

Her mouth snapped open, as if in a convulsion, exposing a toothless purple orifice writhing with slick, fluttering tendrils, and she emitted a prolonged, ear-splitting screech commingled of hate, horror, and hunger. This was her only reply to Remnon.

Then her gown, which Brimm now saw to be made of living skin, parted like a curtain and her true lower half was revealed. In the place of legs were ten mottled gray limbs, now stretching toward them: eight wriggling tentacles bore circular suckers and two longer limbs, equally prehensile, and tipped with dexterous club-shaped appendages.

Perhaps the creature had once been a woman, but it was no longer. What vestiges remained served merely as mocking disguise. This "princess" was wholly monster.

The men backed away—but the tentacles stretched out, longer and thicker than Brimm would have thought possible. Cleito's cephalopodean lower half was disproportionately bigger, far larger than its upper half, and yet perfectly melded with its torso. The slippery-wet squid-like part of it now tilted back, raising up to expose a gigantic beak where the tentacles converged, snapping hungrily at the warriors.

Men screamed in horror; Fress bolted to the doors and pounded on them, squalling in fear. Remnon threw himself face down, babbling prayers.

Suddenly, fast as a striking cobra, Cleito's tentacles whipped round the northern barbarians, lifted them screaming into the air, and drew them near. The monster thrust first one, then the other into the opened beak, which elongated as needed for its feasting. Weapons raised, the warriors reacted with moans and cries of fury.

In seconds, Cleito had sucked the flesh from the northmen—and then the beak opened, spewed out their bones, their armor and leather, the greater part sinking away in the pool. A few bits flew past the edge of the pool so that a fresh skull rolled to thump onto Snoori's boots; with an unmanly yelp he kicked it away into the pool about the throne.

More tentacles surged out, and Brimm dodged this way and that, avoiding flashing tentacles, ducking, striking with his piercer like a stinging wasp as the limbs whipped past. He struck home and black blood oozed, but the limbs did not slow their grasping. He tried frantically to remember a spell he might use against this abomination, but the castings he knew needed concentration and time—he was given no time for anything but dodging and slashing.

Crying out in many languages the warriors backed away from Cleito, waving their blades—but its sucker-lined lower limbs, as much supernatural as fleshly, plucked them one by one; in seconds the mortal flesh was stripped from their bones, spitting out weapons like a man spitting out gristle from his dinner. As the beak drew men in and crushed them, the false princess's scarlet mouth worked in sympathy, as if it were chewing.

The black warrior shouted in defiance and threw his spear hard at the upper parts of creature on the throne—but fast as a darting barracuda, a tentacle bolted out and caught the weapon, reversed it, and sped it neatly back so that it impaled the warrior's neck, splitting his throat. Then as he stood swaying, clutching the spear haft, the other tentacle lashed round his ankles and dragged him, thrashing and gurgling, feet first to its giant beak.

The warriors hacked furiously at the tentacles—one big man with a battleaxe cut partway through a suckered limb and Snoori chopped at the wound with the head of his javelin. The limb fell apart, but another grew quickly in its place.

Faster and faster the limbs flashed, the beak gulped—and soon seven shrieking men were gone. The spear of the black warrior was there, lying on the edge of the pool . . .

A tentacle whipped at Brimm—and with it another, so that they were coming from both sides. Brimm ducked, slashing. "Snoori—help me feed it this old fool!" He bent, dragged the weeping, slobbering old Remnon to his feet; with Snoori's help Brimm heaved Remnon toward the tentacles. The offering was accepted—Remnon was caught up and tucked into the beak.

But the other tentacles reached for new prey. Heart pounding, Brimm used his flexible, razor-sharp piercer to good effect, just managing to deter the undulating limbs.

Only a few of the Ten remained. The warrior of Ur, though darting and spinning adroitly, was next to be caught . . .

"We're the next morsel unless we can find a way out!" Snoori yelled, slashing at tentacles to keep them back.

A club-tentacle shot out wrapping tightly around Snoori's legs and drawing him screaming across the floor toward the great snapping beak.

"Drag your javelin in the floor, Snoori, to slow it down!" Brimm called.

Snoori did as Brimm bid, and the javelin point caught hold a crack in the floor as Brimm ran to the doors. The monster was still chewing the man from Ur, whose armor slowed mastication. The giant squid-beak spat the armor out in several uneven chunks.

Brimm picked Fress up in his arms, ran with the struggling Atlantean to the beak, spun himself to increase his throw . . .

And he cast Fress at the beak.

Fress was caught in the air by a great appendage—and was quickly crammed, howling, into the creature's maw. Snoori was in mid-air himself now, half strangled by another tentacle, throwing the javelin at the creature's bosom. It missed, clacking off the throne.

Brimm caught up the black warrior's spear—and then the tentacle dropped Snoori, as if suddenly disinterested.

Cleito had fed to repletion, Brimm realized. It needed ten men to feed upon, and ten it had consumed.

Laughing hysterically, Snoori thrashed in the pool and Brimm reached out, helped him onto the rim.

The cephalopodic half of Cleito was covering itself now, receding under the gown of skin. The throne was beginning to rumble, to lower once more into the pool. The dreadful "princess" belched hugely, and tittered. Brimm thought to see a febrile misery burning in its eyes.

"No," Brimm snarled.

He aimed the black warrior's spear, and threw it with all his might. Cleito was no longer protected by its tentacles, and the spear flew straight and true to drive itself between the opalescent eyes. It squealed and twisted, spurting black blood; ink gushed from its undersides.

Still the throne drew down, and she vanished with it, in a swirl of black effluvia.

The floor closed—and behind them, the metal doors creaked slowly open. Brimm and Snoori turned away—then Snoori bent down, plucking up a purse that had been spat from the creature's beak. Brimm recalled seeing the purse on Remnon's sash.

They hurried out of the throne room, and were soon gasping in the sweet open air outside the ruined palace.

It was quiet out here. Somewhere, a bird called, the sea surged, and galleys, below them, slid unhurriedly along glassy canals.

"So much for your *princess*," Brimm said, his voice hoarse. "An effective deception to trick foolish men who persist in thinking of women as prizes to be won. As for the treasure—riches are always a ploy that always appeals. Neither ever existed at all."

"Don't be so sure about the riches!" Snoori opened the purse. "Ha! Four pearls and a double handful of gold. Didn't I tell you?"

"Didn't you . . . " Brimm stared at him. "I could still strangle you—with my bare hands."

"Suppose we find an inn, and I buy dinner, would that put you in a better mood?"

"We will split that purse—I'll pay for my own dinner. Come—I see smoke from a far hamlet. Let us find some other realm than Poseidonia . . . And see something better of Atlantis."

"Yes—why not! We can find work here! Make Atlantis our new home!"

"Perhaps. But . . . Did you feel the ground rumbling, just now?"

"Oh that—it happens all the time here. Nothing to worry about. This is Atlantis! What could go wrong?"

And so they set off along the crumbling old cliffside track, until they found a trail that would lead them down into the heart of Atlantis.

⚔

Tempering & Sharpening

"Bluestocking" (also published as "The Adventuress," 1967) is the first, chronologically, of Joanna Russ's (1937–2011) five stories to feature the sword-and-sorcery heroine, Alyx. This, and the next of her adventures, "I Thought She Was Afeard Till She Stroked My Beard," is very much in the vein of Fritz Leiber's Fafhrd and the Gray Mouser. (In fact, Alyx mentions one of Leiber's characters in "Bluestocking." Leiber, in turn, refers to Alyx in two of his tales.) In the final three Alyx stories, the heroine is an agent of the Trans-Temporal Authority in a more science fictional universe.

Working with less than 8,500 words, Russ gives us a remarkably complete protagonist and setting. Even Edarra, the young heiress Alyx aids, develops (somewhat) from a whiny spoiled child into a more self-possessed young woman. If you have never met the smart, competent, skilled, adventurous Alyx before, she may quickly become one of your favorite characters—man or woman—in sword and sorcery.

BLUESTOCKING

Joanna Russ

This is the tale of a voyage that is of interest only as it concerns the doings of one small, gray-eyed woman. Small women exist in plenty—so do those with gray eyes—but this woman was among the wisest of a sex that is surpassingly wise. There is no surprise in that (or should not be) for it is common knowledge that Woman was created fully a quarter of an hour before Man, and has kept that advantage to this very day. Indeed, legend has it that the first man, Leh, was fashioned from the sixth finger of the left hand of the first woman, Loh, and that is why women have only five fingers on the left hand. The lady with whom we concern ourselves in this story had all her six fingers, and what is more, they all worked.

In the seventh year before the time of which we speak, this woman, a neat, level-browed, governessy person called Alyx, had come to the City of Ourdh as part of a religious delegation from the hills intended to convert the dissolute citizens to the ways of virtue and the one true God, a Bang tree of awful majesty. But Alyx, a young woman of an intellectual bent, had not been in Ourdh two months when she decided that the religion of Yp (as the hill god was called) was a disastrous piece of nonsense, and that deceiving a young woman in matters of such importance was a piece of thoughtlessness for which it would take some weeks of hard, concentrated thought to think up a proper reprisal. In due time the police chased Alyx's co-religionists down the Street of Heaven and Hell and out the swamp gate to be bitten by the mosquitoes that lie in wait among the reeds, and Alyx—with a shrug of contempt—took up a modest living as pick-lock, a profession that gratified her sense of subtlety. It provided her with a living, a craft and a society. Much of the wealth of this richest and vilest cities stuck to her fingers but most of it dropped off again, for she was not much awed by the things of this world. Going their legal or illegal ways in this seventh year after her arrival, citizens of Ourdh saw only a woman with short, black hair and a sprinkling of freckles across her milky nose; but Alyx had ambitions of becoming a Destiny. She was thirty (a dangerous time for men and women alike) when this story begins. Yp moved in his mysterious ways, Alyx entered the employ of the lady Edarra, and Ourdh saw neither of them again—for a while.

Alyx was walking with a friend down the Street of Conspicuous Display one sultry summer's morning when she perceived a young woman, dressed like a jeweler's tray and surmounted with a great coil of red hair, waving to her from the table of a wayside garden-terrace.

"Wonderful are the ways of Yp," she remarked, for although she no longer accorded that deity any respect, yet her habits of speech remained. "There sits a red-headed young woman of no more than seventeen years and with the best skin imaginable, and yet she powders her face."

"Wonderful indeed," said her friend. Then he raised one finger and went his way, a discretion much admired in Ourdh. The young lady, who had been drumming her fingers on the tabletop and frowning like a fury, waved again and stamped one foot.

"I want to talk to you," she said sharply. "Can't you hear me?"

"I have six ears," said Alyx, the courteous reply in such a situation. She sat down and the waiter handed her the bill of fare.

"You are not listening to me," said the lady.

"I do not listen with my eyes," said Alyx.

"Those who do not listen with their eyes as well as their ears," said the lady sharply, "can be made to regret it!"

"Those," said Alyx, "who on a fine summer's morning threaten their fellow-creatures in any way, absurdly or otherwise, both mar the serenity of the day and break the peace of Yp, who," she said, "is mighty."

"You are impossible!" cried the lady. "Impossible!" and she bounced up and down in her seat with rage, fixing her fierce brown eyes on Alyx. "Death!" she cried.

"Death and bones!" and that was a ridiculous thing to say at eleven in the morning by the side of the most wealthy and luxurious street in Ourdh, for such a street is one of the pleasantest places in the world if you do not watch the beggars. The lady, insensible to all this bounty, jumped to her feet and glared at the little pick-lock; then, composing herself with an effort (she clenched both hands and gritted her teeth like a person in the worst throes of marsh fever), she said—calmly—

"I want to leave Ourdh."

"Many do," said Alyx, courteously.

"I require a companion."

"A lady's maid?" suggested Alyx. The lady jumped once in her seat as if her anger must have an outlet somehow; then she clenched her hands and gritted her teeth with doubled vigor.

"I must have protection," she snapped.

"Ah?"

"I'll pay!" (This was almost a shriek.)

"How?" said Alyx, who had her doubts.

"None of your business," said the lady.

"If I'm to serve you, everything's my business. Tell me. All right, how much?"

The lady named a figure, reluctantly.

"Not enough," said Alyx. "Particularly not knowing how. Or why. And why protection? From whom? When?" The lady jumped to her feet. "By water?" continued Alyx imperturbably. "By land? On foot? How far? You must understand, little one—"

"Little one!" cried the lady, her mouth dropping open. *"Little one!"*

"If you and I are to do business—"

"I'll have you thrashed—" gasped the lady, out of breath, "I'll have you so—"

"And let the world know your plans?" said Alyx, leaning forward with one hand under her chin. The lady stared, and bit her lip, and backed up, and then she hastily grabbed her skirts as if they were sacks of potatoes and ran off, ribbons fluttering behind her. *Wine-colored ribbons*, thought Alyx, *with red hair; that's clever*. She ordered brandy and filled her glass, peering curiously into it where the hot, midmorning sun of Ourdh suffused into a winy glow, a sparkling, trembling, streaky mass of floating brightness. *To* (she said to herself with immense good humor) *all the young ladies in the world*. "And," she added softly, "great quantities of money."

At night Ourdh is a suburb of the Pit, or that steamy, muddy bank where the gods kneel eternally, making man; though the lights of the city never show fairer than then. At night the rich wake up and the poor sink into a distressed sleep, and everyone takes to the flat, whitewashed roofs. Under the light of gold lamps the wealthy converse, sliding across one another, silky but never vulgar; at night Ya, the courtesan with the gold breasts (very good for the jaded taste) and Garh the pirate, red-bearded, with his carefully cultivated stoop, and many many others, all ascend the broad, white steps to someone's roof. Each step carries a lamp, each lamp sheds a blurry radiance on a tray, each tray is crowded with sticky, pleated, salt, sweet . . . Alyx ascended, dreaming of snow. She was there on business. Indeed the sky was overcast that night, but a downpour would not drive the guests indoors; a striped silk awning with gold fringes would be unrolled over their heads, and while the fringes became matted and wet and water spouted into the garden below, ladies would put out their hands (or their heads—but that took a brave lady on account of the coiffure) outside the awning and squeal as they were soaked by the warm, mild, neutral rain of Ourdh. Thunder was another matter. Alyx remembered hill storms with gravel hissing down the gullies of streams and paths turned to cold mud. She met the dowager in charge and that ponderous lady said:

"Here she is."

It was Edarra, sulky and seventeen, knotting a silk handkerchief in a wet wad in her hand and wearing a sparkling blue-and-green bib.

"That's the necklace," said the dowager. "Don't let it out of your sight."

"I see," said Alyx, passing her hand over her eyes.

When they were left alone, Edarra fastened her fierce eyes on Alyx and hissed, "Traitor!"

"What for?" said Alyx.

"Traitor! Traitor! Traitor!" shouted the girl. The nearest guests turned to listen and then turned away, bored.

"You grow dull," said Alyx, and she leaned lightly on the roof-rail to watch the company. There was the sound of angry stirrings and rustlings behind her. Then the girl said in a low voice (between her teeth), "Tonight someone is going to steal this necklace."

Alyx said nothing. Ya floated by with her metal breasts gleaming in the lamplight; behind her, Peng the jeweler.

"I'll get seven hundred ounces of gold for it!"

"Ah?" said Alyx.

"You've spoiled it," snapped the girl. Together they watched the guests, red and green, silk on silk like oil on water, the high-crowned hats and earrings glistening, the bracelets sparkling like a school of underwater fish. Up came the dowager accompanied by a landlord of the richest and largest sort, a gentleman bridegroom who had buried three previous wives and would now have the privilege of burying the Lady Edarra—though to hear him tell it, the first had died of overeating, the second of drinking and the third of a complexion-cleanser she had brewed herself. Nothing questionable in that. He smiled and took Edarra's upper arm between his thumb and finger. He said, "Well, little girl." She stared at him. "Don't be defiant," he said. "You're going to be rich." The dowager bridled. "I mean—even richer," he said with a smile. The mother and the bridegroom talked business for a few minutes, neither watching the girl; then they turned abruptly and disappeared into the mixing, moving company, some of whom were leaning over the rail screaming at those in the garden below, and some of whom were slipping and sitting down involuntarily in thirty-five pounds of cherries that had just been accidentally overturned onto the floor.

"So that's why you want to run away," said Alyx. The Lady Edarra was staring straight ahead of her, big tears rolling silently down her cheeks. "Mind your business," she said.

"Mind yours," said Alyx softly, "and do not insult me, for I get rather hard then." She laughed and fingered the necklace, which was big and gaudy and made of stones the size of a thumb. "What would you do," she said, "if I told you yes?"

"You're impossible!" said Edarra, looking up and sobbing.

"Praised be Yp that I exist then," said Alyx, "for I do ask you if your offer is open. Now that I see your necklace more plainly, I incline towards accepting it—whoever you hired was cheating you, by the way; you can get twice again as much—though that gentleman we saw just now has something to do with my decision." She paused. "Well?"

Edarra said nothing, her mouth open.

"Well, speak!"

"No," said Edarra.

"Mind you," said Alyx wryly, "you still have to find someone to travel with, and I wouldn't trust the man you hired—probably hired—for five minutes in a room with twenty other people. Make your choice. I'll go with you as long and as far as you want, anywhere you want."

"Well," said Edarra, "yes."

"Good," said Alyx. "I'll take two-thirds."

"No!" cried Edarra, scandalized.

"Two-thirds," said Alyx, shaking her head. "It has to be worth my while. Both the gentleman you hired to steal your necklace—and your mother—and your husband-to-be—and heaven alone knows who else—will be after us before the evening is out. Maybe. At any rate, I want to be safe when I come back."

"Will the money—?" said Edarra.

"Money does all things," said Alyx. "And I have long wanted to return to this city, this paradise, this—swamp!—with that which makes power! Come," and she leapt onto the roof-rail and from there into the garden, landing feet first in the loam and ruining a bed of strawberries. Edarra dropped beside her, all of a heap and panting.

"Kill one, kill all, kill devil!" said Alyx gleefully. Edarra grabbed her arm. Taking the lady by the crook of her elbow, Alyx began to run, while behind them the fashionable merriment of Ourdh (the guests were pouring wine down each other's backs) grew fainter and fainter and finally died away.

They sold the necklace at the waterfront shack that smelt of tar and sewage (Edarra grew ill and had to wait outside), and with the money Alyx bought two short swords, a dagger, a blanket, and a round cheese. She walked along the harbor carving pieces out of the cheese with the dagger and eating them off the point. Opposite a fishing boat, a square-sailed, slovenly tramp, she stopped and pointed with cheese and dagger both.

"That's ours," said she. (For the harbor streets were very quiet.)

"Oh, no!"

"Yes," said Alyx, "that mess," and from the slimy timbers of the quay she leapt onto the deck. "It's empty," she said.

"No," said Edarra, "I won't go," and from the landward side of the city thunder rumbled and a few drops of rain fell in the darkness, warm, like the wind.

"It's going to rain," said Alyx. "Get aboard."

"No," said the girl. Alyx's face appeared in the bow of the boat, a white spot scarcely distinguishable from the sky; she stood in the bow as the boat rocked to and fro in the wash of the tide. A light across the street, that shone in the window of a waterfront café, went out.

"Oh!" gasped Edarra, terrified, "give me my money!" A leather bag fell in the dust at her feet. "I'm going back," she said, "I'm never going to set foot in that thing. It's disgusting. It's not ladylike."

"No," said Alyx.

"It's *dirty*!" cried Edarra. Without a word, Alyx disappeared into the darkness. Above, where the clouds bred from the marshes roofed the sky, the obscurity deepened and the sound of rain drumming on the roofs of the town advanced steadily, three streets away, then two . . . a sharp gust of wind blew bits of paper and the indefinable trash of the seaside upwards in an unseen spiral. Out over the sea Edarra could hear the universal sound of rain on water, like the shaking of dried peas in a sheet of paper but softer and more blurred, as acres of the surface of the sea dimpled with innumerable little pockmarks . . .

"I thought you'd come," said Alyx. "Shall we begin?"

◆ ◆ ◆

Ourdh stretches several miles southward down the coast of the sea, finally dwindling to a string of little towns; at one of these they stopped and provided for themselves, laying in a store of food and a first-aid kit of dragon's teeth and ginger root, for one never knows what may happen in a sea voyage. They also bought resin; Edarra was forced to caulk the ship under fear of being called soft and lazy, and she did it, although she did not speak. She did not speak at all. She boiled the fish over a fire laid in the brass firebox and fanned the smoke and choked, but she never said a word. She did what she was told in silence. Every day bitterer, she kicked the stove and scrubbed the floor, tearing her fingernails, wearing out her skirt; she swore to herself, but without a word, so that when one night she kicked Alyx with her foot, it was an occasion.

"Where are we going?" said Edarra in the dark, with violent impatience. She had been brooding over the question for several weeks and her voice carried a remarkable quality of concentration; she prodded Alyx with her big toe and repeated, "I said, where are we going?"

"Morning," said Alyx. She was asleep, for it was the middle of the night; they took watches above. "In the morning," she said. Part of it was sleep and part was demoralization; although reserved, she was friendly and Edarra was ruining her nerves.

"Oh!" exclaimed the lady between clenched teeth, and Alyx shifted in her sleep. "When will we buy some decent *food*?" demanded the lady vehemently. "When? When?"

Alyx sat bolt upright. "Go to sleep!" she shouted, under the hallucinatory impression that it was she who was awake and working. She dreamed of nothing but work now. In the dark Edarra stamped up and down. "Oh, wake up!" she cried, "for goodness' sakes!"

"What do you want?" said Alyx.

"Where are we going?" said Edarra. "Are we going to some miserable little fishing village? Are we? Well, are we?"

"Yes," said Alyx.

"Why!" demanded the lady.

"To match your character."

With a scream of rage, the Lady Edarra threw herself on her preserver and they bumped heads for a few minutes, but the battle—although violent—was conducted entirely in the dark and they were tangled up almost completely in the beds, which were nothing but blankets laid on the bare boards and not the only reason that the lady's brown eyes were turning a permanent, baleful black.

"Let me up, you're strangling me!" cried the lady, and when Alyx managed to light the lamp, bruising her shins against some of the furniture, Edarra was seen to be wrestling with a blanket, which she threw across the cabin. The cabin was five feet across.

"If you do that again, madam," said Alyx, "I'm going to knock your head against the floor!" The lady swept her hair back from her brow with the air of a princess. She was trembling. "Huh!" she said, in the voice of one so angry that she does not dare say anything. "Really," she said, on the verge of tears.

"Yes, really," said Alyx, "really" (finding some satisfaction in the word), "really go above. We're drifting." The lady sat in her corner, her face white, clenching her hands together as if she held a burning chip from the stove. "No," she said.

"Eh, madam?" said Alyx.

"I won't do anything," said Edarra unsteadily, her eyes glittering. "You can do everything. You want to, anyway."

"Now look here—" said Alyx grimly, advancing on the girl, but whether she thought better of it or whether she heard or smelt something (for after weeks of water, sailors—or so they say—develop a certain intuition for such things), she only threw her blanket over her shoulder and said, "Suit yourself." Then she went on deck. Her face was unnaturally composed.

"Heaven witness my self-control," she said, not raising her voice but in a conversational tone that somewhat belied her facial expression. "Witness it. See it. Reward it. May the messenger of Yp—in whom I do not believe—write in that parchment leaf that holds all the records of the world that I, provoked beyond human endurance, tormented, kicked in the midst of sleep, treated like the off-scourings of a filthy, cheap, sour-beer-producing brewery—"

Then she saw the sea monster.

Opinion concerning sea monsters varies in Ourdh and the surrounding hills, the citizens holding monsters to be the souls of the wicked dead forever ranging the pastureless wastes of ocean to waylay the living and force them into watery graves, and the hill people scouting this blasphemous view and maintaining that sea monsters are legitimate creations of the great god Yp, sent to murder travelers as an illustration of the majesty, the might and the unpredictability of that most inexplicable of deities. But the end result is much the same. Alyx had seen the bulbous face and coarse whiskers of the creature in a drawing hanging in the Silver Eel on the waterfront of Ourdh (the original—stuffed—had been stolen in some prehistoric time, according to the proprietor), and she had shuddered. She had thought, *Perhaps it is just an animal*, but even so it was not pleasant. Now in the moonlight that turned the ocean to a ball of silver waters in the midst of which bobbed the tiny ship, very very far from anyone or anything, she saw the surface part in a rain of sparkling drops and the huge, wicked, twisted face of the creature, so like and unlike a man's, rise like a shadowy demon from the dark, bright water. It held its baby to its breast, a nauseating parody of humankind. Behind her she heard Edarra choke, for that lady had followed her onto the deck. Alyx forced her unwilling feet to the rail and leaned over, stretching out one shaking hand. She said:

> "By the tetragrammaton of dread,
> By the seven names of God.
> Begone and trouble us no more!"

Which was very brave of her because she did not believe in charms. But it had to be said directly to the monster's face, and say it she did.

The monster barked like a dog.

Edarra screamed. With an arm suddenly nerved to steel, the thief snatched a fishing spear from its place in the stern and braced one knee against the rail; she leaned into the creature's very mouth and threw her harpoon. It entered below the pink harelip and blood gushed as the thing trumpeted and thrashed; black under the moonlight, the blood billowed along the waves, the water closed over the apparition, ripples spread and rocked the boat, and died, and Alyx slid weakly onto the deck.

There was silence for a while. Then she said, "It's only an animal," and she made the mark of Yp on her forehead to atone for having killed something without the spur of overmastering necessity. She had not made the gesture for years. Edarra, who was huddled in a heap against the mast, moved. "It's gone," said Alyx. She got to her feet and took the rudder of the boat, a long shaft that swung at the stern. The girl moved again, shivering.

"It was an animal," said Alyx with finality, "that's all."

The next morning Alyx took out the two short swords and told Edarra she would have to learn to use them.

"No," said Edarra.

"Yes," said Alyx. While the wind held, they fenced up and down the deck, Edarra scrambling resentfully. Alyx pressed her hard and assured her that she would have to do this every day.

"You'll have to cut your hair, too," she added, for no particular reason.

"Never!" gasped the other, dodging.

"Oh, yes, you will!" and she grasped the red braid and yanked; one flash of the blade—

Now it may have been the sea air—or the loss of her red tresses—or the collision with a character so different from those she was accustomed to, but from this morning on it became clear that something was exerting a humanizing influence on the young woman. She was quieter, even (on occasion) dreamy; she turned to her work without complaint, and after a deserved ducking in the sea had caused her hair to break out in short curls, she took to leaning over the side of the boat and watching herself in the water, with meditative pleasure. Her skin, that the pick-lock had first noticed as fine, grew even finer with the passage of the days, and she turned a delicate ivory color, like a half-baked biscuit, that Alyx could not help but notice. But she did not like it. Often in the watches of the night she would say aloud:

"Very well, I am thirty—" (Thus she would soliloquize.) "But what, O Yp, is thirty? Thrice ten. Twice fifteen. Women marry at forty. In ten years I will be forty—"

And so on. From these apostrophizations she returned uncomfortable, ugly, old and with a bad conscience. She had a conscience, though it was not active in the usual directions. One morning, after these nightly wrestlings, the girl was leaning over the rail of the boat, her hair dangling about her face, watching the fish in the water and her own reflection. Occasionally she yawned, opening her pink mouth and shutting her eyes; all this Alyx watched surreptitiously. She felt uncomfortable. All morning the heat had been intense and mirages of ships and gulls and unidentified objects had danced on the horizon, breaking up eventually into clumps of seaweed or floating bits of wood.

"Shall I catch a fish?" said Edarra, who occasionally spoke now.

"Yes—no—" said Alyx, who held the rudder.

"Well, shall I or shan't I?" said Edarra tolerantly.

"Yes," said Alyx, "if you—" and swung the rudder hard. All morning she had been watching black, wriggling shapes that turned out to be nothing; now she thought she saw something across the glittering water. *One thing we shall both get out of this*, she thought, *is a permanent squint*. The shape moved closer, resolving itself into several verticals and a horizontal; it danced and streaked maddeningly. Alyx shaded her eyes.

"Edarra," she said quietly, "get the swords. Hand me one and the dagger."

"What?" said Edarra, dropping a fishing line she had begun to pick up.

"Three men in a sloop," said Alyx. "Back up against the mast and put the blade behind you."

"But they might not—" said Edarra with unexpected spirit.

"And they might," said Alyx grimly, "they just might."

Now in Ourdh there is a common saying that if you have not strength, there are three things which will serve as well: deceit, surprise and speed. These are women's natural weapons. Therefore when the three rascals—and rascals they were or appearances lied—reached the boat, the square sail was furled and the two women, like castaways, were sitting idly against the mast while the boat bobbed in the oily swell. This was to render the rudder useless and keep the craft from slewing round at a sudden change in the wind. Alyx saw with joy that two of the three were fat and all were dirty; *too vain*, she thought, *to keep in trim or take precautions.* She gathered in her right hand the strands of the fishing net stretched inconspicuously over the deck.

"Who does your laundry?" she said, getting up slowly. She hated personal uncleanliness. Edarra rose to one side of her.

"You will," said the midmost. They smiled broadly. When the first set foot in the net, Alyx jerked it up hard, bringing him to the deck in a tangle of fishing lines; at the same instant with her left hand—and the left hand of this daughter of Loh carried all its six fingers—she threw the dagger (which had previously been used for nothing bloodier than cleaning fish) and caught the second interloper squarely in the stomach. He sat down, hard, and was no further trouble. The first, who had gotten to his feet, closed with her in a ringing of steel that was loud on that tiny deck; for ninety seconds by the clock he forced her back towards the opposite rail; then in a burst of speed she took him under his guard at a pitch of the ship and slashed his sword wrist, disarming him. But her thrust carried her too far and she fell; grasping his wounded wrist with his other hand, he launched himself at her, and Alyx—planting both knees against his chest—helped him into the sea. He took a piece of the rail with him. By the sound of it, he could not swim. She stood over the rail, gripping her blade until he vanished for the last time. It was over that quickly. Then she perceived Edarra standing over the third man, sword in hand, an incredulous, pleased expression on her face. Blood holds no terrors for a child of Ourdh, unfortunately.

"Look what I did!" said the little lady.

"Must you look so pleased?" said Alyx, sharply. The morning's washing hung on the opposite rail to dry. So quiet had the sea and sky been that it had not budged an inch. The gentleman with the dagger sat against it, staring.

"If you're so hardy," said Alyx, "take that out."

"Do I have to?" said the little girl, uneasily.

"I suppose not," said Alyx, and she put one foot against the dead man's chest, her grip on the knife and her eyes averted; the two parted company and he went over the side in one motion. Edarra turned a little red; she hung her head and remarked, "You're splendid."

"You're a savage," said Alyx.

"But why!" cried Edarra indignantly. "All I said was—"

"Wash up," said Alyx, "and get rid of the other one; he's yours."

"I said you were splendid and I don't see why that's—"

"And set the sail," added the six-fingered pick-lock. She lay down, closed her eyes and fell asleep.

Now it was Alyx who did not speak and Edarra who did; she said, "Good morning," she said, "Why do fish have scales?" she said, "I *like* shrimp; they look funny," and she said (once), "I like you," matter-of-factly, as if she had been thinking about the question and had just then settled it. One afternoon they were eating fish in the cabin—"fish" is a cold, unpleasant, slimy word, but sea trout baked in clay with onion, shrimp and white wine is something else again—when Edarra said:

"What was it like when you lived in the hills?" She said it right out of the blue, like that.

"What?" said Alyx.

"Were you happy?" said Edarra.

"I prefer not to discuss it."

"All right, *madam*," and the girl swept up to the deck with her plate and glass. It isn't easy climbing a rope ladder with a glass (balanced on a plate) in one hand, but she did it without thinking, which shows how accustomed she had become to the ship and how far this tale has advanced. Alyx sat moodily poking at her dinner (which had turned back to slime as far as she was concerned) when she smelled something char and gave a cursory poke into the firebox next to her with a metal broom they kept for the purpose. This ancient firebox served them as a stove. Now it may have been age, or the carelessness of the previous owner, or just the venomous hatred of inanimate objects for mankind (the religion of Yp stresses this point with great fervor), but the truth of the matter was that the firebox had begun to come apart at the back, and a few flaming chips had fallen on the wooden floor of the cabin. Moreover, while Alyx poked among the coals in the box, its door hanging open, the left front leg of the creature crumpled and the box itself sagged forward, the coals inside sliding dangerously. Alyx exclaimed and hastily shut the door. She turned and looked for the lock with which to fasten the door more securely, and thus it was that until she turned back again and stood up, she did not see what mischief was going on at the other side. The floor, to the glory of Yp, was smoking in half a dozen places. Stepping carefully, Alyx picked up the pail of seawater kept always ready in a corner of the cabin and emptied it onto the smoldering floor, but at that instant—so diabolical are the souls of machines—the second front leg of the box followed the first and the brass door burst open, spewing burning coals the length of the cabin. Ordinarily not even a heavy sea could scatter the fire, for the door was too far above the bed on which the wood rested and the monster's legs were bolted to the floor. But now the boards caught not in half a dozen but in half a hundred places. Alyx shouted for water and grabbed a towel, while a pile of folded blankets against the wall curled and turned black; the cabin was filled with the odor of burning hair. Alyx beat at the blankets and the fire found a cupboard next to them, crept under the door and caught in a sack of sprouting potatoes, which refused to burn. Flour was packed next to them. "Edarra!" yelled Alyx. She overturned a rack of wine, smashing it against the floor regardless of the broken glass; it checked the flames while she beat at the cupboard; then the fire turned and leapt at the opposite wall. It flamed up for an instant in a straw mat hung against the wall, creeping upward, eating down through the planks of the floor, searching out cracks under the cupboard door, roundabout. The potatoes, dried by the heat, began to wither sullenly; their canvas sacking crumbled and turned black. Edarra had just come tumbling into the cabin, horrified, and Alyx was choking on the smoke of canvas sacking and green, smoking sprouts, when the fire reached the stored flour. There was a concussive bellow and a blast of air that sent Alyx staggering into the stove; white flame billowed from the corner that had held the cupboard. Alyx was burned on one side from knee to ankle and knocked against the wall; she fell, full-length.

When she came to herself, she was half lying in dirty seawater and the fire was gone. Across the cabin Edarra was struggling with a water demon, stuffing half-burnt blankets and clothes and sacks of potatoes against an incorrigible waterspout that knocked her about and burst into the cabin in erratic gouts, making tides in the water that shifted sluggishly from one side of the floor to the other as the ship rolled.

"Help me!" she cried. Alyx got up. Shakily she staggered across the cabin and together they leaned their weight on the pile of stuffs jammed into the hole.

"It's not big," gasped the girl, "I made it with a sword. Just under the waterline."

"Stay here," said Alyx. Leaning against the wall, she made her way to the cold firebox. Two bolts held it to the floor. "No good there," she said. With the same exasperating slowness, she hauled herself up the ladder and stood uncertainly on the deck. She lowered the sail, cutting her fingers, and dragged it to the stern, pushing all loose gear on top of it. Dropping down through the hatch again, she shifted coils of rope and stores of food to the stern; patiently fumbling, she unbolted the firebox from the floor. The waterspout had lessened. Finally, when Alyx had pushed the metal box end over end against the opposite wall of the cabin, the water demon seemed to lose his exuberance. He drooped and almost died. With a letting-out of breath, Edarra released the mass pressed against the hole: blankets, sacks, shoes, potatoes, all slid to the stern. The water stopped. Alyx, who seemed for the first time to feel a brand against the calf of her left leg and needles in her hand where she had burnt herself unbolting the stove, sat leaning against the wall, too weary to move. She saw the cabin through a milky mist. Ballooning and shrinking above her hung Edarra's face, dirty with charred wood and sea slime; the girl said:

"What shall I do now?"

"Nail boards," said Alyx slowly.

"Yes, then?" urged the girl.

"Pitch," said Alyx. "Bail it out."

"You mean the boat will pitch?" said Edarra, frowning in puzzlement. In answer Alyx shook her head and raised one hand out of the water to point to the storage place on deck, but the air drove the needles deeper into her fingers and distracted her mind. She said, "Fix," and leaned back against the wall, but as she was sitting against it already, her movement only caused her to turn, with a slow, natural easiness, and slide unconscious into the dirty water that ran tidally this way and that within the blackened, sour-reeking, littered cabin.

Alyx groaned. Behind her eyelids she was reliving one of the small contretemps of her life: lying indoors ill and badly hurt, with the sun rising out of doors, thinking that she was dying and hearing the birds sing. She opened her eyes. The sun shone, the waves sang, there was the little girl watching her. The sun was level with the sea and the first airs of evening stole across the deck.

Alyx tried to say, "What happened?" and managed only to croak. Edarra sat down, all of a flop.

"You're talking!" she exclaimed with vast relief. Alyx stirred, looking about her, tried to rise and thought better of it. She discovered lumps of bandage on her hand and her leg; she picked at them feebly with her free hand, for they struck her somehow as irrelevant. Then she stopped.

"I'm alive," she said hoarsely, "for Yp likes to think he looks after me, the bastard."

"I don't know about *that*," said Edarra, laughing. "My!" She knelt on the deck with her hair streaming behind her like a ship's figurehead come to life; she said, "I fixed everything. I pulled you up here. I fixed the boat, though I had to hang by my knees. I pitched it." She exhibited her arms, daubed to the elbow. "Look," she said. Then she added, with a catch in her voice, "I thought you might die."

"I might yet," said Alyx. The sun dipped into the sea. "Long-leggedy thing," she said in a hoarse whisper, "get me some food."

"Here." Edarra rummaged for a moment and held out a piece of bread, part of the ragbag loosened on deck during the late catastrophe. The pick-lock ate, lying back. The sun danced up and down in her eyes, above the deck, below the deck, above the deck . . .

"Creature," said Alyx, "I had a daughter."

"Where is she?" said Edarra.

Silence.

"Praying," said Alyx at last. "Damning me."

"I'm sorry," said Edarra.

"But you," said Alyx, "are—" and she stopped blankly. She said, "You—"

"Me what?" said Edarra.

"Are here," said Alyx, and with a bone-cracking yawn, letting the crust fall from her fingers, she fell asleep.

At length the time came (all things must end and Alyx's burns had already healed to barely visible scars—one looking closely at her could see many such faint marks on her back, her arms, her sides, the bodily record of the last rather difficult seven years) when Alyx, emptying overboard the breakfast scraps, gave a yell so loud and triumphant that she inadvertently lost hold of the garbage bucket and it fell into the sea.

"What is it?" said Edarra, startled. Her friend was gripping the rail with both hands and staring over the sea with a look that Edarra did not understand in the least, for Alyx had been closemouthed on some subjects in the girl's education.

"I am thinking," said Alyx.

"Oh!" shrieked Edarra. "Land! Land!" and she capered about the deck, whirling and clapping her hands. "I can change my dress!" she cried. "Just think! We can eat fresh food! Just think!"

"I was not," said Alyx, "thinking about that." Edarra came up to her and looked curiously into her eyes, which had gone as deep and as gray as the sea on a gray day; she said, "Well, what are you thinking about?"

"Something not fit for your ears," said Alyx. The little girl's eyes narrowed. "Oh," she said pointedly. Alyx ducked past her for the hatch, but Edarra sprinted ahead and straddled it, arms wide.

"I want to hear it," she said.

"That's a foolish attitude," said Alyx. "You'll lose your balance."

"Tell me."

"Come, get away."

The girl sprang forward like a red-headed fury, seizing her friend by the hair with both hands. "If it's not fit for my ears, I want to hear it!" she cried.

Alyx dodged around her and dropped below, to retrieve from storage her severe, decent, formal black clothes, fit for a business call. When she reappeared, tossing the clothes on deck, Edarra had a short sword in her right hand and was guarding the hatch very exuberantly.

"Don't be foolish," said Alyx crossly.

"I'll kill you if you don't tell me," remarked Edarra.

"Little one," said Alyx, "the stain of ideals remains on the imagination long after the ideals themselves vanish. Therefore I will tell you nothing."

"Raahh!" said Edarra, in her throat.

"It wouldn't be proper," added Alyx primly. "If you don't know about it, so much the better," and she turned away to sort her clothes. Edarra pinked her in a formal, black shoe.

"Stop it!" snapped Alyx.

"Never!" cried the girl wildly, her eyes flashing. She lunged and feinted and her friend, standing still, wove (with the injured boot) a net of defense as invisible as the cloak that enveloped Aule the Messenger. Edarra, her chest heaving, managed to say, "I'm tired."

"Then stop," said Alyx.

Edarra stopped.

"Do I remind you of your little baby girl?" she said.

Alyx said nothing.

"I'm not a little baby girl," said Edarra. "I'm eighteen now and I know more than you think. Did I ever tell you about my first suitor and the cook and the cat?"

"No," said Alyx, busy sorting.

"The cook let the cat in," said Edarra, "though she shouldn't have, and so when I was sitting on my suitor's lap and I had one arm around his neck and the other arm on the arm of the chair, he said, 'Darling, where is your *other* little hand?"

"Mm hm," said Alyx.

"It was the cat, walking across his lap! But he could only feel one of my hands so he thought—" but here, seeing that Alyx was not listening, Edarra shouted a word used remarkably seldom in Ourdh and for very good reason. Alyx looked up in surprise. Ten feet away (as far away as she could get), Edarra was lying on the planks, sobbing. Alyx went over to her and knelt down, leaning back on her heels. Above, the first sea birds of the trip—sea birds always live near land—circled and cried in a hard, hungry mew like a herd of aerial cats.

"Someone's coming," said Alyx.

"Don't care." This was Edarra on the deck, muffled. Alyx reached out and began to stroke the girl's disordered hair, braiding it with her fingers, twisting it round her wrist and slipping her hand through it and out again.

"Someone's in a fishing smack coming this way," said Alyx.

Edarra burst into tears.

"Now, now, now!" said Alyx. "Why that? Come!" and she tried to lift the girl up, but Edarra held stubbornly to the deck.

"What's the matter?" said Alyx.

"You!" cried Edarra, bouncing bolt upright. "You; you treat me like a baby."

"You are a baby," said Alyx.

"How'm I ever going to stop if you treat me like one?" shouted the girl. Alyx got up and padded over to her new clothes, her face thoughtful. She slipped into a sleeveless black shift and belted it; it came to just above the knee. Then she took a comb from the pocket and began to comb out her straight, silky black hair. "I was remembering," she said.

"What?" said Edarra.

"Things."

"Don't make fun of me." Alyx stood for a moment, one blue-green earring on her ear and the other in her fingers. She smiled at the innocence of this red-headed daughter of the wickedest city on earth; she saw her own youth over again (though she had been unnaturally knowing almost from birth), and so she smiled, with rare sweetness.

"I'll tell you," she whispered conspiratorially, dropping to her knees beside Edarra, "I was remembering a man."

"Oh!" said Edarra.

"I remembered," said Alyx, "one week in spring when the night sky above Ourdh was hung as brilliantly with stars as the jewelers' trays on the Street of a Thousand Follies. Ah! what a man. A big Northman with hair like yours and a gold-red beard—God, what a beard!—Fafnir—no, Fafh—well, something ridiculous. But he was far from ridiculous. He was amazing."

Edarra said nothing, rapt.

"He was strong," said Alyx, laughing, "and hairy, beautifully hairy. And willful! I said to him, 'Man, if you must follow your eyes into every whorehouse—' And we fought! At a place called the Silver Fish. Overturned tables. What a fuss! And a week later," (she shrugged ruefully) "gone. There it is. And I can't even remember his name."

"Is that sad?" said Edarra.

"I don't think so," said Alyx. "After all, I remember his beard," and she smiled wickedly. "There's a man in that boat," she said, "and that boat comes from a fishing village of maybe ten, maybe twelve families. That symbol painted on the side of the boat—I can make it out; perhaps you can't; it's a red cross on a blue circle—indicates a single man. Now the chances of there being two single men between the ages of eighteen and forty in a village of twelve families is not—"

"A man!" exploded Edarra. "That's why you're primping like a hen. Can I wear your clothes? Mine are full of salt," and she buried herself in the piled wearables on deck, humming, dragged out a brush and began to brush her hair. She lay flat on her stomach, catching her underlip between her teeth, saying over and over "Oh—oh—oh—"

"Look here," said Alyx, back at the rudder, "before you get too free, let me tell you: there are rules."

"I'm going to wear this white thing," said Edarra busily.

"Married men are not considered proper. It's too acquisitive. If I know you, you'll want to get married inside three weeks, but you must remember—"

"My shoes don't fit!" wailed Edarra, hopping about with one shoe on and one off.

"Horrid," said Alyx briefly.

"My feet have gotten bigger," said Edarra, plumping down beside her. "Do you think they spread when I go barefoot? Do you think that's ladylike? Do you think—"

"For the sake of peace, be quiet!" said Alyx. Her whole attention was taken up by what was far off on the sea; she nudged Edarra and the girl sat still, only emitting little explosions of breath as she tried to fit her feet into her old shoes. At last she gave up and sat—quite motionless—with her hands in her lap.

"There's only one man there," said Alyx.

"He's probably too young for you." (Alyx's mouth twitched.)

"Well?" added Edarra plaintively.

"Well what?"

"Well," said Edarra, embarrassed, "I hope you don't mind."

"Oh! I don't mind," said Alyx.

"I suppose," said Edarra helpfully, "that it'll be dull for you, won't it?"

"I can find some old grandfather," said Alyx.

Edarra blushed.

"And I can always cook," added the pick-lock.

"You must be a *good* cook."

"I am."

"That's nice. You remind me of a cat we once had, a very fierce, black, female cat who was a very good mother," (she choked and continued hurriedly) "she was a ripping fighter, too, and we just couldn't keep her in the house whenever she—uh—"

"Yes?" said Alyx.

"Wanted to get out," said Edarra feebly. She giggled. "And she always came back pr—I mean—"

"Yes?"

"She was a popular cat."

"Ah," said Alyx, "but old, no doubt."

"Yes," said Edarra unhappily. "Look here," she added quickly, "I hope you understand that I like you and I esteem you and it's not that I want to cut you out, but I *am* younger and you can't expect—" Alyx raised one hand. She was laughing. Her hair blew about her face like a skein of black silk. Her gray eyes glowed.

"Great are the ways of Yp," she said, "and some men prefer the ways of experience. Very odd of them, no doubt, but lucky for some of us. I have been told—but never mind. Infatuated men are bad judges. Besides, maid, if you look out across the water you will see a ship much closer than it was before, and in that ship a young man. Such is life. But if you look more carefully and shade your red, red brows, you will perceive—" and here she poked Edarra with her toe—"that surprise and mercy share the world between them. Yp is generous." She tweaked Edarra by the nose.

"Praise God, maid, there be two of them!"

So they waved, Edarra scarcely restraining herself from jumping into the sea and swimming to the other craft, Alyx with full sweeps of the arm, standing both at the stern of their stolen fishing boat on that late summer's morning while the fishermen in the other boat wondered—and disbelieved—and then believed—while behind all rose the green land in the distance and the sky was blue as blue. Perhaps it was the thought of her fifteen hundred ounces of gold stowed belowdecks, or perhaps it was an intimation of the extraordinary future, or perhaps it was only her own queer nature, but in the sunlight Alyx's eyes had a strange look, like those of Loh, the first woman, who had kept her own counsel at the very moment of creation, only looking about her with an immediate, intense, serpentine curiosity, already planning secret plans and guessing at who knows what unguessable mysteries . .

("You old villain!" whispered Edarra. "We made it!")

But that's another story.

⚔

In his sword-and-sorcery cycle—Return of Nevèrÿon, eleven stories and one novel published from 1979 to 1987—Samuel R. Delany (1942–) uses language and style to intentionally distance his tales from what he sees as the "adjective heavy, exclamatory diction that mingles myriad archaisms with other syntactical distortions meant to signal the antique: the essence of the pulps." As David G. Hartwell has said, the Nevèrÿon cycle is "a masterpiece of imagination and stylistic innovation." Of the stories collected in Tales of Nevèrÿon, *Delany told me "The Tale of Potters and Dragons" is the one that teachers and students/readers seem to find of interest and like the most. I feel "The Tale of Dragons and Dreamers" best illustrates his use of S&S.*

THE TALE OF DRAGONS AND DREAMERS

Samuel R. Delany

But there is negative work to be carried out first: we must rid ourselves of a whole mass of notions, each of which, in its own way, diversifies the theme of continuity. They may not have a very rigorous conceptual structure, but they have a very precise function. Take the notion of tradition: it is intended to give a special temporal status to a group of phenomena that are both successive and identical (or at least similar); it makes it possible to rethink the dispersion of history in the form of the same; it allows a reduction of the difference proper to every beginning, in order to pursue without discontinuity the endless search for origin . . .

—Michel Foucault, *The Archeology of Knowledge*

1

Wide wings dragged on stone, scales a polychrome glister with seven greens. The bony gum yawned above the iron rail. The left eye, fist-sized and packed with stained foils, did not blink its transverse lid. A stench of halides; a bilious hiss.

"But why have you penned it up in here?"

"Do you think the creature unhappy, my Vizerine? Ill-fed, perhaps? Poorly exercised—less well cared for than it would be at Ellamon?"

"How could anyone know?" But Myrgot's chin was down, her lower lip out, and her thin hands joined tightly before the lap of her shift.

"I know *you*, my dear. You hold it against me that I should want some of the "fable" that has accrued to these beasts to redound on me. But you know; I went to great expense (and I don't just mean the bribes, the gifts, the money) to bring it here . . . Do you know what a dragon is? For me? Let me tell you, Myrgot: it is an expression of some natural sensibility that cannot be explained by pragmatics, that cannot survive unless someone is hugely generous before it. These beasts are a sport. If Olin—yes, Mad Olin, and it may have been the highest manifestation of her madness—had not decided, on a tour through the mountain holds, the creatures were beautiful, we wouldn't have them today. You know the story? She came upon a bunch of brigands slaughtering a nest of them and sent her troops to slaughter the brigands. Everyone in the mountains had seen the wings, but no one was sure the creatures could actually fly till two years after Olin put them under her protection and the grooms devised their special training programs that allowed the beasts to soar. And their flights, though lovely, are short and rare. The creatures are not survival oriented—unless you want to see them as part of a survival relationship with the vicious little harridans who are condemned to be their riders: another of your great-great aunt's more inane institutions. Look at that skylight. The moon outside illumines it now. But the expense I have gone to in order to arrive at those precise green panes! Full sunlight causes the creature's eyes to inflame, putting it in great discomfort. They can only fly a few hundred yards or so, perhaps a mile with the most propitious drafts, and unless they land on the most propitious ledge, they cannot take off again. Since they cannot elevate from flat land, once set down in an ordinary forest, say, they are doomed. In the wild, many live their entire lives without flying, which, given how easily their wing membranes tear through or become injured, is understandable. They are egg-laying creatures who know nothing of physical intimacy. Indeed, they are much more tractable when kept from their fellows. This one is bigger, stronger, and generally healthier than any you'll find in the Falthas—in or out of the Ellamon corrals. Listen to her trumpet her joy over her present state!"

Obligingly, the lizard turned on her splay claws, dragging the chain from her iron collar, threw back her bony head beneath the tower's many lamps, and hissed—not a trumpet, the Vizerine reflected, whatever young Strethi might think. "My dear, why don't you just turn it loose?"

"Why don't you just have me turn loose the poor wretch chained in the dungeon?" At the Vizerine's bitter glance, the Suzeraine chuckled. "No, Myrgot. True, I could haul on those chains there, which would pull back the wood and copper partitions you see on the other side of the pen. My beast could then waddle to the ledge and soar out from our tower here, onto the night. (Note the scenes of hunting I have had the finest craftsmen beat into the metal work. Myself, I think they're stunning.) But such a creature as this in a landscape like the one about here could take only a single flight—for, really, without a rider they're simply too stupid to turn around and come back to where they took off. And I am not a twelve-year-old girl; what's more, I couldn't bear to have one about the castle who could ride the creature aloft when I am too old and too heavy." (The dragon was still hissing.) "No, I could only conceive of turning it loose if my whole world were destroyed and—indeed—my next act would be to cast myself down from that same ledge to the stones!"

"My Suzeraine, I much preferred you as a wild-haired, horse-proud seventeen-year-old. You were beautiful and heartless . . . in some ways rather a bore. But you have grown up into another over-refined soul of the sort our aristocracy is so good at producing and which produces so little itself save ways to spend unconscionable amounts on castles, clothes, and complex towers to keep comfortable impossible beasts. You remind me of a cousin of mine—the Baron Inige? Yet what I loved about you, when you were a wholly ungracious provincial heir whom I had just brought to court, was simply that that was what I could never imagine you."

"Oh, I remember what you loved about me! And I remember your cousin too—though it's been years since I've seen him. Among those pompous and self-important dukes and earls, though I doubt he liked me any better than the rest did, I recall a few times when he went out of his way to be kind . . . I'm sure I didn't deserve it. How is Curly?"

"Killed himself three years ago." The Vizerine shook her head. "His passion, you may recall, was flowers—which I'm afraid totally took over in the last years. As I understand the story—for I wasn't there when it happened—he'd been putting together another collection of particularly rare weeds. One he was after apparently turned out to be the wrong color, or couldn't be found, or didn't exist. The next day his servants discovered him in the arboretum, his mouth crammed with the white blossoms of some deadly mountain flower." Myrgot shuddered. "Which I've always suspected is where such passions as his—and yours—are too likely to lead, given the flow of our lives, the tenor of our times."

The Suzeraine laughed, adjusting the collar of his rich robe with his forefinger. (The Vizerine noted that the blue eyes were much paler in the prematurely lined face than she remembered; and the boyish nailbiting had passed on, in the man, to such grotesque extents that each of his long fingers now ended in a perfect pitted wound.) Two slaves at the door, their own collars covered with heavily jeweled neckpieces, stepped forward to help him, as they had long since been instructed, while the Suzeraine's hand fell again into the robe's folds, the adjustment completed. The slaves stepped back. The Suzeraine, oblivious, and the Vizerine, feigning obliviousness and wondering if the Suzeraine's obliviousness were feigned or real, strolled through the low stone arch between them to the uneven steps circling down the tower.

"Well," said the blond lord, stepping back to let his lover of twenty years ago precede, "now we return to the less pleasant aspect of your stay here. You know, I sometimes find myself dreading any visit from the northern aristocracy. Just last week two common women stopped at my castle—one was a redhaired island woman, the other a small creature in a mask who hailed from the Western Crevasse. They were traveling together, seeking adventure and fortune. The Western Woman had once for a time worked in the Falthas, training the winged beasts and the little girls who ride them. The conversation was choice! The island woman could tell incredible tales, and was even using skins and inks to mark down her adventures. And the masked one's observations were very sharp. It was a fine evening we passed. I fed them and housed them. They entertained me munificently. I gave them useful gifts, saw them depart, and would be delighted to see either return. Now, were the stars in a different configuration, I'm sure that the poor wretch that we've got strapped in the dungeon and his little friend who escaped might have come wandering by in the same wise. But no, we have to bind one to the plank in the cellar and stake a guard out for the other . . . You really wish me to keep up the pretense to that poor mule that it is Lord Krodar, rather than you, who directs his interrogation?"

"You object?" Myrgot's hand, out to touch the damp stones at the stair's turning, came back to brush at the black braids that looped her forehead. "Once or twice I have seen you enjoy such an inquisition session with an avidity that verged on the unsettling."

"Inquisition? But this is merely questioning. The pain—at your own orders, my dear—is being kept to a minimum." (Strethi's laugh echoed down over Myrgot's shoulder, recalling for her the enthusiasm of the boy she could no longer find when she gazed full at the man.) "I have neither objection nor approbation, my Vizerine. We have him; we do with him as we will . . . Now, I can't help seeing how you gaze about at my walls, Myrgot! I must tell you, ten years ago when I had this castle built over the ruins of my parents" farm, I really thought the simple fact that all my halls had roofs would bring the aristocracy of Nevèrÿon flocking to my court. Do you know, you are my only regular visitor—at least the only one who comes out of anything other than formal necessity. And I do believe you would come to see me even if I lived in the same drafty farmhouse I did when you first met me. Amazing what we'll do out of friendship . . . The other one, Myrgot; I wonder what happened to our prisoner's little friend. They both fought like devils. Too bad the boy got away."

"We have the one I want," Myrgot said.

"At any rate, you have your reasons—your passion, for politics and intrigue. That's what comes of living most of your life in Kolhari. Here in the Avila, it's—well, it's not that different for me. You have your criticism of my passions—and I have mine of yours. Certainly I should like to be much more straightforward with the dog: make my demand and chop his head off if he didn't meet it. This endless play is not really my style. Yet I am perfectly happy to assist you in your desires. And however disparaging you are of my little pet, whose welfare is my life, I am sure there will come a time when one or another of your messengers will arrive at my walls bearing some ornate lizard harness of exquisite workmanship you have either discovered in some old storeroom or—who knows—have had specially commissioned for me by the latest and finest artisan. When it happens, I shall be immensely pleased."

And as the steps took them around and down the damp tower, the Suzeraine of Strethi slipped up beside the Vizerine to take her aging arm

2

And again small Sarg ran.

He struck back low twigs, side-stepped a wet branch clawed with moonlight, and leaped a boggy puddle. With one hand he shoved away a curtain of leaves, splattering himself face to foot with night-dew, to reveal the moonlit castle. (How many other castles had he so revealed . . .) Branches chattered to behind him.

Panting, he ducked back of a boulder. His muddy hand pawed beneath the curls like scrap brass at his neck. The hinged iron was there; and locked tight—a droplet trickled under the metal. He swatted at his hip to find his sword: the hilt was still tacky under his palm where he had not had time to clean it. The gaze with which he took in the pile of stone was not a halt in his headlong dash so much as a continuation of it, the energy propelling arms and legs momentarily diverted into eyes, ears, and all inside and behind them; then it was back in his feet; his feet pounded the shaly slope so that each footfall, even on his calloused soles, was a constellation of small pains; it was back in his arms; his arms pumped by his flanks so that his fists, brushing his sides as he jogged, heated his knuckles by friction.

A balustrade rose, blotting stars.

There would be the unlocked door (as he ran, he clawed over memories of the seven castles he had already run up to; seven side doors, all unlocked . . .); and the young barbarian, muddy to the knees and elbows, his hair at head and chest and groin matted with leaf-bits and worse, naked save the sword thonged around his hips and the slave collar locked about his neck, dashed across moonlit stubble and gravel into a tower's shadow, toward the door . . . and slowed, pulling in cool breaths of autumn air that grew hot inside him and ran from his nostrils; more air ran in.

"Halt!" from under the brand that flared high in the doorframe.

Sarg, in one of those swipes at his hip, had moved the scabbard around behind his buttock; it was possible, if the guard had not really been looking at Sarg's dash through the moonlight, for the boy to have seemed simply a naked slave. Sarg's hand was ready to grab at the hilt.

"Who's there?"

Small Sarg raised his chin, so that the iron would show. "I've come back," and thought of seven castles. "I got lost from the others, this morning. When they were out."

"Come now, say your name and rank."

"It's only Small Sarg, master—one of the slaves in the Suzeraine's labor pen. I was lost this morning—"

"Likely story!"

"—and I've just found my way back." With his chin high, Sarg walked slowly and thought: I am running, I am running . . .

"See here, boy—" The brand came forward, fifteen feet, ten, five, three . . .

I am running. And Small Sarg, looking like a filthy field slave with some thong at his waist, jerked his sword up from the scabbard (which bounced on his buttock) and with a grunt sank it into the abdomen of the guard a-glow beneath the high-held flare. The guard's mouth opened. The flare fell, rolled in the mud so that it burned now only on one side. Small Sarg leaned on the hilt, twisting—somewhere inside the guard the blade sheered upward, parting diaphragm, belly, lungs. The guard closed his eyes, drooled blood, and toppled. Small Sarg almost fell on him—till the blade sucked free. And Sarg was running again, blade out for the second guard (in four castles before there had been a second guard), who was, it seemed as Sarg swung around the stone newel and into the stairwell where his own breath was a roaring echo, not there.

He hurried up and turned into a side corridor that would take him down to the labor pen. (Seven castles, now. Were all of them designed by one architect?) He ran through the low hall, guided by that glowing spot in his mind where memory was flush with desire; around a little curve, down the steps—

"What the—?"

—and jabbed his sword into the shoulder of the guard who'd started forward (already hearing the murmur behind the wooden slats), yanking it free of flesh, the motion carrying it up and across the throat of the second guard (here there was always a second guard) who had turned, surprised; the second guard released his sword (it had only been half drawn), which fell back into its scabbard. Small Sarg hacked at the first again (who was screaming): the man fell, and Small Sarg leaped over him, while the man gurgled and flopped. But Sarg was pulling at the boards, cutting at the rope. Behind the boards and under the screams, like murmuring flies, hands and faces rustled about one another. (Seven times now they had seemed like murmuring flies.) And rope was always harder hacking than flesh. The wood, in at least two other castles, had simply splintered under his hands (under his hands, wood splintered) so that, later, he had wondered if the slaughter and the terror was really necessary.

Rope fell away.

Sarg yanked again.

The splintered gate scraped out on stone.

"You're free!" Sarg hissed into the mumbling; mumblings silenced at the word. "Go on, get out of here now!" (How many faces above their collars were clearly barbarian like his own? Memory of other labor pens, rather than what shifted and murmured before him, told him most were.) He turned and leaped bodies, took stairs at double step—while memory told him that only a handful would flee at once; another handful would take three, four, or five minutes to talk themselves into fleeing; and another would simply sit, terrified in the foul straw, and would be sitting there when the siege was over.

He dashed up stairs in the dark. (Dark stairs fell down beneath dashing feet . . .) He flung himself against the wooden door with the strip of light beneath and above it. (In two other castles the door had been locked.) It fell open. (In one castle the kitchen midden had been deserted, the fire dead.) He staggered in, blinking in firelight.

The big man in the stained apron stood up from over the cauldron, turned, frowning. Two women carrying pots stopped and stared. In the bunk beds along the midden's far wall, a red-headed kitchen boy raised himself up on one arm, blinking. Small Sarg tried to see only the collars around each neck. But what he saw as well (he had seen it before . . .) was that even here, in a lord's kitchen, where slavery was already involved in the acquisition of the most rudimentary crafts and skills, most of the faces were darker, the hair was coarser, and only the shorter of the women was clearly a barbarian like himself.

"You are free . . . !" small Sarg said, drawing himself up, dirty, blood splattered. He took a gulping breath. "The guards are gone below. The labor pens have already been turned loose. You are free . . . !"

The big cook said: "What . . . ?" and a smile, with worry flickering through, slowly overtook his face. (This one's mother, thought Small Sarg, was a barbarian: he had no doubt been gotten on her by some free northern dog.) "What are you talking about, boy? Better put that shoat-sticker down or you'll get yourself in trouble."

Small Sarg stepped forward, hands out from his sides. He glanced left at his sword. Blood trailed a line of drops on the stone below it.

Another slave with a big pot of peeled turnips in his hands strode into the room through the far archway, started for the fire rumbling behind the pot hooks, grilling spits, and chained pulleys. He glanced at Sarg, looked about at the others, stopped.

"Put it down now," the big cook repeated, coaxingly. (The slave who'd just come in, wet from perspiration, with a puzzled look started to put his turnip pot down on the stones—then gulped and hefted it back against his chest.) "Come on—"

"What do you think, I'm some berserk madman, a slave gone off my head with the pressure of the iron at my neck?" With his free hand, Sarg thumbed toward his collar. "I've fought my way in here, freed the laborers below you; you have only to go now yourselves. You're free, do you understand?"

"Now wait, boy," said the cook, his smile wary. "Freedom is not so simple a thing as that. Even if you're telling the truth, just what do you propose we're free to do? Where do you expect us to go? If we leave here, what do you expect will happen to us? We'll be taken by slavers before dawn tomorrow, more than likely. Do you want us to get lost in the swamps to the south? Or would you rather we starve to death in the mountains to the north? Put down your sword—just for a minute—and be reasonable."

The barbarian woman said, with her eyes wide and no barbarian accent at all: "Are you well, boy? Are you hungry? We can give you food: you can lie down and sleep a while if you—"

"I don't want sleep. I don't want food. I want you to understand that you're free and I want you to move. Fools, fools, don't you know that to stay slaves is to stay fools?"

"Now that sword, boy—" The big slave moved.

Small Sarg raised his blade.

The big slave stopped. "Look, youth. Use your head. We can't just—"

Footsteps; armor rattled in another room—clearly guards' sounds. (How many times now—four out of seven?—had he heard those sounds?) What happened (again) was:

"Here, boy—!" from the woman who had till now not spoken. She shifted her bowl under one arm and pointed toward the bunks.

Small Sarg sprinted toward them, sprang—into the one below the kitchen boy's. As he sprang, his sword point caught the wooden support beam, jarred his arm full hard; the sword fell clanking on the stone floor. As Sarg turned to see it, the kitchen boy in the bunk above flung down a blanket. Sarg collapsed in the straw, kicked rough cloth (it was stiff at one end as though something had spilled on it and dried) down over his leg, and pulled it up over his head at the same time. Just before the blanket edge cut away the firelit chamber, Sarg saw the big slave pull off his stained apron (underneath the man was naked as Sarg) to fling it across the floor to where it settled, like a stained sail, over Sarg's fallen weapon. (And the other slave had somehow managed to set his turnip pot down directly over those blood drops.) Under the blanketing dark, he heard the guard rush in.

"All right, you! A horde of bandits—probably escaped slaves—have stormed the lower floors. They've already taken the labor pen—turned loose every cursed dog in them." (Small Sarg shivered and grinned: how many times now, three, or seven, or seventeen, had he watched slaves suddenly think with one mind, move together like the leaves on a branch before a single breeze!) More footsteps. Beneath the blanket, Small Sarg envisioned a second guard running in to collide with the first, shouting (over the first's shoulder?): "Any of you kitchen scum caught aiding and abetting these invading lizards will be hung up by the heels and whipped till the flesh falls from your backs—and you know we mean it. There must be fifty of them or more to have gotten in like that! And don't think they won't slaughter you as soon as they would us!"

The pair of footsteps retreated; there was silence for a drawn breath.

Then bare feet were rushing quickly toward his bunk.

Small Sarg pushed back the blanket. The big slave was just snatching up his apron. The woman picked up the sword and thrust it at Sarg.

"All right," said the big slave, "we're running."

"Take your sword," the woman said. "And good luck to you, boy."

They ran—the redheaded kitchen boy dropped down before Small Sarg's bunk and took off around the kitchen table after them. Sarg vaulted now, and landed (running), his feet continuing the dash that had brought him into the castle. The slaves crowded out the wooden door through which Small Sarg had entered. Small Sarg ran out through the arch by which the guards had most probably left.

Three guards stood in the anteroom, conferring. One looked around and said, "Hey, what are—"

A second one who turned and just happened to be a little nearer took Small Sarg's sword in his belly; it tore loose out his side, so that the guard, surprised, fell in the pile of his splatting innards. Sarg struck another's bare thigh—cutting deep—and then the arm of still another (his blade grated bone). The other ran, trailing a bass howl: "They've come! They're coming in here, now! Help! They're breaking in—" breaking to tenor in some other corridor.

Small Sarg ran, and a woman, starting into the hallway from the right, saw him and darted back. But there was a stairwell to his left; he ran up it. He ran, up the cleanly hewn stone, thinking of a tower with spiral steps, that went on and on and on, opening on some high, moonlit parapet. After one turn, the stairs stopped. Light glimmered from dozens of lamps, some on ornate stands, some hanging from intricate chains.

A thick, patterned carpet cushioned the one muddy foot he had put across the sill. Sarg crouched, his sword out from his hip, and brought his other foot away from the cool stone behind.

The man at the great table looked up, frowned—a slave, but his collar was covered by a wide neckpiece of heavy white cloth sewn about with chunks of tourmaline and jade. He was very thin, very lined, and bald. (In how many castles had Sarg seen slaves who wore their collars covered so? Six, now? All seven?) "What are you doing here, boy . . . ?" The slave pushed his chair back, the metal balls on the forelegs furrowing the rug.

Small Sarg said: "You're free . . . "

Another slave in a similar collar-cover turned on the ladder where she was placing piles of parchment on a high shelf stuffed with manuscripts. She took a step down the ladder, halted. Another youth (same covered collar), with double pointers against a great globe in the corner, looked perfectly terrified—and was probably the younger brother of the kitchen boy, from his bright hair. (See only the collars, Small Sarg thought. But with jeweled and damasked neckpieces, it was hard, very hard.) The bald slave at the table, with the look of a tired man, said: "You don't belong here, you know. And you are in great danger." The slave, a wrinkled forty, had the fallen pectorals of the quickly aging.

"You're free!" Small Sarg croaked.

"And you are a very naïve and presumptuous little barbarian. How many times have I had this conversation—four? Five? At least six? You are here to free us of the iron collars." The man dug a forefinger beneath the silk and stones to drag up, on his bony neck, the iron band beneath. "Just so you'll see it's there. Did you know that our collars are much heavier than yours?" He released the iron; the same brown forefinger hooked up the jeweled neckpiece—almost a bib—which sagged and wrinkled up, once pulled from its carefully arranged position. "These add far more weight to the neck than the circle of iron they cover." (Small Sarg thought: Though I stand here, still as stone, I am running, running . . .) "We make this castle function, boy—at a level of efficiency that, believe me, is felt in the labor pens as much as in the audience chambers where our lord and owner entertains fellow nobles. You think you are rampaging through the castle, effecting your own eleemosynary manumissions. What you are doing is killing free men and making the lives of slaves more miserable than, of necessity, they already are. If slavery is a disease and a rash on the flesh of Nevèrÿon—" (I am running, like an eagle caught up in the wind, like a snake sliding down a gravel slope . . .) "—your own actions turn an ugly eruption into a fatal infection. You free the labor pens into a world where, at least in the cities and the larger towns, a wage-earning populace, many of them, is worse off than here. And an urban merchant class can only absorb a fraction of the skills of the middle level slaves you turn loose from the middens and smithies. The Child Empress herself has many times declared that she is opposed to the institution of indenture, and the natural drift of our nation is away from slave labor anyway—so that all your efforts do is cause restrictions to become tighter in those areas where the institution would naturally die out of its own accord in a decade or so. Have you considered: your efforts may even be prolonging the institution you would abolish." (Running, Small Sarg thought, rushing, fleeing, dashing . . .) "But the simple truth is that the particular skills we—the ones who must cover our collars in jewels—master to run such a complex house as an aristocrat's castle are just not needed by the growing urban class. Come around here, boy, and look for yourself." The bald slave pushed his chair back even further and gestured for Small Sarg to approach. "Yes. Come, see."

Small Sarg stepped, slowly and carefully, across the carpet. (I am running, he thought; flesh tingled at the backs of his knees, the small of his back. Every muscle, in its attenuated motion, was geared to some coherent end that, in the pursuit of it, had become almost invisible within its own glare and nimbus.) Sarg walked around the table's edge.

From a series of holes in the downward lip hung a number of heavy cords, each with a metal loop at the end. (Small Sarg thought: In one castle they had simple handles of wood tied to them; in another the handles were cast from bright metal set with red and green gems, more ornate than the jeweled collars of the slaves who worked them.) "From this room," explained the slave, "we can control the entire castle—really, it represents far more control, even, than that of the Suzeraine who owns all you see, including us. If I pulled this cord here, a bell would ring in the linen room and summon the slave working there; if I pulled it twice, that slave would come with linen for his lordship's chamber, which we would then inspect before sending it on to be spread. Three rings, and the slave would come bearing sheets for our own use—and they are every bit as elegant, believe me, as the ones for his lordship. One tug on this cord here and wine and food would be brought for his lordship . . . at least if the kitchen staff is still functioning. Three rings, and a feast can be brought for us, here in these very rooms, that would rival any indulged by his lordship. A bright lad like you, I'm sure, could learn the strings to pull very easily. Here, watch out for your blade and come stand beside me. That's right. Now give that cord there a quick, firm tug and just see what happens. No, don't be afraid. Just reach out and pull it. Once, mind you—not twice or three times. That means something else entirely. Go ahead . . . "

Sarg moved his hand out slowly, looking at his muddy, bloody fingers. (Small Sarg thought: Though it may be a different cord in each castle, it is always a single tug! My hand, with each airy inch, feels like it is running, running to hook the ring . . .)

" . . . with only a little training," went on the bald slave, smiling, "a smart and ambitious boy like you could easily become one of us. From here, you would wield more power within these walls than the Suzeraine himself. And such power as that is not to be—"

Then Small Sarg whirled (no, he had never released his sword)—to shove his steel into the loose belly. The man half-stood, with open mouth, then fell back, gargling. Blood spurted, hit the table, ran down the cords. "You fool . . . !" the bald man managed, trying now to grasp one handle.

Small Sarg, with his dirty hand, knocked the bald man's clean one away. The chair overturned and the bald man curled and uncurled on the darkening carpet. There was blood on his collar piece now.

"You think I am such a fool that I don't know you can call guards in here as easily as food-bearers and house-cleaners?" Small Sarg looked at the woman on the ladder, the boy at the globe. "I do not like to kill slaves. But I do not like people who plot to kill me—especially such a foolish plot. Now: are the rest of you such fools that you cannot understand what it means when I say, "You're free"?"

Parchments slipped from the shelf, unrolling on the floor, as the woman scurried down the ladder. The boy fled across the room, leaving a slowly turning sphere. Then both were into the arched stairwell from which Small Sarg had come. Sarg hopped over the fallen slave and ran into the doorway through which (in two other castles) guards, at the (single) tug of a cord, had come swarming:

a short hall, more steps, another chamber. Long and short swords hung on the wooden wall. Leather shields with colored fringes leaned against the stone one. A helmet lay on the floor in the corner near a stack of greaves. But there were no guards. (Till now, in the second castle only, there had been no guards.) I am free, thought Small Sarg, once again I am free, running, running through stone arches, down tapestried stairs, across dripping halls, up narrow corridors, a-dash through time and possibility. (Somewhere in the castle people were screaming.) Now I am free to free my master!

Somewhere, doors clashed. Other doors, nearer, clashed. Then the chamber doors swung back in firelight. The Suzeraine strode through, tugging them to behind him. "Very well—" (Clash!) "—we can get on with our little session." He reached up to adjust his collar and two slaves in jeweled collar pieces by the door (they were oiled, pale, strong men with little wires sewn around the backs of their ears; besides the collar pieces they wore only leather clouts) stepped forward to take his cloak. "Has he been given any food or drink?"

The torturer snored on the bench, knees wide, one hand hanging, calloused knuckles the color of stone, one on his knee, the fingers smeared red here and there brown; his head lolled on the wall.

"I asked: Has he had anything to—Bah!" This to the slave folding his cloak by the door: 'that man is fine for stripping the flesh from the backs of your disobedient brothers. But for anything more subtle . . . well, we'll let him sleep." The Suzeraine, who now wore only a leather kilt and very thick-soled sandals (the floor of this chamber sometimes became very messy), walked to the slant board from which hung chains and ropes and against which leaned pokers and pincers. On a table beside the plank were several basins—in one lay a rag which had already turned the water pink. Within the furnace, which took up most of one wall (a ragged canvas curtain hung beside it), a log broke; on the opposite wall the shadow of the grate momentarily darkened and flickered. "How are you feeling?" the Suzeraine asked perfunctorily. "A little better? That's good. Perhaps you enjoy the return of even that bit of good feeling enough to answer my questions accurately and properly. I can't really impress upon you enough how concerned my master is for the answers. He is a very hard taskman, you know—that is, if you know him at all. Krodar wants—but then, we need not sully such an august name with the fetid vapors of this place. The stink of the iron that binds you to that board . . . I remember a poor, guilty soul lying on the plank as you lie now, demanding of me: 'Don't you even wash the bits of flesh from the last victim off the chains and manacles before you bind up the new one?'" The Suzeraine chuckled: "'Why should I?' was my answer. True, it makes the place reek. But that stench is a very good reminder—don't you feel it?—of the mortality that is, after all, our only real playing piece in this game of time, of pain." The Suzeraine looked up from the bloody basin: a heavy arm, a blocky bicep, corded with high veins, banded at the joint with thin ligament; a jaw in which a muscle quivered under a snarl of patchy beard, here gray, there black, at another place ripped from reddened skin, at still another cut by an old scar; a massive thigh down which sweat trickled, upsetting a dozen other droplets caught in that thigh's coarse hairs, till here a link, there a cord, and elsewhere a rope, dammed it. Sweat crawled under, or overflowed, the dams. "Tell me, Gorgik, have you ever been employed by a certain southern lord, a Lord Aldamir, whose hold is in the Garth Peninsula, only a stone's throw from the Vygernangx Monastery, to act as a messenger between his Lordship and certain weavers, jewelers, potters, and iron mongers in port Kolhari?"

"I have . . . have never . . . " The chest tried to rise under a metal band that would have cramped the breath of a smaller man than Gorgik. " . . . never set foot within the precinct of Garth. Never, I tell you . . . I have told you . . . "

"And yet—" The Suzeraine, pulling the wet rag from its bowl where it dripped a cherry smear on the table, turned to the furnace. He wound the rag about one hand, picked up one of the irons sticking from the furnace rack, drew it out to examine its tip: an ashen rose. "—for reasons you still have not explained to my satisfaction, you wear, on a chain around your neck—" The rose, already dimmer, lowered over Gorgik's chest; the chest hair had been singed in places, adding to the room's stink. "—that." The rose clicked the metal disk that lay on Gorgik's sternum. 'these navigational scales, the map etched there, the grid of stars that turns over it and the designs etched around it all speak of its origin in—"

The chest suddenly heaved; Gorgik gave up some sound that tore in the cartilages of his throat.

"Is that getting warm?" The Suzeraine lifted the poker tip. An off-center scorch-mark marred the astrolabe's verdigris. "I was saying: the workmanship is clearly from the south. If you haven't spent time there, why else would you be wearing it?" Then the Suzeraine pressed the poker tip to Gorgik's thigh. Gorgik screamed. The Suzeraine, after a second or two, removed the poker from the blistering mark (amidst the cluster of marks, bubbled, yellow, some crusted over by now). "Let me repeat something to you, Gorgik, about the rules of the game we're playing: the game of time and pain. I said this to you before we began. I say it to you again, but the context of several hours" experience may reweight its meaning for you—and before I repeat it, let me tell you that I shall, as I told you before, eventually repeat it yet again: When the pains are small, in this game, then we make the time very, very long. Little pains, spaced out over the seconds, the minutes—no more than a minute between each—for days on end. Days and days. You have no idea how much I enjoy the prospect. The timing, the ingenuity, the silent comparisons between your responses and the responses of the many, many others I have had the pleasure to work with—that is all my satisfaction. Remember this: on the simplest and most basic level, the infliction of these little torments gives me far more pleasure than would your revealing the information that is their occasion. So if you want to get back at me, to thwart me in some way, to cut short my real pleasure in all of this, perhaps you had best—"

"I told you! I've answered your questions! I've answered them and answered them truthfully! I have never set foot in the Garth! The astrolabe was a gift to me when I was practically a child. I cannot even recall the circumstances under which I received it. Some noble man or woman presented it to me on a whim at some castle or other that I stayed at." (The Suzeraine replaced the poker on the furnace rack and turned to a case, hanging on the stone wall, of small polished knives.) "I am a man who has stayed in many castles, many hovels; I have slept under bridges in the cities, in fine inns and old alleys. I have rested for the night in fields and forests. And I do not mark my history the way you do, cataloguing the gifts and graces I have been lucky enough to—" Gorgik drew a sharp breath.

"The flesh between the fingers—terribly sensitive." The Suzeraine lifted the tiny knife, where a blood drop crawled along the cutting edge. "As is the skin between the toes, on even the most calloused feet. I've known men—not to mention women—who remained staunch under hot pokers and burning pincers who, as soon as I started to make the few smallest cuts in the flesh between the fingers and toes (really, no more than a dozen or so), became astonishingly cooperative. I'm quite serious." He put down the blade on the table edge, picked up the towel from the basin and squeezed; reddened water rilled between his fingers into the bowl. The Suzeraine swabbed at the narrow tongue of blood that moved down the plank below Gorgik's massive (twitching a little now) hand. 'the thing wrong with having you slanted like this, head up and feet down, is that even the most conscientious of us finds himself concentrating more on your face, chest, and stomach than, say, on your feet, ankles and knees. Some exquisite feelings may be produced in the knee: a tiny nail, a small mallet . . . First I shall make a few more cuts. Then I shall wake our friend snoring against the wall. (You scream and he still sleeps! Isn't it amazing? But then, he's had so much of this!) We shall reverse the direction of the slant—head down, feet up—so that we can spread our efforts out more evenly over the arena of your flesh." In another basin, of yellow liquid, another cloth was submerged. The Suzeraine pulled the cloth out and spread it, dripping. "A little vinegar . . . "

Gorgik's head twisted in the clamp across his forehead that had already rubbed to blood at both temples as the Suzeraine laid the cloth across his face.

"A little salt. (Myself, I've always felt that four or five small pains, each of which alone would be no more than a nuisance, when applied all together can be far more effective than a single great one.)" The Suzeraine took up the sponge from the coarse crystals heaped in a third basin (crystals clung, glittering, to the brain-shape) and pressed it against Gorgik's scorched and fresh-blistered thigh. "Now the knife again . . . "

Somewhere, doors clashed.

Gorgik coughed hoarsely and repeatedly under the cloth. Frayed threads dribbled vinegar down his chest. The cough broke into another scream, as another bloody tongue licked over the first.

Other doors, nearer, clashed.

One of the slaves with the wire sewn in his ears turned to look over his shoulder.

The Suzeraine paused in sponging off the knife.

On his bench, without ceasing his snore, the torturer knuckled clumsily at his nose.

The chamber door swung back, grating. Small Sarg ran in, leaped on the wooden top of a cage bolted to the wall (that could only have held a human being squeezed in a very unnatural position), and shouted: "All who are slaves here are now free!"

The Suzeraine turned around with an odd expression. He said: "Oh, not again! Really, this is the last time!" He stepped from the table, his shadow momentarily falling across the vinegar rag twisted on Gorgik's face. He moved the canvas hanging aside (furnace light lit faint stairs rising), stepped behind it; the ragged canvas swung to—there was a small, final clash of bolt and hasp.

Small Sarg was about to leap after him, but the torturer suddenly opened his bloodshot eyes, the forehead below his bald skull wrinkled; he lumbered up, roaring.

"Are you free or slave?" Small Sarg shrieked, sword out.

The torturer wore a wide leather neck collar, set about with studs of rough metal, a sign (Small Sarg thought; and he had thought it before) that, if any sign could or should indicate a state somewhere between slavery and freedom, would be it. "Tell me," Small Sarg shrieked again, as the man, eyes bright with apprehension, body sluggish with sleep, lurched forward, "are you slave or free?" (In three castles the studded leather had hidden the bare neck of a free man; in two, the iron collar.) When the torturer seized the edge of the plank where Gorgik was bound—only to steady himself, and yet . . . —Sarg leaped, bringing his sword down. Studded leather cuffing the torturer's forearm deflected the blade; but the same sleepy lurch threw the hulking barbarian (for despite his shaved head, the torturer's sharp features and gold skin spoke as pure a southern origin as Sarg's own) to the right; the blade, aimed only to wound a shoulder, plunged into flesh at the bronze-haired solar plexus.

The man's fleshy arms locked around the boy's hard shoulders, joining them in an embrace lubricated with blood. The torturer's face, an inch before Sarg's, seemed to explode in rage, pain, and astonishment. Then the head fell back, eyes opened, mouth gaping. (The torturer's teeth and breath were bad, very bad; this was the first time Small Sarg had ever actually killed a torturer.) The grip relaxed around Sarg's back; the man fell; Sarg staggered, his sword still gripped in one hand, wiping at the blood that spurted high as his chin with the other. "You're free . . . !" Sarg called over his shoulder; the sword came loose from the corpse.

The door slaves, however, were gone. (In two castles, they had gone seeking their own escape; in one, they had come back with guards . . .) Small Sarg turned toward the slanted plank, pulled the rag away from Gorgik's rough beard, flung it to the floor. "Master . . . !"

"So, you are . . . here—again—to . . . free me!"

"I have followed your orders, Master; I have freed every slave I encountered on my way . . . " Suddenly Small Sarg turned back to the corpse. On the torturer's hand-wide belt, among the gnarled studs, was a hook and from the hook hung a clutch of small instruments. Small Sarg searched for the key among them, came up with it. It was simply a metal bar with a handle on one end and a flat side at the other. Sarg ducked behind the board and began twisting the key in locks. On the upper side of the plank, chains fell away and clamps bounced loose. Planks squeaked beneath flexing muscles.

Sarg came up as the last leg clamp swung away from Gorgik's ankle (leaving dark indentations) and the man's great foot hit the floor. Gorgik stood, kneading one shoulder; he pushed again and again at his flank with the heel of one hand. A grin broke his beard. "It's good to see you, boy. For a while I didn't know if I would or not. The talk was all of small pains and long times."

"What did they want from you—this time?" Sarg took the key and reached around behind his own neck, fitted the key in the lock, turned it (for these were barbaric times; that fabled man, named Belham, who had invented the lock and key, had only made one, and no one had yet thought to vary them: different keys for different locks was a refinement not to come for a thousand years), unhinged his collar, and stood, holding it in his soiled hands.

"This time it was some nonsense about working as a messenger in the south—your part of the country." Gorgik took the collar, raised it to his own neck, closed it with a clink. "When you're under the hands of a torturer, with all the names and days and questions, you lose your grip on your own memory. Everything he says sounds vaguely familiar, as if something like it might have once occurred. And even the things you once were sure of lose their patina of reality." A bit of Gorgik's hair had caught in the lock. With a finger, he yanked it loose—at a lull in the furnace's crackling, you could hear hair tear. "Why should I ever go to the Garth? I've avoided it so long I can no longer remember my reasons." Gorgik lifted the bronze disk from his chest and frowned at it. "Because of this, he assumed I must have been there. Some noble gave this to me, how many years ago now? I don't even recall if it was a man or a woman, or what the occasion was." He snorted and let the disk fall. "For a moment I thought they'd melt it into my chest with their cursed pokers." Gorgik looked around, stepped across gory stone. "Well, little master, you've proved yourself once more; and yet once more I suppose it's time to go." He picked up a broad sword leaning against the wall among a pile of weapons, frowned at the edge, scraped at it with the blunt of his thumb. "This will do."

Sarg, stepping over the torturer's body, suddenly bent, hooked a finger under the studded collar, and pulled it down. "Just checking on this one, hey, Gorgik?" The neck, beneath the leather, was iron bound.

"Checking what, little master?" Gorgik looked up from his blade.

"Nothing. Come on, Gorgik."

The big man's step held the ghost of a limp; Small Sarg noted it and beat the worry from his mind. The walk would grow steadier and steadier. (It had before.) "Now we must fight our way out of here and flee this crumbling pile."

"I'm ready for it, little master."

"Gorgik?"

"Yes, master?"

"The one who got away . . . ?"

"The one who was torturing me with his stupid questions?" Gorgik stepped to the furnace's edge, pulled aside the hanging. The door behind it, when he jiggled its rope handle, was immobile and looked to be a plank too thick to batter in. He let the curtain fall again. And the other doors, anyway, stood open.

"Who was he, Gorgik?"

The tall man made a snorting sound. "We have our campaign, little master—to free slaves and end the institution's inequities. The lords of Nevèrÿon have their campaign, their intrigues, their schemes and whims. What you and I know, or should know by now, is how little our and their campaigns actually touch . . . though in place after place they come close enough so that no man or woman can slip between without encounter, if not injury."

"I do not understand . . . "

Gorgik laughed, loud as the fire. "That's because I am the slave that I am and you are the master you are." And he was beside Sarg and past him; Small Sarg, behind him, ran.

3

The women shrieked—most of them. Gorgik, below swinging lamps, turned with raised sword to see one of the silent ones crouching against the wall beside a stool—an old woman, most certainly used to the jeweled collar cover, though hers had come off somewhere. There was only iron at her neck now. Her hair was in thin black braids, clearly dyed, and looping her brown forehead. Her eyes caught Gorgik's and perched on his gaze like some terrified creature's, guarding infinite secrets. For a moment he felt an urge, though it did not quite rise clear enough to take words, to question them. Then, in the confusion, a lamp chain broke; burning oil spilled. Guards and slaves and servants ran through a growing welter of flame. The woman was gone. And Gorgik turned, flailing, taking with him only her image. Somehow the castle had (again) been unable to conceive of its own fall at the hands of a naked man—or boy—and had, between chaos and rumor, collapsed into mayhem before the ten, the fifty, the hundred-fifty brigands who had stormed her. Slaves with weapons, guards with pot-tops and farm implements, paid servants carrying mysterious packages either for safety or looting, dashed there and here, all seeming as likely to be taken for foe as friend. Gorgik shouldered against one door; it splintered, swung out, and he was through—smoke trickled after him. He ducked across littered stone, following his shadow flickering with back light, darted through another door that was open.

Silver splattered his eyes. He was outside; moonlight splintered through the low leaves of the catalpa above him. He turned, both to see where he'd been and if he were followed, when a figure already clear in the moon, hissed, "Gorgik!" above the screaming inside.

"Hey, little master!" Gorgik laughed and jogged across the rock.

Small Sarg seized Gorgik's arm. "Come on, Master! Let's get out of here. We've done what we can, haven't we?"

Gorgik nodded and, together they turned to plunge into the swampy forests of Strethi.

Making their way beneath branches and over mud, with silver spills shafting the mists, Small Sarg and Gorgik came, in the humid autumn night, to a stream, a clearing, a scarp—where two women sat at the white ashes of a recent fire, talking softly. And because these were primitive times when certain conversational formalities had not yet grown up to contour discourse among strangers, certain subjects that more civilized times might have banished from the evening were here brought quickly to the fore.

"I see a bruised and tired slave of middle age," said the woman who wore a mask and who had given her name as Raven. With ankles crossed before the moonlit ash, she sat with her arms folded on her raised knees. "From that, one assumes that the youngster is the owner."

"But the boy," added the redhead kneeling beside her, who had given her name as Norema, "is a barbarian, and in this time and place it is the southern barbarians who, when they come this far north, usually end up slaves. The older, for all his bruises, has the bearing of a Kolhari man, whom you'd expect to be the owner."

Gorgik, sitting with one arm over one knee, said: "We are both free men. For the boy the collar is symbolic—of our mutual affection, our mutual protection. For myself, it is sexual—a necessary part in the pattern that allows both action and orgasm to manifest themselves within the single circle of desire. For neither of us is its meaning social, save that it shocks, offends, or deceives."

Small Sarg, also crosslegged but with his shoulders hunched, his elbows pressed to his sides, and his fists on the ground, added, "My master and I are free."

The masked Raven gave a shrill bark that it took seconds to recognize as laughter: "You both claim to be free, yet one of you bears the title 'master' and wears a slave collar at the same time? Surely you are two jesters, for I have seen nothing like this in the length and breadth of this strange and terrible land."

"We are lovers," said Gorgik, "and for one of us the symbolic distinction between slave and master is necessary to desire's consummation."

"We are avengers who fight the institution of slavery wherever we find it," said Small Sarg, "in whatever way we can, and for both of us it is symbolic of our time in servitude and our bond to all men and women still so bound."

"If we have not pledged ourselves to death before capture, it is only because we both know that a living slave can rebel and a dead slave cannot," said Gorgik.

"We have sieged more than seven castles now, releasing the workers locked in the laboring pens, the kitchen and house slaves, and the administrative slaves alike. As well, we have set upon those men who roam through the land capturing and selling men and women as if they were property. Between castles and countless brigands, we have freed many who had only to find a key for their collars. And in these strange and barbaric times, any key will do."

The redheaded Norema said: "You love as master and slave and you fight the institution of slavery? The contradiction seems as sad to me as it seemed amusing to my friend."

"As one word uttered in three different situations may mean three entirely different things, so the collar worn in three different situations may mean three different things. They are not the same: sex, affection, and society," said Gorgik. "Sex and society relate like an object and its image in a reflecting glass. One reverses the other—are you familiar with the phenomenon, for these are primitive times, and mirrors are rare—"

"I am familiar with it," said Norema and gave him a long, considered look.

Raven said: "We are two women who have befriended each other in this strange and terrible land, and we have no love for slavers. We've killed three now in the two years we've traveled together—slavers who've thought to take us as property. It is easy, really, here where the men expect the women to scream and kick and bite and slap, but not to plan and place blades in their gut."

Norema said: "Once we passed a gang of slavers with a herd of ten women in collars and chains, camped for the night. We descended on them—from their shouts they seemed to think they'd been set on by a hundred fighting men."

Sarg and Gorgik laughed; Norema and Raven laughed—all recognizing a phenomenon.

"You know," mused Norema, when the laughter was done, "the only thing that allows you and ourselves to pursue our liberations with any success is that the official policy of Nevèrÿon goes against slavery under the edict of the Child Empress."

"Whose reign," said Gorgik, absently, "is just and generous."

"Whose reign," grunted the masked woman, "is a sun-dried dragon turd."

"Whose reign—" Gorgik smiled—" is currently insufferable, if not insecure."

Norema said: "To mouth those conservative formulas and actively oppose slavery seems to me the same sort of contradiction as the one you first presented us with." She took a reflective breath. "A day ago we stopped near here at the castle of the Suzeraine of Strethi. He was amused by us and entertained us most pleasantly. But we could not help notice that his whole castle was run by slaves, men and women. But we smiled, and ate slave-prepared food—and were entertaining back."

Gorgik said: "It was the Suzeraine's castle that we last sieged."

Small Sarg said: "And the kitchen slaves, who probably prepared your meal, are now free."

The two women, masked and unmasked, smiled at each other, smiles within which were inscribed both satisfaction and embarrassment.

"How do you accomplish these sieges?" Raven asked.

"One or the other of us, in the guise of a free man without collar, approaches a castle where we have heard there are many slaves and delivers an ultimatum." Gorgik grinned. "Free your slaves or . . . "

"Or what?" asked Raven.

"To find an answer to that question, they usually cast the one of us who came into the torture chamber. At which point the other of us, decked in the collar—it practically guarantees one entrance if one knows which doors to come in by—lays siege to the hold."

"Only," Small Sarg said, "this time it didn't work like that. We were together, planning our initial strategy, when suddenly the Suzeraine's guards attacked us. They seemed to know who Gorgik was. They called him by name and almost captured us both."

"Did they, now?" asked Norema.

"They seemed already to have their questions for me. At first I thought they knew what we had been doing. But these are strange and barbaric times; and information travels slowly here."

"What did they question you about?" Raven wanted to know.

"Strange and barbaric things," said Gorgik. "Whether I had worked as a messenger for some southern lord, carrying tales of children's bouncing balls and other trivial imports. Many of their questions centered about . . . " He looked down, fingering the metal disk hanging against his chest. As he gazed, you could see, from his tensing cheek muscle, a thought assail him.

Small Sarg watched Gorgik. "What is it . . . ?"

Slowly Gorgik's brutish features formed a frown. "When we were fighting our way out of the castle, there was a woman . . . a slave. I'm sure she was a slave. She wore a collar . . . But she reminded me of another woman, a noble woman, a woman I knew a long time ago . . . " Suddenly he smiled. "Though she too wore a collar from time to time, much for the same reasons as I."

The matted-haired barbarian, the western woman in her mask, the island woman with her cropped hair sat about the silvered ash and watched the big man turn the disk. "When I was in the torture chamber, my thoughts were fixed on my own campaign for liberation and not on what to me seemed the idiotic fixations of my oppressor. Thus all their questions and comments are obscure to me now. By the same token, the man I am today obscures my memories of the youthful slave released from the bondage of the mines by this noble woman's whim. Yet, prompted by that face this evening, vague memories of then and now emerge and confuse themselves without clarifying. They turn about this instrument, for measuring time and space . . . they have to do with the name Krodar . . . "

The redhead said: "I have heard that name, Krodar . . . "

Within the frayed eyeholes, the night-blue eyes narrowed; Raven glanced at her companion.

Gorgik said: "There was something about a monastery in the south, called something like the Vygernangx . . . ?"

The masked woman said: "Yes, I know of the Vygernangx . . . "

The redhead glanced back at her friend with a look set between complete blankness and deep knowingness.

Gorgik said: "And there was something about the balls, the toys we played with as children . . . or perhaps the rhyme we played to . . . ?"

Small Sarg said: "When I was a child in the jungles of the south, we would harvest the little nodules of sap that seeped from the scars in certain broadleafed palms and save them up for the traders who would come every spring for them . . . "

Both women looked at each other now, then at the men, and remained silent.

"It is as though—" Gorgik held up the verdigrised disk with its barbarous chasings "—all these things would come together in a logical pattern, immensely complex and greatly beautiful, tying together slave and empress, commoner and lord—even gods and demons—to show how all are related in a negotiable pattern, like some sailor's knot, not yet pulled taut, but laid out on the dock in loose loops, so that simply to see it in such form were to comprehend it even when yanked tight. And yet . . . " He turned the astrolabe over. " . . . they will not clear in my mind to any such pattern!"

Raven said: 'The lords of this strange and terrible land indeed live lives within such complex and murderous knots. We have all seen them whether we have sieged the castle of one or been seduced by the hospitality of another; we have all had a finger through at least a loop in such a knot. You've talked of mirrors, pretty man, and of their strange reversal effect. I've wondered if our ignorance isn't simply a reversed image of their knowledge."

"And I've wondered—" Gorgik said, "slave, free-commoner, lord—if each isn't somehow a reflection of the other; or a reflection of a reflection."

"They are not," said Norema with intense conviction. "That is the most horrendous notion I've ever heard." But her beating lids, her astonished expression as she looked about in the moonlight, might have suggested to a sophisticated enough observer a conversation somewhere in her past of which this was a reflection.

Gorgik observed her, and waited.

After a while Norema picked up a stick, poked in the ashes with it: a single coal turned up ruby in the silver scatter and blinked.

After a few moments, Norema said: "Those balls . . . that the children play with in summer on the streets of Kolhari . . . Myself, I've always wondered where they came from—I mean I know about the orchards in the south. But I mean how do they get to the city every year."

"You don't know that?" Raven turned, quite astonished, to her redheaded companion. "You mean to tell me, island woman, that you and I have traveled together for over a year and a half, seeking fortune and adventure, and you have never asked me this nor have I ever told you?"

Norema shook her head.

Again Raven loosed her barking laughter. "Really, what is most strange and terrible about this strange and terrible land is how two women can be blood friends, chattering away for days at each other, saving one another's lives half a dozen times running and yet somehow never really talk! Let me tell you: the Western Crevasse, from which I hail, has, running along its bottom, a river that leads to the Eastern Ocean. My people live the whole length of the river, and those living at the estuary are fine, seafaring women. It is our boats, crewed by these sailing women of the Western Crevasse who each year have sailed to the south in our red ships and brought back these toys to Kolhari, as indeed they also trade them up and down the river." A small laugh now, a sort of stifled snorting. "I was twenty and had already left my home before I came to one of your ports and the idea struck me that a man could actually do the work required on a boat."

"Ay," said Gorgik, "I saw those boats in my youth—but we were always scared to talk with anyone working on them. The captain was always a man; and we assumed, I suppose, that he must be a very evil person to have so many women within his power. Some proud, swaggering fellow—as frequently a foreigner as one of your own men—"

"Yes," said Norema. "I remember such a boat. The crew was all women and the captain a great, black-skinned fellow who terrified everyone in my island village—"

"The captain a man?" The masked woman frowned beneath her mask's ragged hem. "I know there are boats from your Ulvayn islands on which men and women work together. But a man for a captain on a boat of my people . . . ? It is so unlikely that I am quite prepared to dismiss it as an outright imposs—" She stopped; then she barked, "Of course. The man on the boat! Oh, yes, my silly heathen woman, of course there is a man on the boat. There's always a man on the boat. But he's certainly not the captain. Believe me, my friend, even though I have seen men fulfill it, captain is a woman's job: and in our land it is usually the eldest sailor on the boat who takes the job done by your captain."

"If he wasn't the captain, then," asked Norema, "who was he?"

"How can I explain it to you . . . ?" Raven said. "There is always a man in a group of laboring women in my country. But he is more like a talisman, or a good-luck piece the women take with them, than a working sailor—much less an officer. He is a figure of prestige, yes, which explains his fancy dress; but he is not a figure of power. Indeed, do you know the wooden women who are so frequently carved on the prow of your man-sailored ships? Well he fulfills a part among our sailors much as that wooden woman does among yours. I suppose to you it seems strange. But in our land, a single woman lives with a harem of men; and in our land, any group of women at work always keeps a single man. Perhaps it is simply another of your reflections? But you, in your strange and terrible land, can see nothing but men at the heads of things. The captain indeed! A pampered pet who does his exercises every morning on the deck, who preens and is praised and shown off at every port—that is what men are for. And, believe me, they love it, no matter what they say. But a man . . . a man with power and authority and the right to make decisions? You must excuse me, for though I have been in your strange and terrible land for years and know such things exist here, I still cannot think of such things among my own people without laughing." And here she gave her awkward laugh, while with her palm she beat her bony knee. "Seriously," she said when her laugh was done, "such a pattern for work seems so natural to me that I cannot really believe you've never encountered anything like it before—" she was talking to Norema now—"even here."

Norema smiled, a little strangely. "Yes, I . . . I have heard of something like it before."

Gorgik again examined the redhead's face, as if he might discern, inscribed by eye-curve and cheek-bone and forehead-line and lip-shape, what among her memories reflected this discussion.

Something covered the moon.

First masked Raven, then the other three, looked up. Wide wings labored off the light.

"What is such a mountain beast doing in such a flat and swampy land?" asked Small Sarg.

"It must be the Suzeraine's pet," Norema said. "But why should he have let it go?"

"So," said Raven, "once again tonight we are presented with a mysterious sign and no way to know whether it completes a pattern or destroys one." The laugh this time was something that only went on behind her closed lips. "They cannot fly very far. There is no ledge for her to perch on. And once she lands, in this swampy morass, she won't be able to regain flight. Her wings will tear in the brambles and she will never fly again."

But almost as if presenting the image of some ironic answer, the wings flapped against a sudden, high, unfelt breeze, and the beast, here shorn of all fables, rose and rose—for a while—under the night.

X

The adventures of Paksenarrion Dorthansdotter began in novel Sheepfarmer's Daughter *(1988). Over the course of three books the peasant girl escapes marriage to a pig farmer to become a mercenary, then a paladin of Gird. She must work, fight, and sacrifice herself to insure a rightful king gains the throne despite various evil forces. Beyond this first trilogy, Elizabeth Moon (1945–) explores Paksenarrion's universe in two prequels, five sequels, and a dozen or so short stories. Moon's novels are epic military fantasy that balances gender and the role of women. There's much more "sword" than sorcery and heroism requires discipline, honor, and self-sacrifice more than derring-do. In "First Blood," set in the Paksenarrion universe, a young squire finds himself riding toward his first battle.*

FIRST BLOOD

Elizabeth Moon

Luden Fall, great-nephew of the Duke of Fall, had not won the spurs he strapped to his boots the morning he left home for the first time. War had come to Fallo, so Luden, three years too young for knighthood, had been give the honor of accompanying a cohort of Sofi Ganarrion's company to represent the family.

The cohort's captain, Madrelar, a lean, angular man with a weathered, sun-browned face, eyed him up and down and then shrugged. "We march in a ladyglass," Madrelar said. "There's your horse. Get your gear tied on and be at my side when we mount up."

The mounted troop moved quickly, riding longer and faster than Luden had before, into territory he had never seen, ever closer to the Dwarfmounts that divided the Eight Kingdoms of the North from Aarenis. His duties were minimal. When he first attempted to help the way he'd been taught at home, picking up and putting in place everything the captain put down, carrying dishes to and from a serving table, Madrelar told him to quit fussing about. Luden obeyed, as squires were supposed to do.

He had hoped to learn much from a mercenary captain, a man who had fought against Siniava and might have seen the Duke of Immer when he was still Alured the Black and an ally, but Madrelar said little to him beyond simple orders and discouraged questions by not answering them. Pastak, the cohort sergeant, said less. The troopers themselves ignored him, though he heard mutters and chuckles he assumed were at his expense.

Finally one evening, when the sentries were out walking the bounds, the captain called Luden into his tent. "You should know where we are and why," Madrelar said. He had maps spread on a folding table. "We guard the North Trade Road, where the road from Rotengre meets it, so Immer cannot outflank the duke's force. It's unlikely he'll try, but just in case. Do you understand?"

Luden looked at the map, at the captain's finger pointing to a crossroads. Back there was Fallo, where he had lived all his life until now. "Yes," he said. "I understand outflanking, and I can see . . . " He traced the line with his finger. "They could come this way, along the north road. But could they not also follow the route we took here, only bypassing us to the south?"

"They are unlikely to know the way," Madrelar said.

"What force might they bring?" Luden asked.

Madrelar shrugged. "Anything from nothing to five hundred. If they are too large, we retreat, sending word back for reinforcements. If they are small enough, we destroy them. In the middle . . . " He tipped his hand back and forth. "We fight and see who wins." He gave Luden a sharp glance out of frosty blue eyes. "Are you scared, boy?"

"Not really." Luden's skin prickled, but he knew it for excitement, not fear.

Madrelar grinned. "That will change."

The next day they stayed in camp. Madrelar told him to take all three of the captain's mounts to be checked for loose shoes. Luden waited his turn for the farrier, listening to the men talk, hoping to hear stories of Siniava's War. Instead, the men talked of drinking, dicing, money, women, and when they would be back in "a real city."

"Sorellin?" Luden asked, having seen that it was nearest on the map.

They all stopped and looked at him, then at one another. Finally one of them said, "No, young lord. Valdaire. Have you heard of it?"

"Of course—it's in the west, near the caravan pass to the north."

"It's our city," the man said. "Any other place we go, we're on hire. But in Valdaire, we're free."

"The girls in Valdaire . . . " another man said, making shapes with his hands. "They love us, for we bring money."

Luden felt his ears getting hot. His own interest in girls was new, and his father's lectures on deportment both clear and stringent.

"Don't embarrass the lad," the first trooper said. "He'll find out in time." His glance quieted the others. "You ride well, young lord. It is an honor to have a member of your family along."

"Thank you," Luden said. He knew the other men were amused, but this one seemed polite. "My name is Luden. This is the first time I have been so far."

Silence for a moment, then the man said, "I am Esker." He gestured. "These are Trongar, Vesk, and Hrondar. We all came south from Kostandan with Ganarrion."

Luden fizzed with questions he wanted to ask—was the north really all forest? Was it true that elves walked there? Esker tipped his head toward the fire. "Janits waits you and the captain's horses. Best go, or someone will take your place in line."

"Thank you," Luden said, and led the horses forward.

When he returned the horses to the hitch-line strung between trees, it was still broad daylight. He glanced in the captain's tent—orderly and empty. The men were busy with camp chores, with horse care, cleaning tack, mending anything that needed it. Luden's own small possessions were new enough to need nothing.

Luden spoke to the nearest sentry. "Would it be all right if I went for a walk?"

The man's brows rose. "You think that's a good idea? You do realize there might be an enemy army not a day's march away?"

"I thought . . . nothing's happening . . . I could just look at things."

The sentry heaved a dramatic sigh. "All right. Don't go far, don't get hurt, if you see strangers, come back and tell me. All right? Back in one sun-hand, no more."

"Thank you," Luden said. He looked around for a moment, thinking which way to go. Little red dots on a bush a stone's throw away caught his eye.

The dots were indeed berries, some ripened to purple, but most still red and sour. Luden ate some of the ripe ones, and brought a neck-cloth full back to the camp. At home, the cooks were always happy to get berries, however few. Here, too, the camp cook nodded when Luden offered them. "Can you get more?"

"I think so," Luden said.

"Take this bowl. Be back in . . . " he glanced up at the sun, "a sun-hand, and I'll be able to use these for dinner."

Luden showed the sentry the bowl. "Cook wants more of those berries."

"Good," the sentry said.

Near the first bush were others; Luden filled the bowl and took it back to the cook. After that—still no sign of the captain—Luden wandered about the camp until he found Esker, the man who had been friendly before, replacing a strap on a saddle.

"If you've nothing to do, you can punch some holes in this strap," Esker said.

Luden sat down at once. Esker handed him another strap and the punching tools, and told him how to space the holes. Luden soon made a row of neat holes. "Good job, lad—Luden, wasn't it? Have you checked all your own tack?"

"It's almost new," Luden said. "I didn't see anything wrong."

"Bring it here. We'll give you a lesson in field maintenance of cavalry tack."

Luden brought his saddle, bridle, and rigging over to Esker where he sat amid a group of busy troopers. Luden had cleaned his tack, but—as Esker pointed out—he hadn't gone over every finger-width of every strap.

"You might think this doesn't matter as much," Hrondar said. Esker's friends had now joined in the instruction. Hrondar pointed to the strap that held a water bottle on his own saddle. "If that gives way and you have no water on a long march, you'll be less alert. Everything we carry is needed. Every strap should be checked daily to see it's not cracked, drying out, stretching too much."

Other men shared their ideas for keeping tack in perfect condition—including arguments about the best oils and waxes for different weather. Luden drank it in, fascinated by details his father's riding master had never mentioned.

Captain Madrelar found him there, two sun-hands later. "So this is where you are! I've been searching the camp, squire." The emphasis he put on "squire" would have sliced wood. "I need you in my quarters."

Luden scrambled to his feet, threw the rigging over his shoulder, put his arm through the bridle, and hitched his saddle onto his hip. The captain had turned away; Esker got up and tucked the trailing reins into the rigging on his shoulder. Luden nodded his thanks and followed the captain back to his tent.

There he endured a blistering scold for his venture out to pick berries and his interfering with the troopers at their tasks. Finally, the captain ran down and left the tent, with a last order to "Put that mess away, eat your dinner without saying a word, and be ready to ride in the morning."

Luden put his tack on the rack next to the captain's, shivering with reaction. He'd been scolded plenty of times, but always he'd understood what he'd done wrong. What was so bad about gathering food for others and learning more that soldiers needed to know? He hadn't been gossiping or gambling.

He looked around the tent for something useful to do. A scattering of maps, message tubes, and papers covered the table. He heard the clang of the dinner gong; he could clear the table before the cook's assistant brought the captain's meal. He'd done that before; the captain never minded.

Luden picked up the first papers then stopped, staring at a green and black seal, one he had seen before. Had the captain found it somewhere? It was wrong to read someone else's papers, but this was Immer's seal. The enemy's seal. The hairs rose on his scalp as he read. Captain Madrelar—the name leapt out at him—was to put his troop at the service of the Duke of Immer, by leading them into an ambush, four hundred of Immer's men, within a half-day's ride of the crossroads Madrelar had shown him. For this Madrelar would receive the promised reward and a command. If he had been able to talk Fallo into sending one of his nephews or grandsons along, then Madrelar should drug or bind the sprout and send him to Cortes Immer.

Luden dropped the paper as if it were on fire and started shaking. It was the most horrible thing he could imagine. The captain a traitor? Why? And what was he supposed to do? He was only a squire, and how many of these men outside, these hardened mercenaries, were also traitors?

He had not understood fear before. He had thought, those times he climbed high in a tree, or jumped from a wall, that the tightness in his belly was fear, easily overcome for the thrill with it. This was different—fear that hollowed out his mind and body as a spoon scoops out the center of a melon. His bones had gone to water. All he'd heard of Immer—the tortures, the magery, the way Andressat's son had been flayed alive—came to mind. As soon as the captain came back and saw that he'd moved things on the desk, he might be overpowered, bound, doomed.

He had to get away before then . . . somehow. Even as he thought that, and how impossible it would be, his hands went on working, shuffling several other messages on top of Immer's, squaring the sheets to a neat stack. He rolled the maps as he usually did, noting even in his haste the marks the captain had made on one of them. They were not two days' ride from the crossroads, but one: the captain had lied to him. He put the maps in the map-stand as always. What now? He glanced out the tent door. No immediate escape: the cook's assistant was almost at the tent with a basket of food, and the captain had already started the same way, talking to his sergeant.

Luden took the dinner basket from the cook and had the captain's supper laid out on the table by the time the captain arrived. When the captain came in, he stood by the table, hoping the captain could not detect his thundering heart. The captain stopped short.

"Who did this?"

"Sir, I laid out your dinner as usual."

"You touched my papers? When?"

"To have room for the dinner." Luden gestured at the stack of papers at the end of the table. "It took only a moment, to stack them and put the maps away. Just as usual."

"Hmph." The captain sat and pointed to his cup. "Wine. And water."

Luden poured, his hand shaking. The captain gave him a sharp look.

"What's this? Still shivering from a scold? I hope you don't fall off your mount with fright if we do meet the enemy." The captain stabbed a slab of meat, cut it, and put it in his mouth.

Madrelar said nothing more in the course of the meal, then ordered Luden to take the dishes back to the cook, and eat his own dinner there. "I will be working late tonight," he said. "It's dry; sleep outside, and don't be sitting up late with the men. They need their rest. We ride early."

Luden could not eat much, not even the berry-speckled dessert. What was the captain up to, besides betrayal? Were the other men, or some of them, also part of it? Was the captain really prepared to sacrifice his own troops? And why? Luden's background gave him no hint. He tried to think what he might do.

Could he run away? He might escape the sentries set around camp on foot, but the horse lines had a separate guard. He could not sneak away on horseback. And even if he did escape afoot, he might be captured before he reached home—they had ridden hard to get here, and going back would take him longer. Especially since he had no way to carry supplies.

What then could he do? He looked around for Esker, but didn't see him, and dared not wander around the camp, in case the captain looked for him. Finally, he went back to the captain's tent. A light inside cast shadows on the wall . . . two people at least were in it.

Outside, near the entrance, he found a folded blanket and a water bottle on top of it. The captain clearly meant for him to stay outside. He picked them up, went around the side of the tent, rolled himself in the blanket, and—sure he could not sleep—dozed off.

He woke from a dream so vivid he thought it was real, and heard his voice saying "Yes, my lord!" He lay a moment, wide awake, chilled by the night air. The dream lay bright as a picture in his mind: his great-uncle, the Duke of Fall, speaking to all the children as he did every Midwinter Feast. It is not for wealth alone, or tradition, that the Dukes of Fall have ruled here for ages past, since first we came from the South. But because we keep faith with our people. Never forget what you owe to those who work our fields, who take up arms to defend us. They deserve the best we have to give them. And then the phrase that had wakened him: Luden, look to your honor.

He was a child of Fallo; he was the only one of that House here, and these men around him—some of them at least, and maybe all but the captain—were being led to slaughter. He still had honor, and the duty that came with honor.

And he badly needed the jacks. He threw off his blanket and stood up.

Overhead, stars burned bright in the clear mountain air; he could see the tips of the tallest mountains, snow at their peaks even in summer, pale against the night sky, and enough silvery light glimmered over the camp to show him the way.

He had taken but ten steps toward the jacks when someone grabbed his arm and swung him round.

"And where d'you think you're going?"

It was Sergeant Pastak. Had the captain set a watch over him? Of course: he would need to, just in case. And so the sergeant was in on it, also a traitor.

"To the jacks," Luden said, glad his voice sounded slightly annoyed.

"To be sure, the jacks," the sergeant said, with a sneer. "Young lads . . . always eager to go to war until they get closer to it. Thinking of that, are you?"

"I'm thinking I ate too many of those berries before I gave the rest to the cook," Luden said. "And I need the jacks."

The sergeant shook his arm; Luden stumbled. "Just know, lad, you're with a fighting troop, not some fancy-boy's personal guards. You're not running off home."

That was clear enough. He stiffened against the sergeant's arm and adopted a tone he'd heard from his elders. "I am not one to run away, Sergeant. But I would prefer not to mark my clothes with berry juice and have someone like you think it was fear."

The sergeant let go of his arm as if it had burned him. "Well," he said. "The young cock will crow, will he? We'll see how you crow when the time comes—if it does." He gestured, the starlight running down his mail shirt like molten silver. "Go on then. To the jacks with you, and if you mark your clothes red and not yellow, I'll call you worthy."

Red could mean blood and not berry juice. Luden held himself stiffly and stalked off to the jacks as if he hadn't thought of that. He was not the only one at the jacks trench, though he was glad to see he had room to himself. He did have a cramp, and what he had eaten the previous day, berries and all he was sure, came out in a rush. He waited a moment, two, and then, as he stood, saw another man nearby.

"All right, Luden?" It was Esker. "The berries were good, but I think they woke me up."

"I ate handfuls raw," Luden said.

"That can do it. These mountain berries—they look like the ones back in the lowlands, but they clear the system, even cooked."

Could he trust Esker? He had to do something, and Esker was the only one he had really talked to. "Esker, I have to tell—"

"I thought I told you to leave the soldiers alone, sprout!" It was the captain. No doubt the sergeant had told him where Luden was. "No chatter. Get to your blanket and stay there. And no more berries on the morrow." Luden turned to go. Behind him, he heard the captain. "Well, Esker? Sucking up to the old man's brat?"

"He had the gripe, captain, same as me. You know those mountain berries. I'd have sent him back in a moment."

Then murmurs he could not hear. Back near the tent, a torch burned; the sergeant stood beside it. Luden returned to his blanket and lay down, feigning sleep. He knew they would not leave him unwatched. Once again, sleep overtook him.

He woke to a boot prodding his ribs. "Hurry up. It's almost daylight."

Stars had faded; the sky glowed, the deep blue called Esea's Cloak, and the camp stirred. Horses whinnied, men were talking, laughing, he smelled something cooking. As he rolled his blanket, the captain stood by, watching. Luden yanked the thongs snug around it, and stood with it on his shoulder.

"Don't forget your water," the captain said. "You'll be thirsty later."

Luden bent to pick up the water bottle.

"Your tack's over there." The captain pointed to a pile on the ground; two men were already taking down the captain's tent.

Luden picked up his tack and headed for the horse lines.

"If you've no stomach for breakfast," the captain said, "put some bread in your saddlebags; you'll want it later."

He saddled his mount, put the water bottle into one saddlebag and then carried the bags to the cook for bread. Troopers were taking a loaf each from a pile on a table.

"Captain thought you'd like this," the cook said, handing him a spiced roll. "Gave me the spice for it special, and said put plenty of honey in it."

Luden's stomach turned. "It'll be too sweet if it's all I have. Could I have some plain bread, as well?"

The cook grinned. "You're more grown up than that, you're saying? Not just a child, to eat all the sweets he can beg?" He handed Luden a small plain loaf from the pile. "There. Eat troops' rations if you'd rather, but don't tell the captain; he only thought to please you."

"Thank you," Luden said. The sweetened roll felt sticky. He put both rolls in the other saddlebag, and then went to the jacks trench a last time. It was busy now; Luden went to one end, squatted, fished in the saddlebag for the roll, sticky with honey, that he was sure had some drug in it. He dropped it in the trench, then stood and grabbed the shovel, and covered it quickly.

"That's not your job," one of the men said. "Go back to the captain, get your gear tied down tight. Here—give me the shovel."

"I'll see him safe," another said. Esker.

Luden glanced in the trench; no sign of the roll. Unless someone had seen him drop it . . . he looked at Esker. "Thank you," he said. All at once it occurred to him that the formality of the duke's house—the relentless schooling in manners, in what his great-uncle called propriety—had a use after all. Underneath, he was still frightened, but now he could play other parts.

"Come on, then," Esker said. When they were a short distance from the trench, Esker said, "There was something you wanted to tell me last night. Still want to tell me in daylight? Is it that you're scared?"

As a rabbit before the hounds he wanted to say, but he must not. Instead, in a rush, he said, "The captain's going to betray you all to Immer's men; four hundred are coming to meet us."

Esker caught hold of his shoulder and swung him around. "Boy. Fallo's kin. That cannot be true, and we do not like liars."

"I'm not lying," Luden said. "I saw it—"

"Or sneaking."

"—a message from Immer, with Immer's seal."

Esker chewed his lip a moment. "You're certain?"

"Immer's seal, yes."

"I am an idiot," Esker said, "if I believe a stripling lad when I have ridden with the captain these eight years and more." He stopped abruptly, then pulled Luden forward. In a low growl: "Do not argue. There's no time; I can do nothing now. If it's true I will do what I can." Luden saw the captain then, staring at them both. Esker raised his voice. "Here he is, captain. Lad had a hankering to fill a jacks trench; Trongar saw him. I'm bringing him back to you." He sounded cheerful and unconcerned.

"I saw you head to head like old friends," the captain said.

"That, captain, was me telling him the second time that he had years enough for filling jacks trenches and you'd be looking for him. He's just young, that's all."

"That he is," the captain said, looking down at Luden. "Did you saddle that horse?"

"Yes, sir," Luden said. "And I thank you for that sweet loaf the cook gave me. Cook said you told him to put spice in it as well as honey."

The captain smiled. "So I did. You can eat it midmorning, when we rest the horses, since I doubt you've eaten breakfast after last night's adventure with berries."

"That's so, sir," Luden said. "It still gripes a bit."

"Today will take care of that," the captain said. "Riding a trot's the best thing for griping belly." He turned to the trooper. "Very well, Esker, I have him under my eye now; get back to your own place."

"Yes, Captain," Esker said. "Not a bad lad, sir. Just eager to help."

"Too eager," the captain said, "can be as annoying as lazy."

"True. So my own granfer told me."

Both men laughed; Luden's heart sank. He did not think Esker was a traitor, but clearly the man thought him just a foolish boy.

They were mounted when the first rays of sunlight fired the treetops to either side. When they reached the North Trade Road, their shadows lay long and blue before them. To either side, the forest thickened to a green wall and rose up a hill on the north side. Luden couldn't see the mountains now, but he could feel the cool air sifting down through the trees, fragrant with pine and spruce. Here and there he saw more bushes covered with berries. The captain pointed out a particularly lush patch.

"Tempted to stop and pick some?"

"No, sir."

"Good. Wouldn't want your belly griping again." A moment later, "Ready for that sweet bread yet?"

"No, sir," Luden said. "It's not settled yet."

"Ah. Well, you'll eat it before it spoils, I daresay."

The sun was high, their shadows shorter, when a man on horseback leading a pair of mules loaded with packs came riding toward them. He wore what looked like merchants' garb, even to the soft blue cap that slouched to one side. But it was the horse Luden noticed. He knew that horse.

That bay stallion with a white snip, uneven front socks, and a shorter white sock on the near hind had been stolen—along with fifteen mares—from a Fallo pasture the year before. Before that, it had been one of the older chargers used to teach Luden and his cousins mounted battle skills. Luden knew that horse the way he would know his own shirt; he had brushed every inch of its hide, picked dirt out of those massive hooves. And so the man riding him must be Immer's agent.

"Sir," he said to the captain. "That man's a horse thief."

"Don't be ridiculous," the captain said.

"I know that horse," Luden said.

"The world is full of bays with three white feet," the captain said. "It's just a merchant. Perhaps he'll tell us if he's seen any sign of brigands or—unlikely—Immer's troops."

"I'm telling you, I know that horse!"

The captain turned on him, furious. "You know nothing. You are a mere child, foisted on me by your great-uncle, Tir alone knows why, and you will be quiet or I will knock you off that horse and you can walk home alone."

Luden clamped his jaw on what he wanted to say and stared at the merchant instead. For a merchant, he sat the stallion very much like a cavalry trooper, his feet level in the stirrups, his shoulders square . . . and what was a merchant doing with the glint of mail showing at his neck? What was that combination of straight lines under the man's cloak? Not a sword . . .

The stallion stood foursquare, neck arched, head vertical, ears pointed forward. Luden checked his memory of the markings. It had to be the same horse.

Luden glanced at the captain, who raised his arm to halt the troop, then rode forward alone. Now was his only chance. Would the horse remember the commands? He held out his hand, opened and closed his fist twice, and called. "Sarky! Nemosh ti!"

At the same moment, a bowstring thrummed; Luden heard the crossbow bolt thunk into the captain's body, saw the captain stiffen, then slide to one side, even as the bay stallion leapt forward, kicking out behind; its rider lurched, dropped the crossbow and grabbed at the saddle.

"Ambush!" Luden yelled, "Ambush—form up!" He drew his sword and spurred toward Sarky; the stallion landed in a series of bucks that dumped its rider on the ground. Its tack glinted in the sun; instead of saddlebags, a polished round shield hung from one side of the saddle, and a helmet from the other. Bolts hummed past Luden; he heard them hitting behind him and kept going. Horses squealed, men cursed. The captain now hung by one foot from a stirrup, one bolt in his neck, two more bolts in his body; he bled from the mouth, arms dragging as his horse shied this way and that.

Luden had no time wonder why the enemy had shot the captain who'd done what he was hired to do. A crossbow bolt hit his own mount in the neck, then another and another. It staggered and went down. Luden rolled clear as the horse thrashed, but stumbled on a stirrup getting to his feet and fell again. He looked around—the old bay stallion was close beside him, kicking out at the fallen rider who now had a sword out, trying to reach Luden.

"Sarky," he called. *"Vi arthrin dekost."* In the old language, "Lifebringer, aid me."

The stallion pivoted on his forehand, giving Luden the position he needed to jump, catch the saddlebow, and scramble into the saddle from the off side, still with sword in hand. The man on the ground, quick witted, grabbed the trailing reins and held off the stallion's lunge with the point of his sword.

"Here he is—Fallo's whelp—help me, some of you!"

Luden scrambled over the saddlebow, along the horse's neck, and sliced the bridle between the horse's ears. The stallion threw his head up; the bridle fell free. The man, off balance, staggered and fell backward. Luden slid back into the saddle just as the horse jumped forward, forefeet landing on the fallen man. He heard the snap and crunch of breaking bones.

Mounted soldiers wearing Immer's colors swarmed onto the road. Ganarrion's smaller troop was fully engaged, fighting hard—and he himself was surrounded, separated from them. He fended off the closest attackers as best he could, yanking his dagger from his belt, though he knew it might break against the heavier curved swords the enemy used. The horse pivoted, kicked, reared, giving him a moment to cut the strings of the round shield and get it on his arm.

He took a blow on the shield that drove his arm down, got it back up just in time, parried someone on the other side with his own blade, and with weight and leg aimed his mount in the right direction—toward the remaining Ganarrion troopers. The stallion, unhampered by bit or rein, bullied the other mounts out of his way—taking the ear off one, and biting the crest of another, a maneuver that almost unseated him. Arm's length by arm's length they forced their way through the enemy to rejoin the Ganarrion troop—itself proving no easy prey, despite losses of horses and men.

"Tir's guts, it's the squire!" someone yelled. "He's alive." A noise between a growl and a cheer answered him.

Luden found himself wedged between two of the troopers, then maneuvered into the middle of the group. He saw Esker; the man grinned at him then neatly shoved an enemy off his horse.

"We need to get out of here!" someone yelled.

"How? Which way? They're all over—!"

"Luden!" Esker shouted over the din. "WHERE?"

He saw other glances flicking to him and away as the fight raged. They were waiting—waiting for him to make a decision. What decision? He was only a squire, he couldn't—but he had to: he was Fallo here. "BACK!" he yelled. "Take word back—warn them! Follow me!"

He put his spurs to Sarky, forcing his way between the others to the east end of the group. Twice he fended off attacks, and once he pushed past a wounded trooper to run his sword into one of the enemy. When he reached the far end of the group, he yelled "Follow me!" again and charged ahead, into a line three deep of enemy riders. Sarky crashed into one of the horses; it slipped, fell, and opened a gap.

For a terrifying time that seemed to last forever, Luden found himself fending off swords, daggers, a short lance, hands grabbing for him, trying to keep himself and his mount alive. He felt blows on his back, his arms, his legs; he could not think but only fight, hitting as hard as he could anything—man or horse—that came close enough. The noise—he had never imagined such noise—the screaming of men and horses, the clash of swords. Someone grabbed his shield, tried to pull him off the saddle; he hacked at the man's wrist with his sword; blood spurted out as the man's hand dropped away.

Always, the stallion pushed on, biting and striking, and behind him now he heard the Ganarrion troopers. One last horseman stood in his way; he felt Sarky's sides swell, and the stallion let out a challenging scream; that rider's mount whirled and bolted.

"Kerestra!" Luden said. Home. Despite his wounds, the stallion surged into a gallop. Behind, more yells and screams and a thunder of hooves that shook the ground. Luden dared a glance back. Behind him were the red and gray surcoats of Ganarrion's troop—more than half of them—and behind them the green and black of Immer's. How far could they run, how far could Sarky run, with blood flowing from a gash on his shoulder, with thick curds of sweat on his neck?

Ganarrion's troops had the faster horses, and opened a lead, but Sarky slowed, laboring. Esker rode up beside Luden. "Only a little farther, and we can give your mount a rest. Were you wounded?"

"I don't think so," Luden said. "I was hit, but it doesn't hurt."

"We'll see when we stop. Where do we go from here?"

"Straight back to Fallo. Tell the first troops we see that Immer's on the way."

"I thank you for the warning," Esker said. "And more, for getting us out of that."

"It was mostly Sarky," Luden said. The stallion flicked an ear back at his name.

One of the troopers in the rear yelled something Luden did not understand; Esker did. "They've halted and turned away," he said. "They may come on later, but it's safe to slow now as soon as they're out of sight. But it's your command."

"Mine?" Luden looked at Esker.

"Of course, sir—young lord—I mean. Captain and sergeant are dead; you're the only person of rank. And you got us out of that."

"Then . . . can we slow down now?"

Esker looked ahead and behind. "I'd say up there, young lord, just over that rise. Shall I post a lookout there?"

"Yes," Luden said, wishing he'd thought of that. By the time they cleared the rise, the old stallion had slowed to an uneven trot. The troop surrounded them as the stallion stood, sides heaving.

"By all the gods, young lord, I thought we were done for!" said one of the men. "Esker told me what you said. I didn't believe it until it happened."

"Kellin, see to his horse. That's a nasty shoulder wound. Hrondar, we need a watch over the rise," Esker said.

Luden slid off the stallion; his legs almost gave way. The smell of blood, the sight of it on so many, men and horses both. Several of the men were already binding up wounds.

"You are bleeding," Esker said to him. "Here, let me see." He slit Luden's sleeve with his dagger, and there was a gash. Luden looked at it then looked away. "That needs a battle-surgeon," Esker said. "But we can stop the bleeding at least. Sit down. Yes, right down on the ground."

He called one of the other men over; for a few moments, Luden struggled to keep from making a noise. Now that he was sitting down, his arm throbbing, he felt other injuries. Esker looked him over, pronounced most of them minor, though two would need a surgeon's care, and offered a water bottle. Luden remembered that his was on the saddle of the horse that had fallen under him. Also that he'd had no breakfast and the loaf in his saddlebag was as distant and unobtainable as his own water bottle. Around him now, the troopers were eating.

"Here," Esker said, tearing off a piece of his own. "Eat this—too bad you lost the one the captain gave you—honey would be good for you about now."

"It was poisoned," Luden said. He bit off a hunk of roll.

"How do you know that?"

"The letter I saw, with Immer's seal. It wasn't just the ambush. He was also supposed to bring a member of Fall's family for them to take back to Cortes Immer."

"You—but he said you were a nuisance he had to bring along."

Luden shrugged. That hurt; he took another bite of bread. The longer he sat, the more he hurt, though bread and water cleared his head. He looked around. Kellin had smeared some greenish salve on Sarky's wounds. "Give me a hand," he said, reaching up.

Esker put a hand down, and Luden stood.

"How long do the horses need to rest?" Luden asked.

Esker stared at him a moment. "You don't want to camp here?"

"We don't know where they are. They could be circling round, out of our sight. We need to move—" He stopped. Sarky's head had come up, ears pricked toward the east. Other horses stared the same way.

"Tir's gut, we didn't need this," Esker said.

A shrill whistle from the west, from the lookout on the rise; Luden tensed. Esker grinned. "It's our folk," he said.

"Our folk?"

"Ganarrion." He leaned closer. "Your command, young lord, but we'd look better mounted and moving. Even slowly."

"I'll need a leg up," Luden said, then, "Mount up! We'll go to meet them." Esker helped him into the saddle; the others mounted, and the lookout in the rear trotted up to join them. Luden's head swam for a moment, but he nudged Sarky into a walk; the troop formed up behind him.

In moments, he could see the banner, larger than the one his own cohort carried: Ganarrion himself was with them. Behind Ganarrion's company came another, Count Vladi's black banner in the lead. Ganarrion rode directly to Luden.

"Boy! What happened? Where's Captain Madrelar?"

Luden stiffened at the tone. "Madrelar's dead. He led us into ambush."

"WHAT?" Ganarrion's bellow echoed off the nearest hill.

"We were led into ambush; the enemy shot Madrelar, and we're all that fought free."

Ganarrion sat his horse as if stunned, then turned to his own company. "Sergeant Daesk, scouts out all sides, expect enemy contact. Cargin, fetch the surgeon; we have wounded." Then, to Luden he said, "You're Luden Fall, is that right? Prosso's son?"

"Yes, sir," Luden said.

"The duke told me to look for you. And that horse—if I'm not mistaken, that's one of the duke's horses, stolen a while back. And, no bridle? How did you—or I suppose the troop surrounded you?"

"No, my lord," Esker said. "Lord Fall warned us of the ambush then led us out, fighting all the way."

Lord Fall? He was no lord; he was barely a squire.

"Barely a squire," Esker continued, echoing Luden's thought, "but he took command when Madrelar and Pastak died, and led the charge that broke us out."

"And it was treachery?"

"Yes."

Ganarrion chewed his mustache for a long moment, staring at Luden then nodded. "Thank you, Esker." He gave a short bow. "Lord Fall, with your permission, I will relieve you of command. You and your mount are both in need of a surgeon's care, and I have need of those of your troop who are still fit to fight. Will you release them to me?"

Luden bowed in his turn; his vision darkened as he pushed himself erect again. "Certainly, Lord Ganarrion. As you wish." Then the dark closed in.

◆ ◆ ◆

He woke in a tent with lamps already lit. When he tried to move, he could scarcely shift one limb, and he hurt all over. The memory of Immer's letter came first, and for one terrifying moment he thought he lay bound, already on his way to the dungeons of Cortes Immer. Then he heard voices he knew—Sofi Ganarrion, Count Vladi, Esker. The events of the day reappeared in memory, hazy as if seen through smoke.

"It's unusual, certainly," Count Vladi was saying. "But I remember a certain young squire dancing with death when I was a captain in Kostandan . . . "

Ganarrion grunted. "I was young and foolish then."

"And brave and more capable than anyone expected. This lad was not foolish, for what other choices did he have? We shall have much to tell Duke Fall when we return."

Luden stood before the Duke of Fall, when he was again fit to ride and fight. Behind him were the men of Ganarrion's company; Sofi Ganarrion stood on his sword-side and his own father on his heart-side.

"Victory is sweet," the old man said, "but honor is bread and meat to the soul. Those who have both, even once in their lives, are fortunate beyond all riches. You won your spurs, Luden; I cannot give them to you. Let us say I found something of mine that I am too old to use, that might be of service to you."

He opened the box on the table between them and turned it around to show Luden. The spurs within were old, the straps burnished with wear. Luden's breath caught. The duke's own spurs? He didn't deserve—

"Men died, my lord," is what came out of his mouth before he could stop it. "Life was enough reward."

Duke Fall nodded. "You are right, nephew. And it is as much for your understanding as for your courage that these spurs are now yours. We will speak more later; for now, let your sponsors perform their duties."

His father and Sofi Ganarrion stepped forward, each taking a spur, then knelt beside him, fastening them to his boots.

⚔

Saladin Ahmed's (1975–) debut novel Throne of the Crescent Moon *(2012) features Doctor Adoulla Makhslood, "the last real ghul hunter in the great city of Dhamsawaat." In the following short story, "Where Virtue Lives"—a prequel to the novel—the doctor meets Raseed bas Raseed who will become his apprentice. Ahmed's modern sword and sorcery in, many respects, resembles traditional S&S: heroes with hearts of gold, magic, monsters, evil to be stopped, plenty of atmosphere and action—but there are also departures. Makhslood is a fat old man who says he prefers sipping cardamom tea and eating pastries rather going on adventures, but still finds them anyway. The diminutive Raseed is a young dervish with a strong sword arm, but his desire to serve God is stronger. Unlike the stereotyped orientalism of the pulps, Ahmed's refreshingly non-Eurocentric fantasy world—the Crescent Moon Kingdoms—draws on Middle Eastern legends and evokes comparison to the mythical Arabia of* The One Thousand and One Nights. *There's room for further novels and the second in the series is set for publication September 2017.*

WHERE VIRTUE LIVES

Saladin Ahmed

"I'm telling you, Doctor, its eyes—its teeth! The hissing! Name of God, I've never been so scared!"

Doctor Adoulla Makhslood, the best ghul hunter in the great city of Dhamsawaat, was weary. Two and a half bars of thousand-sheet pastry sat on his plate, their honey and pistachio glazed layers glistening in the sunlight that streamed into Yehyeh's teahouse. Adoulla let out a belch. *Only two hours awake. Only partway through my pastry and cardamom tea, and already a panicked man stands chattering to me about a monster! God help me.*

He brushed green and gold pastry bits from his fingers onto his spotless kaftan. Magically, the crumbs and honey-spots slid from his garment to the floor, leaving no stain. The kaftan was as white as the moon. Its folds seemed to go on forever, much like the man sitting before him.

"That hissing! I'm telling you, I didn't mean to leave her. But by God, I was so scared!" Hafi, the younger cousin of Adoulla's dear friend Yehyeh, had said "I'm telling you" twelve times already. Repetition helped folk talk away their fear, so

Adoulla had let the man go on for a while. He had heard the story thrice now, listening for the inconsistencies fear introduces to memories—even honest men's memories.

Adoulla knew some of what he faced. A water ghul had abducted Hafi's wife, dragging her toward a red riverboat with eyes painted on its prow. Adoulla didn't need to hear any more from Hafi. What he needed was more tea. But there was no time.

"She's gone!" Hafi wailed. "That horrible thing took her! And like a coward, I ran! Will you help me, Doctor?"

For most of his life men had asked Adoulla this question. In his youth he'd been the best brawler on Dead Donkey Lane, and the other boys had looked up to him. Now men saw his attire and asked for his help with monsters. Adoulla knew too well that his head-hair had flown and his gut had grown. But his ghul hunter's raiment was unchanged after decades of grim work—still famously enchanted so that it could never be dirtied, and quietly blessed so that neither sword nor knife could pierce it.

Still, he didn't allow himself to feel too secure. In his forty years ghul hunting he'd faced a hundred deaths other than sword-death. Which deaths he would face today remained to be seen.

"Enough," Adoulla said, cutting off yet more words from Hafi. "I've some ideas where to start. I don't know if your wife still lives, young man. I can't promise to return her to you. But I'll try my best to do so, and to stop whomever's responsible, God damn them."

"Thank you, Doctor! Um . . . I mean . . . I hereby thank and praise you, and beg God's blessings for you, O great and virtuous ghul hunter!"

Does he think I'm some pompous physician, to be flattered by ceremony? A ghul hunter shared a title but little else with the haughty doctors of the body. No leech-wielding charlatan of a physician could stop the fanged horrors that Adoulla battled.

Adoulla swallowed a sarcastic comment and stood up. He embraced Hafi, kissing him on both cheeks. "Yes, well. I will do all I can, child of God." He dismissed the younger man with a reassuring pat on the back.

O God, Adoulla thought, why have You made this life so tiring? And why so full of interrupted meals? In six quick bites he ate the remaining pastries. Then, sweets in his belly and a familiar reluctance rising within him, he left Yehyeh's teahouse in search of a river boat with painted eyes, a ghul, and a bride whom Adoulla hoped to God was still alive.

Raseed bas Raseed frowned in distaste as he made his way down the crowded Dhamsawaat street his guide called the Lane of Monkeys. Six days ago Raseed had walked along a quiet road near the Lodge of God. Six days ago he'd killed three highwaymen. Now he was in Dhamsawaat, King of Cities, and there were dirty, wicked folk all about him. City people who spoke with too much speed and too little respect. Raseed brushed dust from his dervish-blue silks. As he followed his lanky guide through the press of people, he dwelt—though it was impermissibly proud to do so—on his encounter with the highwaymen.

"A 'Dervish Dressed In Blue,' eh? Just like in the song! I hear you sons of whores hide jewels in those pretty dresses."

"Haw haw! 'Dervish Dressed In Blue!' That's funny! Sing for us, little dervish!"

"What do you think that forked sword'll do against three men's spears, pup? Can your skinny arms even lift it?"

When the robbers had mentioned that blasphemous song, they had approached the line that separates life from death. When they had moved from rough talk to brandishing spears, they'd crossed that line. Three bodies now lay rotting by the road. Raseed tried not to smile with pride at the thought.

They'd underestimated him. He was six-and-ten, though he knew he hardly looked it. Clean-shaven, barely five feet, and thin-limbed as well. But his silk tunic and trousers—the habit of the Order—warned most ruffians that Raseed was no easy target. As did the curved sword at his hip, forked to "cleave the right from the wrong in men," as the Traditions of the Order put it. The blade and silks inspired respect in the cautious, but fools saw the scrawny boy and not the dervish.

That did not matter, though. Soon, God willing, Raseed would find the great and virtuous ghul hunter Adoulla Makhslood. If it pleased God, the Doctor would take Raseed as an apprentice. If Raseed was worthy.

But I am impatient. Proud. Are these virtues? The Traditions of the Order say, "A dervish without virtue is less than a beggar."

The sudden realization that he'd lost sight of his guide pulled him out of his reflections. For a moment Raseed panicked, but the lanky man stepped back into view, gesturing for him to follow. Raseed thanked God that he'd found a reverent and helpful guide, for Dhamsawaat's streets seemed endless. Raseed had been the youngest student ever to earn the blue silks. He feared neither robbers nor ghuls. But he would not know what to do if lost amidst this horde of lewd, impious people.

Life had been less confusing at the Lodge of God. But then High Shaykh Aalli had sent him to train with the Doctor.

"When you meet Adoulla Makhslood, little sparrow, you will see that there are truths greater than all you've learned in this Lodge. You will learn that virtue lives in strange places."

Before him, his guide came to a halt. "Here we are, master dervish. Just over that bridge."

At last. Raseed thanked the man and turned toward the small footbridge. The man tugged at Raseed's sleeve.

"Apologies, master dervish, but the watchmen will not let you cross without paying the crossing tax."

"Crossing tax?"

The man nodded. "And the bastards will charge you too much once they see your silks—they respect neither piety nor the Order. If you wish, though, I will haggle for you. A half-dirham should suffice. Were I a richer man I'd cover your tax myself—it's a sad world where a holy man must pay his way over bridges."

Raseed thanked the man for his kindness and handed him one of his few coins.

"Very good, master dervish. Now please stay out of sight while I bargain. I will return for you shortly. God be with you."

Raseed waited.

And waited.

Adoulla needed information. Ghuls had no souls of their own—they did only as their masters bade. Which meant that a vile man had used a water ghul in his bride-stealing scheme. And if there was one place Adoulla could go to learn of vile men's schemes, it was Miri's. There was no place in the world that pleased him more, nor any that hurt him so.

Though God alone knows when I'll get there. Adoulla walked the packed Mainway, wishing the crowd would move faster, knowing it wouldn't. Overturned cobblers' carts, dead pack animals, traffic-stopping processions of state—Dhamsawaat's hundred headaches hurried for no man. Not even when a ghul stalked the King of Cities.

By the time he reached Miri's tidy storefront it was past midday. Standing in the open doorway, Adoulla smelled sweet incense from iron burners and camelthorn from the hearth. For a long moment he stood there at the threshold, wondering why in the world he'd been away from this lovely place so long.

A corded forearm blocked his way, and another man's shadow fell over him. A muscular man even taller than Adoulla stood scowling before him, a long scar splitting his face into gruesome halves. He placed a broad palm on Adoulla's chest and grabbed a fistful of white kaftan.

"Ho-ho! Who's this forgetter-of-friends, slinking back in here so shamelessly?"

Adoulla smiled. "Just another foolish child of God who doesn't know to stay put, Axeface."

The two men embraced and kissed on both cheeks. Then Axeface bellowed toward an adjoining room, "The Doctor is here, Mistress. You want me to beat him up?"

Adoulla could not see Miri, but he heard her husky voice. "Not today, though I am tempted. Let the old fart through."

For one moment more, though, Axeface held him back. "She misses you, Doctor. I bet she'd still marry you. When're you gonna wake up, huh?" With a good-natured shove, he sent Adoulla stumbling into the greeting-room.

One of the regular girls, wearing a dress made of sheer cloth and copper coins, smiled at Adoulla. The coins jingled as she shimmied past, and he tried to keep from turning his head. *Just my luck*, he thought not for the first time, *that the woman I love runs the whorehouse with the city's prettiest girls.*

Then she was there. Miri Almoussa, Seller of Silks and Sweets, known to a select few as Miri of the Hundred Ears. Her thick curves jiggled as she moved, and her hands were hennaed. Adoulla had to remind himself that he was there to save a girl's life. "When one is married to the ghuls, one has three wives already," went the old ghul hunter's adage. *O God, how I wish I could take a fourth!*

Silently, Miri led him to a divan. She glared at him and brushed her hand over his beard, ridding it of crumbs he hadn't known were there. "You're a wonderful man," she said by way of greeting, "but you can be truly disgusting sometimes."

A man's slurred shouts boomed from the next room. Irritation flashed across Miri's face, but she spoke lightly. "Naj is usually so quiet. Wormwood wine makes him loud. At least he's not singing. Last week it was ten rounds of 'The Druggist, the Draper, and the Man Who Made Paper' before he passed out. Name of God, how I hate that song!" She slid Adoulla a tray with coffee, little salt fish, and rice bread. Adoulla popped a fish into his mouth, the tiny bones crunching as he chewed. Despite the urgency of his visit he was hungry. And Miri was not a woman to be rushed, no matter what the threat.

She continued. "Unlike *some* people, though, Naj can be counted on to be here every week, helping to keep me and mine from poverty. It's been a while, Doullie. What do you want?" She set her powder-painted features into an indifferent mask.

"I'm wondering, pretty one, if you've heard anything about a stolen bride in the Quarter of Stalls."

Miri smiled a disgusted smile. "Predictable! Of course you already have your gigantic nose in this nonsense! Well. For the usual fee plus . . . five percent, I might remember something my Ears have heard."

"A price hike, huh?" Adoulla sighed. "You know I'll pay what you ask, my sweet."

"Indeed you will. We may be more than friends here and there, 'my sweet,' but we're not man and wife. *Your* choice, remember? Our monies are separate. And this, Doullie, is about money. Now, according to my Ears . . . "

A name would've made Adoulla's task easier, but Miri's information was almost as good. A red riverboat with eyes painted on the prow had been spotted only two hours ago at an abandoned dock near the Low Bridge of Boats. And Hafi's wife may not have been the first woman taken by the ghul. Two of Miri's Ears said the ghul served a man, one said a woman, but none had gotten a close look.

Still, Adoulla had a location now. Enough to act on. And so, calling himself mad for the thousandth time in his life, Adoulla prepared to leave a wonderful woman's company to chase after monsters.

Raseed approached the well-kept storefront and allowed himself to hope. This was not Adoulla Makhslood's home, but after Raseed's "guide" had absconded, an old woman had led Raseed to this storefront, insisting that she had just seen the Doctor enter.

Raseed paused at the threshold. He had journeyed far, and if it pleased God he'd have a new teacher. *If* it pleased God. He took a measured breath and stepped through the doorway.

Inside, the large greeting-room was dim. Scant sunlight made its way through high windows. Tall couches lined the wall opposite the door, and a few well-dressed men sat on them, each speaking to a woman. And at the center of the room, on a juniper-wood divan, sat a middle-aged woman and an old man in a spotless kaftan. They stared as a massive man with a scar ushered Raseed in. Raseed looked at the man in white. *Doctor Adoulla Makhslood?*

It had to be him. He was the right age, though Raseed had expected the Doctor to be leaner. And clean-shaven. This old man had the bumpy knuckles of a fist-fighter. *Can this rough-looking one really be him?*

Raseed bowed his head. "Begging your pardon, but are you Doctor Adoulla Makhslood? The great and virtuous ghul hunter?"

The man snorted a laugh. " 'Great and virtuous'? No, boy, you're looking for someone else. I'm Doctor Adoulla Makhslood, the best belcher in Dhamsawaat. If I see this other fellow, though, I'll tell him you're looking for him."

Raseed was confused. *Perhaps he's testing me somehow.* He spoke carefully. "I apologize for disturbing you, Doctor. I am Raseed bas Raseed and I have come, at High Shaykh Aalli's bidding, to offer you my sword in apprenticeship." He bowed and waited for the Doctor's response.

Old Shaykh Aalli? The only true dervish Adoulla had ever known? Adoulla had assumed that ancient Aalli had gone to meet God years ago. Was it really possible this Raseed had been sent by the High Shaykh? And might the boy be of some help? The Doctor sized up the five-foot dervish. He was yellow-toned with tilted eyes and a clean-shaven face. He looked like one who had killed but did not yet value life.

A scabbard of blue leather and lapis lazuli hung at the boy's waist. Adoulla smiled as he thought of the bawdy song that poked fun at an "ascetic" dervish's love for his jeweled scabbard. The tune was as catchy as the words were blasphemous. Without meaning to, Adoulla started humming "Dervish Dressed In Blue." The boy frowned, then bit his lip.

God help me, he looks so sincere. Adoulla sighed and stood, avoiding Miri's glare. "We'll talk as we walk, boy. A girl's life is in danger and time is short." He paid Miri her fee, mumbled his inadequate goodbyes, and herded the boy out onto the street.

A dervish of the Order. Adoulla decided he could not ignore the advantages of having such a swordsman at his side. After all, who knew what awaited him at the Low Bridge of Boats? He was easily winded these days, and he had no time to stop by his townhouse for more supplies. He needed help, truth be told. But first the boy had to be set straight.

"The name of Shaykh Aalli goes far indeed with me, boy. You may accompany me for now. But we're not in a holy man's parable. We're trying to save a poor girl's life and keep from getting ourselves killed. God's gifts and my own study have given me useful powers. But I'll kick a man in his fig-sack if need be, make no mistake. A real girl has been stolen by a real monster. God forbid it, she may be dead. But it's our job to help however we can."

The boy looked uncomfortable, but he bowed his head and said "Yes, Doctor." That would be enough for now.

The thoroughfare the Doctor called the Street of Festivals was lined with townhouses separated by small gardens. A girl hawked purple pickles from a copper bowl. Raseed smelled something foul, but it wasn't the pickles.

Two houses down a human head had been mounted above the doorway.

The Doctor spat. "The work of 'His Greatness' the Khalif. That is the head of Nassaar Jamala. Charged with treason. He made a few loud speeches at market. Meanwhile, young brides are abducted by ghuls and the watchmen do nothing."

"Surely, Doctor, if the man was a traitor it was righteous that he should die," Raseed said.

"And how is it that *you* are a scholar of righteousness, boy? Because you're clean-shaven and take no wine? Shave your beard and scour your soul?" The Doctor squinted at Raseed. "Do you even need to shave yet? Hmph. What trials has your mewling soul faced, O master dervish of six-and-ten-whole-years? O kisser of I-am-guessing-exactly-zero-girls?"

The Doctor waved his big hand as if brushing away his own words. "Look. There are three possibilities. One, you're a madman or a crook passing yourself off as a dervish. Two, you are a real Lodge-trained holy man—which in all likelihood still makes you a corrupt bully. Three—" he gave Raseed a long look. "Three, you are the second dervish of the Order I've ever met who actually lives by his world-saving oaths. If so, boy, you've a cruel, disappointing life ahead."

" 'God's mercy is more powerful than all the world's cruelties' " Raseed recited. But the Doctor merely snorted and walked on.

As Raseed followed through the throngs of people, his soul sank. Despite years of training he felt like a small boy, lost and about to cry. His long journey was over. He had made it to Dhamsawaat. He had found the man Shaykh Aalli named the Crescent Moon Kingdoms' greatest ghul hunter.

And the man was an impious slob.

Doubt began to overwhelm Raseed. What would he do now? He knew that he needed direction—he wasn't so proud that he couldn't admit that. But what could he learn from this gassy, unkempt man?

And yet Raseed could not deny that there was something familiar about Adoulla Makhslood. A strength of presence not unlike High Shaykh Aalli's that seared past the Doctor's sleepy-seeming eyes. Perhaps . . .

He didn't realize he'd come to a halt until a beggar elbowed past him. The Doctor, a dozen yards ahead, turned and hollered at him to hurry. Raseed followed, and they walked on into the late afternoon.

It was nearly evening when they finally approached the abandoned dock near the Low Bridge of Boats. *There should be watchmen here, keeping the street people from moving in*, Adoulla thought. But neither vagrants nor patrols were in sight. *Bribery. Or murder.*

"Doctor!" The boy's whisper was sharp as he pointed out onto the river.

Adoulla saw it too: the red riverboat. He cursed as he saw that it was already leaving the dock. The owner had seen their approach—a lookout spell, no doubt. Adoulla cursed again. Then two figures stepped out from behind a dockhouse twenty yards ahead.

They were shaped vaguely like men, but Adoulla knew the scaly grey flesh and glowing eyes. *Water ghuls. And not one of them, but two!*

Adoulla thanked God that he had the little dervish with him. "Enemies, boy!"

The ghuls hissed through barb-toothed leech-mouths, and their eyes blazed crimson. It was no wonder Hafi had run from them. Any man in his right mind would have.

Adoulla dug into his kidskin satchel and withdrew two jade marbles. He clacked the spheres together in one hand and recited from the Heavenly Chapters.

"God the All-Merciful forgives us our failings."

The jade turned to ash in Adoulla's palm, and there was a noise like a crashing wave. The water ghul nearest him lost its shape and collapsed into a harmless puddle of stinking liquid, twitching with dead snakes and river-spiders.

The drain of the invocation hit Adoulla and he felt as if he'd dashed up a hill. *So much harder every year!*

The other ghul came at them. Raseed sped past Adoulla, his forked sword slashing. The creature snaked left. The boy's weapon whistled through empty air. The ghul drove its scaly fist hard into the boy's jaw. It struck a second time, catching Raseed in the chest. Adoulla was amazed that the boy still stood.

Regaining his own strength, Adoulla reached back into his satchel. He'd had only the two marbles but there was another invocation . . . *Where is that vial?* The ghul struck at Raseed a third time—

And the boy dodged. He spun and launched a hard kick into the ghul's midsection. Its red eyes registered no pain, but the creature scrabbled backward.

Adoulla marveled at the boy's speed. Raseed's sword flashed once, twice, thrice, four times. And Adoulla saw that his other invocation would not be needed.

Ghuls fell harder than men, but they fell all the same. The boy had finished this one. Its hissing shifted into the croaks and buzzes of swamp vermin. Its claws raked the air. Then, its false soul snuffed out, the thing collapsed in a watery pile of dead frogs and leeches.

Adoulla smiled at the puddle. *So he's not all bravado, then. Ten-and-six years old!* "Well done, dervish! I've seen stone-hard soldiers run the other way when faced with those glowing eyes. But you stood your ground and you're still alive!"

"It . . . it wouldn't die!" the boy stammered. "I cut it enough to kill five men! It wouldn't die!"

"It was a ghul, boy, not some drunken bully! Let me guess: for all your zeal, this is the first time you've faced one. Well, I won't lie. You did brilliantly. But our work isn't done. We've got to find that boat."

"Brilliantly," he said. Raseed sheathed his sword, trying not to feel pride. He had killed a ghul!

"Thank you, Doctor. I hope—"

He heard a noise from the dockhouse. To his surprise, a scrawny young woman stepped from the shadows. Except that there was not enough shadow there to have hidden her. *How could I not have seen her? Impossible!* The girl wore a dirty dress with billowy sleeves. Her face was a small oval, her left eye badly bruised.

"You killed them," she said. "You *killed* them!"

The Doctor smiled at her. "Well, not killed, exactly, dear. They never truly lived. But we stopped them, yes." He bowed slightly, like a modest performer.

"But he said they couldn't be killed! He swore it!"

The Doctor's expression turned grim. "Who swore it? Are you not Hafi's wife? Did these creatures not attack you?"

The girl frowned. "Attack me? I . . . he *swore*," she said dazedly. "They . . . gave me time." She shook her head, as if driving some thought away, and raised a clenched fist. As she did, Raseed saw that she held two short pieces of rope, one white, one blue. His keen eyes noted intricate knots tied at the end of each. The girl raised the white rope—tied with a fat, squarish knot—to her mouth.

"Damn it! Stop her!" the Doctor shouted. There was an unnaturally loud whispery sound as the girl blew on the white rope. As Raseed stood there confused, Adoulla's shout twisted into a scream. The Doctor hunched over, gripping his midsection in agony. He spoke around gritted teeth. "Get. Ropes."

The girl blew on the knot again, and Raseed heard another whispery puff-of-air sound. The old man screamed again and dropped to his knees.

Knot-blowing! Raseed had never seen such wicked magic at work, but he'd heard dark stories. He charged as he saw the girl raise the blue rope—tied with a small, sleek knot—to her lips. *That one's for me*, he realized. But Raseed was too swift. He crossed the space between them and palm-punched the woman flat on her back. The little ropes flew from her hand. Before she could get to her feet, Raseed's sword sang out of its scabbard. He held its forked tip to her throat.

The Doctor shuffled up beside him, panting and still wincing with pain. "Let her stand," he said, and Raseed did so. The Doctor's tone was hard but strangely courteous. "So. Young lady. Blower-on-knots. Were these *your* pet ghuls we destroyed?"

The girl sounded half asleep. "No. Pets? No. Zoud said that . . . Said that . . . " She eyed Raseed's sword fearfully and trailed off.

The Doctor took a deep breath and gestured to Raseed, so he brought the blade away from the girl's throat. But he did not sheathe it.

The Doctor's voice grew infuriatingly gentle. "Let's begin again. What's your name, girl?"

The girl's eyes lost a bit of their glaze. She had the decency to look ashamed. "My name's Ushra."

"And who has hurt you, Ushra? The magus who made these ghuls? What's his name?"

The girl looked at the ghuls' puddle-remains. "He . . . my husband is called

Zoud. He sent me to stop you while he got away. I'm his wife. First wife. I've . . . I've helped him catch others. Four . . . five now?"

Wickedness, Raseed thought. *This one deserves death.*

"Well, his girl-stealing days are over," the Doctor said. "Whatever's happened, we'll help you, Ushra, but we also need your help."

Raseed could not keep his disapproval to himself. "And why have you never run away, woman? Or used your knots on this Zoud?"

"I would never! I *could* never. You shouldn't say such things!" Ushra looked terrified, and for a moment Raseed almost forgot that she was a wicked blower-on-knots who had just made the Doctor helpless with her magic. For a moment.

"I must go back!" she said. "He'll find me. He'll make more ghuls! He'll feed my living skin to them! He did it with his stolen wives . . . "

The Doctor sucked in an angry-sounding breath. "We'll stop him, Ushra. Where is he going in that riverboat? Where can we find him?"

Raseed could not let this interrogation continue. "With apologies, Doctor, this one has worked wicked magics and must be punished. It is impermissible, according to the Traditions of the Order, to twist information from one who must be slain."

The Doctor threw his hands up. "God save us from fanatical children! We're not going to slay her. We're going to stop this half-dinar magus Zoud, and save Hafi's wife. Whatever your Shaykhs taught you, boy, if you wish to study with me you will—"

The puff-of-air sound again.

Another rope. She had another rope hidden in those sleeves! As Raseed thought it, his vision went black.

Blinded! It was so sudden that he cried out in spite of himself. He felt a soft hand on his face. Then his stomach twisted up and his mind stopped working properly. All around him was darkness and his thoughts seemed wrapped in cotton. **What is this? What foul magic has she worked on me?**

Raseed could not ask the Doctor, because the Doctor was not there.

Adoulla heard the puff-of-air sound again, and suddenly he was alone on the dock. The girl had disappeared and, along with her, Raseed.

Damn me for a fool! A whisking spell, no doubt, used to travel from the location of one object to another. Adoulla had seen such magic before—leaving an ensorcelled coin at home and carrying its counterpart to provide a quick escape—but he hadn't known knot-blowing could be used the same way. *She must have touched the boy, too.* The girl's power was great, if feral. Adoulla himself avoided such spells. It only took one bad whisking to break a mind, and the caster never knew when it was coming. No quick trip home was worth a lifetime of gibbering idiocy.

He had to find them, and fast. Praise God, he had a name now. A crude tracking spell, then. He would have a splitting headache the next day from the casting, but it was his only choice. Standing on the still-quiet dock, Adoulla dug charcoal and a square of paper from his satchel. After writing the Name of God on the front of the paper and "Zoud" on the back, he pulled forth a platinum needle, pricked his thumb, and squeezed one drop of blood onto Zoud's name. He rolled the square into a tube and placed it in his pocket. The mental tug he felt meant God had deemed Adoulla's quarry cruel enough to lead His servant to the man. He followed it eastward, the half-sunk sun at his back.

He cursed himself five times as he crossed Archer's Yard. Adoulla had shown mercy, and the girl had betrayed him. The dervish had been right. Adoulla was a soft old man who called for tea when he should be calling for the blood of his enemies. The Yard's hay training targets stood abandoned now, a few arrows still sticking out of them. To Adoulla's mind the arrows seemed accusatory fingers pointing at him—a fuzzy-headed fool whose weak heart had killed a boy of six-and-ten.

No. Not if he could help it. He had brought the boy into this mess. Now, if Raseed still lived, Adoulla would get him out of it.

Raseed awoke blindfolded, gagged, and bound. During his training he'd learned to snap any bonds that held him, no matter how well tied. But something was wrong here. He was bound not with rope or chain, but with some fiendish substance that burned hotter the harder he tried to escape.

His struggles caused him a slicing pain in his wrists and ankles, but for an uncontrolled moment he thrashed like a madman.

Calm yourself! He was disgusted at how easily he lost a dervish's dignity. He went into a breathing exercise, timing his inhalations and exhalations. The first thing was to figure out where he was. They had blindfolded him, which meant that the knot-blower's blinding curse was not permanent. *Praise God for that.* Adapting quickly, Raseed let his other senses take over. He heard the cries of rivergulls and a splashing sound against one wall. He smelled water and felt himself swaying. A boat. *Zoud's. The one we saw leaving.* Raseed was captive on a boat, and bleeding.

He wondered where the Doctor was. *I should not have listened to him. He is old and grown soft.* Raseed could have ended the girl's life and ought to have done so. Now it was too late. Impermissible panic began to rise in him.

Inhale . . . exhale. He would not feel fear. He would find a way out.

Suddenly Raseed heard a sobbing sound. A young woman crying as she spoke. "I'm sorry, holy man. So sorry. The whisking spell could have killed you."

Ushra. Perhaps a yard away from him. From the same direction he heard glass clink and smelled something acidic.

"What can I do?" the girl continued, her voice moving about. "I'm damned. I didn't want to be his wife, master dervish. He . . . he took me and he made me need him. But the things he did to the other wives . . . " The girl wept wordlessly for a moment, then took a deep breath. "Please don't scream," she whispered, pulling down Raseed's gag.

Talk to her!

Raseed felt that God was with him, for the words came quickly. "You can correct your wickedness, Ushra. You can make amends for your foulness. 'In the eyes of God our kindnesses weigh twice our cruelties.' "

She untied his blindfold, and Raseed blinked at the dim lantern-light. Ushra crouched before him, a long glass vial in the crook of her arm. The look on the girl's face gave him hope. *'Our kindnesses weigh twice our cruelties.'* The scripture echoed in Raseed's head.

"Zoud's gone now, master dervish, but he'll return soon. He left me to guard you." She took a breath and closed her eyes. "I know I can't fix everything. But I freed the girl, his new wife. That will weigh well with God, won't it?"

Raseed would not presume to speak for Him. He said simply, "God is All-Merciful."

The girl opened her teary eyes and spoke more swiftly. "He bound you with firevine. It can't be untied. I've poisoned it, but it'll take an hour to die. God willing, it'll die before he returns." More weeping. "I *am* foul, holy man. My soul is dirty. But, God forgive me, I want to live. I have to go. You don't know the things he can do, master dervish. I have to go."

Ushra went.

But she's freed Hafi's wife! Raseed praised God as he lay there captive, bleeding, alone.

The red riverboat had docked near the High Bridge of Boats. Adoulla found the hatch open and thanked God. He made his way into the cabins without being discovered, which meant that this Zoud was either blessedly overconfident or waiting for him. For a moment Adoulla half-hoped that he'd find Raseed and the magus's "wives" before Zoud found him.

But then, as he came to the threshold of a cabin that seemed impossibly spacious, he heard whistling. It was "The Druggist, the Draper, and the Man Who Made Paper," Miri's least-favorite song. *Not a good omen.*

The room *was* impossibly spacious, Adoulla realized. A magically-enlarged cabin, grown to the size of a tavern's greeting-room. In a far corner the dervish lay bound on the floor. *Firevine!* Dried blood ringed Raseed's wrists and ankles.

Between Adoulla and the boy stood Zoud.

The magus was gaunt and bald with a pointed beard. Raseed's sheathed sword lay at Zoud's feet, and beside the magus stood an oaf whose size made his purpose obvious—*bodyguard*. There was no way Adoulla could reach the dervish before those two did.

Zoud, disturbingly unsurprised at Adoulla's entrance, stopped whistling and gestured toward Raseed. "He is in great pain."

Adoulla frowned. "Why stage this gruesome show for me?"

Zoud smiled. "Simple. I'm no fool—I know your sort. I don't want you as an enemy. Hounding me across the Crescent Moon Kingdoms on some revenge-quest. No. All I ask is your oath before God that you'll leave me in peace. I'd hoped to take the boy with me—the Order has enemies who'd pay well for a live dervish. But if you'll be reasonable you may walk off this ship, and we'll put the boy off as well. That's fair, isn't it? You've taken much from me already. My new wife. Even my first wife."

Ushra's not here? And Hafi's wife is free? How? Adoulla could find out later. What mattered now was that his options had just increased. In the corner behind the magus and his henchman, Adoulla saw a small flicker of blue movement. *Impossible!*

He smothered a smile and silently thanked God.

"So," Zoud said. "Do I have your oath, Doctor?"

Adoulla cleared his throat. "My Oath? In the Name of God I swear that you, with your tacky big-room spells, are but a half-dinar magus with a broken face coming to him!"

Everything happened at once.

He heard a snapping noise and the boy was free. It was impossible to snap firevine. But Adoulla adapted quickly to impossibilities. As Raseed leapt to his feet Zoud darted behind his bodyguard and screamed "Babouk! Kill!" The magus clapped twice.

Oh no.

The flash of red light dazzled Adoulla for a moment. But his eyes knew and adjusted to the glamour-glimmer of a dispelled illusion well enough. Adoulla had to give this fool Zoud his due. The big bodyguard was gone. In his place was an eight-foot-tall cyklop.

This is not good.

A blue streak darted at the one-eyed, crimson-scaled creature. *Raseed!* The dimwitted monster grunted as the dervish barreled into it and knocked the mighty thing off its clawed feet.

Adoulla stood there for a stunned half-moment. *Half the monster's size, yet he topples it!* Dervish and furnace-chested cyklop wrestled on the ground until the monster wrapped its massive arms around the boy. Adoulla took a step toward the pair and shouted "Its eye! One sword-stroke through its eye!"

Then he whirled at the familiar sound of blade leaving sheath. Zoud stood before him with a hunted look on his face and a silver-hilted knife in his hand. *All out of tricks, huh? And now you think to buy your freedom with a knife?* Adoulla cracked his knuckles and took a step toward the magus.

Raseed wriggled free of the cyklop's crushing hug. The monster pressed him again, closing its clawed hands around Raseed's fists. His wounds from the firevine burned, but he pushed the pain away.

As part of his training, Raseed had once wrestled a northern bear. This creature was stronger. Still, Raseed thought, as impermissible pride crept in, he would slay it. Then he'd know that he had fought a cyklop and won. He twisted his powerful arms, trying to get the leverage to free himself. But the cyklop held him fast. And the pain in Raseed's wrists and ankles grew worse.

Then he heard a small sound and his left hand blazed with pain. His little finger was broken. Another sound. His index finger. The rest would follow if he did not get free. But how?

The cyklop decided for him. Shifting, it hoisted Raseed aloft like a doll. The monster tried to dash Raseed's brains out on the floorboards.

Raseed twisted as he fell, somersaulting across the room. His sword hand was unharmed. He thanked God and forced away the pain of his wounds. He scooped up the blue scabbard, rolled to his feet, drew.

The cyklop grunted. It blinked its teacup-sized eye as Raseed rushed forward. With eagle-speed Raseed leapt, sword extended. He thrust upward.

With an earsplitting howl, the cyklop fell, blood seeping from its single eye. Watching the monster die, Raseed felt more relief than pride.

Adoulla charged Zoud, making sure that his robed shoulder was his opponent's most prominent target. A sneer flashed on Zoud's face. The fool thought Adoulla was blundering into his dagger-path.

The silver-handled blade came down.

And glanced off the blessed kaftan, as surely as if Adoulla were wearing mail. Zoud got in one more useless stab before Adoulla let loose the right hook that had once made him the best street fighter on Dead Donkey Lane. With a girlish cry, the magus crumpled into a heap. Somewhere behind Adoulla, the cyklop howled its death-howl.

His tricks gone and his nose broken, Zoud lay bleeding at Adoulla's feet. The magus whimpered to himself like a child yanked from a good dream. Before Adoulla knew what was happening, Raseed was at his side.

"Magus!" the dervish said. "You have stolen and slain women. You dared demand an oath before God to cover your foulness. For you, there can be no forgiveness!" Raseed sent his blade diving for Zoud's heart. In a breathspace, the forked sword found it. The magus's eyes went wide as he gurgled and died.

Adoulla felt ill.

"What is wrong with you, boy? We had the man at our -" He fell silent, seeing the boy's firevine wounds.

Raseed narrowed his tilted eyes. "With apologies, Doctor, I expected Adoulla Makhslood to be a man who struck swiftly and righteously."

"And instead you've found some pastry-stuffed old fart who isn't fond of killing. Poor child! God must weep at your cruel fate."

"Doctor! To take God's name in mock is imper—"

"Enough, boy! Do you hear me? Fight monsters for forty years as I have—cross the seas and sands of the Crescent Moon Kingdoms serving God—then *you* can tell *me* what is 'impermissible.' By then, Almighty God willing, I'll be dead and gone, my ears untroubled by the peeps of holy men's mouths!" The tirade silenced the dervish, who stood looking down at the magus's bleeding corpse.

The problem was, Adoulla feared that the boy's way might be right. Adoulla thought of the girl, Ushra. And of Raseed's pain as the firevine had tortured him. And of Zoud's dead "wives." He sighed.

"Oh, God damn it all. Fine, boy. You're right. Just as you were about the blower-on-knots." Adoulla sat down with a grunt, right there on the bloody floorboards. He had fought a dozen battles more difficult than this over the decades, but he did not think he'd ever felt so weary.

Raseed spoke slowly. "No, Doctor. *You* were right. About Ushra, at least. She did what she did from weakness and fear of a wicked man. Yet I would've killed her." The dervish was quiet for a long moment. "It was her, Doctor. Ushra. She poisoned the firevine. She freed Hafi's wife. I'm ashamed to say it, but I must speak true—I wouldn't have escaped if not for her."

Adoulla was too tired to respond with words. He grunted again and clambered to his feet.

Yehyeh's teahouse buzzed with chattering customers. Raseed tried to ignore the lewd music and banter. Hafi and his tall, raven-haired wife sat with her grateful parents on a pile of cushions in the far corner. At a table near the entrance, Raseed sat with the Doctor, who was nursing what he had called a "God damned gruesome tracking spell headache". Lifting his head from his hands slowly, the Doctor fixed a droopy eye on Raseed.

"How many men have you killed, boy?"

Raseed was confused—why did that matter now? "Two. No . . . the highway-men . . . five? After this villain last night, six."

"So many?" the Doctor said.

Raseed did not know what to say, so he said nothing.

Adoulla sighed. "You're a fine warrior, Raseed bas Raseed. If you're to study with me, though, you must know your number and never forget it. You took a man's life yesterday. Weigh that fact! Make it harder than it is for you now. Remember that a man, even a foul man, is not a ghul."

Again, Raseed was confused. "'Harder,' Doctor? I've trained all my life to kill swiftly."

"And now you will train to kill reluctantly. *If* you still wish an apprenticeship."

"I do still wish it, Doctor! High Shaykh Aalli spoke of you as—"

"People speak of me, boy, but now you've met me. You've fought beside me. I eat messily. I ogle girls one-third my age. And I don't like killing. If you're going to hunt monsters with me, you must see things as they are."

Raseed, his broken fingers still stinging, his wrists and ankles still raw, nodded and recalled the High Shaykh's words about where virtue lives. *Strange places indeed.*

A quiet settled over the table and Adoulla devoured another of the almond-and-anise rolls that Yehyeh had been gratefully plying him with. As he ate he thought about the boy sitting across from him.

He did not relish the thought of a preachy little dervish in his home. He could only hope the boy was young enough to stretch beyond the smallness that had been beaten into him at the Lodge. Regardless, only a fool would refuse having a decades-younger warrior beside him as he went about his last years of ghul hunting.

Besides, the dervish, with his meticulous grooming, would make a great house-keeper!

He could hear Miri's jokes about boy-love already.

Miri. God help me.

Raseed lifted his bowl of plain limewater and sipped daintily. Adoulla said nothing to break the silence, but he slurped his sweet cardamom tea. Then he set his teabowl down, belched loudly, and relished the horrified grimace of his virtuous new apprentice.

⚔

The novels of Scott Lynch's The Gentleman Bastard series—starting with The Lies of Locke Lamora *(2006)—combine crime with sword and sorcery. The "Gentle Bastard" protagonists are a pair of thieves, rogues who use elaborate cons to swindle the rich. (Think: a swashbuckling* Oceans Eleven *fantasy.) A seven-book series, we are still awaiting the fourth volume, but I'm confident the wait will be worth it. In "The Effigy Engine" Lynch introduces the Red Hats, "a tight-knit pack of lunatics, misfits, and idealists, [that] somehow always manage to find themselves in the service of the smaller, weaker party in any given disagreement"—according to the author—and wars are waged with musketry and magic. (Lynch's even more S&S-ish novelette "In the Stacks" will be reprinted next month in my anthology* Ex Libris: Stories of Librarians, Libraries, and Lore.*)*

THE EFFIGY ENGINE: A TALE OF THE RED HATS

Scott Lynch

11TH MITHUNE, 1186
PAINTED SKY PASS, NORTH ELARA

"I took up the study of magic because I wanted to live in the beauty of transfinite mathematical truths," said Rumstandel. He gestured curtly. In the canyon below us, an enemy soldier shuddered, clutched at his throat, and began vomiting live snakes.

"If my indifference were money you'd be the master of my own personal mint," I muttered. Of course Rumstandel heard me despite the pop, crackle, and roar of musketry echoing around the walls of the pass. There was sorcery at play between us to carry our voices, so we could bitch and digress and annoy ourselves like a pair of inebriates trading commentary in a theater balcony.

The day's show was an ambush of a company of Iron Ring legionaries on behalf of our employers, the North Elarans, who were blazing away with arquebus and harsh language from the heights around us. The harsh language seemed to be having greater effect. The black-coated ranks of the Iron Ring jostled in consternation, but there weren't enough bodies strewn among the striated sunset-orange rocks that gave the pass its name. Hot lead was leaving the barrels of our guns, but it was landing like kitten farts and some sly magical bastard down there was responsible.

Oh, for the days of six months past, when the Iron Ring had crossed the Elaran border marches, their battle wizards proud and laughing in full regalia. Their can't-miss-me-at-a-mile wolf-skull helmets, their set-me-on-fire carnelian cloaks, their shoot-me-in-the-face silver masks.

Six months with us for playmates had taught them to be less obvious. Counter-thaumaturgy was our mission and our meal ticket: coax them into visibility and make them regret it. Now they dressed like common officers or soldiers, and some even carried prop muskets or pikes. Like this one, clearly.

"I'm a profound disappointment to myself," sighed Rumstandel, big round florid Rumstandel, who didn't share my appreciation for sorcerous anonymity. This week he'd turned his belly-scraping beard blue and caused it to spring out in flaring forks like the sculpture of a river and its tributaries. Little simulacra of ships sailed up and down those beard strands even now, their hulls the size of rice grains, dodging crumbs like rocks and shoals. Crumbs there were aplenty, since Rumstandel always ate while he killed and soliloquized. One hand was full of the sticky Elaran ration bread we called corpsecake for its pallor and suspected seasoning.

"I should be redefining the vocabulary of arcane geometry somewhere safe and cultured, not playing silly buggers with village fish-charmers wearing wolf skulls." He silenced himself with a mouthful of cake and gestured again. Down on the valley floor his victim writhed his last. The snakes came out slick with blood, eyes gleaming like garnets in firelight, nostrils trailing strands of pale caustic vapor.

I couldn't really pick out the minute details at seventy yards, but I'd seen the spell before. In the closed ranks of the Iron Ring the serpents wrought the havoc that arquebus fire couldn't, and legionaries clubbed desperately at them with musket-butts.

As I peered into the mess, the forward portion of the legionary column exploded in white smoke. Sparks and chips flew from nearby rocks, and I felt a burning pressure between my eyes, a sharp tug on the strands of my own magic. The practical range of sorcery is about that of musketry, and a fresh reminder of the fact hung dead in the air a yard from my face. I plucked the ball down and slipped it into my pocket.

Somewhere safe and cultured? Well, there was nowhere safer for Rumstandel than three feet to my left. I was doing for him what the troublemaker on the ground was doing for the legionaries. Close protection, subtle and otherwise, my military and theoretical specialty.

Wizards working offensively in battle have a bad tendency to get caught up in their glory-hounding and part their already tenuous ties to prudence. Distracted and excited, they pile flourish on flourish, spell on spell until some stray musket ball happens along and elects to take up residence.

Our little company's answer is to work in teams, one sorcerer working harm and the second diligently protecting them both. Rumstandel didn't have the temperament to be that second sorcerer, but I've been at it so long now everyone calls me Watchdog. Even my mother.

I heard a rattling sound behind us, and turned in time to see Tariel hop down into our rocky niche, musket held before her like an acrobat's pole. Red-gray dust was caked in sweaty spirals along her bare ebony arms, and the dozens of wooden powder flasks dangling from her bandolier knocked together like a musical instrument.

"Mind if I crouch in your shadow, Watchdog? They're keeping up those volleys in good order." She knelt between me and Rumstandel, laid her musket carefully in the crook of her left arm, and whispered, "Touch." The piece went off with the customary flash and bang, which my speech-sorcery dampened to a more tolerable pop.

Hers was a salamandrine musket. Where the flintlock or wheel mechanism might ordinarily be was instead a miniature metal sculpture of a manor house, jutting from the weapon's side as though perched atop a cliff. I could see the tiny fire elemental that lived in there peering out one of the windows. It was always curious to see how a job was going. Tariel could force a spark from it by pulling the trigger, but she claimed polite requests led to smoother firing.

"Damn. I seem to be getting no value for money today, gents." She began the laborious process of recharging and loading.

"We're working on it," I said. Another line of white smoke erupted below, followed by another cacophony of ricochets and rock chips. An Elaran soldier screamed. "Aren't we working on it, Rumstandel? And by 'we' I do in fact mean—"

"Yes, yes, bullet-catcher, do let an artist stretch his own canvas." Rumstandel clenched his fists and something like a hot breeze blew past me, thick with power. This would be a vulgar display.

Down on the canyon floor, an Iron Ring legionary in the process of reloading was interrupted by the cold explosion of his musket. The stock shivered into splinters and the barrel peeled itself open backward like a sinister metal flower. Quick as thought, the burst barrel enveloped the man's arm, twisted, and—well, you've squeezed fruit before, haven't you? Then the powder charges in his bandolier flew out in burning constellations, a cloud of fire that made life immediately interesting for everyone around him.

"Ah! That's got his attention at last," said Rumstandel. A gray-blue cloud of mist boiled up from the ground around the stricken legionaries, swallowing and dousing the flaming powder before it could do further harm. Our Iron Ring friend was no longer willing to tolerate Rumstandel's contributions to the battle, and so inevitably . . .

"I see him," I shouted, "gesturing down there on the left! Look, he just dropped a pike!"

"Out from under the rock! Say your prayers, my man. Another village up north has lost its second-best fish-charmer!" said Rumstandel, moving his arms now like a priest in ecstatic sermon (recall my earlier warning about distraction and excitement). The Iron Ring sorcerer was hoisted into the air, black coat flaring, and as Rumstandel chanted his target began to spin.

The fellow must have realized that he couldn't possibly get anymore obvious, and he had some nerve. Bright blue fire arced up at us, a death-sending screaming with ghostly fury. My business. I took a clay effigy out of my pocket and held it up. The screaming blue fire poured itself into the little statuette, which leapt out of my hands and exploded harmlessly ten yards above. Dust rained on our heads.

The Iron Ring sorcerer kept rising and whirling like a top. One soldier, improbably brave or stupid, leapt and caught the wizard's boot. He held on for a few rotations before he was heaved off into some of his comrades.

Still that wizard lashed out. First came lightning like a white pillar from the sky. I dropped an iron chain from a coat sleeve to bleed its energy into the earth, though it made my hair stand on end and my teeth chatter. Then came a sending of bad luck I could feel pressing in like a congealing of the air itself; the next volley that erupted from the Iron Ring lines would doubtless make cutlets of us. I barely managed to unweave the sending, using an unseemly eruption of power that left me feeling as though the air had been punched out of my lungs. An instant later musket balls sparked and screamed on the rocks around us, and we all flinched. My previous spell of protection had lapsed while I was beset.

"Rumstandel," I yelled, "quit stretching the bloody canvas and paint the picture already!"

"He's quite unusually adept, this illiterate pot-healer!" Rumstandel's beard-boats rocked and tumbled as the blue hair in which they swam rolled like ocean waves. "The illicit toucher of sheep! He probably burns books to keep warm at home! And I'm only just managing to hold him—Tariel, please don't wait for my invitation to collaborate in this business!"

Our musketeer calmly set her weapon into her shoulder, whispered to her elemental, and gave fire. The spinning sorcerer shook with the impact. An instant later, his will no longer constraining Rumstandel's, he whirled away like a child's rag doll flung in a tantrum. Where the body landed, I didn't see. My sigh of relief was loud and shameless.

"Yes, that was competent opposition for a change, wasn't it?" Tariel was already calmly recharging her musket. "Incidentally, it was a woman."

"Are you sure?" I said once I'd caught my breath. "I thought the Iron Ringers didn't let their precious daughters into their war-wizard lodges."

"I'd guess they're up against the choice between female support and no support at all," she said. "Almost as though someone's been subtracting wizards from their muster rolls this past half-year."

The rest of the engagement soon played out. Deprived of sorcerous protection, the legionaries began to fall to arquebus fire in the traditional manner. Tariel kept busy, knocking hats from heads and heads from under hats. Rumstandel threw down just a few subtle spells of maiming and ill-coincidence, and I returned to my sober vigil, Watchdog once more. It wasn't in our contract to scourge the Iron Ringers from the field with sorcery. We wanted them to feel they'd been, in the main, fairly bested by their outnumbered Elaran neighbors, line to line and gun to gun, rather than cheated by magic of foreign hire.

After the black-clad column had retreated down the pass and the echo of musketry was fading, Rumstandel and I basked like lizards in the mid-afternoon sun and stuffed ourselves on corpsecake and cold chicken, the latter wrapped in fly-killing spells of Rumstandel's devising. No sooner would the little nuisances alight on our lunch than they would vanish in puffs of green fire.

Tariel busied herself cleaning out her musket barrel with worm and fouling scraper. When she'd finished, the fire elemental, in the form of a scarlet salamander that could hide under the nail of my smallest finger, went down the barrel to check her work.

"Excuse me, are you the—that is, I'm looking for the Red Hats."

A young Elaran in a dark blue officer's coat appeared from the rocks above us, brown ringlets askew, uniform scorched and holed from obvious proximity to trouble. I didn't recognize her from the company we'd been attached to. I reached into a pocket, drew out my rumpled red slouch hat, and waved it.

About the hats, the namesake of our mercenary fellowship: in keeping with the aforementioned and mortality-avoiding principle of anonymity, neither Tariel nor myself wore them when the dust was flying. Rumstandel never wore his at all, claiming with much justice that he didn't need the aid of any particular headgear to slouch.

"Red Hats present and reasonably comfortable," I said. "Some message for us?"

"Not a message, but a summons," said the woman. "Compliments from your captain, and she wants you back at the central front with all haste at any hazard."

"Central front?" That explained the rings under her eyes. Even with mount changes, that was a full day in the saddle. We'd been detached from what passed for our command for a week and hadn't expected to go back for at least another. "What's your story, then?"

"Ill news. The Iron Ring have some awful device, something unprecedented. They're breaking our lines like we weren't even there. I didn't get a full report before I was dispatched, but the whole front is collapsing."

"How delightful," said Rumstandel. "I do assume you've brought a cart for me? I always prefer a good long nap when I'm speeding on my way to a fresh catastrophe."

Note to those members of this company desirous of an early glimpse into these, our chronicles. As you well know, I'm pleased to read excerpts when we make camp and then invite corrections or additions to my records. I am not, however, amused to find the thumbprints of sticky-fingered interlopers defacing these pages without my consent. BE ADVISED, therefore, that I have with a spotless conscience affixed a dweomer of security to this journal and an attendant minor curse. I think you know the one I mean. The one with the fire ants. You have only yourself to blame. – WD

Watchdog, you childlike innocent, if you're going to secure your personal effects with a curse, don't attach a warning preface. It makes it even easier to enact countermeasures, and they were no particular impediment in the first place if you take my meaning. Furthermore, the poverty of your observational faculty continues to astound. You wrote that my beard was "LIKE the sculpture of a river and its tributaries", failing to note that it was in fact a PRECISE and proportional model of the Voraslo Delta, with my face considered as the sea. Posterity awaits your amendments. Also, you might think of a more expensive grade of paper when you buy your next journal. I've pushed my quill through this stuff three times already. – R

13TH MITHUNE, 1186
SOMEWHERE NEAR LAKE CORLAN, NORTH ELARA

Rumstandel, big red florid garlic-smelling Rumstandel, that bilious reservoir of unlovability, that human anchor weighing down my happiness, snored in the back of the cart far more peacefully than he deserved as we clattered up to the command pavilion of the North Elaran army. Pillars of black smoke rose north of us, mushrooming under wet gray skies. No campfire smoke, those pillars, but the sigils of rout and disaster.

North Elara is a temperate green place, long-settled, easy on the eyes and heart. It hurt to see it cut up by war like a patient strapped to a chirurgeon's operating board, straining against the incisions that might kill it as surely as the illness. Our trip along the rutted roads was slowed by traffic in both directions, supply trains moving north and the displaced moving south: farmers, fisherfolk, traders, camp followers, the aged and the young.

They hadn't been on the roads when we'd rattled out the previous week. They'd been nervous but guardedly content, keeping to their villages and camps behind the bulk of the Elaran army and the clever fieldworks that held the Iron Ring legions in stalemate. Now their mood had gone south and they meant to follow.

I rolled from the cart, sore where I wasn't numb. Elaran pennants fluttered wanly over the pavilion, and there were bad signs abounding. The smell of gangrene and freshly amputated limbs mingled with that of smoke and animal droppings. The command tents were now pitched about three miles south of where they'd been when I'd left.

I settled my red slouch on my head for identification, as the sentries all looked quite nervous. Tariel did the same. I glanced back at Rumstandel and found him still in loud repose. I called up one of my familiars with a particular set of finger-snaps and set the little creature on him in the form of a night-black squirrel with raven's wings. It hopped up and down on Rumstandel's stomach, singing:

Rouse, Rumstandel, and see what passes!
Kindle some zest, you laziest of asses!
Even sluggard Red Hats are called to war
So rouse yourself and slumber no more!

Some sort of defensive spell crept up from Rumstandel's coat like a silver mist, but the raven-squirrel fluttered above the grasping tendrils and pelted him with conjured acorns, while singing a new song about the various odors of his flatulence.

"My farts do not smell like glue!" shouted Rumstandel, up at last, swatting at my familiar. "What does that even mean, you wit-deficient pseudo-rodent?"

"Ahem," said a woman as she stepped out of the largest tent, and there was more authority in that clearing of her throat than there are in the loaded cannons of many earthly princes. My familiar, though as inept at rhyme as Rumstandel alleged, had a fine sense of when to vanish, and did so.

"I thought I heard squirrel doggerel," our captain, the sorceress Millowend, continued. "We must get you a better sort of creature one of these days."

It is perhaps beyond my powers to write objectively of Millowend, but in the essentials she is a short, solid, ashen-haired woman of middle years and innate rather than affected dignity. Her red hat, the iconic and original red hat, is battered and singed from years of campaigning despite the surfeit of magical protections bound into its warp and weft.

"Slack hours have been in short supply, ma'am."

"Well, I am at least glad to have you back in one piece, Watchdog," said my mother. "And you, Tariel, and even you, Rumstandel, though I wonder what's become of your hat."

"A heroic loss." Rumstandel heaved himself out of the cart, brushed assorted crumbs from his coat, and stretched in the manner of a rotund cat vacating a sunbeam. "I wore it through a fusillade of steel and sorcery. It was torn asunder, pierced by a dozen enemy balls and at least one culverin stone. We buried it with full military honors after the action."

"A grief easily assuaged." My mother conjured a fresh red hat and spun it toward the blue-bearded sorcerer's naked head. Just as deftly, he blasted it to motes with a gout of fire.

"Come along," said Millowend, unperturbed. This was the merest passing skirmish in the Affair of the Hat, possibly the longest sustained campaign in the history of our company. "We're all here now. I'll put you in the picture on horseback."

"Horseback?" said Rumstandel. "Freshly uncarted and now astride the spines of hoofed torture devices! Oh, hello, Caladesh."

The man tending the horses was one of us. Lean as a miser's alms-purse, mustaches oiled, carrying a brace of pistols so large I suspect they reproduce at night, Caladesh never changes. His hat is as red as cherry wine and has no magical protections at all save his improbable luck. Cal is worth four men in a fight and six in a drinking contest, but I was surprised to see him alone, minding exactly five horses.

"We're it," Millowend, as though reading my thoughts. Which was not out of the question. "I sent the others off with a coastal raid. They can't possibly return in time to help."

"And that's a fair pity," said Caladesh as he swung himself up into his saddle with easy grace. "There's fresh pie wrapped up in your saddlebags."

"A pie job!" cried Rumstandel. "Horses and a pie job! A constellation of miserable omens!"

His misgivings didn't prevent him, once saddled, from attacking the pie. I unwrapped mine and found it warm, firm, and lightly frosted with pink icing, the best sort my mother's culinary imps could provide. Alas.

Would-be sorcerers must understand that the art burns fuel as surely as any bonfire, which fuel being the sorcerer's own body. It's much like hard manual exercise, save that it banishes flesh even more quickly. During prolonged magical engagements I have felt unhealthy amounts of myself boil away. Profligate or sustained use of the art can leave us with skin hanging in folds, innards cramping, and bodily humors thrown into chaos.

That's why slender sorcerers are rarer than amiable scorpions, and why Rumstandel and I keep food at hand while plying our trade, and why my mother's sweet offering was as good as a warning.

In her train we rode north through the camp, past stands of muskets like sinister haystacks. These weren't the usual collections with soldiers lounging nearby ready to snatch them, but haphazard piles obviously waiting to be cleaned and sorted. Many Elaran militia and second-liners would soon be trading in their grandfatherly arquebuses for flintlocks pried from the hands of the dead.

"I'm sorry to reward you for a successful engagement by thrusting you into a bigger mess," said Millowend, "but the bigger mess is all that's on offer. Three days ago, the Iron Ring brought some sort of mechanical engine against our employers' previous forward position and kicked them out of it.

"It's an armored box, like the hull of a ship," she continued. "Balanced on mechanical legs, motive power unknown. Quick-steps over trenches and obstacles. The hull protects several cannon and an unknown number of sorcerers. Cal witnessed part of the battle from a distance."

"Wouldn't call it a battle," said Caladesh. "Battle implies some give and take, and this thing did nothing but give. The Elarans fed it cannonade, massed musketry, and spells. Then they tried all three at once. For that, their infantry got minced, their artillery no longer exists in a practical sense, and every single one of their magicians that engaged the thing is getting measured for a wooden box."

"They had fifteen sorcerers attached to their line regiments!" said Tariel.

"Now they've got assorted bits of fifteen sorcerers," said Caladesh.

"Blessed pie provisioner," said Rumstandel, "I'm as keen to put my head on the anvil as anyone in this association of oathbound lunatics. But when you say that musketry and sorcery were ineffective against this device, did it escape your notice that our tactical abilities span the narrow range from musketry to sorcery?"

"There's nothing uncanny about musket balls bouncing off wood and iron planking," said Millowend. "And there's nothing inherently counter-magical to the device. The Iron Ring have crammed a lot of wizards into it, is all. We need to devise some means to peel them out of that shell."

Under the gray sky we rode ever closer to the edge of the action, past field hospitals and trenches, past artillery caissons looking lonely without their guns, past nervous horses, nervous officers, and very nervous infantry. We left our mounts a few minutes later and moved on foot up the grassy ridgeline called Montveil's Wall, now the farthest limit of the dubious safety of "friendly" territory.

There the thing stood, half a mile away, beyond the churned and smoldering landscape of fieldworks vacated by the Elaran army. It was the height of a fortress wall, perhaps fifty or sixty feet, and its irregular, bulbous hull rested on four splayed and ungainly metal legs. On campaign years ago in the Alcor Valley, north of the Skull Sands, I became familiar with the dust-brown desert spiders famous for their threat displays. The scuttling creatures would raise up on their rear legs, spread their forward legs to create an illusion of bodily height, and brandish their fangs. I fancied there was something of that in the aspect of the Iron Ring machine.

"Watchdog," said Millowend, "did you bring your spyflask?"

I took a tarnished, dented flask from my coat and unscrewed the cap. Clear liquid bubbled into the air like slow steam, then coalesced into a flat disc about a yard in diameter. I directed this with waves of my hands until it framed our view of the Iron Ring machine, and we all pressed in upon one another like gawkers at a carnival puppet-show.

The magic of the spyflask acted as a refracting lens, and after a moment of blurred confusion the image within the disc resolved to a sharp, clear magnification of the war machine. It was bold and ugly, pure threat without elegance. Its overlapping iron plates were draped in netting-bound hides, which I presumed were meant to defeat the use of flaming projectiles or magic. The black barrels of two cannon jutted from ports in the forward hull, lending even more credence to my earlier impression of a rearing spider.

"Those are eight-pounder demi-culverins," said Caladesh, gesturing at the cannon. "I pulled a ball out of the turf. Not the heaviest they've got, but elevated and shielded, they might as well be the only guns on the field. They did for the Elaran batteries at leisure, careful as calligraphers."

"I'm curious about the Elaran sorcerers," said Rumstandel, twirling fingers in the azure strands of his beard and scattering little white ships. "What exactly did they do to invite such a disaster?"

"I don't think they were prepared for the sheer volume of counter-thaumaturgy the Iron Ringers could mount from that device," said Millowend. "The Iron Ring wizards stayed cautious and let the artillery chop up our Elaran counterparts. Guided, of course, by spotters atop that infernal machine. It would seem the Iron Ring is learning to be the sort of opponent we least desire . . . a flexible one."

"I did like them much better when they were thick as oak posts," sighed Rumstandel.

"The essential question remains," I said. "How do we punch through what fifteen Elaran wizards couldn't?"

"You're thinking too much on the matter of the armored box," said Tariel. "When you hunt big game with ordinary muskets, you don't try to pierce the thickest bone and hide. You make crippling shots. Subdue it in steps, leg by leg. Lock those up somehow, all the Iron Ring will have is an awkward fortress tower rooted in place."

"We could trip it or sink it down a hole," mused Rumstandel. "General Alune's not dead, is she? Why aren't her sappers digging merrily away?"

"She's alive," said Millowend. "It's a question of where to dig, and how to convince that thing to enter the trap. When it's moving, it can evade or simply overstep anything resembling ordinary fieldworks."

"When it's moving," I said. "Well, here's another question—if the Elarans didn't stop it, why isn't it moving now?"

"I'd love to think it's some insoluble difficulty or breakdown," said Millowend. "But the telling fact is, they haven't sent over any ultimatums. They haven't communicated at all. I assume that if the device were now immobilized, they'd be trying to leverage its initial attack for all it was worth. No, they're waiting for their own reasons, and I'm sure those reasons are suitably unpleasant."

"So how do you want us to inaugurate this fool's errand, captain?" said Rumstandel.

"Eat your pie," said my mother. "Then think subtle thoughts. I want a quiet, invisible reconnaissance of that thing, inch by inch and plate by plate. I want to find all the cracks in its armor, magical and otherwise, and I want the Iron Ring to have no idea we've been peeking."

ENCLOSURE: The open oath of the Red Hats, attributed to the Sorceress Millowend.

To take no coin from unjust reign
Despoil no hearth nor righteous fane
Caps red as blood, as bright and bold
In honor paid, as dear as gold
To leave no bondsman wrongly chained

And shirk no odds, for glory's gain
Against the mighty, for the weak
We by this law our battles seek

ADDENDUM: The tacit marching song of the Red Hats, attributed to the Sorcerer Rumstandel, sometimes called "The Magnificent".

Where musket balls are thickest flying
Where our employers are quickest dying
Where mortals perish like bacon frying
And horrible things leave grown men crying
To all these places we ride with haste
To get ourselves smeared into paste
Or punctured, scalded, and served on toast
For the financial benefit of our hosts!

13TH MITHUNE, 1186
MONTVEIL'S WALL, NORTH ELARA
ONE HOUR LATER

Cannon above us, cannon over the horizon, all spitting thunder and smoke, all blasting up fountains of wet earth as we stumbled for cover, under the plunging fire of the lurching war machine, under the dancing green light of hostile magic, under the weight of our own confusion and embarrassment.

We had thought we were being subtle.

Millowend had started our reconnaissance by producing a soft white dandelion seedhead, into which she breathed the syllables of a spell. Seeds spun out, featherlike in her conjured breeze, and each carried a fully realized pollen-sized simulacrum of her, perfect down to a little red hat and a determined expression. One hundred tiny Millowends floated off to cast 200 tiny eyes over the Iron Ring machine. It was a fine spell, though it would leave her somewhat befuddled as her mind strained to knit those separate views together into one useful picture.

Rumstandel added some admittedly deft magical touches of his own to the floating lens of my spyflask, and in short order we had a sort of intangible apparatus by which we might study the quality and currents of magic around the war machine, as aesthetes might natter about the brushstrokes of a painting. Tariel and Caladesh, less than entranced by our absorption in visual balderdash, crouched near us to keep watch.

"That's as queer as a six-headed fish," muttered Rumstandel. "The whole thing's lively with dynamic flow. That would be a profligate waste of power unless—"

That was when Tariel jumped on his head, shoving him down into the turf, and Caladesh jumped on mine, dragging my dazed mother with him. A split heartbeat later, a pair of cannonballs tore muddy furrows to either side of us, arriving just ahead of the muted thunder of their firing.

"I might forward the hypothesis," growled Rumstandel, spitting turf, "that the reason the bloody thing hasn't moved is because it was left out as an enticement for a certain band of interlopers in obvious hats."

"I thought we were being reasonably subtle!" I yelled, shoving Caladesh less than politely. He is all sharp angles, and very unpleasant to be trapped under.

"Action FRONT," cried Tariel, who had sprung back on watch with her usual speed. The rest of us scrambled to the rim of Montveil's Wall beside her. Charging from the nearest trench, not a hundred yards distant, came a column of Iron Ring foot about forty strong, cloaks flying, some still tossing away the planks and debris they'd been using to help conceal themselves. One bore a furled pennant bound tightly to its staff by a scarlet cord. That made them penitents, comrades of a soldier who'd broken some cardinal rule of honor or discipline. The only way they'd be allowed to return to the Iron Ring, or even ordinary service, was to expunge the stain with a death-or-glory mission.

Such as ambushing us.

Also, the six-story metal war machine behind the penitents was now on the move, creaking and growling like a pack of demons set loose in a scrapyard.

And then there were orange flashes and puffs of smoke from the distances beyond the machine, where hidden batteries were presumably taking direction on how to deliver fresh gifts of lead to our position.

Tariel whispered to her salamander, and her musket barked fire and noise. The lead Iron Ringer was instantly relieved of all worries about the honor of his company. As she began to reload, shrieking cannon balls gouged the earth around us and before us, no shot yet closer than fifty yards. Bowel-loosening as the flash of distant cannonade might be, they would need much better luck and direction to really endanger us at that range.

I enacted a defensive spell, one that had become routine and reflexive. A sheen appeared in the air between us and the edge of the ridge, a subtle distortion that would safely pervert the course of any musket ball not fired at point-blank range. Not much of a roof to shelter under in the face of artillery, but it had the advantage of requiring little energy or concentration while I tried to apprehend the situation.

Rumstandel cast slips of paper from his coat pocket and spat crackling words of power after them. Over the ridge and across the field they whirled, toward the Iron Ring penitents, swelling into man-sized kites of crimson silk, each one painted with a wild-eyed likeness of Rumstandel, plus elaborate military, economic, and sexual insults in excellent Iron Ring script. Half-a-dozen kites swept into the ranks of the charging men, ensnaring arms, legs, necks, and muskets in their glittering strings before leaping upward, hauling victims to the sky.

"Hackwork, miserable hackwork," muttered Rumstandel. "Someday I'll figure out how to make the kites scream those insults. Illiterate targets simply aren't getting the full effect."

The cries of the men being hoisted into the air said otherwise, but I was too busy to argue.

The war machine lurched on, cannons booming, the shot falling so far beyond us I didn't see them land. So long as the device was in motion, I wagered its gunners would have a vexed time laying their pieces. That would change in a matter of minutes, when the thing reached spell and musket range and could halt to crush us at leisure.

"We have to get the hell out of here!" I cried, somewhat suborning the authority of my mother, who was still caught in the trance of seed-surveillance. That was when a familiar emerald phosphorescence burst around us, a vivid green light that lit the churned grass for a thirty-yard circle with us at the center.

"SHOT-FALL IMPS," bellowed Caladesh, which is just what they were; each of the five of us was now beset by a cavorting green figure dancing in the air above our heads, grinning evilly and pointing at us, while blazing with enough light to make our position clear from miles away.

"Here! Here! Over here!" yelled the green imps. The reader may assume they continued to yell this throughout the engagement, for they certainly did. I cannot find the will to scrawl it over and over again in this journal.

Shot-fall imps are intangible (so we couldn't shoot them) and notoriously slippery to banish. I have the wherewithal to do it, but it takes several patient minutes of trial and error, and those I did not possess.

Fire flashed in the distance, the long-range batteries again, this time sighting on the conspicuous green glow. It was no particular surprise that they were now more accurate, their balls parting the air just above our heads or plowing furrows within twenty yards. This is where we came in after the last intermission, with the enemy bombardment, the scrambling, and the general sense of a catastrophically unfolding cock-up.

Rumstandel hurled occult abuse at the penitents, his darkening mood evident in his choice of spells. He transmuted boot leather to caustic silver slime, seeded the ground with flesh-hungry glass shards, turned eyeballs to solid ice and cracked them within their sockets. All this, plus Tariel's steady, murderous attention, and still the Iron Ringers came on, fierce and honor-mad, bayonets fixed, leaving their stricken comrades in the mud.

"Get to the horses!" I yelled, no longer concerned about bruising Millowend's chain of command. It was my job to ward us all from harm, and the best possible safeguard would be for us to scurry, leaving our dignity on the field like a trampled tent.

The surviving penitents came charging up a nearby defile to the top of Montveil's Wall. Caladesh met them, standing tall, his favorite over-and-under double flintlocks barking smoke. Those pistols threw .60 caliber balls, and at such close range the effect was . . . well, you've squeezed fruit before, haven't you?

The world became a tumbling confusion of incident. Iron Ring penitents falling down the slope, tangled in the heavy bodies of dead comrades, imps dancing in green light, cannonballs ripping holes in the air, a lurching war machine —all this while I frantically tried to spot our horses, revive my mother, and layer us in what protections I could muster.

They weren't sufficient. A swarm of small water elementals burst upon us, translucent blobs the color of gutter-silt, smelling like the edge of a summer storm. They poured themselves into the barrels and touch-holes of Caladesh's pistols, leaving him cursing. A line of them surged up and down the barrel of Tariel's musket, and the salamander faced them with steaming red blades in its hands like the captain of a boarded vessel. The situation required more than my spells could give it, so I resolved at last to surrender an advantage I was loath to part with.

On my left wrist I wore a bracelet woven from the tail-hairs of an Iron Unicorn, bound with a spell given to me by the Thinking Sharks of the Jewelwine Sea, for which I had traded documents whose contents are still the state secrets of one of our former clients. I tore it off, snapped it in half, and threw it to the ground.

It's dangerous arrogance for any sorcerer to think of a fifth-order demon as a familiar; at best such beings can be indentured to a very limited span of time or errands, and against even the most ironclad terms of service they will scheme and clamor with exhausting persistence. However, if you can convince them to shut up and take orders . . .

"Felderasticus Sixth-Quickened, Baronet of the Flayed Skulls of Faithless Dogs, Princeling of the House of Recurring Shame," I bellowed, pausing to take a breath, "get up here and get your ass to work!"

"I deem that an irretrievably non-specific request," said a voice like fingernails on desert-dry bones. "I shall therefore return to my customary place and assume my indenture to be dissolved by mutual—"

"Stuff that, you second-rate legal fantasist! When you spend three months questing for spells to bind me into jewelry, then you can start assuming things! Get rid of these shot-fall imps!"

"Reluctant apologies, most impatient of spell-dabblers and lore-cheats, softest of cannon-ball targets, but again your lamentably hasty nonspecificity confounds my generous intentions. When you say, 'get rid of', how exactly do you propose—"

"Remove them instantly and absolutely from our presence without harm to ourselves and banish them to their previous plane of habitation!"

A chill wind blew, and it was done. The shot-fall imps with their damned green light and their pointing and shouting were packed off in a cosmic bag, back to their rightful home, where they would most likely be used as light snacks for higher perversities like Felderasticus Sixth-Quickened. I was savagely annoyed. Using Felderasticus to swat them was akin to using a guillotine as a mousetrap, but you can see the mess we were in.

"Now, I shall withdraw, having satisfied all the terms of our compact," said the demon.

"Oh, screw yourself!" I snarled.

"Specify physically, metaphysically, or figuratively."

"Shut it! You know you're not finished. I need a moment to think."

Tariel and Caladesh were fending off penitents, inelegantly but emphatically, with their waterlogged weapons. Rumstandel was trying to help them as well as keep life hot for the Iron Ring sorcerer that must have been mixed in with the penitents. I couldn't see him (or her) from my vantage, but the imps and water elementals proved their proximity. Millowend was stirring, muttering, but not yet herself. I peered at the towering war machine and calculated. No, that was too much of a job for my demon. Too much mass, too much magic, and now it was just two hundred yards distant.

"We require transportation," I said, "Instantly and—"

"Wait," cried my mother. She sat up, blinked, and appeared unsurprised as a cannon ball swatted the earth not ten feet away, spattering both of us with mud. "Don't finish that command, Watchdog! We all need to die!"

"Watchdog," said Rumstandel, "our good captain is plainly experiencing a vacancy in the upper-story rooms, so please apply something heavy to her skull and get on with that escape you were arranging."

"No! I'm sorry," cried Millowend, and now she bounced to her feet with sprightliness that was more than a little unfair in someone her age. "My mind was still a bit at luncheon. You know that flying around being a hundred of myself is a very taxing business. What I mean is, this is a bespoke ambush, and if we vanish safely out of it they'll just keep expecting us. But if it looks as though we're snuffed, the Iron Ring might drop their guard enough to let us back in the fight!"

"Ahh!" I cried, chagrined that I hadn't thought of that myself. In my defense, you have just read my account of the previous few minutes. I cleared my throat.

"Felderasticus, these next-named tasks, once achieved, shall purchase the end of your indenture without further caveat or reservation! NOW! Interpreting my words in the broadest possible spirit of good faith, we, all five of us, must be brought alive with our possessions to a place of safety within the North Elaran encampment just south of here. Furthermore—FURTHERMORE! Upon the instant of our passage, you must create a convincing illusion of our deaths, as though . . . as though we had been caught by cannon-fire and the subsequent combustion of our powder-flasks and alchemical miscellanies!"

I remain very proud of that last flourish. Wizards, like musketeers, are notorious for carrying all sorts of volatile things on their persons, and if we were seen to explode the Iron Ringers might not bother examining our alleged remains too closely.

"Faithfully shall I work your will and thereby end my indenture," said the cold voice of the demon.

The world turned gray and spun around me. After a moment of disjointed nausea I found myself once again lying under sharp-elbowed Caladesh, with Rumstandel, Tariel, and my mother into the bargain. Roughly 600 pounds of Red Hats, all balanced atop my stomach, did something for my freshly eaten pie that I hesitate to describe. But, ah, you've squeezed fruit before, haven't you?

Moaning, swearing, and retching, we all fell or scrambled apart. Guns, bandoliers, and hats littered the ground around us. When I had managed to wipe my mouth and take in a few breaths, I finally noticed that we were surrounded by a veritable forest of legs, legs wearing the boots and uniform trousers of North Elaran staff officers.

I followed some of those legs upward with my eyes and met the disbelieving gaze of General Arad Vorstal, supreme field commander of the army of North Elara. Beside him stood his general of engineers, the equally surprised Luthienne Alune.

"Generals," said my mother suavely, dusting herself off and restoring her battered hat to its proper place. "Apologies for the suddenness of our arrival. I'm afraid I have to report that our reconnaissance of the Iron Ring war machine ended somewhat prematurely. And the machine retains its full motive power."

She cleared her throat.

"And, ah, we're all probably going to see it again in about half an hour."

ENCLOSURE: Invoice for sundry items lost or disposed of in Elaran service, 13th instant, Mithune, 1186. Submitted to Quartermaster-Captain Guthrun on behalf of the Honorable Company of Red Hats, countersigned Captain-Paramount Millowend, Sorceress. 28th instant, Mithune, 1186

ITEM VALUATION:

Bracelet, thaumaturgical . . . 1150 Gil. 13 p.
Function (confidential)
Spyflask, thaumaturgical . . . 100 Gil. 5 p.
Function (reconnaissance)
Total Petition . . . 1250 Gil. 18 p.
Please remit as per terms of contract.

WATCHDOG—Actually, I picked up your spyflask when you rather thoughtlessly dropped it that afternoon. I did mean to return it to you eventually. These minor trivialities of camp life do elude me sometimes. I hadn't realized that the company received a hundred gildmarks as a replacement fee. Do you want me to keep the flask, or shall I write myself up a chit for the hundred gildmarks? I am content with either. – R

13TH MITHUNE, 1186
SOMEWHERE NEAR LAKE CORLAN, NORTH ELARA

But they didn't come. Not then.

Afternoon wound down into evening. Presumably, the Iron Ring thought it too late in the day to commence a general action, and with all of their sorcerous impediments supposedly ground into the mud, one could hardly blame them for a lack of urgency. The war machine stood guard before Montveil's Wall, and behind it came the creak and groan of artillery teams, the shouts of orders, and the tramp of boots as line regiments moved into their billets for the night. The light of a thousand fires rose from the captured Elaran fieldworks and joined in an ominous glow, giving the overcast the colors of a banked furnace.

In the Elaran camp, we brooded and argued. The council ran long, in quite inverse proportion to the tempers of those involved.

"It's not that we can't dig," General Alune was saying, her patience shaved down to a perceptibly thin patina on her manner. "For the tenth time, it's the fact that the bloody machine moves! We can work like mad all night, sink a shaft just about the right size to make a grave for the damn thing, and in the morning it might spot the danger and take five steps to either side. So much for our trap."

"Have you ever seen a pitfall for a dangerous animal?" said Tariel, mangling protocol by speaking up. "It's customary to cover the entrance with a light screen of camouflage—"

"Yes, yes, I'm well aware," snapped General Alune. "But once again, that machine is the master of the field and may go where it pleases, attacking from any angle. We have no practical means of forcing it into a trap, even a hidden one."

"Has the thing truly no weak point, no joint in its armor, no vent or portal on which we can concentrate fire? Or sorcery?" said Vorstal, stroking the beard that hung from his craggy chin like sable-streaked snow. "What about the mechanisms that propel it?"

"I assure you I had the closest look possible," said Millowend. "It was the only useful thing I managed to do during our last engagement. The device has no real machinery, no engine, no pulleys or pistons. It's driven by brute sorcery. A wizard in a harness, mimicking the movements they desire the machine to make, a puppeteer driving a vast puppet. You might call it an effigy engine. It's exhausting work, and I'm sure they have to swap wizards frequently. However, while harnessed, the driver is still inside the armored shell, still protected by the arts of their fellows. It's as easy to destroy the machine outright as it is to reach them."

"How many great guns have we managed to recover since yesterday's debacle?" said General Vorstal.

"Four," said General Alune. "Four functional six-pounders, crewed by a few survivors, the mildly injured, and a lot of fresh volunteers."

"That's nothing to hang our hopes on," sighed Vorstal, "a fifth of what wasn't even adequate before!"

"We could try smoke," said Rumstandel. While listening to the council of war he'd added flourishes to his beard, tiny gray clouds and twirling water-spouts, plus lithe long-necked sea serpents. Life had become very hard for the little ships of the Rumstandel Delta. "Or anything to render the hull uninhabitable. Flaming caustics, bottled vitriol, sulfurous miasma, air spirits of reeking decay—"

"The Iron Ring sorcerers could nullify any of those before they caused harm," I said. "You and I certainly could."

Rumstandel shrugged theatrically. Miniature lightning crackled just below his chin.

"Then it must be withdrawal," said Vorstal, bitterly but decisively. "If we face that thing again, with the rest of the Iron Ring force at its heels, this army will be destroyed. I have to preserve it. Trade territory for time. I want 100 volunteers to demonstrate at Montveil's Wall while we start pulling the rest out quietly." He looked around, meeting the eyes of all his staff in turn. "Officers will surrender their horses to hospital wagon duty, myself included."

"With respect, sir," said General Alune, "you know how many Iron Ring sympathizers . . . that is, when word of all this reaches parliament they'll have you dismissed. And they'll be laying white flags at the feet of that damned machine before we can even get the army reformed, let alone reinforced."

"Certainly I'll be recalled," said Vorstal. "Probably arrested, too. I'll be counting on you to keep our forces intact and use whatever time I can buy you to think of something I couldn't. You always were the cleverer one, Luthienne."

"The Iron Ring won't want easy accommodations," said Millowend, and I was surprised to notice her using a very subtle spell of persuasion. Her voice rang a little more clearly to the far corners of the command pavilion, her shadow seemed longer and darker, her eyes more alight with compelling fire. "You've bled them and stymied them for months. You've defied all their plans. Now their demands will be merciless and unconditional. If this army falls back, they will put your people in chains and feed Elara to the fires of their war-furnaces, until you're nothing but ashes on the trail to their next conquest! Now, if that war machine were destroyed, could you think to meet the rest of the Iron Ring army with the force you still possess?"

"If it were destroyed?" shouted General Vorstal. "IF! If my cock had scales and another ninety feet it'd be a dragon! IF! Millowend, I'm sorry, you and your company have done us extraordinary service, but I have no more time for interruptions. I'll see to it that your contract is fully paid off and you're given letters of safe passage, for what they're worth."

"I have a fresh notion," said my mother. "One that will give us a long and sleepless night, if it's practicable at all, and the thing I need to hear, right now, is whether or not you can meet the Iron Ring army if that machine is subtracted from the ledger."

"Not with any certainty," said Vorstal, slowly. "But we still have our second line of works, and it's the chance I'd take over any other, if only it were as you say."

"For this we'll need your engineers," said Millowend. "Your blacksmiths, your carpenters, and work squads of anyone who can hold a shovel or an axe. And we'll need those volunteers for Montveil's Wall to screen us, with their lives if need be."

"What do you have in mind?" said General Alune.

"A trap, as you said, is wasted unless we can guarantee that the Iron Ring machine moves into it." Millowend mimicked the lurching steps of the machine with her fingers. "Well, what could we possibly set before it that would absolutely guarantee movement in our desired direction? What challenge could we mount on the field that would compel them to advance their machine and engage us as directly as possible?"

After a sufficiently dramatic pause, she told us.

Then the real shouting and argument began.

14TH MITHUNE, 1186
SOMEWHERE NEAR LAKE CORLAN, NORTH ELARA

Just before sunrise, the surviving Elaran skirmishers fell back from Montveil's Wall, their shot-flasks empty, their ranks scraped thin by musketry, magic, and misadventure in the dark. Yet they had achieved their mission and kept their Iron Ring counterparts out of our lines, away from the evidence of what we were really up to.

Behind them, several regiments of Elaran foot had moved noisily throughout the night, doing their best to create the impression of the pullback that was only logical. A pullback it was, though not to the roads but rather to a fresh line of breastworks, where they measured powder, sharpened bayonets, and slept fitfully in the very positions they would guard at first light.

We slept not at all. Tariel and Caladesh passed hours in conference with the most experienced of the surviving Elaran artillery handlers. Rumstandel, Millowend and I spent every non-working moment we had on devouring anything we could lay our hands on, without a scrap of shame. My mother's plan was a pie job and a half.

The sun came up like dull brass behind the charcoal bars of the hazy sky. Fresh smoke trails curled from the Iron Ring positions, harbingers of the hot breakfast they would have before they moved out to crush us. General Vorstal had reluctantly sentenced his men and women to a cold camp, to help preserve the illusion that large contingents in Elaran blue had fled south during the night. We sorcerers received our food from Millowend's indentured culinary imps, their pinched green faces grotesque under their red leather chef's hats, their ovens conveniently located in another plane of existence.

As the sun crept upward, the Iron Ring lines began to form, regimental pennants fluttering like sails above a dark and creeping sea. A proud flag broke out atop the war machine, blue circle within gray circle on a field of black. The symbol of the Iron Ring cities, the coal-furnace tyrants, whose home dominions girded the shores of vast icy lakes a month's march north of Elara.

By the tenth hour of the morning, they were coming for us, in the full panoply of their might and artifice.

"I suppose it's time to find out whether we're going to be victorious fools, or just fools," said Millowend. We had taken our ready position together, all five of us, and rising anxiety had banished most of our fatigue. We engaged in our little rituals, chipper or solemn as per our habits, hugging and shaking hands and exchanging good-natured insults. My mother dusted off my coat and straightened my hat.

"Rumstandel," she said, "are you sure now wouldn't be an appropriate time to rediscover that chronically misplaced hat of yours?"

"Of course not, captain." He rubbed his ample abdominal ballast and grinned. "I much prefer to die as I've always lived, handsome and insufferable."

My mother rendered eloquent commentary using nothing but her eyebrows. Then she cast the appropriate signal-spell, and we braced ourselves.

Five hundred Elaran sappers and work-gangers, already drained to the marrow by a night of frantic labor, seized hold of ropes and chains. "HEAVE!" shouted General Alune, who then flung herself into the nearest straining crew and joined them in their toil. Pulleys creaked and guidelines rattled. With halting, lurching, shuddering movements, a fifty-foot wood and metal tripod rose into the sky above the Elaran command pavilion, with the five of us in an oblong wooden box at its apex, feeling rather uncomfortably like catapult stones being winched into position.

We leveled off, wavering disconcertingly, but more or less upright. Cheers erupted from thousands of throats across the Elaran camp, and musketeers came to their feet in breastworks and redoubts, loosing their regimental colors from hiding. Our North Elaran war machine stood high in the morning light, and even those who'd been told what we were up to waved their hats and screamed like they could hardly believe it.

It was all a thoroughly shambolic hoax, of course. The Iron Ring machine was the product of months of work, cold metal plates fitted to purpose-built legs, rugged and roomy, weighed down with real armor. Ours was a gimcrack, upjumped watch-tower, shorter, narrower, and wobbly as a drunk at a ballroom dance. Our wooden construction was braced in a few crucial places with joints and nail-plates improvised by Elaran blacksmiths. Our hull was armored with nothing but logs, and our only gun was a cast-iron six-pounder in a specially rigged recoil harness, tended by Caladesh and Tariel.

"Let's secure their undivided attention," said Millowend. "Charge and load!"

Tariel and Caladesh rammed home a triple-sized powder charge, augmented with the greenish flecks of substances carefully chosen from our precious alchemical supply. Rumstandel handed over a six-pound ball, laboriously prepared by us with pale ideograms of spells designed to ensure long, straight flight. Caladesh drove it down the barrel with the rammer while Tariel looked out the forward window and consulted an improvised sight made from a few pieces of wood and wire.

"Lay it as you like, then fire at will," said Millowend.

Our gunners didn't dally. They sighted their piece on the distant Iron Ring machine, and Tariel whistled up her salamander, which was taking a brief vacation from its usual home. The fire-spirit danced around the touchhole, and the six-pounder erupted with a bang that was much too loud even with our noise-suppression spells deadening the air.

Ears ringing, nostrils stinging from the strange smoke of the blast, I jumped to a window and followed the glowing green arc of the magically enhanced shot as it sped toward the enemy. There was a flash and a flat puff of yellowish smoke atop the target machine's canopy.

"Dead on!" I shouted.

We had just ruined a cannon barrel and expended a great deal of careful sorcery, all for the sake of one accurate shot at an improbable distance. It hadn't been expected to do any damage, even if it caught their magicians by surprise. It was just a good old-fashioned gauntlet across the face.

"They're moving," said Caladesh. "Straight for us."

The Iron Ringers answered our challenge, all right. It was precisely the sort of affair that would appeal to them, machine against machine like mad bulls for the fate of North Elara. Hell, it was just the sort of thing that might have appealed to us, if only our "machine" hadn't been a shoddy counterfeit.

"Forward march," said my mother, and I resumed my place at her side along with Rumstandel. This part was going to hurt. We joined hands and concentrated.

We hadn't had time to devise any sort of body harness for the control and movement of our device. Instead we had an accurate wooden model about two feet tall, secured to the floor in front of us. On this we could focus our sorcerous energies, however inefficiently, to move corresponding pieces of the real structure. Ours was, in a sense, a true effigy engine.

Imagine pulling a twenty-pound weight along a chain in hair-fine increments by jerking your eyebrow muscles. Imagine trying to push your prone, insensate body along the ground using nothing but the movements of your toes. This was the sort of nightmarish, concentrated effort required to send our device creaking along, step by step, shaking like a bar-stool with delusions of grandeur.

The energy poured out of us like a vital fluid. We moaned, we shuddered, we screamed and swore in the most undignified fashion. Caladesh and Tariel clung to the walls in earnest, for our passage was anything but smooth. It was a bit like being trapped inside a madman's feverish delusion of a carriage ride, some fifty feet above the ground, while a powerful enemy approached with cannons booming.

We had to hope that our Elaran employers had strictly obeyed our edict to clear our intended movement path. There was no chance to look down and halt if some unfortunate soul was about to play the role of insect to our boot-heel.

Iron Ring cannonballs shrieked past. One of them peeled away part of our roof, giving us a ragged new skylight. Closer and closer we stumbled, featherweight frauds. Closer and closer the enemy machine pounded in dread sincerity. Even fat and well-fed sorcerers were not meant to do what we were doing for long; our magic grew taut and strained as an overfilled water-sack. It was impossible to tell tears from sweat, for it was all running out of us in a torrent. The expressions on the faces of Tariel and Caladesh struck me in my preoccupation as extremely funny, and then I realized it was because I had never before seen those consummate stalwarts look truly horrified. Another round of fire boomed from the charging Iron Ring machine. Our vessel shuddered, rocked by a hit somewhere below. I tried to subdue my urge to cower or hide. There was nothing to be done now; a shot through our bow would likely fill the entire cabin with splinters and scythe us all down in an instant. In moments, we must also come within range of the wizards huddled inside the enemy machine, and we were in no shape to resist them. Luck was our only shield now. Luck, and a few seconds or yards in either direction.

"They're going," cried Tariel. "THEY'RE GOING!"

There was a sound like the world coming apart at the seams, a juddering drum-hammer noise, sharpened by the screams of men and metal alike. Everything shook around us and beneath us, and for a moment I was certain that Tariel was wrong, that it was we who'd been mortally struck at last, that we were on our way to the ground and into the history books as a farcical footnote to the rise of the Iron Ring empire.

The thing about my mother's plans, though, is that they tend to work, more often than not.

Given luck, and a few seconds or yards in either direction.

I didn't witness it personally, but I can well imagine the scene based on the dozens of descriptions I collected afterward. We had barely thirty more yards of safe space to move when the Iron Ring machine hit the edge of the trap, the modified classic pitfall scraped out of the earth by General Alune's sappers, then concealed with panels of canvas and wicker and even a few tents. A thousand-strong draft had labored all night to move and conceal the dirt, aided here and there by our sorcery. It wasn't quite a ready-made grave for the war machine. More of a good hard stumble of about thirty feet.

Whatever it was, it was sufficient. In clear view of every Iron Ring soldier on the field, the greatest feat of ferro-thaumaturgical engineering in the history of the world charged toward its feeble-looking rival, only to stumble and plunge in a deadly arc, smashing its armored cupola like a crustacean dropped from the sky by a hungry seabird. A shroud of dust and smoke settled around it, and none of its occupants were left in any shape to ever crawl out of it.

Millowend, Rumstandel and I fell to our knees in the cabin of our hoax machine, gasping as though we'd been fished from the water ten seconds shy of drowning. Everything felt loose and light and wrong, so much flesh had literally cooked away from the three of us. It was a strange and selfish scene for many moments, as we had no idea whether to celebrate a close-run tactical triumph, or the simple fact of our continued existence. We shamelessly did both, until the noise of battle outside reminded us that the day's work was only begun. Sore and giddy, we let Rumstandel conjure a variation of his kites to lower us safely to the ground, where we joined the mess already in progress.

It was no easy fight. The Iron Ringers were appalled by the loss of their war machine, and they had deployed poorly, expecting to scourge an already-depleted camp in the wake of their invincible iron talisman. They were also massed in the open, facing troops in breastworks. Still, they were hard fighters and well-led, and so many Elarans were second-line militia or already exhausted by the long labors of the night.

I'll leave it to other historians to weigh the causes and the cruxes of true victory in the Battle of Lake Corlan. We were in it everywhere, rattling about the field via horses and sorcery and very tired feet, for many Iron Ring magicians remained alive and dangerous. In the shadow of our abandoned joke of an effigy engine, we fought for our pay and our oath, and as the sun finally turned red behind its veils of powder smoke, we and 10,000 Elarans watched in exhausted exaltation as the Iron Ring army finally broke like a wave on our shores, a wave that parted and sank and ran into the darkness.

After six months of raids and minor successes and placeholder, proxy victories, six months of stalemate capped by the terror of a brand-new way of warfare, the Elarans had flung an army twice the size of their own back in confusion and defeat at last.

It was not the end of their war, and the butcher's bill would be terrible. But it was something. It meant hope, and frankly, when someone hires the Red Hats, that's precisely what we're expected to provide.

In the aftermath of the battle I worked some sorcery for the hospital details, then stumbled, spell-drunk and battered, to the edge of the gaping pit now serving as a tomb for the mighty war machine and its occupants.

I have to admit I waxed pitifully philosophical as I studied the wreck. It wouldn't be an easy thing to duplicate, but it could be done, with enough wizards and enough skilled engineers, and small mountains of steel and gold. Would the Iron Ring try again? Would other nations attempt to build such devices of their own? Was that the future of sorcerers like myself, to become power sources for hulking metal beasts, to drain our lives into their engines?

I, Watchdog, a lump of coal, a fagot for the flames.

I shook my head then and I shake my head now. War is my trade, but it makes me so damned tired sometimes. I don't have any answers. I keep my oath, I keep my book, I take my pay and I guard my friends from harm. I suppose we are all lumps of coal destined for one furnace or another.

I found the rest of the company in various states of total collapse near the trampled, smoldering remains of General Vorstal's command pavilion. Our options had been limited when we'd selected a place to build our machine, and unfortunately the trap path had been drawn across all the Elaran high command's nice things.

Caladesh was unconscious with a shattered wagon wheel for a pillow. Tariel had actually fallen sleep sitting up, arms wrapped around her musket. My mother was sipping coffee and staring at Rumstandel, who was snoring like some sort of cave-beast while miniature coronas of foul weather sparked around his beard. In lieu of a pillow, Rumstandel had enlisted one of his familiars, a tubby little bat-demon that stood silently, holding Rumstandel's bald head off the ground like an athlete heaving a weight over its shoulders.

"He looks so peaceful, doesn't he?" whispered Millowend. She muttered and gestured, and a bright new red hat appeared out of thin air, gently lowering itself on to Rumstandel's brow. He continued snoring.

"There," she said, with no little satisfaction. "Be sure to record that in your chronicles, will you, Watchdog?"

The reader will note that I have been pleased to comply.

⚔

Steven Erikson (1959–) says of his beginnings as a writer:

> *In my youth, I sidestepped Tolkien entirely, finding my inspiration and pleasure in the genre through Howard, Burroughs, and Leiber. And as with many of my fellow epic fantasy writers, our first experience of the Tolkien tropes of epic fantasy came not from books, but from* Dungeons & Dragons *roleplaying games . . . As my own gaming experience advanced, it was not long before I abandoned those tropes . . . Accordingly, my influences in terms of fiction are post-Tolkien, and they came from conscious responses to Tolkien (Donaldson's Thomas Covenant series) and unconscious responses to Tolkien (Cook's Dread Empire and Black Company series)."*

The Malazan world was created in 1982 by Erikson and Ian Cameron Esslemont as a backdrop for role-playing games. The main series, Malazan Book of the Fallen, consists of ten novels (1999-2011) by Erikson. He has also published two Malazan prequel novels with a third slated, and six novellas. Esselmont has authored another six novels and started another related prequel trilogy. Luckily, we can offer a short *story that gives you a taste of the sword and sorcery of Malazan.*

GOATS OF GLORY

Steven Erikson

Five riders drew rein in the pass. Slumped in their saddles, they studied the valley sprawled out below them. A narrow river cut a jagged scar down the middle of a broad floodplain. A weathered wooden bridge sagged across the narrow span, and beyond it squatted a score of buildings, gray as the dust hovering above the dirt tracks wending between them.

A short distance upriver, on the same side as the hamlet, was a large, unnatural hill, on which stood a gray-stoned keep. The edifice looked abandoned, lifeless, no banners flying, the garden terraces ringing the hillsides overgrown with weeds, the few windows in the square towers gaping black as caves.

The riders rode battered, beaten-down horses. The beasts' heads drooped with exhaustion, their chests speckled and streaked with dried lather. The two men and three women did not look any better. Armor in tatters, blood-splashed, and all roughly bandaged here and there to mark a battle somewhere behind them. Each wore a silver brooch clasping their charcoal-gray cloaks over their hearts, a ram's head in profile.

They sat in a row, saying nothing, for some time.

And then the eldest among them, a broad-shouldered, pale-skinned woman with a flat face seamed in scars, nudged her mount down onto the stony descent. The others fell in behind their captain.

The boy came running to find Graves, chattering about strangers coming down from the border pass. Five, on horses, with sunlight glinting on chain and maybe weapons. The one in the lead had long black hair and pale skin. A foreigner for sure.

Graves finished his tankard of ale and pushed himself to his feet. He dropped two brass buttons on the counter and Swillman's crabby hand scooped them up before Graves had time to turn away. From the far end of the bar, Slim cackled, but that was a random thing with her, and she probably didn't mean anything by it. Though maybe she did. Who could know the mind of a hundred-year-old whore?

The boy, whom Graves had come to call Snotty, for his weeping nose and the smudges of dirt that collected there, led the way outside, scampering like a pup. To High Street's end, where Graves lived and where he carved the slabs he and the boy brought down from the old quarry every now and then.

Snotty went into the tiny one-stall stable and set about hitching up the mule to the cart. Graves tugged open the door to his shed, reminding himself to cut back the grass growing along the rain gutter. He stepped inside and, though his eyes had yet to adjust, he reached with overlong familiarity to the rack of long-handled shovels and picks just to the left of the door. He selected his best shovel and then the next best one for the boy, and finally his heavy pick.

Stepping outside, he glared up at the bright sun for a moment before walking to where Snotty was readying the cart. The three digging tools thumped onto the bed in a cloud of dust. "Five you say?"

"Five!"

"Bring us two casks of water."

"I will."

Graves went out back behind the shed. He eyed the heap of slabs, dragged out five—each one dressed into rough rectangular shapes, sides smoothed down, one arm's-length long and an elbow-down wide—and he squatted before them, squinting at the bare facings. "Best wait on that," he muttered, and then straightened when he heard the boy bringing the cart around.

"Watch your fingers this time," Graves warned.

"I will."

Graves moved the pick and shovels to the head of the cart bed to make room for the slabs. Working carefully, they loaded each stone onto the warped but solid planks. Then Graves went around to the mule's harness and cinched the straps tighter to ease the upward pull on the animal's chest.

"Five," said the boy.

"Heavy load."

"Heavy load. What you gonna carve on 'em?"

"We'll see."

Graves set out and Snotty led the mule and the creaking cart after him, making sure the wooden wheels fell evenly into the ruts on the road, the ruts that led to the cemetery.

When they arrived, they saw Flowers wandering the grassy humps of the burial ground, collecting blossoms, her fair hair dancing in the wind. The boy stopped and stared until Graves pushed the second-best shovel into his hands.

"Don't even think about it," Graves warned.

"I'm not," the boy lied, but some lies a man knew to just let pass. For a time.

Graves studied the misshapen lumps before them, thinking, measuring in his head. "We start a new row."

Shovels in hand, they made their way into the yard.

"Five, you said."

"Five," answered the boy.

It took most of the morning for the riders to reach the floodplain. The trail leading down into the valley was ill-frequented and there had been no work done on it in decades. Seasonal runoff had carved deep, treacherous channels around massive boulders. Snake holes gaped everywhere and the horses twitched and shied as they picked their way down the slope.

The cooler air of the pass gave way to cloying heat in the valley. Broken rock surrendered to brambles and thickets of spike-grass and sage. Upon reaching level ground, the trail opened out, flanked by tree stumps and then a thin forest of alder, aspen, and, closer to the river, cottonwoods.

The approach to the hamlet forked before reaching the bridge. The original, broader track led to a heap of tumbled blackstone, rising from the bank like the roots of shattered teeth with a similar ruin on the other side of the river. The wooden bridge at the end of the narrower path was barely wide enough to take a cart. Built of split logs and hemp rope, it promised to sway sickeningly and the riders would need to cross it one at a time.

The man who rode behind the captain was squat and wide, his broad face a collection of crooked details, from the twisted nose to the hook lifting the left side of his mouth, the dented jawline, one ear boxed and looking like a flattened cabbage, the other clipped neatly in half with top and bottom growing in opposite directions. His beard and mustache were filthy with flecks of dried spit and possibly froth. As he guided his horse over the bridge, he squinted down at the river to his left. The remnants of the stone pillars that had held up the original bridge were still visible, draped in flowing manes of algae.

Horse clumping onto solid ground once more, he drew up beside his captain and they sat watching the others cross one by one.

Captain Skint's expression was flat as her face, her eyes like scratched basalt.

"A year ago," said the man, "and it'd take half the day for alla us t'come over this bridge. A thousand Rams, hard as stone."

The third rider coming up alongside them, a tall, gangly woman with crimson glints in her black hair, snorted at the man's words. "Dreaming of the whorehouse again, Sarge?"

"What? No. Why'd ya think—"

"We ain't Rams anymore. We're goats. Fucking goats." And she spat.

Dullbreath and Huggs joined them and the five mercenaries, eager for the respite the hamlet ahead offered them—but admitting to nothing—fell into a slow canter as the track widened into something like a road.

They passed a farm: a lone log house and three stone-walled pens. The place stank of pig shit and the flies buzzed thick as black smoke. The forest came to a stumpy end beyond that. A few small fields of crops to the left, and ahead and to the right stood some kind of temple shrine, a stone edifice not much bigger than the altar stone it sheltered on three sides. Surrounding it was a burial ground.

The riders saw a man and a boy in the yard, digging pits, each one marked out with sun-bleached rags tied to trimmed saplings. A mule and cart waited motionless beneath an enormous yew tree.

"That's a few too many graves on the way," Sergeant Flapp muttered. "Plague, maybe?"

No one commented. But as they rode past, each one—barring the captain—fixed their attention on the two diggers, counting slow to reach . . . five.

"Five flags." Flapp shook his head. "That's probably half the population here."

A small girl walked the street a short distance ahead of the troop, clutching in one hand a mass of wildflowers. Honeybees spun circles around her tousled head.

The riders edged past her—she seemed oblivious to them—and cantered into the hamlet.

Slim came back from the doorway and slid along the bar rail to lurch to a halt opposite Swillman. "Give us one, then. I'll be good for it."

"Since when?"

"Them's soljers, Swilly. Come from the war—"

"What war?"

"T'other side of the mountains, o'course."

Swillman settled a gimlet regard on the ancient whore. "You hear anything about a war? From who? When?"

She shifted uneasily. "Well, you know and I know we ain't seen traffic in must be three seasons now. But they's soljers and they been chewed up bad, so there must be a war. Somewhere. And they came down from the pass, so it must be on t'other side."

"On the Demon Plain, right. Where nobody goes and nobody comes back neither. A war . . . over there. Right, Slim. Whatever you say, but I ain't giving you one unless you pay and you ain't got nothing to pay with."

"I got my ring."

He stared at her. "But that's your livelihood, Slim. You cough that up and you got nothing to offer 'em."

"You get it after they've gone, or maybe not, if I get work."

"Nobody's that desperate," Swillman said. "Seen yourself lately? Say, anytime in the last thirty years?"

"Sure. I keep that fine silver mirror all polished up, the one in my bridal suite, ya."

He grunted a laugh. "Let's see it, then, so I know you ain't up and swallowed it."

She stretched her jaw and worked with her tongue, and then hacked up something into her hand. A large rolled copper ring, tied to a string with the other end going into her mouth, wrapped around a tooth, presumably.

Swillman leaned in for a closer look. "First time I actually seen it, y'know."

"Really?"

"It's my vow of celibacy."

"Since your wife died, ya, which makes you an idiot. We could work us out a deal, y'know."

"Not a chance. It's smaller than I'd have thought."

"Most men are smaller than they think, too."

He settled back and collected a tankard.

Slim put the ring back into her mouth and watched with avid eyes the sour ale tumbling into the cup.

"Is that the tavern?" Huggs asked, eyeing the ramshackle shed with its signpost but no sign.

"If it's dry I'm going to beat on the keeper, I swear it," said Flapp, groaning as he slid down from his horse. "Beat 'im t'death, mark me." He stood for a moment, and then brushed dust from his cloak, his thighs, and his studded leather gauntlets. "No inn s'far as I can see, just a room in back. Where we gonna sleep? Put up the horses? This place is a damned pustule, is what it is."

"The old map I seen," ventured Wither, "gave this town a name."

"Town? It ain't been a town in a thousand years, if ever."

"Even so, Sarge."

"So what's it called?"

"Glory."

"You're shitting me, ain't ya?"

She shook her head, reaching over to collect the reins of the captain's horse as Skint thumped down in a plume of dust and, with a wince, walked—in her stockings as she'd lost her boots—to the tavern door.

Huggs joined Wither tying up the horses to the hitching post. "Glory, huh? Gods, I need a bath. They should call this place Dragon Mouth, it's so fucking hot. Listen, Wither, that quarrel head's still under my shoulder blade—I can't reach up and take off this cloak—I'm melting underneath—"

The taller woman turned to her, reached up, and unclasped the brooch on Huggs's cloak. "Stand still."

"It's a bit stuck on my back. Bloodglue, you know?"

"Ya. Don't move and if this hurts, I don't want to have to hear about it."

"Right. Do it."

Wither stepped around, gripping the cloak's hems, and slowly and evenly pulled the heavy wool from Huggs's narrow back. The bloodglue gave way with a sob, revealing a quilted gambeson stained black around the hole left by the quarrel. Wither studied the wound by peering through the hole. "A trickle, but not bad."

"Good. Nice. Thanks."

"I wouldn't trust the bathwater here, Huggs. That river's fulla pig shit and this place floods every spring, and I doubt the wells are dug deep."

"I know. Fucking hole."

The others had followed Captain Skint into the tavern. There was no shouting from within—a good sign.

The shorter, thinner woman—whose hips were, however, much broader than Wither's—plucked at the thongs binding the front of the gambeson. "Sweat's got me all chafed under my tits—lucky you barely got any, Withy."

"Ya. Lucky me. Like every woman says when it's hot, 'Mop 'em if you got 'em.' Let's go drink."

The soldier woman who walked into the bar didn't look like the kind to give much away. She'd be a hard drinker, though, or so Swillman judged in the single flickering glance he risked taking at her face. And things could get bad, because she didn't look like someone used to paying for what she took; and the two soldier men who clumped in behind her looked even uglier to a man like Swill—who was an honest publican just trying to do his best.

The woman wasn't wearing boots, which made her catlike as she drew up to the bar.

"Got ale," said Swillman before she could open her mouth and demand something he'd never heard of. The woman frowned, and Swill thought that maybe these people were so foreign they didn't speak the language of the land.

But she then said, in a cruel, butchered accent, "What place is this?"

"Glory."

"No." She waved one gauntleted hand. "Kingdom? Empire?"

Swillman looked over at Slim, who was watching with a hoof-stunned expression, and then he licked his lips and shrugged.

The foreign woman sighed. "Five tankards, then."

"Y'got to pay first."

To Swillman's surprise, she didn't reach across and snap his neck like a lamp taper. Instead, she tugged free a small bag looped around her throat—the bag coming up from between her breasts somewhere under that chain armor, and spilled out a half-dozen rectangular coins onto the countertop.

Swillman stared down at them. "That tin? Lead?"

"Silver."

"I can't make no give-back on silver!"

"Well, what do you use here?"

He reached down and lifted into view his wooden cash tray. Its four sculpted bowls held seven buttons in three different sizes, a few nuggets of raw copper, a polished agate, and three sticks of stale rustleaf.

"No coins?"

"Been years since I last seen one a those."

"What did it look like?"

"Oblong, not like yours at all. And they was copper."

"What was stamped on 'em?" asked the short, bearded man who'd sidled up between the woman and Slim. "Whose face, I mean? Or faces—three faces? Castle in the sky? Something like that, maybe?"

Swillman shrugged. "Don't recall."

"One of these should do us for the night, then," said the woman, nudging one of the silver coins in Swill's direction.

"A cask of ale for you and meals, too, that would be about right."

He could see that the woman knew she was being taken, but didn't seem much interested in arguing.

The bearded man was eyeing Slim, who was eyeing him back.

The other man, leaning on the rail on the other side of the stocking-footed woman, was big and stupid-looking—Swillman could hear his loud breathing and the man's mouth hung open.

Probably too dumb to understand what was going on about anything, from that empty look in his eyes and those snaggled teeth, yellow and dry jutting out like that.

Drawing the first three tankards, Swillman served them up. A moment later, two more women soldiers clumped in.

Slim scowled and did her usual shrink-back when people she thought of as competition ever showed up, but the bearded man just went and moved closer. "Keep," he said, "give this sweet lass another one."

Swillman gaped, and then nodded. He was already drawing two more tankards for the new women—gods, they were all cut up and bruised and knocked about, weren't they just? All five of 'em. Addled in the heads, too, he suspected. Imagine, calling Slim a sweet lass! Bastard was blind!

The loud breather startled him by speaking up. "Seen no stables—we need to put up for the night. Horses need taking care of. We want somewhere to sleep under cover. We need food for the ride, too, and clean, boiled water. Is there a drygoods here? How about a blacksmith? Anyone work leather and hide? Is there a whetstone? Anyone selling blankets?"

Swillman had begun shaking his head with the very first query, and he kept shaking it until the man ran down.

"None of that?"

"None. Sorry, we're not on, uh, any road. We see a merchant once a year, whatever he don't sell elsewhere by season's end, we can look at."

Slim drained her tankard in one long pull and then, after a gasp, she said, "Widow Bark's got some wool, I think. She spins something, anyway. Might have a blanket to sell. The stable burned down, we got no horses anyway. We got pigs, and sheep a walk south of here, near the other end of the valley, but all that wool down there goes into the next valley, to the town there—to Piety."

"How far away is Piety?" the bearded man asked.

"Four days on foot, maybe two on horseback."

"Well," the breather demanded, "where can we sleep?"

Swillman licked his lips and said, "If it's just a dry roof you're looking for, there's the old keep on the hill."

They'd dug one of the pits too close to a barrow, and from one end of the rectangular trench old bones tumbled out in lumps of yellow clay. Graves and Snotty stared down at them for a time. Splinters and shards, snapped and marrow-sucked, and then Graves scooped up most of them with his shovel.

"We'll bore a hole in the mound," he said.

Snotty wiped his running nose and nodded. "I'm thirsty."

"Let's break, then."

"They going up to the keep?"

Graves lifted the mud and bones and tipped the mess onto the ground opposite the back pile. "I expect so." He set the shovel down and clambered out, then reached back to pull the boy out of the hole.

"They was looking at us as they went past."

"I know, boy. Don't let it bother you."

"I don't. I was just noticing, that's all."

"Me too."

They went over to broach the second cask of water, shared the single tin cup back and forth a few times. "I shouldn't have had all that ale earlier," said Graves.

"You wasn't to know, though, was you?"

"That's true. Just a normal day, right?"

Snotty nodded. "A normal day in Glory."

"I'm thinking," mused Graves, "I probably shouldn't have put up the rags, though. Soldiers can count that high, mostly, if they need to. Wonder if it got them thinking."

"We could find out, when we get back to the bar."

"Might be we're not done afore dark, boy."

"They're soljers, they'll stay late, drinking and carousing."

Graves smiled. "Carousing? That's quite the imagination you got there."

"Taking turns with Slim, I mean, and getting drunk, too, and maybe getting into a few fights—"

"With who?"

"With each other, I guess, or even Swillman."

"Swillman wouldn't fight to save his life, boy. Besides, he'll be happy enough if the soldiers pay for what they take. If they don't, well, there's not much he can do about it, is there?" He paused, squinting toward town. "Taking turns with Slim. Maybe. Have to be blind drunk, though."

"She shows 'em her ring and that'll do."

Graves shot the boy a hard look. "How you know about that?"

"My birthday present, last time."

"I doubt you is—"

"That's what her tongue's for, ain't it?"

"You're too young to know anything about that. Slim—that wretched hag, what was she thinking?"

"It was the only present she had t'give me, she said."

Graves put the cup away. "Break's over. Don't want them t'drink up all the ale afore we get there, do we?"

"No, sir, that'd be bad."

The sun was down and the muggy moon yet to rise when Flapp went off with Slim into the lone back room behind the bar.

Huggs snorted. "That man's taste . . . can you believe it?"

Shrugging, Wither drained her tankard and thumped it down on the bar. "More, Swilly!" She turned to Huggs. "He's always been that way. Picks the ugliest ones or the oldest ones and if he can, the ugliest oldest ones if the two fit the same whore."

"This time he's got it all and no choice besides. Must be a happy man."

"I'd expect so."

Captain Skint had gone to one of the two tables in the bar and was working hard emptying the first cask all by herself. Dullbreath sat beside her, mouth hanging open, staring at not much. He'd taken a mace to the side of his head a week back, cracking open his helmet but not his skull. Hit that hard anywhere else and he'd be in trouble. But it was just his head, so now he was back to normal and his eyes didn't cross no more. Unless he got mad. As far as Wither could tell, there'd be no reason for Dullbreath to get mad here and on this night. This place was lively as a boy's Cut Night after three days of fasting and no booze.

She and Huggs glanced over when a man and a snot-faced boy came into the bar.

"He ain't so bad," Huggs said. "Think he's for hire?"

"Y'can ask him."

"Maybe I will. Get his face cleaned up first, though."

"Them two was the diggers."

Huggs grunted. "You're right. Could be we can find out who did all the dying."

Wither raised her voice, "You two, leave off that table and come here. We're buying."

The older man tipped his head. "Obliged. And the lad?"

"Whatever he wants."

Sure enough the boy moved up to stand close beside Huggs, wiping at his nose with a dirt-smeared forearm. His sudden smile showed a row of even white teeth. Huggs shot Wither a glance and aye, things were looking up.

A life on the march sure messed with the bent of soldiers, Wither reflected.

Camp followers were mostly people with nothing left to lose and lives going nowhere, and plenty of scrawny orphans and bastards among 'em, and so a soldier's tastes got twisted pretty quick. She thought the older man looked normal enough. A grave digger like every other grave digger and she'd met more than a few. "Swilly, more ale here."

The digger was quiet enough as he drank and he showed plenty of practice doing that drinking.

Wither eyed him a moment and then said, "Five graves. Who up and died?"

He glanced at her, finished his tankard, and then stepped back. "Obliged again," he said. "Snotty, you coming?"

"I'll stay a bit, Graves."

"As you like."

The man left. Wither stared after him, and then turned to say something to Huggs, but she had her hand down the front of the boy's trousers and he was clearly old enough to come awake.

Sighing, Wither collected her cup and went over to join Skint and Dullbreath. "A piss pit of a town," she pronounced as she slumped down in a chair. "Captain, you scrape an eye o'er that keep on the hill? Looks like it's got a walled courtyard. Stables."

Dullbreath looked at her. "It's a Jheranang motte and bailey, Wither. That conquest was a thousand years ago. The Jheran Concord's been dust half that long. I doubt a single inner roof's standing. And since we're on the border to the Demon Plain, it was probably overrun in the Birthing Wars. Probably stinks of ghosts and murder, and that's why it stays empty."

"It stays empty because this valley's been forgotten by whoever rules the land, and there's nothing to garrison or guard. Upkeep on a pile like that is a pig."

Dullbreath nodded. "That too. Anyway, it should do us fine. Nice and quiet."

"For a change."

Skint stirred. "One more round for the lot," she said, "and then we ride on up."

Wither rose. "I'll tell Huggs t'get on with it, then. Boys that age it's short but often—she'll just have to settle with that."

The Broken Moon dragged its pieces above the horizon, throwing smudged shadows on the empty street, as the troop dragged themselves back into their saddles and set off for the ruin.

Graves stood in the gloom between two gutted houses and watched them pass, his shoulders hunched against the night air. He heard a noise behind him and turned. Herribut the blind cobbler edged closer, and behind him was a half-dozen villagers—most of the population, in fact.

"Y'think?" Herribut asked.

Graves scowled. "Ya, the usual. First pick's mine, as always."

Herribut nodded. "Lots drawn on after ya. I won." He grinned toothlessly. "Imagine that! I never had a touch of luck in my whole life, not once! But I won tonight!"

"Happy for ya, cobbler. Now, alla you, go get some sleep, and be sure to stopper your ears. Nobody's fault but your own if you're all grainy-eyed and slow come the morning pickings."

They shuffled off, chattering amongst themselves.

Exciting times in Glory, and how often could anyone say that without a bitter spit into the dust and then a sour smile? Graves stepped out into the street. The soldiers had reached the base of the hill, where they had paused to stare up at the black, brooding fortification.

"Go on," Graves whispered. "It's quiet. It's perfect. Go on, damn you."

And then they did, and he sagged in relief.

Nobody invited any of this, so nobody was to blame, not for anything. Just came down to making a living, that's all. People got the right to that, he figured. It wasn't a rule or anything like it, not some kingly law or natural truth. It was just one of those ideas people said aloud as often as they could, to make it more real and more true than it really was. When the fact was, people got no rights to anything. Not a single thing, not air to breathe, food to eat, ale to drink. Not the sweet smile between the legs, not a warm body beside you at night. Not land to own, not even a place to stand. But it made it easier, didn't it, saying that people got the right to a living, and honest hard work, like digging graves and carving capstones, well, that earned just rewards because that's how things should be.

The boy came out from the bar, weaving his way into the street. The woman had gotten him drunk besides stained in the crotch.

Graves set out to collect Snotty and take him to his solitary shack close to his own house. Couldn't be nice, he imagined, to end up just being abandoned by his ma and da when they were all passing through, and left to survive on his own. That was three years back, and Graves knew the boy had latched on to him to fill the holes in his growing up, and that was all right. To be expected. The boy would be in no shape for anything come the morning, but Graves would pluck a thing or two for him anyway. It was the least he could do.

The cobbled ramp climbed the hillside in three sharp switchbacks that would have cramped any supply wagon and likely made a mess of stocking the keep. The path was overgrown and cluttered with chunks of masonry, but otherwise picked clean.

Sergeant Flapp shifted uncomfortably in the saddle as his horse clumped up the sharp incline. That whore still had teeth, damn her, and that ring had been way too small. His snake felt strangled. He noticed, in passing, that all the anchor rings on the walls to either side had been dug out and carried off, leaving rusty-ringed holes. "They stripped this place right down," he said. "Doubt we'll find a single door, a single hinge or fitting. And now they'll probably sneak up and try and rob us tonight."

"They wouldn't be that suicidal," Wither said.

Flapp belched. "Maybe not. That Slim was one eager whore, though."

They rounded the last turn and came within sight of the gate. The portcullis was gone, as expected, all that iron, and the arched passageway yawned black as a cave mouth. Flapp followed Skint in. The drop chutes and murder holes were all plugged with muddy, guano-streaked martin nests, and they could hear the birds moving restlessly as they rode past.

The passage opened out to a yard overgrown with brambles. A stone-lined well marked the center, all its fittings removed. To the right was a low building running the length of one high wall. "Stables," Flapp said. "But we'll have to use the last of our fodder."

Skint pointed to a stone trough close to the stables. "Wither, check that, make sure it's not cracked. Huggs, collect up the water gourds and rig up a rope—let's see what we can scoop from the well. Flapp and Dullbreath, you're with me. Let's check out the main house."

That building was built to withstand its own siege. No windows on the lower floors, a narrow aperture preceding the doorway, arrow slits on the two squat towers flanking the inner facing. The slanted roof, they saw, was slate-tiled and holed through here and there.

"I'd wager the towers are solid and probably cleaner than anywhere else," said Flapp.

They dismounted. Walked toward the entrance.

The slow drumbeat of horse hoofs on the cobbles had awakened them, and now, in scores of chambers in the keep, figures stirred. Long, gnarled limbs unfolded, slitted eyes glittered as heads lifted, jaws stretching open to reveal rows of thin, vertical fangs. Twin hearts that had thumped in agonizingly slow syncopation for months now thudded faster, rushing blood and heat through tall, rope-muscled bodies. Talons clicked at the ends of unfurling hands.

The slaughterers of the garrison five hundred years ago, demons from the cursed plain beyond the mountains, awoke once more. A night of swift blood awaited them. A few soft-skinned travelers, such as haplessly sought shelter in this place every now and then. Food to share out, a mouthful of pulped meat—if that—and there would be fierce struggle over even such modest morsels. They'd eat everything but the bones and they'd split the bones and suck out the marrow and then leave the rubbish outside the gate before dawn arrived.

The imp commanding the demons ate its way out from its woven cocoon of human hair and scrambled, claws skittering, on all fours down the south tower's spiral staircase. Nostrils flaring at the sweet scent of horse and human meat, it clacked its teeth in hungry anticipation. Shin-high, the creature wore a tiny hauberk of scaled armor, a belted sword at its hip not longer than a bear's canine and nearly as dull. Its head was bare, victim to vanity, permitting its bright stiff shock of white hair to stand fully upright. Its eyes, a lurid yellow, flared with excitement.

Its fiends were awake, but the time for summoning must wait. The imp needed to see the victims with its own eyes, needed to feast on their growing fear. Needed them, indeed, trapped and then devoured by that terrifying realization. A silent command unveiled dark sorcery, swallowing the gatehouse in a swirling miasma of foul vapors, vitriolic and deadly. No, there would be no escape. There never was.

Soon, so very soon, the slaughter would begin. First the humans, and then the horses.

Dullbreath halted in the center of the broad, high-vaulted, pillar-lined hallway just inside the keep's narrow entrance. He sniffed the air. "Ghosts," he muttered. "This place was overrun, Captain. Plenty died in here."

Skint glanced back at the man, studied him for a moment, and then turned her attention once more to the far wall with its row of gaping doorways.

Flapp scanned the mosaic floor and frowned at the black, crumbly streaks all over it. He looked up to peer at the ceiling, but it was too dark to see much of anything up there—no obvious gap open to moonlight, though. "Smells kinda scaly in here."

Huggs stumped in. "Captain, we got a problem."

"What?"

"Horses getting edgy. And some kind of ward's sprung up at the gate. Stinks, burns the eyes and throat just getting close. Probably kill us if we tried to push through."

"Someone wants us to stay the night," Dullbreath said, his breathing loud and whistling in the chamber.

"Lonely ghosts?" asked Flapp.

Dullbreath shrugged. "Could be."

"All right," Skint said, "we pick us a room with one way in and one way out—"

"Ghosts go through walls, Captain—"

"Huggs, how's the wound?"

"Wither dug it out. It'll do."

Skint nodded and looked around once more. "Fuck ghosts," she said, "this ain't ghosts."

"Shit," said Huggs, and she walked back outside.

"Stay here, Dull," ordered Skint. "Sergeant, fire up that lantern and let's go find us a room."

"Never thought you cared, Captain."

The first three chambers along the row in front of them were dark, stinking hovels with passages through to secondary rooms—and those rooms opened out to both sides, their facing walls revealing the keep's heavy stones where rotted sheets of plaster had peeled away. The two mercenaries did little more than peer into those back chambers. The fourth room was an old armory, picked bare.

Flapp lifted the lantern and said, "See that? There, far corner—a trapdoor."

They walked to it. The brass ring was gone and the wood looked rotted through. "Give it a prod with your sword," Skint said.

"You sure?"

"Do it."

He handed her the lantern and withdrew his long blade of blued Aren steel. As soon as he touched the tip to the door, the planks crumpled, fell in a cloudy whoosh through the hatch. They heard sifting sounds from below.

"That ain't been used in a long time," Flapp observed.

Skint edged closer and brought the lantern over the hole. "Iron ladder, Sergeant. Looks like the looters lost their courage."

"I'm not surprised," he replied.

"Still drunk, Sergeant?"

"No. Mostly . . . no."

"We might want to take a look down there."

He nodded.

"I think," she said slowly, turning to face him, "we got ourselves a demon."

"That's the smell all right."

They heard clattering from the main hall.

Skint led the way back to the others.

Wither and Huggs had brought in the crossbows and dart-bags and were pulling and dividing up quarrels. Dullbreath was ratcheting tight the cords on the all-metal fist-punchers, smearing gobs of grease into the thick braids.

"Light the rest of the lanterns, Sergeant," said Skint, tightening the straps of her gauntlets. "Where's my helmet, Withy?"

"Behind Dullbreath, Captain."

"Everybody suit up. The night's gonna start with a bang. Then we can get some rest."

"I thought we'd left crap-face demons behind us," griped Huggs.

"One got out and squirreled up here, that's all."

"A magic-shitter, too."

"It'll show, we drive it back, corner it, and kill the fucker."

The others nodded.

High in the rafters, the imp stared down at the five fools. Soldiers! How exciting. They had managed well reining in their panic, but the imp could smell their acrid sweat, that pungent betrayal of terror. It watched as they assembled their weapons, went over each other's armor—what was left of it—and then, arranging the five lanterns in a broad circle, they donned their helmets—one of those badly cracked, the one on the taller of the two men—and, slotting quarrels into the crossbows, settled into a circle well inside the ring of fitful light.

Sound defensive positioning.

The demon they were now discussing could come from anywhere, after all, any of the doorways, including the one leading outside. Could come from the ceiling, too, for that matter. And the imp grinned with its needle teeth.

All very good, very impressive.

But there wasn't just one demon, was there?

No. There were lots. And lots. And lots.

The imp awoke sorcery again, sealing the keep's doorway. One of the women caught the stench of that and she swore. That one had a nose for magic, she did. Too bad it wasn't going to help.

Still grinning, the imp summoned its fiends.

In the stable, the horses, sensitive to such things, began shrilling and screaming.

Flapp saw the captain lift her head, as if trying to hear something behind the maddened horses. A moment later, she straightened. "Collect up the lanterns. Time to retreat to our room."

Burdened with gear, crossbows cradled, the lanterns slung by their handles over the stirrups, the group moved in a contracting circle toward a lone gaping doorway.

Flapp was the first through. A quick scan, and then a grunt. "Clear."

The others quickly filed in.

Huggs made to speak, but the captain silenced her with a gesture, and then, when Skint had everyone's attention, she hand-talked, fast, precise. Nods answered her all around. Lanterns clunked softly on the floor.

Gray-scaled, trailing cobwebs and shedding mortar dust, the demons poured like foul water down a cataract, round and round the spiral stairs of the north tower. Ten, twenty, thirty, their jaws creaking, fangs clashing, lunging on all fours, tails slithering in their wake. They spilled out onto the landing, talons screeching across the tiles as they rushed the single lit doorway two-thirds of the way down the corridor.

Cries of rising bloodlust shrilled from their throats, a frenzied chorus that could curdle a lump of lard and set it quivering. The imp dropped down from the rafters and scurried into their wake, in time to see the first of the demons plunge through the entrance.

It howled—but the cry was one of blunted frustration.

The imp slipped under, over, and around the mob clamoring at the doorway, leapt through to find itself in a room with naught but demons lashing about, gouging the walls in fury.

The lanterns had been kicked against the walls.

The five humans were gone.

Where?

Ah—the imp caught sight of a gaping hole in the floor.

With frantic screeches, it commanded the demons to pursue, and the one closest to the trapdoor slithered through, followed quickly by the others.

Clever humans! But how fast could they run?

Not fast enough!

The imp awakened the rest of its children, and curdling howls erupted from countless chambers.

The first demons swarmed down the ladder to the first subterranean level—there were a half-dozen such levels, a maze of narrow, low-ceilinged, crooked passageways bored in the hill's enormous mound. Storerooms, cisterns, armories, cutter surgeries, and wards. It had been centuries since the demons last scoured these tunnels.

The imp sensed their sudden confusion—the stench of the humans went off in each of the three possible directions, and then two more at a branch ten strides along the main corridor. They had panicked! Now each fool could be hunted down, dragged to the grimy, greasy cobbles in a burst of blood and entrails.

Chittering with excitement, the imp sent demons after every one of the pathetic, wretched things.

A demon slunk noiselessly down a cramped passage, nostrils glistening, dripping in answer to the sour smell of a human hanging like mist in the dark air. Jagged black jolts ripped through its brain in waves, a jarring hunger that trembled through its elongated torso, shivering down its gnarled limbs to softly clatter its claws and talons.

The long sleep was an ugly, cruel place, and awakening was painful with savage need.

It came upon a foul woolen cloak, lost in the quarry's frantic flight. The demon crouched and breathed deep, stirring memories of centuries-old slaughter. Lifting its head, it reflexively spread wide its jaws, and crept forward.

At a sound behind it the demon spun around.

A studded, gauntleted fist smashed into the demon's face, crushing its snout, sending shards of splintered fangs into the back of its throat. The fist drove home again, snapping the demon's head against the wall. And again, and again.

Sergeant Flapp's fist was a blur, a rapid mallet that repeatedly pounded the pulped mess that was the demon's head while his other hand held the thing up by the neck. When the meaty, crunching sounds gave way to the hard impact of a skull plate driven flat against the stone of the wall, he stepped back and let the twitching fiend slide to the floor.

He could hear more coming up the corridor.

Flapp collected his cloak and set off down the narrow side passage he had been hiding in—watching the demon sidle past—only moments earlier.

Three demons skidded around at the intersection and sprinted on all fours, voicing deep growls that would shiver the hair off a pack of wolves. The lead one's head exploded in a spray of blood and bone as Wither's quarrel took it between the eyes. Sprawling, its limbs entangled the demons behind it and they howled in fury.

Ten loping strides down the passageway, Wither stepped back out of sight, into the side corridor—a narrow chute barely wide enough to let her pass. Wedging the crossbow crossways at chest height just within the entrance, she took two steps back, drawing her two longswords, and waited.

The first demon's forelimbs wrapped claws around the corner to slow it down as it lunged into the chute.

The iron crossbow brought it up short, clipping its lower jaw and snapping its head down.

Wither selected that inviting bald pate as a suitable target and swung down with both blades.

Brains splattered the walls.

The demon suddenly crowding behind it shrieked as a quarrel tore through its neck from farther up the main corridor. Gasping red froth, it staggered back and decided on a noisy death.

Wither kicked the virtually headless demon away and, sheathing one sword, wrenched loose her crossbow, and then set out down the chute.

Twenty paces along the main corridor, Huggs dropped the crossbow stirrup, set her boot toe on it, and tugged the cord into lock, wincing as the wound in her shoulder flared with pain. Slotting a new quarrel, she plunged into the gloom. Of course, demons could see in the dark, and some of them could see any hot-blooded beastie, but when hungry, they preferred to follow their noses and that was a savage yank on their leashes (not that they had leashes, not these ones anyway).

And their eyes, why, they blazed and made perfect targets.

She could hear more coming. Some would take off after Wither. The rest would latch on to her tail. She hurried off.

Crowded by four of its fellows, a demon crouched in an intersection. Human trails led into opposing corridors. It hesitated. The one behind it snarled and darted to the left, and then skidded to a halt as it stumbled on a discarded cloak. It grunted in confusion, and then whirled—

The man with the jutting yellow teeth launched himself from the corridor to the right, throwing all his weight behind a sword thrust that punched through the demon in the intersection, piercing both hearts, the hilt slamming hard against ribs. Leaving the weapon there, he ducked down, twisting to drive one scale-armored elbow into the next closest demon, caving in its forehead.

The remaining two demons collided with each other in their eagerness to reach him.

Dullbreath stepped back, and then drove a boot into the heavy balls dangling between the legs of one of the creatures. As it sank back with a grinding groan, the last demon was suddenly unimpeded and with a shriek it flung itself at the man. He caught its throat with both hands and squeezed in a single lightning-quick clench that crushed the demon's windpipe. Throwing the twitching thing aside, Dullbreath drew his hunting knife and sliced open the throat of the demon he'd kicked, since he was feeling merciful.

Sheathing the knife, he tugged loose his sword, collected up his crossbow, and set off, snagging up his cloak along the way.

One hand trailing along a wall—keeping herself straight as she ran mostly blind in the darkness—Huggs felt the sudden gap to her right. Sliding to a halt, she backed up—fighting sounds from somewhere down there. Savage-sounding stuff, maybe even desperate.

She knew she had a few and maybe more coming up behind her. Whoever she helped out might curse Huggs if she led them down after her—trapping Huggs and whomever else between two slavering mobs.

Oh well. She hefted her crossbow and darted down the side passage.

She heard a solid thunk—like the world's biggest crossbow—and that worried her, until she heard demonic shrieks of agony and rage.

Someone's found a new toy?

Clattering claws behind her, closing fast, and that wasn't good.

Huggs halted, crouched, raised her weapon, and waited until she saw the gleam of the first demon's eyes. Took that one down easy. Dropping the crossbow, she drew her sword into her right hand, her crack-finder into her left.

Four more sets of blazing eyes rushed upon her.

"Drop flat!"

Huggs did.

A thunderous whoosh raced over her. Sudden mayhem up the corridor, as a huge pig of a barbed quarrel ripped through three of the damned things, gouging a shoulder of the fourth one. Laughing, Huggs leapt to her feet and charged it.

With a squeal, the demon fled as fast as three working limbs could take it.

"Shit." Huggs halted, jogged back, peered in the darkness. "Who?"

"Wither—listen, found a whole storeroom of these fuckers. Siege arbalests."

"Lead the way, darling."

"Watch your step up here. Lots of bodies."

"Right."

Captain Skint shoved the faceless mess aside and pushed through the doorway, stepping clear and then turning to meet the first of the demons that lunged into view at the threshold. Her sword tip opened a wide grin in its throat. The next one, clambering over its fallen kin, lost the top of its head, bisecting its relatively small brain, which stopped working in any case.

Three more squeezed through and Skint took a step back to clear some room and let them in.

Talons slashed with murderous intent, but caught empty air. Jaws snapped on nothing. Surges to close and grapple missed again and again. The woman was a blur of motion to their eyes. A demon's head jumped free of the rest of it, and the stumpy neck poured blood everywhere. Another shrieked as something kissed its belly and it looked down to see its intestines tumbling out—withered, empty things, like starving worms. Collecting them up, it waddled to the doorway—but that was blocked as dozens of demons struggled to press through the doorway. The disemboweled demon snarled and took two fatal talons to its eyes for its ill manners.

Skint helped a demon leap into a wall, and when it fell to the floor, she stamped her heel into its throat, then jumped away to avoid its thrashing.

She cast a gauging regard upon the swarm of gleaming eyes jammed in the doorway, and then stepped forward and began hacking with her sword. Sometimes, finesse was just stupid.

Flapp balanced on the crossbeam and watched as the third and last demon passed underneath. His quarrel buried itself in the back of the thing's head, and as it fell, the sergeant flung the crossbow at the nearest beast—which had twisted around, eye flaring like coals—and saw it bounce from the demon's flat fore-head even as Flapp plunged off the edge to land on the floor, two short swords snapping out but held points-down.

He rushed the demons. Blades slashed, intersecting wrists and forearms, slashed some more, cutting through hamstrings and other assorted, necessary tendons. He drove his head forward. Helmed bridge guard slammed with a happy crunch into a forehead, and then Flapp was past them both—they flopped and writhed behind him all messy with blood. He spun around and made quick work of them, and then retrieved his crossbow, only to snarl when discovering its bent arm. Flinging it away, he trundled down the corridor.

He could hear fighting.

He went to find it.

They could make out a mob of the bastards swarming a doorway, which meant someone was cornered, or, rather, had let themselves get cornered, which meant it was the captain. Grunting beneath the weight of the arbalests both women held, they sent two bolts tearing into the crowd. Torn bodies and pieces of meat flew.

And then, with a scream, Huggs charged the rest. Cursing, Wither dropped her arbalest and unsheathed her swords, setting off after her. By the time she reached the writhing mound, Huggs was buried somewhere beneath the heaving press of snarling demons.

Wither started chopping off limbs, heads.

She saw the captain's sword tip lunge from the doorway, driving deep between two widening eyes, and a moment later Skint kicked her way into view.

The demons broke, a half dozen bolting with shrieks up the corridor.

Where someone else hit them.

Wither started dragging bodies off Huggs, and found her pounding on a knife she'd driven through the top of a demon's head, but its jaws were still clamped tight around her left thigh.

"You idiot!" snapped Wither, "get your hands away so I can pry it loose. Gods below, we could have stood back and cleared the whole mess with a couple more bolts!"

Huggs spat blood. "Why should Skint get all the fun? Get this fucking thing off my leg!"

"I'm trying—sit still!"

Sergeant Flapp arrived. "Three got away!"

"There's more," said Skint.

"You said one!" Wither hissed, finally loosening the demon's death-bite.

"So I was off by a few. Where's Dullbreath? Anyone see him?"

"Not since we split," said Flapp.

"Same here," added Wither, and Huggs nodded as she sat up.

Skint swung her sword to shed gore and blood from the blade. "They're on the run now. So we hunt."

Her soldiers checked their weapons.

Flapp saw one of the arbalest bolts and kicked at it. "Nice."

"Got a whole room of the damned things."

"I need me a replacement."

"We'll take you there, Sergeant—"

"Take us all there," said Skint. "Then we split up again. Rendezvous in the main hall up top, and don't dally. Someone's running this army, and I want it skewered."

"Follow me," said Wither.

Whimpering, the imp picked its way around yet another heap of demon corpses. Poor children! This was a slaughter, a terrible, grievous, dreadful slaughter!

And now they were hunting the survivors down—nowhere to hide!

Human stench everywhere, down every passage, every twisting, turning corridor, every cursed chamber and rank room. There was no telling where they were now, no telling what vicious ambushes they'd set up.

The imp crouched, quivering, hugging itself, and crooned its grief. Then it shook itself, drawing free its tiny sword. Enough of these evil tunnels and warrens! To the ladder! Flee this cruel place!

With renewed determination, and a healthy dose of terror, it scampered.

Breathing hard, the demon froze, nose testing the pungent, bitter air. Its eyes were wide, seeking the telltale bloom of body heat—those cursed cloaks, they'd been sopping wet, cold to the touch, blind to the demon's eyes; and the iron chain wasn't much better. Even so, there was no way a human could sneak up on it. No way.

It needed to find somewhere to hide. A privy hole, maybe. A crack in a wall. Anywhere.

The demon edged forward, and suddenly the human stench was overpowering. Mewling, it slowly straightened—and then turned around.

The bearded face hovering a hand's width in front of its snout elicited a piercing scream of horror from the demon.

"Looking for me?" And then a red-stained studded fist rammed into its face. Twice, thrice, eight, nine, twelve times.

As the demon crumpled at his feet, Flapp grunted and said, "Didn't think so."

The two demons, boon companions for centuries, clutched each other, sharing a puddle of rank piss pooling around them, as two female humans stepped into view. Ferocious barbed bolts flung the two demons apart like rag dolls.

Wither began working the crank to reload her weapon, whilst Huggs limped forward. "You see them? Fucking pathetic."

"You're getting soft, Huggs."

"Loaded?"

"Yes."

"My turn. Keep an eye peeled, Withy."

"Count on it."

The imp could hear random death-cries echoing down the corridors, each one trembling through its scrawny, puny form. Reaching the iron ladder, it clambered upward as fast as its little limbs could carry it.

Not fast enough.

"Got ya."

A mailed hand snatched the imp up, plucked it from the railing.

The imp squealed and thrashed about, but it was no use. It struggled to bring its sword to bear, but the man reached with his other hand and broke the imp's sword arm. Snap, like a twig. Broke the other one, too, and then both legs. That really hurt!

Helpless, the imp dangled limp in the man's grip. He stared down at it, breathing loud, mouth hanging open.

And then he bit down on the imp's head and held it in his mouth as he climbed the ladder.

That breath! The imp cringed, even through its agony of broken bits everywhere. That breath!

As soon as they reached the top, and the man walked out of the armory, along the corridor, and out to the main chamber, the imp sent forth a frantic cry, a sorcerous plea bristling with desperate power.

Mommy! Mommy! Help me!

None left. Of course they could not be entirely certain of that, but they'd scoured every possible hiding place, rooting out the snarling oversized rats and chopping them to pieces.

Skint led them back to the arbalest armory, where they loaded up on bolts, including the assault quarrels with their looped ends, as well as bundles of thick cables. The walk back to the ladder was slow and awkward, with all the blood, corpses, and gore cluttering the passageways. By the time they strode out into the main chamber, Dullbreath was waiting for them. He nodded to a small figure pinned by a tiny sword to the floor in the center of the room.

"Still breathing?"

"Hard to say. Hard to kill for real, those things."

"All right. Good work, Dullbreath. Let's get ready then."

The girl who walked in through the keep's doors clutched a bundle of plucked flowers, her blond hair drifting like seed fluff. Her large eyes settled on the tiny figure of the imp nailed to the floor, and she edged closer.

Her expression fell as she looked down on her dead child. Kneeling, she set aside her flowers and reached out to brush that tiny, cold forehead.

Then, as she straightened, five soldiers stepped out from behind pillars, each bearing loaded arbalests.

The girl raised her scrawny arms and vanished inside a blurry haze. Spice-laden clouds rolled from where she stood, and the soldiers stared as she awakened to her true form, burgeoning, towering at almost twice the height of an average man, and easily twice as wide. Fangs as long as short swords, a mass of muscles like bundles of rope, hands that could crush armored soldiers as if they were frail eggs.

Huggs snorted. "A demon, huh? That's not just a demon, Captain. That's a fucking Harridan!"

"Commander of a legion," added Dullbreath. "What were they thinking?"

The demon opened its maw and howled.

The sound deafened them, shook plaster loose from ceiling and walls.

The soldiers lifted their weapons. And fired.

The bolts pounded deep into the giant beast, and each dart snaked cables behind it—cables bound around the base of a pillar. The hinged barbs on the heads snagged deep in the demon's flesh. Shrieking, it sought to pull away, but the thick ropes snapped taut—to tear loose of any one of the quarrels would break bones and spill out organs and who knew what else.

"Reload," growled Skint.

And so they did.

Dawn's light slowly stole in through the entrance, crept across the floor of the main chamber.

"Last crate," said Flapp in a ragged, exhausted voice.

He went around, passing out the last of the bolts. Cranks clanked, but slowly.

Wither stepped up to squint at the pin-cushioned heap of mangled flesh huddled in the center of the chamber, and then shrugged and returned to her arbalest.

Five weapons clanged. Five bolts sank into the body.

"Quivered some," observed Flapp.

"So would you," said Huggs. "No whimpers though. Those stopped some time ago." She turned to the captain. "Could be it's finally dead."

"Prod it with your sword," Skint commanded.

"Me and my big mouth." But Huggs drew her weapon and edged closer. She gave the thing a poke. "Nothing." She poked harder. Still no response. So she stabbed. "Hah! It's dead all right."

Arbalests dropped from exhausted arms.

"Saddle us up, Withy. Let's get the fuck out of here."

"You got it, Captain."

Graves had been up all night. No amount of beeswax could have stoppered up that seemingly endless chorus of screams and howls from the keep. It had never been so bad. Ever. Those soldiers, they'd died hard. Damned hard.

He rigged up his mule and cart and led the procession—a quiet bunch this morning, for sure—up to collect the remains and whatever loot came out with it. Work was work, wasn't it just. People did what they did to get by, and what else was life all about? Nothing. That was it. It and nothing more. But, dammit, he didn't want the boy to spend his whole cursed life here in Glory, didn't want him taking over when Graves gave it up, not stepping in when Slim finally swallowed her ring and choked to death—the gods knew she wasn't going to die naturally. Didn't want any of that, not for the boy.

After sending a few scowls at the bleary-eyed but ever-greedy faces arrayed behind him, he tugged the reluctant mule up to the first of the hillside's switchbacks.

And then stopped.

As the first clump of horse hoofs sounded up ahead.

The captain was in the lead. The others followed. Every one of them. Five, aye, five one by one by one by one by one.

Graves stared.

As she passed him, Skint flung a bloody mass of something at him. Reflexively, he caught it and looked down at the wilted remnants of flowers. Dripping red.

The sergeant was next. "Five graves? Not enough, sir, not by a long shot."

Wither added more as she rode past, "Try about ninety-five more."

Huggs snorted. "And a big one, too, and I mean big. Oh, and a tiny one, too."

Dullbreath halted opposite Graves and looked down at him with jaded eyes. "For fuck's sake, Graves, we kill those fuckers for a living."

He rode on. They all did.

Graves looked down at the flowers in his hand.

People do what they do, he reminded himself. To get by. Just that, to get by.

"Two days to Piety," said Flapp as they rode along the track on the slow climb to the distant valley mouth.

"And then—"

"Captain," called out Dullbreath from the rear.

They all reined in and turned.

Slim was riding a mule after them, the old whore rocking back and forth like she'd never learned how to ride, and that struck Flapp as damned funny. But he didn't laugh.

"We got us a camp follower," said Wither. "I don't believe it."

Flapp opened his mouth and was about to say something, and then he stopped—he'd caught a glint of metal—from way up the trail they'd come down yesterday. "Captain! I saw a flash of steel! Halfway up to the pass!"

Everyone stiffened. Stared, breaths held.

"There! You seen it?"

And the look Skint turned on him was twisted into a mask of unholy terror. "He's still after us! Ride, soldiers! To save your lives, *ride*!"

⚔

*Reviewer Liz Bourke has written that Elizabeth Bear's (1971–) Eternal Sky trilogy [*Range of Ghosts *(2012),* Shattered Pillars *(2013), and* Steles of the Sky *(2014)] "subverts the expectations of epic fantasy even as it uses them to create a narrative with mythic resonance and force." The trilogy is filled with "wonder, amazing world-building, heroism, and tragedy—and also filled with grit, emotional realism, and a light, ironic, humane sense of humor. . . . [its] world [is] inspired by Central Asia and the Silk Road, by the Chinese kingdoms and Tibet and the Mongolian steppe and the caliphates of Turkey and Iran." Bear's characters "feel like real people with real motivations and desires and complexities." A sequel trilogy, The Lotus Kingdoms, launches this fall with* The Stone in the Skull. *Its protagonists—the Dead Man, an exiled royal guard, and the Gage, a wizardly automaton—are introduced in "The Ghost Makers."*

THE GHOST MAKERS

Elizabeth Bear

The faceless man walked out of the desert at sunset, when the gates of the City of Jackals wound ponderously closed on silent machinery. He was the last admitted. His kind were made by Wizards, and went about on Wizards' business. No one interrogated him.

His hooded robe and bronze hide smoked with sun-heat when the priest of Iashti threw water from the sacred rivers over him. Whether it washed away any clinging devils of the deep desert, as it was intended, who could have said? But it did rinse the dust from the featureless oval of his visage so all who stood near could see themselves reflected. Distorted.

He paused within and he lowered the hood of his homespun robes to lie upon his shoulders. The gates made the first sound of their closing, a heavy snap as their steel-shod edges overlapped and latched. Their juncture reflected as a curved line up the mirror of the faceless man's skull. Within the gates, bars as thick as a man glided home. Messaline was sealed, and the date plantations and goats and pomegranates and laborers of the farms and villages beyond her walls were left to their own devices until the lion-sun tinted the horizon again.

Trailing tendrils of steam faded from the faceless man's robe, leaving the air heavy with petrichor—the smell of water in aridity—and the cloth over his armored hide as dry as before. His eyeless mask trained unwaveringly straight ahead, he raised his voice.

"Priest of Iashti." Though he had no mouth, his voice tolled clear and sonorous.

The priest left his aspergillum and came around to face the faceless man, though there was no need. He said, "You already have my blessing, O Gage . . . of . . . ?"

"I'd rather information than blessings, Child of the Morning," said the Gage. The priest's implied question—to whom he owed his service—the faceless man left unacknowledged. His motionlessness—as if he were a bronze statue someone had draped in a robe and left inexplicably in the center of the market road—was more distressing than if he'd stalked the priest like a cat.

He continued, "Word is that a poet was murdered under the Blue Stone a sennight since."

"Gage?"

The Gage waited.

The priest collected himself. He tugged the tangerine-and-gold dawn-colored robed smooth beneath his pectoral. "It is true. Eight days ago, though—no, now gone nine."

"Which way?"

Wordlessly, the priest pointed to a twisting, smoky arch towering behind dusty tiers of pastel houses. The sunset sprawled across the sky rendered the monument in translucent silhouette, like an enormous, elaborate braid of chalcedony.

The faceless man paused, and finally made a little motion of his featureless head that somehow still gave the impression of ruefully pursed lips and acknowledgment.

"Alms." He tossed gold to the priest.

The priest, no fool, caught it before it could bloody his nose. He waited to bite it until the Gage was gone.

The Gage made his way through the Temple District, where great prayer-houses consecrated to the four major Messaline deities dominated handfuls of lesser places of worship: those of less successful sects, or of alien gods. Only the temple to the Uthman Scholar-God, fluted pillars twined about with sacred verses rendered in lapis lazuli and pyrite, competed with those four chief temples for splendor.

Even at dusk, these streets teemed. Foot traffic, litter bearers, and the occasional rider and mount—mostly horses, a few camels, a mule, one terror-bird—bustled through the lanes between the torch bearers. There were soldiers and merchants, priests and scholars, a nobleman or woman in a curtained sedan chair with guards crying out *"Make way!"* The temples were arranged around a series of squares, and the squares were occupied by row upon row of market stalls from which rose the aromas of turmeric, coriander, roses, sandalwood, dates, meat sizzling, bread baking, and musty old attics—among other things. The sweet scent of stitched leather and wood-pulp-and-rag paper identified a bookseller as surely as did the banner that drifted above his pavilion.

The faceless man passed them all—and more than half of the people he passed either turned to stare or hurried quickly along their way, eyes fixed on the ground by their shoes. The Gage knew better than to assign any quality of guilt or innocence to these reactions.

He did not stay in the temple district long. A left-hand street bent around the temple of Kaalha, the goddess of death and mercy—who also wore a mirrored mask, though hers was silver and divided down the center line. The temple had multiple doorways, and seemed formed in the shape of a star. Over the nearest one was inscribed: IN MY HOUSE THERE IS AN END TO PAIN.

Some distance behind the temple, the stone arch loomed.

At first he walked by stucco houses built cheek to cheek, stained in every shade of orange, red, vermilion. The arches between their entryways spanned the road. But soon the street grew crooked and dark; there were no torch-bearers here. A rat or two was in evidence, scurrying over stones—but rodents went quickly and fearfully here. Once, longer legs and ears flickered like scissors as a slender shadow detached itself from one darkness and glided across the open space to the next: one of the jackals from which Messaline took its epithet. From the darkness where it finished, a crunch and a squeak told of one scurrying at least that ended badly for the scurrier.

In these gutters, garbage reeked, though not too much of it; things that were still useful would be put to use. The people passing along these streets were patch-clothed, dirty-cheeked, lank of unwashed hair. Many wore long knives; a few bore flintlocks. The only unescorted women were those plying a trade, and a few men who loitered in dark doorways or alleys drew back into their lairs as the Gage passed, each footstep ringing dully off the cobbles. He was reminded of tunnel-spiders, and kept walking.

As he drew closer to one base of the Blue Stone, though, he noticed an increase in people walking quickly in the direction opposite his. Though the night sweltered, stored heat radiating back from the stones, they hunched as if cold: heads down and shoulders raised protectively.

Still no one troubled the faceless man. Messaline knew about Wizards.

Others were not so lucky, or so unmolested.

The Gage came out into the small square that surrounded one foot of the

Blue Stone. It rose above him in an interlaced, fractal series of helixes a hundred times the height of a tall man, vanishing into the darkness that drank its color and translucency. The Gage had been walking for long enough that stars now showed through the gaps in the arch's sinuous strands.

The base of the monument separated into a half-dozen pillars where it plunged to earth. Rather than resting upon a plinth or footing, though, it seemed as if each pillar had thrust up through the street like a tree seeking the light—or possibly as if the cobbles of the road had just been paved around them.

Among the shadows between those pillars, a man wearing a skirted coat and wielding a narrow, curved sword fought silently—desperately—valiantly—for his life.

The combat had every appearance of an ambush—five on one, though that one was the superior swordsman and tactician. These were advantages that did not always affect the eventual result when surrounded and outnumbered, but the man in the skirted coat was making the most of them. His narrow torso twisted like a charmed snake as he dodged blows too numerous to deflect. He might have been an answer to any three of his opponents. But as it was, he was left whirling and weaving, leaping and ducking, parrying for his life. The harsh music of steel rang from the tight walls of surrounding rowhouses. His breathing was a rasp audible from across the square. He used the footings of the monument to good advantage, dodging between them, keeping them at his back, forcing his enemies to coordinate their movements over uneven cobblestones.

The Gage paused to assess.

The lone man's skirts whirled wide as he caught a narrower, looping strand of the Blue Stone in his off hand and used it as a handle to swing around, parrying one opponent with his sword hand while landing a kick in the chest of another. The kicked man staggered back, arms pinwheeling. One of his allies stepped under his blade and came on, hoping to catch the lone man off-balance.

The footpad—if that's what he was—huffed in pain as he ran into the Gage's outstretched arm. His eyes widened; he jerked back and reflexively brought his scimitar down. It glanced off the Gage's shoulder, parting his much-patched garment and leaving a bright line.

The Gage picked him up by the jaw, one-handed, and bashed his brains out against the Blue Stone.

The man in the skirted coat ran another through between the ribs. The remaining three hesitated, exchanging glances. One snapped a command; they vanished into the night like rain into a fallow field, leaving only the sound of their footsteps. The man in the skirted coat seemed as if he might give chase, but his sword was wedged. He stood on the chest of the man he had killed and twisted his long, slightly curved blade to free it. It had wedged in his victim's spine. A hiss of air escaping a punctured lung followed as he slid it free.

Warily, he turned to the Gage. The Gage did not face him. The man in the skirted coat did not bother to walk around to face the Gage.

"Thank . . . "

Above them, the Blue Stone began to glow, with a grey light that faded up from nothingness and illuminated the scene: glints off the Gage's bronze body, the saturated blood-red of the lone man's coat, the frayed threads of its embroidery worn almost flat on the lapels.

"What the—?"

"Blood," the Gage said, prodding the brained body with his toe. "The Blue Stone accepts our sacrifice." He gestured to the lone man's prick-your-finger coat. "You're a Dead Man."

Dead Men were the sworn, sacred guards of the Caliphs who ruled north and east of Messaline, across the breadth of the sea.

"Not anymore," the Dead Man said. Fastidiously, he crouched and scrubbed his sword on a corpse's hem. "Not professionally. And not literally, thanks to you. By which I mean, 'Thank you.' "

The faceless man shrugged. "It didn't look like a fair fight."

"In this world, O my brother, is there such a thing as a fair fight? When one man is bestowed by the gods with superior talent, by station with superior training, by luck with superior experience?"

"I'd call that the opposite of luck," said the faceless man.

The Dead Man shrugged. "Pardon my forwardness; a true discourtesy, when directed at one who has done me a very great favor solely out of the goodness of his heart—"

"I have no heart."

"—but you are what they call a Faceless Man?"

"We prefer the term Gage. And while we're being rude, I had heard your kind don't leave the Caliph's service."

"The Caliph's service left me. A new Caliph's posterior warms the dais in Asitaneh. I've heard *your* kind die with the Wizard that made you."

The Gage shrugged. "I've something to do before I lie down and let the scavengers have me."

"Well, you have come to the City of Jackals now."

"You talk a lot for a dead man."

The Dead Man laughed. He sheathed his sword and thrust the scabbard through his sash. More worn embroidery showed that to be its place of custom.

"Why were they trying to kill you?"

The Dead Man had aquiline features and eagle-eyes to go with it, a trim goatee and a sandalwood-skinned face framed by shoulder-length ringlets, expensively oiled. Slowly, he drew a crimson veil across his nose and mouth. "I expected an ambush."

Neither one of them made any pretense that that was, exactly, an answer.

The Gage reached out curiously and touched the glowing stone. "Then I'm pleased to see that your expectation was rewarded."

"You discern much." The Dead Man snorted and stood. "May I know the name of the one who aided me?"

"My kind have no names."

"Do you propose then that there is no difference between you? You all have the same skills? The same thoughts?"

The Gage turned to him, and the Dead Man saw his own expression reflected, distorted in that curved bronze mirror. It never even shivered when he spoke. "So we are told."

The Dead Man shrugged. "So also are we. Were we. When I was a part of something bigger. But now I am alone, and my name is Serhan."

The Gage said, "You can call me Gage."

He turned away, though he did not need to. He tilted his featureless head back to look up.

"What's this thing?" The Gage's gesture followed the whole curve of the Blue Stone, revealed now as the light their murders had engendered rose along it like tendrils of crawling foxfire.

"It is old; it is anyone's guess what good it once was. There used to be a road under it, before they built the houses. A triumphal arch, maybe?"

"Hell of a place for a war monument."

The Dead Man's veil puffed out as he smothered a laugh. "The neighborhood was better once."

"Surprised they didn't pull it down for building material."

"Many have tried," the Dead Man said. "It does not pull down."

"Huh," said the Gage. He prodded the brained man again. "Any idea why they attacked you?"

"Opportunity? Or perhaps to do with the crime I have been investigating. That seems more likely."

"Crime?"

Reluctantly, the Dead Man answered, "Murder."

"Oh," said the Gage. "The poet?"

"I wonder if it might have been related to this." The Dead Man's hand described the arc of light across the sky. The glow washed the stars away. "Maybe he was a sacrifice to whatever old power inhabits . . . this."

"I doubt it," said the Gage. "I know something about the killer."

"You seek justice in this matter too?"

The Gage shrugged. "After a fashion."

The Dead Man stared. The Gage did not move. "Well," said the Dead Man at last. "Let us then obtain wine."

They chose a tavern on the other side of the block that faced on the Blue Stone, where its unnerving light did not wash in through the high narrow windows. The floor was gritty with sand spread to sop up spilled wine, and the air was thick with its vinegar sourness. The Gage tested the first step carefully, until he determined that what lay under the sand was flagstone. As they settled themselves—the Dead Man with his back to the wall, the Gage with his back to the room—the Gage said, "Did it do that when the poet died?"

"His name was Anah."

"Did it do that when Anah died?"

The Dead Man raised one hand in summons to the serving girl. "It seems to like blood."

"And yet we don't know what they built it for."

"Or who built it," the Dead Man said. "But you believe those things do not matter."

The girl who brought them wine was young, her blue-black hair in a wrist-thick braid of seven strands. The plait hung down her back in a spiral, twisted like the Blue Stone. She took the Dead Man's copper and withdrew.

The Dead Man said, "I always wondered how your sort sustained yourselves."

In answer, the Gage cupped his bronze fingers loosely around the stem of the cup and let them lie on the table.

"I was hired by the poet's . . . by Anah's lover." The Dead Man lifted his cup and swirled it. Fumes rose from the warmed wine. He lifted his veil and touched his mouth to the rim. The wine was raw, rough stuff, more fruit than alcohol.

The Gage said, "We seek the same villain."

"I am afraid I cannot relinquish my interest in the case. I . . . need the money." The Dead Man lifted his veil to drink again. The edge lapped wine and grew stained.

The Gage might have been regarding him. He might have been staring at the wall behind his head. Slowly, he passed a brazen hand over the table. It left behind a scaled track of silver. "I will pay you as well as your other client. And I will help you bring her the Wizard's head."

"Wizard!"

The Gage shrugged.

"You think you know who it is that I hunt."

"Oh yes," the Gage said. Scratched silver glittered dully on the table. "I can tell you that."

The Dead Man regarded his cup, and the Gage regarded . . . whatever it was.

Finally, the Gage broke the impasse to say, "Would you rather go after a Wizard alone, or in company?"

Under his veil, the Dead Man nibbled a thumbnail. "Which Wizard?"

"Attar the Enchanter. Do you know where to find him?"

"Everyone in Messaline knows where to find a Wizard. Or, belike, how to avoid him." The Dead Man tapped the nearest coin. "Why would he kill a *poet*? Gut him? In a public square?"

"He's a ghost-maker," the Gage said. "He kills for the pleasure it affords him. He kills artists, in particular. He likes to own them. To possess their creativity."

"Huh," said the Dead Man. "Anah was not the first, then."

"Ghost-makers . . . some people say they're soulless themselves. That they're empty, and so they drink the souls of the dead. And they're always hungry for another."

"People say a lot of shit," the Dead Man said.

"When I heard the manner of the poet's death, and that Attar was in Messaline . . . " The Gage shrugged. "I came at once. To catch up with him before he moves on again."

"You have not come about Anah in particular."

"I'm here *for* Anah. And the other Anahs. Future and past."

"I see," said the Dead Man.

His hand passed across the table. When it vanished, no silver remained. "Is it true that darkness cannot cloud your vision?"

"I can see," said the faceless man. "In dark or day, whether I turn my head aside or no. What has no eyes cannot be blinded."

"That must be awful," the Dead Man said.

The lamplight flickered against the side of the Gage's mask.

"So," said the Gage, motionless. "When the Caliph's service left you, you chose a mercenary life?"

"Not mercenary," the Dead Man said. "I have had sufficient of soldiering. I'm a hired investigator."

"An . . . investigator."

The corners of the Dead Man's eyes folded into eagle-tracks. "We have a legacy of detective stories in the Caliphate. Tales of clever men, and of one who is cleverer. They are mostly told by women."

"Aren't *most* of your storytellers women?"

The Dead Man moved to drink and found his cup empty. "They *are* the living embodiment of the Scholar-God."

"And you keep them in cages."

"We keep God in temples. Is that so different?"

After a while, the Dead Man said, "You have some plan for fighting a Wizard? A Wizard who . . . killed your maker?"

"My maker was Cog the Deviser. That's not how she died. But I thought perhaps a priest of Kaalha would know what to do about a ghost-maker."

"Ask the Death God. You are a clever automaton."

The Gage shrugged.

"If you won't drink that, I will."

"Drink it?" the Gage asked. He drew his hands back from where they had embraced the foot of his cup.

The Dead Man reached across the table, eyebrows questioning, and waited until the Gage gestured for him to tilt the cup and peer inside.

If there had been wine within, it was gone.

When the lion-sun of Messaline rose, haloed in its mane, the Gage and the Dead Man were waiting below the lintel inscribed, IN MY HOUSE THERE IS AN END TO PAIN. The door stood open, admitting the transient chill of a desert morning. No one barred the way. But no one had come to admit them, either.

"We should go in?" the Dead Man said.

"After you," said the Gage.

The Dead Man huffed, but stepped forward, the Gage following with silent precision. His joints made no more sound than the massive gears of the gates of Messaline. Wizards, when they chose to wreak, wrought well.

Beyond the doorway lay a white marble hall, shadowed and cool. Within the hall, a masked figure enveloped in undyed linen robes stood, hands folded into sleeves. The mask was silver, featureless, divided by a line—a join—down the center. The robe was long enough to puddle on the floor.

Behind the mask, one side of the priest's face would be pitted, furrowed: acid-burned. And one side would be untouched, in homage—in sacrifice—to the masked goddess they served, whose face was the heavy, half-scarred moon of Messaline. The Gage and the Dead Man drew up, two concealed faces regarding one.

Unless the figure was a statue.

But then the head lifted. Hands emerged from the sleeves—long and dark, elegant, with nails sliced short for labor. The voice that spoke was fluting, feminine.

"Welcome to the House of Mercy," the priestess said. "All must come to Kaalha of the Ruins in the end. Why do you seek her prematurely?"

They hesitated for a moment, but then the Dead Man stepped forward. "We seek her blessing. And perhaps her aid, Child of the Night."

By her voice, perhaps her mirrors hid a smile. "A pair of excommunicates. Wolf's-heads, are you not? Masterless ones?"

The supplicants held their silence, or perhaps neither one of them knew how to answer.

When the priestess turned to the Gage, their visages reflected one another—reflected distorted reflections—endlessly. "What have you to live for?"

"Duty, art, and love."

"You? A Faceless Man?"

The Gage shrugged. "We prefer the term Gage."

"So," she said. She turned to the Dead Man. "What have *you* to live for?"

"Me? I am dead already."

"Then you are the Goddess's already, and need no further blessing of her."

The Dead Man bit his lip and hid the hand that would have made the Sign of the Pen. "Nevertheless . . . my friend believes we need her help. Perhaps we can explain to the Eidolon?"

"Walk with me," said the priestess.

Further along the corridor, the walls were mirrored. The priestess strode beside them, the front of her robe gathered in her hands. The mirrors were faintly distorted, whether by design or flaw, and they reflected the priestess, the Gage, and the Dead Man as warped caricatures—rippled, attenuated, bulged into near-spheres. Especially in conjunction with the mirrored masks, the reflections within reflections were dizzying.

When they left the corridor of mirrors and entered the large open atrium into which it emptied, the priestess was gone. The Dead Man whirled, his hand on the hilt of his sword, his battered red coat swinging wide to display all the stains and shiny patches the folds of its skirts hid.

"Ysmat Her Word," he swore. "I hate these heathen magics. Did you see her go? You see everything."

The Gage walked straight ahead and did not stop until he reached the middle of the short side of the atrium. "I did not see that."

"A heathen magic you seek, Dead Man." A masked priestess spoke from atop the dais at the other end of the long room.

It was unclear whether this priestess was the same one. Her voice was identical, or nearly so. But she seemed taller and she walked with a limp. Of course, it would be easy to twist an ankle in that trailing raiment, and the click of wooden pattens as she descended the stair said the truth of her height was a subject for conjecture.

She came to them through shafts of sunlight angled from high windows, stray gleams catching on her featureless visage.

"Forgive me." The Dead Man inclined his head and dropped one knee before her. "I spoke in haste. I meant no disrespect, Child of the Moon."

"Rise," said the priestess. "If Kaalha of the Ruins wants you humbled, she will lay you low. The Merciful One has no need of playacted obeisance."

She offered a hand. It was gloved, silk pulled unevenly over long fingers. She lifted the Dead Man to his feet. She was strong. She squeezed his fingers briefly, like a mother reassuring a child, and let her grip fall. She withdrew a few steps. "Explain to me your problem, masterless ones."

"Are you the Eidolon?" the Gage asked.

"She will hear what you speak to me."

The Gage nodded—a movement as calculated and intentional as if he had spoken aloud. He said, "We seek justice for the poet Anah, mutilated and murdered nine—now ten—days past at the Blue Stone. We seek justice also for the wood-sculptor Abbas, similarly mutilated and murdered in his village of Bajishe, and for uncounted other victims of this same murderer."

The priestess stood motionless, her hands hanging beside her and spread slightly as if to receive a gift. "For vengeance, you wish the blessing of Rakasha," she said. "For justice, seek Vajhir the warrior. Not the Queen of the Cold Moon."

"I do not seek vengeance," said the Gage.

"Really?"

"No." It was an open question which of them was more immovable. More unmoving. "I seek mercy for all those this murderer, this ghost-maker, may yet torture and kill. I seek Kaalha's benediction on those who will come to her eventually, one way or another, if their ghosts are freed. As you say: the Goddess of Death does not need to hurry."

The priestess's oval mask tilted. On her pattens, she was taller than both supplicants.

The Gage inclined his head.

"A ghost-maker, you say."

"A soulless killer. A Wizard. One who murders for the joy of it. Young men, men in their prime. Men with great gifts and great . . . beauty."

Surely that could not have been a catch of breath, a concealed sob. What has no eyes cannot cry.

The Gage continued, "We cannot face a Wizard without help. Your help. Please tell us, Child of the Moon: what do you do against a killer with no soul?"

Her laughter broke the stillness that followed—but it was sweet laughter, glass bells, not sardonic cruelty. She stepped down from her pattens and now both Men, Faceless and Dead, topped her by a head. She left the pattens lying on the flagstones, one tipped on its side, and came close. She still limped, though.

"Let me tell you a secret, one mask to another." She leaned close and whispered. Their mirrored visages reflected one another into infinity, bronze and silver echoing. When she drew back, the Gage's head swiveled and tilted to acknowledge her.

She extended a hand to the Dead Man, something folded in her fist. He offered his palm. She laid an amethyst globe, cloudy with flaws and fracture, in the hollow. "Do you know what that is?"

"I've seen it done," said the Gage. "My mistress used one to create me."

The priestess nodded. "Go with Kaalha's blessing. Yours is a mission of mercy, masterless ones."

She turned to go. Her slippered feet padded on stone. She left the pattens lying. She was nearly to the dais again when the Dead Man called out after her—

"Wait!"

She paused and turned.

"Why would you help us?" the Dead Man asked.

"Masterless ones?" She touched her mask with both hands, fingertips flat to mirrored cheeks. The Dead Man shuddered at the prospect of her face revealed, but she lifted them empty again. She touched two fingers to her mask and brushed away as if blowing a kiss, then let her arms fall. Her sleeves covered her gloved hands.

The priestess said, "She is also the Goddess of Orphans. Masterless Man."

The Dead Man started to slip the amethyst sphere into his sash opposite the sword as he and the Gage threaded through the crowd back to the street of Temples. Before he had quite secured it, though, he paused and drew it forth again, holding it up to catch the sunlight along its smoky, icy flaws and planes.

"You know what this is for?"

"Give it here."

Reluctantly, the Dead Man did so. The Gage made it vanish into his robe.

"If you know how to use that, and it's important, it might be for the best if you demonstrated for me."

"You have a point," the Gage said, and—shielded in the rush of the crowd—he did so. When he had demonstrated to both their satisfaction, he made it vanish again and said, "Well. Lead me to the lair of Attar."

"This way."

They walked. The Gage dropped his cowl, improving the speed of their passage. The Dead Man lowered his voice. "Tell me what you know about Messaline Wizards. I am more experienced with the Uthman sort. Who are rather different."

"Cog used to say that a Wizard was a manifestation of the true desires, the true obsessions of an age. That they were the essence of a time refined, like opium drawn from poppy juice."

"That's pretty. Does it mean anything?"

The Gage shrugged. "I took service with Cog because she was Attar's enemy."

"Gages have lives before their service. Of course they do."

"It's just that you never think of it."

The Dead Man shrugged.

"And Dead Men don't have prior lives."

"None worth speaking of." Dead Men were raised to their service, orphans who would otherwise beg, whore, starve, and steal. The Caliph gave them everything—home, family, wives. Educated their children. They were said to be the most loyal guards the world knew. "We have no purpose but to guard our Caliph."

"Huh," said the Gage. "I guess you'd better find one."

The Dead Man directed them down a side street in a neighborhood that lined the left bank of the river Dijlè. A narrow paved path separated the facades of houses from the stone-lined canal. In this dry season, the water ran far down in the channel.

The Gage said, "I told you I chose service with Cog because she was Attar's enemy. Attar took something that was important to me."

"Something? Or someone?"

The Gage was silent.

The Dead Man said, "You said Attar kills artists. Young men."

The Gage was silent.

"Your beloved? This Abbas, have I guessed correctly?"

"Are you shocked?"

The Dead Man shrugged. "You would burn for it in Asmaracanda."

"You can burn for crossing the street incorrectly in Asmaracanda."

"This is truth." The Dead Man drew his sword, inspected the faintly nicked, razor-stropped edge. "Were you an artist too?"

"I was."

"Well," the Dead Man said. "That's different, then."

Before the house of Attar the Enchanter, the Dead Man paused and tested the door; it was locked and barred so soundly it didn't rattle. "This is his den."

"He owns this?" the Gage said.

"Rents it," the Dead Man answered. He reached up with his off hand and lowered his veil. His sword slid from its scabbard almost noiselessly. "How much magic are you expecting?"

"He's a ghost-maker," the Gage said. "He travels from murder to murder. He might not have a full workshop here. He'll have mechanicals."

"Mechanicals?"

"Things like me."

"*Won*derful." He glanced up at the windows of the second and third stories. "Are we climbing in?"

"I don't climb." The Gage took hold of the knob and effortlessly tore it off the door. "Follow me."

The Gage's footsteps were silent, but that couldn't stop the boards of the joisted floor from creaking under his armored weight. "I hate houses with cellars," he said. "Always afraid I'm going to fall through."

"That will only improve once we achieve the second story," the Dead Man answered. His head turned ceaselessly, scanning every dark corner of what appeared to be a perfectly ordinary, perfectly pleasant reception room—unlighted brass lamps, inlaid cupboards, embroidered cushions, tapestry chairs, and thick rugs stacked several high over the indigo-patterned interlocking star-and-cross tiles of that creaking floor. Being on the ground floor, it was windowless.

"We're alone down here," said the Gage.

The staircase ascended at the back of the room, made of palm wood darkened with perfumed oils and dressed with a scarlet runner. The Gage moved toward it like a stalking tiger, weight and fluidity in perfect tension. The Dead Man paced him.

They ascended side by side. Light from the windows above reflected down. It shone on the sweat on the Dead Man's bared face, on the length of his bared blade, on the bronze of the Gage's head and the scratched metal that gleamed through the unpatched rent at his shoulder.

The Gage was taller than the dead man. His head cleared the landing first. Immediately, he snapped—"Close your eyes!"

The Dead Man obeyed. He cast his off hand across them as well, for extra protection. Still the light that flared was blinding.

The Gage might walk like a cat, but when he ran, the whole house shook. The creak of the floorboards was replaced by thuds and cracks, rising to a crescendo of jangling metal and shattering glass. The light died; a male voice called out an incantation. The Dead Man opened his eyes.

Trying to focus through swimming, rough-bordered blind spots, the Dead Man saw the Gage surrounded by twisted metal and what might be the remains of a series of lenses. Beyond the Faceless Man and the wreckage, a second man—broad-shouldered, shirtless above the waist of his pantaloons, of middle years by the salt in his beard but still fit—raised a flared tube in his hands and directed it at the Gage.

Wood splintered as the Gage reared back, struggling to move. The wreckage constrained him, though feebly, and his foot had broken through the floor. He was trapped.

With his off hand, the Dead Man snatched up the nearest object—a shelf laden with bric-a-brac—and hurled it at the Wizard's head. The tube—some sort of blunderbuss—exploded with a roar that added flash-deafness to the flash-blindness that already afflicted the Dead Man. Gouts of smoke and sparks erupted from the flare—

—the wall beside the Gage exploded outward.

"Well," he said. "That won't endear us to the neighbors."

The Dead Man heard nothing but the ringing in his ears. He leaped onto the seat of a Song-style ox-yoke chair, felt the edge of the back beneath his toe and rode it down. His sword descended with the force of his controlled fall, a blow that should have split the Wizard's collarbone.

His arm stopped in mid-move, as if he had slammed it into the top of a stone wall. He jerked it back, but the pincers of the steam-bubbling crab-creature that grabbed it only tightened, and it was all he could do to hold onto his sword as his fingers numbed.

Wood shattered and metal rent as the Gage freed his foot and shredded the remains of the contraption that had nearly blinded the Dead Man. He swung a massive fist at the Wizard but the Wizard rolled aside and parried with the blunderbuss. Sparks shimmered. Metal crunched.

The Wizard barked something incomprehensible, and a shadow moved from the corner of the room. The Gage spun to engage it.

The Dead Man planted his feet, caught the elbow of his sword hand in his off hand, and lifted hard against the pain. The crab-thing scrabbled at the rug, hooked feet snagging and lifting, but he'd stolen its leverage. Grunting, he twisted from the hips and swung.

Carpet and all, the crab-thing smashed against the Wizard just as he was regaining his feet. There was a whistle of steam escaping and the Wizard shouted, jerking away. The crab-thing's pincer ripped free of the Dead Man's arm, taking cloth and a measure of flesh along with it.

The thing from the corner was obviously half-completed. Bits of bear- and cow-hide had been stitched together patchwork fashion over its armature. Claws as long as the Dead Man's sword protruded from the shaggy paw on its right side; on the left they gleamed on bare armature. Its head turned, tracking. A hairy foot shuffled forward.

The Gage went to meet it, and there was a sound like mountains taking a sharp dislike to one another. Dust rattled from the walls. More bric-a-brac tumbled from the shelf-lined walls. In the street or in a neighboring house, someone screamed.

The Dead Man stepped over the hissing, clicking remains of the crab-thing and leveled his sword at the throat of the Wizard Attar.

"Stop that thing."

The Wizard, his face boiled red along one cheek, one eye closed and weeping, laughed out loud. "Because I fear your sword?"

He grabbed the blade right-handed, across the top, and pushed it down as he lunged onto the blade, ramming the sword through his chest. Blood and air bubbled around the blade. The Wizard did not stop laughing, though his laughter took on a . . . simmering quality.

Recoiling, the Dead Man let go of his sword.

Meanwhile, the wheezing armature lifted the Gage into the air and slammed him against the ceiling. Plaster and stucco-dust reinforced the smoky air.

"You call yourself a Dead Man!" Attar ripped the sword from his breast and hurled it aside. "This is what a dead man looks like." He thumped his chest, then reached behind himself to an undestroyed rack and lifted another metal object, long and thin.

The Dead Man swung an arc before him, probing carefully for footing amid the rubble on the floor. Attar sidled and sidestepped, giving no advantage. And Attar had his back to the wall.

The Gage and the half-made thing slammed to the floor, rolling in a bear hug. Joists cracked again and the floor settled, canting crazily. Neither the Gage nor the half-made thing made any sound but the thud of metal on metal, like smith's hammerblows, and the creak of straining gears and springs.

"I have no soul," said Attar. "I am a ghost-maker. Can your blade hurt me? All the lives I have taken, all the art I have claimed—all reside in me!"

Already, the burns on his face were smoothing. The bubbles of blood no longer rose from the cut in his smooth chest. The Dead Man let his knees bend, his weight ground. Attar's groping left hand found and raised a mallet. His right hand aimed the slender rod.

"ENOUGH!" boomed the Gage. A fist thudded into his face; he caught the half-made thing's arm and used its own momentum to slam it to the ground.

The rod detonated; the Dead Man twisted to one side. Razors whisked his face and shaved a nick into his ear. Blood welled hotly as the spear embedded itself in the wall.

With an almighty crunch, the Gage rose from the remains of the half-made thing, its skull dangling from his hand. He was dented and disheveled, his robe torn away so the round machined joints of knees and elbows, the smooth segmented body, were plainly visible.

He tossed the wreckage of the half-made thing's head at Attar, who laughed and knocked it aside with the hammer. He swung it in lazy loops, one-handed, tossed it to the other. "Come on, faceless man. What one Wizard makes, another can take apart."

The Gage stopped where he stood. He planted his feet on the sagging floor. He turned his head and looked directly at the Dead Man.

The Dead Man caught the amethyst sphere when the Gage tossed it to him.

"A soul catcher? Did you not hear me say I am soulless? That priest's bauble can do me no harm."

"Well," said the Gage. "Then you won't object to us trying."

He stepped forward, walking up the slope of the broken floor. He swung his fist; Attar parried with the hammer as if the blow had no force behind it at all. The Gage shook his fist and blew across it. There was a dent across his knuckles now.

"Try harder," the Wizard said.

He kept his back to the corner, his hammer dancing between his hands. The Gage reached in, was deflected. Reached again. "It's not lack of a soul that makes you a monster. That, beast, is your humanity."

The Wizard laughed. "Poor thing. Have you been chasing me for Cog's sake all these months?"

"Not for Cog's sake." The Gage almost sounded as if he smiled. "And I have been hunting you for years. I was a potter; my lover was a sculptor. Do you even remember him? Or are the lives you take, the worlds of brilliance you destroy, so quickly forgotten."

The Wizard's eyes narrowed, his head tipping as if in concentration. "I might recall."

Again the Gage struck. Again, the Wizard parried. His lips pursed as if to whistle and a shimmer crossed his face. A different visage appeared in its wake: curly-haired, darker-complected. Young and handsome, in an unexceptional sort of way. "This one? What *was* the name? Does it make you glad to see his face one last time, before I take you too? Though your art was not much, as I recall—but what can you expect of—"

The Gage lunged forward, a sharp blow of the Wizard's hammer snapping his arm into his head. The force knocked his upper body aside. But he took the blow, and the one that followed, and kept coming. He closed the gap.

He caught Attar's hammer hand and bent it back until the bones of his arm parted with a wet, wrenching sound.

"His name was Abbas!"

The Wizard gasped and went to his knees. The Dead Man stepped in with a hard sidearm swing, smashed the amethyst sphere against his head, and pressed it hard.

It burst in his opening hand, a shower of violet glitter. Particles swirled in the air, ran in the Wizard's open mouth, his nostrils and ears, swarmed his eyes until they stared blank and lavender.

When the Dead Man closed his hand again, with a vortex of shimmer the sphere re-coalesced.

Blank-faced, Attar slumped onto his left side, dangling from his shattered arm. The Gage opened his hand and let the body fall. "He's not dead. Just really soulless now."

"As soon as I find my sword I'll repair that oversight," the Dead Man said. He held out the amethyst. Blood streaked down his cheek, dripped hot from his ear.

"Keep it." The Gage looked down at his naked armature. "I seem to have left my pockets on the floor."

While the Dead Man found his blade, the Gage picked his way around the borders of the broken floor. He moved from shelf to shelf, lifting up sculptures, books of poetry, pottery vases—and reverentially, one at a time, crushing them with his dented hands.

Wiping blood from his sword, the Dead Man watched him work. "You want some help with that?"

The Gage shook his head.

"That's how you knew he didn't live downstairs."

"Hmm?"

"No art."

The Gage shrugged.

"You looking for something in particular?"

"Yes." The Gage's big hand enfolded a small object. He held it for a moment, cradled to his breast, and bowed his scratched mirror over it. Then he pressed his hands together and twisted, and when he pulled them apart, a scatter of wood shreds sprinkled the floor. "Go free, love."

When he looked up again, the Dead Man was still staring out the window. "Help me break the rest of these? So the artists can rest?"

"Also so our friend here doesn't grow his head back? Soul or no soul?"

"Yeah," the Gage answered. "That too."

Outside, the Dead Man fixed his veil and pushed his dangling sleeve up his arm, examining the strained threads and tears.

"Come on," the Gage said. "I'll buy you a new coat."

"But I like this one."

"Then let's go to a tavern."

This one had better wine and cleaner clientele. As a result, they and the servers both gave the Dead Man and the Gage a wider berth, and the Dead Man kept having to go up to the bar.

"Well," said the Dead Man. "Another mystery solved. By a clever man among clever men."

"And you are no doubt the cleverest."

The Dead Man shrugged. "I had help. I don't suppose you'd consider a partnership?"

The Gage interlaced his hands around the foot of his cup. After a while, he said, "Serhan."

"Yes, Gage?"

"My name was Khatijah."

Over his veil, the Dead Man's eyes did not widen. Instead he nodded with satisfaction, as if he had won some bet with himself. "You're a woman."

"I was," said the Gage. "Now I'm a Gage."

"It's supposed to be a selling point, isn't it? Become a Faceless Man and never be uncertain, abandoned, forsaken again."

"You sound like you've given it some thought."

The Dead Man regarded the Gage. The Gage tilted his featureless head down, giving the impression that he regarded the stem of his cup and the tops of his metal hands.

"And yet here you are," the Dead Man said.

"And yet here I am." The Gage shrugged.

"Stop that constant shrugging," the Dead Man said.

"When you do," said the Gage.

⚔

A reviewer of Kameron Hurley's novel, The Mirror Empire *(2014, the first of The Worldbreaker Saga), wrote that it sometimes reads "like a mirror version of a Robert E. Howard sword-and-sorcery tale, complete with childlike men waiting for their rescue by muscle-bound females ready to rip their clothes off and mount up on their throbbing manhood." Well, there's more human dimension than that, but yes, Hurley intentionally challenges dominant cultural assumptions to allow readers to think about the traditional roles fantasy has typically portrayed. It makes some people uncomfortable or distracts them from the story—much like the old tropes make other folks too uncomfortable to enjoy the tales. Personally, I don't feel* thinking *limits the entertainment value; it heightens it. Hurley tells a fine story and Bet, the protagonist of "The Plague Givers," is a true, if reluctant, hero in this machete-and-sorcery tale.*

THE PLAGUE GIVERS

Kameron Hurley

She had retired to the swamp because she liked the color. When the Contagion College came back for her thirty years after she had fled into the swamp's warm, black embrace, the color was the same, but she was not.

Which brings us here.

The black balm of dusk descended over the roiling muddy face of the six thousand miles of swampland called the Freeman's Bath. Packs of cannibal swamp dogs waded through the knobby knees of the great cypress trees that snarled up from the russet waters. Dripping nets of moss and tangled limbs gave refuge to massive plesiosaurs. The great feathered giants bobbed their heads as the swamp dogs passed, casual observers in the endless game of hunter and hunted.

Two slim people from the Contagion College, robed all in black muslin, poled their way through a gap in the weeping moss and brought their pirogue to rest at the base of a bowed cypress tree. Light gleamed from openings carved high up in the tree trunk, far too high to give them a view of what lay within. There was no need. This tree had been marked on a map and kept in the jagged towers of the Contagion College in the city for decades, waiting for a day as black as this.

"She's killed a lot of people," the smaller figure, Lealez, said, "and she's been wild out here for a long time. She may be unpredictable." The poor light softened the contours of Lealez's pockmarked face. As Lealez turned, the lights of the house set the face in profile, and Lealez took on the countenance of a beaked fisher-bird, the large nose a common draw for childhood bullies and snickering colleagues at the Contagion College who had not cared much for Lealez's face or arrogance. Lealez suspected it was the arrogance that made it so easy for the masters to assign Lealez this terribly dangerous task, rushing off after some wild woman of legend at the edge of civilization. They were always saying to Lealez how important it was to know one's place in the order of things. It could be said with certainty that this place was not the place for Lealez.

Lealez's taller companion, a long-faced, gawky senior called Abrimet, said, "When you kill the greatest sorcerer that ever lived, you can live wild as you like, too."

Abrimet's hair was braided against the scalp in a common style particular to Abrimet's gender, black as Lealez's but twice as long, dyed with henna at the ends instead of red like Lealez's. Lealez admired the shoman very much; Abrimet's older, experienced presence gave Lealez some comfort.

Full dark had fallen across the swamp. Swarms of orange fireflies with great silver beaks rose from the banks, swirling in tremulous living clouds. Far off, something much larger than their boat splashed in the water; Lealez's brokered mother had been killed by a plesiosaur, and the thought of those snaky-necked monsters sent a bolt of icy fear through Lealez's gut. But if Lealez turned around now, the Contagion College would strip Lealez of title and what remained of Lealez's life would be far worse than this.

So Abrimet called, "We have come from the Contagion College. We are of the Order of the Tree of the Gracious Death! You are summoned to speak."

Inside the tree, well-insulated from the view of the two figures in the boat, a thick, grubby woman raised her head from her work. In one broad hand she held the stuffed skin of an eyeless toy hydra; in the other, a piece of wire strung with a long white matte of hair. An empty brown bottle sat at her elbow, though it took more than a bottle of plague-laced liquor to mute her sense for plague days. She thumbed her spectacles from her nose and onto her head. She placed the half-finished hydra on the table and took her machete from the shelf. The night air wasn't any cooler than the daytime shade, so she went shirtless. Sweat dripped from her generous body and splattered across the floor as she got to her feet.

Her forty-pound swamp rodent, Mhev, snorted from his place at her feet and rolled onto his doughy legs. She snapped her fingers and pointed to his basket under the stairs. He ignored her, of course, and started grunting happily at the idea of company.

The woman rolled her brown, meaty shoulders and moved up to the left of the door like a woman expecting a fight. She hadn't had a fight in fifteen years, but her body remembered the drill. She called, "You're trespassing. Move on."

The voice replied—young and stupidly confident, maybe two years out of training in the city, based on the accent, "The whole of this territory was claimed by the Imperial Community of the Forked Ash over a decade ago. As representatives of the Community, and scholars of the Contagion College, we are within our rights in this waterway, as we have come to seek your assistance in a matter which you are bound by oath to serve."

The woman did not like city children, as she knew they were the most dangerous children of all. Yet here they were again, shouting at her door like rude imbeciles.

She pushed open the door, casting light onto the little boat and its slender occupants. They wore the long black robes and neat purple collars of the Order of the Plague Hunters. When she had worn those robes, long ago, they did not seem as ridiculous as they now looked on these skinny young people.

"Elzabet Addisalam?" the tall one said. That one was clearly a shoman, hair twisted into braided rings, ears pierced, brows plucked. The other one could have been anything—man, woman, shoman, pan. In her day, everyone dressed as their correct gender, with the hairstyles and clothing cuts to match, but fashions were changing, and she was out of date. It had become increasingly difficult to tell shoman from pan, man from woman, the longer she stayed up here. Fashion changed quickly. Pans dressed like men these days. Shomans like pans. And on and on. It made her head hurt.

She kept her machete up. "I'm called Bet, out here," she said. "And what are you? If you're dressing up as Plague Hunters, I'll have some identification before you go pontificating all over my porch."

"Abrimet," the shoman said, holding up their right hand. The broad sleeve fell back, exposing a dark arm crawling in glowing green tattoos: the double ivy circle of the Order, and three triangles, one for every Plague Hunter the shoman had dispatched. Evidence enough the shoman was what was claimed. "This is Lealez," the shoman said of the other one.

"Lealez," Bet said. "You a shoman or a neuter? Can't tell at this distance, I'm afraid. We used to dress as our gender, in my day."

The person made a face. "Dress as my gender? The way you do? Shall I call you man, with that hair?" Bet wore nothing but a man's veshti, sour and damp with sweat, and she had not cut or washed her hair in some time, let alone styled her brows to match her pronouns.

"It is not I knocking about on stranger's doors, requesting favors," Bet said. "What am I dealing with?"

"I'm a pan."

"That's what I thought I was saying. What, is saying neuter instead of pan a common slur now?"

"It's archaic."

"We are in a desperate situation," Abrimet said, clearly the elder, experienced one here, trying to wrest back control of the dialogue. "The Order sent us to call in your oath."

"The Order has a very long memory," Bet said, "I am sure it recalls I am no longer a member. Would you like a stuffed hydra?"

"The world is going to end," Lealez said.

"The world is always ending for someone," Bet said, shrugging. "I've heard of its demise a dozen times in as many years."

"From who?" Lealez grumbled. "The plesiosaurs?"

Abrimet said, "Two rogue Plague Givers left the Sanctuary of the Order three days ago. *Two* of them. That's more than we've had loose at any one time in twenty years."

"Sounds like a task that will make a Plague Hunter's name," Bet said. "Go be that hero." She began to close the door.

"They left a note addressed to you!" Abrimet said, gesturing at the pan. "I have it," Lealez said. "Here."

Bet held out her hand. Lealez's soft fingers brushed Bet's as per put the folded paper into Bet's thick hands.

Bet recognized the heavy grain of the paper, and the lavender hue. She hadn't touched paper like that in what felt like half a lifetime, when the letters came to her bursting with love and desire and, eventually, a plague so powerful it nearly killed her. A chill rolled over her body, despite the heat. The last time she saw paper like this, six hundred people died and she broke her vows to the Order in exchange for moonshine and stuffed hydras. She tucked the machete under her arm. Unfolded the paper. Her fingers trembled. She blamed the heat.

The note read: *Honored Plague Hunter Elzabet Addisalam, The great sorcerer Hanere Gozene taught us to destroy the world together. You have seven days to save it. Catch us if you can.*

The note caught fire in her hands. She dropped it hastily, stepped back.

The two in the boat gasped, but Bet only watched it burn to papery ash, the way she had watched the woman with that same handwriting burn to ash decades before.

The game was beginning again, and she feared she was too old to play it any longer.

II.

Thirty years earlier . . .

The day of the riots, Hanere Gozene leaned over Bet's vermillion canvas, her dark hair tickling Bet's chin, and whispered, "Would you die for me, Elzabet?"

Bet's tongue stuck out from between her lips, brow furrowed in concentration as she tried to capture the sky. For six consecutive evenings she had sat at this window, with its sweeping view over the old, twisted tops of the city's great living spires, trying to capture the essence of the bloody red sunset that met the misty cypress swamp on the city's far border, just visible from her seat.

The warm gabbling from the street was a prelude to the coming storm. Tensions had been hot all summer. The cooler fall weather moved people from languid summer unrest to more militant action. Pamphlets littered the streets; the corpses of dogs had been stuffed with them, as protest or warning, and by which side, Bet did not know or care. Not then. Not yet. She cared only about capturing the color of the sky.

Bet was used to Hanere's flare for the dramatic. Hanere had spent the last year in a production of *Tornello*, a play about the life and death of the city's greatest painter. She had a habit of seeking out and exploiting the outrageous in even the most mundane situations.

Hanere twined her fingers into Bet's apron strings, tugging them loose.

Bet batted Hanere's hands away with her free one, still intent on the painting. "You want to date a painter because you're playing one," Bet said, "I have to give you the full experience. That means I work in this light. Just work, Hanere."

"Sounds divine," Hanere said, reaching again for the apron.

"I'm working," Bet said. "That's as divine as it gets. Have some cool wine. Read a book."

"A book? A book!"

Bet would remember Hanere just this way, thirty years hence: the crooked mouth, the spill of dark hair, eyes the color of honey beer widened in mock outrage.

The lover who would soon burn the world.

III.

"Hanere Gozene," Bet said, waving the two Plague Hunters inside. The name tasted odd on her tongue, like something both grotesquely profane and sacred, just like her memories of that black revolution.

Mhev barked at the hunters from his basket. Bet shushed him, but his warning bark convinced her to look over her young guests a second time. The appearance of Hanere's letter had shaken her, and she needed to pay attention. Mhev didn't bark at Plague Hunters, only Plague *Givers.*

"Neither of us is used to company," Bet said. When she was younger, she might have forced a smile with it to cover her suspicions, but she had given up pretending she was personable a long time ago.

Abrimet sat across from her at the little table strewn with bits of leather and stuffing from her work on the hydras. The younger one, the pan, stood off to the side, tugging at per violet collar. Bet slumped into her seat opposite. She didn't offer them anything. She picked up the half-finished hydra and turned it over in her hands. "City people buy these," she said. "I trade them to a merchant who paddles upriver to sell them. No back country child is foolish enough to buy them and invite that kind of bad luck in, like asking in a couple of Plague Hunters."

Lealez and Abrimet exchanged a look. Abrimet said, quickly, "We know Hanere left twelve dead Plague Hunters behind her, when she last escaped. If she's out there mentoring these two rogues—"

"I'm over fifty years old," Bet said. "What is it you hope I'll do for you? You're not here to ask me to hunt. So what do you want?"

Mhev stirred from his basket and snuffled over to Abrimet's boots. He licked them. Abrimet grimaced and pulled the boots away.

"Did you step through truffled salt?" Bet asked, leaning forward. She used the shift in her position to push her hand closer to the hilt of the machete on the table. They were indeed Givers, not Hunters. She should have known.

Abrimet raised hairless brows. "Why would—"

"It is a common thing," Bet said, "for Plague Givers to walk through truffled salt to neutralize their last cast, or to combat the plain salt cast of a Plague Hunter, which of course you would realize. It ensures they don't bring any contagion from that cast with them to the next target. Mhev can smell that salt on you. It's like sugar, to him. Regular salt, no. Truffled salt? Oh yes."

"Abrimet is a respected Hunter," Lealez said, voice rising. "You accuse Abrimet of casting before coming here, like some rogue Giver? Abrimet is a Hunter, as am I."

"You're here for the relics," Bet said, because most of the company who came here wanted the relics, and though these two had a fine cover story and poor ability to hide what they were, they would be no different.

"You *did* use them, then," Abrimet said, leaning forward. "To defeat Hanere."

Mhev nosed under Abrimet's boot. Abrimet toed at him.

"Not every godnight story is entirely rubbish," Bet said. She still held the bottle, though it was empty. Flexed her other hand, preparing to snatch the machete. "We went south, to the City by the Crushed Lake where Hanere learned all of her high magic. The relics assisted in her capture, yes."

"We'll require the relics to defeat her students," Abrimet said, "just as you defeated her."

Mhev, sated by the salt, sat at Abrimet's boot and barked.

Bet made her choice.

She threw her bottle at Abrimet. It smashed into Abrimet's head, hard. Bet grabbed her machete and drove the machete through Abrimet's right eye.

Lealez shrieked. Raised per hands, already halfway into reciting a chant. Mhev's barking became a staccato.

Bet grabbed one of the finished hydras on the shelf and pegged Lealez in the head with it. A puff of white powder clouded the air. Lealez sneezed and fell back on the floor.

"No spells in here," Bet said to her. "That's six ounces of night buzz pollen. You won't be casting for an hour."

Bet pulled the machete clear of Abrimet. Abrimet's face still moved. Eye blinked. Tongue lolled. The body tumbled to the floor. Mhev squeaked and went for the boots.

"How were you going to do it?" she asked Lealez.

"I don't, I don't understand—" Lealez sneezed again, wiping at per face.

Bet thrust the bloody machete at per. "I have hunted Plague Givers my whole life. You thought I could not spot one like Abrimet? Did you know they cast a plague before they came here? Why do you think they stepped through truffled salt?"

Lealez considered per position, and the fine line between truth and endangering per mission. Bet's face was a knotted ruin, as if she had taken endless pummeling for decades. Her twisted black hair bled to white in patches. She was covered in insect bites and splattered blood. The spectacles resting on her head were slightly askew now. She stank terribly. The little rat happily gnawed at Abrimet's boots. Lealez had a terrible fear that this would all be blamed on per. Cities would die, the Order would be disbanded, because per had been too arrogant, and gotten perself into this horrible assignment. Abrimet, a Plague Giver? Impossible. Wasn't it? Lealez would have seen it.

"I didn't know what Abrimet was," Lealez said. "I just want to make a name for myself the way you did. I was the best of my class. I've . . . I've already killed three givers!"

"If that's true you should have a name already," Bet said.

"If they find that you killed Abrimet, you will be stung to death for it."

"A very risky venture, then, to let you go," Bet said, and was rewarded with a little tremble from Lealez.

Lealez wiped the pollen from per robe. It made per fingers numb. As per straightened per robe, Lealez wondered if Bet knew per was stalling, and if she did, how long she would let per do it before stabbing Lealez, too, with a machete. "I can speak for you before the judges, in the end," Lealez said. "You'll need someone to honor you. Another hunter. We can't hunt alone."

"A smart little upstart with no talent," Bet said.

"It's true I'm an upstart," Lealez said, "but you can't legally hunt without another hunter." Per smirked, knowing that even this old woman could not stand against that law.

Bet lowered her machete. "I'd have guessed the story you sold me was as fake as your friend, but I knew the paper, and I knew the signature. If I find you faked that too, you'll have more to worry about than just one dead Plague Hunter."

"It's very genuine," Lealez said. "We only have four days. They'll kill tens of thousands in the capital."

"The note said seven days."

"It took us three days to find you."

"I'll hide better next time."

Lealez got to per feet. Lealez found per was trembling, and hated perself for it. A woman like Bet looked for weakness. That was Abrimet's flaw; their fear made them start to cast a plague, instead of waiting it out. A dangerous tell in front of a woman like this. Lealez needed to seal perself up tight.

Insects whispered across the pier. "Bit of advice," Bet said. "The Order forgives a great deal if you deliver what it wants."

"You need me."

"Like a hole in the head," Bet said, "But I'll take you along. For my own reasons."

"What's more important than eliminating a threat to the Community?"

"You don't get it," Bet said. "The last time I got a note on paper like that, it was from Hanere. It's not just two rogues you're dealing with."

"There must be any number of stationery shops where—"

"That was Hanere's handwriting."

"That isn't possible."

"I turned Hanere over to the Order three decades ago, and read about her death on all the news sheets and billboards."

"She was drawn and quartered," Lealez said.

"And burned up in the searing violet flame of the Joystone Peace," Bet said. "But here she is. And why do you think that is, little upstart?"

Lealez shook per head.

"Somehow she survived all that, and now she's back to bite the Community."

"So where do we start?" Lealez asked.

"We start with the sword," Bet said. "Then we retrieve the shield. Then we confront Hanere."

"How will we know where to find her?"

Bet pulled her pack from a very high shelf. "Oh, we won't need to find her," she said. "Once the objects of power are released, she'll find us."

IV.

The Copse of Screaming Corpses loomed ahead of Bet and Lealez's little pirogue. Great, knotted fingers, black as coal, tangled with the fog, poking snarling holes in the mist that hinted at the massive shapes hidden within. Sometimes the waves of gray shifted, revealing a glaring eye, a knobby knee, or the gaping mouth of one of the twisted, petrified forest of giants, forever locked in a scream of horror.

The copse was a good day's paddle from Bet's refuge. When she told Lealez the name, Lealez thought Bet was making fun.

"That isn't the real name," Lealez said. The dense fog muffled per words.

"Oh, it is," Bet said. "It's aptly named."

"Does the name alone scare people off?"

"The smart ones, yes," Bet said.

Ripples traveled across the bubbling water.

"What are these bubbles?"

"Sinkhole," Bet said. "They open up under the swamp sometimes. Pull boats under, whole villages. We're lucky. Probably happened sometime last night."

"Just a hole in the world?"

"Had one in the capital forty years ago," Bet said. "Ate the Temple of Saint Torch. Those fancy schools don't teach that?"

"I guess not," Lealez said. Per gazed into the great canopy of dripping moss that covered the looming giants above them. Their great, gaping maws were fixed in snarls of pain, or perhaps outrage. Lealez imagined them eating per whole. "Why put it here?" per said. "This place is awful."

"Would you come here for any other reason but retrieving an object of power?"

"No."

"You have your answer."

Bet poled the pirogue up to the edge of a marshy island and jumped out. She tied off the pirogue and pulled a great coil of rope over her shoulder. She headed off into the misty marsh without looking back at Lealez. Lealez scrambled after her, annoyed and a little frightened. Bet's generous shape was quickly disappearing into the mist.

Lealez yelped as per brushed the knobby tangle of some giant's pointing finger.

When Lealez caught up with Bet, she was already heaving the large rope over her shoulder. She sucked her teeth as she walked around the half-buried torso of one of the stricken giants. Its hands clawed at the sky, and its face was lost in the fog.

Bet tossed up one end of the rope a couple of times until she succeeded in getting it over the upraised left arm of the giant. She tied one end around her waist and handed Lealez the other end.

Lealez frowned.

"Hold onto it," Bet said. "Pull up the slack as I go. You never climbed anything before?"

Lealez shook per head.

Bet sighed. "What do they teach you kids these days?" She kicked off her shoes and began to climb. "Don't touch or eat anything while you're down here."

Lealez watched, breathless. Bet seemed too big to climb such a thing, but she found little hand and footholds as she went, jamming her fingers and toes into crevices and deviations in the petrified giant.

Lealez held tight to the other end of the rope, pulling the slack and watching Bet disappear into the fog as she climbed up onto the giant's shoulder. Lealez glanced around at the fog, feeling very alone.

Above, Bet took her time climbing the monster. She had been a lot younger when she did this the first time, and she was already resenting her younger self. Warbling hoots and cries came from the swampland around her, distorted by the fog. Her breath came hard and her fingers ached, but she reached the top of the giant in due course.

She knew there was something wrong the moment she hooked herself up around the back of the giant's head. The head was spongy at the front, as if rotting from within. The whole back of it had been ripped open. Inside the giant's head was a gory black hole where the sword had been.

She pulled the knife from her hip and hacked into the back of the head, peering deep inside, scraping away bits of calcified brain matter. But it was no use. The head was empty. She traced the edges of the hole carved in the giant's head. Someone had hacked out the great round piece of the skull that she had mortared back into place with a sticky contagion years ago. Only she and her partner Keleb had known about the contagion. They would be the only two people capable of neutralizing it before removing the relic.

"Briar and piss," she muttered.

Below, Lealez screamed.

Bet sheathed her knife as she scrambled back down the giant, aware that her rope had gone slack. Foolish pan, what was the point of a rope if Bet cracked her head open on the way down?

Lealez screamed and screamed, horrified by the rippling of per skin. Lealez had tilted per head up to follow Bet's progress and left per mouth open, and a shard of the great giant's skin had flaked off and fallen into per mouth.

Lealez gagged on it, but it went down, and now per body was . . . growing, distending; Lealez thought per would burst into a thousand pieces. But that, alas, did not happen. Instead, Lealez grew and grew. Arms thickened with muscle. Thighs became large around as tree trunks.

When finally Lealez saw Bet sliding down the tree, Lealez's head was already up past Bet's position.

Bet swore and leapt the rest of the way down the face of the giant. She took a fistful of salt from the pouch at her hip and threw it in a circle around Lealez's burgeoning body. Lealez's clothes had burst, falling in tatters all around per. Bet muttered a chant, half-curse, half-cure, concentrating on the swinging arms above her. Bet pulled a bit of tangled herb from another pouch, already laced with contagion. She breathed the words she had last spoken in a dusty library in the Contagion College and let the plague free.

All around them, biting flies swarmed up from the swampland, drawn by her cast. They ate bits of the contagion and landed onto Lealez's body, which was now nearing the height of the petrified giants around them. Per skin was beginning to blacken and calcify around per ankles.

The swarm of flies covered Lealez's body like a second skin. Lealez squealed and swatted at them, per movements increasingly slow. The flies bit Lealez's flesh again and again while Bet squatted and urinated on the salt circle.

All at once the flies fell off Lealez. The pan's skin began to flake away where it had been bitten. The body contracted again, until it was half the size it had been, still giant. Then Lealez fell over with a great thump.

Bet ran to Lealez's side. The skin had turned obsidian black, hard as shale. Bet took her machete from her hip and hacked at the torso until great cracks opened up in the body. Then she pulled the pieces away.

Lealez was curled up inside the husk of per former self, arms crossed over per chest, shivering.

"Get out of there now," Bet said, offering per an arm.

Lealez tentatively took her hand, and Bet pulled per out. "Dusk is coming soon," Bet said, "I don't want to get caught out here."

It was warm enough that Bet wasn't too worried about Lealez being naked, but Lealez seemed to mind, and went searching for per pack, which had been ripped from Lealez's body. It was a stupid search, Bet thought, because the fog was getting denser, and they were losing the light, and Lealez's things could have gone anywhere.

Finally Lealez found the remains of per haversack, and pulled on a fresh robe. But the rest of per things were scattered, and Bet insisted they move on and not wait.

"The College will be angry," Lealez said. "My books, my papers—"

"Books and papers? Is that all you can think about? Hurry. Didn't I tell you not to touch or eat anything?"

"You didn't say why!"

"I shouldn't have to say why, you dumb pan. When I was your age I did whatever my mentor said."

"Are you my mentor now? You aren't even officially a Hunter. You would never be approved as a mentor by the college."

"Is everything joyless and literal with you?"

"You don't know how the college is now," Lealez said. "Old people like you tell us how things should be, how we should think, but this is a new age. We face a different government, and new penalties after the Plague Wars. We can't all go rogue or shirk our duties. We'd be kicked out. The college is very strict these days. People like you would never make it to graduation. You would end up working in contagion breweries."

"I'm sure you'd like to continue on with that fantasy awhile longer," Bet said.

Once they were in the pirogue and had cast off, Lealez finally roused perself from misery and asked, "What about the artifact?"

"Someone got to it first," Bet said.

"Hanere?"

"Only one other person knows where these are. I expect they were compelled to get it."

"Your partner?" Bet nodded.

"You think they are still alive?"

"No," Bet said.

At least Lealez said nothing else.

V.

Bet's partner Keleb, too, had retired, but had chosen a canal that acted as a main trading thoroughfare into the city instead of a hard-to-find retreat like Bet's. It took a day and a half to reach the shoman's house, and Bet found herself counting down the time in her head. Lealez, too, reminded her of the ticking chirp of time as they poled downriver. The current was sluggish, and the weather was still and hot.

Despite the stillness, Bet smelled the smoke before she saw it. Lealez sat up in per seat and leaned far over the prow, knuckles gripping the edge of the craft.

The guttered ruin of Keleb's house came into view as they rounded the bend. The shoman had built the house with Bet's help, high up on a snarl of land that hardly ever flooded. Now the house was a charred wreck.

Bet tied off the pirogue and climbed up the steep bank. She counted three sets of footprints along the bank and around the house. They had stayed to watch it burn.

Bet poked around the still smoking house and found what was left of Keleb's body, as charred and ruined as the house.

"Help me here," Bet said to Lealez.

Lealez came up after her. "What can we do?" Lealez said. "The shoman is dead."

"Not the body I'm here for," Bet said. She walked off into the wood and chopped down two long poles from a nearby stand of trees. She handed a pole to Lealez. "Help me get the body rolled back, clear the area here."

Lealez knit per brows, but did as per was told. They heaved over Keleb's body to reveal a tattered hemp rug beneath. Bet yanked it away and used the pole to lever open a piece of the floor. Peeling back the wood revealed a long, low compartment. Lealez leaned over to get a better look, but it was clearly empty.

Bet sucked her teeth.

"What was here?" Lealez asked.

"The cloak," Bet said.

"I thought there were two relics, a sword and a shield."

"That's because that's all we reported," Bet said. "Because we knew this day would come." Bet saw the edge of a piece of paper peeking out from the bottom of the cache and picked it up. It was another note, made out to her in Hanere's handwriting.

"What does it say?" Lealez asked.

Bet traced the words and remembered a day thirty years before, rioting in the streets, a plump painter, and a future she had imagined that looked nothing like this one.

Bet crumpled up the note. "It says she will trade me the objects in return for something I love," Bet said. "Good thing I don't love anything."

Nothing but Hanere, of course. But that was a long time ago. Bet hardly felt anything there in the pit of her belly when she thought of Hanere. It was the time in her life she longed for, not Hanere. That's what she told herself.

"What a monster," Lealez said, staring at Keleb's charred body.

"None of us is a sainted being, touched by some god," Bet said. "But she's missing the third relic. She'll need that before she can end the world."

Lealez shivered. "We don't have much time left."

"There's a suspension line that runs up the river near here," Bet said.

"Let's see if we can find you some clothes."

"There are only shoman's clothes here," Lealez said.

"We all have to make sacrifices," Bet muttered.

They walked away from Keleb's house; two people, a woman and a pan dressed in shoman's clothes, the vestments smoky and charred. Bet expected Lealez to talk more, but Lealez kept the peace. Lealez found perself following after Bet in a daze. For years Lealez had wanted nothing more than to prove perself to the Contagion College. It was beginning to dawn on Lealez just what per had to do to achieve the honor per wished for, and it was frightening, far more frightening than it had seemed when Lealez read all the books about Plague Hunters and Plague Givers and how the Hunters tracked down the Givers and saved the world. No one spoke of charred bodies, or what it was like to be cut out of one's own plague-touched skin.

The great suspension line ran along the Potsdown Peace canal all the way to the Great Dawn harbor that housed the city. Bet sighed and paid their fare to the scrawny little pan who lived in what passed for a gatehouse this far south of the city.

"College better reimburse all this," Bet said, and laughed, because the idea that she would be alive to get reimbursed in another day was distinctly amusing.

Bet and Lealez climbed the stairs up to the carriage that hung along the suspended line and settled in. Lealez looked a little sick, so Bet asked, "You been up before?"

"I don't like heights," Lealez said.

The gatekeeper came up and attached their carriage line to the pulley powered by a guttering steam engine, which the pan swore at several times before the carriage finally stuttered out along the line, swinging away from the gatehouse and over the water.

Lealez shut per eyes.

Bet leaned out over the side of the carriage and admired the long backs of a pod of plesiosaurs moving in the water beneath them.

After a few minutes, Lealez said, "I don't understand why you didn't tell the College there were three objects."

"Of course you do," Bet said.

"It doesn't—"

"Don't pretend you're some fool," Bet said. "I haven't believed a word you've said any more than I believed your little friend."

Lealez stiffened. "Why keep me alive, then?"

"Because I think you can be salvaged," Bet said. "Your friend couldn't. Your friend was already a Plague Giver. I think you're still deciding your own fate."

They rode in silence after that for nearly an hour. Lealez was startled when Bet finally broke it.

"Keleb and I couldn't defeat Hanere ourselves," Bet said. "I'd like to tell you we could. But she's more powerful. She has a far blacker heart, and a blacker magic. We went south, Keleb and I, and got help from sorcerers and hedge witches. They were the ones who created the objects of power. The sword, the shield, and the cloak."

"How do they work?" Lealez asked.

"You'll know soon enough," Bet said. "Not even Keleb knew where I kept the shield, though."

"But, the other weapons—"

The carriage shuddered. Lealez gave a little cry.

"Hold on, it's just—" Bet began, and then the carriage hook sheared clean away, and they plunged into the canal.

VI.

Thirty years earlier . . .

Hanere had always loved to watch things burn. Bet sat with her on the rooftop while riots overtook the city. They sipped black bourbon and danced and talked about how the world would be different now that the revolutionaries had done more than talk. They were burning it all down.

"If only I could be with them!" Hanere said.

Bet pulled Hanere into her lap. "You are better off here with me. Out there is a world of monsters and mad people."

Hanere waggled her brows. "Who's to say I'm not a bit of both? Come with me, we are out of bourbon!" She held up the empty bottle.

"No, no," Bet said. "Stay in. We'll sleep up here."

Bet had gone to sleep while the world burned. But that wasn't Hanere's way. While Bet slept, Hanere went out into it.

It was the edge of dawn when Bet finally woke, hung over and covered in cigarette ash, hands smeared in paint from her work earlier in the day. It was not until she sat up and saw the paint smearing the roof that she thought something was amiss. Her gaze followed the trail of paint that was not paint but blood to its origin. Hanere stood at the edge of the rooftop, wearing a long white shift covered in blood.

Bet scrambled up. "Are you hurt? Hanere?"

But as Hanere turned, Bet stopped. Hanere raised her bloody hands to the sky and her face was full of more joy than Bet had ever seen.

"The government is nearly toppled," Hanere said. "We will be gods, you and I, Bet. There's no one to stop us. It's delightful down there. You must come."

"What did you do, Hanere?"

"I am alive for the first time in my life," Hanere said. She opened her hands, and salt fell from her fingers. She murmured something, and little blue florets colored the air and passed out over the city.

"Stop it," Bet said. "What are you doing? You can't cast in the city outside the College!"

"I cast all night," Hanere said. "I will cast all I like. Come with me. Bet, come with me, my Elzabet. My love. We can take this whole city. We can burn down the college and those tired old people and repaint the world."

"No, Hanere. Get down from there."

The joy left Hanere's face. "Is that what you wish for us?" she said. She came down from the rooftop and walked over to Bet. She placed her hands on Bet's stomach. The blood on her hands was still fresh enough to leave stains. "Is that what you wish for our child?"

VII.

Bet sucked in water instead of air, and paddled to the surface, kicking wildly. She popped up in the brown water and took in her surroundings.

Lealez was nowhere in sight. She dove again into the water, feeling her way through the muck for Lealez. Opening her eyes was a lost cause; she could see nothing. Her fingers snagged a bit of cloth. She grabbed at it and heaved Lealez to the surface.

Lealez coughed and sputtered. Bet kept per at arm's length, yelling that all per splashing was going to drown them both.

"Head for the shore," Bet said.

Lealez shook per head and treaded water using big, sloppy strokes. Bet followed per gaze and saw the hulking shapes of the plesiosaurs circling the carriage.

"They eat plants," Bet said. "Mostly."

Bet hooked Lealez under her arm and paddled for the shore. The plesiosaurs kept pace with them, displacing great waves of water that made it more difficult to get to the shore.

Lealez gasped. "They'll crush us!"

"More worried about the lizards on the shore," Bet said.

"What?"

Two big alligators lay basking along the shore. Bet made for another hollow a little further on, but they were closer than they should be.

"They only eat at night," Bet said, reassuring herself as much as Lealez. "Mostly."

Bet and Lealez crawled up onto the bank and immediately started off into the brush. Bet wanted to put as much distance between her and the lizards as possible. Massive mosquitoes and biting flies plagued them, but Bet knew they were close enough to the city now that they might find a settlement or—if they were lucky—someone's spare pirogue.

Instead, they found the plague.

The bodies started just twenty minutes into their walk to the shore, and continued for another hour as they grew nearer and nearer the settlement. Soft white fungus grew from the noses and eyes and mouths of the dead; their fingers and toes were blackened. Bet stopped and drew a circle of salt around her and Lealez, and sprinkled some precautionary concoctions over them.

"Do you know which one it is?" Lealez whispered.

"One of Hanere's," Bet said. "She likes to leave a mark. She's expecting us."

"Is this where you left the shield?"

"Hush now," Bet said as the swampland opened up into a large clearing. Nothing was burning, which was unlike Hanere.

Bet stopped Lealez from going further and held up a finger to her lips. Two figures stood at the center of the village, heads bent in deep conversation. One wore a long black and purple cloak. The other carried a sword emblazoned with the seal of the Contagion College.

"Stay here," Bet said to Lealez. She pulled out her machete and stepped into the clearing.

The two figures looked up. Bet might have had to guess at their gender if one of them wasn't so familiar. She knew that one's gender because she'd been there during the ceremony where he'd chosen it. It was her and Hanere's own son, Mekdas. The other was most likely female, based on the hairstyle and clothing, but that didn't much concern Bet.

A trade for something Bet loved, that's what Hanere had written.

"So it was you who broke away from the Contagion College," Bet said.

Mekdas stared at her. He was nearly thirty now, not so much a boy, but he still looked young to her, younger even than Lealez. He had Hanere's bold nose and

Bet's straight dark hair and Hanere's full lips and Bet's stocky build and Hanere's talent and impatience.

"I left you with the college so you could make something of yourself," Bet said. "Now here you are disappointing me twice."

"That's something Hanere and you never had in common," Mekdas said. "She was never once disappointed in me."

Bet searched the ground around them for the shield. If they had gotten this far they must have found that too, no matter that Bet was the only one who was supposed to know where it was. Had Hanere used some kind of black magic to find it?

"Give over the objects," Bet said, "and we can talk about this."

"Have you met my lover?" Mekdas asked. "This is Saba."

Saba was a short waif of a woman, a little older than Mekdas. As much as Bet wanted to blame this all on some older Plague Giver, she knew better. She had done her best with Mekdas, but it was all too late.

Bet held out her hand. "The cloak, Mekdas."

"You're an old woman," Mekdas said. "Completely useless out here. Go back to your swamp. We are remaking the world. You don't have the stomach for it."

"You're right," Bet said. She didn't know what to say to him. She had never been good with children, and with Hanere dead, she had wanted even less to do with this particular child. He reminded her too much of Hanere. "I don't have the stomach for many things, but I know a plague village when I see one. I know where this goes, and I know how it ends. You think you can take this plague all the way to the city?"

Saba raised the sword. "With the relics, we will," she said, and smirked.

"Hanere tell you how they work, did she?" Bet said. "The trouble is Hanere doesn't know. There is one person alive who knows, and it's me."

"Hanere will show us," Saba said.

"You shut the seven fucking hells up," Bet said. "I'm not talking to you. Mekdas—"

"Why are you even here?" he said.

"Because Hanere invited me," Bet said.

That got a reaction from him. Surprise. Shock, even.

Bet already had a handful of salt ready, but so did they. The shock was all the advantage she had. Bet flicked the salt in their faces and charged toward them. She bowled over Saba and snatched the sword from her. They were Plague Givers, not warriors, and it showed.

Mekdas had the sense to run, but Bet stabbed the sword through his cloak and twisted. He fell hard onto a body, casting spores into the air.

Bet yelled for Lealez.

Lealez bolted across the sea of bodies, hand already raised to cast.

"Circle and hold them," Bet said.

Lealez's hands trembled as per made the cast to neutralize the two hunters.

Bet tore the cloak from Mekdas's shoulders and wrapped it around her own. She dragged the sword in one hand and crossed to the other side of the village. Bet found the tree she had nested her prize in decades before and hacked it open to reveal the shield, now buried in the heart of the tree. Sweat ran down her face so heavily she had to squint to see. She picked up the shield and marched back to where Saba and Mekdas lay prone inside the salt circle.

"Now you'll see all you wanted to see," Bet said to Mekdas. "You will see the world can be made as well as unmade, but there are sacrifices." She raised the sword over her head.

"No!" Lealez said.

"Please!" Mekdas said.

Bet plunged the blade into Saba's heart and spit the words of power that released the objects' essence. A cloud of brilliant purple dust burst from Saba's body and filled the air. Lealez stumbled back, coughing.

Bet quickly removed the cloak and draped it over Saba. All around the village, the bodies began to convulse. White spores exploded from their mouths and noses and spiraled toward the cloak, a great spinning vortex of contagion.

Lealez watched the cloak absorb the great gouts of plague, feeding on it like some hungry beast. A great keening shuddered through the air. It took Lealez a moment to realize it was Saba, screaming. And screaming. Lealez covered per ears.

Then it was over.

Bet stepped away from Saba's body, but tripped and stumbled back, fell hard on her ass. She heaved a great sigh and rested her forehead on the hilt of the sword.

"What did you do?" Mekdas said. His voice broke. He was weeping. Bet raised her head.

All around them, the plague-ridden people of the village began to stir. Their blackened flesh warmed to a healthy brown. Their plague-clotted eyes cleared and opened. Soon, their questioning voices could be heard, and Bet got to her feet, because she was not ready for questions.

"They're alive!" Lealez said, gaping. "You saved them."

Bet pulled the cloak from Saba's body. Saba's face was a bitter rictus, frozen in agony. "They only save life by taking life," Bet said. "Now you know why I separated them. Why I never kept them together. Yes, they can give life. But they can take it, too. It's the intent that matters."

"We have one of them, at least," Lealez said. "We can take him to the Contagion College."

"No," Bet said. She raised her head to the sky. "This is not done." While the people of the village stirred, the insects in the swampland around them had gone disturbingly quiet.

"What is—" Lealez began.

"Let's get to the water," Bet said. "Take Mekdas. We need to get away from the village."

"But—"

"Listen to me in this, you fool."

Lealez bound Mekdas with hemp rope rubbed in salt and pushed him out ahead of them. Lealez had to hurry to keep up with Bet. Carrying the objects seemed to have given her some greater strength, or maybe just a sense of purpose. She forged out ahead of them, cutting through swaths of swampland, cutting a way for them all the way back down to the water on the other side of the river.

Lealez stared out at the water and saw two pirogues attached to a cypress tree another hundred steps up the canal. "There!"

"Take my machete," Bet said. "You'll take one boat on your own. Follow after Mekdas and I."

Lealez took the machete. "You're really going to turn him in?"

Bet glared at per so fiercely Lealez wanted to melt into the water.

"All right," Lealez said, "I wasn't sure what I was thinking." Lealez waded out toward the pirogue. Lealez noticed the ripple in the water out of the corner of per eye and turned.

Bet saw the ripple a half moment before. She yelled and raised her sword, but she was too slow.

A massive alligator snatched Lealez by the leg and dragged per under the water. Bet saw Lealez's upraised arms, a rush of brown water, and then nothing.

Mekdas ran.

Bet swore and scrambled after him. She fell in along the muddy bank, and then something else came up from the water for her.

Hanere emerged from the depths of the swamp like a creature born there. She head-butted Bet so hard Bet's nose burst. Pain shattered across her face. Bet fell in the mud.

Muddy water and tangles of watercress streamed off Hanere's body. Her hair was knotted and tangled, and her beard was shot through with white. She grabbed hold of Bet's boot and dragged Bet toward her.

Bet held up the sword. "Revenge will get you nothing, Hanere!"

"It got me you," Hanere said, and wrenched the shield from Bet's hand and threw it behind her.

"You feel better with me here?" Bet said, gasping. "A bit, yes."

"And when your son is dead? If I don't kill him, someone else will."

"They were in love, like we were," Hanere said. "It was easy to convince them to burn down a world that condemned them, and me. Even you. This world cast even you out, after all you did."

"Not like us. They're both criminals."

"You became a criminal when you fucked me, and kept fucking me, even when you told them you were hunting me. You and your soft heart."

Bet kicked herself further down the bank, holding the sword ahead of her. "I thought you dead," Bet said. "For thirty years—"

"That's a bunch of shit," Hanere said. "You know they'd never kill someone like me. You know what they did to me for thirty years? Put me up in a salt box and tortured me. Me, the greatest sorcerer that ever lived."

"How did you—"

"Does it matter?" Hanere said, and her tone softened. She crawled toward Bet and took hold of the end of the sword. She pressed it to her chest and said, "Is this what you wanted? To do it yourself? Or did you wait always for this day, when we could take the world together?"

Tears came, unbidden. Bet gritted her teeth in anger. Her own soft heart, betraying her. "You know I can't."

"Even now?" Hanere said softly, "after all this time?"

Bet shook her head.

Hanere reached out for Bet's cheek, and though it was mud on Hanere's fingers and not blood, the memory of Hanere's bloody hands was still so strong after all these years that Bet flinched.

"We are done," Bet said, and pressed the sword into Hanere's heart.

Hanere did not fight her. Instead, she pulled herself forward along the length of the blade, closer and closer, until she could kiss Bet with her bloody mouth.

"I will die in your arms," Hanere said, "as I should have done."

Mekdas screamed, long and high, behind them. Bet sagged under Hanere's weight.

Mekdas bolted past her and ran toward the two pirogues.

Bet turned her eyes upward. Soft while clouds moved across the purple- blue sky. She wanted to be a bird, untethered from all this filth and sweat, all these tears. Thirty years she had hid, thirty years she had tried to avoid this day. But here it was. And she had done it, hadn't she? Done everything she hoped she would not do.

She heard a splashing from the water, and heaved a sigh. The lizard would take her. Gods, let the lizard take her, and the relics, and drown them for all time.

When she opened her eyes, though, it was Lealez who stood above her, dripping water onto her face. The pan was covered in gore, and stank like rotten meat. Lealez held up the machete. "Told you I was the best in my class," Lealez said.

"Didn't know you learned how to kill lizards," Bet said. Lealez gazed at Hanere's body. "Is she really dead?"

"I don't know that I care," Bet said. "Is that strange?"

Lealez helped her up. "The boy is trying to figure out the pirogue," Lealez said. "We aren't done."

"You take him."

"He's your family," Lealez said. "My responsibility?"

"I just thought . . . You would want to take the credit."

Bet huffed out a laugh. "The credit? The credit." She heaved herself forward, slogging toward the pirogue.

Mekdas saw her coming and pushed off. As she approached he stood up in the little boat, unsteady already on the water.

Behind him, Bet could just see the lights of the city in the distance. Did they all know what was coming for them? Did any realize that there were Plague Givers out here who wanted to decimate the world and start over? Would they care, or would they be like Hanere, and wish for an end?

"You must kill me to save that city, then, mother," Mekdas said. "Will you kill me like you did Hanere? You won't bring me in alive. You must make the—"

Bet threw her sword. It thunked into her son's belly. He gagged and bowled over.

Lealez gaped.

Bet waded out to the pirogue and pulled it back to shore. "You killed him," Lealez said. "I thought—"

"He's not dead yet," Bet said, but the words were only temporarily truth. He was gasping his last, drowning in his own blood.

"I've heard ultimatums like that before," Bet said. "Hanere gave me one, and when I hesitated, I lost her. You only make a mistake like that, the heart over reason, once. Then you take yourself away from the world, so you don't have to make decisions like that again."

"But—"

"Blood means little when there's a city at stake," Bet said. She gazed back out at the city. "Let's give them to the swamp."

"But we have to take the bodies back to—"

Bet raised the sword and pointed it at Lealez. It was only then that she realized Lealez was favoring per right leg; the lizard had gotten its teeth in per, and Lealez would get infected badly, soon, if they didn't get per help in the city.

"We do the bodies my way," Bet said, "then we get you back to the city." When they came back to Hanere's body, it was encircled by a great mushroom ring. Green spores floated through the air.

"Is she dangerous?" Lealez said.

"Not anymore," Bet said.

Together, they hauled the body through the undergrowth, avoiding the snapping jaws of swamp dogs and startling a pack of rats as big as Bet's head. Bet was aware of Hanere's stinking body, the slightly swelling flesh. When they dumped her into the hill of ants, Bet stood and watched them devour the woman she had spent half her life either chasing or romancing.

"Are you all right?" Lealez said.

"No," Bet said. "Never have been."

Mekdas was next.

While they stood watching the ants devour him, Lealez glanced over at Bet and said, "I know this is a hard profession, but there's honor in it. It does a public good."

"No, we just murder people."

"We eliminate threats to—"

"Can you even say it? Can you say, 'We murder people.' "

"This is a ridiculous conversation."

"On that, we can agree," Bet said. She glanced over at Lealez. "Something I noticed back there, in the Copse of Screaming Corpses. You never showed me your credentials."

"Don't be ridiculous."

Bet grabbed per arm and yanked back per sleeve before Lealez could pull away. There was the double ivy circle of the order, but no triangles.

Bet released her, disgusted. "What happened to being best in your class? Apprehending three Plague Givers? That's what your duplicitous friend Abrimet said, wasn't it?"

"I came out here to make a name for myself."

Bet stared down at the little pan, and though she wanted to hate Lealez more than anything, she had to admit, "I suspect you have indeed done that."

VIII.

Lealez smoothed per coat and mopped the sweat from per brow. The great Summoning Circle of the Contagion College was stuffed to bursting with fellow

Plague Hunters. The map case Lealez carried over per shoulder felt heavier and heavier as the afternoon wore on to dusk. The initial round of questions had worn down into a second and then third round where Lealez felt per was simply repeating perself. Not a single apprentice or hunter with fewer than three triangles was allowed into the space. By that measure, Lealez wouldn't have been able to come to per own trial just a few days ago. Lealez swallowed hard. In front of per lay the relics per and Bet had spent so much effort retrieving.

Lealez knew it was a betrayal, but per also knew there was no triangle on per arm yet, and this was the only way.

The coven of judges peered down at Lealez from the towering amber dais. The air above them swarmed with various plagues and contagions, all of them meant to counteract any assaults coming from outside the theater. But the swarm still made Lealez's nose run and eyes water. Lealez felt like a leaky sponge.

"Where are the bodies?" Judge Horven asked, waggling her large mustache.

"We disposed of them," Lealez said. "Elzabet was . . . understandably concerned that Hanere Gozene could rise again. As she had risen once before."

"Then you have no proof," Judge Horven said.

Lealez gestured expansively to the relics. "I have brought back the relics that Elzabet Addisalam and Keleb Ozdanam used to defeat Hanere Gozene," Lealez said. "And you have the testimony of the two of us of course."

Judge Rosteb, the eldest judge, held up their long-fingered hands and barked out a long laugh. "We are former Plague Hunters, all," they said. "We know that testimony between partners can be . . . suspect."

"I stand before you with all I have learned," Lealez said. "Abrimet was unfortunately lost to us along the way, through no fault of either Elzabet or myself. Their death was necessary to our goal. I regret it. You all know that Abrimet was my mentor. But we did as we were instructed. We stopped Hanere and the other two Plague Givers. I retrieved the relics. Both of those things cannot be contested. Because even if, as you say, you see no body, I can tell you this—you will never see Hanere again upon this soil. That will be proof enough of my accomplishments."

The judges conferred while Lealez sweated it out below them. Not for the first time, Lealez wished they had let Bet inside, but that was impossible, of course. Bet had murdered Abrimet, and done a hundred other things that were highly unorthodox in the apprehension of a Plague Giver. The judges would already worry that Bet had been a terrible influence on Lealez. Lealez would be lucky to get through this with per own head intact. At least Lealez would die in clean clothes, after a nice cold bath, which was the first thing per had done on entering the city.

Finally, the judges called Lealez forward.

"Hold out your arm," Judge Rosteb said.

IX.

Bet waited for Lealez outside the great double doors of the theater. Plague Hunters streamed past Bet as they were released from the meeting, all pointedly ignoring her. No one liked a woman who could kill her own family, no matter how great a sorcerer she was. The better she was, the more they hated her.

And there was Lealez. Lealez walked out looking dazed. Bet frowned at per empty hands. Lealez had gone in with the relics to make per case for destroying them, but Bet had a good idea of what had happened to them.

"Let's see them," Bet said, and snatched Lealez's arm. They had tattooed the mark of three successful hunts there. Bet snorted in disgust. "All three, then. You really learned nothing at all, did you? I could kill you too, but there are hundreds, thousands, just like you, crawling all over each other to do the bidding of the City Founders. You're like a hydra, spitting up three more scaly heads for every one I hack off."

"You don't know how difficult it is to rise up through the college now," Lealez said.

"You kids talk like it was any easier. It wasn't. We got asked to make the same stupid choices. They wanted the relics when Keleb and I came back, too. But we held out."

"You were already famous! Your reputation was secured!"

"Shit talk," Bet said. "You're just not tough enough to give up your career so young. I get that. But think on this. It's easy to destroy a country with plague, but how do you save your own from it? You'll all unleash something in the far empires and think we're safe, but we aren't, not with a thousand relics. All killing gets you is more killing. You pick up a machete, kid, and you'll be picking it up your whole life."

"None of it matters now," Lealez said, and sniffed. Lealez pulled a cigarette from a silver case, but for all per insouciance, Bet noted that per hands trembled. "They have the relics. What they do with them now doesn't concern me."

"Dumb kid," Bet said.

Lealez lit per cigarette with a clunky old lighter from per bag, something that would have weighed per down by an extra pound in the swamp. Lealez took a long draw. "I gave them the sword and the shield," per said, "just so you know."

"The . . . sword and shield. That's what you gave them?"

"Yeah, like I said." Lealez pulled a leather map case from per shoulder. "Here's the thing I promised you," Lealez said.

"I see," Bet said. She took the case from per. "You know the relics don't work unless they're all together?"

"Don't know about that," Lealez said. "I'm just a dumb kid, remember?"

"I'm sorry," Bet said.

Lealez shrugged. "Just get out of here. You aren't suited to the city."

Bet tipped her head at Lealez. "I don't want us to meet again," Bet said. "No offense meant."

"None taken," Lealez said. "If we meet again it means I'm not doing my job. I know how to play this game too, Bet." Lealez handed Bet the lighter and walked back into the college.

Bet pocketed it and watched per go. Lealez did not look back. When Lealez opened the great door of the College to go back inside, per hand no longer trembled. That pan was going to make a good Hunter someday, like it or not.

Bet shouldered the map case and began her own long walk across the city. It took nearly two hours to cross the dim streets, navigating her way based on which roads had functioning gaslights. She went all the way to the gates of the city and into the damp mud of the swamp before she risked opening the map case.

Inside, the cloak artifact was rolled up dry and tight. Bet rented a skiff upriver and spent the next week trudging home on foot and by whatever craft she could beg a ride up on.

When it came time to do what needed to be done, she wasn't sure she could do it. What if there was another Hanere? But so long as the relics existed, the world wasn't safe.

Bet burned the cloak there in the canopy of the cypress trees while swamp dogs snarled and barked in the distance. She watched the smoke coil up through the dense leaves and moss, and let out a breath.

It was decided. For better or worse.

X.

She had retired to the swamp because she liked the color. The color was the same, but she was not.

Bet leaned over the dim light of her firefly lantern, pushing her stuffed hydra into its glow. She eased the big sewing needle through its skin with her rough, thick fingers. On the shelves behind her were dozens of cast-off hydras, each defective in some way that she could not name. The College knew where she was now, and it made her work more difficult to concentrate on in the many long months back at her damp home. She sweated heavily, as the sun had only just set, and the air would keep its heat for a long time yet. She was tired, but no more than the day before, or the day before that. She had made her choices.

Mhev snorted softly in his basket with a litter of four baby swamp rodents, all mewing contentedly out here in the black. She wished she could join them, but her work was not done.

Outside, the insects grew quiet. Bet had been waiting for them. The waiting was the worst part. The rest was much easier. Whether it was child or Hunter or Giver or beast who stilled their call, she had made her choice about how to defend her peace long before, when she first condemned Hanere to death. She had already killed everything they both loved then.

That left her here.

Bet took hold of the machete at her elbow, the machete she would be taking into her hands for the rest of her life, and opened the door.